QUALIFY
(The Atlantis Grail, Book One)

Vera Nazarian

Copyright © 2014 by Vera Nazarian
All Rights Reserved.

Cover Design Copyright © 2014 by James, GoOnWrite.com

Additional Cover Layout Copyright © 2014 by Vera Nazarian

ISBN-13: 978-1-60762-134-8
ISBN-10: 1-60762-134-7

Trade Paperback Edition

December 20, 2014

A Publication of
Norilana Books
P. O. Box 209
Highgate Center, VT 05459-0209
www.norilana.com

Printed in the United States of America

Qualify

The Atlantis Grail: Book One

Norilana Books

Science Fiction

www.norilana.com

QUALIFY

THE ATLANTIS GRAIL
Book One

VERA NAZARIAN

Chapter 1

March, 2047.

Today is a day like any other day. Only it's not.

Today the Qualification tests begin—at all designated schools, and public sites in remote places where they don't have schools, all across the country and around the world—and everyone in my family is trying to pretend things are as usual.

I am at the messy kitchen counter chewing the breakfast scrambled eggs while the smart wall TV is blaring in the living room. Mom has her back turned and she is leaning over the stove making another skillet, which apparently is burning. I watch Mom's fragile stooped back, the collar of the flannel pajama top, and the yellow cotton scarf covering her head, bald from the most recent round of chemo. The air is thick with garlic and scalded toast and things unspoken. No one else is up yet.

"Need some help burning the house down, Mom?" I say, in-between tasteless bites. Normally I love cheesy garlic eggs, but not today. Today, nothing has a taste. Especially not my forced humor.

"Thanks," she says, without turning around. "But no, I think I am managing just fine with the arson."

"M-m-m-m," I say. The skillet makes another grand hiss.

Voices of various morning news show talking heads sound from the living room TV smart wall. "Qualify or die" is repeated often. I imagine there's a running marquee with that phrase, interspersed with stock tickers and national weather and the continuing coverage of the mystery of a missing plane that disappeared thirty-three years ago, while the footage of the asteroid and then the Atlantis ships hanging in the skies like balloons among the clouds is running on repeat in a small lower window of the screen. Unfortunately that's the spot of the smart wall surface with the greatest number of bad pixels. Our old wall needs an upgrade, but it's not going to happen now that the world is about to end.

They've been showing the same footage for the last three months. The asteroid is dramatic, a blazing white monster against black space. It's hurtling at us head-on. And then it's always followed by the video clip of the same famous spaceship disk, silvery metallic monolith, miles above the New York skyline. Most of Manhattan ground level is two feet underwater these days, but the skyscrapers remain active centers of business and make for a dramatic backdrop amid the street canals congested with taxi speedboat traffic. There are hundreds of other spaceships of course, all around the country and the world, but they only show the definitive New York one, with the Empire State Building in the frame. The ones here in Vermont, over Burlington, Montpelier, and St. Albans, don't warrant national coverage.

George comes into the kitchen. His dark brown hair is sticking up more than usual, which means he's been tossing and turning all night, and probably had very little sleep, much like me. He looks bleary-eyed too, and his good-looking angular face is stuck in a frown. He's wearing black jeans and a grey hoodie.

"Hey," I mumble at my seventeen-year-old older brother, and he only gives me the hard thoughtful look. How well I know it, since it's the same look that I've seen in the mirror this morning as I tried to comb the snags out of my own brown hair, long, wavy and unruly, and stared into my hard blue eyes. Grumpy and thoughtful runs in our family. Or at least with some of us. George and I are alike that way, prone to serious, prone to scary quicksilver moods interspersed with sarcasm. And now that Mom's really sick, we stopped laughing altogether.

Good thing our two younger siblings don't particularly share this hang-up. Twelve-year-old Grace has always been a giggle machine and chatterbox—though lately she gets weird anxiety attacks at night and has trouble falling asleep, then can't wake up on time in the morning, and is always late. Dad thinks it's because she is right on the border of the cutoff age for the Qualification, and it can go either way for her today. So she's been quietly freaking out.

As for Gordon, fourteen and sure of himself, he just hums whatever's playing in his earbuds, and smirks a lot, also quietly, even when he fiddles with his art and woodcrafts stuff. Gordie is convinced he will not Qualify, but he claims he does not care—which is of course crazy, but if it makes it easier for him to deal, then what can be said?

"Have some eggs, George," Mom says. "Grab a plate."

"I'm not hungry." My brother pours himself a glass of cheap apple juice.

"Yes, you are. You'll need it. You can't run all day on that sugary swill. And it's going to be a *very* long day." Mom turns around and grimaces, looking at the transparent yellowish baby-food liquid that George loves so much. Mom's skin has an unhealthy grey tint, and at the same time her face is reddened by the heat of the kitchen stove. Both her hands are shaking slightly with the usual tremors. But there is determined focus in her watery blue eyes. I stare at her and see the effort she is making. Margot Lark, my mother, is the strongest person I know.

"You shouldn't be doing this. You shouldn't be cooking." George frowns and gulps down half a glass of juice at once. I watch his Adam's apple move with each swallow, in tandem with the muscles of his lean neck.

"I am not cooking. You call this cooking?" Mom smiles, throwing me a wink, in an attempt to get me to make my usual sarcastic commentary that indicates I still have a pulse.

"It's pretty good, actually," I say, making a show of forking a large piece and chewing and swallowing with enjoyment, even though I am tasting *nothing* and my insides are filled with rocks. "Where's everyone else?"

"I heard Gee Three flush the toilet." George reluctantly takes a plate and Mom dumps half a skillet of cheesy yellow eggs onto it.

In case it's unclear, we're the Four Gees, in order of birth: George, Gwenevere, Gordon, Grace. I still don't get it why our parents decided to use names starting with the letter "G" for naming all their kids. Mom says she wanted a neat musical pattern to it, and for us to sound "elegant." Mom is a classical opera singer—or was, before she got sick—so "elegant" is important to her. Dad says it was an old tradition on his mother's Italian side of the family to use the same initial letter. Honestly, whatever. But everyone in school now calls us the Four Gees, and we're stuck with it.

"Gracie still in bed?" Mom continues, without glancing at George.

"You bet. Want me to go drag her out?"

Mom shakes her head, wipes a dot of skillet splatter off her nose with the back of her hand, still holding a greasy spatula. "No, let her sleep a bit longer. Your father will get her when he comes down. Give them another fifteen minutes. And now I want you to eat."

George shrugs. "Whatever. She'll make everyone late again."

"No. You'll be fine."

I am still chewing the eggs, swallowing them dutifully like lumps of unknown stuff, and now I feel a familiar pang of fear twist my guts.

We'll be fine. Somehow hearing this makes it worse, brings it all home.

Today's the day. The day we've been prepping ourselves for, emotionally, psychologically, for weeks and months. And when I say "we," that's pretty much everyone on this planet. Teens and their parents. And all the people who care about them. And really, everyone else too, since they get to watch. They get to find out—even though they themselves are out of the picture, out of the running—they get to witness us make it or fail.

Today we Qualify for rescue, for Atlantis.

Or we don't—which means we'll die together with all the rest of the world when the asteroid hits Earth, in about nineteen months from now. . . .

There's no way to stop it.

But at least for some of us, there is Atlantis.

Turns out, Atlantis is not a myth. It's ancient history. There really *was* a great continent by that name in ancient times, somewhere in the middle of what we now call the Atlantic Ocean, spanning the infamous Bermuda Triangle, the Bahamas, and beyond, and it was home to a very advanced high-tech civilization that stretched around the globe. Supposedly, they had computers, the internet, super-medicine, weapons of mass destruction, probably gaming consoles, and all kinds of other incredible or obnoxious stuff even more sophisticated than our own modern equivalents.

And then *something* happened. Maybe they did it to themselves—basically ruined the planet, kind of like what we're doing now with the environment and other species, the out-of-control pollution, carbon dioxide imbalance and resulting cascade of climate change. Or maybe it was Mother Nature, at least in part.

Because at some point more than twelve thousand years ago, something huge and terrible took place—a mega-cataclysm on such a scale that it caused a whole continent to disappear without a trace, in earthquakes and floods and who knows what—and wiped the high-level civilization off the face of the planet. To escape this global disaster—we are told—the people of Atlantis used their advanced technology to leave Earth and flee to the stars. They eventually established a human colony on a habitable planet.

They called this colony planet "Atlantis," or whatever's the equivalent in their language, in memory of their own ancient roots on Earth, to honor their native civilization and the terrestrial continent of their birth that started it all.

And now, after all these thousands of years, they're back. They returned to Earth, their ancient home world, and they are here to help. That is, the distant descendants of the original Atlantean colonists are here to help. They claim to be one hundred percent human and supposedly *not all that different from ourselves*—if you don't count the thousands of generations of separate evolution and branching off to live in an alien environment. Yeah, right.

Anyway, the Atlanteans share our DNA and they're our cousins. And, just like cousins, it makes them either weird or welcome guests.

Right now, they are desperately welcome and desperately needed. The asteroid brought them here—or, like some paranoid people in the media say, maybe "they brought the asteroid."

Whichever it is, at this point, Atlantis is all we've got.

When the news of the lethal asteroid first broke, months ago, almost simultaneously the Atlantean spaceships appeared in the skies all over the world. It's as if they've been watching us, and waiting to make first contact. The asteroid just gave them the excuse.

Okay, at first it was a huge global mess. World governments going into panic mode and military overdrive, people on the streets screaming about alien invasions, religious fundamentalists having a field day, scientists having aneurisms, stock markets crashing worldwide, to the tune of billions.

But once the Atlantean shuttles landed, and we saw them to be human and not little green men or big green lizards, it was okay. They met with representatives of governments, the United Nations, and were received with caution and eventually with open arms. "We are you," they told us in various languages of Earth. How they knew our languages is unclear, but it's probably some kind of advanced tech, or they've been listening in on us for far longer than we know. They explained who they were—which is kind of insane if you think about it, all that mythic stuff that Plato wrote about is mostly true—and demonstrated some of their amazing technology.

Only it wasn't all that amazing when it came to the asteroid.

Yes, they tried moving it and changing the path of its trajectory, and all kinds of other advanced science stuff, in conjunction with global space agencies and the three International Space Stations we currently have—the largest one in Earth orbit, a second small one on the surface of the Moon, and the barely functional newest one on Mars. They even landed on the asteroid's surface and drilled and took samples. But nothing worked, at least not enough to make a difference. The asteroid is going to hit Earth and it is going to cause nuclear winter at best. And at worst—well, let's just say there may not be much of this planet left after the impact. . . .

However, not all is lost. Because the Atlanteans are going to save as many of us as possible and take us back with them—back to the colony planet Atlantis, a fertile blue-green world that's supposed to be beautiful beyond belief, with a golden-white sun and not one but three moons.

To that effect, they have brought enough spaceships to carry millions of people—ten million, to be precise. It sounds great but means they can only rescue a very small portion of the general Earth population of eight point five billion—no more than can fill their present fleet of monolith silver ships, since there is no time for multiple trips between Earth and Atlantis before the asteroid strikes.

There is only one condition for rescue. Those lucky few that get to board the Atlantis ships have to be young people between the ages of eleven and twenty—teenagers.

Capable, talented, special teenagers.

The best of the best on Earth.

And the only way to determine who these teens will be is to make them pass Qualification. . . .

Qualify or die.

The smart wall in the living room is playing TV snippets of a canned interview with the President. Later tonight she will address the nation live. . . . But for now it's old footage. President Katherine Donahue is speaking in her usual droning and soothing voice that's powerful and at the same time conciliatory, in that nasty mixture that only politicians manage. "Our children and we must be brave together, but rest assured, no one's giving up" and "we hold them in our prayers as Qualification looms" and "the ultimate survival and benefit of humanity might ultimately depend on well-orchestrated air strikes" are some of the phrases heard.

Same old junk they've been saying for months, as soon as they figured out that nothing substantial could be done to stop the asteroid, and that the Atlanteans are not all-powerful after all, despite what everyone hoped.

Thing is, the governments, the global leaders, the media, the scientists, the talking heads—they all feel the guilt-ridden need to keep talking, keep trying, even up to the last, even as the world goes up in flames or ash clouds or whatever. "Vaporware Hope," as Dad calls it, is one way to fill up the void between *now* and *the end.*

Sure, there's Qualification. But for the human spirit that's just not good enough. To that end, there are also numerous space missions being prepped by the United Nations and private conglomerates, by individual governments and science agencies. Everyone's building shuttles, rockets and "payload delivery systems," whatever that means, to see if they can blast the asteroid into manageable bits or move it out of the fatal earth-contact trajectory. Meanwhile, others are building spaceship arks, just to get off the planet—kind of like the ancient Atlanteans themselves did, thousands of years ago. I guess they think, maybe if they can just get far enough away from the blast and resulting atmospheric turbulence, the Atlanteans might guide them the rest of the way?

The Atlanteans observe these various efforts sadly, and have indeed volunteered to assist to the best of their abilities. But the reality remains grim, there's not all that much that can be done, at least not for the majority of living beings on Earth. The asteroid is huge and supposedly made up of mostly heavy metals and some other newly discovered stuff that makes it pretty much impossible to move or damage—or so they say. And as for escape, there are simply too many people, animal species, and too few ships.

President Donahue's words are cut off briefly with video-bytes of breaking news, basically public unrest worldwide, demonstrations around school buses that are supposed to take us all to the Qualification sites, various local police forces in riot gear, and people screaming and throwing rocks and demanding justice. "Please! Just save my baby!" a woman somewhere in the Midwest is crying in a crazed voice of despair. "What good are my tax dollars with all your idiot scientists and useless military and failed national defense? Why can't you nuke that space rock and save us!"

The stairs creak softly under Dad's familiar steady footsteps. He comes down, fully dressed in his nice beige blazer, black shirt, brown slacks, tweed vest. And he's wearing a tie, which is a rare thing. My father, Charles Lark, is the epitome of academia, with his rimless spectacles, somewhat tousled, wavy brown hair and greying temples. He is a professor of classics and history at the local University, and is exactly what you might think that means. Smart, and a little eccentric, and living mostly inside his head, his lesson plans, and research, with plenty of oddball stories and trivia to tell to his kids.

"Let's please turn the awful TV off," Dad says tiredly. He is bleary-eyed too, and he is immediately looking at Mom.

"Good morning!" Mom throws him a cheerful look and turns her back again. "I thought all of you might want some real breakfast today. Coffee's ready."

"How are you feeling? You really shouldn't be up so early, straining yourself." Dad goes directly for the coffee maker.

"Are you kidding? This is good for me. Besides, I would never miss seeing all of you off today, of all days."

"Why, what's today?" George says grimly.

From the living room now comes the familiar voice of the Atlantean Fleet Commander giving his now famous inspirational speech to the United Nations. The voice is soft, rich and musical. It is pleasant in timbre despite the strange lilting accent, and the Atlantean is speaking perfect English. Which is all kind of amazing. And yet it makes my skin crawl with new pangs of fear. Because there's all that strange, leashed power in that voice, and it's held back somehow. How do I know this? I don't, I have no idea. But Commander Manakteon Resoi (try saying that three times) with his pleasant, sonorous voice, his fixed handsome face, metallic-golden blond hair and contrasting black eyebrows that seems to be typical of his ethnicity, gives me the creeps. Especially when he talks about "humanitarian efforts amid failure of hope" and "technological impetus" and "a new era for Earth and Atlantis."

"I hate that Goldilocks guy and his BS," George mumbles.

Goldilocks. That's the derogatory term being used lately to refer to Atlanteans, because supposedly they all color their hair metallic gold, which is a fashion statement. Or maybe it's an indicator of rank. No one's sure. Apparently, gold's so common and abundant on Atlantis, that it's considered a base metal. . . .

In that moment, the stairs groan as Gracie and Gordie come downstairs one after the other, Gracie trailing. My younger brother Gordon is slight and skinny, lacking the sinewy strength and height of George, and with brown hair that's several shades lighter and so short it's almost buzzed. He's wearing his usual dingy jeans and faded black sweatshirt with paint stains on it. And his rimless glasses have dirty finger spots you can see from several feet away.

Gracie is last. She is a younger version of me, tall and slim, except without any curves and with straight long hair that's dirty blond instead of dark like mine. Gracie is dressed up in pastel pink skinny jeans and a black sweater with sequins. She is wearing black eyeliner, mascara and lip gloss, and gaudy plastic bangles on her wrists. Normally Mom would say something about the eye junk and the lip gloss, but today Grace Lark gets to wear whatever she likes—whatever gives her strength.

"All right," Mom says. "Everyone, get plates, these cheesy eggs are pure magic!"

"Thanks, Mom. Pile it on." Gordie heads right for the kitchen counter and pulls up a chair, while Gracie stops in the middle of the kitchen and stares. Her face is very pale, and she looks sickly, despite her mascara and lip gloss. Or maybe because of it.

"Gracie, honey, don't waste time, please." Mom picks up a clean plate and starts filling it.

"I don't want any eggs."

Dad sits down nearby at the small side table with his mug of coffee and a plate of eggs. "Your Mom got up early and made the breakfast, and you should eat it."

Grace is frowning. "I hate eggs, and I'm not really hungry."

"Okay." Mom sighs. "How about a banana and toast? You need to eat something today. You know you do."

"We're out of bananas," I recall. "Gracie, come on, why don't you just eat the eggs, just this once, okay? They're really good! Yummy-yum-yum! Protein and fuel!"

Gracie shrugs. I can't believe she is this quiet. She's not even calling me an idiot.

"We have ten minutes," George says. "Move it, Gee Four."

Gracie silently slips onto a chair at the counter and reaches for a slice of toast.

A few minutes later we're in the old minivan, headed for school, with Dad at the wheel. We still feel Mom's tight desperate hugs and ringing-hard kisses on our cheeks. In my mind, she's still standing at the porch, waving, and her eyes are red and swimming in tears as she watches us drive away. If we Qualify, this will be the last time we ever see Mom. Already I am fixing this image of her, searing it into memory.

Usually George drives us in his peeling truck, but today Dad is bringing us in, as if to make sure we are delivered properly in time for the Qualification tests. All our duffel bags are packed in the trunk, in addition to the usual school backpacks. Everything's according to the official Qualification instructions that have been handed out, weeks in advance, by the schools that are designated RQS, or Regional Qualification Sites. Our bags contain a basic travel kit, a change of clothing, and a few personal items that are up to us. The assumption is, if we advance in the Qualification preliminary stage, we will be taken directly to the Regional Qualification Centers where the next stage of the process will take place. And we don't get to say goodbye to anyone.

My duffel bag has a few of my favorite books including *The Iliad*, *The Odyssey*, *The 101 Dalmatians*, and *The Birthgrave*. Okay, it has a lot of books, and is heaviest, almost exceeding the forty pounds limit. That's because these are actual honest-to-goodness *books*, printed on paper. Yeah, you heard that right. Some of them are rare collector editions from Dad's library. Dad often says that an electromagnetic pulse or EMP disaster can strike any moment and destroy our digital information storage capability, so he's been hoarding the paper print editions like precious treasure for most of his life. His personal library is amazing. And now here's my chance to save some of those classics before the asteroid takes them first.

In addition to the load of books, my bag also has a small pouch of trinkets. There are family photos, a tiny rose crystal Pegasus figurine, and a sterling silver dancing fairy locket my parents gave me for my sixteenth birthday a few months ago. It's not electronic-enhanced smart jewelry, but it has heart.

George has chosen to pack close to nothing of personal value, only an extra pair of running shoes and some flat rectangular thing wrapped in brown paper, plus a bunch of paper books for Dad's sake. In contrast, Gordie's duffel has micro-bead CDs, rare sheet music, and his skinny Backpacker travel guitar, in addition to his favorite weird quartz pieces from his extensive rock collection, a purple geode, a Swiss Army knife, a portable color pen-and-pencil art box, and a sketchbook. As for Gracie, she has taken her costume jewelry including a pair of latest version smart earrings, a cosmetics pouch, and her flute. And yeah, more of Dad's books.

I stare outside the window at the bleary landscape. It's March, but snow is still on the ground, and the sky is overcast.

However, as I stare southeast, the Atlantean ship in the sky over St. Albans can be seen in the corner of the window, through the tall pine and maple trees. From this distance it looks like a flattened weather balloon, silvery metal. In reality, I know it is massive, almost a mile in diameter. It hovers, motionless, silent, eternal.

Gordie, Gracie, George, my Dad, all of us glance at it periodically.

George is up in the front passenger seat next to Dad, and he voice commands the car radio on. Immediately there is a blast of riot noise, and the radio deejay comes on with frenzied commentary. The mayors of Chicago, St. Louis, Dallas, and Inland Los Angeles are being interviewed about the ramifications of crowd control and widespread urban looting, and next up, expert practical advice from a pop psychologist at something dot com: "Five Tips for Teens—how to maximize your chances to Qualify today."

"Oh great, do we have to listen to this?" Dad says.

George invokes the scan function on the radio and it jumps to a music station.

"No, don't turn it off!" Gracie clutches the back of George's seat. "I want to hear the five tips!"

"No, you don't."

"Yes I *do!*"

George groans.

Gordie just stares out the window with blissful indifference and his earbuds are crackling with his own entertainment.

"All right." Dad is turning off the main highway onto a smaller road that's near our high school and Gracie's middle school, both in the same complex. Our schools are a designated Regional Qualification Site. The traffic is busier than usual, as parents from other school districts are dropping off their children, and everyone wants to be on time. Car horns are blaring. We make the turn into school grounds and the rows of yellow buses are already lined up in the parking lot, ready to take those of us who are lucky enough to pass the preliminaries on to the next stage of Qualification, hours later.

"You want five tips?" Dad says seriously. "I'll give you five tips. Number one—"

"I don't want *your* tips! I want what that program was going to say!" Gracie's voice rises in that same whiny awful noise that has been produced by her for weeks now, whenever something doesn't go her way.

"Oh, jeez—" George shakes his head.

"I want to hear Dad," I say.

Gracie turns around and glares at me. Her hand is still clutching the back of the seat in front of her with a white-knuckled grip.

"Speak fast, Dad, because we're almost here."

I see my father's sad, drawn expression reflected in the rear view mirror. He looks old suddenly, old and exhausted. He takes a silent breath and pushes his spectacles up his nose. "Tip number one—be yourself. Number two—do the best you can under the circumstances and never let fear control you and make you freeze. Number three—okay—" He pauses and I see him make the tired effort to say something constructive and hopeful. "Number three—listen to your gut instinct, always. Your gut is one smart buddy there. Listen to it. Number four—never give up. Never, ever, ever, times infinity. Number five—make the choice that will ultimately make you feel good inside about yourself—as a human being. That's always the right choice."

"Are you done?" Gracie says.

Dad sighs. "You know how hard it is for all of us, Grace. Take a big breath. All right, we're almost there."

"Thanks for the words of wisdom, Dad. That's actually gold in thar' them hills. I bet you wrote it up last night in your lecture notes. Am I right?" George mumbles while looking straight ahead, as he begins to get ready to unbuckle his seatbelt even before we are parked.

"Yeah, well," Dad says. "What if I did? Couldn't let you all go without saying something brilliant to help you remember your old man by. There's actually more, but I thought the 'five tips' gave me a nice excuse to summarize. Want to hear the rest? No? I didn't think so. It was worth a try."

The minivan is still crawling along in a line of cars through the parking lot and onto the football field that has been designated as supplementary parking. Security guards stand, waving the cars into parking spots or designated drop-off points. There are also several media news vans and vehicles with video and sound equipment. Even now, they are filming us live. It's weird to think, but all that's happening right now is being recorded, is breaking news. . . .

We stop not too far from the side entrance to the main school building, in the yellow zone. Kids and parents are everywhere, opening cars, carrying bags. Many people are crying.

We get out, and Dad pops the trunk, which sails open slowly.

Shivering in my jacket from the chill morning air, I stand waiting for George to get his duffel bag, while Gordie has his already. Grace stands right behind me, breathing down my neck.

Dad stops the engine and comes around to help us. Or more likely he is gathering himself for the big goodbye.

I glance around, seeing students I know, other classmates, heading up the stairs and inside, past security. Carrie Willis, a girl from my class rushes by with tear-reddened eyes, dragging a bulky, ugly purple-and-orange travel bag that's rolling along on squeaky wheels. Her mom and some other relatives watch below, waving and sobbing.

Gordie watches her also, shakes his head and adjusts the strap of his heavy duffel bag, then pulls his knitted ski hat over his reddened ears. "This is all seriously messed up."

"Yeah, that one there seriously needs new luggage." George steps back, shouldering his bag and his backpack with muscular ease.

"No, I mean, *this*, all of this situation—she, they, us, everyone, the world," Gordie says.

I lean forward and take my turn with my stuff. It feels surreal, like someone else is going through the motions. My backpack is hoisted up and lands on my back with a thud that's lessened by the stuffed lining of my winter jacket. I adjust the straps on both arms, then reach for the heavier duffel.

Gracie is starting to sniffle behind me, and I hear Dad embrace her in a bear hug.

Well, this is it.

I suddenly feel a burning in my eyes. In the back of my throat a huge horrible lump is gathering. No, I am not going to cry.

But the pressure is building in my sinuses, and as I keep my eyes open wide, afraid to blink, already I can feel the first stupid fat teardrop starting to well in one eye, as my vision gets blurry. I back away from the minivan, while Gracie disengages from Dad's hug, wipes her face with the back of her hand—which smears her eyeliner on one side—and goes for her bag with trembling hands.

I stand watching the peeling spots of paint on the wall of the school building, while blurs of students are going past me up the stairs. I am momentarily distracted from needing to bawl by the familiar faces. Mindy Erikson walks by with her stuff, and her flaming red hair. . . . There goes football jock Nick Warren and his younger brother, whatshisname.

"Gwen, honey . . ." Dad's voice cuts through everything, and it makes me turn around and look at him, and face him at last.

"Here, my sweet girl, there you go," Dad says, reaching out for me, and I meet his eyes, and it breaks me completely. *Dad. . . . This is my dad, and he is going to die.*

I am glad that next comes the great big hug so he doesn't see me start to lose it. Instead I lose myself in his chest, and crush my face against the beige blazer, and think about how he'll have to have it dry cleaned to get my stupid tears and snot off the fabric. I stay that way for several moments, shaking silently, feeling Dad's powerful embrace and smelling the faint aftershave and wool scent of his clothes.

"My brave, smart Gwen," Dad says in my ear. "Love you, honey, stay strong! Promise me, never give up! Watch out for your sister and brothers—"

"Love you, Dad, I will. . . ."

I let go, and stand back, and smear my face with the back of my hand, and that's it.

I watch Dad take Gordie in a quick tight hug, and pat his back, and then George, who evades the hug and instead gets a grownup handshake.

"Well, this is it," Dad says. He takes a symbolic step back and nods at us, and says, "God speed, go on, all of you! I promise you, the Lark family will Qualify, hands down, all four of you!" I see Dad's eyes are sort of red too, as he just stands there, looking at us through his spectacles.

George nods briefly, and just for a moment he is suspended, motionless, like a post. He turns and gives the rest of us a serious look. "Okay! Let's do this. See you on the flip side." And George heads up the stairs.

Gordie follows, trudging silently.

Gracie and I take a moment longer, to give Dad another last

look.

"Go on!" he says. "Don't be late now, hurry! Your Mom and I are rooting for you one hundred percent. Go!"

And so I take my sister by the arm, and pull her along, and we start up the steps.

We enter the school building without looking around again at Dad.

It's easier this way.

Chapter 2

In the hallway, the crowds are insane, with many unfamiliar faces from other neighboring schools. The Qualification instructions say we are supposed to report to our own homerooms. Meanwhile the strangers are assigned as extras to our own classrooms and herded around campus by teachers, to begin the Qualification process.

In moments the Lark siblings are all separated. Gracie gives me a deer-in-the-headlights last look as she is made to go to an adjacent building with other middle schooler seventh graders. George's a senior, so he heads upstairs to his own homeroom. Gordon's freshman class homeroom is far down the hall to the right on the ground floor.

I'm a junior and my homeroom is downstairs in the basement floor past the rows of lockers. Just as the bell rings, I move quickly down the stairwell, jostling past classmates and trying to keep my head down, out of years of habit. Nerds and smart "achiever" kids like me have learned it's best to minimize eye contact, because we get punished for it by the usual suspects.

I enter the classroom, grab my seat in the second row near the front, stuff my bags under my feet, and watch others start filling their seats. My homeroom teacher, Mrs. Grayland, is already at her desk, looking anxious and exhausted, and it's not even 8:00 AM yet. Next to her, some unfamiliar woman administrator is standing at the board, dressed in a suit jacket and skirt. She has a red-green-blue-yellow striped armband wrapped around her sleeve, which is the familiar color swatch of Atlantis. She is in no way Atlantean herself—no, she looks too bland and homegrown-stocky to be anything but local Earth material. I'm guessing she is simply a designated representative. However her expression is stone-blank and authoritative.

"Hey, Gwen. . . ." Ann Finnbar takes the seat next to me. I glance at Ann's freckled nose and stressed expression. I am glad my closest friend shares homeroom with me this semester, because I really don't want to be alone right now.

"Hey. . . . So—ready for this thing?" I try to speak lightly. "It's not like you can prepare or study for it."

Ann shakes her head and grimaces painfully, then bends down and starts messing with her bags on the floor. I notice her hands are shaking.

A boy I don't recognize sits down on the other side of me. The classroom is filling up quickly. There are additional chairs that have been brought in, and I see many completely unfamiliar faces of students from other schools. There are more desk rows than usual, so everyone is packed closer together, and for once every seat is taken. At some point they run out of desks and chairs and, a few latecomer students end up in the back of the classroom and at the sides, sitting on the floor against the walls. Voices are high-strung, angry, and there are a few nervous giggles.

"Good morning, everyone, for those of you not from Mapleroad Jackson High School, I am Mrs. Grayland." Our homeroom teacher clears her throat to silence the noise and talk. "All right, I am going to take roll call, so please everyone find your seats and keep your desks clear. The faster you settle down, the faster we can begin. When I say your name, listen closely, because I will read your next designated classroom number. That's where you will be going to take the next portion of the Qualification test. Write it down. Now, let's begin. Abbott, Gary—"

"Here!"

"You'll be going to room 115-B. Andrew, Nancy—room 25-C."

My eyes switch back and forth from Mrs. Grayland as she reads names, and the other woman, who is standing motionless, holding her hands together behind her back. The white board behind them has the words "Qualification Day" written in large letters. I stare at the letters and almost start to space out.

" . . . Lark, Gwenevere. Room 217-C."

"Here!" My normally low voice sounds abrupt, breathless and squeaky. For a moment even I don't recognize it. As I turn slightly,

I see Mark Gardner give me a hard and obnoxious smirk from a seat in the back. Big and burly, good looking and popular a-hole Mark's one of my regular tormentors. You'd think that today of all days he'd have other, more pressing things on his mind, but I guess bullying does not take vacations, not even for end-of-the-world stuff.

Next to Mark, there's Jenny Hawls, his most recent girlfriend, equally bitchy and popular. She stares at me with her model-perfect pretty face, then flips her long honey-blond hair. She and Mark and another guy, Chris Jasper, exchange mocking looks and then cover their mouths. They'd started in on me early, at the end of the first semester of our freshman year, when they first "noticed" how I always raised my hand in class and spoke up, and seemed to know all the correct answers.

I try not to think of them as I repeat in my mind, "Room 217-C," over and over, even though I'd just jotted it down in my notebook.

Mrs. Grayland is done with roll call. She turns to the woman in the suit and introduces her as Ms. Wayne, from Qualification, who is going to administer this first portion of the test.

Ms. Wayne steps forward and begins with a canned introduction about Atlantis, our long-lost earth colony, the asteroid situation, and how "the best and brightest" of us have been given this lucky chance to save our lives in the face of this global misfortune, and how we are the hope of humanity. "Qualification is for your own benefit," she says with a stone face. "It is the most fair method of choosing the next generation, and instead of a chance lottery you have the opportunity to prove yourself and showcase your talents."

The students around me stare, and again furious whispers are heard.

"Settle down," Mrs. Grayland says, then nods to Ms. Wayne to continue.

"This is the most important day of your life." Ms. Wayne looks around the room. "You will be tested in more ways than you or I can imagine, and some of these tests may not seem to make sense. Please understand that we are only administering them as instructed by the Atlantis Central Agency, in cooperation with the federal government. All interpretation of the final results for each stage of Qualification will be made according to Atlantean criteria. We have no control whatsoever over test results or the final outcome. Nor have we set any of these criteria ourselves."

"What's that mean? What criteria?" a boy interrupts from the back.

"It means, we don't know what kind of test answers are 'correct' and we don't know what they are looking for."

"So how are we supposed to do the test?" says another student, and her voice cracks with a hint of tears.

"Do your best. That's all anyone can expect of you. Do the best you can, take your time with your answers, and good luck to all of you! And now, I am sorry, but I cannot answer any more questions. We need to begin." Ms. Wayne sighs, checks the clock, and suddenly she is no longer just an automaton in a suit but a tired ordinary woman.

She turns to Mrs. Grayland, and they both begin passing out test booklets, answer sheets, and number two pencils.

"Clear your desks of everything, and please put away all phones and electronic devices—that includes smart jewelry—keep it turned *off*. And—" Ms. Wayne pauses meaningfully—"Please don't bother cheating. Truth be told, this is one test on which you cannot cheat."

There are more whispers throughout the classroom.

"Now," Ms. Wayne continues, coming around the room. "This is the general knowledge portion of Qualification. It includes math and science and history and spelling and analytical sections. And yes, it is long. We do not know how much weight it carries in the overall examination. Format is standardized multiple choice, intentionally low-tech paper and pencil, because no computer use was designated for this portion. However you should all be sufficiently familiar with this. Be sure to use your pencils to fill in the bubbles in their entirety."

Groans are heard all around the room. "Excuse me, how do I use a pencil?" someone cracks.

"Easy! Just stick it in your—"

Snickers start in waves.

"Why on *Earth* do I need to take the SAT to get to Atlantis?" someone else whispers behind me. More snickers, quickly stifled.

Mrs. Grayland stops by my desk and hands me the test materials, then moves over to Ann's, and then the next person.

I stare at the super-thick text booklet. It's so thick it's ridiculous. It's got a pale blue cover and a printed Atlantis logo of some kind of cube. I've seen this stupid logo before on TV, together with the four-color swatch. Supposedly it represents the Great Square in the constellation of Pegasus—the general region in space where the star system with the planet Atlantis is located.

"Everyone, please open your booklets and turn to the first page of the test. You have exactly an hour and forty-five minutes. This is critical—be sure to fill out your name portion in the front of the answer sheet before you do anything else. And now, begin."

An hour and a half later, I fill in the last answer bubble, put down my pencil and look up. Most everyone else is still marking their answer sheet.

The test was easy. At least I think it was. I feel confident about ninety percent of my answers, and if anything about this is an indicator of what's to come, this bodes well for me totally acing Qualification.

Yeah, right.

Next to me Ann is still biting her pencil and has a few pages of the booklet to go. She gives me a dazed look then returns to her answer sheet.

Ms. Wayne, who is pacing quietly through the rows of desks, and watching us like a hawk, immediately notices I am done, and comes up to me. I silently hand her my finished test.

As I turn to watch Ms. Wayne's retreating back, I see Jenny Hawls glare at me, before returning to her test. Jenny's a dim bulb when it comes to schoolwork, so I am sure she is having a rotten time with the test material. If I weren't so generally stressed, I'd feel a rare moment of satisfaction. But honestly, this is not the time for petty stuff—we're all in this sorry mess together.

Soon, the bell rings. The teachers tell us to put down our pencils. We are reminded that our names should be clearly marked on the answer sheets in order to get proper credit, and that we're supposed to go on to our next designated classroom.

"Crud, I couldn't even finish. It was so long!" Ann is frowning as we grab our things and head outside into the hallway.

"How did you do?"

"Okay, I guess, sort of. Some of the questions were super hard." I feel bad for Ann, so I underplay it. Ann's smart and a good student, but she doesn't always do all that well when it comes to timed, standardized tests. And this one's life-and-death, *literally*.

"Easy for you to say. You always ace these things. I panicked. My brains turned to mush and left the building, right in the middle of it." She fiddles with her navy blue backpack and travel bag nervously, adjusting the shoulder strap. I wonder what she chose as her personal stuff to put in that duffel. What special items, to keep with her as mementoes of Earth, if she Qualifies and makes it to the stars? As though reading my mind, she glances meaningfully at her bag. "I took antique family photo albums and two of my Grandpa's wood carvings. And Mom's pearl necklace—with an added smart phone bead, since Mom insisted. And my skating trophy."

"That's great," I say. "I'll show you the stuff I'm taking, during lunch."

"You think they'll let us break for lunch?"

"I don't see why not—"

"Hey, move it, Finnbar and dork." Jeremy Carverson is shoving past us, and he snaps the strap of my maroon backpack. "Stop taking up the hallway!"

"Dork" doesn't even rhyme properly with "Lark," but I am used to it.

We break away and I mutter "good luck, see you soon" to Ann, then hurry upstairs to the second floor, to room 217-C. That's three long flights of stairs from the basement, and by the time I get to the final landing, carrying both my heavy backpack and the book-stuffed duffel, I'm somewhat winded, to put it mildly. Okay, I am kind of dead. It occurs to me that if any part of Qualification involves going up many stairs while carrying luggage, I could be screwed.

The classroom is one of the larger ones, and it's already halfway full. It's divided into rows of desks and additional chairs and a strange partitioned area that has a sign posted "Testing Area. Do Not Enter." Two women teachers stand near the partition, and again one of them is wearing the four-color Atlantis armband.

Since I don't know either one of them, I am guessing the one without the armband is just faculty from another school, and the other's from Qualification.

The teachers watch us dispassionately as we enter the classroom. It's the same beaten-down, resigned look in their eyes that most grownups have these days—a sad mixture of weary despair and grim acceptance. I am reminded once again that, as adults, they've had weeks and months of agonized panic, denial, and eventually resignation with impending death, to deal with. At least *we* have a shred of hope, while they're all living on death row. They get to stay *here* on our doomed planet, and the best they can hope for is, if they have teenage children, maybe their kids might Qualify, so their DNA gets to be saved.

"Take your seats, please," one of them says in a voice with little inflection. "When I call your name, you will come up here and be tested. This is an individual portion of the test. It is not timed, but should take no longer than five minutes per person. The rest of you please remain in your seats until your name is called. And no talking!"

I find an empty seat near the middle in the fourth row, between an unfamiliar round-faced girl with dark hair and some skinny kid in a grey hoodie, both of whom look way younger, like freshmen. And it occurs to me that this is a mixed classroom, not just juniors like me. Pretty weird to be taking a test with people from other grades.

I look around the room and I see some familiar people I know from my class, and a few seniors and sophomores. Everyone's muttering, whispering, students are looking around warily, and I see fear and uncertainty in their eyes.

And then my stomach drops out from under me, and suddenly I am ice-cold and scalding-hot at the same time. Logan Sangre is sitting only a few seats in front of me and to the right, in the second row.

Logan Sangre. . . .

Dark hair, longish and wavy, a rare black with rich brown highlights. Olive skin, chiseled angular features, dreamy hazel brown eyes, and the longest dark lashes I've ever seen on a boy. Add to that, wide shoulders, muscled arms underneath his black hoodie, long and powerful runner's legs encased in black jeans, and perfectly defined abs that belong on a classical Greek statue.

Logan Sangre, a senior, the hottest guy in Mapleroad Jackson High, and an all-around amazing combination of track star athlete and honor roll student. Beauty and brains. He can have his pick of any girl, any time. And as far as I know, he does, because they're always falling all over him—though I think he might be between girlfriends now, since I haven't seen him hanging around Joanie Katz, his latest GF, for more than a week. . . . And, oh yeah, he's got time to play lead guitar in a band. Just kill me now.

It's such a cliché to say it, but Logan Sangre is completely out of my league. Like, miles-to-the-Moon out of my league. And he doesn't know that I exist. I've been crushing on Logan since my first month of freshman year, which makes it three years now—from the very start when we first moved to Vermont from California to get away from the West Coast and all its disastrous mess. Pacific coastal radiation was determined to be the primary cause of Mom getting sick, so Dad got his University of Vermont faculty position, and we all ended up attending Mapleroad Jackson School.

Anyway, Logan Sangre. What really got to me from day one was not so much his amazing hotness and good looks, but his confident coolness. Okay, that does not make sense, but see, there I go already, losing IQ points just thinking about him. And the fact that he regularly wins academic competitions makes it even worse. Sure he also brings in track-and-field trophies for our school, but come on, there are plenty of hot jocks out there. But how many of them are also "mathletes" and National Merit Scholars?

So, yeah, Logan Sangre. Whenever I'm in the same room with him, I lose about 20 points off my IQ score and acquire a speech impediment and, I bet, a permanent skin rash from blushing so much. I pretty much cannot function within a twenty-foot radius of him. The funny thing is, we've never spoken a word. . . . Okay, except maybe once there was a "sorry" exchanged in the cafeteria when I nearly ran into him with my tray, my sophomore year. That was the one time he met my gaze and looked into my eyes directly with his dreamy dark ones, and of course that was precisely when I tripped on my own shoelaces and spilled milk all over my best pair of sneakers.

The fact that Logan is in the same classroom with me *now* makes me crazy. How in the world will I be able to concentrate, to deal with Qualification and not make some kind of stupid klutz mistake? Logan Sangre is going to ruin everything.

I take deep breaths and try to stare straight ahead and not to look at him, even though I am aware with every cell of my body that he's *right there*, at the edge of my peripheral vision.

Mrs. Bayard, the teacher with the Atlantis armband on her sleeve, calls the first name, and it doesn't seem to be in alphabetical order, probably some kind of freaky Atlantis-only-knows order. I watch Mindy Clarence, a fellow junior, get up with a very pale face, and hesitate. "Should I leave my bags here?" she asks timidly.

"Up to you, sweetie. Go ahead and bring your things, if you like. But you won't need them for the test. You can collect them on your way out."

Mindy nods and leaves her bags lying under her desk. She walks through the classroom, then steps behind the partition with Mrs. Bayard.

For a few seconds there's silence. Then the whispering begins. The remaining teacher whose name I missed sits down in a chair right before the partition and watches us blandly, but does not shush us yet. She periodically checks the paperwork in her lap, then the clock on the wall.

"What's happening there?" a boy whispers behind me. "What if it's some kind of alien brain experiment thing where they take over your body and suck out your grey matter?"

A few nervous titters sound.

"They're not aliens, stupid, they're humans just like us, only from an ancient genetic branch—" says a girl's voice, also from the back.

"How do *you* know?"

The teacher up in the front looks up and says, "Quiet, please."

I sit and mostly stare ahead of me, running my fingers against the surface of my desk, sticky in places with old gum residue. And I throw occasional glances at Logan Sangre. He is leaning on one elbow and his posture is relaxed and casual, as if he's not nervous in the least. He turns his head occasionally, and his gorgeous face is almost sleepy looking, that's how calm he seems. His grey outer jacket is off, hanging from the back of his chair.

I examine his long black sports bag on the floor next to his backpack, and wonder what personal things are inside. One of his guitars? If my baby brother managed to stuff his skinny portable guitar in a duffel, I wouldn't be surprised if Logan did the same thing.

A couple of minutes later, a funny noise comes from beyond the partition. Everyone immediately stares and the classroom goes really, really quiet as we all strain to listen.

The weird noise comes again and it sounds like Mindy Clarence's voice. She is saying "Eeee" or maybe singing. Weird! "Eeeee, eeee-eeee-eee, eee-eee. . . ."

"What did I tell you?" the same boy hisses from the back. "They're sucking her dry!"

"Shut up!" someone else says in a genuinely frightened voice.

The silence in the classroom is overpowering. Even the teacher in the front frowns and turns her head, appearing to listen.

I watch and listen, transfixed. Even now I cannot help noticing the angular lines of Logan's profile as he partially turns around then looks forward again. Just for a moment, our eyes seem to meet. . . .

Mindy's voice stops. A few seconds later, Mindy Clarence emerges from the partition, looking ordinary, if somewhat troubled, and heads back toward her empty desk. She picks up her stuff, shoulders the backpack and heads out the classroom door without a glance.

The teacher up in the front marks down something on her paper, then calls out the next name.

The next student to go up is an unfamiliar guy, probably a senior, and probably from another school. He walks with a swagger, but you know it's all for show. He disappears behind the partition and again everyone's staring and the whispers are down to a minimum. About two minutes into his test, we hear the boy's voice. It cracks on a laugh at first, then he sings badly, "Eeeee-eeee, eee-eeee."

Someone in the back of the class snickers, and it starts a minor wave.

A few girls in the front turn around with affronted looks.

Soon the senior comes out, with a sheepish expression, then also goes for his bags and leaves the classroom.

The next name is called. This goes on for about forty minutes, maybe an hour, maybe more, like an eternity—I can't tell since the classroom clock is out of my line of sight—and by now the room is getting sparse, as people take the test and leave somewhere. The general classroom whispering resumes, but it keeps to regular levels. Except for a few stifled giggles, there's no unusual reaction whenever a student being tested sings "Eeee-eeee" in a particularly awful way.

I tense up when I hear the name "Logan Sangre" getting called. He gets up, tall and sleek, and calmly walks to the partition. Wow, I so envy him. If only I could bottle all that cool attitude and smear it all over me. . . .

A few minutes pass and I hear Logan's voice. It is confident and smooth, and has a nice velvety quality of a real practiced singer. It actually sounds *good*. I remember that Logan not only plays guitar but frequently sings vocals for his band, taking turns with the regular lead singer and his good bud, Josh Merrow.

If Logan doesn't ace Qualification, I don't know who can.

Soon Logan is done and I am gifted with the sight of him standing there for a moment as he emerges and looks around the classroom, then goes for his seat to grab his things. I watch him put on his grey windbreaker jacket, and sweep the black hair out of his eyes as he moves. He carries the large sports bag with ease, and for another moment I again wonder what's inside.

Logan's gone and the room suddenly loses all its leashed electricity, like an energy balloon deflating in my mind. I am suddenly bored, and the nervous worry surges back full force, to sweep me in its relentless ocean. I return to staring at the front of the classroom, and listen to some poor girl sing "Eeeee-eeee," terribly off-key.

In some ways this feels like the longest class period of my life.

At last, when the room is nearly empty, my name is called.

Chapter 3

My heart starts hammering as I walk behind the partition. Mrs. Bayard is sitting at a large table that appears to have all kinds of things and equipment on it. "Gwenevere Lark?" she confirms, glancing at a sheet.

"Yes."

"Take a seat please, right here, and try to relax. This will be very quick and painless, I promise. I will ask you to perform several brief tasks, some of which may seem a little odd or unusual. Just do them to the best of your ability."

"Okay. . . ." I head over to the empty chair across from her. My hands rest in my lap, and I feel them clamming up.

Mrs. Bayard places a blank sheet of paper on the table in front of me, and a pencil. "Please write your full name on top of the page, on the left."

I do as she asks, making a painful effort to print my name as clear and large as possible, since usually my handwriting is messy and kind of unreadable.

When I look up, Mrs. Bayard is holding up a white plastic object in her palm. I recognize it as some kind of geometrical 3-D shape.

"This is a regular dodecahedron," says the teacher, putting the object down on the table before me. "It's a polyhedron with twelve faces, each face being a pentagon. Basically, it's just a shape with five sides, rendered in three dimensions."

"Okay," I say. "Yes, I know."

"Good. Now, I want you to draw it."

"What?"

Mrs. Bayard sighs. I imagine she's had to deal with a similar reaction far too many times today.

"Simply think of it as art class. Just draw this item the best you can, a quick sketch."

"I am not a good artist—"

"It doesn't matter. Just do the best you can."

"Okay."

I glance at the dodecahedron, and feel a burst of panic. Drawing is just not my strength, although I don't suck at it completely. I try to imagine my brother Gordie in my place, and how he would smile and sketch a masterpiece in thirty seconds.

I try to channel Gordie as I draw a five-sided figure, then awkwardly try to add 3-D sides at various angles, and then some shading to it to make it fancy.

"That's fine now." Mrs. Bayard reaches forward and takes the paper away from me as I am still shading a side. In its place she slides a tablet computer before me.

"Now, I want you to look at some pictures on the touch screen. There are four images displayed at a time. Quickly choose one of these images that appeals to you most. Keep going until the program ends."

I see the screen is divided into four, and each quadrant shows a natural landscape in distinct colors. There's a turquoise-blue island beach scene, a green forest meadow, an orange sunset, and a rosy mist-covered mountain range. I pick the sunset, and the screen shuffles and displays a new set of four images. I pick a moonlit night. Another four pops up, I choose the shady forest. Then, I pick a red canyon.

This keeps going for at least a minute. Series of landscapes with different color schemes, sunset, night, green forest, blue sky, ocean, all come at me in a barrage. Finally the screen goes blank grey and it's done.

Mrs. Bayard removes the tablet and pushes a strange piece of equipment before me.

I stare at it, and suddenly I get the strongest feeling it is *not from Earth*.

I've never seen any Atlantean technology up-close in real life, only whatever occasional gadgets they show on TV. This gadget before me is definitely alien looking.

First of all, the thing is a shapeless lump. It's about ten inches wide and five inches tall, and perfectly seamless. It's all smooth, silvery rounded surfaces, and an incomprehensible irregular shape, somewhat like a naturally occurring water-smoothed rock with bumps and ridges and indentations.

In the middle there's a flat spot that appears somewhat translucent. As I stare closer, it's as if some kind of faint light source is hiding just underneath the surface of an iced-over frozen pond.

Mrs. Bayard watches tiredly as I try to make sense of this thing. "I am not sure what it is either," she says, "except it's some kind of audio recording equipment. It's a sound test."

As she speaks, I notice how the frosted light in the middle of the object pulses suddenly, coming alive like a heartbeat, responding in time to the words. The light pulses pale ghostly white, then subsides as Mrs. Bayard goes silent.

"Oh . . . what should I do?" I say.

The light immediately responds to my voice and fluctuates at my words.

"Touch it with your hand until you see the light flare up blue. That means it's ready for you. It will then play a series of very simple musical tones. You need to repeat each one of them exactly as played, and watch the color of the light. As you sing back the notes, be sure to use the vowel "E." If it's red, you are doing something wrong. If it turns green, then it's correct, and it will play the next one. Keep going until it stops and the light turns blue once again."

I nod, then reach for the silvery object with my finger.

The moment I touch it, it vibrates under my fingertips. The center of it flashes a bright circle of blue under the frosty surface. And then three very soft notes sound. I take a breath and sing back, "Eeee-eee-eeeee."

The object lights up reddish as my first note is a bit flat, and then it goes green as I improve. From there on it's easy. I sing the simple notes and think how the remaining students on the other side of the partition are probably snickering nervously at the stupid sounds I'm making.

"Eeee-eeee-eeeeee. Eeee-eeee-eeeee." Over and over, my voice is generally clean and steady, and I am green all the way.

Eventually the light goes blue. I am apparently done.

"Good," says Mrs. Bayard, removing the weird Atlantean

sound gadget out of the way. "Now, just one more thing for you to do, and you'll be done."

I watch as she fumbles around with some stuff on the table, and takes things out from silvery anti-static bags that crinkle as she rummages inside.

I am absolutely fascinated as she places four very unusual things on the table surface before me.

The first is a hunting knife. It is long, scary looking, with an eight-inch serrated blade and a wood-and-metal studded handle. The second item is a pen, thick-barreled, elegant and expensive looking, with a roller ball tip and a gold and pearl inlay. Next comes a weird, round flattened plate-like thing that has a handle grip on the interior, and is reinforced metal on the outside. It looks like a small old-fashioned shield that I recognize from history books as a medieval buckler. Last of all, the teacher places on the table a folded rectangle of paper that looks like some kind of map.

"Weird . . ." I mutter.

Mrs. Bayard nods sympathetically. "Yes, honey, I know. All right, this is the last part. I am supposed to ask you the following. *You are alone in a strange location. Choose one of these four objects.*"

I stare at the things before me.

"Um . . ." I say. "What kind of location?"

The teacher sighs. "They don't tell us. Just pick one, please."

"Okay. . . . Well, it really depends on what it's all about. This is very strange. I mean, if I knew I was lost in the wilderness or something, it would be one thing. But if I was stuck in a shopping mall elevator—" My attempt to be sarcastic is pretty much lost on the very tired teacher.

And so I take a big breath and try to think what this is really about. I remind myself that when it comes down to it, this really is life and death.

Qualify or die.

I consider the knife, the pen, the shield, and the map. I try to think as the Atlanteans might think—or as they might *want* me to think. Do I need to think Darwinian, survival of the fittest? Or altruism? Or what's honorable? Or—drat, okay I honestly have no frigging idea what they're looking for.

If it's cutthroat survivor instinct they want, I need to take the knife. I really, really *should* take the knife.

On the other hand, if everyone else decides it's a deadly jungle out there and arms themselves, I might be better off with a shield. Because honestly, I have no idea how to fight with a knife. At least with a shield I might keep myself intact, and save my hands from getting all cut up.

Now, if it's a civilized situation, I might be considerably better off with a pen. I could use it to keep records, to write down important things, to communicate. And if I am stuck alone on a desert island, I could even entertain myself.

But, what about the map? If I'm genuinely lost, then wouldn't a map be the most logical and useful thing to have with me? Not to mention, it's reading material.

I bite my lower lip, and pick the map.

The teacher nods and records my answer on her papers.

"That's it," she says. "You are all done with this portion of Qualification. You can take your things and proceed to the auditorium for the next part. If you're unfamiliar with the school, any teacher or security guard in the hallway can guide you."

I pick up my stuff and head for the auditorium. On my way out of the classroom I look up and finally find the wall clock, which shows 1:45 PM. Wow, so we don't get a lunch break after all. This is hardcore.

The hallways are not crowded but they are not empty either. Students are making their way up and down stairs, from room to room, and quite a few are headed my way.

I pass a few familiar people from my class, and finally make it to the auditorium. Inside, I am surprised to see it not set up for assembly, as I thought it might be. All the folding chairs are stacked away, and the large hall is filled with students from all grades, milling about, and it's pretty crowded already. The noise level is unusually subdued, and no one is really laughing. People are seated on the floor against the walls or on top of their bags like weird refugees, and there is plenty of whispering, but it's all hush-hush. A few people are secretly fiddling with micro electronics installed in discreet smart jewelry but the overt standard phones are mostly out of sight because the last thing anyone wants is to have their phone confiscated today of all days. No cell phone use on school premises is a hard rule, and absolutely no hashtagging, even though the wireless internet blocking filter is on in every classroom.

I look around and see a number of teachers, mostly circulating and watching the room, and some of them standing in clusters talking. Armed security guards are pacing quietly. Near the front of the stage, there are a few unfamiliar teachers and other administrators. I recognize Principal Marksen. He is talking to some people whose backs are turned. They are wearing four-color Atlantis armbands. One of them has distinctive golden-blond hair that glitters uncommonly bright under the overhead lights.

A real Atlantean.

My stomach lurches with fear. Again, everything hits home. This is real, this is happening.

Qualify or die.

As I pause for a moment, frozen with the cold incapacitating uncertainty, I hear my name being called.

"Gwen! This way!"

I turn to look, and it's my brother George. He's waving and I see Gracie is with him, looking nervous and wide-eyed. Gordie is there too, sitting hunched forward on the floor, surrounded with bags.

I head over to them. "How did you do? What did you think of it?" Gracie pounces all over me with stress questions.

"I don't know," I say. "Probably okay on the written stuff, but maybe not so well on the weird stuff. How did *you* do?"

"I don't know!" Gracie gesticulates with her hands in frustration.

"Yeah, that's the idea." George glances around the auditorium as he is speaking. He is probably looking for his friends. "No one knows anything."

"Wasn't the 'Eeee' test fun?"

"Oh yeah. That was amazingly stupid."

"Hey, what object did you pick?" Gordie looks up from the floor with a dorky half-smile. "I picked the pen. I wonder what that was about. It was kind of interesting."

"That was crazy!" Gracie stares suddenly intense and wild-eyed. "I picked the knife!"

George stops scanning the room and looks at her. "No way, Gee Four."

"That's badass!" Gordie snorts.

"Yes it is, and I am willing to use it."

"No, you're not." George raises one brow and smiles.

"You have no idea!"

For the first time, seeing the serious intensity in my sister, I can believe it. Something has happened to Gracie, because she is scaring me.

I tell them I chose the map, because it was kind of the reasonable thing to do.

"So much like you, Gee Two," George says casually. "If anyone's going to be reasonable, it's you—"

The bell rings, and suddenly the auditorium is full of extra noise that surges in waves. Someone in administration picks up and tests a microphone. "Please settle down and pay attention, everyone," a voice says. "We'll begin shortly, in about ten more minutes as we wait for more people to arrive. There are no chairs because we need you to clear the center of the auditorium. Soon we are going to be full to capacity. Everyone please move off to the sides and near the walls. You can sit on the floor, but only close to the walls. Also, please do not leave any bags unattended and lying underfoot—"

In the chaotic mess of people, we pick up our stuff and approach the walls. Some guy who is a friend of George's joins us, and then another, and together we all jostle, but George sticks with us. Usually during school, George would never be seen with the other "Gees." He'd go off to hang with his friends instead of his uncool younger siblings, but this is different. This is family protective instinct kicking in. Possibly it's the last time we might all be together in one room, and George understands this. So he stands next to us and keeps one eye on us, even as he chats and smirks and acts all senior-cool with his buddies, and talks trash about Qualification and the Atlanteans and the impending destruction of the Earth as if it's just last night's basketball game.

"It's almost two, and no lunch," someone says. "This really blows. How much longer is this going to be? I need a smoke."

"So, yeah, I'm bored." George turns around, glancing once at me and Gracie, then turns away again, speaking to his bud whose name I think is Eddie. I know for a fact he is not bored and freaking nervous, but there's no way he or his buddies would stop to admit it—that all of this is *terrifying*.

"Are they gonna feed us, ever? Someone order a pizza!" Eddie cracks, drumming his fingers like crazy against the strap of his backpack. "Maybe starvation is part of Qualification."

I try to ignore Eddie and watch my sister.

Gracie has a few girlfriends who are BFFs, but right this moment she does not bother to search the crowd for anyone. She just stands there dejectedly, even after I try to say something typical to make her crack a smile. Gordie the loner is happily oblivious as usual. And as for me, I momentarily give up on Gracie and look around the room to see if Ann Finnbar is anywhere, but don't see her. And then I automatically do the other *secret visual scan* that I always do at school mass gatherings, for a glimpse of Logan Sangre.

About five minutes later Principal Marksen gets up on stage. He's wearing a headset mike, and he looks frustrated and tough at the same time. The stage smart wall behind him remains off, so apparently it's all going to be live and we're not getting a thrilling instructional video.

"May I have your attention," he says and his voice booms through the packed auditorium. "Please move as far as you can to the right and left walls, and clear the center. I repeat, clear the center. And please form rows."

As the Principal is speaking, I see security guards and teachers start herding us closer to the walls, until there is a long narrow path of about twenty feet across, stretching from the stage to the back of the large auditorium space. We are pressed closely so it's standing room only, and those of us who are shorter have to stand up on tiptoe to see what's in front. Good thing I'm reasonably tall, and so is Gracie, and so are my brothers.

A few minutes later, gym mats are brought out, with the P. E. teachers and sports coaches directing. Several other teachers and administrators work together to unroll mats and place them in a long strip in the center of the cleared space, all the way from the beginning of the stage to the back of the auditorium.

"Oh, !@#$%!, it's gonna be a P. E. test," a boy whispers

behind me.

"We better not have to do forward rolls to Qualify for Atlantis, cause then I'm toast . . ." a girl's voice sounds.

"Hey, check this out—" I can hear one of George's friends speaking—"they can't even fit everyone in this auditorium. There are people spilling over into the hallway, and it looks packed there too, from what I can tell. Man, must be at least five schools packed in here. . . ."

"This is the final part of Qualification for today," the Principal says. "It determines whether you will get on a bus and be taken to the Regional Qualification Center in the next few hours—or, if you get to go home. Your tests that you took earlier today are being scored and analyzed right now, even as I speak, and the results should be ready by the time we are done here. The total scores will be combined and tallied, and you will be informed immediately after this final portion of preliminary Qualification. For those of you who will be told to go home, I am very deeply sorry. There are no words adequate to express how much I wish all of you could Qualify uniformly. The unfortunate reality is, less than one tenth of you gathered in this room will Qualify. And now, I will let the Atlantis representative Ligerat Faroi explain to you this last portion for today."

The Principal remains standing on the stage, and now a slim tall man in dark form-fitting clothing and with bright hair that is a shocking metallic yellow joins him. He looks gaunt and it's hard to tell how old he is because his features look somewhat peculiar. But it's hard to place a finger on it, what exactly is it about him that makes him weird.

And then it strikes me and Gracie at the same time. "The dude looks kind of Egyptian!" Gracie whispers loudly. "And I don't mean like some guy from Cairo, but from King Tut's tomb! He looks as if that bust of Nefertiti came to life, sort of chiseled and pretty and weirdly *plastic*. Maybe he needs a tall rounded helmet thing to cover his head like some kind of ancient pharaoh with, supposedly, an elongated skull—except he definitely doesn't have an elongated skull—"

I stare, and although she is being silly, Gracie is amazingly spot-on. The Atlantean looks to be a living version of someone from an Ancient Egyptian burial site. Even his skin is deeply bronzed, and his prominent eyebrows and eyes appear to be darkly outlined. Not sure if it's natural or makeup. Except for his metallic hair, which has to be dyed. Weird! None of the other few Atlanteans I've seen on TV make you think so strongly of old Egypt like this guy does. Maybe the others were made to look more "contemporary Earthlike" to appear on camera?

The Atlantean is holding some kind of long, flat object upright in one hand, resting it against the floor. It's hard to tell what it is from the distance, but it looks like a board of some sort. It is nearly as tall as he is, about two inches thick and perfectly flat.

"Good afternoon, everyone," the Atlantean says. He is speaking calmly and does not raise his crisp, smooth voice, yet it carries particularly well because of its precision. "I am pleased to be with you, and I want to see you succeed. This part of the Qualification process involves seeing how well you can handle and how familiar you can become with a very important tool of daily life which is extremely common in our society on Atlantis."

He easily moves the object forward, turning it on its vertical axis so that the true width of the board becomes apparent, about twelve inches across. It appears to be lightweight, made of matte, non-reflective material, charcoal grey. The top and bottom do not extend straight across into a cutoff like a rectangle but instead are curved smoothly, oval and tapered off, so there are no hard edges.

"This," Ligerat the Atlantean says, "might seem familiar to some of you, especially here in Vermont. Yes, it looks very much like your own snowboard."

Waves of interested whispers run through the auditorium.

"However, it is not the same thing. This is a *hoverboard.*"

The voices in the auditorium become louder, exploding into more waves of excited whispers.

Ligerat takes the board and suddenly lets it fall flat before him, at the same time as he says a hard verbal command: "Ready!"

The board falls forward, then immediately an amazing thing happens. Just before it hits the floor of the stage, it bounces up six inches from the surface of the floor.

And it stays there, sitting suspended in the air, without any support or power source, perfectly soundless.

It *levitates* in place.

The auditorium erupts in hoots and whistles and applause. For a moment, everyone has forgotten what is happening on this day, because this thing is just so unbelievable, so awesome!

My brother George forgets himself and cusses. Gracie laughs and exclaims, "Oh my God, how cool!" And Gordie just stares with a big grin and says, "Whoa!"

Everyone around us is chattering, while Ligerat stands motionless, letting us have our crazy reaction. Then Principal Marksen has to cut in with an "All right, everyone, quiet please!"

"The hoverboard has been programmed with simple commands in English." Ligerat takes a step with his left foot onto the board near the front of its nose. He pushes down to demonstrate. The board gives slightly under his weight, maybe a fluctuation of half an inch, but remains airborne and supports him. He steps on with his other foot, so that he is standing in a loose snowboarder or skateboarder balancing stance, legs slightly apart . . . and now he is suspended in the air.

"Notice, please, there are no bindings to hold my feet and shoes in place. I must stand lightly to keep my balance and be ready to jump off at a moment's notice. In that sense this is more like your Earth surfboard or skateboard than a snowboard. Now, I will use a few simple commands. To make it move forward, simply say 'Go!'"

As soon as the word is spoken, the hoverboard begins to float forward, still soundless, and very slow, at about the speed of a person walking. As the auditorium watches in transfixed fascination, the board floats past the edge of the stage, and suddenly it is eight feet over the auditorium main floor. The Atlantean is sailing gently and effortlessly like a cloud over the gym-mat-lined empty strip that had been cleared of all people. Students in rows stare up at the board's underside as it passes them smoothly.

"Descend!" says Ligerat. And the board starts to come down at a very gradual slope incline of descent. All the while it remains perfectly horizontal and is still continuing to advance forward, until he is only five feet, then three, then just a foot above the mat-lined floor. "Level!" And the board tapers off at about six inches from the surface of the mat and continues moving forward until it passes the last mat and reaches the bare linoleum floor tiles.

All this time, the board has moved along the entire length of the auditorium. Just before it approaches the rear doors, Ligerat says, "Stop!"

The board freezes and levitates in place.

Everyone claps and hoots loudly.

Ligerat raises one hand for silence and then says with precision and in staccato, "Reverse, Rise, Return!"

The board does a smooth 180, and he is turned around. He is once more rising in the air and moving back toward the auditorium stage. Seconds later, the board is back in its starting position six inches above the stage floor. The Atlantean hops off lightly and stands next to the Principal.

"Now," he says. "This is your last portion of Preliminary Qualification for today. Each one of you will come up here on the stage, next to Principal Marksen. He will hand you a token pin with your name and other test scores flash-encoded. The token is your new identification. You must keep the token with you, attach it anywhere on your person, such as your clothing, and do not drop or lose it.

"Next, you will step on the board and simply ride it across the length of this room, using the four simple commands—'Go,' 'Descend,' 'Level' and 'Stop.' When you reach the end of the room, step off and direct the board to perform the 'Reverse, Rise, Return' sequence, without you. It will return here on its own and wait for the next person. Meanwhile you will come up to me, as I will be standing at the desk in the back near the exit, evaluating your performance. I will scan your ID token with the final score. At this point you will take the token with you, pick up your bags, and exit the auditorium.

"Once you are outside this room, you are permitted to find out your final Preliminary Qualification score. Simply place your fingers on the token pin and say "Display Test Score." The token will turn one of two colors. *Green* means you have passed Preliminary Qualification and are advancing to the next stage of the process. *Red* means you have not passed, and you are returning home. Note—we ask you to please respect your fellow classmates and *not* attempt to learn your score while still inside this auditorium. You may activate your score only after you exit into the hallway. If you are green, please proceed outside to any of the designated buses in the parking lot, and board, first come, first served. Do not hesitate, and do not be late, otherwise you will miss the bus and your opportunity to Qualify. Final note—if anyone else *other* than yourself handles *your* token and attempts to activate or display *your* score, the token will turn yellow. Do not attempt to cheat this process, it will not work."

Ligerat pauses, and observes the turbulent auditorium. "And now, please proceed." He nods to Principal Marksen to begin. While several administrators carry a series of large plastic containers up the stage stairs, the Principal calls us to order once again.

I watch the Atlantean descend the stage and walk toward the back of the auditorium, moving through the empty strip in the center, along the edge of the mats, past all the rows of students staring at him from both sides.

"All right, everyone, line up in rows! Start moving, please, use both sides of the stage, and wait your turn."

Next to me, Gracie is whimpering.

I turn to stare into her tear-streaked face. "What, Gracie?"

"I can't!" She wipes her nose, and she is terrified. "I can't do it! You know I don't know how to balance or ride any snowboard thing or anything, and especially not like this! You know I'm afraid of heights! At least you used to ride that little plastic skateboard back in California—"

I feel my breath catching in my throat and I am very, very cold . . . I am numb. Both for Gracie's sake and for myself. Yes, I used to ride a little kiddie skateboard, *badly*. Back when I was ten. And these days I am the last person people pick for team sports. Klutz has become a part of my daily persona, together with bad stooping posture, hunched shoulders and general physical awkwardness.

Furthermore, I am out of shape. I get winded when I try to run around the track, even after just fifty paces. And I am terrified of heights, probably even more so than Gracie.

"Are you guys okay?" George has put his hands on both our shoulders.

"I don't know." I look at my brother. "What are we going to

do?"

"Remember what Dad said? We're going to try, do the best we can, and never ever give up."

"Huh!" I say. "So you were paying attention."

"Naturally."

"But I just can't do it!" Gracie clutches her hands together and wipes them against her jeans. I take her hand with my own shaking clammy one, and press it really hard.

As we are shuffled into some semblance of a line, and start moving, Gordie kicks his bags along the floor. "I've never ridden any board either," he says. "Never really wanted to. But this is totally different. This is intense! It's like flying! I want to do it."

I glance at him, and Gordie has a blissful grin on his face.

"Please try to keep in a straight line," says a teacher, passing our row.

"What—what if I fall?" Gracie whispers, pulling my hand. "From that height? I have no balance!"

To be honest, I am pretty terrified right now myself, so I have very little with which to respond. "Okay . . . they do have mats. So even if you fall, it shouldn't be so bad."

"Just stay on the board," George says evenly to everyone in general, glancing from us to his buddy before him. "No one says we have to look pretty doing it. Just hold on somehow, and stay on the damn board."

"Good point," Gordie says. "For that matter, do we even have to stand up straight? I bet you can just crouch down and hold on to it with both hands, all the way!"

"But—" Gracie turns to him, "don't you think that will mean some points taken off or something? They will probably reduce your score for bad form and posture!"

"Says who?" I press her hand again, with sudden relief. "That's a great idea! It's definitely better than not trying at all, and way better than falling off because you try too hard to balance like you're a snowboarding pow pro, 'tearing it up' and 'shredding the gnar.'"

Gracie finds enough energy to roll her eyes at me.

While we are saying all this stuff to keep the nerves down, people up in the front of the line are already up on stage. The Principal asks their name, grade level, school of origin. An assistant teacher reaches in a box to pick up a blank token, which is basically a round colorless plastic button with a chip, and it gets scanned with a special encoder machine to transfer the student ID and test score data. Then the girl student—an unfamiliar middle school seventh grader—gets the button.

This girl is up first, and she looks just as terrified as Gracie. Her hands are shaking as she attaches the token button to her shirt. She then stands there and stares down at the hoverboard. She takes a deep breath and puts her foot up on the surface of the board. The board wobbles, and immediately the girl gives a small shriek.

"Steady, honey, you're doing fine," a sympathetic woman teacher says. "Just put your other foot up there and relax, take a few breaths, and don't look down."

The girl takes a few seconds, then puts her other foot on the board and balances with both hands. "Go!" she says in a thin raspy voice that carries all the way across the very silent auditorium.

The hoverboard begins to float forward. The girl squeezes her eyes, utters another shriek, then a few stifled noises, and then fixes herself in the posture stiffly. She is floating eight feet over the floor mats, her hands balancing outward like airplane wings, but she manages to remain standing. "Descend!" Again, her tiny voice sounds. The board obeys and begins the incline.

The girl suddenly wobbles and exclaims, "Stop!" The board freezes in the air, in the middle of its gradual descent. She is suspended halfway between the floor and the stage, flailing her hands wildly. And in the absolute silence she begins to cry.

The auditorium is silent as the grave. I stare with transfixed sympathy, and see the equally emotional faces of those around me—students, teachers, security guards, everyone.

A few seconds later the girl steadies herself somehow, stops the sniffles and with another determined breath says, "Go!" The board resumes moving, and this time she says "Descend!" in a more steady voice.

When almost on the mats, she says, "Level!" and continues floating silently to the end of the line. "Stop!" She steps off and stands in one spot, dazed. She looks around. "Um, what do I say now?"

"Reverse, Rise, Return . . ." someone whispers.

"Reverse, Rise, Return!" the seventh grader repeats in a voice of relief. The hoverboard rises and floats away while the girl heads to the back desk toward Ligerat Faroi. The Atlantean nods at her and scans her token, as everyone watches.

Oh, to be her at this point! I think with envy. *To just be done with it!*

"See, that wasn't so bad," George whispers to Gracie. "Look at her, she's a bigger wimp than you. . . . You can do it!"

Meanwhile the next kid is already up in the front of the stage, his ID token scanned. The moment the board arrives, he hops on with a practiced snowboarder stance and with a grin makes a shaka hand sign, then says, "Go!" In moments he sails past the stage, descends smoothly, levels off, and then jumps off at the stop. As the board returns, the kid stares after it with admiration and says, "That was sick! I want that board." He is then ID-scanned at the desk in the back.

"Okay, this is looking more and more like it's gonna take forever," mumbles Gordie.

Suddenly everyone is itching to advance, to get it over with. We move forward a few steps and wait, and watch teens of all ages and from all the schools get onto the board. Some are terrified, others absolutely loving it. Most are more or less in-between, cautious, but grimly determined, since after all, it's *Qualify or die.*

It gets sad however, a few times. A few of the younger kids, both girls and boys, and even a few of the older ones, balk completely as they stand next to the board. Two end up bawling, and just shake their heads negatively and refuse to get up on the hoverboard, even after a teacher comes to hug them and takes them off to the back of the stage to try to speak to them quietly. One girl is unable to put her second foot up. She just stands there, and then a teacher says, "why don't you take a few minutes, try again later?"

And the next name gets called.

I watch the whole thing, as I slowly inch closer to my turn. Gracie is very quiet and subdued, and she keeps grabbing my hand, then letting go.

"Oh man! Oh no! Look!" George's bud Eddie says, and we all stare as Archer Richards, an older boy from our school, my year, suddenly slips and ends up hanging off the board with both hands. . . .

Just wow.

Archer is hanging by his hands then arms, hugging the board, and he cries out, "Stop!" The board freezes eight feet up in the air, just a few feet away from the stage. All Archer needs to do is just let go and he'll be standing on the mat. It's only a few inches to the floor from where he is hanging.

But somehow Archer Richards knows. If he lets go now, he fails the stupid hoverboard test.

And so everyone holds their breath and watches as Archer grunts and switches his grip with both hands, and then suddenly he pulls himself up and lies on his stomach on top of the board.

There are whispers of relief.

Archer lies there for a few seconds. He's a short, stocky guy with powerful arms that look like he works out regularly, and obviously it has helped. He then carefully stands up and resumes the movement of the board, finishing his pass without further mishap. When he gets off, everyone claps and hoots. And apparently the Atlantean in the back has noticed too, and looks well pleased as he scans Archer's token.

"I bet that guy just Qualified," says Gordie, as we take another few steps closer to the stage.

And then, a few minutes later, just as it looks like it can't get any more heartbreaking, I look up on stage and there's a kid in a wheelchair.

Chapter 4

"Oh, no, just *no!*" Gracie mutters, staring with great big eyes at the student in the wheelchair, who has been somehow lifted up onto the stage. It's a dark-haired boy I've never seen before, probably from another school, and he looks frail.

"Poor guy. . . ." George frowns. "This must really blow for him."

"It's really unfair." I stare, while a weird numbing sense fills me. Regret or pity, or I don't know what. Maybe this is what resigned despair feels like. Whatever it is, it makes my gut cold.

The auditorium has once again grown really quiet.

Principal Marksen stands looking at the disabled boy, and for the first time his tough face has cracked and he looks really uncomfortable.

A woman teacher comes up to the wheelchair, leans forward gently and speaks something to the boy. After a pause the boy nods. The teacher then reaches into the box and hands a blank token to the Principal who frowns, then encodes the ID data.

The Principal leans down and hands the token to the boy.

The kid looks up, and I watch his skinny neck move, and the tightening of his lips. He takes the button and pins it to the front of his sweatshirt.

The teacher then pushes the wheelchair closer to the hoverboard.

I hold my breath as the boy lifts himself off the wheelchair with his hands and arms, and then drags himself along the floor. Then he pulls himself up with unexpected strength, lifting his body onto the hoverboard, lies there on his stomach for a few seconds, then manually pulls up his legs, adjusting them to lie along the length of the board.

"Wow! No way!" Gordie opens his mouth.

Everyone else is making noise too.

"Go!" says the kid without the use of his legs. His voice is calm, he is holding on with both hands, while lying on his stomach, and the board sails forward over the stage. He soon moves into a smooth descent and finishes at the end of the run with a confident "Stop!"

Here, he lifts himself onto the linoleum near the edge of the mat, and ends in a sitting position on the floor. He commands the board to return.

As the board is flying back, the teacher who had assisted him on the stage has picked up the wheelchair and is hurrying it down the stairs with the help of someone, and then pushing it through the auditorium in a hurry.

As the kid waits for the chair to be brought to him, the Atlantean in the back leaves his desk and approaches the student. Ligerat stops before the seated boy and shakes his hand. He then scans his token and for the first time there is a smile on his weirdly Egyptian face.

The auditorium erupts in applause, and it's pretty much a standing ovation. A few of the teachers and even the students are wiping their eyes.

"Wow! That was sick! Amazing! Man, that kid, what he did—just wow!"

George turns to look at Gracie. "Now you have no excuse whatsoever, Gee Four. If that poor kid in a wheelchair can do it, so can you! That was awesome!"

But Gracie does not need to be convinced. She is holding her head up and she is suddenly calm. "I know," she says. "I *can* do it."

"Exactly," I say. "We can all do this thing."

And just for a moment I believe it. *Thanks, kid in a wheelchair. I might not have done it without you.*

As I think it, I'm not even kidding.

About forty minutes later, we make it to the front of the stage, at long last. Holy moly. That's what Dad says when things are weird, and now I repeat it in my head, like a calming mantra. "Holy moly." We leave our bags below in a pile, right near the corner where the stage stairs are, as all the other students have been doing before going up. We'll come back for them after this is over.

So far, we've seen it all. The good, the bad, and the seriously pitiful. My friend Ann Finnbar up there, standing up awkwardly but okay, as she manages to ride the board without any problem. A whole bunch of my classmates winging it, one way or another. The popular in-crowd bullies Mark and Chris and Jenny mostly doing well and staying on. But no sign of Logan Sangre—I'm guessing he's still in line somewhere behind us. And then there are students of all ages freaking out over the hoverboard, and a few even manage to fall off the board onto the mat below. No one gets hurt, thank goodness.

And now, here we are.

Eddie is right before George, and he takes his turn in a mediocre way. He stays up, and that's pretty much what counts.

When the board returns, George, who is getting his ID token scanned by Principal Marksen, is up next. He turns to look at us as we stand near the front, waiting, and he smiles and winks.

George then gets up on the hoverboard and rides it, balancing decently considering he's never ridden any kind of board before in his life, and flailing his hands only once in the middle of the auditorium. He makes it to the end safely, and I let myself breathe in relief.

Gordie is next. Okay, my younger brother is just nuts. I watch him put on the token pin, then smile and step on the board, testing its give with his foot with a kind of dazed loony pleasure. He mutters something unintelligible, then puts his other foot up and balances. He says, "Go!" and as the board moves, lets out a woot of excitement, while I put my hand to my mouth and Gracie lets her jaw drop.

We watch Gordie sail all the way across the auditorium, and make it safely and amazingly to the end. He jumps off, and turns to wave at us from a distance, as though he's just taken an amusement park ride.

"That boy is crazy," I say with a smile. "Eh, Gracie? Our little bro is nuts!"

But now the board has returned, and Gracie turns to me and suddenly she is serious and wide-eyed again.

"You can do it, easy!" I squeeze her hand, and nod at her. My lips are mouthing "wheelchair kid" and I watch her nod at me. Then my sister steps to the front of the stage.

I ball up my hands and hold my breath again, as Gracie gets her token.

She pauses next to the hoverboard. From where I'm standing I can only see her back and her long dirty-blond hair, and can just imagine her face. . . .

She places one foot on the board, testing it. Then she brings up the other foot, and she is balancing. Arms are flailing. She steps off, losing her balance.

Oh damn.

Gracie tries again. She steps onto the board and again, flails. Seconds tick. Everyone is watching her.

And then Gracie slowly gets down in a crouch, and places one leg flat down on the charcoal grey hoverboard surface. Then she puts her other leg, knee first. She reaches with both hands and grips the board along the edges on both sides.

She freezes in this position, her long hair spilling over her face and her back. I hear her trembling voice say, "Go!"

And the board begins to carry my sister, on her hands and knees, through the air across the auditorium.

I blink, and I am still not breathing, as I hear her give the other commands.

Then, Gracie reaches the end. She gets off the hoverboard, pretty much tumbling onto the linoleum floor. And she just remains there for a few seconds before going to the desk in the back.

Meanwhile, the board is returning, and so is my breath that I can finally exhale and inhale normally.

Except . . . the board is now here, for *me*.

Did it just get brighter in here? I feel like a stage spotlight is shining on me from overhead, and suddenly I am lightheaded.

Everyone in the world is looking at me.

I walk up to Principal Marksen and he gives me my token. I pin it onto my purple sweater front with icy cold fingers, since I had taken my outer jacket off and it's lying on top of my bags somewhere below stage.

Why am I thinking about my jacket?

The hoverboard is before me. I take a deep breath and let it out. I then put my right foot on the front of the board, trying to remember the feel of the little orange skateboard I rode as a kid. This one feels more resilient, kind of like stepping onto a water surface.

This hoverboard is also so much wider than a kiddie skateboard. It's pretty comfortable actually. I bring up my left foot in the back, and stand, *levitating*. The rubber soles of my sneakers cling to the surface of the board. And it occurs to me for a moment that I ride "goofy," or what the boarders refer to as using my right foot to lead in the front instead of my left which is "regular" or "standard." Yeah, I'm goofy, all right.

Now the worst part remains. The part that has me eight feet above the ground and in the air. I am terrified of heights. I can easily balance this board, but I just don't see myself staying up on it *mentally*, simply because of the height factor. It's going to mess with me too much, the fear of heights. . . .

I think of the amazing kid in the wheelchair.

And then I do a "Gracie." Sort of. I get down in a crouch and hold the board on both sides with my hands. My fingers grip the cool surface of the hoverboard and I will myself to just hold on for dear life and *not let go* and *not look down*.

The worst part will come once I am high above the floor, so I resolve to look directly ahead as much as possible. I'd probably prefer to squeeze my eyes shut, but I need to see where I'm going.

"Go!" My voice sounds weird in the silence of the auditorium.

The board underneath me begins to move forward.

I focus on looking at it mostly, at my fingers gripping the sides, at the curving oval nose of the board. I also let my eyes spot the back doors, far ahead. There is no sound as I advance past the edge of the stage, and suddenly my brain is telling me I'm falling off a cliff, the edge of the world—screw you, brain—and I am now *high up*. Out of my peripheral vision, I see student faces staring at me from both sides of the aisle.

Don't look down.

When I am a third of the distance across the auditorium, I make myself speak the next command. "Descend!"

And then for an instant I feel the floor drop out from under me . . . but it's only a tiny lurch, kind of what an elevator makes. Which I usually hate.

The ride itself is smooth and mind-blowing, and as I am descending gradually and approaching the gym mat surface, my fear of heights is also falling away. For the first time I can truly appreciate the amazing *alien* thing I am riding, this hoverboard. But the feeling lasts only a few seconds.

"Level!" I say before I hit the mat.

Again, a tiny lurch, and the board is moving once more in a line horizontal to the floor. Then the end of the mat looms. I pass over and beyond it, a few extra inches for good measure, then say, "Stop!"

The board freezes.

Slowly my fingers let go their white-knuckled grip. I stand up, and step off the hoverboard.

I did it.

Relief hits me full blast. I am lightheaded and suddenly kind of hungry, as I walk to the back and approach the Atlantean at the desk.

Up-close, he is tall, young-old in a sense that I cannot be sure what age he really is. I am again fascinated by the unreality of his chiseled features, Ancient Egypt come to life. I glance at his sculpted eyebrows and wonder if they are real painted hairs or lapis lazuli inlay. . . . His eyes are black, irises and pupils appearing to run together. And, I swear, he has to be wearing kohl eyeliner.

"Your name?" Ligerat picks up a small hand-held device and looks at me.

"Gwenevere Lark."

He passes the gadget over the ID token pinned to my sweater.

"Thank you," I say as I meet his very dark eyes.

"Good luck," he replies gently.

And that's it.

Somehow I manage to collect my backpack and duffel, then get out of the auditorium into the hallway. I attempt to look around past other jostling students to see where my brothers and sister are. The hallway is jammed with people, and there is a lot of emotional talk.

Some people are still standing in line to do the hoverboard test. Others are done like me, trying to get out. People are sitting on the floor with their feet sticking out, among bags. Some girls and guys are hugging each other, their friends, even just strangers, people they barely know or don't know at all, people from other schools—and they are all crying.

I stare, and see a whole lot of tokens on people's chests already lit up. And they are mostly shining *red*.

Oh no. . . . Well, it's not exactly surprising. They did tell us that very few people would pass even this preliminary stage of Qualification.

Fear returns, gripping me in its cold abyss like an ocean wave pressing from all sides. . . . I look down at my own inactive token and feel sick to my stomach. Should I activate it? But no, I think I'll wait to find out my stupid fate once I see a familiar face at least.

I walk a few steps and there's Ann Finnbar. Her expression is heartbreaking. My best friend is red-eyed, and so is her token, flaming merciless red. I remember seeing Ann up there on that hoverboard half an hour ago, and she looked like she was doing so much better than me. At least she had been standing up.

"Ann!" I say, and then I am hugging her, feeling her skinny shaking form in my arms. We stand there, holding each other, and I say over and over, "Crap, crap, crap, I am so sorry!"

We break apart, and she glances at my own dead token.

"I am going to wait and do it with my sister and brothers there." I feel guilty and rotten and I don't even know why. "I'm sure mine will be red too, I just don't want to find out just yet. Not until I see Gracie at least."

"I get it," she says. "Okay, I'm going home now. My parents are probably worried, or whatever. Yeah, they're not going to be too surprised to see me. At least I can give my Grandpa back his wooden carvings and my Mom gets her necklace back. Yeah, whatever. Anyway, you go on. . . ."

"Look, I'll definitely see you later!" I purse my lips. "When we get home—"

"Oh, stop it." Ann looks at me with an intense expression. "You are probably green." And then she pats me on the shoulder and turns away.

Several minutes later I run into my siblings. "George!" I cry, seeing the back of my brother's head in the crowd.

"There you are!" George looks grim as he waves to me, and Gracie and Gordie are right behind him. It's like a family funeral.

I notice that all their tokens are not lit up yet. So, they waited for me. GMTA. "Gee" minds think alike.

"You waited." I look at Gracie's pained face.

"Yeah," Gordie says, pulling out his earbuds. "We're gonna do it together. Right, Gee One?"

"Larks gotta stick together," George says.

"All right." I look at each one of them, and feel my breath stilling. "Let's do it."

"Ready?" George looks at Gracie. She nods.

We all put our fingers on the tokens. And we speak pretty much in unison. "Display Test Score."

As we speak, Gracie squeezes her eyes shut. I am watching her token, not mine, and I am the first to see Gracie's token turn a blessed *green.*

At the same time, I see my own light up, and it is green also. . . .

George's is green.

Gordie's is green.

Wow.

Holy amazing wow!

Gordie looks down at his chest and says, "Whoa . . ." He's somewhat stunned. He really honestly didn't think he was going to pass even the first stage of Qualification.

"Open your eyes, Gracie!" I exclaim. "You're green! You made it! We all did!"

George makes a stifled sound that resembles a woot, but he's just too cool to exclaim. Instead, grinning for the first time in days, he pounds Gordie on the back.

Gracie opens her eyes and squeals, and then she's hanging around my neck.

"We need to call Mom!" I say, smiling, while we're all still basking in waves of unbelievable relief. Other people in the hall are staring at us, some with open hostility.

"All right, but let's first get out of here." George shoulders the strap of his backpack and duffel. "We need to hurry and get outside."

"Yeah, we don't want to miss the *bus!*" Gracie whispers loudly, while I shove her in the arm.

"Hush! Let's not be rude to other people, okay, let's just go, Gracie." I push strands of her hair behind her ears, and she jokingly wiggles away. Then I rearrange my backpack and duffel straps.

"Oh, and keep your jackets over the tokens, at least for now." George is ever the careful one. He knows that some people are not going to react well to seeing anyone be green right now.

"Gotta stop by the bathroom first," Gordie says. And we do.

Then we start walking and finally exit the building.

Outside the air is cold, the wind biting, and it's early twilight. Have we been cooped up in school all day long? This is just nuts. No lunch, and now no dinner—we haven't eaten.

As if reading my mind, Gordie says, "I'm starving."

"We all are. Doesn't matter. Let's go!"

In the parking lot several school buses wait for us, and they are filling up with students. They—we—are the lucky ones.

Several teachers and security guards stand in clusters, directing us to form another line, this one much shorter, as we board the buses.

"Your tokens, please! Make sure that we can see them," a teacher says. She glances at each person, verifying the green color of their ID token.

In the gathering twilight, it occurs to me that, as we stand there in this new snaking line, that we all wink with green dots of light, as our tokens illuminate the evening.

Like weird green fireflies. . . .

The parking lot lights come on, flaring bright and fluorescent. Then the football field lights up. It has to be past 7:00 PM.

Finally we get on the third bus, just as it's getting cold and true dark, and we stow away our bags under seats and under our feet. Gracie takes the window seat, and I end up in the aisle one next to her, while George and Gordie get the next bench in front of us, with George at the window. The bus seats are narrow and not particularly comfortable, so good thing we are all slim and don't take up much room, though the guys' longer legs are sticking out into the aisles. I notice a few of the larger kids are much less happy to be squeezed in the hard seats. As I look around I see hardly anyone from my class or even from our school on this bus.

Our driver is a big thickset man in a union standard uniform and cap, but he's wearing the Atlantis four-color armband. "Congratulations, you're all Preliminary Qualified. Now, please keep the middle walkway clear. All your things should be out of the way, so that nobody trips, okay," he tells us in a thick tired voice. "This is going to be a rather long drive, at least four, maybe five hours or even more—"

Groans are heard throughout our bus.

"Yeah, I know, I'm sorry," he says. "We'll have several short bathroom breaks at a convenience store, and you can probably grab something to eat then. First break coming up in about an hour. I know it's late, and you're all hungry and tired, and I am sorry about this, but we have an end-of-the-world schedule to keep—literally."

The driver chuckles ruefully, in a weak attempt at a morbid joke, and no one reacts. "You can sleep if you like, but the seats don't adjust, sorry again. Also, try to keep the phone and electronic device use to a minimum, okay? Keep it quiet. If I hear you hashtagging or bothering others, I confiscate it."

More groans.

"Can we get some water at least? Really dehydrated here," a girl near the front says.

"Sorry, dear, you should've had some before you got on the bus. So you'll need to wait till the first bathroom break."

"Man, this just blows!"

"Unbelievable!"

The driver ignores us, as he is starting the bus engine, and the doors whoosh shut.

"Where are we going anyway? Where's this Regional Qualification Center?" a boy asks, as we start to pull out, past the football field, and the rows of trees, in the wake of another bus directly ahead of us.

The driver makes a funny sound. "Pennsylvania!"

Chapter 5

As soon as we're on the road, I pull out my tiny pocket phone and call Mom, holding my hand over my mouth to speak as quietly as possible and not disturb the others on the bus or provoke the ferocious gadget-confiscating wrath of the driver.

"Good news! We all Preliminary-Qualified! All four of us!" I say, the moment I hear her voice. It's important I say it first and up-front, because I know Mom's been going insane all these daylight hours that we were taking the tests. And Dad too, though he's off at the University today, so at least he didn't have to think about us non-stop, only between his lectures.

"Oh, honey! Oh, thank God! Oh, what a blessing!" Mom's warm exhale of relief is a joy to hear. Her voice is exultant but weak, and she is speaking with effort, so I know she's had a pain episode today—not surprising, considering she forced herself to get out of bed for us, to cook our so-called "last breakfast" at home.

"We're all on the bus now, headed to the Regional Qualification Center. In Pennsylvania," I add.

Gracie pulls the phone away from me. "Mom, we made it! Yes, love you too! Nope, no lunch, so we're starving, but it's okay! Here, will let you speak to George and Gordie too—"

The phone gets passed around the Lark siblings. We whisper and chortle, tell Mom about the hoverboard test, the "eeee" nonsense, the interesting stuff of the day. Then it's Dad's turn.

I notice we're not alone in this. Everyone on the bus is calling family and friends. The first hour is full of good news being passed on to loved ones at a time when there is so little good news left.

And then we start spacing out. Some people fall sleep. A few turn on their tablet computers, or enable their smart jewelry. A few water bottles get passed around.

It's a dark and boring drive to Pennsylvania.

I doze through the endless bus ride, coming alive during the bathroom breaks. We don't have much money on us, but enough to buy a few bags of chips and candy bars, and some bottled water and juice, which we consume hungrily in the dark.

We've left Vermont a while ago. It's late, and the buses and occasional delivery trucks and semis are the only things on the road. At some point it starts to rain lightly, a cold mixture of sleet and drizzle. The road is poorly lit and the countryside is all unrelieved darkness on both sides as we move south through Upstate New York, passing through occasional urban centers.

Gracie has fallen asleep against the window. As I stare past Gracie through the glass, I notice that there are more buses now, merging onto the highway from other roads all along the route, so I know it's not just from our school district. In fact, we appear to be a many-mile-long bus cavalcade, a "snake" made of bus segments, that just keeps growing.

All of us, going to this Regional Qualification Center in PA. Or maybe some are going to some other RQC. Who knows? I try to remember and I cannot seem to recall how many RQCs there are in total, all across the country. Did they even tell us when they were building them? And even if they did mention it at some point, with all the eerie horrible things happening, who really paid attention?

It's after 2:00 AM when our bus crosses the New York state line into Pennsylvania. Then it turns east, heading lord knows where in the dark.

And then, another forty minutes later, we arrive at the gates of some kind of impossibly huge gated compound that resembles a military base. It is lit up like a holiday tree, even from a mile away, and we can see the guard towers and the barbed wire fence, and lots of concrete walls. Somewhere in the distance are the looming black shadows of the Appalachian Mountains.

The buses start pulling up to the gates one by one, and we again end up waiting in line, like planes stuck on a runway.

When it's our turn, we pass the checkpoint and the driver is directed by security guards to turn right past the gates then park in the great parking lot that's filling up with school buses and other types of buses. I have never in my life seen so many frigging buses in one place, not even at a bus depot. Seems like the whole world has converged here. . . .

"Everyone, make sure you have your ID tokens ready," the driver tells us. "Don't forget to take all your bags, jackets, bottles, trash, and any other items when you exit the bus. Go directly to the large building to your left with the square Atlantis logo on the front. You will be given instructions from there on. Just follow the others. Good luck, now!"

"Are we there yet?" Gordie turns to us and stifles a crocodile yawn.

"Yeah, we're there, Gee Three, wherever 'there' is." George is lifting his bags from under the seat.

Gracie is still tangled up in her jacket which she'd been using as a blanket.

Other boys and girls around us are blinking sleepily and nervously, picking up their things, and everyone's got the stressed look again.

We get off the bus and cold night air hits us with a blast.

"Oh lord, I am sooooo tired . . ." Gracie mumbles. "I just want to collapse and sleep."

"Me too." I huddle in my own jacket and shoulder my bags. We start walking, and it's one big crowd of teenagers.

Moments later we're at the doors of the building with the square Atlantis logo. Each corner of the square is tinted one of the four "psychological" primary colors in a fading gradation toward the center, until they blend in the middle into white. Red, green, blue, yellow—these are called "psychological primary" as opposed to the real primaries, which are red, green, and blue—something I remember from science class.

Another line is waiting for us. A row of four desks is set up at each side of the double doors. Officials in charcoal grey uniforms with armbands are manning each desk. Each person approaches, gives their token, gets scanned, gets instructions.

A friendly looking woman administrator, also wearing the grey uniform, paces the line and smiles at us gently. "Tokens ready, please!" she says. "You're about to be assigned your permanent dormitories and Color Quadrant assignments."

"Our color *whats?*" a tall lanky boy asks with a frown.

But the woman has already passed down the line.

The line moves surprisingly fast, and soon I'm at one of the four desks, and my siblings at the three others, just ahead of me.

"Name, please," says the official, holding a tablet and a scanning device.

"Gwenevere Lark." I pull open the jacket to reveal my sweater and he passes the scanner over my token pin.

The token has been lit up green all this time, and suddenly it turns bright yellow.

"Oh no," I say. "Sorry. . . . Did I do that? Did something happen? Should I be touching it? Did you touch it by accident and make it go yellow—"

The official looks up at me and he is stone-faced. "No," he says in a curt voice. "Everything's correct. You have been assigned to the Yellow Quadrant. From now on your token will stay yellow throughout the rest of Qualification."

"Oh. . . ."

He looks down again and checks the tablet. "Gwenevere Lark, Yellow Quadrant, Dormitory Eight. Please proceed inside, and look for any Dorm Leader holding a yellow placard with your number on it. They will take you to your Dorm."

I open my mouth, but the man has already turned to the next teen in line, a kid who looks like he is ready to fall into bed.

I turn away and walk inside, seeing Gracie up ahead through the open doors. The hallway is wide, sterile looking, and brightly lit, and there's George and Gordie and my sister, waiting for me, looking a bit perplexed. While other teens are bumping past them, I look at my siblings, and see the problem.

Each one of us has a token that now shows a different color. Gordie is blue. Gracie is red. George is the only one whose token is still green. They are all staring at my own yellow.

"Well, this is just great." Gracie flips strands of hair from her eyes in resignation. "Whatever this color coordinated stupid stuff is, now we can't even stay in the same Dorm! I'm in Dorm Five."

"They frigging separated us," Gordie says. "I'm in Two."

"Dorm Eleven here," George says.

"I'm in Eight," I say. "This kind of sucks."

Gracie looks at me sadly, but exhaustion wins over. "Hug time, then we probably should go find our beds," she mutters and wraps her arms around me. I squeeze her briefly and pat her backpack, since I can't reach her actual back.

"Good deal." George nods. "Lets go find a sack to hit and then tomorrow, whatever, we'll deal with it. It's been—a day. What did they say, look for Dorm Guides or Leaders or what—"

We move forward through the hall, and there are several young people our age, wearing grey uniforms, with armbands that are, unlike the general striped Atlantis one, a solid color. The color of their armband also matches the numbered signs they are holding up. They stand near the walls, and there are small groups of teens already gathering around each one.

Gordie stops when he sees a tall boy with a blue sign that has a number "2" on it. There are at least five teens standing with him, and all their tokens are glowing blue. He glances at us sheepishly, then steps up to the Dorm Two Leader who nods at him and says something. Gordie mumbles back, then glances at us and waves. He then stands there and breaks out in a huge mellow yawn. Typical Gordie.

I bite my lip and keep moving, staring at the colored signs.

"Oh, there's mine!" Gracie points anxiously at a big and burly boy holding up a red "5." She turns to me and George with a lost look, and I squeeze her arm.

"Go on, girl, it's gonna be okay! See you tomorrow!" I say. And Gracie detaches herself from us. One wistful last look, and she turns her back and starts talking to whoever's in charge of the red group.

A few more steps and I see a tall willowy African American girl my age, holding a yellow sign with my number on it, a big fateful "8." Her hair is twisted and braided in cornrows and she looks either very intense or very bored, one arm folded at her chest, the other propping up the number sign. There are a few teens clustered behind her, talking softly.

I look at George and again bite my lip nervously, hesitating. Then I smile at my brother as he makes a wiggle thing with his eyebrows and says in a mocking whine, "So, it's just little ole me left, all alone now, while you get to go and be with your new friends. Why, Gee Two, *why*?"

"Shut up!" I punch George's arm, and he smirks.

"See you. Okay, I think mine's right there, down the line. Later, sis!"

And suddenly I am all alone.

I approach the Dorm Eight Leader and she gives me a no-nonsense look, and notes my yellow token.

"Hi, I guess I am supposed to be here, Yellow Dorm, number Eight. Right?"

"You've come to the right place," she says. "We're waiting for a few more people here, then we'll proceed to the Dorm. Formal introductions will happen later. For now, I am Gina Curtis, your DL. Wait here with us."

"Okay. . . ."

I step back a little, finding myself next to a kid who looks younger, maybe a freshman, stocky and olive skinned with dark wavy hair, maybe Latino, maybe Middle Eastern. Next to him is another boy, medium-built, brown skinned and also dark, who looks like he is from India or Pakistan. Behind them are two girls, probably my age—one pale and slight, with mousy brown hair gathered in a ponytail, and the other with curves, a golden tan coloration, various piercings, long dark hair, and very sultry Latin looks.

It occurs to me, it's kind of cool—after the overly white ethnic concentration of Vermont—to see people of color other than shades of eggshell-white, pasty, or wintry no-tan. In California we were much more used to ethnic diversity, so this colorful people mix is immediately comforting to me, on a basic human vibe level.

"Hi," I say to them, shifting the straps of my heavy book-filled duffel from one shoulder to the other.

"Hey," says the Indian-looking boy with a sudden friendly smile that flashes bright white teeth. "Welcome to the Yellows. My name is Jaideep Bhagat. Just call me Jai."

"Thanks. I'm Gwen Lark."

"Hey, Gwen."

Five minutes later we sound like an AA meeting. Not that I've been to one, but it's kind of like those TV crime dramas—where they go around introducing themselves in a circle and the perp is usually one of the people in the support group looking all innocent and harmless. Except we're not alcoholics but asteroid wannabe refugees, and I kind of doubt any one of us is a serial killer in hiding. Though, anything's possible I suppose. For example, that Jai is smiling so hard he has to be hiding some kind of freaky evil side.

The stocky Latino boy says he's Mateo Perez, and he's not smiling at all. Unlike Jai, he is grim and serious, standing slouched and huddling in his black, worn looking jacket. The mousy-haired ponytail girl is Janice Quinn, and she looks dazed and very, very tired. The curvy raven-haired one is Claudia Grito, with multiple piercings and what looks like a boatload of expensive smart jewelry. She gives me an evaluating long scrutiny.

Meanwhile other teens arrive, an endless stream of people passing through the hall, and quite a few remain, joining our Yellow number Eight party. We give up trying to talk to everyone in our group because there's just too many of us now to remember who's who. Gina Curtis, the Dorm Leader, herds us into a compact growing crowd away from other similar groupings all around the endless hall as far as the eye can see. A girl of few words, she simply stands there looking no-nonsense and telling everyone to wait. "Just a few more minutes," she repeats every few more minutes.

"Not too long, girlfriend, or I am going to pass out on the floor," says an African American girl who's one of the later arrivals, with short relaxed hair that's bobbed and tinted with blond highlights. She stops next to me and plops her stuff down on the floor near my own bags. I look down at her bags and she just shrugs at me with a crooked grin. "Sorry, hope my bag didn't crush yours. I'm Laronda."

"No prob. My stuff's not breakable, it's mostly books," I say.

"Oh yeah?" She looks at me sideways. "What kind of books? Are you a smarty-pants?"

Before I can answer, Dorm Leader Gina starts to wave her Number Eight sign. "All right, may I have your attention, everybody! It's time! We're going to our Dorm now, please follow me. If you're Yellow, Dorm Eight, come along now! I repeat, Yellow, Dorm Eight!"

"Jesus, we heard you the first time . . ." Laronda makes a face, then flips her head back and forth and crosses her eyes at me.

I cannot help it, I break out in a smile. Then, just as we start picking up our stuff and moving out, I turn my head and my stomach immediately does a flip-flop.

Logan Sangre is walking by, in a large group of teens. His token is flaming red, and his Dorm Leader is holding up a red sign with a number "1."

"Hey . . . who's that hot piece of man-meat?" Laronda nudges me mercilessly. I guess she saw me drool and stare at him and heard the "ding-ding-ding" of falling IQ points raining from my brain.

"Huh?"

"You know that guy? I can tell, yeah! He's oozing-hot!"

"No . . . I mean, yeah, he's just someone from my school back in Vermont. I don't really know him."

"Big fat liar!"

I flare with indignation, but before I have the chance to say something awful and ruin things with this Laronda chick after only a five-minute acquaintance, she is grinning at me. She then punches me in the arm. "Nah, just messin' with you. It's okay. I can tell you're into him."

"You can? I'm not!" But I am biting my lip. I really wish Ann Finnbar was here. . . . She'd have my back. Or, maybe not—not in this situation. She'd probably join Laronda and make me cringe and blush about Logan. I can't believe I am so ridiculously obvious.

"All right, so," Laronda says. "Nothing wrong with lusting after such a hunkalicious boy toy. What's his name?"

"Logan . . . Logan Sangre." I speak his name in a whisper.

"Ni-i-ice. Okay," Laronda is looking at me closely as we start walking down the hall in our big Yellow group. "Now that I know the name of your lust object, what's yours?"

"What? Oh . . . I'm Gwen. Gwenevere Lark." I throw her a sideways glance as we all pass through the hall into another long corridor, and turn right.

"Nice to meet you, Gwen Lark. I'm Laronda Aimes. And I'll be your server tonight. I mean, your captain tonight. I mean—" And Laronda crosses her eyes and sticks out her tongue and raises her hands slightly apart and to the sides, to mimic a passenger aircraft.

I snort.

A few moments later we end up outside in the cold night, as our group rapidly walks through the brightly lit compound toward a building somewhere in the back. Other kids are moving toward other buildings past us. There are over a dozen structures in this place. Most of them have at least four floors, and some bear the large square four-color logo, while others display solid-colored squares. I assume those are the dorms.

Eventually our Dorm Leader stops before a building with a large yellow square.

"This is Dorm Eight, Yellow Quadrant, everyone. We go inside! Follow me!"

Then we are indoors again, and pleasant warm air hits us, unlike the other building, which was unheated. We are in a large room that resembles a hotel lobby, with several sofas and comfortable chairs scattered all throughout.

"First floor ground level," Gina, the DL, says, pausing as we come inside and mill around her, a group of at least seventy people, likely more, since more teens are still pouring in. "Common Area and Cafeteria. We'll see more of it tomorrow. Second floor is Boys' Dorm. Third floor is Girls' Dorm. Fourth floor is Classrooms. And basement, one floor below ground level is Physical Training Area."

Gina puts down her yellow sign and looks around her.

A sea of teenagers watches back. We're all exhausted.

"Tomorrow morning, at eight o'clock exactly, I want to see all of you here, for Orientation—"

Groans of protest are heard. "No way, it's three AM now!" someone says.

Gina ignores them and raises one hand for silence, at the same time raising her voice into an authoritative command. "But now, you're all going upstairs, to your designated floor—boys go to second floor, girls to third—and find a bed. *Any* bed. First come, first served. Choose wisely since this will be your bed for the duration of your stay here. There is bedding and other basics available, including a change of clothes for training. The bathrooms are marked clearly, two on each floor, with twelve toilet stalls, and twelve shower stalls each, so you will have to take well-timed turns tomorrow—but more on that later, during Orientation. Tomorrow, the morning dorm alarm will sound precisely at seven and you will wake up and get dressed and come to eat breakfast in the Cafeteria, all before Orientation. Understood? All right, now, we need to clear this room—the Common Area Lobby—because, believe it or not, there are two more groups of just as many people coming in here in the next few minutes. We're simply the first in the building. Now, go everyone! Hurry, grab your beds, you're lucky you get first dibs—go!"

There's a stampede.

We run up the stairs and the boys remain on the second floor while we keep going.

The third floor landing double doors open into a huge hall. And I mean, *huge*. It's the size of the entire building, and it is filled with rows and rows of narrow beds. They are simple, like cots in a shelter. Each cot is made with military neatness, pristine white sheets, a neutral beige-colored blanket pulled tight, a single pillow. There is also a grey uniform folded nearly on top of every bed, consisting of a buttoned tunic shirt and pants, kind of like a martial arts sparring outfit. The uniform is extra-large, generic. The beds are spaced three feet apart, with just enough space to walk around, and there's a small aisle of about five feet between the foot of each bed and the head of the next, so that you can walk quickly through the hall without bumping into beds.

"Wow," says a blond girl behind me as we pause at the doors. "This is like summer camp."

Laronda turns around and grimaces at her. "Honey, you *wish*. This is end-of-the-world asteroid camp, and I don't even want to know what kind of scary-evil "camp activity" junk awaits us tomorrow.

"It's best to grab a bed toward the center of the room," I say, glancing around, and start walking quickly past rows of cots.

Laronda follows me. Not sure why she's decided to latch onto me. "How come?" she asks.

"Because if we're too close to the doors or the bathrooms, then everyone will be passing by our beds all night long. Plus, doors banging, other noise."

"You really are a smarty-pants."

"Heh," I say as we reach the middle of the hall, and I pick a bed directly under one of the large overhead lights that's probably the very middle one.

"What are you looking at?" Laronda looks up to see why I am staring to mark the spot.

"See that lamp?" I glance up. "It's in the center of the room. Easy to remember the exact place where the bed is."

Laronda dumps her bags on the bed next to mine. "Wow, okay. But what about the bright light? Won't it be a problem to sleep right under it?"

I give her a brief smile. "It's gonna be lights out for sleeping anyway. But when the light is on, I might as well have a reading light directly overhead."

"You're a total nerd, you do know that?" Laronda shakes her head at me, but I know it's good humored and harmless.

"I know." I bite my lip, and then head for the bathroom.

Chapter 6

The morning alarm claxon blares through my thick sleep and I swear, I just about fly out of my bed at the noise. I sit up, bleary eyed, heart pounding, and every girl around me is also groaning. Last night, it was chaos long after I got into my bed and pulled the covers over my face, as everyone was still arriving, claiming beds, going to the bathroom. They didn't turn the lights out until almost four. Hardly enough time to get any sleep.

"Oh no, noooo . . ." Laronda in the bed to the left of me is turning over, and trying to cover her head and ears with the blanket.

On the other side, in a bed to the right of me is a brown haired girl whose name I don't know—I guess she must have arrived in a different group later. She is looking dazed and kind of scared.

I don't blame her.

"Bathroom stampede!" someone exclaims a few beds down.

And it happens. I rush to dig in my bag and pull out a toothbrush, soap, and a change of underwear, then hurry along with everyone else for one of the two bathrooms on each side of the hall. We stand in line.

"What time is it?"

"Seven-fifteen. What happens if we're late?"

"I don't plan to be late. Do you?" says a girl with a confident voice. I recognize Claudia Grito from last night, with her multiple piercings. She's several people in line ahead of me, and she sees me staring.

"What are you looking at?" She directs a hard frown at me.

I say nothing; quickly look away. But it's too late. I see her still watching me, with my peripheral vision. There's a slow-burn sense of impending horrible familiarity about this. It's the way bullies usually latch on to me at school, as soon as they notice I exist. I don't know what it is about me that makes me such a bully magnet, besides being a know-it-all in classes—maybe the way I sometimes space out and look at things with drawn-out curious intensity. . . .

Laronda notices. She raises one brow, glances back and forth between Claudia and me, and gives me a questioning look. I don't respond.

Few minutes later, we hit the toilets and the showers. The bathrooms are equally sterile and pristine, and there are stacks of clean towels, not to mention little bars of soap for everyone.

"Welcome to Hotel Qualification!" exclaims a skinny little girl with freckles and reddish hair as she grabs a towel and stuffs two soaps in her pocket.

"Hey, no hogging stuff!" Another girl pulls her sleeve.

"Says who?"

I try to ignore them as I attempt to take care of my own business in a hurry and try to get out of the crowded bathroom. As I back out of the shower stall, freshly showered, barefoot, wearing only a bra and underwear and still carrying my clothes and a towel, I slip on the wet tiles and collide with Claudia Grito, of all people.

"Hey, watch it, loser!" She turns from brushing her silky wet black hair that clings to her dark T-shirt, and elbows me in the gut.

"Sorry!" I manage to say, as I back away from her. Claudia is a little shorter than me, but she is powerfully built, sinewy muscle. She whips her hair out of her face, and her nose piercing flashes silver. She glares at me, looks me up and down, and mutters something in Spanish that I don't want to know, but unfortunately I am in Honors Spanish class, so I know exactly what she said, and it's ugly.

I break eye contact and get out of the bathroom without another word. I stand outside leaning against the dormitory wall and pull on my old jeans and purple sweater, then my socks and sneakers. When I am done, making sure my yellow ID token is still attached to the front of my sweater, I move past the crowds of girls running around getting dressed and head out the main double doors and down the stairs.

The first floor Common Area is a zoo. There are teens everywhere, looking worried, making noise, lazing around on the sofas, and heading to get breakfast. I follow them toward the cafeteria noise and smell of food that comes from the back, and into the huge room that has a food bar stretching along one wall, together with stacked trays, plates and servers. Meanwhile long tables and benches fill the middle.

"Hey, wait up!" Laronda Aimes is right behind me, and we enter together.

"What happened in there?" she asks. "I saw you and the pierced chick talking. Is she being a *bruja* with you?"

"Nothing, I have no idea. Don't worry about it." I shrug, and pick up a tray, while a server in a hairnet gives me a plate with something on it that looks like hash browns.

"This is free food, I guess they're feeding us." I change the subject.

"Yeah, don't see a cash register, thank you Lord. Cause I am all out of money. So, load up, girlfriend, while you can." Laronda picks up her plate and also a glass of milk and another one of orange juice.

We plop down on one of the long tables and eat as quickly as possible, watching the room. There are a few people from my own school that I recognize, but only a handful.

"You know, I tried calling my Auntie Janice," Laronda says, chewing hash browns. "But I couldn't get a signal. Really annoying."

"Weird," I mumble, looking around to note the time on the wall clock. It's seven minutes before eight. "We'd better hurry up, it's almost time."

We're done eating, empty our trays, and hurry out into the Common Area which is now completely packed.

All the sofa and lounge chair seats are taken, and it's pretty much standing room only. We jostle toward the back, and find a spot with a view of the middle of the room. The noise level is significant.

I see that Dorm Leader Gina Curtis is standing in the middle, in her grey uniform and yellow armband. Next to her are two older boys with equally confident postures of authority, also in uniform, with similar yellow armbands.

When the clock shows eight on the dot, the boy in the middle, between Gina and the other, raises both his hands. "Attention, everyone!"

At the same time Gina blows a whistle.

That makes the room go silent.

"Good morning, Dorm Eight!" the boy says. He is medium height, with light brown hair and regular features, nothing out of the ordinary. "I am John Nicolard, and I am one of the three Dorm Leaders of Dorm Eight, Yellow Quadrant. To the right of me is Gina Curtis. To my left is Mark Foster. After this Orientation, we are here to answer your questions and to help you in any way we can. But first, let's get through this quickly, okay?" He turns to the other boy, who takes over.

"Hi, everyone," Mark Foster says in a loud ringing voice that carries well throughout the room. "Welcome to Orientation. You have all passed the Preliminary Qualification tests yesterday, which means that you are the official Candidates for Qualification. Your ID tokens are lit up yellow, which means your test results have indicated that your personality and talents best fit in the Yellow Quadrant. The Yellow Quadrant is one of the four color Quadrants or Cornerstones of Atlantis society. More on this will be explained later in your Atlantis Culture class in the coming weeks. But for now, all you need to know is that you are a proud part of Yellow which represents four admirable traits—Creativity, Originality, Curiosity, and Inspiration."

A few whispers are heard around the room.

Mark ignores the whispering and continues. "Now, I am sure you are all wondering why you are here in this Regional Qualification Center, or RQC, and what happens next. What will happen is, for the next four weeks you will undergo basic training and education to prepare you for the Semi-Final Qualification test. Those of you who pass the Semi-Finals will advance on to the Finals which will take place in another four weeks after, at which point you will either Qualify for Atlantis, or you will return home."

"What kind of tests?" a boy exclaims. "How many more crazy things do they need from us?"

Mark turns in the direction of the speaker. "Questions will be answered at the end, please do not interrupt me again." His voice is hard and commanding so that the teen almost flinches.

"However, I will answer this one," Gina Curtis speaks up. "Because it is relevant. I'll be honest—the tests are grueling. They are physical and psychological, and they will challenge your mind and body equally. They are specifically designed to weed most of you out, I am sorry to say. More will be said later, as you get to train and learn. Now, back to you, Mark."

Mark Foster nods and picks up. "The Semi-Finals will take place in four weeks. Incidentally, it will be televised. It will be shown on national television and live-streamed on all media. Yes, your parents will be watching you, and people all around the world will be watching—"

Excited whispers pass the room like a fretful breeze.

"—Each day leading up to it, you will spend in class. Classes will consist of four categories of training—Agility Training, Combat Training, Atlantis Tech, and Atlantis Culture. Each of these is equally important. Your daily progress and performance will not only determine your performance on the Semi-Finals, but it will also be closely monitored by your Instructors all throughout the process. In fact, their final recommendations will be added to your Semi-Final score. So, don't think you can slide by in any of these types of classes."

Mark grows silent, and now John Nicolard speaks. "All right. The following is your schedule. Your day will be divided thusly. Rise at 7:00 AM and breakfast. Starting at 8:00 AM will be your first two classes, then lunch from 12:00 noon to 1:00 PM, followed by two more classes, then dinner at 6:00 PM, followed by rest hour at 7:00 PM. Finally, from 8:00 PM you do homework or practice, and lights out at 10:00 PM. You get limited allowance for going outside after 8:00 PM homework hour, and absolutely no going outside your Dorm after 10:00 PM, that's the curfew. I realize this is highly structured, and leaves you little time for anything personal. But all of you here understand that this is not fun and games, this is deadly serious. It bears repeating that you are all fighting for your lives here. Your actions and personal achievements will determine your fate."

"And speaking of personal," Gina Curtis interrupts. "Your presence here in this compound is contingent on your good behavior. Basic rules of courtesy and cooperation will be observed, and anyone found fighting, stealing or vandalizing property, or trespassing or engaging in other unacceptable behavior—such as hooking up, for example, yeah, sorry, no dating or intimate 'socializing' beyond normal public conversation—anyone found doing this will be immediately dismissed and sent home. Besides, there are surveillance cameras all over, so you cannot hide your behavior. No girls on the boys' floor after lights out, and vice versa. Why, you might ask? Because there's just no time for this kind of distraction and nonsense in your intense schedule. Anything that distracts you from your training will not be tolerated."

The room is filling with waves of anxious whispers and a few stifled giggles.

"You think this is funny?" Mark Foster says in his powerful ringing voice. "Let me reassure you that after your first full day of classes you will be glad to fall into bed at 10:00 PM, and you will have no thought of anything else. How do I know this? Because as a Dorm Leader I went through a two-week crash course of precisely the same kind of training that you will be going through. We all did. Dorm Leaders were pre-selected on our merits, maturity, and leadership skills, basically upon recommendations of various school districts—a kind of trial group of teenage test subjects—before the general teen population was to be subjected to this training. You might say we were guinea pigs on your behalf."

John Nicolard nods with a rueful smile. "These last two weeks were pure unadulterated hell. We did it, we survived, and now we want to help you make it too."

"As far as your classes and class Instructors," Gina says, "they are going to change and rotate on a weekly basis. Some of the classes will taught by specialists and designated Earth experts. But many more of the classes will be taught by Atlanteans. Many of them are amazing at what they do and what knowledge they will share with all of you. My strong recommendation is that you listen with all you've got and pay attention. The skills you will learn will save your life, literally."

"We are almost done with Orientation." John Nicolard looks around at our faces with a kind of hard fervor of a preacher— definitely someone older than his seventeen or eighteen years. "The last thing you need to know is that there are about five hundred people here in Dorm Eight. And there are twelve such dorms in this RQC. Three dorms each are allocated to the Yellow,

Red, Blue, and Green Quadrants. That's a whole lot of people. About six thousand Candidates in all, which could be the population of a sizeable small town. And that's not counting Dorm Leaders, Instructors, Administration, Security Guards, Techs, Maintenance, Atlanteans, and other personnel. That's just *one* RQC. Now, multiply that by thousands, all across the country and the entire world. You are each other's competition, and it's only going to get more and more brutal as the ranks are weeded down. The crash-course training that we, the DLs, went through is nothing compared to what lies ahead. And by the way, *none* of us DLs are guaranteed Qualification either. We have to compete for the coveted spots on the Atlantis ships also, and we must continue to prove ourselves, all the way up to the last minute, even as we continue to help you. Talk about killer brutal!"

"One last thing before you go." Gina Curtis raises her hand for attention, because the room is once again filling with noise. "As of this morning, all electronic signals to and from outside the RQC are being blocked by industrial strength e-dampers. Your electronic and smart devices are functional, but you will not be able to call out and contact anyone outside the e-damper firewall range. Nor will you be able to hack through the firewall, so don't bother. There are two good reasons for this. We need to maintain the atmosphere of focus and no external distraction on your behalf. And we need to limit sensitive information that might be inappropriate for the fragile mental climate of the outside world. The only exceptions to this two-way 'wall of communication silence' will be extreme emergencies—as determined by RQC officials—and the specially authorized media televised events for the Semi-Finals and Finals."

"That's pretty much it," Mark Foster says. "Your schedule starts today, with your first class in twenty minutes. To find out your specific order of classes for this week, check with any official with an ID reader handheld like this one here—" He holds up a small gadget—"or any of us, your DLs, and we will scan your ID tokens and let you know where you need to go. Most of your classes are held in this same exact building, either upstairs on the fourth floor, or downstairs in the basement floor. Some classes will be held elsewhere in the RQC, including other dorms, and you will be informed well in advance, in each case. Between classes you are free to go anywhere you like on the RQC grounds, including the large Arena Commons super structure, but you may not leave the compound or you will be Disqualified immediately."

Gina Curtis speaks up: "And now, we have about five minutes for questions."

A bunch of hands fly up.

"How do we find you DLs in the middle of the day?"

"Come to the Common Area and ask at that info desk in the corner. There will be a guard posted and he will contact us as needed." Gina points to the farthest wall near the cafeteria.

"What if there's an emergency? What if I get sick or someone gets hurt?"

"Same thing—info desk."

"What if I need something else—"

This time half the room repeats, in a choir, *"Info desk!"*

"All right, we're done here!" Gina Curtis blows her whistle.

The noise level returns, and the three Dorm Leaders are swarmed by teens all trying to get their ID tokens scanned for their schedules.

I look around and notice a woman official near the front entrance, and she has the same ID reader gadget and no one is mobbing her. So I calmly head in her direction.

Naturally, Laronda is right behind me.

I get my ID token scanned without the hassle of a line, and according to my schedule I have Agility and Atlantis Tech followed by lunch, then Atlantis Culture and Combat. Which means my first class is down in the basement.

Laronda gets hers scanned and she has a different class order except for Atlantis Culture which we both share at 1:00 PM. "I guess I'll see you then, or for lunch, eh? Wonder what kind of new torture they'll be putting us through today!"

I mumble something at her then head downstairs in a hurry. I have no idea what Agility Training is, but I am already numb with fear, because it kind of sounds terrifying and precisely the *opposite* of what I'm normally good at, which would be ordinary schoolwork. Agility and me don't really work well together in the same sentence. Maybe it would if I were a dog?

The basement floor is deep below ground—once again, way too many stairs. The landing is brightly lit, and it opens into another large hall similar to our sleeping dorm floor. Except, the Training Hall is pretty much one huge gym, and it has an extra-tall cathedral ceiling. How do I know it's a gym? Because to one side of the hall is an area of about fifty feet filled with weights, stationary bikes, treadmills and other workout equipment which I know nothing about because, yes, if you haven't figured it out by now, I don't exactly work out. But okay, I *have* seen some of these things on late-night TV infomercials.

The rest of the hall is empty, except for strange, stacked metal structures against three of the walls—structures that resemble weird, massive gymnastic monkey bars, except they are made for full-sized grownups, not little kids. Some of the structures consist of multi-tiered scaffolding resembling a metal truss bridge, and things a trapeze artist might use for practice. And these bizarre scaffoldings go all the way up to the ceiling. The fourth wall is a climbing wall, with footholds and protruding ledges.

Lord help me.... I absolutely suck at climbing, and have never been able to do even a single complete pull-up—at least the last time I tried to do one, which was two years ago. Honest, I've only survived P.E. by the sheer grace of the Almighty, and even so it's been touch and go quite a few times.

Did I mention I'm afraid of heights?

And oh yeah, the worst part is, I see no safety mats anywhere.

Let me repeat that, *no safety mats*.

I look around the room, and there are already about twenty teens gathered, girls and boys of various ages, just standing around looking dazed. Some have the deer-in-the-headlights look. I recognize a few faces. There's even one girl from my school. I think her name is Theresa something or other. Also, I quickly recognize Jaideep Bhagat, the friendly-smile guy, and Janice Quinn, the girl with a mousy brown ponytail, both of whom I've met briefly last night as we waited for others from Dorm Eight.

Jai sees me and immediately waves, and again, that big smile. "Hi, Gwen!" Holy wow, he is so sugary nice that I again wonder if maybe he's really a serial killer....

A few more people come down into the Training Hall. We

mill around for a couple of minutes, glance at each other, at the weirdly equipped walls.

"Okay, who's teaching this class anyway?" a girl asks.

"*I* am."

I, and everyone, turn to stare, and immediately it gets kind of surreal. Seriously, it's no wonder.

The speaker is a girl our age, or maybe slightly older—it's hard to tell, really—because she is Atlantean. Metallic blond hair down to her shoulders, beautifully defined curving eyebrows, steely eyes of a strange almost turquoise blue, outlined in smoky black kohl. Features so perfect they appear somewhat doll-like, too sharply chiseled. . . . She is about my height, with a body that's to die for, a combination of spare curves and muscular strength. The grey uniform neatly follows the willowy lines of her hourglass waist, her long legs, and tapers at her calf-high combat boots. She could be wearing Earth military fatigues, she'd fit right in.

The Atlantean girl must have come up from behind, silently, and now stands before us, giving us all a close silent scrutiny, with her arms folded at her chest in a confident stance.

"I am Oalla Keigeri," she says in a strong voice. Even the sound of her name is exotic, pronounced in that strange subtle accent that I am beginning to pick up when I hear Atlanteans speaking English. "You may call me Oalla. I am from Atlantis, and I am one of your Instructors. Today I will be teaching you Agility. Welcome. Please gather closer, and first I want you to go around and give me your names."

We do as we're told. Some of the boys continue to stare so blatantly they should probably wipe some drool.

"Now, I will be scanning you each time at the beginning of the class to mark your attendance." Oalla passes a handheld gadget over each one of our ID tokens. "I will also scan you for merit or demerit, as applicable."

Nervous looks fill the semi-circle. Even Jai's smile is pretty much erased.

"You have all managed to ride the hoverboard during Preliminary Qualification, which is good. It landed you here—"

Oalla is interrupted in her intro speech by the arrival of a latecomer. Standing in a semi-circle around her we all stare as a guard approaches. He is pushing a familiar boy in a wheelchair.

I catch my breath as I recognize him, the same kid who rode the board yesterday at my school, while lying down on his stomach, after pulling himself onto it by the arms.

Oalla looks on while the guard leaves the boy in place at the edge of the semi-circle, nods, then exits the gym.

"You are late," she says to the seated boy. "Next time, please make sure you are here on time with the others. Name?"

"Blayne Dubois . . ." the boy says, gripping the sides of the wheelchair. His voice is soft, slightly reedy. "Sorry."

I frown, noting the reaction of the rest of the teens. One girl drops her jaw and makes a weird face. Another boy looks on with pity. Pretty much everyone is showing surprise. Unlike me, they have no idea about the amazing way Blayne Dubois can ride the hoverboard.

But Oalla must know. Because she turns away from him calmly, showing no inkling of surprise, and continues where she left off. "As I was saying, you all handled the hoverboard halfway decently. Get ready—you will be doing a *lot* of hoverboard riding in the coming days. Now I need to find out what else you can or cannot do. Before we begin real training, I want to see you run, climb, and exercise."

Oh, no, I knew it. . . . This is P.E. of the worst possible kind. *I am going to die.*

My gut is churning with a very sick feeling. And somehow, even though I've seen Blayne on the hoverboard, I just cannot imagine what *he* must be feeling right now about all the rest of it.

As I'm thinking all this, Oalla motions with her hand, palm up, and suddenly makes a very strange noise that sounds like a single long musical note—a G note, I think. She looks up, continuing to hold the note, and suddenly from overhead, we see a hoverboard flying toward her. It has taken off from one of the tall scaffolding levels, about twenty feet up, and has sailed at a horizontal line, stopping directly above the spot where Oalla and the rest of us are standing.

Oalla motions us to step back, while continuing to sing the note. She then changes the G to a falling major scale, ending on another G, only an octave lower. As she does that, the hoverboard descends gradually, then stops six inches away from the floor.

"Whoa," a boy says, impressed.

"This is another way to command the hoverboard." Oalla looks around at us. "Congratulations, you've just learned something new." And then she turns to Blayne, the boy in the wheelchair. "This board is for your use today, Blayne. While the rest of the class does other physical activities, I want you to get onto the hoverboard and practice riding it around the hall. Use the basic verbal commands you learned yesterday. Can you do that?"

Blayne looks up, nodding. His expression shows a keen interest.

Everyone else in the class stares in amazement as he begins to lift himself out of the chair. But Oalla does not allow any one of us to gawk. She claps her hands together, and turns away, saying, "All right, everyone! Your attention! Eyes here! First you're going to run five laps around the room—"

Ten minutes later, I am running in the back of a line of students snaking around the perimeter of the Training Hall. I'm gasping for air, my sides are in stitches, my breath ragged, and my shins hurting.

This is bad, seriously bad. I am the last person in line. Even Jack Carell, the heavy boy with curly blond hair, is ahead of me— red-faced and breathing like a locomotive, but still ahead of me. . . .

Oalla blows the whistle, and we stop in place, and I'm sort of staggering there, seeing spots before my eyes. The Atlantean girl walks our line, making comments here and there. When she comes to the very end and looks at me, seeing what a mess I am, she says with a frown, "You don't know how to run, do you?"

"Not really. . ." I barely gasp out an answer.

She continues her scrutiny. "There's no reason for you to be so out of shape. You simply need to *practice*. Gwenevere Lark, right?"

"Just Gwen."

"Okay, from this day on, I want you to run every day, Gwen. Ten minutes at least, during your homework hours. You can come down here. The Training Hall will be open from seven in the morning until ten each night. Or you can run outside. You can even go to the Arena Commons building and run there along the large track. Either way, you will run."

"Okay . . ." I mumble, while the cold terror is back.

I am going to die.

Oalla must be reading my mind because she gives me a pitying look that's more than a little disdain. She then passes her scan gadget over my ID token. The yellow light pulses once. "That's a demerit," she says. "The person who finishes last each day will get a demerit. Don't let it be you again."

I nod, but she has already turned away.

We spend the next half an hour doing horrible things with our bodies. We line up and climb the first level of the scaffolding, holding on for dear life, and then we stand there on a three-foot narrow strip that is the ledge that hugs the wall, many of us shaking from a combination of terror and the abuse of previously unused muscle groups.

The climb was relatively simple, just rungs and stairs, but the result puts us ten feet above the floor, and my fear of heights kicks in.

Oalla climbs up after us, stepping onto each rung easily with her heavy boots, and amazingly using only a grip of one hand to keep herself anchored on each next rung above. I have no idea how that's even possible, but she must be doing it on purpose to mess with our minds. "Look up," she tells us, once she's up there with us. "These are parallel bars."

We stare directly overhead at the next level of scaffolding, and this one is sheer, made only of parallel rungs, not metal sheets like the one we're standing on now. It's only about three feet overhead, so if the tallest ones of us stand on tiptoes, we can reach it with our fingers.

"Each of you will cross the distance from here to the end using your hands only. When done, you will climb down the rung ladder back to ground level. If you fall at any point in the middle, make sure you land on the floor of this scaffold, or you will end up on the ground. You fall, you walk to the end then climb down. Anyone who does not finish the distance and walks, gets a demerit. Now, form a line starting here against the wall, and begin. First, observe me."

There are noises of protest and whimpers of terror. A few of the younger kids look like they're ready to cry. I am with them.

I remember, when I was a little kid on a playground, I managed to hand-swing the distance of only about three to five rungs on the monkey bars, before dropping down. This thing stretches at least *thirty* across.

Oalla demonstrates the climb by easily reaching upward with both hands. She jumps up, grabbing the first parallel rung. She then moves with effortless strength, swinging her body forward smoothly with each motion and switches hands easily from bar to bar. In seconds she is all the way across the length of the scaffolding. Then she climbs down to the floor and watches us.

A tall athletic boy goes first. His name is Chris, I think. He easily hand-swigs the whole distance, then climbs down from the scaffold, looking calm. The rest of us follow. Some kids slip immediately, barely able to hang on with their hands for only one or two bars. Others struggle a bit longer to reach partway across, until dropping away.

I watch Janice Quinn struggle and slip after about six bars. She lands on the metal ledge flooring awkwardly and it looks like she may have twisted her ankle, because she grips the wall in a panicky way and starts to limp as she makes it the rest of the way across. Jai does okay most of the way with his hands, then slips off, and walks to the end.

My turn. I look up at the bars and my hands are already slippery like eels, just in anticipation. I wipe them against my jeans, then stand up on tiptoe and reach for the metal rungs.

I grip, and then I swing. My arms, already tired from the short climb up the side ladder, are barely obeying me, and there's a stinging pain of uncustomary soreness. I let go of one hand and reach for the next bar . . . grab it. My hand, and then my arm, feels like it's being ripped out of its socket.

I am now stretched out between two bars, and it's excruciating. Gathering all my arm strength, I let go of the first hand and reach for the second rung. I know I should have swung more, aiming for the third rung instead—so that each bodily swing and motion of the hand would propel me onward. But no, I can only do it the stupid hard way. So I merely grip the second rung with both hands and hang on.

A gasp for air, then I reach for the third rung again with my leading hand. Again, I am stretched between two bars, and my arms are ripped apart in agony. . . .

I let go of the back bar, reach in futility for the next one. And then, with a sinking feeling of despair, I feel my fingers slipping. . . . I don't so much let go as I am forced to acknowledge the fact that my body just gave up on me.

At least I land on my feet. There's a small thud, a terrifying moment of vertigo, and then I walk the rest of the way on the metal scaffolding, without looking over the side that's the ledge.

Now, the climb down. Oh, no. . . .

I pause at the end near the downward ladder, feeling faint, then squeeze my eyes shut, breathe, open them again. I turn my back to the precipice, and grip the metal upright corner posts of the scaffolding. They both comprise the side supports for the whole structure all the way up to the ceiling, and they create the ladder. I lower one leg and feel with my foot the first rung on the way down. . . .

Please don't slip. . . . Please don't slip. Somehow I make it to the floor.

Oalla is waiting there for me, and she scans my ID token. "Demerit," she says coldly and looks away.

Yeah, I knew that was coming.

After everyone's down, and two thirds of us have earned demerits, the next phase of torture begins.

At least this one is relatively simple.

Oalla Keigeri calls down six hoverboards. Once again she uses musical tones, singing a pattern of notes that I find curiously pleasing. One by one they come down from the top of the scaffolding near the ceiling, where they are apparently being stored.

Each hoverboard is the same—about six feet long, with tapered oval ends, and made of that same matte charcoal and slate grey material. Oalla directs them into a lineup, side by side, stretching across the hall, at a level "Ready" position six inches off the floor.

"All right. You remember the English commands you were taught yesterday, during Preliminary Qualification?" She points to the boards. "Well, today you will get to use them again. All this week you will be allowed to continue to use verbal commands to control the boards. But, starting next week, you will have to use tones, the same way we do on Atlantis. That would be in a different class. For now, English is fine. Now, I want you to get on a board and ride all the way to the end of the room and back on this horizontal starting level. For now, I want to observe your posture, so we will not lift the boards any higher.

Janice Quinn, who is standing up with difficulty while favoring one foot, raises her hand. "I am sorry, but I think my ankle got hurt. . . . What should I do?"

Oalla turns in her direction, and there's silence.

"After class, you may go to get a bandage and medical care. There's a doctor on the first floor near the Cafeteria. Ask at the info desk."

"But—" Janice looks frightened. "What should I do *now?*"

The Atlantean girl gets a cold, blank expression. No sympathy, no emotion, nothing. "Do you want to Qualify?" she asks. "If so, then get on a board and ride. Or get a demerit. Your choice."

Janice bites her lip and nods.

"Bitch . . ." someone mutters quietly.

Oalla pauses, then slowly turns in the direction of the whisperer. "Who said that? If I hear another such outburst from any one of you, that person will be *Disqualified immediately.*"

Silence. You can hear a pin drop. Suddenly everyone is looking down and away.

"Now then, I want to see you all ride. Prove to me that you are half as good as Blayne Dubois who's been hoverboarding all the while we were doing the laps and the climbing." Oalla turns as though nothing happened. She glances around then spots him and points to the other end of the hall. There we see the "wheelchair kid" lying on his stomach atop a board and gliding smoothly around in laps, six inches above the floor.

We line up behind each board and take the basic "Go! Stop! Reverse! Go! Stop!" two-way ride along the Training Hall. Even Janice Quinn with her sprained ankle manages somehow—though her face is deathly pale, and a sheen of pain-sweat covers her forehead.

By the time my turn comes, I am shaking in exhaustion, but

maybe it's what makes it easier, since by this point my muscles are too tired to be stiff—which in my experience is normally the cause of all my "clumsy." I put my right foot up on the board, then the left one behind me in my usual "goofy" stance, and balance without much difficulty. Since no heights are involved, I feel no need to crouch down, so I ride upright all the way, balancing on my feet, and amazingly I don't fall off.

I also don't get a demerit.

"Class dismissed," Oalla tells us soon enough. "See you next time. Be warned, you will be very sore tomorrow."

Chapter 7

My second class is Atlantis Tech. I wonder what in the world that means as I climb up the stairs all the way to the fourth floor, pretty much dying on the way, after the physical exertion I've just endured. Admittedly, it's not really that bad—at least not for a normal athletic teen. But I've managed to avoid P.E. or take the easiest classes possible, for years. And now it's all catching up with me . . . at the worst time possible.

The fourth floor landing is identical to the others, brightly lit and sterile. But instead of double doors leading to one ginormous room the size of the Training Hall or the sleeping floor, this one leads into a corridor with many classroom doors on all sides. My schedule said "Room 17," and so I go down the hall past a stream of other students—no, wait, I need to stop thinking of everyone here as just students. No, we're Candidates. Candidates for Qualification, fighting for our lives. And we are all sporting our yellow tokens, which suggests to me that our classes are likely going to be Yellow-Quadrant-only, or maybe even limited to our own Dorm Eight, whatever it really means.

And for a brief moment I wonder how my brothers and sister are doing. . . . I'll have to go look for them as soon as the classes for the day are over. My chest feels a sudden constriction, a pang of nerves on their behalf.

But first, Atlantis Tech.

Inside, the classroom is filled with Candidates. I am one of the last arrivals, so I get a lousy seat in the back. The front of the class has a usual teacher's desk and on it is some kind of equipment. There is also a large whiteboard.

The Instructor is a middle-aged man, definitely not Atlantean. He's wearing a plain grey suit and a yellow armband. He has a balding head and a mild and somewhat abstracted expression.

"Good morning everyone, I am Mr. Warrenson. I will be one of your Atlantis Tech Instructors." His voice is pleasant and he looks over the packed room kindly. "I'm sure you're all wondering what this is all about. Well, to be honest, when I got the intensive crash course on the basic principles of their technology, I was pretty much stunned—all the scientific community was. But their technology is so different from our own, so original, the principles of physical interactions of wave and particle mechanics, heat and energy transfer—"

I see the kids' eyes starting to glaze over. At the same time I watch the excitement gathering in the way this man is starting to slur his speech together, and recognize he is a nerdy science type who got tasked with teaching us some advanced stuff that's unfortunately going to go over many of the teens' heads.

But not mine!

"Anyway, the main initial point I'm trying to get across," Mr. Warrenson says, motioning with his hand at the spread of unrecognizable objects on the desk before him, "is that Atlantis technology is *based on sound*. To be precise, it is based on the interactions of various tones and frequencies and the opposing bombardment of sound waves from different directions in order to conduct, transfer and convert sound energy and in the process create physical movement and other tangible manifestations in the physical world."

Mr. Warrenson pauses and stares at us, as if to give us time to let it sink in.

Everyone mostly kind of stares back at him, blank faced, expectant, uncertain.

"Huh?" a boy mumbles.

Me? I'm kind of getting blown away.

Disappointed in our lack of reaction, the Instructor continues. "Let me put it this way. It's sound, it's music!—tones and notes—that make those amazing hoverboards levitate! Sound is what makes the bulk of their technology work! It's mind-blowing! Oh, if only we had more time! More time to get a thorough in-depth look at the functionality, the things I could tell you—But in any case, what's important is that the one solid reason why you all passed Preliminary Qualification, a reason I can reveal to you now, is that all of you here can more or less *carry a tune*. Or at least you can replicate auditory signals correctly. Which means you are prime Candidates for being able to use Atlantis technology!"

This time the class is paying a bit more attention.

"So." Mr. Warrenson picks up one of the weirdo gadgets on the table. "What we're going to do in the very brief time we have, is learn how to use their technology, their computers, their engines, their mechanisms. We—or better to say, *you*—won't know how or why it works, but at least, by the time we're done here, you will all know how to use it!"

A curly-haired girl raises her hand. "Okay, does this mean we're going to be singing in this class?" she quips.

"Actually—" Mr. Warrenson smiles. "You're not too far off."

And then he kind of launches into a rambling lecture on music theory. In a nutshell—and believe me, even I am a little bored with the thick overload of *theory* and mega-rambling in this one—in a nutshell, different notes, scales, tones, and progressions of sound waves create real usable energy.

"The Yellow Quadrant," Mr. Warrenson tells us, "is directly related to sounds and musical notes that are classified as *sharp*. That's one of the four sound divisions within their system—with the Green Quadrant representing *flat* notes, Red Quadrant referring to *major* musical keys, and Blue Quadrant related to *minor* musical keys. Supposedly they all have special functions and very important roles and meanings in Atlantean science and physics. But all we need to know is how to make the correct musical sounds at the appropriate times and in the right places."

So, we are going to be singing indeed.

I feel myself freezing up on the inside. . . .

I haven't mentioned it previously, but *I don't sing.*

And I don't mean I cannot form notes—I can, reasonably well, otherwise apparently I wouldn't have passed Preliminary Qualification. What I don't do is sing for pleasure or for entertainment or for *anything*. I used to love to sing, when I was younger, a tiny little kid, singing along in delight to her opera singer Mom's arias and solo repetitions. If I can even remember any of it, I think I was even kind of good at it. . . .

But none of it matters.

Not anymore. Not since Mom got cancer and it metastasized

to her lungs, and caused her to stop being able to make the gorgeous mezzo-soprano notes, and forced her to quit her musical career and then stop working altogether. At that time something weird happened to me also. I don't know what it is, and no, I am not being dramatic or a pretentious jerk.

It's just . . . something.

So, I don't sing. My brothers and my sister, sometimes they still sing a little, the way we used to do all together, and they still play their instruments—but I don't.

And so, as Mr. Warrenson starts explaining Atlantean audio gadgets to us, and then makes us echo the notes he makes in a chorus, demonstrating random levitation and other fascinating mechanical functionality, I keep as still as possible, and barely open my mouth.

This class is going to be hell after all.

A t noon, we break for lunch.
        I get up and follow the stream of jostling Candidates downstairs. Some of us stop at the girls or boys dormitory floors to grab our stuff, or a fifteen minute nap, or check our belongings to make sure nothing has been taken from our beds, whatever—not that it would be, considering the immediate threat of Disqualification, and all the supposed security cameras (I haven't seen any beyond ordinary yet, but it doesn't mean they're not there).

I don't bother. As if anyone is going to steal my books or my cheap trinkets. And I've never been one for naps, not even when dead-tired.

Instead, I go directly to the Common Area on the first floor. On impulse I consider skipping lunch and instead heading out in search of Gracie and my brothers right now, right this moment, to see how they're all doing. Poor Gracie, I can't imagine how she must be dealing with Agility Training. . . .

As I come down the last flight and enter the landing, still thinking about taking off, I notice a freight elevator right around the corner. It dings, its wide door swings open and I see Blayne Dubois in his wheelchair. There's no one else in the elevator with him. He uses his hands to rotate the wheels but a wheel appears to get stuck on the small ledge between the elevator and the ground floor.

He looks up, and I see his intense expression.

Normally I'm the last person to stick my nose into other unfamiliar kids' business, but something prompts me to pause. Especially since in that moment, no one else is around in this spot—all the noise is coming from the Common Area and the cafeteria, and there's a brief lull as, in the last thirty seconds, no one else has come down the stairs behind me. . . .

"Hi," I say, and start moving toward him. "Need some help?"

His gaze flits in my direction, and I meet his dark blue eyes.

"No!" he says, just as my hands connect with the back of his chair at the handles.

I freeze, and at the same time the heavy elevator door starts closing in on us, then bobs open again.

"No! I don't need any help!" he repeats, with a frown. His voice is stubborn, not at all faint or reedy. It sounds stronger than I remember from the auditorium last night, or the Training Hall gym an hour earlier. Since I am already halfway in the elevator, and this is a weird situation, I say, "Oh. . . ."

And then, because the elevator starts to close again, I grip the wheelchair from the back, and give it one small shove. "I'll just push it over this part here," I say.

He bites his lip, and up-close I see his angular chin, his pale skin, and the brown wisps of hair falling over his eyes. He appears my age or a little younger, but I'm not sure.

The wheelchair snags momentarily, then we're out of the elevator.

"Thanks," he says coldly. "But I can get around by myself. Really."

Now I bite my lip, then mumble something like, "Sorry, yeah, I know. You're Blayne, right?"

"Yes." He looks up at me. "You can *let go now*."

"Oh yeah, okay." I smile nervously, step back, then add, "I saw you ride the hoverboard yesterday in my school back in Vermont, that was amazing—"

Blayne stares at me, and his frown deepens. "Oh, yeah? What's so amazing about not wanting to die?"

"Oh, no, I mean, you were really inspirational, and it helped me and my sister, and a whole lot of other people, I bet, seeing you there—"

I should just shut up now, because I am only digging myself in deeper.

"So, it's inspirational to see a loser cripple crawl onto that board and barely hang on?" He smirks. "Some inspiration! Why are you talking to me anyway?"

"Sorry," I say. "I was only trying to help—"

Blayne says nothing. He looks away from me, and I briefly see the hard flash of his blue eyes before his hair falls in his face. He then furiously starts turning the wheels with his hands, and the wheelchair rolls along the floor, away from me.

Other people finally come down the stairs and pass us on the way to the cafeteria, and I am still paused like a fool, blocking traffic. I stand and watch his retreating shoulders and arms moving powerfully, and notice that they are more muscular up-close than I thought. I guess they have to be, since it's how he gets around.

Well, apparently Blayne Dubois is a bit of a jerk.

Or maybe he's not. I immediately feel rotten for thinking it. He's probably just pretty much sick of people treating him this way. Kind of like how I just did, without meaning to.

Yeah, I screwed up.

I bite my lip and continue into the Common Area, past a whole bunch of people I don't know. I doubt I'll have time now to search for Gracie and our bros. It'll have to wait till later tonight. For now, best to just grab some food before the next class.

As I make a beeline for the cafeteria, keeping myself as small as possible out of habit, and looking mostly straight ahead, I hear a minor commotion just off to the side near the lounging area. Loud guy voices, harsh female laughter, and a general hard tone I am used to associating with danger and in-crowd unpleasantness. It almost always means someone is getting picked on—or about to be—and it's usually me.

There's a cold sinking feeling in my gut as I pass the source of the noise, the loud group of teens who have taken over the lounge chairs. These are exactly the kind of loud popular crowd that terrifies me, so I try not to look at all. . . . Until I hear what they're saying.

"Hashtag wheelchair. Hashtag effed-up-loser. Hashtag how-long-will-he-last. Hashtag Atlantis-meals-on-wheels. Hashtag send. Okay pretend I just sent it to you, since the !@#$% stupid crap e-damper is on." The guy who is speaking is an older teen, a big muscular jock type with dark blond hair and a thick neck. He's sitting with one foot up on the sofa armrest and wearing the yellow token on one shoulder in a kind of careless show of contempt, while he's got a sports team pin on the other. I'm guessing it's a smart-pin.

"Oooh, good one, Wade!" The speaker is also an older girl, sleek and auburn-haired, perched up on the sofa's back, with her tight hip-hugging jeans showing off her curves. She's leaning over him with her big chest pushed forward provocatively, and using a high giggly voice that tells me she is flirting hard. I vaguely recognize her from the girls' dorm floor, and I think her name is Olivia.

There are five other guys and three girls gathered around, variously spread out on the sofas and chairs. One of them, I notice, is Claudia Grito, who immediately glares at me. Great. Do I have some kind of nerd alert cowbell round my neck that announces my arrival to the haters?

"Okay, my turn," says another guy, dark-haired and hard-faced, with a prominent tattoo on his equally thick neck. "Hashtag wheelchair. Hashtag total-waste-of-space. Hashtag he-needs-to-go-pronto. Hashtag Atlantis-qualification-fail. Hashtag screw—"

They're not supposed to be hashtagging. And apparently the smart devices being rendered non-functional by the e-dampers is not stopping them from messing around anyway. Except, in some ways this is even worse. Normally, hashtagging is just a stupid online thing. It raises the popularity of a keyword phrase transmitted by a bunch of people and gets it trending across the various social networks, for various reasons, mostly stupid harmless ones. But it can be used as a personal assault bomb—in order to devastate some poor victim of the online mass attack. Since it is a known bully tactic, hashtagging is strictly forbidden in school, even though it happens all the time anyway, being the latest hot teen trend. But this—this "pretend hashtagging" done verbally in the person's hearing is especially devastating.

Because I see Blayne Dubois just a few feet away, paused

near the wall. He is staring straight ahead, and not moving. His wheelchair is blocked by the extended legs and feet of four guys who have cleverly positioned themselves to surround him. Their feet are stretched, sticking out, or otherwise dangling off furniture just so that he cannot maneuver past them.

I pause, freezing up completely, as fear renders me useless for about ten seconds.

And then something crazy happens. I turn and walk toward Blayne in his wheelchair. It's as if I have nothing to lose. Claudia's been staring at me for all these long seconds anyway, so screw everything. I move past everybody's legs sticking out, bumping them casually while saying, "Sorry, oops, sorry. . . ."

"Hey," I say, stopping next to Blayne, as if we know each other well and he's expecting me. "Sorry it took me so long, let's go in to eat." I take hold of the back of his wheelchair, and before Blayne even opens his mouth, I start pushing him through the people's feet-and-legs barricade, while everyone kind of goes really quiet and stares at me, stunned.

"What the f—" A boy cusses at me as the wheelchair hits his leg.

"Watch it, bitch!" says another guy. "Who says you can walk here?"

But I keep going. Blayne only turns his head and looks at me, but smartly says nothing. I think he's kind of stunned too.

We roll several feet past the lounge area, and then we're less conspicuous, since there's people traffic here as most everyone is heading to the cafeteria.

"Okay, why the hell did you do that?" he says, putting his arm down hard to stop the wheels from moving, and we are paused near the cafeteria entrance. Teens are jostling past us, and the smell of fries and cooked burger is overpowering.

"I thought you were . . . well, stuck, and needed a reason to get away." I let go of the wheelchair and look at him, attempting a friendly expression, but managing only slightly sour.

"Seriously?" He cranes his neck to the side to better look at me. His hair falls from his forehead and eyes, and I see he is *furious*.

I am kind of amazed, and this time I am getting ticked off too.

"I told you before," he says, "*I don't need your help.* What part of 'I don't need your help' did you not understand? Are you an idiot?"

"Jeez, thanks a lot. . . ." I start to say something awful, then bite my lip. "Look, I just got you out of a crappy situation that was about to get ugly. The least you can do is say thanks!"

But Blayne continues to look at me as if I am the one who'd just cornered him and called him a waste of space. "You really are stupid," he says. "If you think they were going to do anything. It's just words. And words don't hurt me. And they know better than to do anything that could compromise their place here, their precious chances to Qualify."

"It sure didn't look like that to me. Trust me, I personally know how it is, how these a-holes operate. Things can deteriorate—just like that. And no one would notice, not even with all the security cameras. . . . Oh yeah, and thanks for calling me stupid, so much appreciated."

"You still don't get it." He shakes his head at me with a cold expression. "I had it under control. I *know* how to deal with it. I've been dealing for years. And now you've only made it worse."

"Worse? Worse—how? Okay, I am sorry—sorry if I insulted you somehow," I say, stumbling on words. "But I just couldn't watch them do it to you."

"Here's what. Before you interfered, they were just bored, just venting. But now, they are pissed. And they've noticed *both* of us. That's how worse."

I shrug, and my frown is back. "Okay then. I don't know what to say. . . ."

Blayne suddenly relaxes his face. He is not exactly smiling, but at least he doesn't look like he is going to lash out and scorch me. "That's the first intelligent thing you've said," he mutters.

I let out a breath. I should be pissed at him, and in some small way I still am. But I also suddenly understand. And somehow that makes it okay.

My gaze falls down momentarily at his legs. They are thin, stick-like, encased in blue jeans. His feet, looking oversized in comparison, in white tube-socks that are folded neatly around his ankles, are stuck in a useless pair of sneakers. It occurs to me that his sneakers are so pristine, so clean.

"Since we're here," he continues, "I'm going in, to eat."

And Blayne starts rolling his wheelchair through the cafeteria entrance.

I follow him.

I watch Blayne collect a tray and start putting stuff on it with skill born of practice. A plate with a burger, some fries, coleslaw, a dish of orange jello. He is balancing the tray on his lap and pouring a glass of milk from the dispenser and I don't dare help him. As I get my own plate, and ask the server for extra fries, I see Laronda. She's carrying an overloaded tray and motioning with her head at me toward an empty table.

"Hey, Gwen! Over here, girlfriend!"

I turn and see Blayne has disappeared. A quick scan of the busy room reveals him at a distant table near the wall, alone. His wheelchair is positioned so that his back is turned to the rest of the hall.

"Gwen! Wake up! You coming?" Laronda's making googly eyes.

"Why don't we go sit over there?" I say, and carry my tray to Blayne's table.

Laronda's right behind me.

"Hey," she says, as we stop near Blayne and his wheelchair. "Who's your friend?"

Blayne reacts by tightening his shoulders and staring at me. The half-eaten burger is suspended in his hands, and his mouth is full, so I simply put my tray down next to his, and pull up a chair.

I realize I'm acting a little crazy-weird even for me. Why am I doing this? He's clearly not interested in human contact. And normally, neither am I.

Blayne continues chewing and stares in fascination as Laronda plunks down her tray, making dishes and plasticware rattle, and sits down on the other side of him. "Hi, I'm Laronda."

He finally swallows, looks at her once then completely ignores her, and gives me a sideways glance. "Did I say you could sit here? No? What makes you think I want to—"

"Well, I wouldn't want to eat alone," I mumble.

"Then *don't*. There's another empty table over there. Or that one, with people on it." He points with the hand that's holding the burger, and takes another bite. He's no longer looking at us but at his plate.

"Hey, hey! Hold your seahorses!" Laronda opens her mouth and puts her hand palm down. "We just want to eat lunch, okay? Not date you. Gwen, how come we're sitting with this guy? I thought he was your friend or something."

"He's definitely something," I say, while my cheeks are turning red in angry embarrassment.

And then I glance at Blayne and he is silent, hunched over, and something about him twists me on the inside. I see the yellow token on the front of his shirt, lit up brightly, as a strange reminder of everything, of this impossible situation we are all in.

"Look," I say. "I completely understand you want to be alone, but it's probably better you're not, at least not right now. Those—those *mean* people out there, they could come in here any moment and bother you again and do something *bad.*"

"So?" Blayne tips his glass to wash down the burger. "Big bad meanies are gonna get me. What's it to you? Why are you taking to me like a three-year-old?"

"I'm not—I mean, sorry. It's nothing. Nothing, I guess, but—" He's got a point. Why am I talking like that? What's wrong with me?

"Okay, what's going on?" Laronda says, starting her own lunch, jello-first. "Big bad who?"

"I'll tell you later." I glance at Laronda. And then I continue to Blayne. "Sorry—and I—I'm not sure. It kind of really upsets me, I guess. No—I don't just *guess,* I am pretty certain it upsets me. Really sorry for being annoying and possibly weird. I'm not stalking you or anything. I mean, I don't even *know* you."

"Okay." Blayne is done eating the burger and his fingers are drumming on the table. He looks at me, and his expression is direct and sarcastic. "So what do you want? My irresistible self? My four-wheel drive wheelchair?"

"Jeez, you some kind of jerk . . ." Laronda mutters with a mouth full of jello and frowns at him.

"He's not!" I say quickly, turning to her, then back to Blayne. "It's not you, it's *them.* They're the jerks."

"Thanks." Blayne is watching me expectantly. "So, answer

the question."

"What I want? I guess I want to make sure you're going to be okay, at least short-term—at least before that asteroid hits Earth. So let's just start over, please." I meet the gaze of his very blue eyes. "Hi, my name is Gwen Lark. I go to school in Northern Vermont, snow country. I'm guessing you do too. Nice to meet you."

Not sure what's happened, but a few minutes later we're all still talking, and Blayne is no longer trying to get rid of me—at least not actively—although he still has a closed-off expression. Laronda has taken it in stride and just as quickly seems to have forgotten the initial person-to-person weirdness. Now she is complaining loudly about her Atlantis Combat class that she just had before lunch, and for once both Blayne and I are interested in hearing this.

"Okay, I have no clue why we need to learn their fighting stuff. Like, are we expected to enlist in some kind of Atlantis army, or what? Do they have street fighting there? Space gangs? Anyway, first there was all this funky *rope* and netting stuff. I can't even begin to describe—well, then they made us line up and throw these martial arts punches! Whoa! Whoa!" Laronda makes a wild slash motion with one hand and then a dance move with the other. "Okay, no, actually they didn't, but it was something called *forms*, and it wasn't exactly punches, but what do I know, right? I have *no idea* what it was, but it was c-raaazy! Like real King Fu or Karate, kick-boxing stuff you only see in those action movies! I mean, girlfriend, I can't do that! Mama help me, I almost had my eye poked out by this one guy who was supposed to be my partner. He did this coo-coo twirly thing, and I did that—" She again motions with one hand and then the other, and almost knocks over her glass.

"Did you say rope? Martial arts? Wow. Ugh. I have that class last today," I say while a new pang twists my stomach. "So, Combat is going to suck. Though I can't imagine it's any worse than Agility." I explain to Laronda what happened in our first class. "Blayne and I both had it first thing. At least he got to use the hoverboard while I died and went to gym hell."

"I actually like the hoverboard," he says softly. "It makes me feel like I can get around for once. Kind of evens the playing field."

"Oh, yeah?" I lean my head to the side, watching him.

Blayne glances sideways at me then looks away and fiddles with the plastic spoon on his empty plate.

"I wouldn't mind having a hoverboard instead of this stupid wheelchair," he says. "Then I wouldn't need disabled access. I could just fly around on it, upstairs or anywhere I like. It's amazing."

"You could take it to the bathroom with you," Laronda jokes.

But he's all serious. "Yeah, I could."

"You know, that's not a bad idea." I bite my lip thoughtfully.

"What, a hoverboard in the bathroom?" Laronda snorts, enjoying this.

"No, but he could ask for one. Maybe the Atlanteans would let him borrow one for the duration of this Qualification thing."

Blayne shakes his head. "I doubt it."

"You should ask them, at least."

But he only shrugs.

At the same time a claxon alarm sounds, and suddenly everyone in the cafeteria is getting up. It's five minutes till our 1:00 PM classes.

"See you later, Blayne. . . ." I pick up my tray.

"Yeah, good luck in crappy Combat, hope they give you a hoverboard," Laronda tells him, since it's his next class.

He gathers his tray with one hand and mutters a short and sardonic "Yeah, sure, whatever. . . . Bye."

Then the two of us head to our mutual Atlantis Culture class up on the third floor.

As we're walking up the stairs, Laronda says, "Well, this Blayne guy's a piece of work. But I like him."

I smile slightly. "I do too. Don't know why, though. He's got an attitude."

"Well yeah, wouldn't you? Poor guy's stuck in a wheelchair. Do you know what's wrong with his legs?"

"No. . . ."

"You gonna ask him about it?"

"Probably not. It's kind of rude, at this point."

"Too bad. Well, maybe I'll ask him—later, eventually, don't worry. He's kind of cute. In a pitiful puppy sort of way." Laronda waves her hand and casually slaps the stairwell banister.

"Pitiful? I don't know about that. Asocial, maybe, but I wouldn't call him pitiful. I don't think he is at all. I think—"

"He could be kind of hot, if he moved all that hair out of his face, so you could see his eyes." She winks at me. And then she remembers. "Hey! So have you seen your hunky Logan yet? What's the name, Logan Sangre?"

"Not today." We turn onto the fourth floor landing, both already out of breath, and my heart skips an additional beat at the thought of Logan Sangre. "He's probably in his own dorm, Number One, I think. He's in the Red Quadrant, like my sister Gracie."

"Same dorm?"

"I wish. No, she's in Five. I'm going over to see her tonight after dinner—that is, if I survive two more classes." I laugh bitterly.

We go down the long, now familiar fourth floor hall, in search of Room 9.

Chapter 8

The room where they are going to teach us Atlantis Culture is blessedly just a regular classroom with desks and a whiteboard up in front. The Instructor's desk is yet unoccupied and mostly empty of gadgets. However, there are, what appear to be, several very old looking books and long cylinders that may or may not be *real* ancient scrolls. The classics and history professor's daughter in me is starting to geek out at the possibility.

The room is getting filled up quickly, so Laronda and I take two seats close to the front in the second row. If possible, I would've taken first row, following my usual nerdy habit in school, but Laronda is a little more hesitant to be noticed by the teacher. Therefore, row two, where you don't get to be seen as much while you still get a decent view of the board, is a nice compromise.

At the height of the classroom noise an Atlantean walks in quietly, and continues past the seated Candidates, stopping at the teacher's desk. He seems to be an older teen, not unlike Oalla Keigeri. Or possibly he just looks that way, generally youthful, because we still don't have an accurate sense of the Atlanteans' aging rate compared to our own. And, just like Oalla, he is wearing the grey uniform with a yellow arm-band. His blazing-gold hair is trimmed shorter than most other Atlanteans I've seen, but his face is typically handsome in the general way of their ethnicity—not that we really know the full range of ethnic diversity on Atlantis, but so far we've seen a pattern that seems to point more and more to Ancient Egypt, or even India, at least in this bunch. Well-balanced features, a somewhat blunt chin with a single dimple, prominent brows, and eyelids decorated in lapis and kohl. The only difference is, his skin is a few degrees darker, a hue somewhere between olive and sienna, so that it is reminiscent of red river clay.

He is carrying a small tablet-like device that looks vaguely alien in the same way that I've come to recognize Atlantis tech—the overall shape is imperfect, asymmetrical, unlike the tech gadgets designed on Earth which are usually polished and balanced to appear aesthetically pleasing, smooth, trendy objects.

He places the Atlantean tablet on the desk next to the books and scrolls.

And then he speaks.

"Good afternoon, Candidates. I am Nefir Mekei. I am from Atlantis, and I am going to teach you Atlantis Culture."

As his words flow, it seems a soft, lilting, almost subliminal buzzing hum has entered the classroom, and echoes are reverberating along the walls. Immediately I feel goose bumps. The fine hairs along my arms begin to stand up on end from the strange tangible sensation of this guy's amazing voice. It's grazing along my skin and smoothing it down at the same time, as though honey is being poured over every inch of me, making me alert and receptive at the same time. . . .

I glance to my side and Laronda is equally affected. She is staring at the Atlantean with wide eyes and parted lips. And, it seems, so is everyone else in the room.

Nefir Mekei looks around at us, his unblinking gaze sweeping the classroom. There is a shadow of a smile on his face.

"What you are hearing now is the voice of a Storyteller. It is one of many things you will learn about us, your distant ancient relatives. In our society on Atlantis we cultivate very special *voices*—voices that are imbued with power, to a varying degree. Voices that in their inflection have a purpose and a specific task attached. There are voices of Creation, of Force, of Movement, of Command, of Desire. Voices that build skyscrapers, and navigate ships, and dig canals, and heal whatever ails the body. There are so many voices that it would take me several days to tell you the function of each. Suffice it to say, they are voices for everything you can imagine, and even for things you have no words for."

"Wow," someone says in the back of us.

"Wow is a good way to sum it up," Nefir says, turning to the speaker. "You will learn much more in the coming days, but for now, be aware of the Storyteller voice, because you will come to know it very well."

"What else can you do?" says the boy.

Nefir looks at him and smiles. "I was taught a number of different voices. We all were, since infancy. However, most of us retain the mastery of only a few. Usually we excel at one in particular. It becomes our specialty. Mine is this one."

A chubby girl with curling red hair raises her hand nervously. "Are you gonna teach us these—voices?"

"I will try. In the very short time we have, you may not be able to learn this skill that takes many years to cultivate. Yes, a few of you might be fortunate enough to discover a basic ability to do a voice or two. But at least all the rest of you will know about it. And you will have some idea of how to defend yourself from—its unwanted effects."

"Oh, yeah?" a brown-skinned Latino boy says, running fingers through his black hair. "What kind of effects? Are you talking about some kind of *mind control?* Like making people do things?"

The Atlantean pauses. "You might call it that, yes—perhaps. But rest assured, mind control is completely illegal in Atlantis, and misuse of voice is strictly punished and enforced. Potentially dangerous forms of power voice may only be used with the consent of others. Also there are defense techniques that are taught—which I will teach you, as I said. But first—today, our first day, I will tell you some general things you need to know about Atlantis. You might want to take notes—"

The shuffling of papers is heard as Candidates take out notebooks and writing implements, while some people reach out to touch-enable their smart jewelry recording functions.

"—Atlantis is a planet very similar to Earth, technically larger in circumference, but only by a negligible number of your Earth units of distance. It is located in the area of your sky that you know as the constellation of Pegasus, or the Great Square. The sun of Atlantis is slightly bigger and brighter than Earth's Sol, so daylight is more blazing, and the seasons are longer due to a longer orbit and hence year, the equivalent of 417 Earth days. The day is slightly longer also, the equivalent of Earth's 27 hours, because Atlantis rotates along its axis a bit slower than Earth.

"The atmosphere is oxygen rich, similar to Earth. Now, we

have somewhat less surface water on Atlantis, so there are only two large oceans that cover about one half of the planet, and the rest is mostly green forests and tall snow-covered mountains. Other animal species are abundant. However, unlike Earth, Atlantis is very sparsely populated, with fewer than a billion human beings on the planet, and fewer than seventy national boundaries. There are several main cities—"

I take my usual excessive notes while the general geography lesson goes on. Each time I glance at him, Nefir appears to be speaking eloquently about the most fascinating things ever, and the classroom is hanging on to his every word. Okay, even I know that's not natural. No one is *that* interested in surface temperatures and demographics. *No one.* Especially not some of the less brainy kids . . . not to mention, the jocks, or the obvious junkies. (Because, yeah, I can see some of them in this room. I've no idea how they managed to pass Preliminary Qualification while being high on some crap.)

Must be his compelling Storyteller voice that's causing us to pay such super attention.

Before I know it, the hour is up and class is over.

"We will continue tomorrow." Nefir picks up his tablet device and lightly touches its surface with his fingertip. Immediately all our tokens emit a single bright pulse of yellow light, like a flash, then return to steady yellow. Gasps are heard around the classroom.

"Relax, I've just taken your attendance," he says. His face again registers the same light smile. It's both wise and curious. And yet I find it slightly obnoxious because it manages to come across as superior.

"Yeesh! Could've used a warning!" Laronda blinks, staring at her own token.

"I bet he did it on purpose to mess with us," I say lightly, putting away my notes. I'm still feeling the happy buzz of intellectual excitement from the lecture I've just heard.

And then just as quickly it dissipates. Because I suddenly realize what's my next and last class for the day.

Atlantis Combat.

My stomach is in knots as I head back down to the basement Training Hall gym. I've only been here once previously, and I already hate this room with a passion.

This time I notice the presence of mats on the floor—which is both a good thing and a bad thing. Good, because at least if we fall down, there will be padding to break the fall. Bad, because, well, there's gonna be *falling* going on.

Ugh. . . .

I stare around the room and see the weights training equipment in the front near the entrance, and the now familiar multi-story scaffolding where somewhere up on top the hoverboards are stashed away. There are about thirty people here so far, and more are coming in behind me. We all look sheepish, stressed, scared—or at least most of us do, and after a quick glance I see there are no familiar faces.

No, I take that back. There's at least one. Claudia Grito is standing with her arms folded, looking fearless and bored. Her long black hair has been gathered into a sleek ponytail and she's changed into a tight black tank-top and skin-tight jeans. The bright overhead lights catch like fire in the metal stud piercings in her nose and ears.

Just as I think it can't get any worse, I see several of the popular hashtaggers from the lobby who had ganged up on Blayne. There's curvy Olivia and the dark-haired guy with the neck tattoo, and the big blond jock Wade.

The moment they see me they all turn like vultures. I feel the weight of their stares, hear smirking whispers, while a cold numbing thing starts to build and fill me up like a brick. How well I know that cold slimy resident of my gut.

While I freeze, they start casually moving in my direction. Meanwhile, the neck tattoo guy shapes his mouth into a nasty kiss, then licks his lips and gives me a sneer, all without taking his eyes off me. I think that's gotta be the creepiest worst.

Before any of them reach me however, I am saved by the arrival of Oalla Keigeri. The gorgeous Atlantean girl comes into the gym hall walking in her swift brusque manner. She is followed by two others.

"Attention, Candidates!" Oalla claps her hands together and starts speaking before she even reaches the middle of the room.

"Line up!"

Everyone's milling about, but her ringing drill sergeant voice compels us, so that for a moment I wonder if she's using a *power voice*, now that I know about it. The bullies forget me for the moment, and everyone moves in toward her.

"Two lines, one to my right, one to my left! Starting here, now! *Move!*"

We hurry to do what she says, in a brief stampede. I swear, it feels like army basic training. In seconds I find myself in a lineup with some skinny African American guy with locks I don't know to my right, and a young Asian girl I've never seen before on my left. Meanwhile, across from me are other unfamiliar, frightened faces.

Basically we've just formed a gauntlet line. Or maybe a line dancing line. Whatever. There's roughly two rows of us, facing each other, separated by about ten feet.

Oalla stands at the start of the line between our two rows, and two other Atlanteans are behind her.

"Stand up straight! Feet together! Hands down at your sides! Eyes on me!"

We shuffle and pull ourselves up as straight as possible. I press my fingers against my sides and notice from the corner of my eye the Asian girl to my left is shaking.

Oalla takes a step aside, and the Atlantean immediately behind her walks forward so that at last we can see him. He is very tall, ebony-black, with the darkest skin I've seen so far in their kind, but his tightly curled short hair is colored the same molten gold. He is slightly older or possibly our age, extremely good looking, with a slightly heavier cast to his features, and a beautifully toned muscular body encased in the grey uniform that looks tailored on him. Curiously, the armband he is wearing is blue, not yellow.

"Good afternoon," he says in a deep gorgeous voice. "I am Keruvat Ruo, and I am from Atlantis. Some of you know me already from an earlier Agility class, just as you know Oalla Keigeri who also teaches Agility. Together, we will be teaching Combat."

"But first—" He nods to Oalla who picks up speaking after

him.

"First, before we begin," she says loudly, "we are fortunate to have with us today an important visitor."

Keruvat and Oalla both take a step to either side, and we all stare while a third Atlantean walks past them and stops in the middle.

He is not nearly as tall as Keruvat, but now that he is here, his presence overwhelms. Light bronze skin, striking chiseled features. Longish golden hair, of a washed-out metallic hue that seems a shade lighter than the others. He is probably the same age as Keruvat and Oalla, an older teen, or the Atlantean equivalent. His expression is a perfect blank mask, hard and impassive. His eyes, framed by dark brows and a fine tracing of kohl, are fierce blue lapis. His lips are held in a tight slightly disdainful line.

The grey uniform sits well on his toned body, compact, muscular. And yes, it must be said, there is something about him overall—maybe the confident way he stands, the way he holds himself—that makes him strangely, undeniably *hot.*

Okay, I can't believe I just said that. But it's true. . . .

This guy is *attractive*, and I bet he knows it.

As I am thinking this, I notice also that he's wearing an armband that is neither yellow, nor blue, red, green, or even rainbow.

It is black.

"This is Command Pilot Aeson Kass, one of the highest ranking officers of our Fleet, and *astra daimon*. Remember well his name, for you will come to know it, even among the other *daimon*. He is here to observe our class, to observe all of you. This is an honor!" Oalla speaks, glancing around the room, and then looks back at Aeson Kass with a tiny light smile. This is the first time I've seen Oalla smiling, and it makes her face more open, more beautiful, if such a thing is even possible.

It occurs to me for just a moment, that Oalla is deferring to him, and it's a strange thing to see. Meanwhile, Keruvat is looking from her to Aeson, and there's also a tiny shadow of a smile just wanting to break out.

But Aeson Kass does not smile. "Thank you, Oalla, Keruvat." His voice is pleasantly low, but very soft, almost tired-sounding, which is probably deceptive. "And now, please proceed."

Aeson Kass then moves aside and barely nods to the other two Atlanteans. He simply stands, watching us.

Oalla and Keruvat take us through some kind of a warm-up drill. I honestly don't even know what is happening, but it's hell and there are just no words. . . . My body is like a puppet, and I am told to move this way and step that way . . . jump up and down, and raise both hands and arms . . . extend my torso and bend forward, then back, and rotate from the waist . . . crane my neck, then drop to the floor and do something else physically unspeakable. A few minutes later I am panting hard, and so are many of the teens around me.

It really sucks to be out of shape. And we haven't even started anything real yet, this is just warm-up!

"Enough! Now stand! Line up!" Oalla says at last.

I crawl up from some kind of messy sit-up, and stand, breathing hard. My weak knees are buckling under me, still traumatized and shaking from the physical effort of this morning's Agility Training ordeal. The guy with African locks next to me is rubbing his elbow and I see sweat glistening on his face. He mouths some kind of complaint and grins painfully at me, while I nod back and roll my eyes.

As I'm still struggling to calm my breath, Keruvat goes to an equipment cabinet near the wall and motions to one of the Candidates in line to follow him. The teen and the tall black Atlantean both return carrying a large bulky athletic bag which they deposit in the middle of the room.

Keruvat nods for the Candidate to fall back in line. He then unzips the huge bag, and turns it over to dump out what looks like a whole bunch of netting. Ropes and nets and cords of all sizes and lengths, some twisted, some in great spools. There's metallic and plastic, and ordinary coarse natural rope, and everything in-between.

"Candidates, take a good look," he says, pacing around the mountain of netted and loose strands on the floor. "These nets and cords are the basic weapon of the Yellow Quadrant. If you want to Qualify, you will learn to use them to your advantage, in addition to the hand-to-hand combat forms of Er-Du which is our traditional martial art."

Oalla approaches and picks up a short net, and snaps it open. Turns out, it's a two-meter wide round woven piece resembling a spider web, with sizeable gaps between each segment, big enough to draw your hand and arm through it. "This alone," she says, "can be used to kill your opponent."

Keruvat meanwhile reaches into the pile of netting to select a single long cord. "And this," he says, "can serve you equally well."

Oalla picks up the net and with a lightning motion she flings it at Keruvat, who stands still to allow her the demonstration. "The net is an ancient traditional weapon of Poseidon, the great city of Atlantis, and its origins are the sea," Oalla says, as she tightens a single rope segment, and suddenly Keruvat is immobilized in an impossible net cocoon. His entire body is encased to his ankles, and his hands and feet bound. "Fishermen used nets to harvest the waters of ancient Earth oceans, and then the tradition was continued on Atlantis. First, they harvested fish, then they learned to harvest men."

A few surprised exclamations are heard in our rows.

"Now, admittedly, the net and cord of the Yellow Quadrant is impressive on its own," Keruvat retorts. "But it is a weak weapon against the edged blade weapon of the Red Quadrant, the *sword*." Still bound, he makes an equally blazing-fast move, despite his confined state, and retrieves a previously invisible short dagger from his sleeve. He slashes a few times, and in seconds he is free of the net, which now lies in torn pieces on the floor.

"Whoa!" some kid gasps in the line nearby.

"Yes, the Red Quadrant sword cleaves the Yellow Quadrant cord," Oalla says, with a blank, hard expression. "But it, in turn, is a weak weapon against the Blue Quadrant *firearm*." She draws like quicksilver, and from a hidden holster on her leg comes a small object resembling an Earth handgun. She fires, there's a soft pop, and Keruvat's dagger goes flying out of his hand from the force of the projectile striking the blade perilously near the grip.

This time there are loud hoots of appreciation all around the gym hall. Some of the guys clap. A few of the younger boys and girls hold their hands to their mouths.

But Oalla and Keruvat ignore the noise around them. Their gazes are locked, and now they are circling each other, in loose sleek fighter stances.

"As you see, the Blue Quadrant firearm trumps the Red Quadrant blade," Keruvat says, without taking his eyes off Oalla. "However, it happens to be a weak weapon against the Green Quadrant *shield*."

I have no time to blink because Keruvat's hand streaks for his own hidden gun holster on his thigh. He fires at Oalla—not once, but in a series of sharp staccato pops and the volley fills the hall with recoil echoes.

Holy crap! I cringe, wanting to cover my eyes. . . .

But amazingly, Oalla is standing unharmed. Each time Keruvat fires, she as quickly moves her forearms in a strange shielding stance between her and the bullet projectiles. And now I see her long grey uniform sleeves are riddled with holes going up her arm and all the way to her shoulder.

Okay, *what is she*, some kind of freaky comic book heroine? Super duper bullet-resistant wonder? She should be seriously hurt, maybe even dead!

But Oalla raises her hands and arms to show us the torn sleeves and bullet holes, and then she pulls up her uniform sleeves, rolling them up past the armband, to her shoulders.

Her arms, from the wrists up to just below her armpits, are encased in some kind of skin-tight braces, made of a silvery metallic material. I am guessing it is not ordinary fabric. However, it is discreet, and amazing in the sense that it can be worn easily and inconspicuously underneath long sleeves, like body armor. The bullets—small round pellets of metal—are stuck like pearls to the material of the braces.

This time most of us are too stunned to make a sound.

The African locks guy next to me silently mouths, "Oh, f— me!"

"As you can see, I am unhurt," Oalla announces in a loud voice, still holding up her hands and arms to the room. "Every bullet has been stopped and adhered to the arm shield. Underneath, my skin might show a few light impact bruises tomorrow, but that's about it."

"Before you lose your nerve completely," Keruvat speaks up, starting to circle Oalla once again, "you need to realize that while the Green Quadrant shield might defeat the Blue Quadrant gun, it is a weak weapon and no match for your own Yellow Quadrant *cord!*"

Keruvat flings himself toward Oalla, and this time the cord is back—the same one he's been discreetly holding all along, apparently balled up in one fist. He makes a series of strange coordinated hand and finger movements and the cord becomes a sequence of short loops that he'd single-handedly shaped and twisted with the fingers of one hand, because there's no other explanation for it.

In seconds, the loops are thrown then tightened around Oalla's arms in their braces, and her hands are effectively tied together before her in an intricate net-like knot.

She stands with a shadow of a smile, hands bound, while Keruvat holds the end of the cord and nods at her. He then flicks his wrist and the cord handcuffs come apart with a single tug. Must be sleight-of-hand, because honestly, even looking at it, I have no idea how he did that!

This time everyone in the room is clapping.

Off to the side, Aeson Kass claps also. He then continues to observe, arms folded at his chest. I glance at him and note the continued impassive expression, hard and cold and impenetrable like a wall.

Oalla rubs her arms lightly along the bullet-covered braces, then pulls down her sleeves. "You have just learned the basic tenet of Atlantis weapons combat. Yellow cord trumps Green shield trumps Blue firearm trumps Red blade, which in turn trumps Yellow cord. It's an eternal circular balance—a Great Square. Somewhat like your Earth game of *paper-scissors-rock*. We in Atlantis study all four weapon forms, but ultimately specialize in one, depending on which Quadrant we embrace."

She paces between our rows, fierce and commanding.

A frightened girl raises her hand. "Seems amazing, all of this. How much of the weapon fighting are we supposed to learn? I mean, there's so little time. . . ."

Oalla turns to look at her, and the poor girl almost cringes. "A valid question. And yes, there's hardly enough time to master weapons and combat techniques in just a few weeks. For that, you will need *years*. But there is enough time to determine if you have the potential to become proficient. Those of you who can prove your potential, will Qualify."

"But suppose for a moment—what if you have no weapon?"
Keruvat speaks in turn. "What if there's no netted cord, no gun, no
sword, no shield at your disposal? Then all you have are your bare
hands, your body, your speed, strength, and stamina. And, don't
forget, your *voice* and your mind."

"And that's where the ancient martial art of Er-Du comes in,"
Oalla says. Unexpectedly she turns around and her gaze seeks
Aeson Kass. With a bow of her head and a smoothly gliding hand
movement, she motions to him. "With your permission, Command
Pilot Kass, may I have the honor, *daimon?*"

We all stare.

Aeson's face does not show any reaction, not even a motion
of an eyelid, not a blink. A pause. And then he nods lightly. And
he approaches.

For some reason I find that my breathing has pretty much
stopped. I stare, mesmerized, as I see Aeson and Oalla fall
seamlessly into a pliant combat stance. Although Aeson is much
taller, they appear evenly matched. Feet are slightly apart, knees
loose, backs straight. Their hands start at their sides, then sweep
upward like wings, then fall back to float in the air at shoulder
level, in a strangest kind of warrior dance.

They circle each other and take wide steps, parallel and
opposite to each other like chess pawns starting out their strategic
movement across a chessboard. Their fingers make complex signs,
hands and arms continue moving with strange grace, from unfurled
wings to snakes, to swans, shaping intricate figures in the air
before them.

In the next instant, Oalla strikes. She is a serpent, or a
scorpion bringing down its tail. Her hands flash forward, and are
met and blocked effortlessly by her opponent. Aeson seems to be
barely moving, so casually and lightly he steps, and his hands flash
out, arms bent at the elbows, then twisting to escape impossibly,
coming together and apart in intricate contortions, easily avoiding
Oalla's fierce hand strikes.

I bite my lip and continue to hold my breath.

Their hand strikes rain down, faster and faster. . . . And now,
kicks are added to the mix. Oalla takes a running leap and does a

roundhouse kick, narrowly missing his chest, while Aeson lunges to the side and away like an eel, then returns with his own kick. It lands and sends Oalla flying along the slippery floor, away from the safe landing area of the mats. She recovers easily with a back flip, and springs back up. Immediately she goes into a spin series of kicks and punches that move so fast she appears to be spinning into invisibility like a top.

Aeson Kass matches her effortlessly, strike for strike. . . .

It is all happening so fast now, faster than any martial arts combat sequence I've ever seen, even in those SFX-enhanced ancient Hong Kong action movies where people fly on hidden wires, seemingly by magic. I can no longer tell what's going on.

I also momentarily wonder if either of these Atlanteans is actually *human*.

No way on God's green Earth—or on Atlantis—will I, or for that matter any of the Candidates, ever be able to do anything even remotely close to what's being demonstrated here before our eyes. This is insane!

Then just as unexpectedly they come to a stop. Their feet are planted in wide stances, hands held in pliant beautiful final forms, palms of one hand touching their opponent's while the other hand floats. Their gazes are unblinking and they stand looking at each other, with only slightly elevated breathing to mark their impossible exertions.

A pause.

Then Oalla breaks away, lowers her palm and then lowers her head in a small bow, then steps backward. "My profound thanks, *astra daimon*."

Aeson Kass nods to her, and straightens, stepping out of his own final form. "A pleasure as always, *daimon* Oalla."

"Wait, what? She's a *daimon* too? What's a *daimon* again?" The locks guy next to me whispers, and I throw him a quick glance, raising my eyebrows and widening my eyes to indicate cluelessness.

Bad move.

All three Atlanteans turn in our direction, and suddenly the locks guy and I are both being scrutinized by three intense stern gazes.

"You ask what is a *daimon*," Keruvat says. "We are *astra*

daimon. We are the elite of the Star Pilot Corps, who have mastered our disciplines and excelled beyond the highest expectations of our rank."

Oalla glances at Keruvat, followed by a fleeting glance at Aeson. Then she again looks at us—at *me* in particular. "The *astra daimon* answer to no one but their own. We are a brotherhood and sisterhood, the best of the best. To be chosen as one of our brethren, a Pilot must earn the honor. The *astra daimon* have mastered the disciplines of at least one of the Four Quadrants. See this band on my arm?" She points to the yellow armband on her sleeve. "These are not mere 'dorm colors' as you might have seen on some of the other Instructors. It is a symbol of my chosen discipline and Allegiance to the Yellow Quadrant."

"As mine is to the Blue Quadrant," Keruvat says, pointing to his own blue armband sleeve.

"And what about him?" the guy with locks next to me speaks up suddenly, motioning at Aeson Kass. "Is he some kind of black ninja?"

A few stifled giggles and nervous titters are heard.

Aeson's expression does not change. Everyone stares at the black armband on his sleeve.

Oalla addresses locks. "Your name, Candidate?"

"Who? Me?" the kid with the locks says. "Yeah, okay. I'm Tremaine—Tremaine Walters."

"Tremaine Walters, you think this is funny?" Oalla says. Her voice is hard as flint.

"Um, no . . . sorry."

"The black color of his armband means that this *astra daimon* has *died* on our behalf. He has given his life once for the Fleet and his brethren, and he was brought back, and we are forever indebted to him—all of us, indeed, all of Atlantis."

Keruvat adds, "A black armband is the highest honor, and is usually earned posthumously—after death. Command Pilot Aeson Kass is a rare exception. He is one of the few in our history who has the right to wear the black armband while living."

I hold my breath, and so does, it seems, everyone else in the gym hall. Tremaine's jaw drops.

"All right, any more questions, before we proceed?" Oalla

scans the room, glancing down the two rows of Candidates.

In that moment, some crazy brain thing makes me open my big fat mouth.

"Yes, I have a question..." I say, raising my hand tremulously. And then the words just come pouring out, because I am in the blab zone. "Why? Why all this? Why must there even *be* Combat? Why do we need to learn to fight, and hurt, and possibly kill other people, in order to Qualify for just being alive? Doesn't Atlantis have some kind of organized legal system so that the average citizen doesn't need to engage in violence? I mean—"

It's gotten so quiet you can hear the hum of the air conditioning.

Everyone is staring at me.

And I mean, *everyone*.

Oalla watches me with an intense scrutiny, and Keruvat's expression is curiosity.

But it is Aeson Kass who speaks.

"You ask why we are required to fight?" The Command Pilot looks at me directly, and I feel his gaze like a tangible thing, as though a bright searchlight is suddenly shining at me and through me. "In Atlantis, we believe in taking responsibility for ourselves. As you learn to fight, you learn to defend yourself from physical harm. You acquire a powerful self-preserving skill set, and a specific attitude. This attitude carries across to other aspects of your life. So that you can defend yourself from other *less tangible* but far more dangerous things that can break you—not just your body, but your spirit. Things such as deception, corruption, disparagement, coercion, false accusation and persecution. Subtle evil things that undermine *you*. And if you can maintain the inner ability to defend yourself against influence, you can build a *purpose* in your life that no one can take away from you."

He pauses momentarily, still looking at me, holding me like a fly caught in amber, in the overwhelming power of his gaze. "In Atlantis, we believe that purpose is the most important virtue. You can lose your freedom, your health, your honor, everything you love and care about. And yet, if you still have your purpose, you have lost nothing."

He ends, his words falling like bright ringing things. "Does that answer your question?"

Silently, I nod. . . . For the first time in like *ever*, I, who usually talk in class and competitively argue with all my teachers, I who have geeky amazing opinions to offer and theories to elaborate or dispute—I've been rendered speechless. Why? I'm not sure exactly, but for some reason the things he just said kind of blew my mind. I feel like I suddenly understand *why*—why Combat.

As I stand thinking this, his cool gaze leaves me. Aeson Kass turns away and nods once to Keruvat and Oalla. In the next breath, he has forgotten me and now observes the rest of the Candidates.

I exhale. . . .

Next to me Tremaine raises his eyebrows and gives me a "wow" look. On the other side of me, the Asian girl whose name I don't know makes brief sympathetic eye contact.

And then we forget everything because Oalla Keigeri shouts a command.

"Candidates! You will now learn the basic Forms of Er-Du! Watch and follow me!"

She strikes a simple wide stance opening form, and suddenly we all move, copying her. A few feet down the line, Keruvat falls into the same opening form, moving elegantly like her doppelgänger.

I step forward, and raise my right hand, clumsily trying to repeat what the two Atlantean Instructors are doing. My hand is shaking; my wide stance is unsteady.

I seriously hope that, whatever he might be doing, Aeson Kass is not looking at me right now.

Chapter 9

When Combat Training is finally dismissed, it is close to 5:30 PM.

I think I am dead.

No, really, I am a disembodied spirit dragging around a skinny meat carcass made of Pain and Fail that was just made to do crazy things with itself it has never done before. Almost two hours of lunging forward on shaking legs and unsteady feet, and then trying to do weird stuff with hand motions with the person across from you in the other row.

Lucky me—for the whole afternoon I've been paired up with some small wiry kid who looks like a freshman or even a middle schooler, and oh yeah, he is just a happy athletic bundle of horrid energy.

Damn you, Joshua Bell and your enthusiasm for Tae Kwan Do or whatever martial art you happen to think *you know from your local Philly dojo, and now you think you can kick my useless butt in this Er-Du. . . .*

I grumble to myself as I climb up the stairs to the third floor girls' dormitory, clutching the banister with both hands. My hair is in ratty wet tangles, so—reminder to self—next time, put it up in a ponytail before Agility or Combat Training.

Dinner is at 6:00 PM, so there's time to kind of collapse onto the cot for fifteen minutes, or maybe take a shower, because yeah, I am pouring sweat. Okay, so are most of the other Candidates in my class. (I saw them crawling up the stairs like roadkill all around me, so, yeah.)

I consider the situation, and shower wins out. And so I get in line in the bathroom, and fifteen minutes later I am decent, and wearing my only other change of clothing. Hope there's a laundry room on premises.

As I'm rummaging through my bag next to my cot, looking for a spare hair rubber band for dealing with my wet hair, I see Claudia Grito and next to her Olivia and another one of the bully girls, and they are just a few cots away, and heading toward me. . . .

I quickly look back down at my stuff, and pretend very hard I don't see them, as if that might steer them away. But, no such luck.

"Hey, what's this I see, a little drowned rat?" Olivia says with a smirk, stopping right in front of me and taking hold of my hairbrush that's lying on top of my blanket.

I look up. Olivia's looking all perfect and cleaned up after our Combat class, down to the freshly applied makeup and blow-dried auburn hair.

Meanwhile Claudia comes up on the other side of me and she is a little sweaty, but negligibly so, in a sexy bitch kind of way, with a few strands of her black hair loosened. She should be reeking, but instead there's a deep musky perfume scent coming from her, which I bet guys just go crazy for. She leans in on me and says, "So, Gwen Lark. . . . What are we gonna do about you? You've been a bad girl. You know that, don't you? A very bad girl."

"They have cameras here . . ." I say, and my voice sounds wimpy and pathetic.

"Of course." Olivia moves in closer, and she then sits down right next to me on the cot, still holding my hairbrush. "But all they can see is how we're all just friends, and hey, we're smiling, right?"

"That's right." Claudia starts to smile too, and then she's running her hand through my hair. I feel a slow steady tug that becomes intense then painful.

"And hey, look, we're such good friends that we're gonna brush your hair for you," Olivia says. She picks up the hairbrush and presses it hard against my scalp, then starts pulling it down, so that the pins dig into me, hard, and at the same time they snag on the kinks in my wet unbrushed hair. . . .

I freeze, in agony. Mostly, because I am used to freezing in such situations, and because I am terrified.

Small clumps of my hair are torn out, as Olivia brings the

brush down again, even harder.

"Hey now, you better start smiling, girlfriend," Claudia says through her teeth.

The third girl with them meanwhile opens my bag, and starts taking things out. I stare helplessly as she takes out a book, one of my Dad's precious rare editions.

"No!" I say.

"What's she got there, Ashley?" Claudia lets go of my hair and looks closer at Ashley, a skinny blonde, who's holding up a leather-bound precious copy of *Consuelo* by George Sand— possibly my favorite book in the whole world—by its front hardcover cardboard plate.

"Put that down, please," I say.

"Oh, yeah? Or what?" Ashley holds the book carelessly and gives it a shake, so that a fragile, age-yellowed page falls out from the middle, and the cover itself starts to rip and come apart at the binding. . . .

I feel a fierce burning at the back of my throat, and the stifling thickness that comes just before tears. I am about to bawl, like a pathetic loser coward, both from the pain and the humiliation, as I've done before countless times, when cornered at school. . . .

So many times before. . . . *Always.*

But something different happens this time. *This is my favorite book in the world.* My Dad's beloved edition. I am probably not going to Qualify. So, in a few months from now, it's going to burn in asteroid flames as the world ends. Together with me, and probably most other people I love.

What does anything matter?

A weird new sense of calm comes over me. For some reason in that instant, I also remember, of all things, Aeson Kass. I see his steady blue eyes, strangely intense and unblinking. He is speaking to me, in a low soft voice of power, and his words fill my head. *As you learn to fight, you learn to defend yourself. . . .*

The hairbrush that Olivia's holding tangled up in a clump of my hair is ripping my hair out. I lift my hand and take hold of her wrist.

And suddenly I *press hard*—I press with all I've got, feeling the bones in her wrist, so that Olivia exclaims in surprise and lets go of my hairbrush that clatters on the floor. At the same time I use my other hand, balled up in a fist, to slam into Claudia's midriff area.

In the next second, I stand up. I reach out quickly and grab the precious book from Ashley. "Get away from me! Get out!" I say, and my voice, it's different now, as if it's not my own. It's low and hard, and coming through my teeth.

"Get out."

I am standing straight, and my eyes are burning with intensity, tears transformed into fury.

I can see something has clicked, because Claudia's expression is transformed also, and she is frowning, but at the same time she's no longer so sure of herself.

"Did you hear me?" I say, looking at each one of them. "The cameras are on us right now. What are you going to do, if you still want to Qualify?"

"We're not done, chica," Claudia mutters, holding her abdomen. "Don't think we're done. You *touched* me, you're gonna *pay*." But she is up, and she is backing away from my cot casually, and she throws a smile at Olivia, who glares at me. Ashley steps back also, then kicks my bag, hard, as she walks by.

"See you next time, Gwen-baby," Olivia says. "Meanwhile, you'd better watch your back."

I don't answer. I am breathing hard, watching them leave. No one else is in the surrounding area, the nearest cots are vacant and the girls' dormitory floor is nearly empty. The closest girl is more than a dozen cots away, and she has her back turned, straightening her things, likely pretending she heard nothing. I don't blame her.

I stand, holding *Consuelo* in one hand. It occurs to me, *I just defended a book.*

What have I done? I am absolutely insane. They are going to come after me even harder now. They always do. And cameras don't matter—they will find a way.

I go downstairs to grab dinner. In the cafeteria, no one I know is around, not even Laronda. And there's no sign of Blayne's wheelchair. So I eat alone, at a table near the wall, as quickly as possible. I am keeping my head down, and thinking grim thoughts, as I move my fork around some kind of bland, greasy macaroni casserole.

After dinner, I decide, I'm finally getting out of this building. Time to go look for my brothers, for Gracie.

Ten minutes later, as I unload the remnants on my tray into the trash, I turn to see the big scary guy with the neck tattoo walking past me. As he passes, he pinches my rear and then slams his elbow into my side painfully, and keeps walking, without a glance at me.

I wince in pain and almost double over, but hide it, pretending to be checking something at the seam of my jeans near my thigh.

Quickly I head out of the cafeteria, out through the lobby, and outside. The place where the jerk pinched me really smarts, and so does the side where he slammed into me. I wonder how much if anything those supposed surveillance cameras picked up.

The chill evening air strikes me, and I remember I left my sweater upstairs, and I'm only wearing a T-shirt. Whatever, it doesn't matter. I continue outside, after getting a printed page with the map of the campus buildings, up at the info desk.

According to the map, Dorm Five, Red Quadrant, where Gracie's at, is only three buildings away.

The compound grounds are filled with Candidates walking in the twilight. I see small groups of teens whispering nervously, hear occasional bursts of laughter. But mostly, it's just quiet solitary individuals hurrying somewhere.

Dorm Five looms before me, with its red square logo up on top. As I enter the front doors, I am in a Common Area lobby that's an exact copy of my own dorm, down to the layout of the info desk, the stairs, cafeteria doors in the back, and even the lounge furniture. I see teens everywhere, and the only difference is, their tokens are all shining red. A few of them give me and my yellow token hard looks.

I pause, considering what to do next, where to even begin looking for Gracie, when I see a bunch of people gathered on the sofas and chairs. As I scan the company, there's Gracie herself. She is sitting on the sofa, chatting with people on both sides of her, and I can even hear her familiar giggle laughter, all the way to the door. Okay, wow. Gracie hasn't been so cheerful and relaxed in days. What on Earth has happened to my little sis, overnight?

I make a beeline directly for her. Gracie says something to a boy on one side of her, tosses her hair back, slaps her hands together, and then her gaze falls on me.

"Gwen! Oh my gosh, Gwen! Over here!" Gracie jumps up from her seat, and as I approach she throws herself at me. I am hugging my sister, smelling the familiar scent of her hair, soggy from a recent shower. Then we pull apart, and I see her face with its slightly smudged, newly applied eyeliner and globby mascara, and she is glowing with high-energy excitement.

"So, you survived today! How was everything?" I say with a grin. And then, as Gracie opens her mouth and begins to talk, I happen to glance sideways and see . . .

Logan Sangre.

He is sitting on the sofa near the empty spot where Gracie has been.

I feel like someone had just body-slammed me in the gut, and I freeze, while my cheeks are suddenly on fire. Gracie is saying something, and honestly I have no idea what's coming out of her mouth. Could be anything, blah, blah, blah.

". . . and so we had Agility Training first thing after lunch, and it was kinda awful at first, then not so bad!" Gracie is chattering. "I got a demerit because I fell off the monkey bars, and oh, the hoverboards were okay, maybe even fun in a weird way! And our Red Quadrant weapon is the bestest *evar*, a sword!"

"How are your Instructors?" I say, trying to take in a deep calming breath so that I can speak evenly and keep my face from twitching or my teeth from chattering.

"Oh, they were mean and awful! Two of them were these hotshot Atlanteans with a real hard attitude," Gracie exclaims, plopping back down in her seat on the sofa.

As she does so, Logan Sangre, who's been talking to some guy on the other side of him, turns his head to look at me.

"Everyone, this is my sister Gwen!" Gracie looks around and then focuses on Logan, of all people. "Oh hey, Gwen, this is Logan, he's a senior from our school, can you believe that?" Gracie has *no idea* about my crush obsession, naturally, no one does. No one, that is, except my friend Ann Finnbar, the only person I've ever told, back at school. And oh yeah, now there's Laronda who knows too. . . .

"Hi," Logan says to me, with a light smile on his sexy chiseled lips, a smile that makes his already amazing face beautiful beyond belief. "It's a small world. Go, Mapleroad Jackson High Wolf Cubs!"

"Hey," I say, while I drown in his warm hazel-brown eyes with their mile-long lashes. Somehow I manage to make my own lips shape the necessary words, as though I am a wooden puppet. "Yeah, I think I've seen you around. Go, Wolf Cubs!"

"Yeah. . . ." He leans back, and his hair falls in an attractive way over his forehead as he leans his head sideways, looking me over. "I'm sure I've seen you too. Are you a junior?" His eyes, warm, rich, are looking at me directly, and it's *smoking-hot*, and I am just going to stop breathing now. This. Very. Moment.

My temples are pounding. *He knows what year I am!*

"Wanna sit down?" Gracie says, as I nod and mumble some half-baked reply. She then moves off to the side a little, making space for me right between her and Logan.

"Sure," I say, while the whole world is pretty much spinning around me in a crazy carousel.

And then I sit down next to Logan Sangre.

I mean, *flush next to him.* So that we're touching. The entire side of my body, my left hip is pressing against his. I feel the muscular hardness of his body.

And he *doesn't* move away. Instead, he puts his arm around the back, so that if I close my eyes and imagine it, in some alternate dimension or something it could count like he's got his arm around *me!*

It took the end of the world to bring this about.

I am squeezed between my sister and Logan Sangre.

If the asteroid hits us now, I can go out with a smile.

We talk about stuff for the next five minutes, and if you ask me, I wouldn't be able to say what we've been talking about, or for that matter if we've been talking human or dog. This is what the presence of Logan Sangre does to my pathetic brain. I was going to ask Gracie about our brothers, if she'd seen them, but of course now that's all gone out of my mind, together with any semblance of rational thought, motor function, or long term memory.

Seriously, I am fortunate that I can remain seated without keeling over and tripping over my own legs, or my feet snagging on the coffee table before us. It could be worse; I could be having an attack of the hiccups, loss of bladder control, or spontaneous drooling.

Good thing Logan seems to be unaware of my discomfort. Neither is Gracie or anyone else in this lounge group.

"Yeah, can you believe it, we get to fight with swords! Real swords!" a freckled redhead younger boy keeps saying. His name is Charlie Venice, and he is sitting on the other side of Gracie, and sort of hitting on her. And by hitting on her, I mean, he is being loud and saying dumb things in a stupid voice and constantly grinning obnoxiously. His token is glowing red—about as red as his hair and freckles.

Gracie is oblivious, because I notice she is chattering with everyone, and looking over at Logan, and at the guy on the other side of him, who introduced himself as Daniel Tover.

"So, people. We made it this far. Now what are all your plans to make it all the way? To Qualify?" Daniel leans forward, speaking to everyone in general. He's dark haired, older, with a large-featured pleasant face and a slightly crooked nose. His expression is steady and comfortable. "I mean, we passed the initial tests, and now we have all this bizarre training. What do you think it is all leading up to?"

"Yeah, what's up with all that fighting stuff? And the four color Quadrants? It's like we're in a creepy color-coordinated camp," a petite and pretty brown-haired girl says. Her name's Mia Weston, and she is also a Red. As far as I know, I am the only Yellow in the room.

Logan is watching me—I know with my peripheral vision, even though I am trying to look straight ahead while pretending to be fascinated with what Mia is saying. He definitely must be looking at my yellow token. That must be it, there's no other reason for him to be looking at me.

"So, Yellow Dorm," Logan says, turning his face at me, and leaning in closer. "What was your Combat like? I'm curious what's it like to have to work with nets and cords—or whatever they call it. Swords and blades are intuitive, but the Yellow

Quadrant weapons seem very complicated."

"It's pretty weird, I guess," I say, trying not to look directly into his eyes, while my cheeks begin to warm up again. "We didn't get to do anything with them yet, only watched the demo. The two Instructors were showing us all the four types of weapons. I have to admit, they were really something! Amazing moves!"

"Were they also stuck-up a-holes, like our Instructors?" Gracie laughs, nudging me.

"Kind of, yeah," I say. "But then they're *astra daimon*, which I suppose gives them some kind of excuse for having an attitude."

"Oh, really?" Logan looks at me with even more interest. "I've heard that term used today in Culture class. Isn't that supposed to be their highest elite Pilot rank? *Astra daimon* means something like 'star demon?'"

"Is that what that means? I didn't know," I mutter. "Okay, yes, that would make total sense, since Ancient Atlantean shares linguistic roots with Ancient Greek. . . ."

"Yeah, that's their elite fighting forces." Logan pulls out a small knife from his jeans pocket and flicks it open then snaps the blade folded again, with a clever motion of his fingers. I stare at his sleek movements, his strong, well-shaped hand.

"Those hotshot Pilots, I hear they've all got fancy call signs," Charlie says, leaning in over Gracie. "Oh, wait! I was early to Combat class, and heard a couple of Goldilocks Instructors talking quietly out in the hall, before anyone else got there. Get this—apparently their giant motherships are no longer in those low-altitude positions in our skies! You know how they used to be parked right over the cities and stuff, so you could see them when they first showed up? Well, now that we've all been Preliminary-Qualified, those huge ships have gone back up into orbit!"

Daniel Tover leans forward and glances at him. "Since when?"

"Happened overnight! So now instead they've got space shuttles landing and going up all the time. And not just here, but all over! They go back and forth between all the RQC compounds and their starships, on a regular basis."

"I think I saw one launch this morning," Mia says. "We watched it from our dorm windows."

Charlie nods vigorously. "And also today, okay, there was

some kind of extra-VIP shuttle arriving. Some really important Atlantean dude coming down to visit, and he's here in *our* compound. Why, I don't know. Probably to check up on us 'Candies.' You know that's what they call us, right? They and the Dorm Leaders call us behind our back, Candidates—*Candies*. We're all Candies. Oh, and from what I could tell, they used some weird Greek God sounding 'call sign' name for the VIP—"

"Who is it? Do you remember what they called him?" Daniel's gaze follows Charlie's excessive nervous movements.

Charlie shakes his head. "Like I said, some Greek mythology thing. I don't remember that kind of junk."

"Mythology is not junk," I say. "And if it's the same person, I think he was looking in on our Combat Training class. His name's Aeson Kass—he was kind of different from the rest of them. Not just higher ranking but—hard to explain. . . . *Better*, I guess. He was wearing a black armband. But I don't think they mentioned any Greek-sounding 'call sign' or whatever."

Logan's one brow goes up. Charlie and Daniel exchange glances.

Gracie stares at me. "Wow, I wonder what's up? What was he like, exactly?"

I think momentarily. How in the world to describe what I've seen in class—the whirlwind Er-Du fighting demo, the amazing, almost inhuman speed of their moves? Both Oalla and Aeson were incredible, and for that matter, so was Keruvat, during the earlier weapons demo.

But Aeson Kass—okay, there really was something special about him. Just a little more, just a tad extra. If Oalla and Keruvat were blazing hot, then he was the *inferno*. . . .

I think and I say, "All I know is, he's *astra daimon*, and he wears a black armband because he gave his life for Atlantis. I guess that's the VIP part. That's what our Instructor Oalla Keigeri said when she introduced him. I have no idea what any of it really means, or what his story is. That's all I know. And yeah, I realize it makes no sense, actually."

"He gave his life? How? Okay, that's so weird!" Gracie has a big-eyed expression. She stares at me then glances over at Logan.

"Very curious, agreed." Logan watches both of us. "There's

QUALIFY   129

so frigging much about these Atlanteans that we don't know. Makes you wonder about all kinds of other things."

"Personally, I don't trust them," says another girl whose name I didn't catch; I think it's Becca. "It's bad enough we are stuck in this impossible situation, and yeah, I get it, they are offering us our only way out. Great! But what really happens *there?* As in, up there, on those starships, and on Atlantis? Those of us who make it, what happens to us?"

"That's the million dollar question." Daniel slaps his leg and gets up. "You coming?" he says to Logan who nods, stands up also then turns to me and Gracie.

"Well, it was great to meet both of you, Gwen, Gracie," Logan says, and his warm hazel eyes crinkle lightly at the corners. I stare up at his lean and powerful runner physique.

"We've been making the rounds of all the Red Dorms," he continues. "Getting to know our fellow Red Candies. We're from Red Dorm One. But now—time to hit the next one before the 8:00 PM homework hour."

"Red Candies! I like that!" Charlie Venice makes a horse-laugh noise. "Checking out the competition, eh?"

"Yes, you better not miss the curfew," I say, "or they might lock you up in the Big Bad Candy Jar." Wow, okay, did I just make an actual albeit lousy joke in the presence of Logan Sangre?

Logan narrows his eyes mischievously, and I just about melt. "You bet," he says. "See you later, Yellow Candy."

Wow, okay. . . . What was *that?* Was that a flirt?

No way. No. Frigging. Way.

Chapter 10

As Logan and Daniel leave the lobby, Gracie's avid stare follows in their wake. I know that look. When my sister is interested in something, she gets a very focused expression.

Oh no. Oh, shining heaven, no. . . . Please, Gracie, please don't let it be you looking that way at Logan Sangre.

Oh no.

"Did you see that guy?" Gracie whispers to me, turning around suddenly. Her eyes are filled with the essence of champagne bubbles.

"Huh?" I mutter. My cheeks are draining of all color.

"Daniel!" Gracie shoves me in the side. "He is so cute! His friend from our school, Logan, he's way prettier, sure, but Daniel is oozing sexy awesomeness! Yumm! I think I want me some Daniel Tover from Upstate New York!"

"Oh . . . yeah," I say, feeling relief, and all the bazillion little blood vessels in my cheeks open up like floodgates again, and my sub-dermal circulation is instantly restored to normal. "He's kinda way older than you, don't you think? Logan is a senior, and so is Daniel, probably."

"So?" Gracie glares, and her eyes get very wide.

"So he's too old for you, Gee Four!" I say comfortably.

"That's just total BS!" She lets her jaw drop, pausing in an attempt to find words sufficient to express her usual Gracie-caliber outrage. "What does any of that stuff matter now? Who cares how old we are? We could all be dead in a few months, or stuck on some crazy alien spaceship headed to some bizarre planet for lord knows what kind of life—"

"Well—" I play my tongue against my teeth and the inside of my cheeks. What can I say to that? "Well, they do still have laws *here on Earth* against that kind of thing. He's probably over eighteen, and you, my little sis, are twelve."

"Oh, puh-leeeze!"

I let my breath out. "Seriously, Gracie, listen to me, you have no idea about that guy, who he is, anything about him, whatever. Just cool it, okay? Besides, didn't your Dorm Leaders tell you the No Dating rule? There's just no time for that kind of silly stuff when we're all here fighting for our lives. Remember? Qualification, hello? This is not summer camp." I give her a light shove on the arm.

Gracie is frowning and turns her face away from me.

"Okay, have you seen George or Gordie yet?" I change the subject.

"No."

"Want to come with me, now? We can go looking for them, check their dorms? There's still time until curfew."

"No! Leave me alone!"

"Okay. . . ." I pause to consider. Gracie is not looking at me and instead staring at her nails.

A few seconds tick away.

"I want to go *home*," my sister announces suddenly, looking up at me at last. Her eyes are intense.

I bite my lip. Immediately, all traces of frustration at her are replaced by a protective desperate pang in my gut. "I'm so sorry, no, we can't," I whisper, putting my hand on her arm.

Gracie's eyes are suddenly shiny with liquid. "I tried calling Mom," she says. "But the e-dampers are on, and I forgot, I tried over and over, and there was no signal."

"I know. . . ." I press her arm, my fingers feeling her beginning to tremble. We're out in public, so I know Gracie is not going to fall apart on me completely in front of her new Red Dorm Five friends, but it's pretty much touch and go.

"Okay, why don't you go up to your girls dorm floor now and get some rest? What kind of homework did you get? You can look over your Atlantis Culture notes or something."

"I don't know. There's not really any homework on the first day, is there?" Gracie wipes the side of her nose and tries to look normal, because Charlie Venice is looking at her a whole lot, and even Gracie has noticed by now.

I take a deep breath. "Believe it or not, I got assigned running.

The Agility Instructor said I sucked, since I was last during the running laps. So I'm supposed to run every day." I let out a short snort-laugh.

"You, running?" Gracie perks up and starts to grin. "Now, I've got to see that!"

"I know, right?" I laugh again, then get up from the sofa seat next to her and adjust the bottom edges of my T-shirt, tugging at the fabric nervously.

"Wait, where are you going? Are you gonna run now?"

I shrug. "I guess I *could*, since it's my 'homework.' But I am so dead. I don't think I can do it, maybe I can skip it tonight. Ugh!"

Gracie is looking up from the sofa at me. "Don't go yet! Please, Gee Two, don't go!"

"You'll be all right. I'll see you tomorrow, I promise! Bye, everyone, nice meeting you." I wave sheepishly at the people chatting nearest to us. A few heads turn, and a girl and boy nod. Mia Weston looks up with a friendly expression and says, "Bye, Gwen!" Charlie Venice gives me a grin and then looks back at Gracie.

As I walk back out of Dorm Five, it occurs to me that my sister has found some okay people to hang out with, thank goodness.

Outside, the night is dark and cold, and the RQC campus is well lit. I shiver from the blast of chill as I hurry back to my own Yellow Dorm Eight. I suppose I could go and visit George and Gordie, but it's almost 8:00 PM and they did say homework hour is limited curfew.

But seriously, what are they gonna do if they catch me walking outside, put me in an Atlantean jail? On the other hand, I suppose, if they are super harsh, they could just Disqualify me on the spot. . . .

I blink, and suddenly there is a streak of light in the dark indigo of sky, right over the top of the buildings up ahead. . . . It hangs there momentarily, a spot of bluish-violet radiance low in the sky. To my mind it resembles a gaudy winter holiday ornament framed against the velvet box of heaven. And then it sweeps upward at an amazing speed, and there's a brief low harmonic sound that makes the ground rumble. The deep chord is a C Major,

I am almost sure, and I can hear the glass windows all around rattle before it goes ultrasonic. The Atlantean shuttle disappears up in the clouds, shrinking from the size of an ornament to a white dot.

And then it's gone. And the harmonic rumble all around has faded, except for an echo in my mind.

I wonder who it was, in that shuttle. Aeson Kass, maybe? Or some other VIP?

The Lounge Area of Yellow Dorm Eight is filled with people. I make my way casually, not looking around. The sick feeling in my stomach is back as I silently pray the popular crowd is not here. Lucky for me, I see no sign of either Claudia or her friends. A couple of older boys, whom I vaguely recognize as part of the hashtagging crowd, give me nasty looks, which I ignore.

It's almost Homework Hour. Okay, what should I do? Homework for me usually means reading and schoolwork involving books and lessons, not gym class. Ugh. . . .

As I stand there at the edge of the Lounge Area, I see our Dorm Leader Gina Curtis enter. She blows a whistle, and the hum of conversation drops into quiet.

"Attention, Candidates! Okay, time to get to work! You all have things to go over from your classes today. A reminder, the Training Hall gym downstairs remains open until 10:00 PM, so if you need to work out, now's a good time. And now—no more chatting, time to go over your notes! If I hear you talking, demerit! You can stay down here in the lounge, or go up to your dormitory, but stay indoors. Got that? The other Dorm Leaders and I will be checking to make sure—"

A few groans are heard, and then a few people get up from their seats while Gina is still talking.

I briefly consider what to do. I probably should go and try to run a lap or two down in the Training Hall gym. On the other hand, I feel blisters starting on my feet, and my legs are shaky. Truth be told, I am about to keel over.

And so I decide, screw it, it's only day one, and I am going upstairs to bed. I can flip through my Culture class notes instead and review the geography of Atlantis.

I can always run in the morning.

Okay, remember how they told us that we're going to be really sore the next day? And by "they" I mean Oalla Keigeri?

Well, yeah—that was one big, ugly, filthy lie of an understatement.

Sore? *Sore?* The 7:00 AM morning claxon alarm peals, and I am in blazing agony.

As I'm thrown out of a dead dreamless sleep, I realize my body is not my own. In the first moments of consciousness, every muscle I try to move is on fire. I *hurt* all over, in places I didn't think I had nerve endings. I am one sorry human teenage girl-shaped ball of Pain.

"Oww!" I groan as I turn over and carefully contort myself into a fetal position and try to pull the thin blanket over my head. Outside the windows, the morning sky is turning pale blue, plus the dormitory overhead lights are on, killer-bright.

In the cot next to me I hear Laronda. "Oww! Awww! Noooo. . . ."

And over on the other side, the girl whose name I never bothered to ask, is moaning like a beached whale. Okay, honestly, strike that—I have no idea if beached whales moan or even make sounds out of water. But if they did, it would sound something like what that poor girl is doing. . . .

"Rise and shine, girlfriends!" someone says a few cots down the line. "Time to get cracking, Qualify or Die!"

"Screw you . . ." Laronda mutters. "Asteroid! Come to Mama! Just please, take me out of my misery now!"

I drag myself up in a seated position. I wonder how the guys are faring. Not much better than us, I bet. George's probably not at his best this morning, even if he may not admit it to anyone. And oh, my poor little bro Gordie who's about as athletic as a turtle! I really should go find them today. . . . On the other hand, I wonder if Logan Sangre's amazing toned runner body feels even the slightest discomfort as he gets up this morning. Except for these athletic jock types, all the rest of us are all just quivering gelatinous messes.

Somehow I manage to dig in my duffel bag and pick out clean underwear and the same clothes from yesterday. My sneakers and socks sit deep underneath the cot. It hurts just to stretch my arm to reach them. . . .

Laronda watches me with an expression that's part bemused and part tormented. "You know, they gave us those grey uniforms for a reason. I'm pretty sure we should wear them at some point. Now's as good as any."

I pause my rummaging and look up at her. (Oww, my neck!) "Hmm, I don't know. Maybe they're for special occasions? Did they mention anything in Agility or Combat, that we should wear them? I don't remember—"

"Yeah, whatever," Laronda says, still not getting up. "Hey, where were you last night?"

"I went to see my sister in Dorm Five."

"Oh. Next time let me know and I'll tag along."

"Okay." I briefly consider if I really should wear the grey uniform that's lying folded on top of my stuff, where I placed it on the first night here. "You planning to get up any time soon?"

"Nah, I think I'll beauty-sleep in for a few more hours." Laronda rolls her eyes, groans and finally gets up. She's wearing a small pastel pink T-shirt nightie over her underwear bottoms, and her dark brown skin is puckered in goose bumps from the slightly chill room. They must've turned the heat down in the middle of the night. "O-okay." Laronda rubs her arms then leans forward over her own bags. "Where, oh where, are my pants?"

"I need to go run some laps," I admit grudgingly, more to myself than to anyone else in the range of hearing. "Should I bother with a shower now or later?"

Laronda snorts. "What difference does it make? You and I'll be dripping new sweat in another hour or two again after classes. They should just hose us down every few hours all day long."

"Agreed. In that case, I'll go run first, then shower."

And so, I find myself five minutes later, down in the basement Physical Training Hall. I am wearing my jeans and yesterday's T-shirt. And the blisters on my feet, oh, lord, they hurt!

A few other people are in the gym. I see Jai Bhagat, Janice Quinn, and Mateo Perez, all three of them on top of the second level scaffolding, attempting the hand bars. I also see Claudia, on the weights near the front. She is pumping the resistance machine easily, and her muscular sleeveless arms glisten with sweat. Olivia and Ashley are here too.

Great. . . .

"Hi, Gwen!" Jai yells out at me, waving from the scaffolding.

Awesome, now the bullies will see me. Thanks a lot, Jai.

I wave back without much enthusiasm, and then take a big breath, and try not to look at anyone, as I begin to run around the perimeter of the gym. My cheeks are flaming in embarrassment, because I know I look like a total dork who has no idea how to run. Each step I take hits my blisters hard. My leg and thigh muscles are screaming in agony. Moments later my body remembers that I simply cannot do this. I am panting hard as I come around the first lap.

Two more, I think. *Just two more, and that's enough for now.*

After all, talking about "two more," I have to conserve strength for two more hellish gym classes today.

I am on my second lap when I feel that my legs have turned into noodles and are going to buckle. I slow down, and walk a few steps, then bend over, to rub my knees. Then I think, if I cannot do this second lap, what remote chance do I have of Qualifying?

So I force myself to resume running. . . . Past the people on the scaffolding (probably staring down at me in pity—but no, never mind, they're too preoccupied with not falling off the parallel bars themselves). . . . Past the mean girls near the weights equipment (probably pointing at me and snickering). . . . Past lord knows who else might walk in any moment and see Gwen Lark, the saddest klutz in New England, trying to pretend she can do this thing. . . .

By the end of the second lap, I don't think I can feel my legs. I am running very slowly, technically I am barely jogging. Compared to yesterday, I can hardly move. This is terrible! Overnight I've been reduced to a weakling invalid. It seems I am doing *worse* now than yesterday when I got the demerit!

One more. . . . Just one more.

I turn the corner and begin on the third lap, barely dragging each leg and foot forward, arms pumping, lungs choking for air.

About halfway around, I feel someone running beside me, and then a leg flashes in front of me, and my foot snags and trips.

I fall down hard, landing on my knees painfully, and instantly one of my wrists is aching from having reached out clumsily for the floor with my hand. I look up, and see Claudia Grito's retreating back. She is running smoothly and powerfully around the room perimeter, as though nothing has happened. Her silk black ponytail is swinging.

The evil bitch tripped me!

I get up, and my knees are singing an Aria of Pain from the Opera of F— Me. My face is flushed red and my eyes sting with tears of humiliation.

So much for even completing three pathetic laps.

Without looking around me, I half walk, half limp out of the Training Hall.

A shower and fifteen minutes later, I sit in the cafeteria next to Laronda, before a plate of breakfast pancakes drenched in maple syrup. This is the real deal—not artificially flavored sugar goo, but actual maple juice—and I should know, since St. Albans, Vermont is the maple syrup capital of the country, so I know real syrup when I see it.

"This is real maple syrup, you know?" I point with my fork, then swirl a piece of pancake in rich amber goodness so that it makes a slow whirlpool on my plate. "Wonder how come they're giving us the good stuff."

But Laronda is not buying my evasion. "So the *bruja* tripped you. Did you at least tell her off? Listen, you can't just let them walk all over you all the time. Bullies totally feed off that kind of weakness. They're like vampires—they suck your fear and your loser vibes and grow stronger." She stares at me seriously with her head leaning sideways, so that her relaxed hair slides out of place where it's parted to the side today, and goes over her nose.

"Well, what am I supposed to do? What can I do? I admit it, I *am* afraid. My loser vibes are too extra-strength, or something."

Laronda lets out a sigh. "You can start by getting a different attitude."

"Like what?"

"You're the smarty-pants, you figure it out."

"I'll get killed first." I laugh ruefully.

"Nuh-huh. No, you won't." Laronda does a side-to-side thing with her neck and wags her finger in the air then stabs my hand with it. Her nails are painted dark red, and ouch, but they're hard. "Just think, all you have to do is survive this Qualification thing. Nothing else matters. No bullies, no nothing. Who cares what they try to do? You just do your own thing and *live*. Stay out of their way as much as possible and watch those witches screw themselves up. Meanwhile, you figure out their weakness. You know what I'm saying?"

"Okay, O Wise One," I say. "But—"

"But what? Just stay out of their way! But if you can't, figure out how to stand your ground, girlfriend."

We leave the cafeteria, get our tokens scanned for the day's schedule, and looks like both Laronda and I have Atlantis Culture first thing. "Thank God," she and I both mutter. "At least we get to sit on our behinds for an hour."

We go up to the fourth floor and find our classroom, which is already full. As I take a seat close to the front, I notice once again the pile of fascinating old books and scrolls on the teacher's desk. I examine them with hungry curiosity.

Soon, judging by the sudden shift in the noise level, Nefir Mekei, the Atlantean with the mesmerizing voice, enters the room. I hope that today he actually uses the ancient objects in his presentation.

As I continue to stare wistfully at the faded scrolls, the classroom gets noticeably quieter. Laronda sitting next to me nudges my foot with her own, hard.

I tear my eyes away and look backward to where everyone else seems to be staring.

Nefir Mekei stands in the back of the classroom. The expression of his kohl-enhanced eyes is wise, alert, and hard to read. Before him, floating in the air, *levitating* five feet above the floor, is a bright golden object.

It looks like a cup or—the ancient myth and legend aficionado within me cannot help but note—it looks like a *grail*.

Chapter 11

Nefir utters a clean low note, steady and in a perfect pitch, and the cup-shaped object floats before him like a drifting golden cloud. Nefir walks to the front of the class and stands at the desk. He makes another tone, this time brief and falling, and the cup descends gently and rests on the surface of the desk.

We are all staring at him with open-mouthed attention.

"This is a small replica model of a much larger object that can be found on display in Poseidon, the capital city of Imperial Atlantida. The original stands, more than two hundred meters tall, and marks the first landing site of the oldest colony on the surface of the planet Atlantis." Nefir looks at each one of us slowly, and his power voice begins to raise the hairs on our skin. "What is it? It is the Atlantis Grail. A symbol of everything our society stands for. Both ancient tradition and new modern innovation. It embodies the spirit of the New World which we inhabit."

Nefir pauses, then reaches out to draw the tip of one finger against the golden rim of the object. The cup shape itself is wide and somewhat flattened, and appears to be made of smooth solid gold without any distinguishable markings. At Nefir's touch, the metal makes a pleasant ringing tone, like a small bell.

"Can you hear it? The Grail sings. Even this little one, the poor replica I just rendered for you on a 3D printer up in the main offices of the Arena Commons Building, fifteen minutes ago. Even this one has the echo of the power that is contained in the original."

We listen closely. It's true—the echo of the bell tone caused by his touch seems to be still hanging in the air.

Okay, I don't know what's wrong with me. Honestly, I have no idea what makes me do these crazy things that involve me suddenly flapping my mouth open and talking in class—but I take a big breath and raise my hand.

Nefir's general gaze focuses on me. "Yes?"

"Is that material real gold? I mean, this replica, and the original? And if not gold, then what is it? What makes it conduct sound—or react to sound, or—" My questions fade into mutters.

Next to me Laronda is looking at me with her eyes rolling.

"You ask interesting questions. But they are better suited for your Atlantis Tech class," he says. "However, I will answer the first question because it is relevant. Yes, this is the element gold— a gold plate over another substance. And yes, so is the original Grail in Poseidon, great ancient city. . . . You might've heard rumors that there is so much naturally occurring gold on Atlantis that we consider it a base metal—which may seem unusual to you since gold is still so rare and prized on Earth. Well, it is true, gold is overabundant and we do not value it as much as our ancestors valued gold when we still lived on Earth. However we have many uses for it, and it is a profound part of our culture."

"Oh, yeah? Then this homey's coming to Atlantis!" a boy says in the back row. A few snickers are heard.

"First, you must prove yourself. You must Qualify." Nefir looks at the boy with a slow blooming smile.

"You bet!" the kid says with a crooked grin.

"What is your name, Candidate?"

"Dionte Jones, mister teacher. Or you can call me Dion-Z, as in, Zee one and only Diontay, get my parlay?"

More hushed snickers roll through the room.

But the Atlantean is unperturbed. "Qualify, and I will call you what you wish."

And then Nefir looks away and calmly continues his lecture. I watch him, hoping he will reach for one of the ancient books, but no such luck.

"*Atlantida*," Nefir speaks the word so that it sounds truly alien. "*Atlantida* is the word in our core language that means Atlantis. It is the original name of the continent and of our colony planet, and also the first nation that was formed. Your Greeks had remembered the remnants of our language in bits and pieces, and apparently passed it onward into the ages. And now, ancient words and fragments are all that you have to remember us by, the once-great civilization that was Atlantis."

I raise my hand again.

This time Nefir looks at me, and smiles. "Yes?"

"Is the Ancient Atlantean language mostly a predecessor to our Earth Ancient Greek, or are there also some Egyptian influences in the mixture, and possibly Mesopotamian, such as Sumerian or Urartu? Oh, and what about Sanskrit?"

"What is your name, Candidate?"

"Gwen Lark."

"You are observant and certainly show a lot of interest, which is admirable. Unfortunately it's beyond the scope of this class to learn the language or its intricacies, only the most rudimentary basics. However, you are welcome to seek me out and ask me outside of class. The same goes for all of you who have more in-depth questions. Find me in the offices on the upper floor of the Arena Commons building, during your Homework Hour."

I nod. "Okay. . . ."

"To briefly answer—yes, there are many of your ancient Earth languages that carry in them remnants of Atlantean. After all, we ruled your world, our culture and technology permeated all the Earth continents. But today, I will speak of the structure of our governments."

A few sighs are heard. But Nefir's voice picks up in tone, if not volume, to energize and engage. "The oldest nation, Atlantida, is an Imperial Democracy. It is important that you know this, because it tells you about our society and our laws. There are other nations on Atlantis that are pure democracies, or hereditary democratic monarchies, and republics. In nearly every instance, it is important that you understand that our government is formed out of *elected* representatives, and that our rulers—imperial or otherwise—are mostly figureheads, and have no control over the workings of the government or its laws." Nefir pauses, for emphasis. "The Imperator and the Imperial Family, they are inspirational and ceremonial, and they preside over public spectacle and traditional events. Meanwhile, councils of elected officials run the government. We have no tyrants, no despots on Atlantis. Such a thing is considered an ancient barbaric anachronism. We choose our government. And our laws are fair and just, for all citizens."

Laronda makes a small sound that only I can hear. I glance at her, and her lips are mouthing, "Yeah, right. . . ."

Another girl, emboldened by my questions, raises a hand. "So what kind of rights do people have? Will we become full Atlantis citizens if we Qualify?"

Nefir pauses. For a moment, his eyes narrow slightly. He is considering his reply carefully. "No," he says. "Those of you who Qualify for rescue, will not become citizens. Citizenship is not automatic, it is an *earned honor*. You will enter our society as resident aliens coming under humanitarian refugee status."

The classroom comes alive with nervous whispers.

Nefir speaks, ignoring the unrest. "As such, you will have all the basic rights accorded to human beings—they include the rights to basic food, housing, education, healthcare, and a chance to work and socialize. However, you will not have the right to vote or advance to the highest elected offices of government. Only citizens can vote. Only citizens can affect and make laws. Nor will you have automatic access to the more advanced privileges of society."

"Whoa! Whoa!" Dionte Jones speaks up without raising his hand. "Are you telling us we'll be some kind of lower class, second-hand crappy *residents*, just because we weren't born into your society? Are we going to be *slaves?* Oh, hayyyell, no!"

"Rest assured, there are no slaves in our society. But there are those whom we call non-citizens, and whom you would consider as the lower economic class, and the less privileged—something that is not at all unlike what you presently have here on Earth. It is a natural result of a free society, is it not?"

"All human beings are supposed to be equal!"

Nefir stares at Dionte with a hard unblinking stare. "Are they? You have billionaires and you have beggars. Even in this so-called 'more developed' country that you call the United States of America—a one-time superpower that has now slipped in influence to secondary world power status behind your China and United Industan and Great Scandinavia. We are no different. However, we do not pretend to take our natural, native-born privileges for granted."

He pauses, still looking at the boy, and his expression grows more and more derisive. "All of you who are born here are citizens. You can choose to vote or not, to participate in the making of your society or not—and mostly, you don't. You can sleepwalk through life and ignore the greater problems around you, as you steep in your own petty personal issues and pass your time *casually existing.* We, on the other hand, have to prove to ourselves, and to others around us, that we will actively make the effort to shape our society and take responsibility for it, *always.* And only once we do this, are we citizens. In short—everyone has basic rights, but everyone earns their privileges."

I take a deep breath and raise my hand again, for the third time today.

Nefir shakes his head lightly, but his lips appear to relax as he turns to me. "Yes, Gwen?"

Holy moly, has it already come to this? The Atlantean Instructors already know me by name. . . .

"What can I or any of us do to become citizens?" I say. "Full citizens of Atlantis, with all the privileges, such as the right to vote, and so on?"

There's a pause.

The classroom has grown perfectly silent.

Nefir meets my gaze with his unblinking stare. "Nothing," he says after the tiniest hint of hesitation. His voice, if I'm not mistaken, appears to be genuinely sad. "For most of you—or to be precise, for almost all of you—there is nothing you can do to become full citizens of Atlantis. You will arrive on our world, you will integrate into our non-citizen society, and you will live long, average, probably comfortable lives, filled with mediocre achievements. But you will not be stars—you will not shine to the fullest, as would a true citizen for whom there are no limits."

"Okay, that's kind of depressing. Actually, it sucks . . ." a girl mutters. "But I guess it's better than getting hit by the asteroid."

Nefir glances at her briefly. "I am glad you understand."

I am still processing this answer. . . . Something inside me has just died slightly at the thought of . . . enforced mediocrity. I don't know what it is. . . . But it occurs to me, I guess I've always unconsciously thought I'd be doing something a little more important with my life, just even a little! As a matter of fact— *okay, face it, Gwen*—I've aspired for something extraordinary, something that might push the limits, and allow me to use my mind to the fullest. . . .

I am crazy! Since when? I guess—since now!

Come on, Gwen, it occurs to me in this moment of tough self-revelation. *You know you've always wanted to be intellect-smart, and that's what you ended up being.*

Being a physical klutz was a badge of honor. You always cared about learning things. And you didn't care about stuff like sports or gym class because secretly you've thought all of that was useless and a waste of time, not to mention a little beneath you. Stupid physical stuff for dumb jocks . . . while you were going to invent things, learn a hundred languages, or discover ancient mysteries, or somehow change the world. Who needs to maintain a toned body for that? Okay, I know, that last thought is pure irony.

Wow. Maybe the asteroid really should just take me out now. Because if I can't try to do all these amazing things with my life (with or without fully acknowledging the part of me that is my physical body, because yeah, now I get it), then what's the use of anything?

I raise my hand, and begin to speak before Nefir even looks at me.

"You said, 'almost nothing.' Actually, sorry, you said, 'nothing for almost all of us.' So does that mean that for a few of us there's *something?* That a few of us can become citizens? How?"

Nefir exhales a long breath and watches me with his kohl-rimmed lapis eyes.

I watch him back, look straight into those unreadable Atlantean eyes that I've rather grown accustomed to. And I don't blink. Because this is important for me, really important. . . .

"Gwen Lark, ah-h-h. . . . You really do ask some difficult questions." Nefir speaks at last. He begins to pace before the desk, and he looks somewhat uncomfortable.

"Technically," he says, "technically, yes, there *is* a way a non-citizen refugee from Earth can become a full citizen of Atlantis." He glances at the golden cup object. "We have an annual *event*, in honor of the Atlantis Grail. They are Games—Games of the Atlantis Grail. The closest Earth equivalent would be your Olympics. And yet, they are not really the same thing at all. Because the Games of the Atlantis Grail are life-and-death contests of strength, endurance, speed, and pure talent. Contestants compete to win, or to die."

"Not all that different from what we're doing now," I say. "Qualify or die."

"Oh, no!" Nefir makes a short sound that might be a laugh. "If you think your Qualification is even remotely similar—okay, maybe only in the most technical sense of having life-threatening high stakes—in that case, yes, I suppose it is. But, no—the Atlantis Grail is *brutal*. The Games include events and tasks of unspeakable difficulty, contests between world-class competitors, master fighters and athletes, master scientists and artists. People train for years before attempting to enter the Games. If any of you refugees from Earth were to enter, you would first have to train—which would take months, years. And even so, you would *still* lose your lives."

The class has grown so silent that I don't think anyone's breathing.

To bring his point home, the Atlantean finally looks away from me, and now his gaze scans the room. He pauses to consider. "Let's see—next year's Games will take place just as you arrive on Atlantis, which would be about fifteen of your Earth months from now. I suppose you could use the time on-board our starships to train, in time for next year's event . . . in which case, my sympathies are with you in advance."

Nefir pauses again then puts his fingers on the rim of the golden grail. "Natives of Atlantis die every year in the Games. Even though we do everything to actively discourage participation, thousands of them die—people of great talent and resourcefulness. Good, solid non-citizens who sacrifice themselves for a remote wild dream. Because, out of thousands of entrants, only Ten can win each year. Ten lucky winners who are called champions can gain the laurels of citizenship and all the high tech luxuries that come with it. Furthermore, all the champions' wishes are granted automatically—anything within the scope of possibility. To be in the Top Ten each year is the fulfillment of everything imaginable."

"If so many people die, then why do they even bother entering?" someone says from behind me.

"Because the rewards are extraordinary. And because it is human nature—to try and prove yourself." Nefir shakes his head.

"There are exclusive luxuries. There are unique and expensive high-end technologies such as advanced medicine that can work miraculous cures. Basic medical resources for the general population do not offer such treatments. But a champion winner of the Atlantis Grail can demand access to any and all procedures. Some past champions have used their newfound privilege to achieve complete physical transformations, while others have used it to cure family members of all diseases—"

"Can you cure cancer?" I interrupt suddenly. My gut is suddenly churning with a cold strange feeling. . . .

Nefir glances at me. "No. Because what you call 'cancer' is not a true disease. It is DNA-level cell damage, an imbalance. A body's general loss of control over its mechanisms, cell function, and resources. The causes are varied, including genetic predisposition, environmental stressors, and lifestyle choices. But the end result is the same—a body's surrender to itself. There is no 'cure.' What our medical technology can do is remove the cancerous cells already present and then restore your body's control and general immune functionality—you might say, reset the internal immune clock. But the fight against any new damage remains up to the individual."

"Sounds like a cure to me."

"Perhaps." Nefir looks away from me and faces the rest of the class. "Any other questions on the Atlantis Grail?"

Candidates watch him back with dimmed expressions. I glance to one side of me and see Laronda frowning. And on the other side, a boy is shaking his head in disgust. There are many stunned faces. For the first time, it seems we've all suffered a strange blow to our confidence, to our very hope.

This new reality about non-citizenship, now that we know about it, really sucks. I should be dazed and depressed as everyone. And yet—for some reason, my mind is racing. . . .

I am thinking what might happen if my Mom underwent treatment with this advanced medical technology, had all her cancerous cells blasted away, her immunity reset—or whatever it is they would do to renew her body's defenses.

To make it happen, all I'd need to do is first Qualify, then train and enter the Games of the Atlantis Grail.

And then, finally, I would need to beat out thousands of highly skilled native Atlanteans in unspeakable contests of skill, strength, and endurance, and *win* the Atlantis Grail.

Naturally I would also need to do all this *before* the asteroid hits Earth. Then, as a champion, I can make all my demands to have my parents saved and brought over to Atlantis, and Mom can get her treatment.

I start laughing quietly at my crazy self, and end up having to put my hand over my mouth.

The rest of the day is a blur of pain and overextended stretched muscles. After Atlantis Culture I say bye to Laronda who heads to a different class. And then I haul my butt downstairs to the basement for torture—ahem, Agility Training. Here I discover that it is possible to feel even more agony and humiliation.

Oalla Keigeri, the Atlantean drill sergeant, makes us run seven laps instead of five. This time the widely spread-out snake of Candidates barely dragging themselves along the perimeter of the gym is even longer than yesterday. A few athletic types make good time around the room—including Claudia Grito who's once again in my class. I watch her pass me several times—on her third and fourth lap while I am still on my second—and try to keep a wide berth between us. But after this morning's incident she's ignoring me completely, and instead showing off her great runner pace.

Everyone else who is not a jock is barely huffing along, and once again I come in dead last, and earn a demerit.

"Have you been running like I told you?" Oalla asks, scanning my yellow token.

"Yes . . ." I gasp, bending over to catch my laboring breath. "But it's only been . . . one day. I . . . ran this . . . morning."

The Atlantean girl looks at me hard. "You will run again tonight, and then again tomorrow morning."

Then for the next forty minutes we practice a combination of hoverboarding around the room, and climbing the scaffolding.

"You will climb all the way to the top tier, run across it, then climb back down to the ground," Oalla tells us. Then you will climb back up halfway, run across the middle tier to the other end and climb back down. Repeat this until I tell you to stop."

The class groans. Even guys like Chris who are in reasonably good shape, don't look too happy.

We start climbing the scaffolding. It's only been a few moments and I can already barely feel the rungs of the ladder with my fingers as I enter a kind of weird disembodied state of exhaustion. It comes over me as I drag myself up and then barely run across the tall scaffolding strip, trying not to look over the edge down. There are people ahead of me and behind me, and occasionally we collide as someone runs too slow or too fast, and all I see is the back and legs of the person before me. . . .

I lose track of time completely. There is only my labored breathing, a weakness in all my extremities and a dull ache in my gut. At some point I think I am going to throw up, as I stagger and barely hold on to the rungs on my umpteenth way down, almost losing my grip and falling.

Out of the corner of my eye, I suddenly see Blayne Dubois. He is also in this class today apparently, and I haven't noticed, because he is body-surfing the hoverboard high up overhead, higher than the highest level of scaffolding, almost near the ceiling.

Wow. . . . In my daze of exhaustion it occurs to me—how easily he handles the turns, and he is flying *fast*, super-fast, like a pro, easily, fearlessly. His dark hair is sleeked back from air resistance, and I see his body is arranged flat and compact on the hoverboard, his legs and feet fixed straight, without slipping.

For someone who cannot walk, this boy has remarkable balance. And the sleek way his hands extend at his sides resemble an Olympic skeleton rider hugging the sled with his body.

I stare at Blayne flying overhead and almost get knocked off the scaffolding as the person behind me runs into me, because apparently I've stopped to gawk.

"Sorry . . ." I gasp to the boy behind me and then continue my teetering run forward to the end of the scaffolding where the ladder begins.

"No slacking! Keep going, everyone!" On the ground Oalla is looking up at me, and her voice rings through the Training Hall.

This goes on for several more interminable minutes.

Next up, Oalla gathers us on the ground and calls down the hoverboards. We stand upright, some of us looking dazed like zombies. Jack Carell, the large heavy boy with blond curly hair, is wiping rivulets of sweat from his reddened face.

"This time you will ride the hoverboards in a wave pattern," Oalla says, looking at the sorry lot of us, while the hoverboards line up, levitating in rows, six inches above the floor.

"Huh?" Mateo Perez says gruffly, blinking sweat away from his eyes.

"Yesterday you rode the boards along a flat plane, never rising or falling," Oalla says. "Today we ride a vertical wave, constantly rising and descending, so that you learn to keep balance on an incline slope."

Oalla then looks around and up, noting Blayne Dubois who is making a circle pass about twenty feet up in the air, near the ceiling. "Blayne!" she says loudly. "Please come down here for a moment."

We all stare, some in greater amazement than others, as the "wheelchair guy," as some of the whispering Candidates refer to him, calls out a series of confident commands. Suddenly his hoverboard nosedives, at the same time as it is sliding closer to our group. In the next blink he comes to a stop before Oalla.

Blayne raises himself up on his hands, so that his upper body is elevated while his lower body and legs remain stretched flat on the board. I can see the muscles in his upper arms tense up. He then looks up at her in expectancy, head turned to the side, with a cool expression on his face. His hair is falling over his blue eyes, and his breathing is elevated, but only slightly. "Yeah?"

It occurs to me, Blayne does not seem to be particularly affected by the hot Atlantean girl's stunning good looks. . . . He appears to be rather indifferent, and you might even say, annoyed. Not much surprise there—Blayne is apparently annoyed by most people.

"Blayne, please demonstrate the wave pattern as I showed you earlier," Oalla says, looking down at him. Her tone of voice actually goes mild compared to what she uses with the rest of us. Does she feel sorry for him, I wonder?

"Ride the hoverboard from here to the end of the room and back. Use the Rise-Descend-Level command pattern on repeat. Candidates, observe!"

Oh, yeah, the sergeant bark is definitely back in that last sentence.

"Sure," Blayne says. He lowers himself flat, chin to the board, arms and hands stretched out at his sides, tight against his body, assuming an aerodynamic position—and I can see from up-close he is in fact gripping the edges of the board with his fingers.

Then he commands the hoverboard to do a 180 turn to face the back of the room. And then, "Go! Rise!" The board pounces forward and immediately starts sloping up until it is ten feet over our heads—"Descend!" The board is now falling—"Level!" It levitates forward for about five feet.

And then Blayne repeats the command sequence. He is rising and falling like a moving sine wave, a vertically undulating snake, a sleek dolphin gliding through an airy ocean. . . .

Candidates watch with slack jaws as he travels the length of the hall, comes to the end, then returns.

"Nicely done!" Oalla points to the other boards hovering at ready. "Now, all of you, do the same, except you will be standing up."

"Yeah, right," a girl mutters.

The class lines up and we begin. The first few hoverboard riders flail wildly, and there are undignified yells as teens barely hang on during the rising and falling stages.

There's one boy ahead of me in line for the hoverboard, and I stand waiting, with quaking knees, and think about how *I am afraid of heights*.

This is about to get really bad.

My turn is here. I get up on the hoverboard and find my basic stance. The rubber soles of my sneakers dig into the charcoal gray surface of the board, as if that's going to help once I start the up-and-down rollercoaster. . . . Ugh.

I take a deep breath. "Go! Rise!"

The board underneath me lurches, and I feel myself lifting up, and at the same time moving forward. I lean in, pressing forward, with my knees bending to maintain the horizontal balance. Three feet, five feet, eight. My sneakers dig into the board and I am wobbling like crazy, hands apart for balance. "Descend!" I speak through my teeth and at the same time squeeze my eyes, as I feel the floor drop out from under me as the rollercoaster plunges. . . . The rubber soles of my footwear begin to slip. . . .

Hold on, hold on, hold on . . . just hold on!

I open my eyes, and it's a good thing too, because I am about to crash into the floor—"Level!" I cry out in panic, then take deep calming breaths, as I now glide on even ground, six inches above the floor.

And then I do the whole thing over again.

The pattern of rising and falling is strangely hypnotic, and by the fourth time, I still haven't fallen off, and I am almost beginning to relax—*almost*. At the apex of each rise, I simply squeeze my eyes shut every time, then say the "Descend" command, then give myself over to whatever universal deity is watching (and probably laughing its head off—if that particular deity has a head, that is— okay, sorry, I am babbling, as you can tell).

Anyway, somehow I turn myself around, arms and hands flailing wildly, and I come back to the starting spot. I stumble off the hoverboard and let the next person get on. At last I let my intense concentration slip . . . and as I do, suddenly I see that people have fallen off their hoverboards all over the room.

Holy moly! There's Jai, sitting down on a mat and nursing a hurt knee, while his hoverboard levitates crookedly next to him, spun out at a 140-degree angle. A few feet away, further along the mats, I see another kid whose name I don't know, also off his board and rubbing his legs. Across the room, there's a dark-skinned girl with braided cornrows who limps and tries to stand up.

And there's Claudia Grito. She crouches on the edge of a mat, apparently tying her shoelaces, while her board is hovering two feet over her head.

Claudia went down! *Yes!*

Okay, I allow myself one mean moment of triumph, and then I try to look away, but I think there's a little smile now that's stuck on my face.

In that exact moment, Claudia looks up, and I swear, she is staring directly at me. Oh, crud! Did she see me smile?

I pretend I am fiddling with my ponytail, while I notice that Oalla has turned to me with a nod of approval. Amazingly, it occurs to me, I am one of the *few* people who have not fallen off their hoverboard during the wave ride.

A few minutes later, the last person ends their hoverboard turn, and class is dismissed.

"I will see you here tomorrow, and I want you to practice the things that give you the most trouble," Oalla says loudly.

I watch Blayne Dubois come down from riding near the ceiling on the hoverboard, and there's his wheelchair, pushed up against the wall. While the other teens are turning in their hoverboards and walking past him, he directs the hoverboard to stop and levitate higher up than normal, about two feet off the ground and nearly level with the seat of his wheelchair. He pushes himself off the board with both hands, then drops himself into the chair from above, cleverly landing in a seated position.

Next, he arranges his lifeless legs and feet in the chair, and commands the hoverboard away.

I watch as he just sits there, paused, thinking about something. . . .

And then I go up to him. "Hey," I say. "Did you ever ask them about letting you keep that hoverboard outside of class? You really should. . . ."

Blayne looks up at me. His expression is startled, as if I'd woken him up from a daydream. "Hey," he says. "Oh, it's you. Um, no. I am not going to ask."

I feel an immediate jolt of frustration. "Why not?"

"Because it's none of your business!"

Okay, what is it with this guy?

"Sorry," I say. "But—look, all I am saying is, this is a great opportunity. And you are kind of good on this hoverboard thing. I mean, really good. You know, you could maybe ask them to borrow it for a little bit each day—"

"Gwen Lark," he says my name with emphasis, while a frown grows on his face. "You are really getting on my nerves, you do realize? Why don't you get lost and leave me the hell *alone!*"

I bite my lip, and shrug. "Okay, sorry . . . whatever. . . ."

And then, because an unexpected lump starts to form in the back of my throat, and I suddenly feel a familiar pressure in my eyes, I quickly turn around. Before I start crying, I get out of the gym hall and race up the stairs.

Chapter 12

After that, lunch hour pretty much sucks. I find Laronda in the cafeteria, and she's sitting all the way in the back, so that I have to carry my tray with its slice of pizza and glass of juice past several tables filled with the popular mean crowd.

It's only day two, and Yellow Dorm Eight has already established a social pecking order, and they are center stage, here in the cafeteria. All the in-crowd has occupied the best tables. This grouping of alphas now includes in one category the hashtaggers, and a number of other athletic-looking jocks and cheerleader types, or simply big and tough teens, many of whom seem to be well-off, sporting expensive smart jewelry and gadgets. In another category there are the scary street-tough guys and girls that look like they are gang-affiliated.

The rest of us, kids who are ordinary beta types, geeks and nerds, the weirdoes, or the invisible loners, are relegated to the secondary, more-or-less "loser tables" at the periphery, the farthest ends of the room, and pressed against the walls and cafeteria backroom doors.

As I pass the loudest table in the middle, I hear laughter and hoots, and then someone says, "Gwen Lark, baby, why you ask such difficult questions?" I pause and a new wave of laugher hits me.

I turn.

The big dark-haired guy with the creepy neck tattoo, who pinched and elbowed me the other day, is staring directly at me. His grin is hard and terrible. Again, he shapes his lips into an air kiss and I feel a wave of cold fear sweep through me. . . .

"Where you going, baby?" he says loudly, leaning his muscled body in my direction. "Looking for some more Atlantis homework? I got some for you right here!" He makes a gesture at his crotch.

"Owww, Derek! You show her, man!" More hoots, crude gestures, and guffaws break out. There's Olivia, hanging on to Wade's arm, and making more disgusting gestures, then covering his ear with her hands to whisper something. Both of them bust out laughing.

My head feels like it will explode from a mixture of sudden rage and fear. But fear wins out and makes me stiffen and turn away and pretend to ignore them—especially this tattooed Derek guy who scares the crap out of me in a serious way, with his bulk and his hardcore attitude, and the aura of street-tough meanness.

I quickly rush past their table, barely keeping the tray in my hands, and make it to Laronda's table.

"Ooooo, girl, they really have it in for you!" Laronda looks at me worriedly. "See, that's what you get for not keeping your mouth shut and talking so much in class. All these jerks notice you!"

"I know. . . ." I slam my tray down, because I am still shaking in anger. "I can't help it. I *always* talk in class. Way too much."

"Then cut it out!" Laronda nibbles at the crust remains of her pizza slice.

I sit down and stare at her. "It's just how I am. I dunno, I always have this need to answer everything—I know, it's crazy, I guess. It's automatic—"

"See, even now you're talking too much. Just, *zip* it. Shush!"

"Okay . . ."

"Nuh-uh!" Laronda lifts her hand palm up in my face, then mimes closing a zipper with her fingers across her lips.

I take the hint and chew some pizza instead.

Meanwhile Laronda tells me stuff—first about her horrible Combat class over at the huge Arena Commons building, then about her Auntie Janice back in Buffalo with whom she lives, and about how her six-year-old baby brother Jamil loves pizza, any pizza no matter how awful, and too bad she couldn't give him some of this crappy cardboard kind from the cafeteria, because he'd eat it for sure. . . .

I listen and nod, and think about saying something about how sorry I am that her aunt and her brother Jamil cannot be here with us, cannot Qualify, just like my parents cannot be here.

But I say nothing, because, of course speaking about any of it is too horrible. . . .

"So hey, how was Agility?" Laronda twirls and folds a drinking straw wrapper into an accordion on her tray.

I tell her about it, and then mention Blayne last, and how he basically cut me off in the end.

"Boy's got issues, that's for sure." Laronda chews the straw wrapper. "So, you're never going to talk to him again now, right? Right? Cause that would be the smart thing to do."

"I don't know, I guess not. . . . Still, I feel so bad for him, for some reason, as if I am supposed to do something—as if I *could* do something to help him."

"Well, you can't. And he doesn't want help. Stop being a pushy fool, and get it through your thick smarty-pants skull. Some people just don't like it when others fuss at them. Let the man have his pride."

The claxon bell rings to indicate the end of lunch hour and five minutes before next class.

Today Laronda and I share this one also, and it happens to be Atlantis Tech.

"All right, move your booty, girl, time for us to go get all 'techie.'"

I nod and pick up my tray. Then we go to unload the remains of our lunch, and I pause momentarily and take Laronda's elbow. "Wait a little. Let those jerks clear out first, I don't want to pass by that table again. . . ."

Laronda glances to where I am motioning with my eyes, and she sees the alpha crowd near the doors, clearing out their trays and leaving the cafeteria.

"Okay, but you can't just avoid them all the time. Remember what I told you, you gotta cultivate an attitude. And I mean, Attitude with a capital A."

"Yeah, okay. Maybe next time. . . ." And I continue waiting a few more seconds, while the majority of them leave the cafeteria.

"Chicken!" Laronda says.

"And proud of it!" I smile at her.

Mr. Warrenson is already in the classroom when we get there, and he is setting out a bunch of gadgets on the large surface of the teacher's desk.

"Hurry, hurry, take your seats please, everyone!" he repeats every few minutes, as Candidates fill up the empty seats in the classroom. "So much to do today, and no time to waste. . . ."

Laronda knows me well already, because she plunks down on a seat in the second row, giving me the "primo" spot closer to the middle.

I purse my lips to hold back another smile.

And then the nerves kick in again. I remember this is the "singing class."

Mr. Warrenson begins class with a demonstration.

"Today," he says, "is very exciting! As you recall, in yesterday's class I demonstrated to you some basic sound-based levitation. Well, today, you are going to learn how to do it yourself—you'll make the sounds that levitate objects! Yes, all by yourself!"

Okay, Mr. Warrenson is being way too geeky and way too optimistic in thinking we actually "recall" anything from yesterday's class. Because, to be honest, he does ramble on a whole lot, which makes it hard to follow him. And that's saying a lot, coming from *me*.

"OMG!" Laronda whispers. "Isn't it like in those really old kids' books about a boy wizard who goes to magic school and they do all these funky spells? I want me some magic wand!"

"Except, this is not magic," I whisper back. "At least I don't think so. . . ."

"Ladies, quiet, please!" Mr. Warrenson turns in our direction then continues. "Now, the fact that we are using the Yellow Quadrant as our basic approach, makes it a bit more complicated. The Majors and Minors—Red Quadrant and Blue Quadrant—have it easy. Their sound controls are based on common musical scales. Yours, on the other hand, are based on relativity, and so are the Green Quadrant's. Yellow is Sharp, while Green is Flat, so basically you don't really have your own reference points, as much as you have to riff off the others. To put it simply, in a musical piece, Red is the melody line, Blue is the harmony, and Yellow and Green are the counterpoints, with Yellow rising and Green falling. But—we'll get to that later, today is just the general basics common to all Quadrants—"

The class appears somewhat dazed at this musical theory explanation. Seriously, a few people are already flatlining from boredom. And it's only been, like, thirty seconds of class. I mean, we're supposed to be levitating stuff, for goshsakes! Where is Nefir Mekei and his mesmerizing Storyteller voice when you need it?

Fortunately Mr. Warrenson gets a clue and gets practical. He picks up a small lump of charcoal gray material from the surface of the desk and displays it to the class. "This—this right here is the basic metal alloy that Atlanteans have developed to resonate to sound. It's the same material that hoverboards are made of. There are so many other uses—"

"What is it?" a girl asks.

"Aha!" Mr. Warrenson pauses, then scratches his balding head to better consider his answer. "Well, that's the thing. We don't really *know* what it is. And the Atlanteans won't tell us."

The classroom comes awake.

"For lack of a better term, we here in the Earth scientific community, refer to it at present as *orichalcum*. I realize it's a placeholder name, and somewhat trite, since it's the mythic term from ancient writings referring to an unknown, 'magic' Atlantis metal. But until the Atlanteans share with us its atomic structure, we have nothing else to go on. And who knows, maybe that's what the mythic orichalcum is anyway."

I raise my hand. Laronda immediately kicks me underneath the desk, but I ignore her.

"Yes," Mr. Warrenson turns to me. "Your name, please?"

"Gwen Lark. I want to know why can't we simply analyze a sample in a lab and find out for ourselves its atomic structure? Isn't it the normal thing to do with unknown substances? And if we already tried, what happened?"

"Good question, Ms. Lark. We have, in fact, tried. Unfortunately, it turns out we cannot properly break down this material to the atomic level, and none of our lab tests are able to have any conclusive effect on it."

My eyes widen, and I stare. The gears of my mind are turning.

Orichalcum, the fabled metal from myth and legend, is in fact real! And it's super weird!

"We do know," Mr. Warrenson continues, "that it is a metal alloy. It appears to conduct heat—sometimes. Yes, I know that makes no logical sense. We can make an educated guess that part of its elemental makeup is gold, since gold is widely used on Atlantis for practically everything. We have not found its melting point temperature however. And everything else we *think* we know about it is messy science at best. The Atlanteans have not been particularly forthcoming with us about this stuff, nor have they shared with us many raw samples."

Mr. Warrenson turns the lump of orichalcum this and that way in his fingers as we continue to stare. Under the bright overhead lights, it appears to catch fire and sparkle with gold flecks. But as soon as light falls away it goes back to dull grey. "But enough background for now. Watch!"

Mr. Warrenson sings a sequence of notes in a clean tenor voice. It's a sustained major sequence, C followed by short notes E and G and then C again, sustained. He repeats this so that it sounds like he is singing the components of a C Major chord, over and over again.

The lump of orichalcum begins to visibly vibrate in his fingers. When suddenly he takes his hand away, the piece remains in place, floating in mid-air.

"Awesome!" a boy says.

"It sure is. Now, I want all of you to do it. Everyone, turn to the person next to you, who will be your partner."

Mr. Warrenson plucks the orichalcum piece from the air—it continues to vibrate oddly in his hand—and then opens a large box that contains a whole bunch of similar grey lumps. "As you can see, the other pieces of orichalcum in this box are presently inert. That's because the container is soundproof and serves as sound insulation."

With the box, he walks around the classroom, depositing a piece on every desk. "This is for your use today, but you cannot keep it. You will need to return it to me at the end of class. Now, put your hands on your piece, squeeze it, close your fingers all around. Warm it in your palm."

I wrap my palm around the small metal lump that Mr. Warrenson just gave me. It feels cool to the touch at first, then quickly takes on body temperature. Soon, it feels strangely *right*.

Next to me, Laronda is holding up her own piece and examining it closely.

"Now, repeat these notes exactly. C-E-G. And be sure to hold the C longer—"

A very young middle schooler with freckles raises her hand. "Excuse me, I don't know music notes. What's a C-E-G?"

Mr. Warrenson sighs. "What is your name, dear?"

"Jessica Conlett . . ." the girl mumbles.

"That's all right now, Ms. Conlett. I know that not all of you've had music education, or even remember all your notes if you did—and really it's quite a lot to demand of you. But, as you realize, this is not ordinary class, this is Qualification." He sighs again. "So please see me afterwards, or during your Homework Hour. My office is upstairs in the Arena Commons building. I'll catch you up on basic music theory. There are also some books you can borrow. . . . In addition, you can see your Dorm Leaders and they might be able to tutor you a bit."

"Okay," the girl mumbles.

"Now, everyone," Mr. Warrenson continues, "even if you don't know the notes, just sing along with me. Hold your piece up on your palm and sing C-E-G, like this."

We raise our palms up, and echo the Instructor. I take a deep breath. As soon as I make the first C note sound, I feel the vibration in my hand start. The lump of metal comes *alive*, and I feel its strange soothing warmth run like a light charge of electricity up and down my arm, echoing in my body. "C-E-G," I sing, and my voice begins soft and breathy then gets more confident, as I continue the notes. I am focusing so hard that my knuckles pressing against the side of the desk are turning white, while I hold up the other hand, palm up, with the orichalcum.

It's just another note, just another note, a familiar mantra begins in my head. I try to ignore it, *focus, focus*.

At my right, Laronda is singing in a pleasant soprano, smooth as silk. On the other side of me, an older girl sings in a slightly nasal lower soprano, with rich overtones. A boy's light tenor sounds directly behind me . . . then further back, someone else with a deeper voice. There are even a few baritones from the older boys. From everywhere, teen voices rise, repeating the grand C Major chord, eerily beautiful and powerful, until the classroom itself is suddenly buzzing, and all our orichalcum pieces are practically dancing in the palms of our hands, vibrating to the frequency. . . .

Mr. Warrenson raises his hand for silence. "Now, keep your palms up, fingers wide open and slowly lower your hands without holding on to the orichalcum."

I gently remove my palm from underneath the piece in my hand, and it . . . stays floating in the air before me.

My breath catches in my throat with awe.

With my peripheral vision, I see other pieces of metal floating like clouds in front of each Candidate. Laronda is watching her own levitating piece with amazement.

"Good!" Mr. Warrenson smiles at us. "What you've all done just now is *keyed* each piece to your unique voice and specific sound frequency. This means that your own piece will respond to only *your* voice and commands, until another person handles it and repeats the keying note sequence. This assures that there are no conflicting commands being issued. It's truly ingenious how the Atlanteans made it so that you have *inert* and *keyed* states for orichalcum."

I raise my hand again. Laronda rolls her eyes at me.

"Yes, Ms. Lark?"

"This is definitely amazing," I say. "But what if no one touches it, and there are several people all singing different commands at the same time? Will the inert piece respond at all? How will it know what command to 'obey?'"

"An excellent question!" Mr. Warrenson nods eagerly. "That is called *auto-keying*. In a situation where several voices sound together, and there is potential conflict, the orichalcum will indeed pick up and *auto-key* to the frequency of the strongest, loudest, cleanest voice. It will then follow the first complete command sequence issued by that voice. So, the more precise and powerful your notes are, the more likelihood there is that you will key the object to yourself remotely."

"Wow," I say.

"Yes, yes." Mr. Warrenson nods at me then walks to his desk.

"Now, there are two ways of returning orichalcum to its inert state. The first is to place it in a soundproof container. After a sufficient period of continued silence—about fifteen minutes to half an hour—the auditory 'charge' appears to wear out. The second method is to issue a 'turn-off' command by the person to whom the object is keyed. And the way to do it is simple. Just sing a few random notes that are *dissonant*. In other words, notes that sound 'jarring' or weird together, and don't make good harmony or melody. Plenty of flat or sharp notes should do it."

Mr. Warrenson holds up his original piece of orichalcum that is still buzzing in his hand. He opens his palm to show us, then takes his hand away until the piece levitates in front of him above the desk surface. And then he sings four notes that don't sound good together at all.

With a clatter, the orichalcum falls down on the desk.

"Now, the next basic commands you need to know is how to lift objects up from either a stationary or levitating position, and how to bring them back down smoothly."

This time Mr. Warrenson stands back from the desk. He clears his throat, then sings a loud C note and holds it for a few seconds, then sweeps up an octave, and concludes on another C, except one octave higher. As he does so, various loose objects on his desk suddenly begin to rise.

There must be a whole lot of orichalcum there, because in seconds, the contents of the entire desk surface are airborne. They float up slowly, and I remember in that moment how Oalla Keigeri had used a similar octave-jumping sequence to call the hoverboards in gym hall.

Before everything floats away to the ceiling, Mr. Warrenson begins singing the C-E-G looping sequence we already know that makes the objects stop in place and just levitate. He goes silent, and looks around the class to see the Candidates staring intently.

"And now," he says, "the final sequence to bring everything back down again." And he sings a C note, starting in a higher octave, then bringing it down to the lower C. The levitating stuff begins to gently float down, until it is once again resting on top of the desk.

"And that's the basics of Atlantean object movement," Mr. Warrenson concludes. "The only other command you need to know for now is the 'advance forward' command. It is perfectly simple. You hold a single note. Usually it's C, or the first note of the chord you choose to use for your keying command sequence—that's the *tonic* note. As I said before, the Red Quadrant uses Major keys and chords, so we have been using C notes and Major sequences in our demonstration. But you can use any chord sequence, Major or Minor. The Blue Quadrant often uses D Minor, for example. As for Yellow and Green—well, that will come later. For now we're keeping it simple."

Mr. Warrenson pauses, then looks at all of us, at our levitating orichalcum pieces. "Now, I want you all to turn to your partner and you will be practicing moving your pieces across space toward each other. . . . Then you will *reset* each piece back to inert state, then switch and try to key each other's piece remotely. Please begin!"

There's much shuffling and scratching sounds of furniture as the class starts rearranging and pushing desks together. In moments Laronda and I are facing each other across two levitating pieces of grayish metal with gold flecks.

"It's on, girl!" Laronda grins. And then she sings a loud and perfect C—at the same time as other teen voices sound everywhere around us.

Her orichalcum easily floats in my direction.

I watch it for a few seconds, then take a deep breath and begin to sing also.

Chapter 13

I have no idea how, but I survive the rest of Atlantis Tech. I clench one hand underneath my desk, out of sight, where I can squeeze it as much as I need, while my knuckles turn bloodless and my nails bite into my palm . . . all so that I can keep the focus and make the notes without breaking apart.

I sing each note—clean, remote and emotionless, all along imagining myself disembodied, a machine—and move the orichalcum piece forward, reset it, then switch with Laronda. I have very little memory of most of it for some reason. Class is over soon enough, and then there's only one more left for the day, which is Combat.

Relief. . . . I know this is just nuts, but I actually feel relief going back down again to the hateful basement and Training Hall, where I don't have to make another musical sound.

When I get there, the gym is nearly empty, and the Instructors have not shown up yet.

A couple of people are milling around near the workout equipment, watching some guy use a punching bag. . . .

Oh great. It's Wade and Derek with the neck tattoo. Their backs are turned, but I recognize Derek's coiling spiked serpent pattern crawling up his muscular neck and disappearing into the dark short-cropped hair at the base of his head. The two of them stand with arms folded, watching a third, the one's who's working out with the punching bag.

Whoever the guy is, he's moving fast. And I mean, *fast*. He's throwing punches in a volley, right and left hooks, and the shirt portion of the grey uniform he *should* be wearing is lying carelessly discarded on the floor a few steps away. . . .

He's naked to the waist, and he's got an amazing upper body. Meanwhile, his uniform pants, tucked into short boots, show off impressive legs and a tight compact rear.

I gulp. . . .

The guy has long, raven-black hair, very dark and straight. It slides against his back with every movement he makes. His deeply bronzed torso is gleaming with sweat, and now I've stopped in my tracks. I am staring so hard, because, holy lord, what a body! There is so much amazing definition in his triceps and biceps, his deltoids emphasizing the breadth of his shoulders in contrast with the lean waist.

He wears a prominent red armband around his upper arm, right over the sexy bicep.

Okay, this guy has to be Atlantean. Yes, his hair is pure "black-hole" black, with not a trace of gold, but there's just very little doubt he is not from our Earth.

Why? Because he's just too impossibly fast. . . . He moves precisely like the other Atlanteans I've seen so far.

If I'm wrong, I will eat my words. I mean, my thoughts. All right, screw my thoughts—they are kind of making me blush right now.

While I am gawking, more Candidates fill the classroom. Now a small crowd has gathered, watching this guy destroy the punching bag. We all stand in silent admiration.

Finally he is done.

He stops and stands back, bringing his hands down in a stance so smooth that it is worthy of a dancer. His chest rises and falls as he catches his breath. He turns around to face us.

A stone-cold handsome face of lean angles meets us. His brows are well defined and his dark brown eyes are emphasized in kohl. Oh yeah, he's Atlantean.

But, what's with that amazing black hair?

While he stands looking at us, woots of approval follow his performance, and many of the Candidates clap.

At the same time, our Instructor from the day before, Keruvat Ruo, comes into the Training Hall.

"Attention, Candidates!" Keruvat says, then pulls out a whistle and blows it. "Line up! Two rows facing each other! Now!"

While we scramble to form the now familiar double line, the

Atlantean with the long dark hair goes casually to pick up a towel. He wipes the sweat from his chest and arms then nods casually at Keruvat.

"I see you've started early." Keruvat turns to the other, with a light glance, ignoring us for the moment. "No shirt, Xel? Really?"

"Get used to it." The raven-haired Atlantean's voice is low and cool, and fits his icy demeanor exactly.

Keruvat shakes his head, but there's a shadow of a smile there. "Oh, I'm used to it, I just don't think these Candidates should have to be."

In answer, the other only shrugs, then tosses the used towel where his uniform shirt lies. He then turns to us and speaks in a hard voice of command. "Candidates! I am Xelio Vekahat, and I will be one of your two Combat Instructors for today. Your other instructor Oalla Keigeri is teaching Combat at Red Dorm Nine in my place. As you will see in the coming days, we will switch often, so that you will have exposure to a greater variety of instructors and fighting styles from all Four Quadrants."

He then approaches Keruvat, and the two of them walk down the line and count us in both our rows.

"First, warm up exercises! Legs apart. Begin with twenty forward stretches, fingers touching floor—"

I move my feet apart and start bending forward, hands to the floor. On either sides of me the Candidates move in unison. As I come up each time, I glance to see the two Atlanteans walking to the equipment cabinets. By the time we're done with the first set of stretches, they return carrying the familiar equipment bag.

"Now, legs wide, lunge with a twist to your left, ten reps, followed by twist to you right, ten reps. Begin!"

As I widen my stance then lunge, feeling my poor knees wobble, I watch Keruvat and Xelio go through the contents of the bag, removing and counting cords and netting.

"Now, ten deep squats, no stopping!"

I am already breathing hard, and trying to stay on my feet, while the now familiar sensation takes over, and my body has turned to pathetic malleable putty.

A few minutes of this, and we are told to stop and stand upright, and shake out our hands and arms at our sides.

I momentarily glance to the side and note that a much smaller pile of cords is now lying in the middle of the room.

"There are exactly forty-three Candidates in this class," Xelio says.

"And there are exactly forty-two cords and nets in this pile behind you," Keruvat adds.

We all stare in the direction of the pile.

"When you hear the whistle," Xelio says, "you will run and grab a cord or a net. The last person to reach for a piece will end up without one. That person will receive a demerit, and will have to face me as sparring partner for the rest of the class."

"Trust me, you *don't* want him for your sparring partner." Keruvat makes a deep noise that sounds like a snort.

I feel a cold sensation of terror wash over me, while my pulse starts to race wildly. The older teen boy to my right cusses softly.

"Are you ready?" Keruvat blows the whistle.

We all burst forward. It's a stampede.

I am bumped and shoved from all sides, as I hurl myself bodily in the direction of the pile of cords. Fortunately I am not too far away in my original spot in the line, and it's only a few paces. But it's a grinder of bodies in front of me. . . .

I claw and shove and end up painfully knocked in my ribs, then forced backwards, as two large girls shove themselves in front of me. I shove back, then slide between them, and go for the closest piece of netting or cord—a green woven net—clutch it with my fingers, while other pieces are being ripped in all directions by multiple hands.

I've got my hands firmly on the netting and I fall back, clutching it anxiously, trying to find my place back in the line.

I turn, and there's Derek.

He bumps into me, full-body, so that I can smell the musky aftershave along his skin, and his serpent tattoo is practically in my face, looming from above, since he's over six feet tall to my five-feet-nine. His arms widen, come around me. . . . He presses the back of my left shoulder painfully with one hand, while the other clenches my hand holding the net. He crushes my fingers until I let go. Immediately, as if nothing happened, he releases me, and steps aside, holding my hard-won net. With it, he gets back in his distant place in line.

While I stand, my mouth gaping in outrage, I see Derek wink and sneer at me. Watching him, I lose precious seconds. There's no time to try for another piece. The pile is no more, and everyone has either a piece of cord or a net.

I'm the only person stuck with *nothing*.

My mind races wildly, fury mixing with terror. I tremble with it, while I seethe. It is *not fair!* And all of a sudden a genuinely crazy idea comes to me.

I hurry back to my spot in my row. As the two Atlantean Instructors walk down the line toward me—yes, they've seen me with nothing, they *know* I'm the loser about to get a demerit—I crouch down and start untying the laces of my sneakers.

My fingers move, they fly like crazy, and I pull, pull, and in ten seconds I've got the shoelaces out and in my hands, and my sneakers stay open-flapped.

What kind of stupid idiot am I? What is this? What did I just do? I think, as I tie one end of one lace together with the one end of the other lace into a quick knot, so it's a single long piece.

This is completely stupid. But now I have a "cord." A really crappy one, but a cord nevertheless.

Xelio stops before me and looks down at me. I stand, offering him the ridiculous cord I've just laced together. He glances at it, and then directly into my eyes.

I shiver. . . . Up-close, I see the intense darkness of his gaze, the chiseled face with its fine aquiline nose, then glancing down, the sleek contours of his sculpted chest, his tanned skin still sleek with sweat from his pre-class workout.

"What is your name, Candidate?" he says in an unreadable voice. Standing so close to him, I almost feel the buzzing vibrations of his rich timbre along the surface of my skin. And his eyes never leave mine.

"Gwen Lark. . . ."

"Gwen Lark. What—is this?"

I cease breathing. . . . Then somehow find the ability to speak. "A cord."

There's a pause.

I think, for one impossible moment, I've rendered him speechless.

A few feet away, Keruvat makes a stifled noise. It could be

another snort.

"A cord?" Xelio repeats at last, and I see him blink. "And where did you get this—*cord?*"

"I—made it. . . ."

"You made it?"

"Yes."

The entire class of forty-two other Candidates is staring at me—and at him—in stilled intensity.

Another long pause.

And suddenly Xelio exhales and casually reaches for the shoelaces in my hand. "This is not a very good cord," he says, examining it, fingering the material and running his thumb over the knot. "Your knot is loose, and barely adequate. It will not hold. Nor is it thick enough. But—cleverly done. For your quick thinking, you will earn no demerit today."

I let out my breath in relief.

"However—" Xelio continues and again looks into my eyes. "You will still be my sparring partner. And next time—" He turns to look at the double line of Candidates. "Next time, none of you will attempt to be this clever again."

Meanwhile Keruvat shakes his head at me. But I see a bright expression in his very dark eyes. "Nicely played," he says softly, raising one brow. And then the really tall, super-black-skinned Atlantean with the short golden hair winks at me.

But I don't have any time to catch a break, because in the very next instant Keruvat barks out a command for us to take the first fighting form stance and face the person in the row across from us.

While everyone else lines up, Xelio takes me aside, and positions me two feet across from him and his amazing shirtless chest and muscled shoulders and biceps.

"Gwen Lark," he says. "Try not to trip over your untied shoes."

"Okay," I say, and already I can feel my face flushing from a combination of terror and strange excitement. In seconds I am about as red as the armband on his muscular arm.

"I want you to look directly into my eyes. Do not take your eyes away, not even for a moment. Use your peripheral vision instead to see what I am doing, and simply mirror me—follow my movements exactly, with their opposites."

His dark eyed gaze drills into me, unblinking, and he starts to raise his hands into a floating stance.

I follow his lead, and raise my own hands, shaking slightly.

He moves one hand forward at me, fingers angled in a deceptively loose yet precise figure.

I try not to blink, not to look away from him, as I bring my own opposite hand to meet his.

"Good," he says. Then his other hand flashes out and stops inches before my face.

I immediately counter him, with sheer panic reflex.

"And again—" Another swift movement, this time around and from the inside, with a flexing at the elbow.

I mirror him, bringing my own hand up and on the inside, and bent at the elbow, somewhat awkwardly.

"Continue to think of a mirror and its reflection," Xelio says, as he strikes again, and I counter.

I have no idea what I'm doing, or how I am doing it. But somehow the logic of the mirror has really resonated with me. *Just to do the opposite of the other person!* Sounds ridiculously easy in theory, but in practice it requires super concentration, and the ability to anticipate the movements of the opponent.

For several minutes that feel like eternity, I move my hands up and around my face to counter the Atlantean. The world narrows into super-focus, as I try to see him begin each hand motion before it happens. I stop hearing the rest of the classroom, the clumsy lunges and strikes and occasional yelps of pain as people miss and hit each other painfully.

"Stop," he says at last. His dark gaze continues to bore into mine.

I freeze and stand panting. By now I no longer feel my hands or my arms, as they hang limp at my sides.

"Wow . . ." I say, blinking in relief. "That was fascinating! I never thought that martial arts fighting was based on a mirror-image thing!"

"This—is not *fighting*." Is there a shadow of sarcasm in his voice? "These are simply forms-based exercises. You haven't even begun to know the Forms yet. You have been aping my free movements—adequately, for now. And, did I say you could look away from me, or blink?"

"Oh . . ." I say.

"Did I say you could speak?"

This time I know better than to open my mouth. Nor do I blink as I resume looking into his eyes until I can no longer tell if they are brown or black, or the color of the abyss.

A pause. . . . I can hear the rest of the class moving in exercise around me, and Keruvat Ruo's sergeant drill commands in his deep booming voice.

But I neither move nor look around.

Xelio nods. "Good. Now you will learn the first true Form, the basic fighting stance that begins and ends all other Forms. We call it the Floating Swan. Watch carefully. And yes, now you may look away from my eyes so that you can understand and observe the details of the Form."

I allow myself to breathe and glance away, breaking eye contact. It feels almost tangible, the sudden cessation of intensity.

Xelio takes a wide stance with his feet and then raises his hands to float at chest level, one outstretched at a 45 degree angle off to the side, the other hand pointing directly at me, hand bent at the wrist, palm vertical, thumb curving inward. He stills in the stance and I cannot help noting the beautiful definitions of his abdomen and chest, slick and bronzed, the proud lines of his shoulders, the muscles tensing in his powerful neck, and the way his long black mane of hair falls like midnight silk. . . .

Someone, for the love of God, please slap me!

"Now, you," he says. "Keep your body pliant and flowing, and do not tense your limbs. Nothing should be tense. Your muscles should not be locked but relaxed. Knees and elbows bent slightly."

He comes around to check me while I widen my stance on wobbling knees and try to copy his hands. My arms are shaking from tension, muscles unused to so much relentless exercise.

"Keep still," he says, then adjusts the placement of my arms in the Form. At his light touch I feel a blush exploding across my face. I struggle to maintain my stance and my composure.

Okay, what *is* it with these Atlanteans, and the oozing sex appeal?

Half an hour later, it is over. I've been taught five Forms, and I'm to practice and repeat them on my own time, as homework. Somehow I survived Xelio's hot proximity, and managed not to melt into a useless hormonal girl puddle. Lucky me, it occurs to me, I got one-on-one lesson time with an amazing Instructor, while the rest of the class had each other and Keruvat's barking commands.

We are dismissed and it's dinnertime.

As I pitifully stagger up the stairs in exhaustion, and emerge in the Common Area lounge on the first floor, there's my brother George. And Gordie is right behind him.

"George!" I say in surprise, wiping sweat from my forehead and adjusting the wisps of hair sticking out from my messy ponytail. "And Gordie! What are you guys doing here?"

George looks pretty awful himself. His grey T-shirt's got sweat stains and his dark brown hair is sticking up in awful messy spikes as if he hasn't been combing it at all, like *ever*. And Gordie is not much better, a sweaty mess, and in addition he's got a purpling bruise around the bridge of his nose and upper cheek. At least his glasses are in one piece.

"Let me guess, you just had Combat or Agility, Gee Two? You look great, babe. Yeah, I know, we look great too. And, sorry if we reek." George makes a tired half-grin thing with his face.

Gordie just waves, then continues the hand motion to rub his bruised cheek with the back of his hand and finally moves his glasses up his nose. Ah, my baby brother, always the economy of movement.

"You guys are alive," I mutter with relief. "Glad we all made it through day two."

"Yeah, just barely," Gordie says. "Only fifty-eight more days to go."

"What's with the shiner on your cheek, Gordie?"

"Nothing. . . . Accident in Agility Training."

"Oh, yeah?"

"I believe, his face connected with someone's fist," George elaborates. "But—he can tell you all about it at dinner. Let's go grab food, I'm starving, and we can catch up."

I pause in confusion. "How are we going to eat together?

Aren't you guys supposed to eat in your own dorms?"

George raises one eyebrow and wiggles it. "Who's going to notice or care?" And when he sees my doubtful expression, he continues, "No, really, I checked with the Dorm Leaders, they say we can eat in any cafeteria we like, any time, as long as it's within the grounds of this compound. So take your pick, Gee Two—your dorm or mine, or even this pisshead's here—" and George snaps Gordie's forehead with his fingers.

"Hey!" Gordie makes a quick avoidance twisty motion that's actually kind of sleek.

"Whoa!" I say. "You've learned some new moves there, Gordon Lark! Looks like all that Atlantis training's paying off with positive results. Way to go, bro!"

"Yeah, a whole two days' worth of it." Gordie rolls his eyes. But he appears pleased.

As I consider our next move, I see Laronda. She's coming down the stairs, probably from the fourth floor classrooms. She waves at me.

I wave back then turn again to my brothers. "What about Gracie?" I say. "Have you guys seen her? Should we go get her?"

"Gracie's decided to skip dinner and get her beauty sleep." George glances at Gordie. "What did she say to you exactly?"

Gordie shrugs. "I went to her dorm and she was right there, hanging out in the lobby, looking beat. She was just about to go in the Red cafeteria with some people and grab food quickly. Then afterwards she was gonna nap, she told me."

"Okay, so no Gracie," I think out loud.

Laronda comes up to us. There's another girl trailing her, a slim younger teen, probably a freshman, with waist-long black hair, dark eyes and light brown skin. "Hey," I tell Laronda. Then I turn to my brothers and introduce everyone. "This is Laronda Aimes, a friend from my dorm," I say. "Laronda, these are my brothers, George and Gordie Lark."

"And this is Dawn Williams," Laronda tells us. "She'll be hanging with us for dinner. So, where are we eating? Here, or Blue or Green?" She glances at the blue and green tokens lit up on my brothers' shirts.

Dawn says "Hi," in a soft, reserved voice then stays quiet,

leaving the tough decision making to us.

"Hmm." I look at everyone. Great, it's like that eternal "where shall we eat" idiot game that people play when a whole bunch gets together and no one can agree on a restaurant.

"Decisions, decisions," George says, reading my mind. "Shall it be Chez Yellow or Le Bleu, or Frou Frou Greenz, or Trattoria Rouge?"

"How about none of the above?" Gordie swipes his purplish bruise again. "I want to go check out the big Arena Commons building. There's supposed to be a cafeteria there too, I think."

"Hey, not a bad idea," George says. "It's neutral ground, where all the Four Quadrants can come together and mingle in a perpetual bliss state of cease-fire, all hostilities forgotten, everyone all kissy-lovey—"

"George, huh? What are you talking about?" I raise my eyebrows at him. "What hostilities?"

"Oh, come, Gee Two, didn't they tell you all about it in your Culture class yet? The Four Quadrants are all supposed to be rivals, way hardcore. And this super duper rivalry, it's some kind of eternal ongoing thing in Atlantis society. Real classy and honor-bound, sure, but still hardcore."

I blink. "Okay, no. Our class didn't exactly get to it. We're still on the Atlantis Grail part."

"The Atlantis what?"

"*Grail*," I repeat.

"What's that?" George is staring.

"It's a cup, George. A round thing you drink from. King Arthur and the Knights of the Round Table had a holy thing for it. Well, not for *it*, to be precise, but for another grail, but same idea. Except, less holy."

Gordie chuckles, then quickly evades George who once again tries to finger-snap his forehead.

I pause and glance at Laronda. She rolls her eyes then says, "It's the annual Atlantis Olympics. Except, it's not. It's this freakish evil Games-to-the-Death thing, and if you win, you get citizenship and everything else you've ever wanted—you basically hit the life lottery jackpot."

"Yeah, that's one way of calling it."

"And if you lose, you kind of *die*."

George snorts. "Great!"

"We'll talk about it on the way, meanwhile, let's go, I'm starving!"

Right on cue, Gordie's stomach rumbles in confirmation.

We get out of Yellow Dorm Eight and head for the big adventure that's the Arena Commons super structure. It's still light outside, but bluish twilight's starting in the east. The air is cool and crisp, and we're all underdressed in our sweaty T-shirts, but no one absolutely cares.

There are other Candidates walking about, and a few campus guards on patrol, moving to and fro. The Arena Commons looms several buildings ahead. At about six stories, it is considerably taller than the other four-story buildings around it. I squint and see a four-color Square Logo in the distance. The roof of the Arena Commons appears to be a dome made of glass panels, kind of like the ceiling of an enclosed indoor shopping mall.

"Oh, look!" Dawn Williams says suddenly, pointing in the opposite direction, against the sunset sky.

We turn, and there are two dark spots rising in the burning orange sky, as sleek silhouettes of Atlantean shuttles fly upward beyond the outer buildings. The sonic booms hit us right after, and the shuttles disappear above the clouds, briefly becoming points of searing light as the setting sun hits them at the angle when they are no longer in the Earth's shadow.

"Wonder what they're doing?" George says.

"More VIPs?" Laronda, walking in front of me, glances at him. "They're probably checking us out and reporting on our progress back on their Mama Starships."

"Maybe they're just rotating Instructors," I say. "Some finish their shifts and go back up, others come down in their place."

"Yeah," Gordie snorts. "Or maybe they can't digest Earth food or breathe our atmosphere for too long, so they have to go up and replenish their bodies with some kind of special Atlantis nutrients and drugs—"

"That's right, Gee Three," I say. "They probably suck blood up there, or eat big bowls of live crawling worms harvested from the green hills of Atlantis—"

"Hey, you never know." Laronda shrugs.

W e arrive at the Arena Commons and go inside past the tall glass doors, moving through throngs of Candidates wearing token IDs in all four colors.

A comparison with an indoor shopping mall promenade is not at all off base here. At least it seems so for the length of the first small entry corridor, that resembles a mall nook, minus the inviting storefronts.

And then you turn the corner, and whoa! It looks like a small sports stadium.

The bulk of this area, domed off with a glass ceiling, encloses a sizeable oval sports arena, with an Olympic-style running track along the inner perimeter, and various sports scaffolding and truss structures taking up sections of the middle.

The outside walls are taken up with five story-levels of balcony walkways that circle the perimeter, and appear to have offices or other commercial looking doors and window displays running around the entirety of the structure.

"What the heck is this place?" Laronda cranes her head up.

"Better to ask, when did they have time to build this thing?" George retorts, looking around. "Must've taken months! It's like a decent-sized ballpark!"

"Looks like my idea of purgatory," I mutter, glancing at the running track and the various scaffolding in the center. "I'm guessing at some point we Candidates are going to have to go in there and use all that equipment. Otherwise, why else would it be here?"

"Hmmm, you could be right, sis," George says. "For Qualification Semi-Finals, maybe? Or even Finals?"

"Ugh," Dawn says with a shudder. I am guessing she is not all that athletic either—though I could be wrong, since she looks the least sweaty of all of us.

Gordie points to one end of the sports arena, in the very back. "Hey, there's a pool!"

And he's right. Way toward the rear, barely visible through the thicket of metal scaffolding, there's a stretch of shimmering blue that sparkles under the overhead lights. I think I even see a diving board. The pool does not look overly large, but it's probably long enough for some basic twenty-five-yard laps.

"Ya-a-y, pool," George says in a semi-enthusiastic manner. "I could go for a swim later. But first, feed me! Let's go, ladies!"

We follow a minor crowd to the interior wall side of the structure where there's something resembling an open food court. It's definitely another cafeteria, and we get our trays and get in line. They are serving what looks like American diner food basics.

At this point, I find that I'm starving. I point out my choices and the server in a gray uniform with a rainbow armband gives me a burger and a slice of pizza and some mashed potatoes. Then, at the self-serve bar I pile veggies in a salad bowl and get two glasses of some kind of unidentified fruit punch. Gordie is jostling after me, and I see his tray is even more loaded than mine, with corn and coleslaw, a ton of fries, and three burgers.

"Yeah, girlfriend, go for it. We've burned up enough calories to eat a whole cow," Laronda says, seeing my guilty pause at the dessert bar as I consider adding a slice of cherry pie to my tray. I turn and she's got a mountain of food on her tray also.

"Let's find a table," Dawn says, balancing her own full tray with one hand and an ice cream cone in another. "Oh, there's an empty one there. . . ."

We head for the table and park there, before other Candidate groups grab it.

As we settle in, it appears we've picked a busy walk-through area, good for people watching. Our table is at the edge of the food court, close to the overhanging balcony of the first upper level, so we can see the walkways overhead all the way up to the top floor.

"Hey, this is good. . . ." Gordie is speaking with his mouth full of burger.

"Easy there, please chew!" Laronda swallows a long French fry with a ketchup-smeared tip, and raises one brow at Gordie with amusement. Meanwhile on both sides of me my brothers dig into their burgers.

Candidates are walking all around us in large and small groups and it's getting loud, and tables are filling up. I guess everyone else had the same idea and decided to check out this Arena Commons place for dinner. Interesting, looks like many people from the same Quadrants seem to be sticking together—

Green with Green, Red with Red, Yellow with Yellow, et cetera.

As I take a big bite of pizza, I happen to glance up and see a group of teens with mostly Red tokens passing by. I recognize one immediately—the familiar black hair with rare brown highlights, broad shoulders, tall muscular back and toned runner's legs—even before he turns around, and yeah, it's Logan Sangre. . . .

Now I am starting to choke on my pizza—or rather, I've forgotten to chew and breathe, and not sure what's happening in my mouth.

Next to Logan, there's his dark-haired friend, Daniel Tover, with the slightly crooked nose and pleasant face. He's walking with a girl who has long dirty-blond hair and who's hanging onto his arm and giggling in a hyper, slightly unnatural voice.

It's Gracie.

Chapter 14

"Gracie!" I exclaim, and drop my pizza. Fortunately it lands on the plate and not my chest.

Everyone at my table stares as my sister turns at her name being called and kind of freezes. Then she and her friends stop and look in our direction.

They approach. In addition to Logan and Gracie and Daniel, there are several other Reds I've not seen before, and there's Mia Weston, the petite girl from Gracie's dorm.

"Gracie!" I continue to speak. "What are you doing here? We thought you weren't going to eat dinner and take a nap instead."

"Oh, hi!" Gracie has a slightly nervous, sheepish expression, and I notice she has let go of Daniel's arm. "Yeah, well, I changed my mind. Everyone was going to see this Arena place!"

"Okay. . . ."

"Hi, Yellow Candy," Logan says, looking at me with a light smile. His gorgeous warm hazel eyes are trained on me directly. I feel a sudden pang in my chest as my lungs kind of collapse and lose their ability to expand. . . . Just for a single dumb moment.

"Hi," I mutter. "I'm Gwen."

"I know." His smile grows. "We've met yesterday, remember? We're from the same school. You're Grace's big sister."

"Hey, wait, I know you, man," my brother George says. "You're Logan, right? Mapleroad Jackson High, varsity track team? Mr. Borster's AP History class?"

"Yup, that's me—Logan Sangre. You're George Lark?"

Logan leans in and they shake hands over a heaping plate of Gordie's burgers.

Introductions happen all around.

"Want to join us?" Laronda says after a meaningful glance in my direction. "We can make room on the table and 'de-tray.' Go grab your food and come back here."

Gracie looks up at Daniel, and the other Reds glance at each other. "Well," she says. "There's sort of this unwritten rule, we're all supposed to stick together with people of our own Quadrant and build up allegiance or something. So maybe we should just go find a different table—"

"Says who? What rule? No one told *us*. . . . Oh, come on!" Laronda snorts. "What's this, some kind of freaky Atlantis segregation? Seriously? You've got to be kidding me."

"Just set your butt down here, Gracie," I say. "This is silly."

"It's not so much a rule as a guideline," Daniel says diplomatically. The Reds exchange more glances and then look at our table and all our multi-color tokens. Among us we've got three yellows, a blue and a green.

"I'm sure we can safely mingle tonight," Logan says, glancing at me with a wink. "I'll be right back." And he heads for the food court service.

"Okay, I guess. . . ." Gracie nods at me then goes after him. The other Reds follow.

"That's right. You all come back now, we don't have color cooties, jeez!" And Laronda rolls her eyes and picks up her burger.

Five minutes later, our table is overcrowded with the Red Quadrant newcomers, and everyone's trays have been removed and stacked on the floor in order to make room for our individual plates. We've pulled up additional chairs, and it's a tight human pack all around.

"So wait," Logan says to us, as he picks up one of his burgers. "You're the Four Gees, right? I remember that meme going around school."

"That's us, we're a meme," Gordie says with a minor cringe, still speaking with his mouth full.

"Yeah, our parents really did us a favor." George grins.

I consider saying something clever but decide to continue chewing instead, and stare down at my plate, just to be safe. Logan's sitting two seats over from me, next to George and Daniel. Even with the space between us, I am acutely aware of his proximity, and the sure way he handles his burger.

The sure way he handles his burger? Really? What kind of asinine thought did I just have? I glance up and observe Logan's elegant jaw moving as he takes a bite, and the way his throat muscles—

Oh, for crying out loud, what am I, a lovesick cow?

I poke a plastic fork at my mashed potatoes and grow angrier with myself with every passing second.

"So, any news from the outside world?" says one of the Reds, an Asian guy with spiked black hair and high-end smart jewelry around his neck and in his earlobes, whose name is Greg Chee. "We can't get past the e-dampers, though I hear a couple of hacker guys have bypassed and have been able to pick up something on their smart pads."

He leans in, and speaks in a lower voice so that our table grows quiet enough to hear him. "Rumor has it, since we Prelim-Qualified and got bused over to these Centers, and then locked up in here, the whole world's been fixated on us. The media's live streaming all the Centers from outside the fenced in compounds round the clock, and some parents have even camped outside. And then—more major riots happened, huge ones in central China, the EU, and one really serious one here, in the Metro DC area near the Houses of Congress. They had to halt their session and evacuate temporarily. Plus, there are new military curfews all over the world, not just here. As for the President, she's been making grandstanding promises as usual. And the UN is eating it up."

"Yeah well, considering that President Donahue is all in bed with the Goldilocks and their technology, and has been since day one, what else is she going to do?" George puts his food down and looks around, starting to frown.

Daniel looks at my brother closely, evaluating him. "You think so?" he says. "So, you're not a big fan of our fine Atlantean overlords?"

"Not a fan, no." George resumes eating.

"Good to have a clear head about the situation," Greg Chee says to George.

Sitting next to me, Gracie pauses eating her fries and glances at Daniel, then Greg. "You guys remember they said they'll be filming us during Qualification Semi-Finals and Finals. Any idea where that's all going to be held? Is it in this building? Do you think other RQCs have their own Arena buildings like ours, and this is what they're all going to film?" She nods over to the track and interior sports area with the scaffolding.

Greg snorts and shakes his head. "No way! Seriously, you think this, right *here*, is where the Finals will be? Hah! Hah! Hah!" He laughs, looking at Gracie with pity.

"What?" She frowns back at him.

"Look—" Greg leans in toward us. "I hear it's huge. Huge! It's going to be all over! The Finals, especially. They— Goldilocks—they're preparing for something major all over the globe. Huge construction projects going on, on all the coasts, inside major cities. When the time comes, they'll be sending us *outside*—wherever it is. This puny arena here, this is *nothing*."

As Greg is speaking, I feel a growing sense of dread. Looks like I'm not the only one, as we all stop eating and listen to him.

"Oh, no . . ." Dawn says across from me. "That sounds really bad."

Greg turns to her. "Yeah, it is."

"So—what is this place for, then?" I say in confusion. "I thought this is where the Qualification happens eventually."

"It's probably just another big gym hall for more advanced training." Logan tells me. "Of course nothing is certain, this dude could be wrong."

Greg snorts. "I wish! Believe me I want to be wrong about this crap. But it doesn't appear to be that way."

"Hey, guys, look. . . ." Laronda cranes her neck and motions with her head upward. We all look up.

There, on the uppermost level of the walkway, a group of about a dozen Atlanteans walks by, headed toward the far end of the level. Their metallic golden hair picks up the strong overhead lights and shines super-bright in the distance, so that they all appear to have halos of light around their heads. . . . They already stand out from the rest of us by the strange grace of their movements, their general good looks—and now, that beacon-bright hair really brings it all home.

They leisurely walk directly above us, only several levels up. We can barely hear their muted conversation, and I'm quite certain it's not in English. At one point there is soft female laughter.

I stare and recognize Oalla Keigeri, and next to her is Keruvat Ruo, the tallest and darkest of them. A few other Atlanteans I don't know stroll by, and then Nefir Mekei, looking straight ahead, his face impassive. Right after him is the glaring contrast of Xelio Vekahat—the only Atlantean whose hair is not metallic gold but midnight black. I note that this time Xelio is wearing his uniform shirt. He is also talking closely with a short-haired Atlantean girl I don't know, leaning in toward her, so that I cannot see his striking face. . . .

A few more Atlanteans pass, their grey uniforms all the same except for the colored armbands—red, green, yellow, blue . . . *black.*

With a strange pang, I recognize the tall slim form of Aeson Kass. I blink and watch the movement of his toned upper body, the black armband hugging his powerful arm, the angle of his head with its slightly washed out radiant metallic hair, his confident profile. Cool and dispassionate, he turns once to glance over at the panorama of the Arena as he moves by.

I am staring at him, and I swear, for a split second his gaze lands on me, and there is a moment of recognition. . . .

But no, that's just crazy. Why would this hotshot Command Pilot and *astra daimon* bother to recognize or even remember *me*, a nerdy and awkward Earth girl who asked weird questions on her first day of Combat class?

"Looks like the Goldilocks are headed to a big party," one of the Reds says.

"All of our Instructors in one place, eh?" Daniel says. "Oh, to be a fly on that wall."

"Must be important."

"More likely, must be dinner. They do eat, just like us, you know."

"We were just wondering about that earlier." Laronda snorts.

Greg stares hard then turns back to our group and whispers, "Oh, man . . . that's *him*. . . ."

"Who?"

"Black armband—the one they call *Phoebos*."

A few of the Reds in the back of the table exchange glances.

"And who's Phoebos?" Mia Weston asks.

"Their top ranking Pilot," Daniel says. "The same VIP we were talking about yesterday. *Phoebos* is a call sign. He's basically in charge of the Fleet, after their Commander, I believe he's either the third or second ranking officer—in any case, he's a really big deal."

"And what is he doing here?" Laronda looks worried.

"Who knows? Probably checking all of us Candies out. Taking stock of our abilities, making preliminary decisions about which of us will Qualify. I'm sure they discuss us in private, and the Instructors give him detailed reports about us." Greg Chee sneers.

I consider mentioning again that Aeson Kass was the surprise visitor in my Combat class yesterday, but for some reason decide to keep my mouth shut.

"I think their offices are all up there," I say instead. "So probably they'll hang around for a few hours in case we want to go see them with homework stuff."

"Sounds about right." George picks up a glass and drinks his apple juice. "Talking about homework—how are you surviving, Gee Two? I can't imagine what Agility must be like for you. The monkey bars and all that running of laps. I'm pretty beat myself and Gordie here is getting his face slapped around. But Gracie and you especially—my poor sis, you can't even run three feet without keeling over—"

Okay, I love my brother George, but right this moment I want to kill him.

I turn bright red. "Okay, shut it, Gee One. Why don't you humiliate me even more, and make a hashtag of it? It's bad enough I suck at it, with daily demerits to prove it, and now the whole world needs to know it too. Thanks, bro."

By "the whole world" I'm of course thinking of Logan Sangre. The boy's possibly the best runner in our school. And now, *he* of all people will know how badly I suck at his chosen sport. Way to impress.

I laugh self-depreciatingly, glance around the table and there's Logan, looking at me seriously. "You have trouble with running? You know, I can help you."

I meet his eyes, and there's this head-rush thing going on. "What do you mean?"

Yeah, smart, very smart retort, Gwenevere Numbskull Lark.

"I'm on the track team," Logan says. "So I can definitely help you train, if that's the trouble you're having."

"Oh wow, thanks . . ." I mutter. "Yes, the suckage I referred to is me and running. I can use all the help I can get."

Leaning over to Dawn, Laronda whispers something and hides a smile.

"Then it's settled," Logan says. "We'll start running tonight, right here. That's a fine looking track they have here, much better than what's in our dorms."

Half an hour later, our dinner group breaks apart, and we head in different directions. My brothers stick around here, while Daniel and a few of the Reds head out to wander the compound. Gracie tries to tag along after them, but I give her a hard glare and pull her aside for a moment.

"You are twelve, Gracie! *Twelve!* Cut it out. I don't want to see you hanging around that guy," I whisper, holding her arm.

Gracie makes furious eyes at me. "You're not my mother!"

"For as long as Mom is not here to say otherwise, yeah, I am!"

"That's a whole bunch of BS! He's nice, and just a friend, totally platonic—"

"It had better be platonic!"

"I am not doing anything wrong, and it's not like anything's gonna happen anyway, he's got a girlfriend back in New York—"

"Whom he's never going to see again, don't you get it?" I hiss. "It's dangerous, and everything is messed up with the world right now—so please, I am begging you now, Gracie, please, don't—"

"Please don't what?" George has overheard us whispering.

"Nothing!" Gracie says with a frown.

I turn to George. "She's got a crush on a much older guy. I don't want her to hang around him."

George raises one eyebrow. "Who is it?"

"Don't!" Gracie screams at the same time as I say, "Daniel, one of the guys you've just had dinner with."

"Hmmm." George makes a noise and looks serious. "Okay,

yeah. He's definitely too old."

"I hate you! I hate you *both!*" Gracie wails, and suddenly turns around and takes off.

"Gracie! Stop!" I exclaim in her wake. "Please don't be like this. . . ."

But my little sister turns a corner beyond the food court enclosure and walks with long jerking strides and furious determination, her long dark blond hair swinging down her back, until she disappears into a large rowdy group of Candidates with mostly green tokens.

George and I both stand sheepishly staring at her retreat. *What would Mom and Dad want or expect us to do in such a situation?* I think, while this new anxiety rips through me. George's expression seems to say, *Yeah, I've got nothing.*

"All right, what drama did I miss?" Laronda says. She's been chatting with Dawn, Logan, and Gordie, a few steps away near the service cart that we've just loaded with our empty trays.

"You really don't want to know." I sigh, tiredly.

Laronda nods, and looks like she has a pretty good idea.

Meanwhile, I notice Logan has made a point of sticking around with us, instead of heading out with the other Reds. Maybe he just wants to hang out with George whom apparently he seems to know a little from school. That would make total sense.

On the other hand, maybe he really meant it when he said he'll help me train?

"Is it eight o'clock yet?" Dawn Williams rubs her skinny arms and scratches her elbows. "I want to head back to the Dorm before first curfew. Can't afford another demerit. Those things add up."

"How does that weird Homework Hour curfew work anyway?" Gordie pushes his glasses up his nose past the purple bruise that appears to have turned an even darker shade since earlier this evening. "Supposing you have to meet up with an Instructor in this building, but then you need to walk back to your own Dorm later, but you were doing legit homework stuff, so— what's the deal? How do you prove to them you were not goofing off?"

"I have no idea," I mutter. I am still thinking about Gracie. *Maybe I should go after her, look for her all over the place if I have to, right now. . . .*

"The Instructor probably scans your token," Logan answers Gordie, meanwhile coming around to stand next to me. His warm hazel eyes look into mine. "So—you ready to do some running, Yellow Candy?"

"What's with the 'Yellow Candy?' He-he-he!" Gordie says with a snort followed by a small grin. Meanwhile George turns and pauses to look at me for a second longer than usual. Is there a tiny little grin also, on my jerk big brother's face? Ugh. . . .

I blush and blush. . . . No one seems to notice, or if they do, no one's saying anything. So of course I have to open my mouth. "We're all Candies," I attempt to explain. "You know, it's the four color Candies—"

"Yeah, yeah," Laronda says diplomatically. "Dawn, ready to head back to Yellow Dorm Eight? I think I'll do my loser homework down in our own gym on the monkey bars. This Arena place is just too huge. Don't want all those people watching my booty as I make a damn fool of myself."

"And I'm going to go upstairs and check out the Atlantean Instructors offices." Gordie points upward. "Not that I need to, but just because. I want to see what's up there on the top level."

"I'll go with you," George quickly adds, without meeting my eyes. "Okay, later, Gee Two, later, folks!" He and Gordie start walking away.

"Okay . . ." I mutter.

Logan and I are suddenly alone.

Just the two of us.

Chapter 15

Logan Sangre and I walk from the food court to the edge of the gym area where the track begins. The floor of the track is made of some kind of soft and rubbery material. I'm assuming this type of surface is easier on your feet than ordinary flooring. It's brick red in color, with eight painted lanes and other markings in white.

A few Candidates are using the track already, running laps. I see one girl from my Dorm jogging by.

We stand before the track.

"This is so embarrassing," I say, quickly looking up into his eyes, before anything else happens, because my mind is reeling with a combination of terror and excitement. "I suck so badly at this. . . . You're probably going to laugh when you see me run— either that or you'll just want to cry."

Logan exhales. Suddenly I feel his hands come around and squeeze my shoulders, as he moves in and looks at me gently. *Whoa!*

"No problem, Gwen. Nothing to be embarrassed about." His face is so serious in that moment, and oh, so beautiful. "This Qualification—this whole situation is abnormal. No one can expect you to know how to run, to be particularly good at it, or to know how to do any of these other impossible things they expect of us, out of the blue. . . . Do what you can, the best you can. And I will help you. All right?"

I nod. The feel of his strong hands around my shoulders, fingers pressing lightly, has turned me into a puddle, and at the same time I am giddy as if I'm twelve, like Gracie. *If only he knew!*

"And no," he adds, leaning in over me, so that our foreheads are almost touching. "I would never laugh. Not at you. Not at the way you or any other beginner might run. If I did, it would make me the worst kind of jerk. I hope you don't think that's what I am."

"Oh, no! Of course not!"

Logan smiles, and his face just lights up. "Okay! In that case, let's see how 'awful' you really are. Go on and start running. I'll catch up with you in a few, but first I want to watch your form."

"My form? Um, how? What should I do?" I say, like a total dummy.

"Just pick a lane—let's say the middle one—and try to stay in it. Now, go!"

I step onto the track, take a deep breath and start running.

When I say *running*, I mean, I am barely moving at a jog, my arms flailing uselessly every which way, and my wobbly feet striking the surface of the track. Only about thirty paces in, and my breath is already coming in ragged. The compounded exhaustion of the second day of uncustomary physical effort has taken its toll. I am panting like a dog, my knees start to wobble, and the raw blisters on my feet are killing me—you know, all the same horrible stuff that's been happening every time I try to run.

I've barely gone around one fifth of the track, when I hear Logan come up running from behind me. He's moving without any discernable effort, legs pumping evenly, and now he runs at my side. The only sound he's making is the light metal jangle of a key chain in his pocket, attached to a small knife. Not sure why, as I'm fighting to catch my breath, but I think of this knife of his that he'd taken out the other night when we were at Gracie's Red Dorm Five. . . .

Three seconds later I stop and bend over clutching my knees. Feels like the inside of my head's going around in crazy circles, and I am about to die.

"Don't stop moving," he says, slowing down beside me. "Now, just walk. The key to building endurance is regular intervals of running and rest. You run, then you walk to recover. Then you run some more. And repeat. With time you'll be able to run longer, and need fewer intervals of walking. That's all there is to it."

"But there isn't any time . . ." I pant, as we walk side by side. "I kind of need a crash course, *now*."

He shakes his head with a light smile. "It doesn't work that way, unfortunately. The best you can do is improve gradually."

"Oh jeez. . . . I really suck, don't I?"

"Yeah, you do. The good news is, you don't suck as badly as you think. Or as badly as you could possibly suck under the circumstances."

"Thanks—I think? See, there you go, you're laughing at me!" I glance at him, but I am smiling too.

"Key word here is, you can *improve*." He watches me playfully. "Of course, it also depends on the condition of your body and your determination."

I make a grimace and wipe the escaped tendrils of hair off my wet forehead with the back of my hand. "I'm pretty determined, I suppose. As for my body—"

His steady gaze sweeps me up and down, and suddenly I feel a full body flush coming on.

"Your body is—fine," he says after the tiniest pause during which he is looking at me closely and more intensely than before. "You are tall, and have long legs which will always give you the advantage of a longer stride. I have no doubt you will catch up quickly."

"So . . ." I say, because I don't know what else to do in that crazy-intense moment. "What about my 'form,' as you say? What should I do to improve faster?"

"Besides practicing?" Logan continues to watch me with his amazing hazel brown eyes. "I noticed that you either flail your arms too much or keep your hands clenched up, and too close to your chest when you pump your arms. Don't do that. Instead, keep your hands open rather than in fists, your arms loose, and your elbows at a 90-degree angle."

He takes my right arm and flexes it at the elbow gently, making a right angle, then opens my hand, loosening my tense fingers, as his own fingers brush my palm. "Keep it loose and relaxed, like this. Let your arms fall naturally."

I feel electricity and shivers coursing up my arm where he touches me. . . .

"As far as breathing, it should be even and regular. If it helps, count paces as you inhale and exhale." He looks down at my legs again. "Oh, and try to keep an even, regular stride. With your long legs you don't need to compensate. In fact, short and quick strides work better in the long run—pun intended."

He can tell my breathing has slowed down closer to normal. Of course he has no clue how his proximity really affects me. . . . I appear to be holding my breath without meaning to, and it's miles-to-the-Moon far from normal. *Breathe, Gwen, breathe!*

"Ready to run some more?" he says.

I nod. I inhale then exhale.

And I begin to run again.

An hour later, we exit the Arena Commons and head back to our dorms, taking the scenic route around the compound perimeter. Logan is walking me to mine, because it's night and it's after Homework Hour, and yeah, we are risking being out and about during the limited curfew period.

I shiver from the cold in my sweaty thin T-shirt. But Logan's presence at my side adds a strange feverish frisson of energy to my otherwise zombie body. Lord, but I'm tired, after having run then walked, and run then walked, over and over, around that track for who knows how many turns, with him keeping pace, running and walking beside me in absolute patience.

"I am sorry I totally wasted your evening," I say, feeling the guilt bubble up now, feeling the insecurity and the general sense of "what the heck is *he* doing here with *me?*"

"Are you kidding?" Logan's dark eyes sparkle in the bright lights of the compound. "I've had a great workout, and great company."

My cheeks grow hot. Once again I hope he does not notice the rising color in my face. "Not much of a workout, for you," I mutter.

"It's funny," he says. "We both go to the same school. But it took an asteroid, Qualification, basically the end of the world, *and* us getting out of Vermont and ending up in Pennsylvania, before we could meet."

I laugh. "Yeah. Pretty funny."

"Strange how I never ran into you at Mapleroad Jackson High."

Oh yeah, real strange. I think about how I pretty much stalked him from afar, all these past three years. Okay, not really *stalked* for real—since mostly it was all dreamy romantic drama happening in my pathetic mind—but I certainly spent a great deal of my free time at school fantasizing and hoping to catch a glimpse of him on campus.

I say nothing.

We pass some more dorm buildings then a stretch of open space with concrete walls. Then an area opens up that looks like a field—or better to say, a small airfield, because there's something that looks like a short landing strip and several small hangars. A helicopter is parked far away, and beyond it there's open space and darkness interspersed with a few lights in the distance and what is probably a chain link barbed wire fence.

"So how is everything else going for you so far?" Logan puts one hand in his pocket and I hear the key chain jangle again. It must be a habit of his, holding on to that pocket knife.

"Okay, I guess. . . . Barely surviving Combat and Agility, doing reasonably average in Culture and Tech. Wondering how my poor parents are doing. Wondering if there are crazy desperate people camped outside, beyond that fence and trees right now, looking in on us and planning who knows what. . . . And you?" I glance at the airfield then try to look straight ahead and not at him.

He laughs, once. It's a tired, slightly bitter sound. "Mostly same as you. My parents are left behind, back in St. Albans. And my older brother Jeff is in the military. He's just been deployed on his first tour of duty, they don't tell us where. Not much guessing involved however, considering all the places worldwide that peacekeeping forces are needed these days."

I turn to glance at him in surprise. "Oh, I didn't know you had an older brother!" And then I realize how weird that must sound. As far as he's concerned, we've just met a day ago and I'm not supposed to know anything about him or his family.

But Logan does not appear to take my outburst as an oddity, thank goodness. "Yeah. My brother Jeff is twenty-two, and that makes him too old, and ineligible for Qualification. Before shipping out, he told me he does not plan to wait for the asteroid, but to give it his all—take all the risks for the sake of performing his job in an exemplary manner. . . . And if necessary, he said, he wants to go all out with flying colors, in the line of duty."

"Oh . . . I'm so sorry."

"Don't be. If I were in his place, I'd probably do the same thing, go out with a bang, make it mean something. Better to die in a blaze of glory, defending the honor and interests of your country than to rot away waiting for the asteroid to hit. . . . What a damn waste."

I watch Logan's gorgeous face in profile, his dark hair, the high cheekbones and angular jaw. There's a new, withdrawn, reserved feeling about him, as he speaks of his brother.

"It really is so senseless," I whisper. "The only difference between us and all the rest of *them* out there, the whole world, is—hope."

"Hope? Not all that much of it. Mostly it's just illusion and BS. A way to buy time for a huge chunk of the population, keep us all docile as we go through the motions of this craptastic Qualification *farce* while our families watch from the outside and wait, and live vicariously through us for as long as they can. But the truth is, you and I will both very likely end up out of the running, and back home, waiting for the asteroid apocalypse with the rest of them. Think about it—most of us here, most of the Candidates, are going back home in a few weeks. We might as well get used to it."

I am stunned. Logan Sangre, so confident and comfortable, so steady and cool, is having personal doubts?

All right, I mean, he's human—yes, I know it with the rational portion of my mind, sure. But to me he has always seemed perfect and invincible.

"If anyone is going to qualify, Logan, it's *you!*" I say passionately, and just as soon as I say it, I realize how my intensity must be coming across.

Stop it, Gwen, cool it. Stop with the crazy!

Logan pauses walking, and turns to me with a blooming smile. "You don't even know me, but—thanks, Gwen. You make a good cheerleader—in the best sense possible."

"Thanks for what?" I pause also, and now I'm staring up at him. "I'm being practical here. I just think you *seem* to be the kind of guy who—who will Qualify for sure! Maybe I'll be the one heading home, but you definitely won't be. Want to bet on it?"

He smiles. His expression is so gentle, kind, that it's melting my heart completely. "No way. Because I don't want to bet against you, Gwen Lark. So how about this—let's not think about it for now, okay?"

"Okay," I say, thinking that the real Logan Sangre is an even better human being than my *idea* of him has been all these years— way better than I expected him to be.

We resume walking and we're almost at the end of the airfield clearing, approaching another dorm structure, when one of the hangars comes awake with lights, and its wide doors slide open.

We stare, and it's an amazing sight. An Atlantean saucer shuttle pulls out of the hangar, hovering silently about three feet in the air. Considering that it's over a hundred feet away from us, I judge it to be about thirty feet across, flat and slightly oval instead of perfectly round. The material it's made of is dull grey from the distance, and yet the bright hangar lights give it a strange prickling sheen of gold, which—I'm suddenly very certain—makes it orichalcum.

"Oh, wow!" I say.

Logan watches with equal wonder. "So that's how they go up and down," he muses.

As we stare, the shuttle glides away from the hangar, and pauses, then without a sound it seems to pick up a bluish-violet glow around it, and then it streaks upward with impossible speed, and momentarily hangs low above the trees.

At the same time, a second shuttle exits the same hangar.

It too, hovers just off the ground, and pulls away, then pauses. It's as if it's waiting for the first shuttle to move away a sufficient distance before following.

In the next moment, two things happen simultaneously. The second shuttle still on the ground now starts climbing. And the first one that's higher up above suddenly ejects a blinding flash which then turns into a nova. . . .

The night sky is rocked by an explosion.

And the ball of fire that was the first shuttle falls.

As the sonic boom and blast hits, I scream and hide my face, as burning debris rain all over the airfield.

"Oh God! Stay here!" Logan cries to me. He then starts running toward the flaming wreckage in the airfield.

My pulse pounds in my temples and I watch his retreating back, at the same time as I see uniformed guards come running from all directions. A few seconds later, claxons go off and sirens begin to wail. No other Candidates seem to be about, only the guards, converging. . . .

At the same time, I look up, and see the second shuttle. It has barely risen a couple hundred feet above the trees, and its super-violet aura is pulsing, as it seems to stagger horizontally, sweeping wildly back and forth across the sky.

I stare, cringing, in terror, never having seen such impossible lightning-fast patterns of movement of any flying aircraft up-close. Earth planes and helicopters are slow hay wagons compared to this thing.

Oh my God, it suddenly occurs to me. *It's having problems too! It's about to crash!*

I stare helplessly, watching the second shuttle in the sky struggle to stay aloft, and at the same time begin an erratic descent.

Whoever's flying it must be aware of the burning wreck below, and trying to land the craft safely far away from the crash site. . . .

Whatever the Atlanteans inside are doing, is causing the shuttle to lean sideways, favoring one end, then try to right itself horizontally, meanwhile starting to fall faster, losing its normal gliding smoothness that all the Atlantean ships seem to have.

It's out of control completely now, spinning wildly, turning over and over, and oh, God—it's coming down right at me!

I start to back away, then begin to run—even though it's hopeless to try to outrun a falling object the size of a bus—while with each second the shuttle is plummeting down . . . it's now a hundred feet, then fifty, then thirty—so that I can see the pulsing colors of its violet-blue aura. Another second, and it looks like an electric charge has covered the entire shuttle in a cocoon of pulsing energy—

I scream.

And then a crazy, last-second-only, desperate idea strikes me.

The ship is probably made of orichalcum. Which means—

My scream turns into a musical *note*.

I don't know what it is, but I am *singing* and holding a single note, at the top of my lungs.

My voice falls into the specific frequency naturally, and I put all my strength and effort into it, and then mold the vowel from an "a-a-a" into an "e-e-e", which I know is the easiest vowel to sing if you want to make a powerful sound.

The random note that I am holding is a Middle F, and then immediately I follow it with an A and C sequence, to make a major chord progression.

As my voice blasts out in the night air, rising over the crackle of the flames and the claxons and the sirens—cutting through *everything*, because I am singing with every fiber of my being, as loudly and *clearly* as I can—the falling shuttle pauses and comes to a jerking standstill in the air.

It *hovers*, about twenty feet over my head. I see its electric-violet plasma-lit metallic underbelly.

It have *keyed* it—yes, this huge shuttle-sized piece of orichalcum—to *myself*.

"F-A-C," I sing the chord sequence, not daring to stop, else it plummets on my head. . . . Even though I remember in flashes that no, once the levitation state is achieved, it stays in place, on its own, until the next voice command is issued.

And then I feverishly think back on my Atlantis Tech class and recall the other sequence needed to bring objects down.

I desperately continue to sing, even as my mind cringes at the thought of this *monster* of metal levitating overhead, as I run backward, trying not to stumble and accidentally knock out my breath. . . . This gets me sufficiently away from underneath its hover space, a distance of at least thirty feet, so that the ovaloid saucer is no longer directly over me—where it might drop any second and squash me like a bug.

And now I mentally try to "find" F in an octave higher than the one I'm singing now.

Oh crap! That's a pretty high note! What in blazes made me go with the Middle F for my tonic, starting note?

How in the world am I going to hit that note cleanly? I haven't properly sung in ages, in years! My Mom could hit that note just like that, easy as apple pie, make it roll out smooth and rich like honey in butter. . . .

And me? I was just a kid accompanying her in my little kiddie voice.

What's worse, I have no idea how high I can sing these days!

I am singing now . . . I'm actually singing . . . no, do not think . . . just keep singing . . . just sing!

I quickly take a big gasping breath, and aim for the higher octave F. . . .

I hit it, clean on.

Holy lord!

My voice holds and sustains the F easily, and I realize my voice is rich and earthy, even in the upper register, and I am a mezzo-soprano just like my mother.

And then, I bring it down, sliding an octave below, stopping on the first F.

As I end the slide and hold the original tonic note, the shuttle begins to descend smoothly.

It comes down, and hovers barely off the ground, maybe a couple of feet, at most.

The colors pulse around it, then suddenly everything goes dark.

And it drops the remaining distance to the ground.

I go silent, balling my fists at my sides, breathing fast in nervous exertion, while a door appears, cleaving the shuttle surface, and a ladder descends. It must be an automated emergency hatch opening, because no one appears to exit. Inside, is near-darkness, and I see the beginnings of smoke coming out.

With my peripheral vision I note guards running in the distance, heading toward me and this barely landed craft. There are also other Candidates coming from the direction of the dorms.

Meanwhile, black thick smoke is really pouring out from the shuttle door.

Where there's smoke, there's going to be some pretty ugly and certain *fire*.

Ugh! What am I doing now? I think, as I take a big gulp of clean night air and then rush forward, grab the rungs and haul myself up the ladder stair and plunge inside.

Chapter 16

The interior of the Atlantean shuttle looks sterile and at the same time strangely old-fashioned, with wall panels alternating orichalcum and another pale material embossed in decorative ornate spiraling designs. Smoke is pouring from one of the wall panels, and there is a fire burning on the floor and engulfing three side panels in one end, throwing orange-red light at the other walls, the floor, and sloping ceiling. It's a single large chamber, with six central seats in a rotating suspension harness and a control panel hovering before the seventh command chair.

All the seats are empty except one.

I see an Atlantean with pale golden hair, slumped over in the command chair. He is wearing the usual grey uniform, and with an awful sinking feeling, I approach and see the black armband on his sleeve.

It's Aeson Kass.

He appears dead.

My temples are already pounding wildly, with panic. And now they go into overdrive. At the same time, this terrible, indescribable odd sense of *regret* comes over me. . . .

I rush toward him, and I take him by his shoulders, raise him up, push him carefully against the back of his chair, and his head lolls to the side. I see his forehead is covered with blood, and his metallic hair is streaking crimson, demonic in the growing flames.

His eyes are closed . . . even now in these insane moments I notice the dark fringe of lashes and the wonderfully exotic lines drawn around the eyelids in kohl—or something else, whatever it is that they use—darkly outlining his eyes, and the lapis tint over his perfectly shaped eyebrows.

I reach with my trembling fingers and feel for a pulse in his wrists, the muscles of his throat—do Atlanteans even have a frigging pulse in the same places we do? Of course they do, what an idiotic thought. And yet I find nothing, or else I don't know how to properly look for a pulse. At least his skin is warm to the touch. . . .

His chiseled lips are parted slightly, and I place a finger against them, and it seems there might be a very faint breath. . . .

Okay, he just might be alive after all—good! A wild strange relief surges through me at the realization. So now we need to get out of here immediately! The fire is spreading!

I look down, and Aeson Kass is attached to the chair with some kind of seatbelt and shoulder and torso harness, but there appears to be a single spring-button release, which I figure out in three seconds, and push it, until the cords and belts fall away, and his body is free to be moved.

Free of the harness, he starts to slump forward again, and I move in, so he falls against me, and I put my arms around him and start dragging him out of the chair.

He is heavier than I thought, and he is all rock-hard muscle. I strain and barely manage to drag him a few feet, leaning into him with all my strength, and panting hard from the exertion. I am already dead tired, and this—this is just insane.

Furthermore, as the smoke spreads and thickens, it's getting harder to breathe.

Adrenaline and panic give me a burst of energy, because the smoke is engulfing the cabin interior, and I cough, sputter, and continue grasping him around the waist as I drag him . . . A few steps more, just a few steps more, as I back out of the shuttle.

I reach the outside opening and stairs, and now it's just a step to fresh cold air. . . .

I manage to feel for the ladder side-rail with one hand, and step backward onto the first rung by feel alone, supporting his entire weight as I descend. Meanwhile, his long, pale gold hair has fallen into my face, and I am now smeared in his blood.

Another step, and I carefully pull him down after me . . . another step. His weight is pulling me down inexorably, and unless I hold on to him and the ladder both we are going to crash hard.

At last I feel the ground under my feet.

Panting, I get him down the last rung, his feet dragging.

I semi-collapse at the base of the shuttle, on the strip of concrete, hitting my knees painfully, and pulling Aeson right after, so he lands on top of me.

"Gwen! *Gwen!*"

Logan is back. He comes around the shuttle, throws himself down and grabs me, while two uniformed guards are right behind him.

"What happened? Are you crazy? You just disappeared! I turned back and you were gone!" Logan exclaims.

"I'm okay," I pant. "But *he's* hurt! He—he needs help—medical attention, quickly!"

"Oh God, you're bleeding!" Logan's strong arms are still around me. Quickly, but super-gently, he examines my face, while I continue to hold Aeson's limp body to me, keeping his injured head up and away from the hard ground, so that he lies back against my chest. The light of the flaming remains of the first shuttle cast shadows against his hollow cheeks smeared in blood and smoke soot, the angles of his lean jaw and throat, and the faint fluttering pulse-beat there.

"It's not my blood . . . I'm okay," I say to Logan, to the guards, as they come around us and finally take over.

When another one of them starts to go inside the shuttle, I hurry to say, "I don't think anyone else is inside there—"

The guard turns, gives me a hard stare.

"All right! Quickly, everyone get back, as far back as you can from this thing!" an older bearded officer says, coming up behind us. "It can blow at any moment!"

I feel a strange twinge of loss, as Aeson's limp form is moved off my chest. He is hurriedly lifted under the arms and knees and carried by two guards with grim faces away from the airfield and toward the closest building in the compound. I stare, dazed and in shock, coughing, while a medical team appears, rushes to meet them, and the injured Atlantean is carefully placed on a stretcher. . . .

Mesmerized, I continue staring, except that Logan now helps me get up.

"Let's go, Gwen, move it!" He shakes me gently.

I come "awake" and start my feet moving. Together we hurry away from the shuttle. All along he's pulling me by the hand, at the same time as he squeezes my fingers so hard that it hurts.

I nearly stumble then right myself. As I wipe my sweat-and-blood covered face and forehead, my hand comes away covered in black soot.

Logan drags me somewhat, pulls me after him quickly, past a few staring Candidates, and into a narrow alley section between buildings. There is no privacy anywhere, naturally, since cameras are all over. How much of the incident did the surveillance capture?

We stop. I am panting hard, wheezing. I stagger, bend over to hold my knees as I struggle to catch my breath, and cough my irritated lungs out.

"Okay, what exactly happened there?" Logan speaks intensely, leaning into my face. "I told you to stay back, and what did you do? You could've been *killed!*"

"I—I don't know, I am not sure . . ." I meet his troubled earnest expression, and for a few moments I honestly just don't know what to say, or how to even begin.

A noisy roar and crash sounds in the distance.

Logan whirls around us with a frown, glances in the direction of the airfield, where the claxons and sirens are still going off, and there's a distant crackle and roar of flames. I suppose he's expecting the second shuttle to blow up any minute. Considering the kind of huge, scary, blazing-white nova it was that filled the sky for a split second when the first one blew, I am not surprised he's trigger-nervous.

Holy lord, I am too. . . .

"I hope he's okay," I whisper.

"Gwen!" Logan is staring hard at me. "This is bad, really bad. . . . Tell me, what the hell happened there? What—what did you *do?* Did you try to examine his head injury, or touch him without knowing how serious his injury was—"

"What do you mean?" I blink, because the soot is now in my eyes, and they are tearing.

"I mean, that Atlantean is one of their top brass, and he is *badly* hurt—if anything happens to him, if he *dies*, do you have any idea what might happen to you—to all of us? They could blame you for aggravating his injuries, for making things worse!

Now, the best thing for you, for both of us, is to stay far away and out of sight."

"I only got him out of there," I say. "I couldn't just leave him inside with the fire—"

"You *what?*" Logan's face is now stunned. "You mean you went *inside* that shuttle? I thought you only got to him when he was already lying on the ground!"

"No . . . Actually, I kind of—landed it. I brought the shuttle down. So that it wouldn't crash. It was falling—so I *sang* it down. And then I got him out. But please—don't tell anyone!"

Logan stares at me like I'm crazy. Shakes his head. His lips part in shock. I have a feeling he does not believe me. Either that, or he *does not understand* what I just said.

I don't blame him. I am still not sure what happened, and even I don't quite believe any of it myself.

"Okay . . ." he says, after a long pause. "But, that is impossible."

"I know."

"The shuttle—how did you—you say you *sang* it down?"

I rub my elbows and stare at him, biting my lip. "It's orichalcum. I made a wild guess. I used the levitation command from Tech class. Okay, I know it sounds wild, unbelievable, but it was about to fall on my head anyway. . . ."

And now Logan's frowning, staring hard, as though trying to remember. "You know, it's crazy, but—just as I was coming back to look for you, I thought I was hearing things . . . I actually thought I heard someone singing at one point—was that real? Was it you?"

"Yeah."

"Holy—" Logan takes his head in his hands, runs fingers through his dark hair, rubs his temples. He then lets go and looks at me like I am suddenly an *alien*.

A strange dark feeling comes to me. It's a wave of cold, and it engulfs me completely. I look at him defiantly and I begin to frown also, and bite my lip again.

"Look," I say. "Logan—you don't have to believe me, or even understand what happened. But I'd really appreciate it if you kept quiet about this. All of this crazy incident. Everything I told you. Okay?"

"Hey, you don't need to tell me twice." He watches me without blinking. Again shakes his head. "To be honest, I really don't think I *can* believe what you're saying. I want to—but, sorry—it makes no sense. I don't really know what happened with you and *him* back there. But I agree, it's dangerous, and we need to distance ourselves from this incident. Who knows how many people died on that first shuttle that exploded—that's bad enough. . . . There will be investigations, and if anything suspicious is determined to be the cause, they will come down hard, on whoever is responsible. But this other one, with the VIP on board—that one's even worse. Disqualification is the least of our worries if they come after us, or come looking for *you*, because something happens to that Phoebos guy—"

"Then help me keep it quiet." I interrupt him in a hard voice.

Suddenly I am shaking. And I need to get away—as far away from Logan, from everything. . . .

"I'm going back to my dorm," I say. "It's late, close to curfew, and I don't want to get caught with blood and gunk on my face."

"I'll come with you, walk you back, make sure you get inside okay—"

"No." My voice is firm. Even I am amazed at how curt I sound. I am speaking to Logan, of all people!

"Okay . . ." he echoes, suddenly uncertain. "It's probably best we walk back separately."

"Yeah." And I start walking in the direction of my dorm.

"Gwen!" he calls suddenly in my wake.

I turn and look back at him, shivering, holding my arms.

Logan's dark eyes glitter with intensity in the bright illumination of the compound. "I won't say anything to anyone—I promise," he tells me in a soft voice.

"Thanks."

"See you around—later?"

"See you."

"Be safe."

"You too."

And I rush back to my dorm. The alarms and claxons continue to fill the night air.

The lobby area of Yellow Dorm Eight is full of people. Teens are talking worriedly, but fortunately hardly anyone glances in my direction. As I enter, I try to look away and keep my head down, as I rush up the stairs to the girls' dorm floor.

I need to hit the shower, and fast!

On my way here, I've tried to rub away the blood as much as possible from my face, but some of it has already dried, and I realize I look strange and awful.

On the third floor, I don't bother to grab a change of clothing from my cot, and instead turn directly into the bathroom. Fortunately no one is using the sinks, although I hear someone flush one of the toilets in the stalls.

I run the water and soap up my face and neck, hands and forearms, scrub hard, and wash in the sink as much as possible, so that the soot and blood comes off, running down in pink and grey rivulets. The girl staring back at me in the mirror looks skinny, crazed, with a smeared sickly pale face, circles of exhaustion under her eyes, and a tangle of dirty, sweaty hair falling out of her mess of a ponytail. *Ugh.*

My T-shirt is seriously messed up, but I will deal with it later, wash it in the sink. First, I splash water on the front so that the worst of the blood is dissolved, and it just looks like I've had some kind of clumsy stain accident and tried to wash it off.

I get out of the bathroom and walk to my cot, past a few beds that are occupied, and a few girls who glance at me without much curiosity.

Thank goodness, Laronda is not there, in the cot next to mine. I can avoid her questions.

I rummage in my bags, pull out a nightshirt and my last clean pair of underwear, and head back to the bathroom barefoot. Oh, but my blistered feet are in agony!

Fifteen minutes and a shower later—during which I spend a long time scrubbing my hair and face with the shampoo, and then wash my clothes that I had just taken off, under the showerhead—I am clean, dried, and dressed for bed.

And best of all, there's no blood anywhere. . . .

I wring out my hand-washed clothes, and carry them back with me. There's nowhere to hang them up, but I can sort of jam

them in around the edges of my cot on the sides of the metal frame
under the mattress, so that they hang off my bed and air-dry
overnight.

"Gwen! There you are!" Laronda comes up, and plops down
on her own cot beside me. "So, where you been, girl? Hanging out
with that hottie Logan all this time? Oh, lord, did you hear what
happened out there? There was a horrible accident—an Atlantean
shuttle crash!"

I glance up briefly, and try to smile casually, or maybe look
surprised—I still haven't quite decided how to play it. "Oh, yeah,"
I mutter. "We went running around that big Arena track, and he
really helped me train—"

"Did you hear? I said, an accident happened! It was a huge
crash! The blast filled the sky! Atlanteans got hurt!"

"Yeah, I heard. Terrible! We've actually just got back here,
when we heard the explosion." I am making it up as I go.

Laronda rolls her eyes and shakes her head at me. "Hey, you
okay there? You look a little out to lunch. . . . Hello! Yeah, I can
tell, your head's still in the clouds, girlfriend. Must've been one
heck of a dreamy training session, one-on-one with his hotness."
She pauses, while I turn away in haste, and pretend to adjust my
wet laundry.

Laronda nods at my efforts. "Hey, now that's a very smarty-
pants rig. Like the way you've got a laundry clothesline going. I
just might have to do the same thing tomorrow, since I am all out
of fresh undies."

"Good idea," I mutter and then fake a large yawn. "I think I'm
going to bed early, I am so dead after all that running."

"What is it, around 9:30? Yeah, okay. I probably should get
ready too, before they flip the light switch."

And Laronda picks up her toiletry bag and heads for the
bathroom.

I climb in bed and lie there, with the bright overhead light
shining directly into my face. My body aches all over in
exhaustion, but my mind—it is racing, racing. . . .

The girl on the other side of me, the one whose name I still
don't know, quietly slips into her own cot.

I shut my eyes and hear other girls moving around the dorm,

getting ready for lights out. There are many nervous whispers and chatter going across the rows of beds. Everyone's talking about the shuttle accident, rumors and conspiracy theories are flying. The name "Aeson Kass" and "Phoebos" is mentioned. So are the words "sabotage" and "retribution." Two girls argue over what one supposedly overheard, that a whole bunch of Atlanteans got killed on that first shuttle—or maybe it was only five people, or maybe just three. . . .

I pretend to be asleep when Laronda gets back and climbs in her own bed. The metal springs of her cot make a creaking sound as she turns and tries to get comfortable.

A scene of smoke and burning flames inside the shuttle replays in my mind . . . Aeson Kass lies unconscious, head lolling, in a tangle of golden hair and blood . . . fire dances in reflections against his skin, the lean angles of his striking face . . . sharp lines of kohl trace closed eyelids fringed with dark lashes, underneath perfect lapis-hued brows.

I remember my fingertips brushing against his lips, searching for a sign of living breath. . . .

Interspersed with the images of the crash, I see Logan Sangre's intense face, as he stares at me with complete disbelief. His beautiful hazel-brown eyes, so warm earlier, are suddenly closed off and impossible to read.

Somehow I fall asleep eventually, while the claxons and alarms still ring outside, all throughout the compound.

Chapter 17

In the morning, the Dorm Leaders drag us out of bed just as the wake-up alarm claxons go off. I come awake to the loud voice of Gina Curtis and then the additional shrill sound of her whistle, as she's moving through the girls' dorm floor.

"*Attention!* Good morning, everyone! Time to get up now, move it, ladies! Up, up, up! A big day today!"

"Awww, nooooo!" Laronda moans one bunk over. And similar groans of pain can be heard from all around the room.

I shudder, pull the blanket over my head and grimace at the pain that's coming from every single tormented muscle in my body.

And then like a cold pail of water the sobering memory of the previous night hits me hard. . . .

"Move your rear ends, get in the bathrooms, get dressed, and be downstairs by seven-thirty AM! No breakfast! I repeat, no breakfast! Dorm meeting!"

"What's going on?" a girl asks. "Is it something to do with that shuttle crash accident?"

Gina Curtis turns in her direction with an angry frown. "You can bet your sweet ass, it has everything to do with the tragedy of last night! Now, move it!"

I drag myself up and check the condition of my makeshift laundry "clothesline" around the mattress. My underwear managed to dry overnight, but the T-shirt and jeans are still a little wet. I can wear them and let them finish air-drying while on me. My socks however are still soggy, so with a grimace I put on my only other unwashed pair, because there's just no way I'll survive the day of new exercise without socks on my blistered feet.

Why am I thinking about underwear and socks?

I grab my clothes, run to the bathroom past other girls, as we push and shove to take care of our morning business.

I keep my head down and brush my teeth at the sink when I hear some familiar voices.

"I heard that three at least died," Olivia says to another girl whose back is turned. Claudia is next to them, as they stand taking up real estate in front of the mirrors and two sinks.

"Yeah, well, serves the Goldilocks right . . . I won't be shedding too many tears—" the girl hisses, then turns around and sees me staring.

"Shut up!" Olivia nudges her. "Quiet, idiot! Don't let anyone hear you talk that way, or they throw you and me both out of here, and you can kiss Qualification goodbye!"

"You didn't hear anything, Gwen Lark," Claudia says, with an intense glare in my direction. "Unless you want me to brush your hair some more, you get my meaning?"

I shake my head, and look away, and quickly finish my business without saying a word. To be honest, I hardly care. . . . I think I've forgotten to be afraid of these alpha girls because of what has happened overnight, and it has given me a strange, new, serene perspective—a sense of cool desperation that is eclipsing all my other usual emotions that would otherwise be overwhelming me right about now.

My mind is going over and over the events of the previous night. . . .

Emotionally numb and yet clear-headed and focused, I come downstairs, and the first floor Common Area and lobby is packed with Candidates from our dorm. Dorm Leaders Gina Curtis, John Nicolard, and Mark Foster are standing in the middle of the room and they don't look too happy.

"All right, attention!" Mark Foster raises his hand for silence.

"Last night, two Atlantean shuttles were involved in a serious incident here on the airfield," John Nicolard says. His face is grave. "There was an incident on takeoff. One of them, carrying three passengers, exploded in flight, for reasons unknown, killing everyone on board. The second, carrying one pilot, crash-landed. The person in the second shuttle was injured but was fortunately treated by our EMTs on the ground. He was then taken up to the closest Atlantis starship for their advanced medical treatment via an emergency transport that was called down on his behalf. He is expected to survive, but I have no details on his present condition."

"In short, this is a very serious situation," Gina picks up speaking. "The airfield is off limits for the day, for cleanup. Furthermore, they are treating it as a possible crime scene. An investigation is going on right now, and we are told, there's a very good chance that this was not an accident but that the shuttles were tampered with. Which means that this whole RQC compound is going to be under possible criminal investigation—all of us, all of *you*. If it's determined that there was sabotage, and if any of the Candidates are at fault, then let me just say, I would hate to be that person or persons who are the guilty party."

"If any of you here had anything to do with it," Mark Foster says loudly, "they *will* find out. They will find you, and you will face criminal punishment, and an Atlantis trial in addition to Disqualification. You cannot hide. Strong recommendation—turn yourself in now. I sincerely hope none of you in this room were foolish enough to be involved with any kind of terrorist group."

"All right, next order of business is, because of the incident, your schedule for today is rearranged," John Nicolard says. "You will have fifteen minutes to grab some breakfast and then you will have your first two classes as per schedule. However, at one PM, right after lunch, there will be a general assembly for all Candidates in the Arena Commons building. Be there promptly! Now, come up and get scanned for your schedules."

We move in a crowd to get our tokens scanned. I am cold, clear-headed, sharp as a razor. Emotionally detached, I am moving on auto-pilot, as I then do a five-minute breakfast, and head to my first class.

"Passion—Aggression—Anger—Force . . ." Nefir Mekei recites in Atlantis Culture class. "These are the qualities of the *Red* Quadrant. Together they embody the Red Cornerstone of Atlantis. Repeat after me!"

We echo his words, speaking in unison. The entire class is somewhat beaten down this morning, as we are still reeling from the events of the night before and the new vague threat of punishment hanging over our heads.

But the Atlantean Instructor does not show any emotion, or

for that matter any normal living expression on his face. Usually reserved, today he is an absolute blank, as he paces before the desk covered with old scrolls and books that he never bothers to open. Only his Storyteller voice continues to mesmerize and keep us alive and attentive.

"Leadership—Control—Reason—Analysis . . ." he intones calmly. "These are the qualities of the *Blue* Quadrant. Together they embody the Blue Cornerstone of Atlantis."

We repeat in unison.

"Endurance—Patience—Resistance—Strength. . . . These are the qualities of the *Green* Quadrant. Together they embody the Green Cornerstone of Atlantis."

I watch Nefir's composed face, and the unblinking stare of his kohl-rimmed eyes. I wonder if he knew the people who died in the shuttle crash. Of course he had to know them! *Maybe they were his friends. Maybe he is grieving them even now, and does not show it. . . .*

"Creativity—Originality—Curiosity—Inspiration . . ." he concludes. "These are the qualities of the *Yellow* Quadrant—your Quadrant. Together they embody the Yellow Cornerstone of Atlantis."

Nefir pauses.

The class watches him, waiting. No one is asking questions, not even me.

"Your lesson for today is to think about what these qualities of the Four Quadrants really mean, and what makes them Cornerstones. Your homework is to memorize them. That is all."

And with those words, Nefir Mekei grows silent. He then walks out of the classroom, with half an hour of lesson time still remaining, leaving us alone.

For the rest of that class we sit stunned, a few of us whispering nervously.

No one leaves the class early.

My next class before lunch is Combat. I get down to the basement gym hall and stand waiting with the others for our Instructors to arrive. No one's using the exercise equipment.

"Wow, I hope our Instructors are okay," Jai Bhagat says. He comes up to me, and with him is Mateo Perez.

I nod. "Yes. . . ."

"Any news on what actually happened?" Jai asks, pacing anxiously. "Who was on that shuttle?"

"I bet they'll tell us during the assembly," Mateo says.

"Where were you when it happened?"

I start a little. "Who, me?" *Damn . . . why is Jai asking this?* "I just got back to the dorm after running at the big track in the Arena Commons. I barely saw the sky flash white in the window—"

"Oh yeah, it was kind of awesome SFX, in a sick way!"

I frown at Jai and his crazy grin. Is he for real? "Don't say that."

"She's right. Better keep your mouth shut, for everybody's sake." Mateo gives Jai a hard look, and turns away, sticking hands in his pockets.

Jai's face goes serious for a moment. He appears hurt. "Hey, just saying . . . I mean it was like, neat optical effects, that's all I'm saying."

"Just—don't say it out loud, dumbass." Mateo turns back around and glares at him. "People died. And because of it, we might all be screwed now. What if they punish us and auto-Disqualify this whole RQC?"

A new freezing chill runs through me. . . . Mateo is right. The repercussions for what happened might be worse than any of us can even imagine. And it's just the beginning.

Moments later, Oalla Keigeri and Keruvat Ruo enter the Training Hall.

Seeing them I feel a sudden wave of relief. The fact that these two could have been on that first shuttle is hitting me hard.

The two Atlanteans look different today. Their faces are hard and impassive, and Oalla, especially, is cold as ice.

Without any preliminaries, the Atlantean girl blows her whistle and we line up in two opposing rows without needing to be told.

Oalla and Keruvat stand in the middle of the room, looking at us.

It's as if they are trying to see *through* us, to read our thoughts and minds, and learn our deepest secrets.

"Attention, Candidates!" Keruvat says in his deep voice, and it carries in echoes through the very silent gym hall. "Before we exercise or train today, we will observe a Moment of Honor for those who died a senseless death yesterday. In Atlantis, we sing farewells to our dead. Now, listen, and follow us."

And then he sings. It is a simple base note sequence, a low D Minor, and he repeats it, while Oalla sings the same note sequence, only an octave higher.

One by one we echo them, singing the same chord in different octaves, our voices naturally choosing whatever frequency is most comfortable, until the room is filled with one great big sound of harmonic grief.

It is said, D Minor is one of the saddest chords of all, and I agree.

It is also my favorite.

I open my mouth and pretend to make a sound, but today, nothing comes out.

I should be more exhausted than I am after Combat class—but I'm not—as I head upstairs from the basement floor to the first floor Common Area. Maybe all that endless exercise is having a positive endurance effect at last on my untrained wimpy muscles. After all, this is the third day here at the RQC. Or maybe it's the fact that I am still reeling after what happened last night, and what I *did*. . . .

I walk through the lobby wiping my sweaty forehead with the back of my hand and think. I could try to go look for Gracie and the other Gees. Somehow the emo tantrum that Gracie threw last night got completely overshadowed by the *incident* that followed. Normally I would follow up with my kid sister, especially considering I have no idea what happened to her after she took off and left us in the Arena building.

But apparently there are other more pressing concerns. As I glance around the lobby and note quite a few Candidates from my dorm hanging around the sofas—which constitutes half the alpha crowd, including that jerk with the tats, Derek—the outside doors open and I see Logan.

He sees me also and immediately heads toward me.

Logan looks sleek and confident as he walks, and in the first instant my heart constricts painfully at how well built and fine he truly is. Every muscle in his lean powerful body moves like music, and he casually turns his head to glance around the room, before his hazel eyes connect with mine.

I feel my breath catch, but I pause and stand stiffly, waiting for him to approach.

With my peripheral vision I see Olivia and Ashley pause their chatter to glance at me. Then they notice Logan, and immediately stare at him in appreciation. And they're not alone. One by one, other girls look in his direction. Yeah, Logan has that effect on females—all females. And quite a few guys, I might add.

But then Derek with his wide neck and scary tattoo turns around and stares also, and his expression goes stone hard when he notices Logan moving my way.

"Hey, Gwen," Logan says. Almost regretfully I notice his serious expression and the fact that he no longer calls me "Yellow Candy."

"Hi." I look up at him and hastily wipe my sweaty fingers over the front of my T-shirt. "What are you doing here?"

"Looking for you," he says.

"Oh?"

"How are you?" His face is composed, but there is something new there, a repressed anxious expression hiding underneath the casual facade.

"I'm good," I say. "Just had Combat class. And you?"

It's becoming obvious that this is not a simple social call. And when he's asking, *"How are you?"* I think he means, *"Are you okay after last night?"*

"You want to go grab something to eat now?" Logan nods in the direction of our Yellow Dorm Eight cafeteria.

I nod woodenly, and we go inside the noisy food hall with the overpowering smell of chili and hot dogs in the air.

As we stand in line getting our trays, Logan leans down close to my ear and says, "This is probably the easiest place to talk, with the solid noise cover."

I glance up, and our faces end up barely inches away.

"I wanted to make sure you really are okay after yesterday," he says softly, putting a plate with two chili-dripping hotdogs on his tray.

"Thanks." My hand holding my own plate is a little unsteady. "I am fine, really. And I appreciate you asking, but you really didn't have to go out of your way like this—"

"I'm not." He frowns lightly. "This is not me 'going out of my way' bullshit. This is the least I can do, after what you went through. I needed to make sure you are dealing with it."

"Yeah. Well, I am. I mean, what is there to deal with, really? I woke up and my voice is a little hoarse with the smoke inhalation, but that's about it."

We move through the line, loading up foodstuff on our plates, then find an empty table.

"Okay, and you haven't mentioned anything to anyone, right?" He takes the seat next to me.

"Um, no, of course not. . . ." I stiffen up. Seriously, what kind of dork does he think I am? "Remember, I was the one who asked *you* to keep it quiet."

He nods. "I know. But under the circumstances, it helps to have someone else to remind you, *gently*, because this is tough, if you have to bear it all alone."

"Okay, what am I bearing, exactly? I didn't do anything wrong!" I hiss at him through the large bite of hotdog that I've put in my mouth and forgot to chew.

"Sh-h-h-h . . ." he says, with a shadow smile coming to his lips. "Keep it down."

I guess that could refer both to the noise level and to the heaping amount of food that's presently sitting motionless in my mouth. I seriously need to get over this nerd habit already and remember to *chew and swallow* before speaking when I am nervous. At least I didn't spray his face with chunks of hotdog and spittle. Eeeew, me! *So very attractive of you, Gwen Lark. . . .*

But he seems unfazed. "Yeah, you did nothing wrong—in fact, the complete opposite, you did something *amazing.* But remember what I said, you don't want them to associate you with any of it at all, good or bad. It's just as this morning all our Dorm Leaders warned us—there will be witch-hunts. And if we're not careful, they may come for us, for whatever unfounded reason."

I chew and swallow, then hurriedly wipe my mouth with a

napkin. I stare at Logan, and find it hard to respond. "So what should I do—or not do?"

He pauses, looks at me intently. "First, we need to get our story straight."

"What story?"

"The story about what we were doing at the time it happened—where we were, etc."

"Okay. Well, I already told a couple of people here that we just got back to my dorm after using the Arena track, and that we only saw the explosion from the window."

Logan nods thoughtfully. "Okay, that should work. The other thing is, we need to say we walked a different route, without even passing the airfield. Here—I drew this on the map, where we walked." He pulls out a folded sheet that has the familiar map of the RQC campus. Pushing his tray aside, he sets it out on the table and shows me the literal path we took in reality, and then the alternate path we will *tell* people we took—one that bypasses the airfield by three buildings.

I look at the map. "Wow, you really are thorough. And—is this really necessary?"

"Yes, if we want to keep our stories aligned. The key is always in the details. I recommend you memorize this—just in case."

"What about all the surveillance cameras everywhere? Won't they show us . . . not being where we say we were?"

Logan exhales, pausing. "Yeah, that's one possible problem. . . . However, if we stick to the basic story with most people, it may never come to it. So let's not give them any reason to be suspicious in the first place. The good thing is, the alternate route we are going to *say* we took is packed with pedestrian traffic, with tons of Candidates walking there. So, even if they check their footage, it would be hard to be sure if we were there or not. Of course if they check the footage for our actual route, that might be a problem."

"Okay, but what about those guards yesterday?" I whisper. "They will remember *me*, and probably you too—and what about the surveillance cameras around the airfield?"

He shakes his head. "I doubt the guards will have a solid

recollection of us, especially considering your face was a bloody mess, and I came to the scene moments later, so it may not look like we necessarily were together. And as for the cameras there, I've thought of it, yeah—but the super great news for us is, supposedly the first shuttle explosion blast caused a shock wave that took out a lot of electronic equipment nearby, so *nothing* was being recorded from that point on!"

"Wow," I say. "If it's true, that's really good. But—this is still kind of nuts. And you are more than a little paranoid. But, okay."

Logan gives me a crooked and awfully charming smile that does not really disguise his serious eyes.

In that moment, for some reason, the image of the unconscious Atlantean from last night comes to me. . . . The lean face of Aeson Kass, eyes closed, soot and blood everywhere.

"I wonder if he is okay," I say.

Logan knows exactly whom I mean.

"Supposedly he is. But—we should soon find out."

"Find out what?"

Both of us look up, and Laronda is here, and so is Dawn Williams.

How much have they overheard?

The girls put their trays down next to ours, and pull up chairs. So long, private conversation.

"Find out what's going on at that assembly after lunch," I say, and casually stick the campus map in my pocket. I then immediately regret doing it, because Laronda, perceptive girl, gives me a meaningful look and raises one brow. Now she probably thinks we're passing cutesy love notes or something.

I sigh, thinking it's better than the alternative.

Belatedly it occurs to me, *I just had lunch with Logan Sangre*, and it doesn't even count as a date.

After lunch, we all walk en masse to the Arena Commons building. Logan is still with us, so Laronda gives me cute stares, and then exchanges glances with Dawn. Fine, let them think we're turning into a "thing," Logan and I. Yeah, right. . . . Sigh.

It's a bright, sunny March day, with the definite signs of spring thaw in the air.

Endless groups and bunches of Candidates converge from all

directions, and for once their tokens are all mixed up, red, yellow, blue, green.

Just as we approach the Arena Commons super structure, four specks of radiance burst down from the sky, like falling meteors. A few stifled gasps of fear sound all around us. Everyone stares up, mostly in nervous expectation, and watches the Atlantean shuttles decelerate smoothly and then hover down and disappear in the general area of the landing airfield. Fortunately, there is no mishap this time.

"Look at them!" Dawn says. "Coming down in force, I bet. Wonder who it is."

"Probably more VIPs." Laronda shields her eyes from the sun glare, as she stares over the roofs of the buildings.

"Wonder if they have police forces?" I mutter. "Law enforcement. Military or otherwise."

Logan gives me a look. "Considering that human nature is the same screwed up mess on Earth as it is on Atlantis, yeah, they do—or so I hear. Their cops are called Correctors."

"Creepy," Dawn notes.

"Absolutely." Logan glances at her briefly. "I also hear they are far more scary and ruthless than our own homegrown equivalent."

"Great. . . ." Laronda shudders. "Just what we need on this planet, more cops. And not just any cops, but scary *alien* cops."

"We didn't get around to study their legal system yet in Atlantis Culture class," I mutter. "What untold pleasures await us. . . ."

Logan again gives me a brief look.

We enter the Arena Commons and it is packed. Every walkway on all the upper levels, and every square inch of the floor below, including the several sections of bleachers, track, and the areas around the equipment in the middle of the great stadium space, is taken up with Candidates from all the twelve dorms of the RQC.

The crowd is huge, and in many places people in grey uniforms and various colored armbands are seen keeping order— Dorm Leaders, security guards, and various adults who are officials. We are jostled closer inward by the stream of incoming teens, as more and more people arrive in the Arena building.

For the first time, it occurs to me, we are, all of us from this particular region, gathered in one place. Candidates for Qualification, together we can fill an ocean . . . or at least a sizeable lake.

And just to think, this is just one RQC out of thousands across the country and around the world.

Talk about fierce competition for each spot!

Everyone's eyes are eventually drawn to one raised platform near the end of the stadium. On it, a group of Earth officials stands, looking serious, like a bunch of school principals. Someone tests a powerful stadium microphone, and then a man steps forward and speaks, after clearing his throat. The sound of his voice hits the space powerfully and creates a reverb.

"Your attention, please."

Waves of noise pass around the stadium, then quiet down.

"Candidates for Qualification at Pennsylvania Regional Qualification Center Three. You have been asked to gather here upon the request of the Atlantis Central Agency, which has been notified of yesterday's tragic incident. As many of you know already, three Atlanteans lost their lives yesterday, and one was injured. After the investigation conducted immediately following the incident, the ACA has strong reasons to believe the shuttle explosion was not an accident but was in fact an act of sabotage, and hence an act of terrorism against this institution, and indeed against all of you, potential Candidates for Qualification."

Noise rises again in the stadium.

"Oh, crap," Laronda whispers next to me.

The speaker continues. "The ACA will therefore initiate a full high-level investigation starting immediately, and has sent down a special team to that effect." He pauses, and in that moment a group of nine Atlanteans is seen, ascending the stage. Their hair gleams metallic gold from the distance so it is easy to tell them apart from the Earth officials.

I stare intently, watching for familiar faces, and can barely make out maybe one or two Instructors, but mostly these are Atlanteans I have not seen before.

I watch their armbands, an even mixture of yellow, green, blue, and red.

One of them is *black*.

My insides do a kind of painful summersault, and something grips me with an unbelievable wrenching force. . . .

Aeson Kass stands among them, and he is upright, appearing absolutely healthy and unharmed—oh my lord, he is entirely *unhurt*. Indeed, his figure is confident, straight-backed and full of that same familiar leashed power that I've come to associate with him. And his face—from this distance it is hard to tell his expression, but I am willing to bet it is as cold and hard as stone.

My jaws literally fall open. Or is it figuratively? Whatever—in this moment even grammar fails me.

Seems, I am not the only one. . . . Everywhere around me, furiously nervous whispers sound, and I can hear the mutterings of "Phoebos" and "Aeson Kass" and "wait—isn't *he* the one who was injured?"

I feel a squeeze at my arm, and it's Logan. He is holding me, and pressing my arm meaningfully, and his expression is intense.

I nod barely to indicate I get it. *Show no unusual emotion, no response.*

And yet, even Logan cannot keep his face completely straight. A frown and stunned shock is there, somewhere.

While we speculate and stand there, staring in confusion, Aeson Kass steps forward on the platform and takes the microphone.

"Candidates," he says—and his voice is exactly as cold and powerful as I somehow expected it to be. Gone is the soft calm timbre that I first heard during our brief exchange in my very first Combat Class, which he graced with his presence and in which he explained to *me* why Atlanteans must learn fighting and self-defense. Now he is all hardness and force, and for a moment I wonder if he is using a *power voice*.

"You are here because in the coming days not only will you continue your Qualification training, but you will be observed closely for evidence of criminal activity. Yesterday, three brave and remarkable human beings lost their lives. Three of our finest Fleet Pilots. Three of my beloved friends and brothers. They lost their lives, and I regretfully, once again—*lived*. Had I not piloted the second shuttle separately, I too would now be dust in your atmosphere."

Aeson pauses. His words that have been ringing out like falling hammer blows, cease. If I did not know better, I might guess he is having trouble speaking. . . .

The stadium is in silence.

"Their names—their names are *Chiar Nuridat . . . Felekamen Gori . . . Tiliar Vahad.* Remember them well, for they died serving the Atlantis Fleet and serving *you.* Pilot First Rank, Chiar Nuridat, Allegiance to Red Quadrant, nineteen years old, seven years in the Fleet . . . Pilot Second Rank, Felekamen Gori, Allegiance to Yellow Quadrant, sixteen years old, five years in the Fleet . . . Pilot First Rank, Tiliar Vahad, Allegiance to Blue Quadrant, nineteen years old, seven years in the Fleet, *astra daimon*—my brother, not by blood but by *heart.*"

He pauses again. His voice never breaks but he stands up on the platform so motionless he could be an effigy. His face is blank—only his body is frozen in grief.

I glance away and see Logan's face, which shows a wealth of emotion in that instant. It occurs to me, he must be thinking of his own brother Jeff, a real brother by blood, who is soon going to die in the service of his country.

And then Aeson Kass speaks again. "These brave Pilots lost their lives because a tiny crucial part was removed from the flight navigation console on their shuttle. This part is a program chip, smaller than the tip of my finger. We know this because all our vehicles transmit their operational status during flight—and so we knew exactly what was wrong. It was removed, and the shuttle was effectively disabled once it had reached a certain altitude and level of thrust. There were no means of recovery once the critical parameters were reached. A cascade reaction was initiated as a result, and the shuttle exploded.

"The same part was removed from my own shuttle. The only thing that saved it—and me—from a similar cascade and explosion was that I had not yet reached that specific altitude and thrust. And while I tried to regain control of the shuttle, it went into an unrecoverable spin that ended with me unconscious on the ground. I have no recollection, and no explanation, short of a miracle, as to *why* and *how* my shuttle landed without me. But in the process of this investigation, I fully intend to find out."

As I listen to him say this, I find I am trembling with suppressed emotion. What that emotion is, I am unsure. But it makes me want to jump out of my own skin. . . .

Logan notices my state—he can probably feel me shaking, because his hand is still tightened around my arm. And he watches me with concern.

Meanwhile, Aeson Kass continues speaking.

"Know, that whoever is responsible for this coward act of sabotage and blatant murder, will be apprehended. If the persons responsible are present in this room—know that you will be found, and you will have to answer to *me*." His final words fall like blades slicing. Aeson glances behind him and nods to the other Atlanteans standing on the platform. They step forward in unison while he moves aside.

"We are the Correctors assigned to this investigation," one of them says, approaching the microphone. "You will get used to our presence on this campus. If you are stopped and questioned, you may not refuse or resist, on pain of Disqualification and incarceration. If you cooperate and are not found guilty, you will have nothing to worry about. As of this moment, we assume control of this Regional Qualification Center, under the supreme authority of Command Pilot Aeson Kass. He will have final say and final judgment. All else falls within our individual jurisdiction."

The Corrector falls silent and retreats a step from the microphone.

Aeson Kass, who has been watching impassively, moves forward again. He speaks in conclusion—and is ruthless: "Candidates, you are now dismissed."

"**O**kay, that was terrifying." Laronda turns to me as we exit the Arena Commons super structure. "One thing I don't get—how come he looks so strong and healthy?"

"Who?" I glance at her and avoid direct eye contact with Logan.

"He! That scary hottie VIP guy—Aeson Kass, 'Phoebos,' or whatever his nickname is."

"Call sign."

"Whatever."

"Yeah," I say. "I don't know."

"He should be beat up or something, don't you think? Walking on crutches maybe. Bandages, scratches, anything!" Laronda muses out loud. "They say they carried him on a stretcher *yesterday*, all bloodied up. So how come he's all recovered like that? Is that even human?"

I'm wondering the same thing. But then I think of what I know of Atlantean high-end medicine. The kind that's available for their *citizens only*. . . .

"If they took him up to their starship and treated him with their high-tech medical equipment overnight, then it probably explains it. They must be able to work miracles!"

"You're telling me!" Laronda continues to make her eye-popping face.

Logan takes the opportunity to interrupt. "Well, ladies," he says, with a glance at the crowds of Candidates moving past us. "Have to apologize but I need to run. I see some people from my dorm walking right over there who I need to see, and then, my next class—so I will see you all later. All right?"

He looks at me as he ends speaking, and I nod silently.

"Bye, Logan!" Laronda drawls with a smile and a glance from me to him and back again.

I bite my lip. "Sure, see you later."

Dawn just waves at him.

And Logan disappears in the crowd.

I wistfully stare in his wake and wonder what's up.

Chapter 18

Everyone is super high-strung in Agility Training. The only consolation is, because of the assembly time cutting in we get an abbreviated version of the class.

But first, true to her drill sergeant form, Oalla Keigeri makes us run nine laps, which is two laps more than the previous day. We all struggle, and by lap seven hardly anyone is actually running—more like dragging ourselves in a slow walking "jog" around the perimeter of the gym hall.

I come in dead last once again. But at least I make Jack Carell, the heavy kid, really work for his second-to-last spot, locked in a dead heat with Janice Quinn, who manages to beat him at the last minute and comes in barely ahead of both of us.

Oalla approaches me to scan my token for the last-place demerit. For once her face is unreadable, and she barely registers my presence.

She is still grieving. . . .

For some reason I find it more frightening than having her wrath directed at me head-on.

Later, we get out the hoverboards and practice making sharp turns on a flat and level plane, sticking to six inches above the floor—no going up and down, thank goodness, so that my fear of heights gets to take the day off.

I notice Blayne Dubois, riding his hoverboard and generally keeping away from the rest of us, as he is practicing rather advanced maneuvers from his lying-flat position. His form is sleek and he looks focused and confident on that board.

At the end of the class, he once again pushes himself up by his hands and arms into the wheelchair, sends the hoverboard away and instantly becomes the same withdrawn and angry guy who slouches with his hair in his face, and who does not talk to anyone.

Once again I get the crazy impulse to approach him, but think better of it.

Instead I head upstairs to Atlantis Tech.

Mr. Warrenson starts out the class by teaching us a few more musical note sequences to orient and move levitating objects.

Laronda is not in my class today, so I am partnered with an older teen boy, Antwon Marks. Antwon has super dark skin and wears a smart earring in his left pierced nostril that has a gold chain running from it to the one in his ear.

It does not seem to interfere with his ability to make rich tenor notes that sound like honey.

We face each other across our desks, with pieces of orichalcum hovering at eye-level before us.

" . . . Just think of it as playing ping-pong," Mr. Warrenson tells the class. "See if you can attempt an *avoidance exchange* so that your pieces do not collide head-on as they approach, but go around each other smoothly. Remember, three quick staccato notes, followed by one long one, sustained . . . Minor note sequences if you want to maneuver below, Major note sequences to pass above. . . . Half-step up for a sharp note to go around and pass on the right. Half-step down for a flat note to go around and pass on the left."

I face Antwon and try to sing the sequence, while gripping my hands in fists underneath the desk to mentally steady myself. Except, my lungs and throat are still sore from yesterday's smoke inhalation, and I am unable to sing cleanly without breaking out into small fits of coughing after every few notes.

"Are you okay?" Antwon says, as I turn bright red from the effort to suppress the cough, then still end up coughing for yet another time in the span of five minutes.

"Yeah, sorry . . ." I choke out. "I think I might be getting a minor cold."

"Yow, sounds more than minor to me. . . . Get some water." Antwon's expression is sympathetic. He then saves me by taking an extra turn to move his own levitating piece smoothly around the hovering obstacle of mine. His singing voice is beautiful and sends shivers down my back.

Next, Mr. Warrenson starts getting deeper into the physics and theory of it, so the class begins to wilt with boredom.

"The ability to hover its own weight plus carry additional weight is dependent on the mass of orichalcum present. For example, one square inch of pure orichalcum can support up to twenty pounds of weight in Earth's gravity—"

I force myself to focus on what he is saying, because this is suddenly very important.

"Just imagine those hoverboards for a moment," Mr. Warrenson says. "They are approximately seventy-two inches long, twelve inches across and two inches thick. How many pounds can each board support?"

"Oh, no . . . math . . . eeeew . . ." Someone moans from behind me.

I scribble some numbers in my notebook then raise my hand. "That would be 72 times 12 times 2, which is 1,728 square inches per hoverboard. And multiply that by 20 pounds, which makes it 34,560 pounds of weight! Oh, wow! One ton is 2,000 pounds so that makes it—"

"Yes, Ms. Lark, it makes it just over seventeen tons! One hoverboard can carry *seventeen tons* of freight," Mr. Warrenson says with satisfied emphasis.

Next to me, Antwon Marks whistles.

Another boy raises his hand. I glance around and it's Derek. He looks at me briefly with a light smirk then addresses Mr. Warrenson. "Wouldn't that be overkill? Are these hoverboards pure orichalcum or do they make them part orichalcum part something else, to save money and resources?"

"Good question," Mr. Warrenson says. "What is your name, Candidate?"

"Derek Sunder."

"All right, Mr. Sunder, our assumption so far is that hoverboards are pure orichalcum. But as far as I know, no one has tested the specific seventeen-ton weight limit in the lab—at least not when I was on the original Atlantis tech research team. We know for a fact that a hoverboard can easily support several full-grown adults and stacked boxes of heavy equipment. But this is definitely something to consider and to verify. Hoverboards could just as well be made of only thin veneer layers of orichalcum applied over other inert materials."

I raise my hand.

"Yes, Ms. Lark?"

"So, would it be possible to levitate an object with orichalcum that is just a minor part of its overall material, such as a lid on a box, or a piece of rope or something? Or, what about a person? How about an orichalcum belt—or even a belt buckle? Maybe, wrist bracelets or armbands? An orichalcum vest or harness?"

"Sure, and why not orichalcum underwear?" Someone snickers, and the whole class bursts out in nervous laughter.

I stare straight ahead and feel my cheeks begin to burn.

But Mr. Warrenson raises his hand to hush us. "Actually that is one of its experimental uses that we are trying to achieve. Orichalcum, in properly measured weight amounts, strategically worn on the body can theoretically create a commercial *flying suit*."

"Yeah!" a girl says, clapping. "I could definitely use that kind of outfit!"

"We all can." Mr. Warrenson turns to her. "Unfortunately there is one small problem, something I've mentioned before—the Atlanteans are just not willing to part with sufficient amounts of it for us to experiment on a large scale and actually make useful things. Plus, we're unable to properly *break down* orichalcum under lab conditions. The only way we know of using it 'raw' is as the building-block material in their special type of 3D printers. In fact, we have a couple of these 3D printers here in the RQC, in the Arena Commons building, upstairs in the offices. . . ."

I listen with fascination—even managing to ignore Derek's relentless stares in my direction—and now all kinds of weird idea gears are turning in my mind.

As soon as class ends, I decide I am going to go look for Gracie. I head downstairs, first stopping by the girls' dorm floor to grab a sweatshirt for the evening chill. Yeah, I've learned my lesson about walking around in nothing but a sweaty T-shirt at night, and my throat is still sore from breathing in all that smoke yesterday—whatever it is, I cannot risk getting sick, not now, especially since I am expected to sing those dratted notes in class. . . .

On the first floor, Candidates are heading into the cafeteria to eat dinner. I see Laronda and Dawn, and wave to them as I hurry by. "I'm just going to see my sister," I say.

"You go, girl!" Laronda winks at me meaningfully. Dawn, a girl of few words, gives me an amused silent look. I bet they think I'm off to meet up with Logan.

I roll my eyes at them then walk through the lobby and outside.

When I get to Red Dorm Five, and look around their Common Area lounge, Gracie's not there. Neither is she upstairs on the third floor, when I head there. Girls with red tokens stare at me and my yellow token as I wander around past their beds, asking if "Grace Lark is here."

"Her bed's over there," one girl tells me, pointing to an empty bed near the back of the hall. "But I think she's gone to dinner."

I glance at the made-up cot, see a familiar duffel bag of Gracie's then look around the large dormitory hall, which looks exactly like my own dorm floor. "Thanks," I say, and head back downstairs.

I peek inside the noisy cafeteria, and again, no sign of Gracie.

At this point I wonder if she's gone to look for me, or our brothers. Okay, I think, she might be over at George's Green Dorm Eleven which is way in the back of the compound. But Gordie's Blue Dorm Two is closer, so I head there first.

As I walk between buildings in the brightly lit areas filled with other walking Candidates, I see more guards out on patrol tonight. The evening sky is deepening indigo. And from the direction of the airfield I hear the noise of helicopter blades cutting the air. With a sinking feeling, I wonder if those are military or police helicopters, and what they're doing. . . . Are they working with the Atlantean Correctors on the investigation?

Blue Dorm Two has a large blue square logo up above the entrance. I go in, and once again, it looks identical to all the other dorms I've seen so far, down to the furniture and bland floor carpeting in the lobby. The lounge area is half-empty, since most people have gone in to eat. The Blue cafeteria is just as noisy, and I smell meatloaf, the same thing that they're serving to us today in

Yellow and Red.

I mill around, thinking. . . . To be honest, I am getting more and more uneasy. Where is Gracie, is she okay? It's my bad that I didn't immediately go after her when she ran off last night. And yeah, George could've been a teeny-tiny bit more helpful too. Really, what would Mom and Dad think of us, if they knew?

I take a big breath and peek inside the Blue cafeteria, and again, no sign of my sis. And no sign of Gordie either.

So I trudge upstairs to the second floor, boys' dorm. I don't feel comfortable going inside a dormitory possibly full of half-naked teen boys—nor, now that I think about it, am I even allowed to, according to the rules of conduct. So, at the doors, I ask some kid if Gordon Lark's inside.

"Who?" the kid says, squinting at me.

"He goes by 'Gordie,'"

"Okay, let me check." The boy goes back inside while I wait. Then I hear him yelling out, "Yo! Gordie Lark! Hey, loser, some girl's here to see you. Oooh!" And then I hear a few rude hoots and laughter.

Moments later, my younger brother peeks around the door sheepishly, adjusting his glasses over his nose, as usual. He's in his jeans and dingy sweatshirt, with sweat stains around the neck and armpits.

"Gordie!"

"Oh," he says, in some relief, seeing it's just me. "Hey, Gee Two. What are you doing here?"

"Have you seen Gracie?"

"No. . . . Why?"

I exhale. Suddenly I feel a weird cold knot building in my stomach.

"I don't know where she is. And I'm worried. She's not at her dorm."

"So? She's probably just walking around. Have you tried the big Arena building?"

"No, should I?"

Gordie shrugs. He looks exhausted, and his face with its fading bruise on the upper cheek near the eye is extremely pale, except for the bruise itself, which is now turning purple-green. Ugh! Not to mention, he also slightly reeks. Oh, Gordie. . . .

I put my hands on my hips. "Gordon Lark, you look like a disaster. Have you had dinner yet? And a shower wouldn't hurt either."

"Heh? No . . . I've got homework to do. I'm not really hungry."

"Are you kidding me? You're always hungry! Okay, that's it, we're going downstairs right now and eating in your cafeteria."

Gordie frowns . . . kind of freezes for a moment.

I stand at the doors, giving him my meanest older sibling look. "Let's go, Gee Three, don't make me drag your sorry butt," I add. "You know I could, I've been working out!"

"Okay . . ." he mumbles, but he doesn't look all that happy.

"Move it!" I say, and he finally starts walking.

Downstairs in the Blue cafeteria, there's pretty much nobody I know. It's packed and eventually I see a few faces that might be kids from our school back in Vermont, but I'm not one hundred percent sure.

Gordie looks sullen as he pushes his tray along the counter shelf stretching before the food bar. He gets his plate of meatloaf and mashed potatoes from the server and I notice he's keeping his head down and not looking around him at all. I'm right behind him, and finally we make it past the desserts, with cherry pie slices on our tray, and pour our drinks from the dispensers.

"See anyone you'd like to sit with?" I ask.

"No," he replies, without even looking around to check who's in the room.

Okay, now I'm really starting to wonder what's going on.

We find an empty table off to the side and sit down. Without much ado, Gordie digs in hungrily, being entirely his usual, normal, pig-out self. So what was the problem?

"Gordie," I say, lifting a forkful of meatloaf up to my face. "What's up, now? Are you okay? Is everything okay?"

"Uh-uh," he mumbles with his mouth full.

I notice he still looks only at his plate and does not look up or around the room. Even for blissful loner Gordie that's kind of abnormal.

"Wanna tell me how you got that big bruise on your face?" I say. "You never told me yesterday what happened to you."

"It's no big deal."

"Oh yeah? Just tell me."

"This guy and I argued in Combat. It was something stupid. He hit me, I hit him back. The Instructors told us to cut it out. . . . It's over."

I turn my head to the side, looking at him. "Wait, I thought it happened in Agility, not Combat. And is it? Over, I mean?"

"Yeah. . . . Agility, Combat, one of these two, whatever. And yeah, it's over." But Gordie does not meet my eyes.

"So how come you're acting kind of weird? And don't even try to pretend, I know you too well, Gee Three. You're avoiding something or *someone*."

In that moment, two guys with blue tokens, carrying trays with dinner leftovers, pass by our table. One of them looks to be Gordie's age, a freshman with brown hair, and the other is slightly older with darker hair. The brown-haired kid slaps our table with one hand and glares at Gordie. "We're not done, loser," he says, leaning in.

Gordie looks up, and his already pale face goes perfectly still.

The second older kid stares with a hard expression. And then he says a crude obscenity.

"Hey!" I set down my fork and look at them with a frown.

"What, you got your Yellow girlfriend here to fight for you, coward loser?" the freshman says.

Gordie opens his mouth and starts to get up. I grab his arm and push him back down, barely holding him with all my strength.

"You guys want to get Disqualified *right now?*" I say to the other two. "Because they have cameras on us."

"Shut up, bitch." The freshman turns away from Gordie and is now glaring at me.

For some reason I am not particularly fazed. *"Disqualification,"* I repeat a single word in a loud voice, meeting his crazy look calmly. And then I add, "Oh, and all those pissed off Atlantean Correctors are all over this RQC, interrogating—pardon me, *interviewing* people. Just give them a reason! They'd love to have a one-on-one chat with you. Hey, I think I see one now, over there, at the doors. Or maybe that's just another surveillance camera pointing at us."

My words seem to have their intended effect. The two guys

frown and give Gordie mean stares, but then decide to move along.

Only after they exit the cafeteria does Gordie exhale in some relief.

I find I'm still holding his arm. And it occurs to me, that was weird, I just talked down two mean jerks and wasn't scared one tiny bit. What's happening to me?

"Wow," I say, releasing Gordie. "That was really ugly."

Gordie mutters something incomprehensible, and I notice his face is flushing now, a funny delayed stress reaction.

"Gordie, you're gonna be okay. Stay safe by being reasonable." I look at my poor brother. "Remember why we're here. This is not summer camp, and screw the bullies. I've got some of my own, and now that I think about it, it's . . . well . . . *okay*."

Gordie looks at me, and his angry flush is still there, but it's going down. He picks up his fork again and begins shoveling meatloaf and mashed potatoes in his mouth.

I smile; I cannot help it. "You know, there's a good chance those guys will still try to beat the crap out of you," I say with rueful amusement.

"Oh, yeah." Gordie nods, chewing, but this time he's grinning too.

"Just don't make it easy for them. Be smart, kiddo. As smart as you always are. After all, you're in Blue, the Smart Kids Quadrant."

"So are *they*."

"They? Oh, phooey!" I bite my lip. "Nobody beats a Lark when it comes to brain power. Right, Gee Three? Keep that in mind!"

"Okay!" Suddenly Gordie pauses eating, chortles with his mouth full, and says, "Talking about brain power—I heard that some girl in a Yellow Dorm did this really cool thing yesterday in Combat class. Everybody's talking about it, they call her 'shoelace girl!' Supposedly, when they ran out of their net and cord weapons, she ended up without one. And so she pulled out her own shoelaces and tied them together into a cord before the Instructors could catch her and give her a demerit—"

"Gordie," I say, and now my mind is kind of reeling. "Okay,

wow. . . . That was *me*. I'm Shoelace Girl. I had no idea that people are talking about this outside my dorm."

"That was you? No way!" Gordie's jaw drops and now he looks totally impressed.

I laugh, seeing his expression. And then I add, "Hey, see, there you go! That just goes to show what I'm talking about here— Lark brain power! We've got it!"

Gordie looks at me with an expression that approaches normal.

He then tells me proudly that he got to shoot a real gun in Combat class. "It takes brain power too, I guess. We had to shoot at a target fifty feet away, and I hit right near the center at least four times!"

I smile and shake my head at my brother. "Gee Three, you with a gun? Holy moly, amazing! See, Gordie, that's what I'm telling you!"

At last I can see that Gordie relaxes completely, because he's got the dopey grin as he looks at me.

We finish up eating uneventfully, even take time to scarf down that cherry pie, and then I leave Gordie to his "homework"— which is basically him hiding in the corner of the dorm lounge with his nose in his sketch notebook as he pretends to look over notes and instead draws something—and off I go to wander the compound in search of Gracie and George.

An hour later, after checking both the Arena Commons super structure and Green Dorm Eleven at the edge of the RQC compound, and finding neither of my two other siblings, I decide to head back. Short of going inside every dorm, there's no way I am going to find them before first curfew.

Gracie had better not be hanging out with Daniel Tover, lord knows where, I think. Only, I have a very grim idea that it's exactly what she's doing.

Chapter 19

The next morning I wake up to the now familiar 7:00 AM alarm claxons, and I remember that I've forgotten to do my running homework the night before.

Ugh, great. . . .

Everyone's groaning in the dormitory, girls on all sides of me complain, as we start getting out of beds and checking our blisters and pulled muscles.

I turn and look at Laronda who stretches her arms, yawning widely.

"Ready for another day of hell camp?"

"Bring it on!" Laronda replies, with another huge yawn.

On the other side of me, I see the brown-haired girl in the other bed next to mine whose name I still don't know. She looks very sad and kind of sickly. And she is not moving out of bed.

I decide to remedy the situation by introducing myself. "Hi, there," I say. "Good morning! It's funny that we've been neighbors for like four nights now, but I don't think I know your name. I'm Gwen—Gwen Lark."

"Hi," she says, and her voice sounds grainy with sleep. "Sorry—my English is not great—my name is Hasmik Tigranian."

"Oh, yeah?" Laronda says on the other side of me. "Hasmik, that's a pretty name. What kind of name is it?"

"I'm Armenian," the girl says.

"Oh, really? That's pretty cool. I'm Laronda Aimes."

"Wow," I say. "Armenia is such an amazing ancient country! I read about it some, it used to be a huge empire at the time of Babylon and earlier, probably all the way back to the time of the original Atlantis, I wouldn't be surprised. It used to be where Mount Ararat is now, the same famous mountain from the Bible where Noah's Ark landed after the Flood—"

"Yes," Hasmik says, pulling back her blanket, and sits up. "But now I am from Boston." And she gives me a weak smile.

"So, how you surviving this Qualification nightmare?" Laronda is now up and messing around her own makeshift clothesline of hand-washed underwear stuffed around the edges of her mattress that she's copied from me.

Hasmik sighs then swings her legs out of bed. I see skinny feet sticking out from under her long flannel nightgown. One of her ankles has an ugly bruise and swelling.

"Hey, you should go see a doctor," I say, pointing to her ankle. "That doesn't look too good."

"I know," she says, then winces as her foot touches the floor. "I've already go to doctor. He say I need to rest, but I can't do that. He gave me medicine, and so I take it. The swelling goes down, but after Combat and Agility class, it hurts my foot again. No time to heal."

Laronda pauses to stare at Hasmik with sympathy. "That's awful, girl! You must be in crazy pain all the time!"

"*Ayoh, shat tsavumeh . . .* I mean, oh, yes." The girl nods, and now I can see why she looks so pale and sickly. She must be living in agony.

Laronda and I stare at her, pretty much stunned.

Hasmik meanwhile opens a small plastic bag and out comes a medical bandage of sorts. She bends down and starts wrapping her ankle in the bandage, and her face is turning green with pain. Finally she is done, the ankle is secured as much as possible. Hasmik opens a pill bottle and pops one. She then smiles at us. "Okay now."

"Oh, man, how long can you keep this up?" Laronda shakes her head.

Hasmik sighs again, shrugs. "Don't worry, I keep going," she says softly in a steady voice. And amazingly she gets up, without even limping, picks up a change of clothing and heads to the bathroom. "We go to breakfast, okay?" she adds, glancing back at us.

Speechless, we follow her.

After a quick breakfast downstairs with Laronda and Hasmik, we return to the Common Area lounge to get our daily class schedules scanned.

Dorm Leader Mark Foster passes the hand scanner over our tokens and reads our schedules. Weird, but apparently we all have second period Combat together and it's going to be held in the Arena Commons building.

"That's interesting," Laronda says. "Seems like everyone's in the same Combat class today."

"Actually, yes." Mark Foster looks up at her, and his face is serious. "The entire Yellow Quadrant is going to have Combat together today, in the large Arena. Which means, Yellow Dorms Four, Eight, and Twelve."

"Three dorms together, wow. . . . How come?" I say.

"Ask your Instructors," Mark says curtly. "Today, from what we're told, they are doing some kind of hardcore mass Combat training. First period, Blue Quadrant, second period, you guys in Yellow. Then Red and Green. Everyone has to go to the Arena for this mandatory thing. Don't be late to that one. . . ."

"I don't like the sound of that." Laronda bites her lip nervously and looks at us as we step away and let Mark continue scanning other people.

"Yeah, I don't either," I mutter.

Hasmik just sighs.

I sit next to Dawn Williams in Atlantis Culture class. To be honest, this morning the stress level is so high that I have trouble concentrating and hardly remember what the lecture is about, despite the compelling nature of the Instructor's usual Storyteller voice.

This morning Nefir Mekei talks much about something innocuous, such as the kind of food they eat on Atlantis. The main takeaway is that because of the abundance of amazingly rich soil for crop production, Atlanteans have evolved to be mostly vegetarian and vegan, consuming a variety of fruits, vegetables, grains, legumes, and vegetable-based protein, especially the upper class citizens.

It is true, Nefir tells us, the non-citizens in the coastal regions of Atlantis consume some locally obtained seafood, but it is done with some distaste and from poverty. Those who can afford it definitely prefer the vegetable-based healthy proteins. And the wealthy citizens have access to fancy and delicious vegetable protein-based meat substitutes that are practically indistinguishable from what we Earthlings might consider premium quality animal meat.

Furthermore, vegetable protein is considered to be the ethical food choice. To kill an animal for sport is a strictly punishable crime. Even to kill as a necessity is looked down upon.

Derek Sunder raises his hand. "So, the big question remains, does that Atlantis veggie meat of yours taste like chicken?"

Snickers are heard around the classroom.

Nefir Mekei pauses and looks at Derek with his slightly creepy unblinking stare. And when I say "creepy unblinking stare," I mean Nefir, because Derek also has his own creepy stare, except that this time he is getting "out-creeped."

There is a long pause during which I get the satisfaction of seeing Derek blink first and squirm in his seat.

"Your question is not something I can answer," Nefir says at last. "I don't know the taste of your chicken."

A few more giggles sound and are quickly stifled. A few teens hold hands over their mouths.

But the Atlantean does not smile. "If your chicken is a living creature, then you should not take pride in knowing its taste."

"It's just a dumb bird," Derek says.

"And so are you, turkey . . ." Dawn whispers next to me, without looking up. Her face remains deadpan serious.

I fight very hard to keep my expression neutral, but my lips are quivering. *Way to go, Dawn!*

Derek must've heard, because he turns around and glares in our direction, but ignores Dawn and gives me a long evil stare.

I get a sudden jolt of familiar cold fear and no longer feel like laughing.

But Nefir says, "For the most part, we believe it is neither honorable nor fair to make fun of those who are helpless, or take advantage of those who are weak—regardless of what living species they are."

"Yeah, well, here on Earth we raise chickens for food and eggs—what else would you call them? Dumbass birds, useless for anything else," Derek says in an abrasive voice intended to provoke the Atlantean.

Nefir does not take the bait, only watches Derek calmly. "You might consider a living creature a 'dumb bird.' On Atlantis, we think differently." And he does not elaborate.

An older teen girl raises her hand. "Okay, do you have tea and coffee on Atlantis? What do you guys drink? What about soda and carbonated stuff?"

Nefir nods. "Yes, we have similar hot and cold brewed drinks that are made from various plants native to Atlantis. They are not an exact equivalent, but very close. There's even a cocoa-like plant that is similar to Earth chocolate."

"What about alcohol? You know, beer, wine, hard cider, that kind of stuff?"

Nefir glances at her, and his expression relaxes slightly. "What do you think? We are human, after all."

Snickers travel around the classroom once again, and a few guys clap and say, "Yeah!"

Class ends eventually, and we all head downstairs and then outside, toward the Arena Commons building.

I walk in a big crowd of Yellow Quadrant Candidates next to Dawn, and we manage to pick up Laronda and Hasmik along the way, plus Jai and Mateo and a few other guys we know. I look around, squinting from the morning sun, and see Blayne Dubois rolling along in his wheelchair, just a few steps behind us. The muscles of his arms strain as he quickly turns the wheels of his chair and keeps up with the flow of the crowd. Everyone's tokens are lit up yellow, and everyone's way more nervous than usual.

As we approach the AC building, blinking in the sunlight, the ranks of Yellow Candidates swell, as two more dorms join the crowd. At the doors, we see an oncoming opposite stream of Candidates with blue tokens, as they exit the building, making room for us. They look sweaty, dejected, and beaten down after a hard workout. Even the tougher guys among them look worn down. That must've been one helluva Combat class. . . .

"This is going to be super duper bad, with a cherry on top," Laronda mutters.

I glance at Hasmik who's walking next to me, and she looks

pained but quietly determined.

Inside, the stadium portion of the building has been cleared of most of the equipment in the middle, to make room for the Candidates.

Already, double rows are forming, facing each other, stretching from one end of the track to the other. When they come to the end, a new iteration of double rows begins, and then a third one—that's how many Candidates are present.

"Okay, this is huge!" Jai Bhagat exclaims.

We file in place, and stand somewhere in the middle of the second double row.

"I don't want to spar with you guys, cause I don't want to hit you," Laronda says. "So why don't we all just stand in this row next to each other, instead of across from each other? That way we would be partnered with someone else to beat and kick around."

"Good idea," I say.

"I really don't want to 'beat and kick around' anyone," Dawn says matter-of-factly, looking almost sleepy. "Sparring would be okay, though."

"Shut up, girl!" Laronda laughs then punches her in the arm.

"Hey, save it for the actual class," Mateo says, three persons down the line.

As we talk, other people we don't know line up across from us. I end up facing some skinny blond girl my age with a perky short haircut.

Moments later, a familiar whistle blows, and we turn in that direction.

Far down the line, on the other end of the Arena, four Atlanteans stand, dressed in the usual grey uniforms. First is Oalla Keigeri, and her long metallic gold hair shines sun-bright. Next to her is Keruvat Ruo, his own closely-cropped head a golden halo, in contrast with raven-haired Xelio Vekahat who stands next to them.

The fourth one is Aeson Kass. He stands with his arms folded at his chest, watching us with a seemingly casual demeanor. And yet, everything about his posture whispers danger.

I feel an immediate twinge of nerves at the sight of him. I don't know what it is precisely, alarm or terror or something else impossible to define. But immediately I am flashing back to that moment two nights ago . . . his stark bloodied face with its chiseled

angles . . . lowered eyelids outlined in kohl, pale gold hair stained
with soot and more blood . . . a striking profile backlit by the
flames . . . the feel of his hard, muscular body against mine, as I
desperately drag him down the rung stairs of the shuttle. . . .

"Attention, Yellow Quadrant!"

I am jerked back to reality by the deep booming voice of
Keruvat Ruo. It needs no microphone to carry across the Arena.

"Stand up straight! First, we begin with stretching—feet apart,
bend at the waist, touch your toes, then back up, lunge with right
leg forward, repeat twenty times!"

I exhale, inhale, and begin the warm-up exercise.

A few minutes later we are done with several series of combo
reps. I am panting for air, trying to catch my breath, and so is
everyone else around me. But one thing is sure—my muscles feel
alive. Blood and energy is rushing through my veins. And although
the bone-weariness is still there, it has somehow become a
secondary ache, retreating to the background.

A fter all, this is day four of Qualification—could it be that my
body is getting used to the daily punishment?

However, there's no time to ponder, because now Keruvat
grows silent and Aeson Kass takes over.

"Candidates!" he says, as he begins to pace before our three
double rows, while the other three Atlanteans walk behind him.
"Today you will show me what you can do! Show me First Form,
Floating Swan!"

The arena erupts in movement. Candidates, myself included,
scramble to assume the First Position of rest and balance.
Hundreds of feet pound the floor—an almost simultaneous
motion—to take the initial side-step that widens the stance. . . .
Then, arms and hands float, off to the side and straight ahead,
fingers forming the precise curvature and sign.

I stand holding the Floating Swan, while I see with my
peripheral vision to the right, Laronda stilled in hers, and beyond
her, Dawn, Jai, Mateo. On the other side of me to the left is
Hasmik, frozen in her stance that is all clean lines, and no one
would ever suspect how much pain she is in right now. . . . To the
left of her is Tremaine Walters with his long locks. Directly across

from me the blond girl with short hair awkwardly holds her stance, her hand outthrust at me.

Aeson Kass walks the line, still many feet away, and I hear his voice cut like a knife. "Show me Second Form, Striking Snake!"

My extended hand drops away, and I slide into a forward lunge with one foot and at the same time strike forward with the other hand, bringing it around from the side—while all my fingers come together to form the snout of a snake. I feel my thigh muscles quake while my knees wobble. Everyone around me attempts to do the same, and I hear many grunts and shuffles.

Aeson's voice approaches, sounds closer, somewhere only twenty feet behind me. Its hard rich timbre and power sends echoes through the otherwise silent space of the great stadium hall. "Show me Third Form, Spinning Wind!"

Oh lord, no, I really suck at this one. . . .

I force my body to move, and I begin the wide rapid half-turn into a 360-degree spin, arms out-flung to the sides, moving my hands clumsily and trying not to hit Laronda and Hasmik on either sides of me. It's one thing when you're *supposed* to hit someone, but not when you do it unintentionally because you're a dork.

This is where it all falls apart. As I stagger to regain my balance on return, apparently so do most of the Candidates in the hall.

"Halt!" Aeson Kass roars at us, and it's like someone shoots me in the chest. I can *feel* his voice, a tangible weight of fierce intensity.

"Stop, and assume Floating Swan!" he says in barely leashed fury, just a few feet away in the other row behind me. "Shame and disgrace! You are not worthy of being called *Candidates* much less *Atlanteans.* You move like a herd of Earth cattle—broken, weak, useless! How badly out of shape are you, considering you are teenagers? An old man on Atlantis can move his dying carcass better than you!"

He approaches, and somewhere past my back I hear his boots striking the floor with angry impact.

I barely dare to breathe, frozen in the Floating Swan, holding my hands and arms in the floating stance, feeling them begin to quake with muscle tension. . . .

And then I hear him make the selections, as he quickens his pace along the rows.

"You! Take one step forward! You! And you! Step forward! You! Step forward! You! *Move!*"

As he returns to the end of one row and now enters our own row, I hear him say, "Those whom I called forward, will now *stand on one foot* until I tell you otherwise. If you set your other foot down, you will have to repeat, for twice the time. *Now, stand on your right foot!*"

As waves of horrified whispers and discontent race through our rows, Aeson continues walking swiftly past us, and makes his selections. "You! And you! Step forward, stand on your right foot!" he points at seemingly random teens who possibly display a less than perfect Floating Swan stance.

I see him approach from the corner of my eye, and he is like a demon. Blazing metallic hair, ruthless closed expression.

Astra daimon. . . .

"You!" He points at Hasmik. Then he passes me, and for a moment I see the flash of terrible dark-blue that is his eyes, as his gaze sweeps over me, and then continues.

Weirdly it occurs to me, how strange it is to see his eyes being *open* and so alive, as opposed to heavy closed eyelids and soot and blood and smoke. . . .

I blink.

Laronda is safe, and so is Dawn, but Jaideep Bhagat gets to step forward. Poor Jai, he stands on his right foot, awkwardly balancing with his hands.

I glance to my left and suddenly remember—Hasmik, oh no!

Hasmik stands on her one very *hurt* foot, and I see her eyes begin to glaze over with pain, while her hands are forming into fists.

But Aeson Kass has gone far down the line, and more and more Candidates are chosen to step forward in disgrace.

"Now, switch!" he exclaims, having come to the end of our row. "Stand on your left foot!"

I glance at Hasmik with sympathy as she switches to her other foot in major relief. "Hang in there!" I barely mouth the words, while she nods at me. Her expression remains stoic, but a sheen of sweat is starting to cover her face.

But after having made the round of all our rows, Aeson Kass is not done. "Now, Candidates, those of you standing on one foot, continue to do so. The rest of you, resume Forms! Show me Second Form, Striking Snake!"

Again we lunge, forming hands into snakes. And again I hear Aeson's relentless voice start making the cruel selections. "You! Step forward! And you!"

"At this rate," I hiss under my breath, to no one in particular, "all of us will be standing on one foot!"

Laronda silently rolls her eyes in pained agreement.

"Show me Third Form, Spinning Wind! Repeat Form until I tell you to stop! The others—switch and stand on your right foot!"

I gasp for air and move into the 360-degree turnabout. Meanwhile next to me Hasmik makes a single whimper of pain and again puts all her weight on the right foot with its badly swollen ankle.

Again the selections happen, and Aeson Kass stalks our rows like a panther.

"*Damn*, here he comes," someone whispers. "What a prick. . . ."

"You! *Silence* or Disqualification! Step forward!"

I watch, staggering after another turnabout, as the boy who got called out is then told to not only stand on one foot but *jump* up an down *while standing on that one foot.*

Holy lord!

While that's all happening a few feet away, things are even worse right here. . . .

That's because, next to me, Hasmik is turning green, and sweat is pouring down her forehead. *The girl is going into shock.*

I see her begin to sway, and so I pause my Form. . . .

What am I doing? This is crazy!

I casually step forward, pretending I was also called out, and stand on my right foot. Then I slowly reach out with my left hand, and take hold of her clammy hand closest to me. I feel her desperate slippery grip, then just the tips of her fingers touching mine. . . .

Together we stand, hands just barely touching—just enough to keep us both balanced, and her upright.

But it lasts only for about a minute.

Because next thing I know, Aeson Kass stands before me.

Did I really think he wouldn't notice? *Yeah, Gwen, you idiot. . . .*

And then comes the sound of his voice. It cuts through me like fire and ice.

Chapter 20

"You!" Aeson Kass speaks, having stopped directly before me. "What are you doing?"

I continue to stand on one foot—which is starting to acquire a fine muscle tremor—and stare straight ahead, so that his face is just barely out of my line of sight . . . so that I don't have to make contact with his *eyes*. And in that first terrible instant I say nothing, as my pulse races madly in my temples, threatening to jump out of my head, if that even makes any sense. My fingers continue to touch Hasmik's hand.

If it's even possible, but I think *he* is slightly thrown off. Because there is an unusually long pause as he continues to stare at me. Meanwhile I see him indirectly with my peripheral vision, and I think I am about to die. . .

. . . or about to be Disqualified.

"Look at me . . ." he says, seemingly gathering himself after that inexplicable pause. "I *said*, what are you doing?"

Slowly I turn my head a miniscule bit to face him—to face his *eyes*.

"I . . . don't know . . ." I whisper.

The intensity of his gaze is impossible to describe.

"You what? You don't *know?*"

"I am sorry, I don't—"

"I did not tell you to step forward and stand on one foot. So, what are you doing?"

"I—must've misunderstood."

If I'm correct, I think his fury is now white-hot. But oh, he keeps it under such perfect control. . . .

He takes a step closer and slowly looks me up and down. And he looks at Hasmik, who is just about to pass out.

There is perfect silence in the arena, except for a few

shufflings of feet and the lonely sound of one boy jumping up and down, his foot laboriously striking the floor.

If I weren't in the middle of such utter hell right now, I might even find it kind of funny, in a sick, remote, ten-years-later kind of way.

"Your name, Candidate."

"Gwen Lark."

He watches me—for what seems to be another extended moment during which his dark blue eyes bore through me and I am rendered into nothing.

"Do you make it a habit to willfully *misunderstand* instructions?"

My heart is racing so fast it feels like I am going into cardiac arrest.

"No . . . only sometimes."

"And is there a reason you are holding hands with the Candidate next to you?"

I take a deep breath and glance at Hasmik who watches me through narrowed fluttering eyelids, while rivulets of sweat pour down her temples. "She is hurt," I say. "She cannot stand like that on her right leg. . . . At least not for much longer."

"I see. So you think you are helping her?"

"I *am*—helping her."

There is a pause.

"You are *cheating*. The consequence for such action is Disqualification. For *both* of you—"

"No!" I exclaim, and let go of Hasmik's fingers as if burned, while a sudden lump forms in the back of my throat, and I realize helplessly I am about to cry. "No, *she* had nothing to do with it! It was all my idea! Please, she really *is* hurt!"

"—and punishment for disobeying direct orders is also Disqualification," Aeson Kass continues, ignoring my outburst. His voice has grown deceptively soft—it is the silence of a coiling serpent—and for some reason it makes it even more terrible.

I stand, still balancing on one foot, breathing in shallow rapid gasps, while the gathering pressure of tears is overwhelming my eyes.

Well, this is it, I think.

In that exact moment, Hasmik creates a timely interruption by quietly collapsing next to me. One instant she stands upright on one foot, and the next she seems to buckle downward, passing out softly, and lies on the floor at my feet.

I gasp, then immediately move. I crouch before her, reach out to feel her head.

"Candidates, halt!" Aeson's hard impassive voice resounds above my head. "All of you, stop and you may put both feet down."

Someone blows a whistle—I am guessing it's Oalla. It is followed by the shuffle of many feet.

I continue holding Hasmik's forehead, and she is breathing faintly. A few seconds and her eyes flutter open. Her skin is cold and clammy to the touch, and I see Keruvat Ruo approach and squat down next to me. His large hands examine her, feeling her pulse, then come around her from the back as we raise her up into a sitting position on the floor.

"Please . . ." I whisper to the dark Atlantean. "She really needs a doctor!"

"No . . . I am all right," Hasmik barely whispers, as she gets up slowly with our assistance and stands upright in a daze.

Incredibly, she then attempts to once again stand on one leg. She must have missed hearing the halt command when she was passed out on the floor.

"You," Aeson Kass tells her coldly. "For the rest of this class, you are excused. You are also excused from today's Agility Training. Go back to your dorm and see the doctor."

"Am I—Disqualified?" she whispers.

"No. Not *today*."

I take a shuddering breath. "What about me?"

Aeson Kass turns back to me, and again I am seared by the overwhelming intensity of his gaze. It makes me unable to breathe.

"You—I still have not decided."

The rows of Candidates around me have fallen into perfect silence, watching in fear and suspense.

I notice Keruvat glancing at Aeson, and even Oalla has a subdued expression on her chiseled face.

In that moment Xelio Vekahat moves in closer and speaks softly to Aeson.

Aeson Kass breaks away his gaze from me and turns slightly, listens to what Xelio has to say. I watch their heads together, a contrast of metallic gold and midnight black, hear the lilting sounds of their Atlantean language. . . .

I wait and stare helplessly, and at one point notice how they both glance down at my feet—at my sneakers.

Oh, no! Has Xelio just told him about the shoelace incident?

I am so screwed now.

I feel a wave of numbing cold pass through me, as despair settles around my mind.

But Aeson Kass turns back to me, and his hard gaze has become a peculiar neutral thing. It's as if his anger has receded somehow, pulled back behind a curtain, and I sense the lessening of pressure.

"Candidate Lark, for the moment, you are *not* Disqualified. However, you will report here later tonight during Homework Hour, for disciplinary action." He points with a slight motion of his head to the raised platform deck in the back of the stadium. "Be on that deck, on time, at 8:00 PM sharp, to receive further instructions. That is all for now."

He looks away from me. And just like that, I am suddenly a nonentity.

I watch Hasmik leave my row and walk away slowly. The Atlantean Instructors watch her retreating back.

In the same instant Aeson Kass begins to pace our rows once more, raising his voice yet again into a terrible thing of power.

"Candidates! Resume your Forms and Examples! Show me First Form, Floating Swan! The rest of you who are Examples, stand on your right foot!"

It is over eventually, and the Yellow Quadrant is dismissed. We shuffle out of the Arena Commons building, beaten down and so tired that it hurts to think. Outside, it's clear skies. The mid-day sunlight is so bright it is painful to the eyes, as we walk back to our dorms.

"What an absolute evil jerkhole!" Laronda says to me, as soon as we're outside.

"Are you okay?" Dawn adds, in her eternally mild voice, but

the expression of her brown eyes is serious and extra sympathetic as she watches me.

"Yeah, man," Jai says, limping next to us. "Sorry about that, Gwen! Like you need any more punishment! This whole Qualification thing is one Big Punishment! I mean, yeah, and now my feet are super-killing me. . . . At least you only had to stand on one foot for five minutes."

"Hey, girl, you did the right thing there." Tremaine comes up to me and pats my shoulder.

I nod silently. I am completely numb, beaten down.

"What can you expect? He's one of their military big-shots," Mateo says sullenly, walking with his hands in his pockets. "And he is *way* pissed. He thinks it's all our fault, we killed his friends in that damn exploding shuttle, so he's taking it out on us."

"I get it," I say. "But there was no need to be so merciless! Hasmik was genuinely hurt, it's not like anyone was actually cheating!"

"Yeah, well, it doesn't matter. It's how the military is. Typical basic training—a combo of mindless obedience and endurance stuff. It's all a bunch of sadist drills, nonstop." Mateo shrugs.

"I don't care what it is, he's still a scary sadist jerk!" Laronda mutters. "And I am so sorry, girlfriend, you absolutely don't deserve this crap."

"Thanks, I know." I glance at Laronda and make a tired attempt at a smile.

"What's *disciplinary action?* Wonder what kind of punishment it is," Dawn says.

I don't reply. What can I say? That I'm wondering too, that I am terrified, full of cold numbing sickness? Even now, it twists my gut with fear and nerves. . . .

We get back to Yellow Dorm Eight and the Dorm Leaders are in the lobby, waiting for us with grim faces, together with several security guards. Two Atlantean Correctors in grey uniforms stand in the middle of the lounge, holding pieces of unfamiliar scanning equipment in their hands, and talk among themselves softly in Atlantean. They ignore us completely.

How do I know they are Correctors? I vaguely recognize them from the assembly. There are no other distinguishing marks about them, no special police insignia, merely a yellow armband on one of them and a blue one on the other.

Apparently while we were away being tortured in Combat, our dorm has been searched.

"Everyone, you are free to proceed upstairs to your dormitory floors, if you need to," Dorm Leader John Nicolard says. "Your belongings are undisturbed, and everything has been left as before. The search scan is non-intrusive. It is now over."

Candidates throw curious, scared, hostile glances at the Correctors, and many of the teens go upstairs.

I don't bother. Neither does Laronda, or Dawn, who just shrugs.

"They're welcome to go through my underwear," Dawn says, and calmly heads for the cafeteria.

We eat lunch quickly and according to my schedule I get the unlucky class order of having Agility Training right after lunch. Still exhausted from Combat, on all levels, emotional and physical, I trudge downstairs to the Training Hall gym.

All I can think of now is, I really need to conserve my strength . . . for the ordeal later tonight. Whatever it happens to be. . . . Ugh.

Agility Training is the usual painfest. Minor difference is, Oalla Keigeri makes us run *eleven* as opposed to nine laps around the perimeter, and this time I share my demerit with Janice Quinn, as we pathetically tie for last place. We also share a weak smile and then give each other high-fives as we stagger to a stop and bend forward to grasp our knees, while panting for air.

Oalla shakes her head at Janice and me. She then gives me an intent look as she scans my token, but says nothing of a haranguing nature. Probably she pities me, knowing what awaits me later tonight. . . . On the other hand, knowing Oalla, I doubt she's feeling sorry, just being practical and letting me conserve my strength.

Later we ride hoverboards around the perimeter, learning to handle corners and curves at high speed as we practice turns. Blayne is faster than most of us as he handles the turns, and I watch him cruise past others repeatedly.

"Wow, that was awesome!" I tell him at one point as he

passes me from overhead in a very clever maneuver.

Blayne turns his face and merely nods, and I see the flash of his blue eyes, just before the underside of his hoverboard eclipses his face from my vantage point. And he speeds away.

When dinner hour comes, for most of it I am numb. I eat quietly in the cafeteria, tasting nothing, sitting alone, until Laronda and a few others join me, and honestly I don't even remember who's there, or what's in my mouth, that's how numb I am, thinking, thinking, even while they're telling me nice things and being all supportive.

All I can think of is, *how much longer till 8:00 PM?*

Meanwhile, I notice that other Candidates I don't even know are giving me looks today. Everywhere I glance in the cafeteria, people are starting at me, whispering. The alpha crowd bullies stare, and sarcastic laughter bursts out from their tables.

Claudia walks by our table and suddenly leans over and grins at me. "Have fun at eight o'clock tonight, Gwen-baby!" And then she moves away.

"Hey, lay off her!" Laronda calls out in her wake.

"It's okay." I reach out and touch Laronda's arm. "Don't worry about it."

And then I look down at my mostly untouched plate of spaghetti.

Afterwards we go hang out in the lounge area for about half an hour. Even then, everyone, it seems, is staring at me.

The whole Yellow Dorm Eight knows I am going to be punished tonight. What am I saying? The whole *Yellow Quadrant* knows—they all stood witness to it earlier today.

Which means that probably others know too, Gracie, my brothers. What must they be thinking? They must be going crazy, worried sick!

It's seven forty, and before heading out, I drop by the bathroom, where I stare in the mirror for a minute and look at myself—pale face, sunken cheeks, terrified eyes, sweaty tendrils of hair sticking out everywhere from my messy ponytail.

Get a grip, Gwen Lark! I tell myself, splashing cool water in my eyes. *Whatever it is, it couldn't be that bad. You are going to live through it, somehow. Breathe!*

I breathe, deeply. Then I get out of the bathroom and walk

through the lobby, to the outside doors, feeling everyone's eyes on me.

Logan Sangre is standing there, waiting for me.

He is quiet, intense, and his hazel eyes give me a jolt of badly needed warmth.

"Gwen!" he says, and places his steady hand on my arm. "I heard what happened—everything. I am going with you."

Chapter 21

Logan walks with me in the deepening twilight through the RQC compound, and in minutes I start to shiver, having once again forgotten to wear anything warm.

"Here," he says, taking off his windbreaker jacket and handing it to me. "Put this on."

"What about you?" I mumble.

"I'm not the one who's covered in goose bumps." He smiles at me. "Didn't your mother ever teach you to dress warm at night?"

I glance up at him, feeling a surge of warmth in my cheeks. I wrap his great big jacket around me and it covers me with sudden comfort. I inhale its pleasant scent of musky aftershave and something else that is uniquely *him*. "Thanks. I'll give it back when we're indoors."

He only nods.

And in minutes we're at the Arena Commons Building.

We enter through the glass doors into the outer mall-like area. There I note the time on one wall clock—it reads five minutes before eight.

The stadium is sparsely populated with Candidates. Occasional bursts of voices and laughter sounds from small clusters of teens walking by, or going to the track to run laps.

Some people are milling around the "food court" cafeteria.

Red, blue, green, yellow tokens everywhere. If I am not mistaken, some of those people are also staring at me.

Okay, what is it? Does everyone in the world know?

I pause walking and turn around. I blink.

There it is, the platform deck, in the back. It is about a hundred feet away, lit up brightly from the overhead electric lights, and it appears to be empty.

Logan watches me stand there, still shivering. I clutch the edges of his jacket around me with a white knuckled grip. "Gwen?" His voice is gentle. "You will be okay."

I take a very deep breath and then purse my lips and exhale. "Yeah," I say. "I know."

I start walking to the platform with determination.

As I approach, I remove Logan's jacket, and hand it back to him. "Thank you," I say, with a single glance behind me.

"No sweat," he says, receiving it from me, just as we reach the bottom scaffolding and the stairs to the deck that stands at least twelve feet above the floor. "Good luck!"

"Now, please go," I say, looking down at him, as I begin to climb the stairs.

"Are you sure?"

"Yes, I'm sure. I really want to be alone for this humiliation, whatever it is."

He nods, and I watch him from above, midway up the stairs, as he slowly backs away, still looking at me, then begins to walk back the way we came from.

I turn and climb the rest of the way to the deck.

Then I stand there, looking around at the panorama of the stadium arena.

It is eight o'clock and I am completely alone.

"Candidate Gwen Lark, you are on time," a disembodied voice says out of nowhere, and I start somewhat, looking around, and there is still no one there.

And then I realize the voice sounds slightly mechanical, because it's coming from a set of speakers at the base of the platform deck. There's a small crackle, but I recognize it as definitely *his*.

Aeson Kass.

I stare around nervously, then glance up to check the distant glass ceiling of the stadium, like a total idiot.

Then, it occurs to me to look to the upper level walkways. He is probably up there in one of their offices, sitting at an observation console. Of course, that has to be it—there are probably dozens of cameras trained on me right now, and on the whole stadium. . . .

Aeson's voice sounds again. "Your instructions are to step to the middle of the deck. There you will stand on your right foot and count to one hundred, slowly, *out loud.* Then you will switch and stand on your left foot and count to one hundred. Repeat this ten times. When you are done, you will descend to the arena floor, then go directly to the fifth level of this building, office 512, for your next instructions. Begin now."

My lips part, as I consider this, freezing for a moment in a kind of stupor.

"Okay . . ." I mutter. *This is not as bad as I thought it would be.*

I go to the middle and stand there on my right foot.

I try to keep my balance, my hands stretched out to my sides, as I begin counting loudly, "One, two, three, four, five. . . ."

Easier said than done. Yeah, I feel like an idiot, and I can see people down on the floor level below glancing at me as they pass by. But the worst part is, after I get to around fifty-count, my right foot starts to acquire the same fine muscle tremor that I got in Combat earlier today, so it's pure agony trying to stay upright, keep my other foot off the floor, and count at the same time.

Soon my arms are flailing.

I get to one hundred and desperately switch to my left foot. Begin counting again, "One, two, three, four, five. . . ."

Here, I find it suddenly hard to find and keep the new balance on the other leg, and so I wobble wildly, and start to hop on that foot just to keep myself standing.

First one-hundred rep pair is down, only nine more to go. Or is it ten more? Did he mean eleven total? Ugh!

I switch to my right foot. . . .

Then, things become very focused and very intense as I lose track of time, and pretty much everything else around me, as I focus on keeping the count and keeping my individual feet balanced, one at a time.

One second at a time. . . .

The world narrows in on me and there is only *agony* and *intensity* and *numbers.*

About twenty minutes later, with sweat pouring down my forehead, I am done.

My legs and feet are quaking under me, and I stand with both feet on the deck platform and just *breathe*.

Okay, what office did he tell me to go to afterwards? Is it number 512? My thoughts are swimming, as I climb down the scaffolding on legs that feel like limp noodles, and then look around again, glance up to the fifth level walkway. . . . It's somewhere up there.

I make my way to the building stairs, hoping to find an elevator instead. No such luck—it's probably somewhere nearby but I have no time to mess around looking, so I climb the nearest corkscrew staircase wearily, up each level, turn around on the landings, then up again.

On level five, I enter the walkway. The offices that line the perimeter of the building are all numbered. Some of the glass windows are lit, indicating someone's there, but most of them are dark for the evening, shades drawn. I read the numbers, striding along the walkway and occasionally glancing at the view of the great big arena space below. My fear of heights kicks in slightly, but only when I approach the outer railing, so I try not to look or get too close.

Finally, toward the end of the level, I see Office 512. The light is on, but the shades are drawn over the wide glass window.

I knock on the door . . . and hear his voice.

"Come in!"

I open the door and see a large classroom-sized space. It is a roomy, bright office, with several modern desks along one wall, covered with smart-tech consoles and computer screens, some split into four quadrants, and surveillance equipment, just as I suspected. It's a master control center.

There are several tall-backed task chairs and Aeson Kass sits in one of them, staring at one of the displays.

His back is turned to me, so all I see is the fall of his metallic hair against the muscular shoulders clad in the grey uniform. He is entering something at a console.

"Wait there, take a seat, and I will be with you shortly," he says without turning around, simply points with one finger behind him.

I glance, and there is a long fabric-upholstered sofa stretching along the other wall, and several chairs, surrounding in a semi-circle a long coffee table.

That's when I notice we are not alone. Someone else is sitting in the corner.

I blink in surprise because it's Blayne Dubois. He is sitting on the sofa, and his wheelchair is moved off to the side in the corner. In one of his hands there's an inert hoverboard, standing upright, its one end resting on the floor.

Blayne looks at me silently, and I would guess a bit sullenly. Or maybe not, I think he just looks resigned and very tired.

"Hi, Blayne . . ." I nod at him, and sit down on the other end of the long sofa. My expression is just as exhausted as his.

Yeah, it's been a long day. And it's not looking to end any time soon. *What is going on here?*

"Hey," he mumbles in reply.

Meanwhile I glance with nervous expectation at the Atlantean.

Aeson Kass turns to us in that same moment . . . and it's like a tangible blow strikes me suddenly in the chest.

As I meet his gaze directly, and have his full attention, I feel *seared* by an inexplicable force. He is looking at me—and now a crazy uncontrollable warmth rises in me, flooding me with a rush of electricity.

I look back at him and suddenly my head is burning—*I am burning. What is happening, holy lord!* My cheeks are on fire, and *I don't know what the hell is wrong with me.*

"So, Candidate Lark," Aeson says in a steady neutral voice, without seeming to notice my flood of color. "I see you've met Candidate Dubois. Good, it makes things easier."

I frown slightly. "Okay . . . is this—what about my— *disciplinary* action?"

For the first time I see Aeson's face take on a new, previously unseen expression. His brows rise slightly, and there's a shadow of something hovering about his lips. But the next instant it's gone, replaced by an impassive cold demeanor. "You found it insufficient? If the activity you've performed just now in the arena is not enough, then I can accommodate you with more. Would you like to go back on that platform and repeat?"

"Oh, no!"

Again he pauses, momentarily saying nothing, only looks at

me. His dark lapis-blue eyes appear to examine me closely. Is there a hint of sarcasm there? I swear, I have never seen him more *human* than he appears in this one moment.

But it is a brief instant, because he closes up once again, and becomes an unreadable mask.

"Your disciplinary action is done. It has served its purpose, primarily as an example to others, not to be stupid. I expect you have learned something from it—or not. But now you are here for a different reason."

"Oh?" I say, feeling an immediate wave of relief combined with anger that he called my actions stupid. Because of it—and fortunately for me—my crazy blush seems to recede. *Thank you, lord.* "What reason?"

"I need a Candidate as an assistant for a specific task. And though I am not convinced at all that you are the right one for this job, you have been recommended by two of your Instructors."

I stare at him. "Really?"

"Apparently both Nefir Mekei and Xelio Vekahat think you show some kind of promise."

Okay, now I am amazed. . . . Nefir, maybe, since I talk so much in Culture class. But Xelio?

While I sit pondering this, Aeson gets up from his chair and approaches the sofa. He stands before Blayne and me, looking down at us both. But again he speaks to me.

"Lark, you are going to be helping Dubois train on the hoverboard for Combat. Basically he needs a spotter to hold the board and to spar with, in a specialized manner—until he has grasped the ability to throw punches and move in specialized Forms for those with limited mobility. All this needs to happen at the same time as he holds the board in a near vertical position to support himself upright."

"What? Why?" Blayne says, at the same time as I say, "Why me?"

"Because we want you to do the best you can during Qualification, Candidate Dubois. *I* want you to do well. You show some extraordinary promise in certain areas." Aeson takes a step toward Blayne and offers him one hand. "Take the board and hold it before you at a fifteen-degree steep angle away from vertical, like this."

And he pulls the board forward to demonstrate, at the same time as he takes Blayne's hand and pulls him up easily from his seated position, so that the boy falls forward onto the board, and lies on his stomach, wrapping his arms around the board on both sides to support himself.

Aeson hums a few short staccato notes in a rich deep voice that sends strange disturbing resonances through me, and the board comes alive. It hovers in the unusual near-vertical position.

I stand watching, mesmerized.

Aeson comes around Blayne from the back and balances the length of the boy's body against the activated board, arranging his torso and limbs in certain ways.

"How much muscle strength does your lower body have?" he asks Blayne, examining the lines of his posture, and taps the back of his calves with his fingers. "Can you feel that?"

"Yeah, I felt that," Blayne mumbles. "I can press the board with my thighs, but anything below the knees, not so much."

"All right." Aeson now turns to me and beckons me with one hand. "Lark, stand here and hold the board like this."

I get up, and do as I am told. We stand in a strange grouping around Blayne and his hoverboard, and eventually I understand what is expected of me.

"The board is already hovering, but it will wobble strongly from the impact of sparring blows," Aeson tells me, with a single brief glance in my direction. "And until he has figured out how to hold on and keep it perfectly steady and immobilized, he will slip off and end up on the floor. Your task is to make sure the board stays put, for now."

"Wow," I say. "Okay, I think I got it. It's kind of like holding a punching bag in place for someone."

"Good analogy." Aeson nods as I place my fingers on both the edges of the board below Blayne's waist level, as instructed.

"Now what?" Blayne asks.

"Now I am going to show you limited mobility Er-Du Forms. Knowing the LM Forms might mean the difference between life and death for you during the Semi-Finals and hopefully Finals, if you advance."

Saying this, Aeson comes around Blayne's front, and faces

the board, while I stand holding it and slightly off to the side. His body leans in, and he takes a variation of the Floating Swan, but intimately up-close to the board and Blayne.

"Look at me," Aeson says to Blayne, and I watch the super-focused expression on the Atlantean's face that has now become hard and merciless. "I am going to strike at you from both directions, and also from below and above. Your first lesson is to observe and memorize the possible moves that can be made in this position."

"Okay," Blayne whispers, with a frown of concentration.

Aeson's dark blue eyes flash at me. "Lark—get ready, hold the board tight, and do not move unless instructed, or you *will* get hurt."

And then he moves, throwing abbreviated controlled punches like lightning.

Chapter 22

Half an hour later, we are done. Blayne has learned several sparring counter-moves, and I have learned that standing immobile while holding in place a hovering object is hard work, especially when two opponents rain blows at each other inches away from me.

The hoverboard is "springy" when activated, and keeping it still and upright is not too different from trying to keep a highly buoyant object angled oddly while submerged underwater—it fights you every second and requires force and effort to keep it under.

"Good work, both of you," Aeson says, stepping back, and I see the finest sheen of sweat on his forehead. *So,* I think, *Command Pilot Kass is human after all.*

For some reason, my gaze unconsciously slides to the side of his head that I remember being hurt during the shuttle incident, the place where so much blood covered his golden hair. I glance away quickly, but not before he notices me looking there. Or, at least, I think he does?

Oh, crap. . . . No one is supposed to know the exact location of his injury. No one *would* know unless they witnessed it. What if he now suspects me?

I try not to think in that direction. Instead I pretend to look around at the computer center consoles while I wait for what comes next.

Blayne is pouring sweat and his arms are trembling from the effort of alternately gripping the board and using his arms for sparring. He makes it to his wheelchair with the help of the hoverboard and sits down, hard.

There's a brief pause.

Then I ruin things and open my big mouth. "Why don't you

let Blayne borrow the hoverboard all the time? He could get around so much easier if he had it—"

My words fade into silence.

Aeson is using a small towel to wipe his forehead, and now he turns to me with a hard look. "Your suggestion is noted. Unfortunately it is out of the question."

"But why? It would be such a good thing!"

"Candidate Lark, are you questioning me?"

I gulp. And then, yeah, lord help me, I say it. "Yes . . . because there's just no good reason why you should say no! I mean, it makes no sense why it shouldn't be allowed, just a single hoverboard—"

Aeson stares at me, drops the towel on the nearest surface, then takes a step toward me. "Are you always like this?"

"Oh, yeah, she is," Blayne says, shaking his head in mild disgust. He pushes hair from his face and looks down wearily.

I whirl around, to stare at him with a sudden rise of anger. "Oh, yeah? Well, considering I'm doing this for *you*, the least thing you could do is shut up!"

"Oh, jeez. . . ." Blayne puts his head down and passes his hand through his hair. "Please don't do me any favors!"

"I am sorry," I say. I take a deep breath and let the sudden "stupid" deflate out of me. I don't know what it is about this whole Blayne situation that makes me crazy-stupid impulsive and makes me want to meddle and fix things that are not my business and that are beyond my control anyway.

"Look," I add, "I really am sorry, and I know it is not my business to press, but it seems to me the *logical* thing to do, a perfect solution to a *logistics problem*, and maybe that's why it drives me nuts to see a perfectly good tool not being used in a capacity where it can truly help—"

As I speak, Aeson looks at me in what can only be mild amazement. It occurs to me, he is not used to anyone *contradicting* him often, if ever.

Finally he cranes his neck to the side slightly and interrupts my tirade. "*Enough.* You have expressed yourself, and because you are a civilian and don't know better, I have allowed it. And now, you will no longer speak on this subject unless you would like to be disciplined again. Is that understood, Candidate?"

I nod. "Yes."

Aeson's lips curve into a shadow-smile. It is dark, sarcastic, confident, and very scary. "Good. Now, because you *are* in an unusual position of not knowing better, and you've indeed asked me a logical question, I am going to answer you. But only this once." He pauses, examining me, my minute reaction.

I remain still, not giving him any excuse.

"The main reason I cannot permit hoverboard use outside the classrooms and training halls is because we cannot afford to let even one orichalcum-based piece of technology to go missing and fall into the wrong hands, and potentially be stolen from this compound. Yes, I know Candidate Dubois is responsible and would never intentionally misplace or misuse the hoverboard. However, he sleeps at night, and cannot be vigilant around the clock."

I glance at Blayne and he is listening carefully.

"The second reason," Aeson says, "is that there can be no favoritism displayed in the process of Qualification. If I let Dubois fly around on this thing, even with his legitimate need-based reason, I would set a precedent. Other Candidates would make rightful demands to be allowed equal use of hoverboards, and that's something we cannot do. There are other reasons, but these are the main ones, and I hope—Candidate Lark—that I have *satisfied* your need for a *logical* explanation."

He grows silent, and watches me again.

"Yes, thank you," I say in a subdued voice.

"Good. Now, you are both dismissed for today, and I will see you both back here tomorrow night, at the beginning of your Homework Hour. We'll work from eight to eight thirty. In the meantime, you are not to speak of the nature of this activity to anyone, because again, I want no Candidate speculation about preferential treatment. If asked, you may say you are meeting with Instructors to get help with your homework."

Blayne nods, and starts pushing his wheelchair to the door. "Thanks for your time, Mr. Kass," he says.

"Command Pilot Kass is the proper address," Aeson tells Blayne, but without reproach.

"Sorry, Command Pilot Kass," Blayne mutters. "Thank you

for all the work you put in with me. I am sorry to be taking up your time—"

"No problem." And Aeson nods at him curtly with what is nearly a smile.

I see that brief fleeting smile and it is remarkable what a difference it makes to the hard angular lines of Aeson's face. No sarcasm, no provocation, just *openness*. Like a burst of sunlight, just as quickly hidden by the usual cloud-mass. . . .

"If it's permitted to ask," I say, lingering at the door after holding it open for Blayne despite his raised brows. "Why am I here? Why not someone else more suitable to help him train? There are plenty of big strong guys in our dorm who would do a better job."

Aeson turns to me once, before returning to his observation consoles and plural surveillance screens. He is tall, pale, reserved, and there are definite signs of exhaustion on his face. It's the only hint that he'd been seriously injured just recently, and may still be unwell—or at least not one hundred percent, healthwise.

"I could tell you it's to keep an eye on you, Lark," he says in a bland voice. "But really, there isn't a particularly exciting explanation. Don't flatter yourself, you're not that interesting. The simple fact is, you happened to be here already, and you are sufficiently up to the task. As your Instructors say, you might have something—some quirk, some potential. So now, by all means, *show me* you are not merely an unremarkable teenager with an inability to keep her mouth shut, and with poor impulse control. Prove me wrong. Now—dismissed."

And he turns away, leaving me to stare in outrage.

S tunned at his put-down, I exit silently and close the office door behind me. Blayne is nowhere in sight on the walkway. I suspect he found the elevator.

It's getting late, about an hour before final curfew, and I still need to run a few laps for homework.

Numb and beyond exhausted, I frown and think, and mull over what has just happened, as I walk down to the arena level. Crazy events of the last few days, one after another, have taken their toll on me.

And now—now I am so angry. . . .

He thinks I am *unremarkable*, with *poor impulse control*.

I am not that interesting.

For some weird reason, *this*, more than anything, really stings. I take it so personally that it becomes the worst thing anyone has ever told me. Worse than being bullied and persecuted by the alpha crowd, called disparaging names, being kicked and pinched and having my belongings damaged. Worse—because deep inside, my self-worth hinges on being considered *smart* and *capable* and *outstanding*. I can endure being a clumsy laughingstock, but not having my mental achievements put into question.

Let me confess—teachers, adults who know me, have always gushed over my intelligence, my aptitude for leaning, my level of knowledge and critical thinking skills.

I'm an honor student, for the love of Pete! No one, no one has ever called me *unremarkable*.

I seethe, as I get to the running track, and the anger acts as the perfect seasoning to my bitter running mood.

I take off in one of the lanes, and hardly anyone else is there. Maybe two guys and a straggler girl finish up their jogging laps.

Breathing hard in just a few seconds, I pound the floor of the track, feeling my blisters sting with each awkward step.

Another minute and I am lightheaded, as I stop and walk periodically, then run again, dragging myself forcibly forward and forward.

If only I could escape the thing inside me, the new sense of insecurity, of sudden disorientation.

But all I can do is run.

And then I get back to Yellow Dorm Eight, a few minutes before 10:00 PM curfew, and barely manage to crawl into bed, before lights out.

At least I get to avoid everyone's questions.

The next morning I am so sickly-tired and emotionally wrung-out, I can barely get out of bed. The 7:00 AM claxon alarm pounds in my head, and I just lie there while the girls' dormitory comes awake.

"Hey, are you okay there, Gwen?" Laronda leans over me, still in her sleeping shirt, holding her dried-overnight underwear and clothes in a bunch. "What happened yesterday? That awful punishment, what was it? Did you get hurt? What did he do to you?"

I squint and blink up at her and at the overhead light that's shining directly in my eyes. How stupid was that, picking a bed right underneath the overhead light? Did I really think I'd have time for reading in bed?

Disgusted at myself, I moan and mutter something.

"Hey, seriously, girl, are you unwell?" Laronda bends forward over me and puts the back of her hand over my forehead to check for temperature.

"Nah, thanks, I'm okay, just seriously dead after yesterday."

"What happened?"

I turn my head and there's Hasmik, sitting on her bed next to me. She looks tired and unwell, but at least she's not green.

"Gwen," Hasmik says. "Gwen, *akhchik jan*, thank you so much for trying to help me yesterday. I am so sorry you got in trouble. So sorry!" And she leans forward and takes my arm and squeezes it gently.

I smile weakly at her, then make the effort to sit up.

"So, tell us! What happened?" Laronda is relentless.

"I had to stand balanced on one foot and then the other for about half an hour, like an idiot. It was painful hell. And then I had to go up to their offices, was chewed out, and dismissed. Then I stopped by an Instructor's office for help with homework. That's about it. It just seems like it took forever and I did my running homework at the arena track."

"Wow." Laronda shakes her head at me in a motherly fashion. "Poor baby. So how was he? The evil Atlantean prick, whassisname?"

"Aeson Kass." I shrug, and feel a rush of anger return at the thought of him. "Pardon me—*Command Pilot* Aeson Kass," I mock.

"Did he say anything about Disqualification?"

I consider what I should or should not say at this point. "He basically told me to keep my mouth shut and behave in the future. And you're right, he *is* a jerk."

"He's kind of good looking . . ." Hasmik says suddenly. "A

cute jerk."

I look up. "Oh, please. He's just full of himself."

And on that note I pick up my clothes and head to the bathroom.

This is day five of Qualification, and first period Agility class finds me in a rotten mood, a combination of exhaustion, muddled anger, and general nerves. Blayne Dubois ignores me completely as he does his usual hoverboard maneuvers away from the rest of us. It's as if last night never happened.

I climb the different levels of scaffolding and barely make it across a few rungs of the parallel bars before slipping off, and yeah, yet another stinking demerit is mine.

However, a minor moment of triumph happens during our running laps. Oalla increases the number of our laps yet again, from eleven to thirteen. And for the first time, as I stumble to the finish line, I am *not* last. Somehow I manage to pass both Janice Quinn and Jack Carell, and frankly I don't know which one of them gets the demerit.

Wow! It's a strange and amazing small victory. I think Oalla gives me an interesting look as for once she passes me by to scan another person's token.

As a result I feel somewhat better as I head to the next period.

Which is Atlantis Tech, and it starts out really boring. Mr. Warrenson goes on and on about the importance of being *in tune* when making the musical tone commands. He also tests us for pitch perception, using a larger version of the Atlantean sound gadget that was used during Preliminary Qualification back at school to make us repeat the "eeee" sounds. This thing takes up half the desk, and looks like a strange malformed lump of silvery rock on the surface of which occasional colored lights come to life.

"One at a time, please," Mr. Warrenson says. "Come up here and place your fingers on the surface, right here. Then you will sing a scale exactly like the sound unit does. Listen, then repeat!"

We go up there, one by one, and when it's done, Mr. Warrenson tells us that although we can all replicate the sounds very well, only three of us in this class have *perfect pitch*, according to the device.

"Candidates whose names I call, have earned a credit today.

Come up here and I will scan your tokens—Antwon Marks, Claudia Grito, and Gwenevere Lark."

Okay, I admit I did not see that one coming. Especially considering that when it was my turn up there, I barely squeaked out the notes. . . .

But it makes me feel good! Yet another good thing today, to partially make up for all the yuck of the previous days. Not only did I not get a demerit, but a credit—my first one!

I am also majorly psyched on Antwon's behalf—he totally deserves it with his amazing honey voice, not to mention he's a great guy. On the other hand, seeing Claudia swagger up there to get her token scanned with a credit puts a minor damper on things. . . .

Soon, it's lunch hour, and as I walk through the Common Area lounge, my confidence almost back, I see Claudia, Olivia, and Ashley watching me. They balance sitting on sofa backs, legs dangling, and Claudia's piercings glitter metallic as she taps the sofa with the fingers of one hand. Her upper arms are sleek and well-toned and her shoulders look tough in that black tank top she's wearing.

"So, Gwen-baby. Perfect pitch, eh?" she drawls mockingly, craning her neck slightly to cut me down with her tough street look. "How about you and me sing it out, later tonight, to see who's really *perfect?*"

I stop and look at her. "What?"

"What? What? Hard of hearing? I thought you had perfect pitch."

I shake my head, not sure how to respond.

"Cat's got your tongue too?" Claudia is really laughing now, and Ashley and Olivia have their hands up over their mouths in hard, mean giggles.

"She's obviously deaf and dumb, chicas. That stupid Atlantis audio device really screwed up when it picked her. I bet she mewls when she sings."

And Claudia makes cat meowing noises at me. Ashley and Olivia pick it up and echo her.

I stand there, genuinely dumbstruck and the cold sickness is back in my gut, twisting like a knife.

A few other hashtaggers show up, including Wade and Derek. "What's up, what's happening here?" Derek says, walking up from behind me. He's sweaty from class and his sharp scent mixed up with aftershave seems to surround me. I cringe away involuntarily, and he notices it and moves in even closer with his big muscular arms, so that I have to step away, which brings me unfortunately closer to Claudia.

"What's happening," Claudia says, "is that our girlfriend Gwen here doesn't want to sing with me tonight. See, we have perfect pitch, both of us, and we're gonna have us a sing-off."

"No, we aren't . . ." I mutter.

"Oh, yeah?" Derek says. "You're going to sing, Gwen-baby. Because our Claudia says so. And because I say so. You got that?" And he leans in my face with his hard unblinking glare.

"I'm not doing anything," I say softly. "Get away from me."

They exchange glances, and then Derek grins at me, baring his teeth. "You're going to sing, or else. Seven o'clock, outside this dorm, in the back. *Be there.*"

"I don't think so," I say, looking up at him.

"What did you say?"

I feel like I am suddenly short of breath, as they are all closing in on me. Why is there no one else in the lounge when you need it? Where is everyone?

"I said—I cannot sing . . ." I say suddenly. "The audio machine made a mistake. It was an accident."

"Nooooo," Claudia drawls. "You can't take it back, Gwen-baby."

I take a deep breath, because if I don't I will pass out. "You know what?" I say.

"What?"

"Screw you!" And with those words I shove past them all and run up the stairs to the third floor girls' dormitory. I find that I am shaking.

Because of this crappy incident, I end up skipping lunch. I sit on my bed, hunched over, rubbing my arms with both hands, and I think.

Neither Laronda nor Hasmik are around, and there are hardly any other girls on the dorm floor now, since most have gone to the cafeteria.

Oh, how I wish the other Gees were here now! Where are my brothers? Where's Gracie? For that matter, haven't they heard about the awful "disciplinary action" against me yesterday, and why haven't they tried to see me, to make sure I'm okay?

There's no way I am going to sing.

No one, not even the bullies can make me do it. Especially not to prove a stupid point.

But—what's going to happen to me if I don't?

I plop down on the cot and lie there, on top of the covers, with the overhead light glaring directly into my eyes.

The alarm claxons go off indicating time for the 1:00 PM class. It's time for Combat.

Somehow I drag myself downstairs to the basement Training Hall.

The Instructors are not there yet. But, just my luck, all the alpha crowd a-holes are here, waiting for me. Quickly I walk as far away as possible, to join another grouping of Candidates, with Jai and Tremaine and Jack Carell. No one else I know is in this class today.

"Hey, Gwen!" Jai gives me the usual white-toothed grin, and then remembers. "Hey, so how was yesterday, the punishment? Did you get in trouble big-time, or what?"

"Not that bad," I mumble, and tell them the abbreviated version.

"Okay, so it could have been worse," Tremaine says. "At least that Phoebos guy didn't put you in lockup or something."

"Yeah." I roll my eyes.

In that moment, Oalla Keigeri and another Atlantean girl come into the gym hall.

The new Atlantean girl, it occurs to me, is somehow familiar. I recognize her and her super-short, straight, metallic hair. She was there, the night of the shuttle accident, up on that upper level walkway in the Arena Commons building, walking next to Xelio and a whole bunch of other Atlanteans while we Candies were all having dinner at the "food court" cafeteria below.

This girl is taller than Oalla and more bulky-muscular, with a powerful and at the same time curvaceous physique. Her skin is golden-brown, a mid-tone range between that of the fair-skinned Oalla and the very dark Keruvat who is absent from our class today. Her eyes are a pale hazel color, and she has amazing sensuous lips that are full and naturally pouty-sexy. She wears the same grey uniform as the other Instructors, but her armband is green.

"Attention, Candidates!" Oalla claps her hands and blows her whistle. "Line up!"

We do as we're told, forming the two opposing rows.

I notice that the person standing directly across from me as my sparring partner for this class is none other than Claudia Grito.

Oh, great. . . .

Meanwhile Oalla turns to the other Atlantean girl and nods.

"Good afternoon, Candidates!" the short-haired girl says in a deeper sonorous voice. "I am Erita Qwas, and I am going to be working with you today in place of Keruvat Ruo who is teaching Combat at Green Dorm Three."

"All right!" Oalla commands us. "First, we do warm-ups!"

Fifteen arduous minutes of hell later, we are lined up and ready for Forms.

"Today, you will practice actual full-contact sparring Forms which require you to defend yourself and attack your opponent. This means that you will be striking each other *for real* and not by accident," Oalla says in a hard voice, pacing in the middle space between our rows, followed by Erita.

"You will begin with the Floating Swan," Erita responds. "And then you and your sparring partner will take turns with the opposite combination of Second Form, Striking Snake, to attack, and Seventh Form, Running Scarab, to defend yourself."

Oh, no, I think, *Please, lord, no, no! Claudia and I are going to be beating up on each other!*

"Row to my right, show me Striking Snake! Row to my left, show me Running Scarab!" Erita exclaims loudly. "First, watch, then follow our lead!"

And with those words the short-haired Atlantean demonstrates. She and Oalla assume the graceful starting position of Floating Swan, and then Erita attacks. The Snake strikes repeatedly, focused and relentless, while Oalla's Scarab defense involves arms being placed strategically to block each strike, echoing the rapid multi-arm movements of the ancient beetle rolling a ball of dung. They repeat the Form exchange slowly three times, and then speed up. . . . Oh, they're lightning-fast!

First, Erita is the Snake, and then Oalla. They switch several times, and each of them is the Scarab to the other's Snake.

"Candidates, your turn! Rows, approach each other, begin sparring!"

And as I stand in the Floating Swan, before I even have a moment to collect myself, Claudia steps forward with a sneer and strikes me. . . .

Her blow lands, hard, against the side of my face on the left. I feel a blinding pain, and stagger back, but there is no time to recover, because Claudia strikes again.

This time I have enough presence left to recall the defensive hand motions that constitute the Running Scarab. I block Claudia's strike with the back of my arm, and quickly extend my other arm to push her away. My face is still burning with pain while my eyes begin to sting with gathering tears. . . .

"Switch!" Erita yells. "Snake becomes Scarab!"

Which means I am now the attacker. I assume the Striking Snake but my first blow falls on open air, as Claudia dodges my arm without even bothering to counter with her own. "Come on, Gwen-baby . . ." she whispers. "Are you going to cry now?"

In answer I strike with my other arm and quickly extend the hand into the snake. It lands on Claudia's collarbone, and I feel the thud and her cry of pain as she misses the opportunity to block me.

"Feels good?" I say with a sudden crazy little smile. And then I strike again.

What in the world is happening to me? I feel an unexpected immense rush of energy driven by anger. And I no longer care about being afraid.

"Switch!" Oalla cries.

This time Claudia has a grim terrible look on her face. She purses her lips as she strikes at me.

But I am ready for her. There is something that suddenly *clicked into place* in my mind, and I can see the logical relationship between the Snake and the Scarab, how one *fits* into the other. These two Forms, they are mates of each other—like dark and light, yin and yang, melody and harmony.

And suddenly it is so easy and clear, how I need to move.

My defending Scarab is effortless, and Claudia does not come close to touching me even once. I, on the other hand, have hit her on the other side of her neck, this time above the collarbone, then bruised her shoulder, and even her right cheek. . . .

This is unbelievable.

I've just beaten up Claudia Grito.

Chapter 23

Combat class is over and I am breathing hard, while an unbelievable rush of adrenaline and elation is still surging through me.

Claudia, meanwhile, hisses, "You are dead now, bitch." She then turns her back on me and quickly races upstairs past the other Candidates going up.

Okay, that was—I have no words for what just happened.

As I start to walk to the doors, Oalla passes me and nods. "Nice job today, Candidate. Your sparring is good."

And behind her, Erita gives me a faint crooked smile. She then passes a handheld gadget over my token and says, "Credit."

I get out of the Training Hall, and honestly, I don't even know if there's a floor under my feet, or how I'm putting one foot ahead of the other—that's how incredible I feel. For the first time after a *gym class* I am moving with a powerful buzz of energy as opposed to being utterly defeated in body and spirit.

I got a credit in Combat. No. Effing. Way.

The buzz carries me upstairs, but as it wears off slightly, the side of my face starts to make itself felt. I wipe the sweat off my forehead and touch the side of my cheek where Claudia managed to get in one blow and yeah, that's going to bruise, if it hadn't already. I bet I'll look like Gordie now, with my matching shiner.

Last class for the day is Culture. I meet up with Dawn and Laronda and we grab the seats in the second row.

"Wow, look at your face," Laronda says, examining me. "How did that happen?"

"Combat. Claudia," I answer with choppy words, but I am smiling.

"What? Did she hit you? What a b—"

"Not as much as I hit her," I admit, grinning now.

"*What?* Way to go, girlfriend!" Laronda claps, and looks at Dawn.

Dawn raises one brow and calmly nods her approval.

"It appears, an ice rink opened up somewhere in hell, because *I can spar*," I announce. "And I got a credit for the day's class!"

Laronda punches me on the arm and then does a seat dance by wiggling in her desk chair.

I let out a minor squeal and punch back, then lean over and punch Dawn who cringes away mockingly to retain her dignity. Soon we get so loud that some of the other Candidates start glancing our way.

We are interrupted by the arrival of the Instructor.

Nefir Mekei brings a sudden damper to settle over the good mood. Because today's lecture is about the importance of family ties in Atlantis. I don't remember much of what he says, because suddenly I'm thinking of my parents back home, and so it seems does everyone else. We sit and remember the families and relatives left behind. Grim reality washes over us. In less than twenty months, they are all going to be dead. . . .

Everything in the world that we know will be no longer.

"On Atlantis, parents and children have strong traditional ties," Nefir tells us, pacing before the desk. "We honor and respect the older generations, gladly defer to their wisdom and experience. But in turn, the power of society lies with the young."

"Is this why you only take teenagers for Qualification?" someone asks. "How come the strict age restrictions of twelve through nineteen?"

"Yes, a good question." Nefir turns to the speaker, an older girl. "We can only make room for the young who will have time to adjust and contribute to the society. And there are other reasons that you will come to understand later."

I raise my hand. "What about the older adults here on Earth who have proven themselves to be valuable, even indispensable? I'm talking about brilliant scientists, engineers, talented artists, or others who have other worthy things to offer. Why don't you take any of them? It seems illogical to me that you would not make exceptions for them."

"I fully understand your reasoning," Nefir says softly, turning his serpentine gaze upon me. "But unfortunately I cannot give you a good answer now. It is a complex thing and it has to do with certain aspects of our society and the real means at our disposal. Suffice it to say, if we could do it, we would take your adults, as many as possible. But we simply cannot. Nor would they be able to fit in sufficiently well, or integrate into Atlantis."

Okay, that's one mysterious and vague reply, I think.

"One thing I can tell you," Nefir continues, turning away from me and addressing the class in general. "We start on our life journeys very young in Atlantis. For example, children commit to the Fleet at the age of seven. Other professions require similar early commitments. It is a rare teenager who is not yet apprenticed in some field."

Wow, I think. That explains the highly skilled and advanced Atlantean Instructors and Pilots who are hardly older than our own age.

"What about social stuff?" a boy asks with a smirk. "Do you guys have a social life? Like, dating, messing around, and so on? Do you have love and romance and marriage?"

"Obviously there's procreation . . ." another guy in the back mutters, and a wave of nervous laughter passes over the classroom.

"Yes," Nefir says, and his expression lightens somewhat. "Yes, we do. Bonds of love between individuals result in sanctioned unions, similar to your own marriage. Children are born and families grow to prominence. In fact, some families— including the Imperial Family Kassiopei, the oldest one in our recorded history, and a few others from Poseidon—are so ancient that they are said to have roots in the original colony of Atlantis."

"Okay," the boy persists. "But how young do you have to be to begin to date, or get in a union, or whatever?"

"It depends. Some begin what you call 'dating' at sixteen, others later. A few, earlier. However, we do not encourage intimate relations before true physical and emotional maturity."

I raise my hand.

"Yes, Gwen Lark?"

"What determines maturity?"

Nefir suddenly smiles at me. "An excellent question as usual, Candidate. We prefer to consider each individual and their situation on a case-by-case basis."

After class is over, we head down to eat dinner. I am still flying high after my successful day, and according to Laronda my bruised cheek is already turning bluish.

"Heh, badge of honor," Dawn says.

I nod and cannot help grinning.

Before we make it to the cafeteria, which smells like garlic and French fries, I see a familiar face in the lounge.

There's my sister Gracie, sitting in a well-padded chair with her feet up, and looking like a mixture of "determined" and "a little lost." She's wearing her black sequined sweater and dramatic dark mascara. Her token blazes red in high contrast.

"Gwen!" she cries, and waves to me nervously.

"Oh, lord, Gracie! Where have you been?" I exclaim, approaching her in a hurry. "I've been looking for you for days, what happened? How are you? Everything okay?"

But Gracie stares at my bruised cheek. "Yeah, I guess. . . . But oh no, what's that on your face?"

I tell her about Combat. "Just like Gordie, I've got a shiner that matches his own—have you seen his?" I say with a smile, running my fingers through her dirty-blond hair to fix a few loose tendrils around her ear.

She cringes away from me initially. "Hey! Stop fussing like Mom." And then her face takes on a familiar frown as she remembers. . . .

"Sorry," I say, letting my hand fall. But I am still smiling.

We stare at each other, and it's amazing, but my little sister appears almost grown up, with her tired pale face and serious focused look.

"So tell me, how are your classes?" I ask, when I really want to be asking, *Have you been hanging out with that guy Daniel all this time?*

And then, seeing Dawn, Hasmik, and Laronda waving from the cafeteria doors, I add, "By the way, let's head in to grab some food, okay? I skipped lunch, so I'm starving."

Gracie nods, and starts telling me all about their sword fighting Combat class and the weird amazing multiple swords and knives of different shapes and lengths they have over there, as we go in to the cafeteria together.

We occupy a table in the corner, away from the loud alpha crowd tables in the middle of the room.

Today they're serving hot sandwiches. Dawn goes up to the food server and asks for a special plate piled high with just cheesy fries, for all of us to share.

"Ooh, yum-m-m!" Gracie reaches for a very long fry and suddenly points it at me in what looks like a blade weapon position, before reversing and bringing it up to her mouth.

"Look at you!" I say, and my lips curve upward.

"Red Quadrant—we're the warriors!" Gracie announces proudly.

"I can totally see that." Dawn chews her own fry and dips it in ketchup. "And ooh, look, blood."

Gracie starts to giggle and then grows serious. "I really should be eating over at my own Red Dorm, but I suppose it's okay this once," she clarifies. "Did I mention, we're supposed to have strong allegiance to our own Quadrant, and not really associate with others—"

"Yeah, I think you Reds mentioned it before." I nod, lifting my glass of milk to wash down the French fry taste in my mouth. "Seriously, what's all that about? How come no one here in Yellow really makes a big fuss about Candies socializing with other Quadrants?"

Gracie shrugs. And then she remembers something else. "Oh, Gwen! What happened to you yesterday? I heard—Logan said you got punished by that awful scary Atlantean dude who's in charge of everything—he didn't hurt you, did he? I mean, that was you, right?"

"Yeah, that was me." I shrug, and tell her the same abbreviated version of the disciplinary action.

"Your sister got in trouble—she try—she help me, and I'm so sorry," Hasmik says to Gracie with an anxious look, reaching with her hand to pat me on the arm.

"It's over, don't worry about it," I tell her, and change the subject. "So, what else did Logan say? Any other meaningful news?"

Gracie takes another French fry and pokes it into a puddle of ketchup. "They say—" she looks up at me—"I mean, some guys in

Red say that there is good reason to think that the awful shuttle explosion thing was caused by this scary terrorist group called Terra Patria. . . ."

"Oh, yeah?" I glance up at her. I recall that Terra Patria is one of the many fringe groups that had emerged during the early days of this whole asteroid and Atlantis end-of-the-world fiasco. It is strongly anti-Atlantean and has claimed responsibility for quite a few incidents over the past months. Terra Patria is a dangerous mix of home-grown extremists and desperate crazies. Or so we've been told in the media. One thing's for sure, neither the President nor Congress approves of their actions.

"Terra Patria?" Laronda says. "Aren't those guys total loonies?"

"They blow up buildings and vans rigged with explosives, wherever Atlanteans may happen to show up," Dawn adds. "So, yeah. Dangerous hate group."

Gracie glances at Dawn. "Well, maybe they kind of have a good reason for hating? I mean, we're Earth natives, we were here first. And these strangers arrived out of nowhere from the stars, claiming to be ancient Earthlings too, and supposedly they can save us from the asteroid—"

"Why does everyone always think they're the first people at any given place?" Dawn shrugs in minor disgust. "There's always someone who's more *native* than you. It's just how it is."

"How can you say that?" Gracie exclaims. "I mean, obviously people of Earth have more rights to this planet than some unknown strangers! Who can argue that we are real Vermonters or Pennsylvanians or New Yorkers, and not some space-faring creepy *Goldilocks*—"

"Gracie!" I say. "Since when do you use that word, Goldilocks? It's kind of racist."

"I can use it if I want to! I'm an Earth native and proud of it!"

"If you want to talk about being native," Dawn says, "I'm Native. Member of the Oneida Nation, in New York. That goes for all the American Indian Nations—we've been here way before most any of you guys arrived, white, black, polka-dot, whatever. Sure, we're Natives of the land, but we share it with you now."

"Wow, I didn't know you're Native American," I say. "That's really cool!"

"Yeah, whatever." Dawn again shrugs. "My point is, Terra Patria is dangerous, and their extremist ideas mostly suck."

"Not to mention, it's such bad timing, if they're responsible for the shuttle explosion," Laronda adds. "Not only did they kill innocent people in that shuttle and achieved nothing, they also got this whole RQC under suspicion. The other day the Correctors searched our dorm, and who knows what they did or didn't find?"

Gracie glances at Laronda, and I can tell my sister is disturbed, by the way she blinks a few times nervously. "They searched my dorm too . . . all the Red Quadrant dorms, when we were in that horrible mass Combat class in the Arena Commons building."

"So, did they find anything?" I say.

"I've no idea. . . ." Gracie looks at her plate, picks up the remaining half of her roast beef sandwich and bites in.

I wonder what's going through that head of hers.

"I guess we'll find out soon enough." Laronda picks at her straw and slurps the dregs of ice on the bottom of her soda glass.

It's a quarter before 8:00 PM. We've sat around, up on our dormitory third floor, chatting on our beds, but now I say bye to the others and walk with Gracie downstairs. While Gracie heads back to her dorm in the chill evening, I go in the opposite direction toward the AC building to keep my secret appointment with Aeson Kass.

I tell the girls I have running homework to do as usual, and hope to see Logan at the big arena track. Both parts are true, and I really do hope to run into Logan eventually, so it makes my story more plausible.

When I reach the Arena Commons and make my way upstairs to level five, and knock on the door of Office 512, there's no answer. The shades are drawn over the large glass widow but there is no light. No one seems to be there.

I check the closest huge wall clock in the arena below, and according to it I appear to be seven minutes early. Okay. . . .

I mill around for another minute, stare at the dizzying panorama of the stadium, at the small figures of Candidates moving around below.

It occurs to me to try the door handle. It opens at my touch, and I peek inside, into the twilight darkness.

Should I be doing this? I think for a moment. *But hey, the door was open, not my fault.*

Oh, yeah.

I blink, and step inside, and immediately see the lights of the multiple computer active display screens over at the observation center. There's a soft hum of cooling fans and machinery, and the displays are live-streaming various scenes and images, so that the room is faintly lit because of it, with flickering light and shadows moving across the nearest walls.

No one's there, and I have a sinking feeling I probably shouldn't be here by myself, but what the heck.

I approach and take a peek, leaning forward in the half-light. The closest displays, split into quadrants, show the compound, various sections of it. I see the airfield in one. . . . So, they repaired the surveillance cameras in that section, I realize with a jolt in my gut. Either that, or they were never actually damaged in the blast as Logan originally claimed.

I glance over, and other displays show media footage, various news channels from the outside, feeding current events. The sound is off, but the images of burning, looting, police in riot gear, are overwhelming. And the running marquees list locations and events in a perpetual scroll of shame.

I put my hands to my mouth as I see a huge explosion take apart a whole section of a skyscraper in some urban center.

While we've been safely ensconced in the artificial cocoon of the RQC for these past five days, things have gotten really bad out there.

I let out a shuddering breath and continue taking in the various news feeds, local and international. There's some kind of huge demonstration in Moscow's Red Square, and another in London in front of the Buckingham Palace where the King and the British Royal Family are hiding. . . . More demonstrations in the streets of Paris, Barcelona, Beijing, Stockholm, Melbourne. Everywhere, people are holding effigies of dolls in Atlantean metallic gold wigs and paper models of spaceships, and setting fire to them, while police advance in gear and tanks roll in. Other counter-demonstrations have Atlantean mannequins rigged as some kind of messianic figures, surrounded by halos and religious symbols, while people hold up signs and scream at each other across militia lines.

"You are early, Candidate Lark."

His cool voice sounds right behind me and I almost jump at the sound of it. How did he come up on me that I did not hear?

My temples are pounding as I turn around and Aeson Kass stands there, watching me with his intense inexplicable eyes. In the low illumination, the colors are faded but the angles of his face are prominent—lean jaw-line, high cheekbones, chiseled straight nose and barely curving brows.

He is impossibly handsome, I realize suddenly—painfully so. My lungs begin to constrict from the awareness, so that for an instant I cannot breathe at all. How did I not see it immediately? I thought him proud, distant, ruthless . . . strangely *alien* when he was injured and covered in blood during the crash . . . confident and attractive, yes, but most recently, terrifying.

But he is also *beautiful.* . . . From the shape of his sculpted body—concealed by the functional grey uniform, but oh, I can easily imagine it—to the lines of his face and all the way to that telltale metallic hair falling to his shoulders.

"Oh, sorry!" I mumble, because I must say something. "I tried the door and it was open, so I came in, hope that's okay. . . ."

"Good evening," he says. "Yes, that's fine. I left it unlocked for you and Candidate Dubois."

"Oh," I say. And continue staring at him.

I am so glad it's dark and he cannot see my face burning up, again, just as it did yesterday—except yesterday I did not know *why* it was happening and now I kind of do. But I also know that I am still furious at him, for the blunt and devastating things he said the last time. And for the fact that he is so *hot* and yet cold as ice— a paradox.

What's the matter with me?

"It is better that you don't look at those news images," he says softly, putting one hand firmly on my upper arm, to guide me away from the computer screens. "The world—your Earth—it is a sorry place right now, and you do not need the distraction of knowing it, which can throw you off track. The process of Qualification is difficult enough without dealing with any of *this*."

The touch of his strong warm fingers against my arm, it *sears* me. "Okay . . ." I mutter. "I did not mean to look."

"Oh yes, you did," he retorts, and I am not sure if he is mocking me or not. Again I feel a searing sense of being ripped open and consumed by fire, because yet again he can see right through me.

I am saved from needing to formulate a reply by the arrival of Blayne Dubois.

He knocks, fumbles with the door handle.

"Come in!" Aeson tells him. "And turn on the light on your way in."

Blayne manages to open the door and pushes himself inside, struggling momentarily as the wheelchair snags on a small bump in the threshold. He flicks the light switch near the entrance, and I blink as the bright overheads come on.

"Sorry I'm late," Blayne says.

"You're not. She is early."

And then Aeson uses tones to call the hoverboard to him. Standing upright, leaning against the farthest wall, the board rises and comes to a stop accurately before Blayne's wheelchair.

Blayne knows exactly what to do, by habit now. He lifts himself by his hands and arms out of the wheelchair and lies flat on his stomach against the board.

I push the empty wheelchair out of the way, without needing to be told. Meanwhile Aeson makes the board rise and hover nearly upright, at an angle.

"Lark," he says, while Blayne grips the board with his hands to stay on, so that his arms are shaking with the effort. "Come and hold it from this side. Keep it steady."

And as I hold the hoverboard in place, Aeson glances at me briefly. "You've got a bruise. What happened to your face?" he asks, while arranging Blayne's lower limbs against the board.

"Got hit during sparring in Combat," I say, almost proudly.

Aeson nods, without looking at me.

"Put some ice on it. Or a paper towel dipped in cold water should work too."

"It doesn't really hurt anymore."

But he is no longer paying attention to me. His focus is on

Blayne.

"Tonight you are going to learn how to use the hoverboard as a defensive shield," Aeson tells him. "There are three LM Forms involved. First LM Shield Form—using your lower limbs as much as possible to keep it anchored and covering you while you fight with your upper body. Second LM Form—combination of lower limbs and using only one upper limb at a time to position it to your advantage, to block your opponent, here and here, while *one hand* fights."

He pauses, to point out various spots on the board where to maintain a grip. "And finally, Third LM Form uses *both hands* to hold the board while your lower body makes no contact with it at all—which means a great deal of upper body strength, since you will need to be able to support your own weight entirely while you manipulate the board as a shield. Basically you are hanging off the board in an upright position as dead weight and moving it too."

"Okay." Blayne nods and follows the movements with his own hands, testing the grip positions.

"Why are there so many LM Forms?" I ask. "Seems very complicated. . . ."

Aeson throws me a hard glance. "Why? They evolved for a very good reason. Wounded soldiers had to have a means of supporting their injured, variously incapacitated bodies while continuing to fight. The LM Forms of Er-Du are taught to all in the Fleet as part of basic training, because they are *necessary*. Limited Mobility is an honorable aspect of military training for an Atlantis warrior. Every soldier experiences it at some point, and it saves lives."

"So, you fight on hoverboards a lot?" I ask.

"We spend a great deal of time on hoverboards. Fighting is only one of the many things we do. Now—enough questions, pay attention to what you're doing."

I grow silent and continue holding the board. I watch Aeson's precise movements and Blayne following his lead. I try to concentrate, to memorize these new LM Forms, now that I know their importance.

Only . . . my mind keeps flashing back to the moment on the airfield when Aeson lies against me senseless, covered with blood and soot, his face backlit with the flames of the burning shuttle. . . .

The half hour is over, and Aeson Kass curtly dismisses us. "Same thing tomorrow. Be here at eight."

As I glance from the corner of my eye, a soft repeating beep alarm sounds from the direction of the observation console center. A video message has come in on one of the screens, and Aeson turns to it, quickly motioning us out of the room. There's enough time for me to see a caller's face framed by metallic hair, as it appears on screen. I recognize it as belonging to one of the Correctors.

"Go, now!" Aeson raises his voice at us. He shuts the door forcefully, as soon as Blayne's wheelchair clears the threshold. And the next moment, Blayne and I find ourselves outside.

"Okay . . . wonder what that was about," I mutter.

"Atlantis business, not ours." Blayne does not make eye contact as he starts to roll away. However, a few feet later he pauses, then turns back to look at me.

"Thanks for working with me," he says, moving his hair out of his eyes in the usual mannerism, and craning his head slightly to look up. "Sorry you're taking up your own homework time with all this LM stuff that's basically useless to you."

I walk after him. "Hey, it's not useless at all. Didn't you hear him explain it? These LM Forms are super-important!"

"Yeah, well."

"I mean it!" I say. "I'm taking mental notes too, this can come in handy for anyone. Wish I'd known about it before."

And then I add, "We're kind of very lucky to be learning this, actually. *You* are lucky. I think *he* really believes in you."

Blayne continues watching me. "You think so?"

I nod.

"Then he knows nothing." And Blayne turns away, starts moving, and this time does not look back.

Chapter 24

Something has happened.

When I get back to Yellow Dorm Eight, close to 10:00 PM curfew—after running a few homework laps around the Arena Commons building stadium track—it seems like everyone has gathered in the first floor lounge. All the Candidates from our dorm are packed in, and the Dorm Leaders are there too.

"What's going on?" I say, making my way through the crowd.

A girl I don't know turns to me. "They found something. The Correctors were here, searching both the dormitory floors *again*, and looks like they found something. . . . They're about to make some kind of announcement."

I frown. At the same time a strange chill passes through me and takes up residence in my gut, with twisting knives. Why am I even nervous?

I look around to see if there's anyone familiar. I notice Dawn and Hasmik toward the back and push my way toward them. Hasmik's leaning against the back of one of the chairs, and dangling her hurt leg off the ground to relieve pressure on the ankle.

"You missed the excitement," Dawn says, leaning in to my ear. "The Correctors were all over our floor. They kicked us out and did the bed search. Girls underwear all over the place. . . . No idea what else."

"Oh, yeah?" I start to snort then frown instead and momentarily think about my bags and my bed—not that there's anything that can be found there. . . .

Dorm Leader John Nicolard blows a whistle. Faces turn and the whispers and chatter in the lounge simmers down. In that moment we all turn to look, and there are two Atlantean Correctors walking down the stairs, with someone in tow, and behind them is a pair of armed guards.

They reach the bottom landing, and the person they are leading by the arms is pushed forward, so that he or she stumbles slightly, and there's a flip of familiar relaxed blond-tinted hair, and *oh, no, oh dear lord, no!*

It's *Laronda.*

I feel cold. Super-bottomless-pit-cold, and at the same time it's like someone had punched me in the gut. Next to me Dawn makes a sound that's like a growl or an exclamation.

"Oh, no!" Hasmik breathes.

"Let go of me!" After a particularly rough shove from behind, Laronda struggles in the grip of the guards. She's wearing nothing but a tank top and hastily pulled on leggings. Her sockless feet are jammed into sneakers. Her dark brown skinny arms are restrained behind her back and her face is terrified. I have never seen her look so lost—*ever.* "I didn't do anything! *Listen to me!* I don't *know* what that thing is—"

The crowd of Candidates parts to let them pass, and the Correctors are silent and impassive as they walk through the lobby, followed by their detainee, ignoring her pleas and protest. One of the Correctors is holding what looks like Laronda's tattered old denim jacket.

"Laronda!" I say as she passes by, and my voice carries through the room.

Laronda turns back, trains her frightened face in my direction, and I can see her eyes are red with tears and her nose is puffy. "Gwen!" she exclaims, almost choking. "Oh my lord, Gwen! I am innocent, I didn't do anything, I swear! Please tell them! Help me! Someone set me up!"

I make a move toward her, but the nearest guard puts his arm out before me to prevent me from making any contact with her. "Please stay back," he says gruffly, blocking me with his bulk.

"It has to be a terrible mistake!" I exclaim. My pulse is pounding in my temples. "She says she didn't do anything! Where are you taking her?"

"Yeah, there's no way this girl did anything wrong!" Behind me Dawn pushes forward to stand at my side. And Hasmik is right behind her.

One of the Correctors pauses suddenly and turns to look at us.

"This Candidate was found to be in possession of one of the components missing from the shuttles," he says in a chill and composed voice. "She is being detained until we can further determine the extent of her involvement."

"Detained where?" Dorm Leader Gina Curtis says, stepping forward to stand next to us. She has a stern intense expression, and I'd hate to be the one who goes up against her.

"The correctional facility space is in Building Fifteen." The Corrector never blinks as he replies to Gina. "All inquiries may be placed there tomorrow morning after 8:00 AM."

"But that's ridiculous!" Other protesting voices rise in the lounge as teens crowd in closer.

"Please do not interfere," the Corrector says. "Unless you would like to be detained also. Any further interference with this process now will result in your Disqualification."

We pretty much fall silent at this. Everyone, all at once. So much for solidarity in the face of personal survival. . . .

The Corrector turns away, followed by the second one, and Laronda makes a sobbing noise as she is led outside.

I stand watching her being taken away, stunned with disbelief, and my emotions are in crazy horrible turmoil.

One of the Dorm Leaders blows the whistle. "All right, everyone, back upstairs to bed! We'll deal with this tomorrow, now, curfew and lights out!"

I am not sure whether I get any sleep that night, because although I am exhausted, I lie in the darkness of the dormitory, wide-awake for hours, and filled with awful sickening adrenaline rushing through my system. I listen to my own pulse, to the small sleeping noises and bed creaks around me. And the unnerving silence of Laronda's empty cot is there, right next to me.

"I am so sorry . . ." Hasmik mumbles in the dark several times on my other side, and I whisper back, "It's okay . . . everything will be okay . . . somehow."

I don't know whom that's supposed to convince or fool. Not me.

I finally fall into some kind of half-frenzied slumber with nightmares about falling shuttles and levitating pieces of orichalcum and lord knows what other evil junk.

When the 7:00 AM claxons alarms peal, I am pulled out of a B-movie level nightmare.

Everyone's coming awake, and the usual lazy groans are subdued this morning, as we still ponder the events of the previous night. Frightened gossip moves in whispers and waves around the dormitory hall.

"She's going to be Disqualified, of course," a girl says, as she collects her clothes and toothbrush and heads to the bathroom. "But what else? Will they put her in jail or physically harm her?"

"What if they execute people?" another girl squeaks in terror. "Do Atlanteans have capital punishment?"

The sound of that starts another wave of cold fear in my gut. There's got to be something that can be done to help Laronda!

Okay, I decide, *as soon as I am dressed, I will go to that jail building where they're holding her and see if I can talk sense to someone.* Maybe I can find Aeson Kass! I can make him listen at least! He has to be there, right?

As I think this, and get showered and dressed, I see Claudia Grito giving me a snide look as she passes by me on her way downstairs.

Okay, did that bitch have anything to do with whatever happened to Laronda? The thought passes through me like a lightning bolt.

Dawn follows me downstairs as I start following Claudia. "Hey, don't do anything stupid, now," she mutters grimly. "Let's go eat first, there's nothing you can do now. Not before eight."

I nod, and we head into the cafeteria.

"I plan to skip the first part of class," I tell Dawn.

"Yeah, I get it. Me too. I'll go with you."

We finish eating breakfast that tastes like straw, in a hurry. As we stop by the Common Area lobby to get our schedules scanned, I check the clock and it's seven-forty.

"Let's go," I say.

Outside it's an overcast cloudy morning, and I shiver slightly and wrap my bulky winter jacket around me. For once I did not forget to wear something warm over my T-shirt.

We head to Building Fifteen, which according to the campus

map is on the other side of the airfield, three structures behind the Arena Commons Building.

There are few Candidates walking outside, just a few joggers and occasional patrolling guards. The sky is pale as milk and it's starting to drizzle lightly as we pass the tall AC Building, and there's Building Fifteen. It looks like a regular dorm, four floors, but there's a four-color square logo on top.

At the doors, heightened security greets us. Two guards give us hard stares as we pass the glass doors. They scan our ID tokens before allowing us to enter the sterile lobby.

"What is your purpose for being here?" An officer asks us from behind a glass enclosure.

I glance at Dawn then back at him. "We're here for Laronda Aimes. She was wrongfully arrested last night in our Dorm, and we want to talk to whoever is in charge of that."

The guard, an older balding man, looks at us silently, then picks up an intercom handset. "Two Candidates here to discuss the detainee from Yellow Dorm Eight," he tells whomever is on the other end. Then he turns back to us and says, "Names?"

"Gwen Lark and Dawn Williams."

He relays our names, then listens. After a pause he looks at me and says, "Okay, you're Gwen Lark?"

I nod.

"You can go in, but just you alone. The other young lady, you wait here."

I frown, and Dawn gives me a strange look, then shrugs. "I'll be here," she says.

And on that note, the guard buzzes me inside through the second set of glass doors, and into the back office area that contains a small cube farm consisting of about a dozen cubicles separated with short partitions, and then a long corridor with closed doors.

I walk sullenly past several office workers and uniformed officers manning keyboards and special consoles and sitting at their cubicle desks. They stare at me briefly. Everyone's wearing rainbow armbands on their grey uniform sleeves, which I've come to associate with Earth workers affiliated with Atlanteans. Not one of them has the metallic golden-blond hair.

The guard takes me past them and we enter the corridor, and walk all the way to the end, past at least twenty doors on both sides, until we come to a dead end and closed double doors.

An armed guard stands on duty at the doors.

My guard nods to him, and the second man stands aside. The guard who brought me over takes out a card and scans it at the optical reader on the wall. The lock bleeps and the status light turns from red to green.

The door opens.

"Proceed inside," he tells me.

I take a deep breath and walk past the double doors.

The room I enter is huge. It is more than three times the size of Office 512 in the AC Building, and it contains a similar computer surveillance multi-screen center lining one of the walls. Rows of screens stretch wall to wall.

Along the perimeter of the other walls there is other tech equipment that I cannot really explain, because most of it is the strange shapeless lumps of Atlantean technology I've encountered before in the audio tests, except this is all on a grand scale.

In the middle of the room, a large table takes up most of the space, and it is covered with what looks like burned and charred pieces of metal, plastic, and orichalcum. . . . Basically, it is what remains of the first exploded shuttle. Some pieces are bulky and large, most are small shards and lumps fused together. Four Atlanteans are in the room, dressed in white lab coats, moving around the table and engaging various equipment around the perimeter.

The fifth is Aeson Kass.

He stands with his arms folded watching them work.

He looks particularly worn this morning, pale as if he hadn't had any sleep. The hollows of his cheeks and jaw are darkened with a faint growth of stubble. His hair is slightly messy and even tousled on one side. And his eyes, dark lapis lazuli blue, are nevertheless traced with a fine perfect line of kohl that appears unsmudged and unblemished, as if it's a natural part of his skin.

Maybe the eyeliner's permanent, and has been tattooed onto his face? I wonder momentarily and stupidly out of left field.

He sees me in that moment and he frowns. "*You?* What are

you doing here, Candidate Lark? What do you want?" His aggravated voice cuts like a knife.

I take a few steps into the room, and my heart is beating so loudly I can feel it in my temples. *Breathe, Gwen, breathe. . . .*

"Laronda Aimes is innocent," I say. "Whatever you *think* she did, she did *not* do it. She is my friend, and she would never do anything as awful that might hurt other people—"

"Silence!" he blasts me in a hard, implacable voice. "Whatever it is you think you're doing, I suggest you reconsider, *now*. You should not be here. This is none of your business, and by being here you put *yourself* under question."

My jaw falls open. "What?" I say, and I am filled with outrage. "How does trying to help a friend implicate *me?* I am telling you, Laronda is completely innocent, and there is no way she is involved in anything stupid and awful that would *ever* hurt other people much less kill anyone, and undermine her being here in this RQC!"

"How well do you know your friend? You have known her for what, six days? The evidence stands against her." He lets his arms drop, takes a step and another, and approaches me. He stops directly before me and I stare up at him, at the terrible hard gaze, in all its intensity, trained on me.

"I don't need six days to know that she's a *good person*," I say softly, and my voice is breathless with anger. "There are just some things you *know*."

"How?" he says, staring down at me. The sheer power in him, it is a mountain. . . . The force of his gaze is making my lungs close up, choking me with the oppressive weight of *presence*. "With your gut? Your intuition? Your amazing ability to read minds? How well do you really know this Laronda and her motives? How do you explain the shuttle navigation chip component found in the pocket of her jacket?"

"There has to be a good reason. She was set up! Someone planted this thing in her pocket to transfer blame onto her . . . it could be a random mistake, someone put it there by mistake, meaning to put it in someone else's pocket, maybe? Or . . . or it could be—it's got to be malicious—jealousy, rivalry, you name it! Someone trying to weed down the competition, the number of

Candidates?" I speak hurriedly, scrambling for answers, because I sense that he is giving me this brief opportunity to speak, and I should be grateful. . . .

"Or it could be she is working for a terrorist group, and she has been given a specific task, and she has carried it out." He pauses for a moment, to glance at the worktable and the Atlanteans in lab coats. And then his gaze returns to me. "Do you know that we found one of the component chips cleverly attached to the underside of a delivery truck yesterday? We intercepted it before it had a chance to leave the compound. And this second chip in your so-called friend's pocket was likely about to be smuggled out in a similar fashion."

"Have you caught whoever is responsible for the delivery truck thing?" I press on, hanging on to any option I can imagine. "Do you have actual proof Laronda was involved in that?"

Aeson considers me and for a moment I sense a tiny pause of hesitation. "Yes," he says. "We have the persons involved with the truck incident in custody. Two Candidates from another dorm, and they will be Disqualified and prosecuted. Both were linked via surveillance and advanced DNA and resonance scanning to the deliberate attempt to move the chip component. They were also linked to not one but *two* of your extremist Earth terror groups, the Sunset Alliance and Terra Patria."

I stare at him, mind racing, not knowing what else to say.

"Enough," he says abruptly, steadily looking at me then suddenly blinking as though coming awake. "This is far more than you need to know. I should not be telling you any of this, but apparently I've had a very long night and it's affecting my better judgment. And you—you are missing your first period class, for which you've just earned a demerit."

"But what about Laronda? What's going to happen to her?"

He exhales tiredly. Again, a pause as he considers whether to speak, and merely looks at me. "Nothing is going to happen to her. She was found to be clean, no primary DNA match, no resonance match. She had nothing to do with it and she is going to be released in half an hour after some minor questioning while the last portion of scanning is concluded—mostly a formality."

"What? Oh!" I say in amazement, followed by anger. "Wait, why didn't you just say so in the first place? I was going nuts here, and you could've just said you were letting her go! What is *wrong* with you?"

Okay, that last part? I think I've just said too much—even I get it. And my voice, holy crap, I've seriously raised my voice at *him*, at Command Pilot Aeson Kass, the guy who pretty much holds the fate of this whole RQC in his hands. . . .

Aeson's lips part. I think I've managed to stun him sufficiently by my words, my insolent loud tone.

But in the next second, there's a beeping sound, a regular repeating audio tone, and it starts coming from the back of the room, from one of the Atlantean machines.

Aeson turns in the direction of the sound.

One of the lab-coat scientists goes over to check, and then looks around and stares at Aeson and me.

He then approaches. There is a very peculiar look on his face. "There's a match," he says softly, almost hesitantly to Aeson. "Her voice—it just tripped the resonance scanner. *She* is a match."

And he looks at *me*.

Chapter 25

"*What?*" Aeson Kass speaks in a hard voice of amazement. Once again, he's been stunned. "Check again! And then re-check the calibration—" And then he continues the rest of the sentence in an angry torrent of Atlantean language.

Meanwhile, I am standing there in absolute confusion, and also filled with a sudden sense of inevitability.

My voice. . . .

Okay. . . . They've just found out something having to do with my voice. Which means, they have a means of knowing that I had something to do with the second shuttle landing? And maybe more? No, that's impossible, how can they?

But I have no time to think because in the next instant I feel the heavy pressure of his fingers on my upper arm, painful even through the thickness of my jacket. And now I am being propelled forward with great force. Aeson Kass holds me in an iron vise and all three of us walk to the back of the room, while the other Atlanteans gather closer.

"What?" I manage to mutter. "What is happening?"

But he does not look at me, does not answer, merely pushes me roughly before a large piece of equipment that at present is beeping every other second.

The Atlantean scientist leans forward to adjust something on a console and along the lumpy metallic surface with multicolored lights. But Aeson moves him out of the way and takes over the equipment console. He presses things I have no way of describing—buttons, indentations, touch-surface maybe? And then he coldly turns to me.

"Sing the tones that you hear, *now*."

"What? Why?"

"*Sing!*"

VERA NAZARIAN

I hear a series of short notes. I take a breath and sing back what I hear. In the otherwise silent room, my voice suddenly sounds reedy and wimpy.

As soon as I am done, the equipment begins to beep once again.

Aeson frowns. He then does something to the machine, which resets the alarm.

"Again!" he says.

The machine plays notes. I echo them.

The machine beep alarm goes off, unmistakably in response to my voice.

There is a pause.

Aeson then resets the alarm and slowly turns to look at me.

"Candidate Lark," he says in a dead voice, and his face, his eyes—they are terrifying. "You are under arrest for conspiracy, possible terrorist action, and murder."

In the next few minutes I am taken into custody by security guards—after being handed over by the Atlanteans, after having Aeson Kass give me no other glance as he turns his back on me, his bearing hard like stone, and his expression cold as I have never seen it before.

My hands shake as I am led out through the double doors and into the long hallway. Somewhere in the middle of the hallway, the guards pause, and a door is opened.

I am shoved inside, and it's a small holding cell, with bright overhead lights, a small square table and two hard chairs. A surveillance camera points at me from each of the four corners.

The door closes upon me and I am left alone.

For the first five minutes I stand motionless, gasping for air. My hands—my whole body—I am shaking. Fine tremors fill me, and a numbing cold settles inside my gut.

I put my hands over my mouth and press hard, feeling the inside of my lips against my teeth, while emotions fill me to bursting, and the pressure behind my eyes rises, forcing tears.

I am rocked by a mix of anger, terror, an impossible sense of injustice, and behind all things, perfect despair.

Yes, I can explain *everything* to them, or at least, try. I can tell them exactly what happened that night, what I did. How I sang like crazy and landed his shuttle by pure luck and accident. And how I *saved him*, dragged him out of that wreck, through the smoke and flames. . . .

But they're not going to believe me, are they? They are going to interpret everything I say as clever deception, just to cover up something else nefarious on my part.

He is not going to believe me.

He already has a certain misconception of me, or at least what I think is a misconception. Whatever it is, he thinks very little of me and my stupid big mouth.

And oh, lord, what rotten coincidence! With Laronda being my friend, and even our beds being right next to each other, everything is now pointing at *me* as the culprit. Sure, how easy to think that *I* planted that damned chip in her pocket! And that all along I've been playing a clever little game, pretending to be earnest and whatever else they think I am—

I take a deep shuddering breath.

Then I sit down at one of the chairs. And I stare straight ahead of me at the neutral off-white wall, eventually falling into a sickly daydream.

The four cameras, they are all pointing at me. I am being watched even now, for body language, for telltale signs of further deception and playacting. Anything and everything I say or do, even how I move, is going to be processed differently by them.

It occurs to me also, *Among other things, I guess I am now officially Disqualified.*

Half an hour later, the door opens and two Correctors enter the room. Pale metallic hair, unfamiliar faces, usual grey uniforms. One has a yellow armband, the other a red one.

I start to get up from my chair.

"Sit," one Corrector tells me, as he himself sits down in the chair across the table from me.

I sit back down.

The second Corrector places a small tech gadget on the table surface.

"Candidate Gwenevere Lark, you have been voice-matched to the shuttle incident site and materially to the outer surface of one of the shuttles."

"What does that mean?" I say.

"As such, you are under suspicion for various criminal acts including conspiring against Atlantis, malicious tampering, and disrupting the lawful proceedings of the Qualification process."

"Before I say anything, am I entitled to a lawyer?" I whisper.

The Corrector across the table from me pauses. "No," he says in an impassive voice. "You are entitled to nothing. This is the jurisdiction of Atlantis, and you can only speak to answer questions, and it is your *only option* if you want to clear yourself."

I take a deep breath, and release it with a shudder. "Very well. I am innocent of any wrongdoing. And I am going to answer all your questions."

"Very well. Where were you on the night of the incident?"

I tell them. I describe having dinner with a crowd of friends at the Arena Commons, then running around the big track, then finally walking back to my dorm. Although I am being honest, I manage not to mention Logan, at least not directly. Not sure why, but it just seems best that I don't bring him into this.

"So you were passing the airfield when the incident happened?"

"Yes."

"Where exactly were you?"

I describe my location the best I can.

"What did you see after the explosion of the first shuttle?"

"The second one was halfway above the trees. It did not rise far. It was flying all over the place, streaking across the sky. . . . Hard to explain, but it was fast."

"Would you say it was out of control?"

"Yes."

"Please elaborate."

I frown. "I am not sure. It looked like it was moving aimlessly, I guess."

"And then what?"

"And then it started sort of falling, directly at me."

The Corrector across the table from me pauses. He and the one standing next to him exchange glances.

"Continue. What happened next?"

I purse my lips and take a deep breath. "I started to run . . . I don't know, it was kind of crazy, everything happening at once. . . . I ran, but it was still falling right at me. It was going to crush me. So I screamed."

"Go on."

"Then I had an idea. . . . It was from my Atlantis Tech class, about levitating orichalcum objects. I remembered the note sequence. So I started to sing."

The Corrector watches me in tense silence. "Impossible. . . . What did you sing?"

I tell them the notes I used, a major sequence starting with F, then A, and C.

The Correctors look at each other then stare at me.

I stare back.

There is a very long pause. . . .

"All right. Assuming what you say is true, describe exactly what happened," the seated Corrector says.

"After I sang the sequence, the shuttle stopped falling and hovered over my head. I continued singing, because I was too afraid to stop. Then I moved out of its way. And then I sang the notes to make levitating objects come down. It came down."

"How?"

"I don't know, it just *did*. And then, just as it stopped a few feet above the ground, all the lights suddenly went out, and it went dead. And it sort of fell the rest of the way down. . . ."

"And then?"

I take another deep breath with a shudder. "Some kind of hatch opened. There was a stair that descended. And then there was a whole bunch of black smoke."

"Did you at any point attempt to call for help?" The Corrector watches me with an unblinking gaze that is somehow more horrible because it is so bland, so perfectly neutral.

"There was no time. I saw people running in my direction but I didn't think they would reach the shuttle in time. . . . So I went in."

"So you went inside the shuttle that you yourself brought down in order to finish what you had started—to kill the occupants? Or was it to steal more navigation equipment? Or simply to cover your tracks?"

"No!" I feel despair and anger rising in me. "No, I went inside to see if I could *help* someone—anyone!"

"What was—inside?"

"*He* was inside! Your Command Pilot Aeson Kass! He was out—unconscious . . . in his chair, covered in blood . . . his head, the side of his face, his hair, everything . . . and there was a fire . . . burning in the back . . . near the floor, I don't know . . ." I speak in quick chopped sentences, as an emotion I have no words for is rising up to choke me, and I have no air in my lungs. My hands are squeezed into fists under the table, and now I am shaking full body.

"What happened next?"

"I got to him . . . got him out of the chair, dragged him outside."

The Corrector leans forward closer to me across the table. "Are you saying that you, a slender girl with no muscle mass, was able to carry a tall muscular young man almost twice your size, and then get him down the stairs on your own, in a matter of minutes?"

"Yes!" I gasp, while tears begin running down my face, and suddenly everything is swimming in my field of vision, and the world blurs, like rain outside the window. . . . "And no, I did not *carry* him, I dragged him! Do *not*—do not put words in my mouth! I pulled and dragged him outside the best I could, yes! And he was heavy, yes, but I wasn't going to just leave him—"

In that moment the door opens and Aeson Kass storms into the room.

"*Enough,*" he says in a hard voice, looking at the Correctors. "Outside, both of you, *now*. I will handle the rest of this *interview*."

There is a pause. The Correctors then incline their heads in acquiescence and depart the room.

As soon as the door shuts behind them, Aeson turns to me. He places both hands on the table, slamming them down, and he stands, looking at me like a demon.

I tremble. . . . Tears are now pouring down my face in a torrent, and I take a few shuddering gasps of air.

"Tell me *exactly* what you did."

His voice—it is soft and precise and devastating.

I look up at him, my eyes held wide and motionless by sheer willpower. I raise one hand, still clenched into a white-knuckled fist, to wipe my red running nose and cheeks with the back of it.

"What I *did?*" I say and my voice breaks. "I hauled your damn, bloody, passed-out ass out of that burning shuttle, is what I did!"

He watches me and does not blink. Several seconds pass.

"Tell me how you found me. Where was I in the shuttle?"

"You were in a chair. In some kind of harness. You were slumped over."

"And how was I hurt?"

I stare at him, and my gaze automatically slides to the place on the side of his head where I remember seeing all that blood. "Your head. It was on that side, and there was a lot of blood."

"Where? Show me. . . ."

I hesitate.

His hand slams the table, hard. *"Show me!"*

I partially rise from my seat and extend my right hand, moving my trembling fingers to point to the spot. His metallic hair, it is falling forward as he leans over me . . . and so I touch it lightly, feeling its strange alien texture.

"Here . . ." I say. "And here. . . . There was so much blood, and it stained all of your face, and your hair too."

He blinks. Just once, at the lightest touch of my fingers against the blond tendrils. . . . But his lips are held in an implacable line.

"Why should I believe you?" he says suddenly. "Why should anything you tell me exonerate you?"

"Because it's the truth!"

His eyes narrow in fury. "Oh, it's *truth*, you claim? How well you are playing me even now—have been playing me all along, with your little innocent act!"

I stop sniffling and my mouth falls open as anger rises to drown out the despair and the fear.

But he continues, and his face hovers above mine as he leans in yet closer, full of dark sarcasm. "It becomes clear now, how you've insinuated yourself with all the Instructors. . . . Such a clever little teacher's pet! So creative, so many bright ideas! Sweet little girl with such pretty earnest eyes . . . such sweet rosy lips . . .

except when they're spouting pure bullshit!"

I make a stifled sound, in a helpless mix of outrage and terror. Both wild horrible feelings are warring inside me, and it's like I am temporarily set on "pause" until I can resolve what emotion is uppermost.

Meanwhile, he steps around the table and suddenly pulls me up out of my chair. His grip on my bare wrist is painful, and my jacket slides down and ends up halfway off my shoulders as he holds me there with his other hand, scalding fingers digging into my bare skin, bruising my shoulder.

I stumble backwards, and he pushes me hard against the wall, breathing into my face. "Tell me, *Gwen Lark*, what group are you affiliated with? Terra Patria or the Sunset Alliance? Or wait, let me guess, neither—for you are far too clever to be a pawn of such narrow-minded small-scale idiots. So I am guessing you are working with some bigger fish. So tell me, which is it?"

"I am not!" I gasp, half-turning my face away as his warm breath washes over my cheek, my neck. "I am not working with anyone!"

In answer, his grip on my shoulder hardens, at the same time as he squeezes my wrist until I cry out in pain. . . . Like a serpent his voice hisses in my ear. "Who trained you?"

"No one! No one trained me! Stop it! Let *go* of me!"

Just as suddenly, he releases his hold and steps back away from me. He is breathing hard, and his eyes are strangely dilated, dark pupils overtaking the blue.

But in seconds he composes himself. His body straightens and he is again remote, and cold as ice, as he stands watching me.

I, too, strand up straight, move away from the wall, and pull up my jacket back over my T-shirt and my bare arms. I glare at him.

"What can I say to make you believe I did nothing wrong?" I say in despair. "What kind of proof do you need?"

"There is nothing you can do or tell me now that I will believe ever again," he says. "Not until I can discover hard undeniable facts that point otherwise. Can you give me such facts?"

"I—I don't know. I don't even know what you're talking about."

"Ah. . . . Then, keep playing," he says softly.

"Holy lord!"

But he shakes his head in disgust.

My hands form into fists. "What are you going to do to me? Am I Disqualified?"

But he says nothing and starts to turn from me.

"Wait!" I exclaim. "What is going to happen?"

"You are going to be questioned continually until we have the information you are withholding."

"You mean, interrogated until I 'confess' to something?"

"Yes. You will remain here in custody until you do."

I begin shuddering again as another wave of emotion strikes me, overwhelming with cold.

He starts to go, then pauses for some reason, and turns again to look back at me. "Tell me one thing at least," he says. "When you got me out of the shuttle chair, how did you release me from the flight harness?"

"What?" I frown. "The what? Oh—there was a weird button. I squeezed it together, and it collapsed the harness."

He cranes his neck slightly and his gaze stills on me. "Thank you—for telling me at least one honest thing."

And then he leaves me alone in the sterile chamber.

Moments later two guards return and I am taken outside into the empty hallway, and made to walk about fifty feet to another door. A guard opens it, and I am pushed inside.

This room is a replica of the first, an exact square, except it has a narrow cot against one wall, topped only with a thin mattress, a pillow and blanket. A toilet stands in the corner.

The door shuts behind me.

Oh, great, this is my first actual, honest-to-goodness real prison cell. *Congratulations, Gwen Lark, terrorist conspirator and Criminal Mastermind—at last, you've arrived.* So, looks like I am going to be here for a while.

I sit down on the cot and stare at the four walls around me. I rub the back of my hand across my nose and wipe the sticky residue of drying tears and yeah, snot. So not attractive.

Then, it occurs to me, pretty soon, at some point, I am going to have to pee. In the presence of surveillance cameras. . . . Ugh.

I have no idea how much time passes, but it feels like at least an hour.

All along, my thoughts race deliriously, and I think of my brothers and Gracie, and Mom and Dad. . . . I guess I'll be going home now. Or, maybe not—Disqualification is only one of my current problems; I might be greeting the asteroid apocalypse in a prison cell.

Or worse—depending on the severity of the Atlantean criminal system and corresponding punishment for my alleged crimes, I might not even live long enough to see it.

Shivering, I get up, trying to shake off the despair. I stand, stomp my feet, move around, sit back down again. There are absolutely no sounds outside the long hallway corridor, not even rare footsteps.

What feels like another hour passes. Or maybe it's only been fifteen minutes. I have no idea—it's all hell.

At last there are footsteps and someone comes to the door.

The door opens, and a guard walks in, followed by my brother George. "You have ten minutes," he says, then steps outside again, locking us both in.

George looks nervous and very grim, as he immediately moves toward me.

"George!" I exclaim. And then my tears start pouring again, like a gusher.

My older brother puts his arms around me and I smell the sweat and faint aftershave from his familiar clothes as I bury my face against his jacket front.

"Okay, Gee Two, what the *hell* is going on?" he mutters. "What have you done? Or better to say, what did you get yourself into?"

"Nothing! *Nothing!*" I say, moving back to wipe my face again with both hands. And then I grab George by the jacket front and hold on for several breaths until I regain my ability to speak instead of blubbering like an absolute wreck.

"What's that on your cheek?" He frowns, examining the side of my face with its dark bruise. "Did they do this to you?"

I shake my head. "No, it's just from sparring in Combat. It's nothing. Just stupid—"

"Okay, let's breathe. . . . And tell me."

We take deep breaths. Or I take deep breaths and George just stands there and lets me recover. Then we both sit down on my cot.

"Okay, listen. . . . I did absolutely nothing wrong. But—but—they think I am a terrorist of some kind, because they matched my voice to—to—"

"To what?" George stares at me in confused worry. "Look, I don't know what's going on, and when your dorm friends came running to get me, they weren't making much sense either, except that you got arrested somehow. And now Gracie's freaking out—she's back at her dorm and swears she cannot deal—you know how she can be, total drama queen. But anyway, right now, we're all here, your friends, Gordie, everyone's outside the building. . . . We wanna see if there's anything we can do to help. But—but you need to explain what happened, okay? Why on earth would they arrest you? Surely not for mouthing off to their big shot VIP, or whatever you did in that Combat class to get you disciplinary action? Is that it?"

"No . . . no, it's not." I move in closer to George and speak in a high whisper. I don't know why I am bothering to whisper, since every movement, every sound is being observed and recorded. But it just feels better somehow to speak that way, a weird illusion of privacy, maybe?

"Okay, I have to tell you something," I begin. "On the night of the shuttle incident, I was—I was *there*."

"What?" George's eyes widen. He slants his head and stares hard at me.

I start talking. I am babbling, but somehow I manage to tell him the entirety of the incident.

"Wait, you *sang* and the shuttle levitated?" His jaw drops. "You *sang?* No way, that's crazy! How can it do that? How's that even possible?"

"I know it's crazy," I mutter hurriedly. "I know, I still can't believe it when I think back, but it was a split-second reaction—it just came out!"

"But how did you make it hover? That ship must weigh a ton! It's not like some skinny hoverboard! I mean—how loud did you even sing? You must have been really loud—"

"Top-of-my-voice loud! I started out screaming, like I just

told you, and then I just flipped it around into a note. . . ."

"But you—" George hesitates at this point. "But you *don't* sing. . . ."

"I know."

"You haven't sung for ages! Not since Mom—"

"Yeah. I didn't even know what I sounded like any more. It was like someone else's voice. It was *unreal*—"

As I recall and describe the moments, I feel a gathering of something painful in my throat, as a lump returns to choke me. I shake my head and put my palm flat against his jacket again in a gesture to make him stop.

George nods, understanding me immediately.

"Okay," he says gently. "Enough of that. So then what next?"

I tell him how I got Aeson Kass out of the shuttle. When I am done, my brother remains silent, thoughtful, as though considering what to say.

"Gwen," he says. "You saved his life. And this is his crazy way of thanking you? He should be giving you a medal or something!"

I bite my lip and shake my head. "There's more. . . ."

And I tell him about Laronda's arrest and the missing chip that was found in her pocket.

"So, wait, how does that connect to you?"

"Her dorm bed is right next to mine. And we're friends. We hang out together a lot."

"So? Could still be a coincidence. Only remotely suspicious."

I shrug. "I am guessing that *anything* suspicious is enough for them to connect the dots. And you must admit, it does look kind of bad. Even I get that."

"So their machine recognized your voice, and your BFF was found with the chip." George exhales loudly and shifts around in place, making the flimsy cot underneath us creak. He puts his head down and runs his fingers through his messy dark hair, then looks up at me again. "Yeah, this is bad," he says. "But there's got to be something we can do. Find whoever's really responsible. . . ."

I sit with my hands digging into the blanket on both sides of me. I am numb and there is really nothing that comes to mind. But seeing George of all people look this crestfallen and glum, I have to at least pretend.

"Yeah, there has to be something. And if there is, I will find a way, Gee One," I say, putting one hand on his shoulder and squeezing. "Meanwhile, you tell Gracie and Gordie I'm okay. Tell Gordie—tell him we have matching shiners now, he'll love it. It's kind of funny!"

Moments later the guard returns to take my brother away.

And again, I am all alone, with the four walls closing in on me.

Chapter 26

I have no idea how much more time passes, and I am getting hungry and thirsty. And yeah, I manage to use the toilet while awkwardly covering myself up with my jacket.

Eventually I lie down on the cot, on top of the blanket, and stare up at the ceiling.

At some point, the door opens again, and guards come to escort me outside.

This time I am led back through the corridor toward the front portion of the building. We pass the cubicle farm, where again every office worker stares at me, this time with reproach. Or at least it seems that way, from what I see in their eyes. We go through the glass double doors and outside into the very front portion, and then the lobby.

"Where are you taking me?" I ask, but the guards do not reply, only propel me by the arms, onward, and out through the main glass doors of the building.

Outside it is late afternoon. There is no sign of the morning overcast and drizzle, and except for a few patchy clouds, the sky is bright blue and turning to gold on the western horizon. Looks like I've been detained for most of the day.

As I look around, I see a bunch of people I know milling around. Both my brothers stand propped against the walls, and there's Dawn and Laronda sitting on a ledge nearby. Hasmik is sitting down on the floor concrete slab with her feet stretched out before her next to Janice Quinn. Jai, Mateo and Tremaine and even Jack Carell are standing up talking in a semi-circle. My heart lurches because there's Logan, next to my brothers, and some other guy and a few girls I barely know are with them, many of them sitting all along the side of the building with their backs to the wall.

Laronda sees me first. "Gwen! Oh, my God, are you okay?" She springs up, followed by Dawn and pretty much everyone else. They turn toward me, people scrambling to get closer.

But the guards stand between them and me, and they continue propelling me forward. "I'm okay, guys!" I say hastily, glancing back at everyone.

"Hey, where are you taking her?" George says loudly to the guards. "That's my sister, where are you taking her? We have a right to know what's happening!"

"I don't know!" I cry back. "They won't tell me—"

"No talking," says one guard. "Keep moving. The rest of you, please stay back."

But my brothers and my friends are now walking alongside us, and behind, keeping a short distance but keeping up—all of them, everyone's coming along. In fact, other Candidates who are outside are beginning to stare. Some are starting to follow along also.

We walk past several buildings at a rapid pace, so that I almost stumble a few times to keep up with the guards, and each time it happens my brothers' voices are heard from the back, "Hey! Slow down, don't push her!"

Way to go, George and Gordie! I think gratefully, wanting to bear-hug them. But then I think of where I might be going, and my gut grows numb with cold.

We pass one more building, and there's the airfield.

About a hundred feet into it, in the middle of the clearing, an Atlantean shuttle sits on the ground.

I stare, and there's a group of people gathered around it. Some of them are clearly Atlanteans, judging by the radiant metallic hair that shines from this distance in the setting sun.

Before the guards even direct me toward the shuttle, I start to get an inkling of what might be going on here.

We enter the airfield that has been swept clean and pristine of any earlier debris from the disaster of a few days ago. "Keep going," one guard tells me, propelling me firmly toward the grouping of individuals around the shuttle.

I step upon the special surface-treated concrete and walk forward. Behind me I can hear my brothers and friends walking. No one is stopping them at least, and for that much I am grateful.

Yeah, I think with a burst of morbid humor, *if they were going to have me face a firing squad, I don't think this would be the best place for it.* So at least I am not getting executed—just yet.

On the other hand, I could be facing a trip "upstairs"—up to the closest mothership for some kind of special Atlantis brand of judgment and/or punishment. Well then, on the bright side, I would at least get to see one of their great ships up-close and personal, before I am Disqualified or worse.

We approach the shuttle and the people near it. With a sinking feeling, fueled to a significant degree by embarrassment—for what, I don't know, but I do tend to become particularly ashamed of being reprimanded by authority figures, especially teachers, maybe because it happens so rarely—I recognize most of them.

Nefir Mekei stands next to Xelio Vekahat, talking softly. The sun shines with molten metal reflecting off Nefir's hair, but disappears into the black-hole abyss that is Xelio's black mane. A few steps away are the two Correctors who interrogated me, silent and impassive, heads glinting with halos of light like stern angels of judgment, observing me approach, with unblinking eyes. Then there's Mr. Warrenson, of all people, appearing both out-of-place ordinary in this gathering of Atlanteans, and also nervous and somewhat curious at the same time. Next to him, Oalla Keigeri and Keruvat Ruo look at me with undisguised disapproval.

Last of all, there is Aeson Kass. He stands silently watching me approach, with his arms folded at his chest in his typical stance. The wind moves strands of his long hair, and he too seems to have a halo of light about him—only *his* light is all implacable merciless brightness, scalding like the sun.

I get it, suddenly. . . .

Phoebos Apollo.

I am made to stop before these people—my Instructors, and now apparently my judges. The guards stand aside and retreat, and I am left alone. Somewhere behind me, I hear my siblings and friends, gathered to support me in whatever this thing is.

I *feel* them with the back of my head like a sixth sense.

Or I merely tell myself that's how it is.

"Candidate Gwen Lark, today you made a claim that you were able to safely levitate and then land a shuttle just like this one,

purely with your voice—a voice that is mechanically unassisted."
Aeson Kass looks into my eyes as he speaks, and his gaze is
neutral and impassive, or maybe it is veiled in so many layers that
it's impossible to fathom. "I do *not* for a moment believe that you
have this exceedingly rare ability. However, before further
measures are taken against you, I have been advised to allow you
to prove yourself one way or another."

He pauses, and I can hear a wave of voices swell behind me,
as Candidates suddenly understand what is going on here, what is
about to happen.

And I too understand at last. *Holy lord!*

This is a demonstration. A demonstration of me being a liar,
or not.

A public shaming and humiliation, before the rest of whatever
it is they have in store for me.

Immediately I am overwhelmed by a general numbing sense.
It is pure terror and panic and it blankets me with weakness.

They want me to *sing*. And not just sing, but sing loudly, at
the top of my voice, sing with all I've got. . . .

Mr. Warrenson anticipates my thoughts and says gently, "Ms.
Lark, if you might recall from our class, please sing the initial
sequence that keys an object to yourself. Follow it up by a
sequence to lift an object vertically. And—only if you manage to
do such a thing, naturally—once the shuttle is airborne, let's say at
just about the height of the nearest building, about fifty feet up
should do it, then you sing the hover sequence. That is—if you
manage it, of course—"

At which point I hear a soft sound of disdain. It comes from
Aeson Kass. I glance briefly at him and see that he shakes his
head, while his lips curve into a dark smile.

A jolt of anger strikes me in the pit of my stomach. It acts as a
strangely energizing force, and suddenly I am *burning* with
something—a sense of rightness, of injustice that needs to be
rooted out.

"Now, I suggest you use a C Major sequence for your tonic
starting point, since it's easiest," Mr. Warrenson continues.

"Well, Candidate?" Aeson Kass says. "Any time now is good.
So—will you grace us with your demonstration, or are we to
conclude correctly that your claim is a sham, and return you to

your confinement?"

"Can I have some water first?" I say, as I begin to hear a pulse racing in my temples. "I've not had anything to drink since morning. Can't sing with a parched throat." And saying this, I stare directly at him.

In response he makes another mocking sound. But he turns to one of the guards and indicates for him to bring what I ask.

"Oh! Gwen, *janik*, wait! I have a bottle here!" I hear from behind me, and it's Hasmik. I turn to look and she is waving at me and raising a water bottle.

I look at Aeson and he nods.

The guard goes over and brings me Hasmik's water bottle. I unscrew the cap with trembling fingers—trembling with energized fury and not fear—and I take a sip then a few deep gulps. The cool water runs down my throat and dribbles down my chin, but I don't care that I look like a fool while a whole crowd of people is watching me drink from a bottle—talk about a moment of crazy zen.

"Had enough?" Aeson says.

"Yeah . . ." I reply, wiping my mouth with the back of my sleeve, as I hand the water bottle back to the guard.

And then I turn to the shuttle, take a deep breath and remember the desperate scream I made, back when what now seems to be so many days ago. . . .

I close my eyes to focus, and my eyelids flutter momentarily as the same terrible haunting *note* issues out of me.

Middle F, weird comfortable middle of my vocal range. I belt it out, gripping my hands into fists at my sides, and the pure fierce note blasts through the air. . . . I quickly follow it up with A and C, and then repeat the three-note keying sequence.

The shuttle before me lurches slightly and then it floats up about a foot off the ground, lighter than a cloud.

In the stunned silence all around me, I continue to sing. And then I think of the F note that's an octave higher, knowing that this time I need to do a *rising* octave slide, the opposite of what I did that last time. . . . Can I aim that high and make it stick?

My voice sweeps up an octave into heaven, effortlessly reaching the high F.

And so does the shuttle—it lifts up, and rises with amazing speed, and it is suddenly far above the building and racing into the clouds.

"Stop! Enough, bring it back down!" Mr. Warrenson exclaims, and I hear him with the back of my mind as I concentrate. And then I sing the levitating hover sequence "F-A-C."

The shuttle stops in the air. Like a dark weather balloon it hovers in silhouette against the setting sun. It is so far up that I have no idea if my voice would even reach it now.

Crud! What have I done?

"Oh dear! Now bring it down! Gently, gently!" Mr. Warrenson mutters again with excitement in the general silence, and he is the only one speaking.

I take another deep breath and this time start with the high F that blasts through the clearing and resounds into the sky. Then I drop it down an octave into an object *lowering* slide.

My voice ends back on the Middle F.

And amazingly, the shuttle responds. Even from that impossible distance, it starts coming back down. . . .

I watch its plasma underbelly glowing faintly in the daylight, and just before it's about to hit the ground from twenty feet above, I sing the hovering "F-A-C."

The shuttle stops and hovers two feet above the ground.

I grow silent. And then, with an insolent triumphant glare of perfect *disdain* of my own, I turn to look at Aeson Kass.

I look directly into his eyes.

And I barely hear the wild woots and catcalls and clapping from my friends behind me, as the crowd of Candidates acknowledges what I've just done.

Because the look on Aeson's face is priceless.

And now everyone is coming toward me. "Amazing, absolutely amazing! I never thought I'd live to see something like this in action!" Mr. Warrenson is speaking excitedly. "What I don't understand is, why haven't you demonstrated the strength of your voice in Tech class, my dear? You were competent, but never particularly loud or unusual, and yes of course, you did earn a credit that one time for having perfect pitch—"

Nefir Mekei stops before me and there is an out-of-the-ordinary *living* expression on his normally reserved face. "Gwen, you have a remarkable voice," he says, placing one hand lightly on my shoulder. "You have no idea how rare it is."

"How?" I say, while I am still riding high with the emotion.

And then for the first time today Nefir smiles. "In Atlantis," he says, "such a natural *power singing voice* is only found among the most ancient families. And these days, only the members of the Imperial Family still wield the ability to sing like that. In the early days, thousands of years ago, they sang to move rocks and mountains, to align things of immense weight, to move and build pyramids and erect cities. *Logos anima mundi* you later came to call it here on Earth, forgetting the original meaning. But the Logos voice is not only the soul of the world, it is the ancient voice of creation. . . ."

I stare in new wonder, as it all begins to sink in, the weird things he just said.

"How is it," Keruvat says, "that *she* can have the Logos voice, here on Earth?" He comes to stand on the other side of us. "We thought it was extinct, the genetic code long gone from the Earth *homo sapiens* DNA. How is it possible? We might need to retest samples of the population—"

"If only there was time," Oalla says. And she looks at me with new appreciation.

All this while I keep glancing at Aeson. He stands off to the side, for some reason—away from me and the others as they surround me—and he is looking away into the distance.

I don't understand if he's stunned, or angry, or both.

Or maybe it's something else.

Because when he finally moves toward me, his face has a strange exalted look of wonder—a peculiar vulnerability almost—before it becomes veiled once more with composure.

"Candidate Lark," he says, facing me at last. "This changes everything."

"Command Pilot Kass—how so?" I stare back at him—still half-insolent in the way I dare to address him, almost a parallel taunt to what he just called me—but also I am curious. "What will you do now? What happens to me?"

"Because of your voice, its intrinsic value to us, we cannot simply set you aside. Therefore, we cannot Disqualify you or proceed with the normal course of legal actions," he says coldly. "However, don't think for a moment that you are relieved of suspicion of wrongdoing. The investigation into your role in the tragic sabotage will continue. But for the moment, you are no longer in custody."

"What? You're letting me go?" I say, amazed. *Okay, I did not see that coming.*

"You may return to your Dorm and your classes. You will continue in the Qualification process, but you will be watched closely." He pauses, and his lips form a severe line. Once again there's the sense that he is looking *through me*, drowning me with the pressure of his gaze in order to force the truth from me. "In addition, it gives me no pleasure, but you will be working with me from now on. We will work on your voice. I will also train you in other things you will need to know, to improve your chances for Qualification."

"So . . . what does that mean?"

"It means, I will see you in my office at eight, starting today. You know where it is. Now, dismissed." And speaking curtly, Aeson Kass turns his back on me.

I pause momentarily, still feeling the echoes of his voice cutting through me, and watch him move away and speak in even cool tones of Atlantean with the two Correctors. Nefir and Oalla join them, and they all begin walking from the airfield, while the others also start dispersing.

I turn, and in that moment George and Gordie are at my side. "Wow, Gwen, what was that? That was incredible!" George says, putting his arm around me. "I had no idea you had a voice like that! When did that come about?"

"Yeah, it was like Mom's! Like you were singing an opera aria, Gee Two! And then you levitated an effing shuttle! Whoa!" Gordie says, with a big smile and slaps me on the back of the neck around the collar of my jacket, then pats my shoulder awkwardly. Gordie's never been much for hugging or physical contact, so coming from him this is huge.

Laronda and Dawn and the others surround me also. Laronda squeezes past Gordie and throws herself around my neck in a crazy embrace. She hugs me till it hurts and says, "Wow, girl, what a day! You and me both locked up! And why didn't you tell me you could sing like that? Holy cannoli, what was it that you did to make the shuttle go up like that? I've never seen anything like it in my life! Oooh, they must really be making plans for you now!"

"Well, they let her go, didn't they!" Dawn says, and I swear, I have never observed Dawn crack a full-blown smile, but here she is, smiling wide at me, and patting my arm.

"Oh! Thank you for the water, Hasmik!" I turn around and see the girl, and she waves with her hand like it was nothing, and finally gives me a big hug.

In the next couple of minutes I give and receive a bunch of hugs and pats and squeezes and other good things from these people who, I can pretty much say, are all my friends, in one way or another.

I turn with a smile and there's Logan. He stands before me, hands in the pockets of his windbreaker, and his warm hazel eyes never leave my face. A light beautiful smile dances on his lips, and then he leans in close to my ear and says softly, "Thank God that's over. . . ."

His breath gently tickles my cheek and immediately I get swept into a warm rising ocean. I am filled with a sensation like champagne bubbles, and I can only whisper back, "Thank you for being here for me."

"You bet," he says. "How are you feeling?"

I smile up at him. "Okay, I guess. . . . *Better*—now that you and everyone are here, and I am not locked up."

"Okay, Gwen, you must be starving," Laronda interrupts our moment of reverie.

"Oh, yeah!" I say. "I could eat an elephant! Not that I would *want* to eat an elephant, poor elephant, but you know what I mean—"

Logan smiles.

"Yeah, yeah! Now, shut it, girl!" Laronda chatters. "The cafeteria is still open, but just barely, if we hurry we can make it to the nearest dorm!"

"That would be my Green Dorm Eleven," George says and points to a nearby building across the airfield.

"Okay, let's go!" And Laronda pulls me by the hand.

We eat a last-minute dinner at George's dorm, all of us packed around a small table in the nearly empty cafeteria, while they close down the place around us. After everything that's happened, I am ravenous, and wolf down whatever mysterious macaroni casserole the cafeteria's serving today.

My brothers sit on both sides of me, and we elbow each other in friendly banter. It feels really strange and amazingly good to have my bros here like this, protective and comfortable. I briefly wonder if Gracie is okay, and if she is still freaked out about what happened to me. I probably should go see her after all this. . . .

Meanwhile, Logan is only one seat away, on the other side of George. They talk among themselves, but often I find, as I sneak peeks in his direction, that Logan is also glancing at me. And whenever our gazes meet, *he does not look away* and smiles.

Okay, that makes me feel amazing and incredibly giddy. I constantly forget to chew and swallow my food and blush a whole lot so that Laronda gives me funny googly-eyed looks across the table.

"So when did they let you out, Laronda?" I say in order to say something. "What time was it?"

"Not too long after they got you locked up instead." Laronda glances at Dawn who has her mouth full of casserole. "What was it, Dawn, around nine AM?"

Dawn nods at me, swallows. "Uh-uh, yeah. I was still waiting for you when I saw Laronda was released. Then we both asked about you and they told us you're arrested. That's when everything got really crazy. . . . Yeesh."

"So, Gwen," Logan says suddenly. "Any plans to go running tonight? I was thinking to do some laps at the AC building track."

"Oh . . ." I say. "Oh, yeah, sure. After all that lazing around in my four-star jailhouse hotel room, I could use some exercise. Except I have that thing at eight—you know—the evil appointment. I have to be over at *his* office—for whatever training or torture *Command Pilot Kass* has planned for me."

"Okay," he says. "But we could fit in a few laps for fifteen minutes before you have to be there, right?"

"I guess! Okay, then!" I smile shyly.

"Great!" And Logan finishes the rest of the juice in his glass.

After everyone disperses, Logan and I head over to the Arena Commons super structure. As we walk, I notice how a few Candidates who are also out and about, stare at me.

In fact, I should mention, this staring phenomenon started as soon as we got back from my "demonstration" ordeal at the airfield and went to eat dinner—news must have spread fast around the dorms, and everyone in the lobby of Green Dorm Eleven was watching and talking about me in quiet and not-so-quiet ways, as soon as they saw us coming.

"Gwen, how are you holding up?" Logan says, as he matches his longer stride to mine and then suddenly places his arm around my shoulders. His touch is light but tangible enough to send jolts of electricity racing all throughout my body. His arm is pressed around me and I look up at him with a quick shy glance, then immediately look straight ahead, while I feel like my lungs are about to burst.

"Well," I say, "it's been both terrifying and sort of cathartic. It's weird to have people think I'm either some kind of criminal terrorist or freak of nature—or both. But it's a relief to have the whole thing out in the open—even though they still suspect me of horrible things I didn't do."

"Yeah, I can see how it's both." He nods. "As for your voice—it really is something else. Kind of mind-blowing. I have to tell you, when you first explained to me that night how you sang and landed the shuttle, I did not believe you. I just couldn't. To my mind, it made no sense. But now that I actually saw and *heard* you do it—just, *wow.*"

I glance at him quickly, and the damned smile just does not want to leave my face.

"I can only begin to imagine," he continues, "the kind of things you can do with that voice of yours. Furthermore, with enough orichalcum at our disposal, we can do some groundbreaking major stuff—think about it, construction, engineering, technology, other industries. The applications here on Earth are limitless. The drilling industries alone—"

"What do you mean?"

"Well, think about it." He lets go of my shoulder and turns to me, and his expression is intensely focused. "What if Earth had access to all this orichalcum voice tech? Assuming, of course, that the asteroid threat was no longer there?"

"What? How can it be? I thought the asteroid is going to make impact regardless of what we do? Earth's official expiration date is what, in November of next year?"

"Yeah, of course it is. The dreaded November 18, 2048, at around 2:47 PM Eastern Time, plus or minus a few minutes, is when we go Boom." He recites the now-famous date and time of anticipated impact in a dramatic tone then shakes his head tiredly. "What I meant was, *what if* these circumstances were different? What if we had all the time in the world, and all the means to make something of ourselves in this new world of shared Atlantis-Earth cooperation?"

"I'm not sure it's any good thinking of what-ifs," I say. "It's super depressing."

"You're right." And then he shrugs it off lightly. "I was kind of carried away by the amazing potential of your voice. Sorry if it made you uncomfortable or bummed you out."

"Thanks, and no, I'm fine."

His hand is back around my shoulder, and I feel a gentle squeeze on my upper arm. "Good, because the last thing I want you to do is be upset over stupid stuff, after the kind of day you've had."

"It's not exactly over yet," I mutter. "I still have to deal with *him*."

Logan pauses walking and turns and looks at me, bringing himself to stand before me. His dark eyes glitter with intensity, reflecting the fluorescent lamps of the brightly lit walkway on which we happen to be—it's a portion of the RQC compound just a building away from the Arena Commons Building, since we're almost there.

"Gwen, you only have to deal with him for a short period of time. Go in there, stay smart, keep cool and use your head. Do nothing to provoke him in any way. All you need is to survive Qualification. And for that you need this Atlantean's special training. Whatever he teaches you—take it! Don't think about anything else. *Use him* as a resource."

"You're right," I say in turn, and gaze up into his warm, bewitching hazel eyes.

His chiseled lips curve upward. "Okay then, here's the plan—first, we run a few laps before eight, then you go in and see him. . . ."

I nod, unable to move away from him, from this incredible proximity and sensation of intimacy. And I think he kind of knows it. . . .

Because he leans in closer to me, so that I can almost feel his breath washing over my lips as he finishes: ". . . And after you get back, I'll be waiting for you."

Before I can say anything in reply, he suddenly closes the distance between us, puts his strong hand on my cheek and turns my head to the side slightly.

I am already reeling a little from the impossible touch of his fingers on my skin.

It's then that Logan Sangre *kisses* me . . .

On my mouth.

Chapter 27

Let me repeat that.

On my mouth.

I've just been kissed by Logan Sangre, full-on, lips against lips.

I've been dreaming of this moment for the last three years. No, strike that—I've been unknowingly *dreaming of this moment* for as long as I can remember, since I first became conscious that there was such a thing as girls and boys and kisses, and that I was a girl and that somewhere out there was the one perfect boy for me. . . .

Talk about uber-pathetic, I know. . . . The idea of the one perfect soul mate—whether it be girl, boy, or flying chipmunk—is right out of an old-fashioned romance novel (okay, maybe not the chipmunk part, unless he's a shape-shifting paranormal chipmunk who turns into a sexy tattooed hunk when the moon is full—yeah, you can tell I'm babbling even in my thoughts). Honestly, I should know better. But I can still dream. . . .

Furthermore, I've been dreaming of that one perfect boy seeing me and naturally falling in love with me at first sight. And then I visualized what it would be like to have that first magical kiss.

And now, the impossible has come true. My first kiss happened with Logan Sangre, the perfect guy of my dreams.

Okay, no, strike that again. This, just now, was my first *real* kiss.

Because there was another awful stupid kiss in first grade, a kiss that doesn't really count except in the technical sense. It happened when a bunch of class bullies gathered around me and another nerdy loser kid—the wimpiest, skinniest, shortest little boy in class, the one who had the huge glasses and the stick arms and whose name I don't remember—and they chanted "Kiss! Kiss! Kiss!" as they crowded around us and pushed and shoved the two of us together until the poor boy reluctantly planted a sloppy fish-wet smooch on my mouth. I remember shoving him away immediately and then spitting in disgust, wiping his disgusting saliva from my lips while saying "Eeeew, gross!"

That was my one and only "kiss" experience before the real thing just happened, seconds ago.

Wow....

I had no idea that a boy's lips could be so soft.

Because *his* lips that are so beautiful and naturally well-shaped are also soft as a dream as they press against mine with gentle sensuality, sending all kinds of electrical impulses coursing down my body.... My lips are now the center of the universe—all feeling, all sensation and focus is there.

Logan draws back, and his hazel eyes never look away. Meanwhile I exhale in wonder, and find that I am trembling.

"What—what was that?" I say like a total fool, even as my lips still remain parted.

He looks at me and then the faintest shadow smile comes to him. "I thought you might like a little support.... I felt like it—and like it was what you needed. I hope I didn't screw up just now? Please let me know if I did!"

"Oh, no!" I blink rapidly, and my lips are still ringing like silent bells from the touch of his against mine. "That was—that was good! Thank you! I mean, it was amazing, and it was—"

"Gwen," he says. "I really *like* you."

I stare, just dumbstruck.

"And maybe I'm wrong," he continues, "but I think there's something there too on your end, something between us. I get the sense that you—"

"Yes!" I say. "I do!"

And then I realize how idiotic that sounds—it's like I just said a formal marriage wow! And now he is probably going to be all disgusted and turned off by my needy clingy response. *Oh lord, what have I done?*

But apparently I have nothing to worry about.

"Oh, phew!" he says with a laugh, and makes a gesture of

wiping fake sweat from his forehead. "Was worried you might not take it well. Or that you may not be interested."

"I—I really like you too! I'm just amazed you don't already have a girlfriend or something."

He shrugs lightly. "I did. Back in St. Albans. She went to our school too, might have been in your class, even. But we broke up a while ago. It was just not working."

"Oh . . ." I say.

"But, forget her, I want to get to know *you*."

"Okay."

"You're not with anyone, are you?"

I shake my head side to side negatively, like a giddy fool. *Oh, if only he knew!*

We resume walking, and Logan's hand slips into mine.

It feels like lightning has struck me, and it's coursing back and forth between us, in the spot where our palms and fingers touch. . . .

I am not exactly sure what happens for the next fifteen minutes. It's all kind of a crazy happy blur. We get to the Arena Commons Building. . . . We run around the track, and we laugh as he pulls me by my hand at some point when I begin to collapse.

I end up in stitches, gasping from running and laughing at I don't know what, while he grins and tells me silly funny things as we again race each other.

And then it's almost eight o'clock.

"Ugh," I say, with a glance up at the fifth level walkway of the stadium arena, "I have to go."

He nods. "Go. I'll be here."

"Are you sure? It might take a while."

"Yeah, I'm sure." There's a determined light in his eyes that makes my heart warm.

And so I leave him at the track and head upstairs to Office 512 and my grim fate.

When I reach the upper walkway and knock on the office door, I am worn out from having just run laps. It's actually good that I am almost too tired to care what Aeson Kass will think or expect of me, because I am still riding the emotional high from hanging out with Logan.

And yet . . . my pulse goes erratic, begins to sound once again in my temples, this time from nerves as opposed to exertion. But my agitation is relatively dull and not as bad as it could be.

Yeah, it really *has* been a very long day.

No one answers the door, but the light inside is on, visible through the shades. Once again I simply turn the handle and enter.

This time the office is lit up brightly, but although the various consoles and surveillance screens are live, there's no one at the computer area. I look around and there's Blayne Dubois on the sofa. He's holding the familiar hoverboard, while his wheelchair has been moved neatly out of the way against the wall.

Okay, I wasn't sure what to expect after today's intense events, but it looks like our secret training arrangement with Blayne is still on. . . .

"Hey." I approach the sofa lounging area and take a seat next to him. "Where is he?"

Blayne gives me a brief look. "He's in the other room. Got some kind of important call, had to take it, said he'll be back in a few."

"What other room?"

Blayne points.

I stare where he's pointing and for the first time notice a very discreet doorway that almost looks like it's a part of the wall, or maybe a utility closet near the end of the sofa.

"Oh," I say. "I didn't notice that door. What is it?"

"I've no idea. Probably more office space. Maybe it's his private rooms."

"I see. . . . Interesting."

"Not really." And Blayne turns away from me, flipping his hair out of his eyes.

"Okay—did he say what we're supposed to do until he gets back?"

"No."

Well, this is going to be awkward.

I sit, drumming my fingers against the sofa upholstery. Minutes pass.

"I heard what happened today," Blayne says suddenly. He is

still not looking at me but staring at the surface of the hoverboard that he's holding upright. "Is it true that you actually levitated a whole shuttle just with your singing?"

"Yeah."

"How'd you do it?"

"No idea. But, I'm hoping that *he* will explain it to me at some point. That is, if he ever shows up."

"That's kind of mind-blowing."

"Yeah. . . ."

Another long pause.

Blayne stops fiddling with the hoverboard and glances at me. "Did you have anything to do with whoever blew up that other shuttle?"

I frown at him. "No! Of course not! Do you seriously think I'd be involved in something awful like that? Jeez!"

He shrugs. "Whatever. Just had to ask."

"Did Command Pilot Kass put you up to this?" I say with beginning irritation.

"No, he didn't have to. It's just me asking. Not that I really think you did it. If you did, it would be completely unlike you." And Blayne's lips curve into the faintest smile.

My mouth falls open. "Okay, what's that supposed to mean?"

"It's a good thing, Lark. Means I don't think you're an a-hole capable of evil villain deeds. You're pushy and annoying, but not malicious."

My jaw drops even more, and my eyebrows go up. "Oh, really?" I snort. "How well you know me! Jeez, thank you for the compliment from hell!" But I'm grinning.

"Any time," he says.

"So, how are you doing?" I decide to change the subject and use this opportunity—since Blayne's not in an entirely asocial mood—to talk to him.

"Fine, great. Insert your own adjective." He runs his fingers against the matte surface of the hoverboard.

"Have you been practicing any of this stuff back at the dorm?" I say it and immediately realize how stupid my question is.

"How? I don't have a hoverboard. The best I can do on my own is the hand Forms. But there's no one to practice sparring with outside of class."

"We can practice together," I say.

He shrugs.

"No, seriously!" I lean forward. "I need someone to practice with anyway, since looks like I will be doing some extracurricular voice stuff or something. And this way we can keep it low-key and won't have to explain things to anyone else. How about it?"

Blayne pauses, then after an exhalation, says, "Sure . . . okay."

"Cool!" I smile at him.

The inner door opens and Aeson Kass comes in from the other room.

Immediately my heart does this weird, hard somersault-lurch-jerk in my chest and the pulse in my temples starts pounding. . . .

Oh, crap! Considering how I react to him, at this rate this guy is going to kill me. . . .

But Aeson does not seem to notice how I stiffen up, nor does he seem to care. His expression is indifferent and he appears very, very tired, judging by the hollows around his eyes.

"All right, let's get started," he says to both of us, never looking at me directly.

"So," I blurt. "Does this mean I am still going to continue helping out with Blayne's practice?"

"Yes, you are." His answer is crisp and emotionless.

"What about my own practice? You said—"

"After this." He interrupts me in a hard voice and turns to Blayne.

I get up and stand ready to assist with holding the board. I am mostly ignored.

It is very strange to be in such near proximity with someone who actively does not want to be around you. As I stand holding the board, watching Aeson and Blayne throw exquisitely precise form-based punches, inches away from my face, I cannot help feeling the new distance between me and the Atlantean.

He never once glances in my direction. All his instructions to me are spoken in a bland voice and accompanied with minimal gestures. At one point when I move in too closely, he stops and tells me to keep back. And again I only see his profile.

Ten minutes later, they finish sparring, and Aeson pauses, while Blayne is trying to catch his breath.

"There is one more thing I need to show you for today, and then we're done." This time Aeson turns to me also and I see his gaze flicker over me as he includes us both.

"At some point when you are on a hoverboard or anywhere else you find that you have to support or *carry* another person in mid-air—especially if the person is hanging off the board and you can only reach and grab them by the hand—we use a technique we call the Grip of Friendship."

I watch in curiosity as Aeson then demonstrates. "Put out your hand," he tells Blayne. "Like this, palm down. And you—" he turns to me. "You reach underneath, to clasp his arm above the wrist. The insides of your arms touch. Both of you hold the other's arm above the wrist."

I do as I am told. I reach out and take Blayne's warm hand, slightly slippery with sweat.

"Clasp firmly, and remember well," Aeson says, looking at our arms and hands held together, and then at our faces. "This hold is similar to what your trapeze artists and acrobats use here on Earth when they hold each other up with arms and hands alone as they swing. It can save your life, and prevent a fall. No other mutual hold or grip is as secure as this one."

"Got it," Blayne says, flexing his fingers in the grip then releasing my arm.

I nod. "Okay."

"Good," Aeson says to Blayne. "That's it for today, Candidate Dubois, you can go."

"Thanks," Blayne mutters, then turns to his wheelchair.

I watch the now familiar maneuver with which Blayne switches over from hoverboard to the chair. And then he heads out.

I am suddenly alone with Aeson Kass.

My face hurts from trying to keep it motionless, not even twitch a muscle, as I wait for Aeson to give me his attention.

"What now?" I say finally, while he goes to the console surveillance area and checks the various multi-screens.

He says nothing. Moments pass.

Finally he returns to me, and I notice that he is carrying

something in one hand. His gaze is steady and unblinking as he looks at me coldly, stands before me, then opens his palm at chest level before him.

On it, are two small pieces of orichalcum.

"Your first lesson," Aeson Kass says, and his eyes narrow with the finest trace of hostility that breaks through his otherwise impeccable composure, "is to be able to fine-tune and control the *focus* of your voice to such a degree that you can perform actions selectively on one object and not the other."

I frown. "What does that mean?"

His gaze bores into me with a dark relentless force that makes me want to retreat—to step back, to blink and look away.

I clutch my fingers slowly, and *don't.*

"Levitate only *one* of these two pieces," he says.

I suddenly begin to understand. "But—is that even possible? I thought that the keying sequence affects everything made of orichalcum within hearing distance."

"Normally yes, that would be the case. But an advanced user of the voice is able to selectively manipulate one or more objects without affecting any of the others. Like this—"

Aeson glances down at the two pieces of gold-flecked grey metal. He parts his lips and turns his head slightly toward one of the two. He sings a single, very precise note, followed by two others in a minor chord keying sequence.

Like an ocean swell, the rich deep sound of his voice rolls through me . . . and suddenly it makes my fine hairs stand on end, while I feel goose bumps rising along my skin.

He grows silent then slowly lowers his open palm. I shiver, the echoes of his voice still caressing me along my nerve endings. And I see that only one of the two pieces is indeed hovering in the air before him. The second piece remains inert on his open palm.

"Okay, wow." I say. "How did you do that?"

"I narrow-focused my sound output. Think of a narrow beam of light, sharp like a laser. Now do the same thing to sound. Each note you make is directed at an object, 'thrown' at it." He points to the sofa. "Here, take these two pieces, go sit over there, and practice for ten minutes."

I raise one brow, then take the orichalcum from him, and

momentarily our fingers touch. At the instant of contact he flinches. And then he turns away and returns to the console surveillance area.

I watch him briefly, but his back is to me and it's as if I am no longer in the room. So I sit down on the sofa, open my palm and begin singing to the orichalcum.

For several embarrassing minutes I feel like a dork because I am only able to do an all-or-nothing kind of levitation. Both pieces levitate, then I re-set them to "inert" so they drop on my palm, and I start over . . . and over . . . and over.

My voice sounds small and tired. I frequently glance up to see what Aeson is doing, but he is busy with the consoles.

At one point he receives a video call and briefly speaks in cold, authoritative tones in Atlantean with a pale-metallic haired girl. She wears an expensive and exotic looking outfit, against a background of waterfalls and rich emerald greenery that I can just barely see from where I'm sitting. Her tone seems upper-class and bored, and the lilting sounds of her voice are like a sweet running stream. It occurs to me, she is *on* Atlantis. Right now. *She is calling from Atlantis.*

The realization acts to stun me briefly. I remember seeing brief video propaganda images of Atlantis shown to us on TV, and the amazing scenery and nature shots. But it had all seemed unreal—until now.

Furthermore, how is that even possible? Shouldn't there be some kind of time delay? And I am talking *major* time delay!

I pause momentarily, gathering my thoughts, then resume the singing exercise.

After the face-to-face call is over, another comes in, and this time it's some Atlantean in uniform against a neutral background. Aeson talks with this guy quickly, and his cool commanding tone does not change. However when the second call is done, there is a sense of something grim and unpleasant that lingers like a foreboding.

Curious, I really wish I knew what they were saying.

Aeson gets up in that moment and approaches.

He stands looking down at me. "Time's up. How are you doing?"

"Not too good." I glance up at him, trying not to blink as I hold his icy gaze. "I can make both pieces levitate but not just one."

"You will keep practicing until you are able to do it. We will continue tomorrow. Now, you may go."

"Oh, okay. Can I take these back with me to practice in my dorm?"

He makes a sound of disdain. "Nice try. No, Candidate, you are the last person who might be permitted to take anything made of orichalcum anywhere."

My lips harden into a straight line. "Okay. But how am I supposed to practice without—"

"That would be *your* problem."

Anger rises in me, until my head is ringing with it. Oh, the things I could say now! But I don't. I stiffen, and then I stand up and silently offer up the contents of my palm to him.

He takes the orichalcum from me, making a subtle point of not touching my fingers.

"If working with me is such a hassle for you," I say suddenly, "why do you do it?"

"It is not a hassle," he replies, and his gaze pierces me like a hard beam of light passing through glass. "It is a necessity."

"But you kind of hate me. Why not get someone else to do it?"

His expression is closed up completely, and I cannot read anything in his eyes. "There is nothing personal here, Candidate Lark," he says after a brief pause. "You are a valuable asset. And as such, you are treated accordingly."

I snort. "Okay, you know what? What a farce! This whole thing is! If I am so valuable, why don't you just Qualify me automatically? Pass me up to the front of the line and just Qualify me already."

He watches me, composed and blank. "That's not how it works. It is not up to me. I have no final say on the Qualification process. I can make strong recommendations which carry some weight toward your passing score, but that's all. You still have to go through the Semi-Finals and then, if you advance, the Finals."

"And who makes these determinations in the first place? Who decides?"

But he shakes his head. "No. We are done talking. You need to go now. Besides, you friend is waiting for you downstairs in the arena."

I crane my head slightly. "Um . . . who?"

Aeson watches me and there's the slightest hint of something dark and intense underneath the composed surface. "That boy. The one you've been running with, and who came with you at least one other time. Who is he?"

"Oh," I say, and a slightly weird sensation awakens inside me. "That's Logan. He's from my high school and he's helping me run better."

Aeson nods. "Fine. I'll see you tomorrow."

And on that note we're done.

When I get to the first floor arena level, Logan Sangre is waiting for me. He sees me, and he smiles, and immediately warmth surges through me. It's as if everything is right with the world, if only for a brief moment.

"How did it go?" he asks, as we start walking together back to our dorms.

"Better than I thought," I say with an exhalation of relief. My pulse begins racing once more, but with a giddy *good* feeling, as it occurs to me yet again, here is Logan, walking next to me, and he kissed me, and he actually *likes* me! *Holy moly!*

And then I tell Logan an abbreviated version, because I am not supposed to be mentioning Blayne and his training. Instead I make it out as though my own voice exercises took up all this time.

"He didn't threaten you with anything else, did he?" Logan touches my back lightly with his palm, sending sweet shivers along my nerve endings, even through the layers of jacket and T-shirt.

"Oh no. Though I did ask him, how come, if I am so valuable to them, do I have to go through all this extended training bull. Why not just Qualify me automatically?"

"And what did he say?"

"Not much. Said it was not up to him."

Logan raises one brow. "Interesting."

I get back to Yellow Dorm Eight and say bye to Logan who presses my slightly trembling hands in his capable strong fingers and leans in closer to my ear.

I think he is going in for another kiss, but he only whispers, while his breath tickles my neck, "Sleep well . . . Yellow Candy." It occurs to me, he knows we are directly in the line of sight of multiple surveillance cameras, so best to tone it down so as not to provoke any anti-dating reprimands.

My heart is racing as I make my way past many staring Candidates in the lounge. I remember once again that yeah, I am kind of famous now, in a weird way, not only among my dorm-mates but probably all around the RQC, as word of my weird voice and shuttle levitation demo is spreading.

It's been one helluva day.

Upstairs, the girls' dormitory floor is no different. Girls glance and whisper and stare at me as I walk past the rows of beds.

"Gwen!" Hasmik waves to me enthusiastically. Laronda and Dawn are sitting on her bed wearing sleeping shirts and undies. They stop chatting and attack me with questions.

"Are you okay, girl? OMG, what happened?"

I smile and tell them, meanwhile noticing how other girls from distant beds look at me as if I'm some kind of alien zoo specimen. Even the alpha mean girls stop their own chatter and glare at me. I can see Ashley and Claudia giving me long killing looks, and then Olivia gets up and purposefully walks by in nothing but a sleek nightshirt and sleeping bra over her super-well-endowed chest, her smooth long legs glistening with newly applied lotion.

"Nice rack on that chick," Dawn quips when Olivia's far away and out of hearing. Laronda rolls her eyes and punches Dawn on the arm.

"What?" Dawn says. "I like boobs. Even on a-hole bitches." And then she gives Olivia another glance.

"Since when do you check out other girls, girlfriend?"

Dawn shrugs. There's a little shy smile on her face. "Since always."

Laronda gives a loud snort-laugh and puts her hand to her mouth. "Wait, are you—"

"Yeah."

I get into bed while they're all still talking and giggling.

Suddenly I am deathly tired. But my mind is swimming with so many conflicting emotions—joy and stress, exuberance and the ever-present old twinges of despair that comes from the knowledge of impending apocalypse.

When the dormitory lights go out, I am already on the edges of a fragile dream.

Chapter 28

The next morning I wake up to claxons and day seven of Qualification. It's hard to believe it's been a whole week at the RQC.

Suddenly everything is racing, it seems—events, levels of stress, difficulty of classes. Things good and bad, mixed up together.

It's actually hard to describe that day—and now that I think about it, most of the following days—because after that first week, nothing drastically weird happens, and it all kind of runs together and becomes a blur of general routine.

Everything, all the three weeks of Qualification that remain to us, are leading up to the day of Semi-Finals.

And that time goes by quickly and uneventfully for the twenty-one days that follow.

We attend classes where we learn more about Atlantis and how to fight and defend ourselves with hand-to-hand combat and with weapons of the Four Quadrants, particularly our own nets and cords. We hone our singing with complicated note sequences. We tone our bodies. Yeah, even those of us who are nerdy klutzes such as yours truly, improve. . . . And while my body still hurts constantly all over with a dull neverending ache, it slowly lessens every night as my endurance increases and my muscles get stronger.

In Agility Training I still get occasional last place demerits for running laps, but only three times in week two and twice in week three. On the fourth week of Agility Training, to my own amazement, I manage to squeak by without a single running demerit. As far as climbing and monkey bars, yeah, I barely learn to hand swing halfway across the scaffolding by the middle of week two, and finally cross the whole distance with my hands by the end of the third week, though inconsistently, four times out of seven. And on week four I make it six times out of seven. Oalla Keigeri gives me a nod of approval the first time I do it. And it feels kind of amazing!

Talking about amazing—turns out, I am actually pretty good in Combat. After that first time when I held my own against Claudia Grito, I find that I am quick and steady with strikes, punches and parries, which more than makes up for my untrained muscle weakness. Er-Du Forms become relatively comfortable if not easy after I learn to hold each precise position, because they make good natural sense, and there's a logic and beauty to the combinations of movement. When the Instructors start scoring us, I generally find myself in the top third of my class when it comes to Forms. Of course it helps that I get that extra lesson time every night from watching Aeson Kass and Blayne in the evening sparring sessions—but more on that in a moment.

Combat classes get more interesting on week two when we are taught how to use cords and nets as true weapons. The key to our native Quadrant weapon, Keruvat Ruo tells us, is the potential for *entanglement* of the opponent.

"Think of a spider weaving a web," he says. "The strands stick together and bind the prey with a combination of adhesiveness and tight bonds. The spider also injects a paralytic to render the prey unconscious. In your case, all you have is one out of three—the ability to create tight restraining bonds. Your opponent is neither paralyzed, nor is there sticky glue involved. All you have on your side is speed and the ability to tie knots and otherwise shape the cord to restrain your opponent's mobility."

For all of week two we practice a variety of intricate knotting techniques, so that Tremaine walks around whistling sailor tunes. "We're in the navy, man!" he drawls. "I'm gonna start tying my locks together in new combo knots!"

After the fancy knots, we are taught combinations of loops and string figures that feel like a complex version of the "cat's cradle" game, using finger agility. On the first day of week three, Oalla Keigeri shows us how to "hand-crochet" a net using nothing but string and our fingers. It is amazing, because it really does resemble crocheting with yarn, except there is no crochet hook, and in its place you use your index finger to pull the string into loops.

"At last, I am a certified ninja granny," Laronda says on the first night of week three, sitting on her dormitory cot, as she finger-manipulates coarse rope into a net that has grown to a radius of five feet around her—and I'm right next to her, doing the same thing on my cot. We race each other as our nets grow, and when we run out of string from the balls given us, we let it all out and start again.

"I love knitting and crochet," Hasmik says from her cot on the other side of me, as her fingers fly in the making of her own net. "In Yerevan, Armenia, we all knit and crochet all the time. My grandmother teach me and my mother too. When we first came to Boston and started to learn English, I tell people I like to work with crochet hook, that I was a good hooker. Okay, they tell me, 'No, no, hooker is a bad word, don't say that!' Oops! See, this is fun!" Admittedly, Hasmik has a point, because her nets are consistently the best in our class, and she has the fastest hands and fingers you can imagine.

During week four, Combat becomes truly intense. Because for the first time we are allowed to interact with Candidates from the other Quadrants, and their own native weapons are pitted against ours.

Mixed classes are taught in the Arena Commons Building. There we go up against the Reds and their sword and knife blade techniques, the Greens and their shields and bucklers and body armor, and the Blues with their projectile weapons and firearms which for now employ safety rounds, rubber bullets, and paintball pellets.

"Each Quadrant weapon presents a natural advantage and disadvantage," Oalla Keigeri tells us, while Keruvat Ruo demonstrates.

"Blue holds the immediate advantage from a distance over everyone except Green and their shields. Yellows—do not let yourself get shot in the first few seconds. Move in quickly, and narrow the distance between you and Blue. Then you can overpower the Blue with your net and cord, up-close and personal."

"Red is the exact opposite," Xelio Vekahat tells us. "Yellow needs to stay as far away as possible, because you will be cut up with the blades, and your cord weapons rendered useless. However, you can still trap Red and render your opponent harmless if you cast your nets and cords in such a way as to disarm them."

"Green is tricky," Erita Qwas says. "Neither distance nor proximity is best when it comes to Yellow fighting Green. Instead, you need to maintain a middle distance and use speed and entanglement, while faced with the blunt force of their shields used as impact weapons to attack you."

And then they bring out the hoverboards.

Oh, yeah. *We get to learn to fight while airborne.*

It amazes me what a difference a few weeks makes when it comes to learning to keep balance on top of a hovering flat surface. By week two, we no longer use English commands to control the hoverboards in Agility training, and have switched to musical note sequences—since by then we've also become proficient in the Atlantis Tech classes with the basic levitation commands.

Week two is all about going up and down on the hoverboard and varying heights. Week three is all about *speed*. First we race along the perimeter of the basement Training Hall in our dorm. Then the later classes are taken to the Arena Commons where we are told to race around the entire arena track, moving as fast as we can without falling off. Many board riders capsize on that third week, and that's when most of the more serious injuries begin to happen. . . . And yes, unfortunately people are Disqualified on that basis, as they get taken out of the RQC in medical ambulances.

By week four, my fear of heights is still there, but it has become a numb secondary thing that I overpower somehow every day, keeping it under tight control. I am never too fast on the hoverboard, but neither am I the slowest one. Instead, I clench my hands and maintain control, and breathe, *breathe*, as I make my flying laps sharp and effective, making each second count.

That way, by the time hoverboards are introduced in Combat, it's no longer a shock.

Meanwhile, in all these days of training, there's Logan Sangre. He's what keeps me sane in all this pressure-cooker atmosphere of the RQC, as we meet every day, as many times a day as possible. Seems like wherever I turn, there's Logan. We train together every night during Homework Hour. We eat lunch and when possible, dinner together. He walks me back from the evening training at the Arena Commons every night. And sometimes, when we get to a certain spot between two buildings where there's no sign of surveillance cameras—at least not any we can humanly imagine in such a tight place—sometimes Logan and I make out.

Yeah, it's mostly very intense and brief kissing, with me propped up against a wall and Logan's hands supporting me as we struggle against each other in sweet crazy heat. His lips crush my mouth, and his tongue enters, hungrily, and I get my first taste of tongue kissing. His mouth tastes sweet, and there is nothing really I can compare it to. . . .

A few seconds in, he presses his body tight against me, and his arms and hands go around my back as he just holds me, very very tight, breathing hard in my throat, and I can hear the wild beating of his strong heart through all the layers of our clothing.

But we cannot linger, so with a shudder we come apart, and sort of straighten our clothes in place, calming our breathing for a few seconds. He gently strokes my long strands of hair and I run my fingers through his tousled own, and we are like two thoroughbreds on a hair-trigger, calming each other down, or we explode. . . .

"Okay?" he whispers and his hazel eyes are at the same time clear and deep and murky with suppressed desire.

"Yeah . . ." I nod, while my pulse beat slowly calms.

And then we continue walking to our dorms, not even holding hands.

By the third week of Qualification, pretty much everyone has an idea that we're a "thing," including my brothers and Gracie.

"He is really nice and cute," Gracie says about Logan, halfway into week three.

I smile at her, and thankfully don't mention that I am glad she hasn't been spending all her time with Daniel Tover—only half of her time. And honestly, there's not all that much that can be done about it, since I can neither supervise nor control my sister's every move. Daniel seems to be mature and reasonable, and as far as I know he really is like an older friend treating Gracie and her childish crush decently.

Basically Gracie's made a bunch of friends in her Red Quadrant, and Daniel's at the center of a widespread group. At least that's what I can glean from asking Logan about it, diplomatically—since Logan is friends with Daniel. For now at least, I'm keeping an open mind and trusting Gracie to behave and the older boy to not take advantage.

As for my brothers, George likes Logan and approves outright, especially since we're all from the same school, so it makes it somehow even better, closer to home—if that makes any sense. Gordie seems to have no strong opinion, which, when it comes to Gordie, is normally a perfectly okay thing.

For the most part, my siblings are handling Qualification training reasonably well. Gracie loves swordfighting and knife throwing and brags about it every time we see each other. According to Gracie, Red Quadrant Atlanteans fight with multiple swords at once, two being the default, and they manage to incorporate additional smaller daggers and micro-blades in every maneuver. Then she shows me a neat trick with her fingers, opening and closing her empty palm and suddenly razor-fine micro-blades are bristling from between each finger digit like claws. "We are supposed to practice hiding and transferring blades between fingers until we get it right, so it's like second nature."

But Gordie wows me even more, because the boy's become a very solid marksman. During week three, my nearsighted baby brother with his permanently smudged glasses and a chronic inability to notice things past his nose, takes me and George to the Arena Commons firing range where he calmly shoots every target in the precise center, and then switches to his left hand and *does it again.*

"Wow, that's crazy good, Gee Three!" I say. "You're awesome! How'd you do it?"

"Thanks." Gordie beams. "It's actually not that hard once they explained how to properly aim at stuff."

"What do you mean? How are you supposed to aim?"

Gordie turns his head slightly and gives me his typical slow crooked smile. "That's the thing," he says. "You don't really aim at all. You sort of *know* where the target is with your mind, beforehand. And then when the time comes to fire, you just let your body's reflexes naturally point to it, on the fly. . . . You *never* aim. You *find* it."

I am not sure I get it completely, but whatever it is, it seems to be working out great for Gordie. And even George admits that our little Gee Three seems very grown up these days. He also thinks Gracie's doing pretty well too, all things considered. At least there's less whining.

George himself is somewhat harder to read. Whatever it is they teach him at the Green Quadrant is not as clearly definable, not as clear-cut. In some ways, Green and Yellow are very similar—both are equally subtle, murky and complicated, in direct contrast to Red and Blue's straightforwardness.

"Our basis is resistance, stability achieved through balance, and defense," George says thoughtfully, trying to put complex notions into words. "With shields, *strength* is used differently. You mostly learn to block, anticipate your opponent, aspire to be where they will be in the next instant. First, you *anchor* yourself . . . and then you become very flexible and 'all over the place.' You surrender your own position and self—in order to retain it. Like a rubber band snapping. Does that even make sense?"

"Yeah, strangely enough, it kind of does." I nod.

George laughs uncomfortably. "Glad you don't think I'm crazy, Gee Two. Because sometimes I think Green is a little crazy. . . . Shields are crazy. Everything, this whole thing is— letting go and holding back. . . . *Sacrifice*."

And when he says this, it makes me think of what's going on outside, beyond the secure fence of the RQC in the greater world . . . which, it turns out, is falling apart more and more every day.

Because although they don't tell us, some news gets in, in one way or another. Over the entire four weeks we learn of new escalations—mass riots on a daily basis, new wars on five continents, and even a brief nuclear threat from one crazy small nation that decided they wanted to go out with a bang *on their own terms* and take the whole world with them before the asteroid makes impact. . . .

I feel utter numbness come over me every time I think of our parents all alone, in our small house back in Highgate Waters, rural northern dairyland Vermont, a few miles from the Canadian border. The closest large city is St. Albans, and I can only imagine the kind of unrest that has reached even these peaceful communities by now. I have no idea if Dad even bothers to commute to his job at the University further south. Or if Mom can get the regular medical supplies she needs. . . .

Honestly, I don't *want* to know. I don't think I can bear it.

Finally, with all that's been going on, there's the situation with my alleged criminal status and my special training. In that sense nothing has changed. I am still under suspicion for the shuttle incident, and over the three weeks, I am questioned at least five more times by the Correctors, as I am called in briefly to Building Fifteen to "verify" certain facts and renew my alibis, and basically reiterate everything I've already told them. Except for the two Candidates who were arrested on the same night as Laronda, in connection with trying to smuggle out one of the navigation chips on the underside of a delivery truck, they still haven't found whoever is responsible for the main sabotage. And so the investigation continues, including random dorm searches. By now, everyone's been "interviewed," some people multiple times.

And then there's my training. Apparently, the power singing voice—the Logos voice—that got me into this mess in the first place, is even more important in its potential than I thought. I still get plenty of curious stares around the RQC compound from Candidates who think of me as the weirdo with the "super voice." Unfortunately, over the three weeks following, I find out that except for my ability to belt out the keying sequence that levitates a shuttle, I am unable to do much of anything else with it—yet.

At least I tell myself the "yet" part because it gets harder and harder to face Command Pilot Aeson Kass and his subtle mocking indifference every night and produce little to no results.

Blayne Dubois, on the other hand, is making amazing progress. By the end of the second week of their sessions, I find that I no longer have to hold the hoverboard for him, as he has figured out a means of keeping the board vertically upright with a combination of upper body balance and his own partial leg muscle strength.

Instead, I now get to help out only occasionally and mostly observe and wait while their sparring is done, and then it's my turn after Blayne leaves. I should mention that Blayne and I have been discreetly practicing LM Forms sparring on our own time, in an empty classroom on the fourth floor of our dorm, with him in his wheelchair and me sitting down across from him to maintain eye-to-eye level. It's not easy to do real LM Forms without a hoverboard, but we do get some extra time in.

But the most oddly unbearable moments happen in Office 512, after Blayne's training is over for the night and Aeson Kass and I are left alone.

That's when Aeson asks me about my progress from the night before, looking at me steadily with his unreadable eyes that appear to see right through me. I cringe inside with embarrassment and tell him that nothing new happened, and I am still unable to perform this task or that.

"Keep practicing," is usually all he says, without any inflection, as he drops pieces of orichalcum into my palm. "Modulate your voice in as many ways as you can—tone, volume, intensity. You have the means to do it. It is up to you to discover how."

And sometimes I retort in frustration, "But I have no idea what I'm doing! Is there anything you can suggest?"

"No," he replies. "It is all practice and insight. I cannot teach you insight, only tell you what may or may not be done."

And that's when I really want to reach out and slap him on his perfectly shaped sarcastic mouth.

There are a few things I do manage to get right, eventually. By the end of week two, I am able to do the selective focus levitation of only *one* orichalcum object out of several.

But the most important assignment he gives me I finally perform by the end of week four, only a few days before our looming date of Semi-Finals.

It's the ability to *override* and temporarily *nullify* other people's keying status in relation to a given orichalcum object. In other words, not only can I re-key objects to myself remotely that have been already keyed and claimed by other people, but I can make it so that the orichalcum receives such a strong charge of my own vocal resonance that *other people cannot* key it back again for a long time. . . .

Basically it means I can step in and take control from others. It is called an Aural Block. And Aeson warns me that I am not to tell anyone about it—about what I can now *do*. . . .

It's my secret weapon for Qualification.

At last, it's day twenty-seven at the RQC, with only one other day remaining before the Semi-Finals. We still don't know *what* the Semi-Finals will actually be—that announcement comes tomorrow.

But today?

Today's the day our official Standing Scores are posted in each of the twelve dorms.

The 7:00 AM claxon alarms go off and I open my eyes, blinking from the bright overhead lights. By now I am used to these rude awakenings, but this one in particular gives me a sinking sense of dread.

"Oh, no . . . noooooo . . . Sweet lord help us . . ." Laronda moans from her own bed, as everyone in the girls' dormitory comes awake to this new frightening day.

"I don't want to go downstairs," Hasmik says from the other side. "I can't bear it."

"I know," I mutter, sitting up.

"Our Scores. . . . Do you think they're already up?" a girl wonders several beds down.

"Probably," another one replies.

"Rise and shine, girlfriends! Get your butts downstairs, sooner not later! *Move!*" Dorm Leader Gina Curtis pops her head in from the double doors and begins yelling at the whole room in her brash voice.

"Yeah, yeah. . . . Ready?" Dawn mutters, holding her change of clothes and underwear as she waits for us to get our own morning stuff together.

"As ready as I'll ever be . . . let's go." Taking a deep breath of resignation, Laronda grabs her clothes and things.

Running on nerves, we hit the bathrooms and already the gossip is non-stop. Everyone has a theory about these dratted

Scores, and some are pretty wild.

As we've been told earlier, our performance over the past four weeks has been evaluated by all of our Instructors. Various achievement factors—some that we might guess, such as "voice," "agility," "weapons combat," and others that we probably can't even imagine—are all added up into an overall combined Achievement Total for each Candidate. These Achievement Totals are then ranked in order. And this is what determines each Candidate's standing in the whole RQC—the Standing Score.

Since there are 6,023 Candidates in the Pennsylvania RQC-3, the highest possible Standing Score is #1 and the lowest Standing Score is #6,023.

What does that mean?

Let's just say that if you are the Candidate whose Standing Score is #1, then you are probably going to Qualify (and most of the rest of us are going to hate your guts).

And if you're that pathetic last-place Candidate #6,023 with the really lousy overall combined AT score, then there is very little chance that you will get through the Semi-Finals unscathed.

However—we are also told—these Standing Scores are only valid *before* the Semi-Finals.

They determine the *entry order*, not the final outcome.

So, yeah, there's still hope, even for that poor Candidate who is ranked dead *last*.

Only—what the heck is this entry order, and why it matters so much, we still don't know.

But we're about to find out.

Chapter 29

When we get downstairs to the Yellow Dorm Eight lounge, there's already a crowd. A line of anxious Candidates has formed before a smart-board that has been set up on one wall.

The board touch-screen displays all our names alphabetically in an endless scroll on the bottom strip. Apparently it's not only the people in our Dorm but the whole RQC.

Each name is followed by a number, like this: *Doe, Jane – #123*. In case of duplicate names, the Dorm is also listed.

Meanwhile, the upper portion of the board lists our own Dorm residents only, in vertical columns of five, and three across.

If you don't see your name, you swipe the screen for more, and keep going until you find it. Then, press your name, and it displays your Standing Score in a large font. Below it is another smaller number that represents the Achievement Total. Press the AT, and you get the detailed breakdown of all the achievement factors that went into that sum.

"Oh, great," Laronda says. "Just what we need, public humiliation. Now everyone can see each of my ultra-lousy scores."

"Wonder why they didn't just scan our tokens and tell us privately?" I say.

"Too much hassle, I bet," Dawn says. "I imagine they don't want to read off every single detail to six thousand people. Besides, this is public knowledge anyway, might as well know our competition."

We get in line. Good thing today is not a full day of classes, otherwise we'd be late. Each Candidate at the board takes their sweet time, it seems, jotting down their scores and taking notes, and probably looking up other people they know in other dorms. Good thing they don't give you the whole RQC's detailed breakdown data, else we'd be here forever.

"Please don't take up too much time, Candidates! Look up your own info only, and stand aside—be considerate of others. You can come back later in the day to see it again, this board is not going away anytime soon. Talk to us if you have any questions," John Nicolard says. The Dorm Leaders are standing off to the side watching this zoo.

About twenty minutes later, I finally get my turn at the board. I swipe, and there's *Lark, Gwenevere – #4,796*. And below it is the AT score: 77.

I press the AT score and the screen reforms to show me the breakdown. Fifteen achievement factors are displayed in three columns of five items:

Agility – 3
Voice – 10
Forms – 6
Weapons – 5
Culture – 7

Creativity – 7
Intelligence – 7
Strength – 3
Speed – 4
Flexibility – 4

Balance – 4
Cooperation – 6
Assertion – 5
Endurance – 3
Leadership – 3

Below it also lists the Average of all the fifteen items, which for me is: 5.13. And considering what that means . . . it means I'm pretty much *just barely squeaking above average* even in my Average—if that makes any sense, sorry about the bad attempt at pathetic verbal humor. Furthermore, if not for my one single stratospheric Voice score, I'd be way below average.

I quickly jot down the numbers into my notebook, and get out of the way for the next person in line—who happens to be Laronda.

As I stand waiting for the others, I ponder my kind-of-not-so-hot Standing Score.

By now, the Dorm Leaders are surrounded by Candidates who have picky specific questions about their scores, and it gets so crazy that Mark Foster puts his hands up. "Whoa!" he says loudly. "Okay, I'm kind of getting tired of saying 'I don't know' so listen up, everyone! All the rest of your detailed questions will be answered today at the 1:00 PM assembly over at the Arena Commons Building. Be there on time and everything will be explained!"

"What about the fifteen achievement factors?" an older boy asks. He's one of the alpha crowd jocks, a friend of Wade and Olivia. "Can't you at least say what those little numbers mean? I got 'Strength – 6' so what does that mean? Is '6' good or bad?"

"Higher numbers are better," Gina Curtis says. "It's 1 to 10, with 10 being best. Okay? Are we clear now?"

"Yeah, but is '6' a good score? It's kind of in the middle, and I am way strong, I'm telling you! I mean—"

"Safe bet—that boy did not get anything above a '5' in Intelligence," Laronda whispers, rolling her eyes.

We get out of the dorm lounge eventually, after getting our daily schedules scanned by a very harassed looking officer at the info desk. Everyone's classes are short today, due to the assembly.

"So what Standing Score did you guys get?" Hasmik says. "I get #5,023. Not really good . . . I think?"

"Mine's not that far off," I say, and I tell them my own score.

Laronda shrugs. "These things are really stupid and sad. I got #3,704, which is nonsense, because I suck at everything."

"Hey, I suck more." I grin.

"It's okay, you all suck," Dawn says.

Laronda punches Dawn in the arm. "Okay, so then what did *you* get?"

Dawn shrugs. "Nothing. Same suckage as everyone."

"No, tell us!"

But Dawn just turns around and waves, as she heads to her first period class.

"Wow, wonder what she got. . . ." Laronda frowns with concern. "Hope it's not too awful. Poor thing."

There's not that much time to blab, so I make my way to my first period, which is Atlantis Culture. This is the last Culture class before Semi-Finals, since tomorrow is actually a free day.

Yeah, imagine that, insane, I know. . . . The Atlanteans actually allocated us a whole free personal day, a sort of mini-vacation before we get to fry in the unholy purgatory that is Semi-Finals. It's supposed to be a day of rest, a day for us to recuperate . . . pray maybe . . . or party . . . or maybe just sleep in. Tomorrow we get to do whatever it is that will help each one of us prepare for the *ordeal*.

But first, this class.

Nefir Mekei comes into the classroom and we all stare at him, expecting some last-minute words of wisdom. But all he says is, "Good luck to all of you, Candidates. It has been a pleasure having you in my class and sharing my native world with you."

He stands before the desk that is filled with scrolls and old books—things he never once referred to or even acknowledged, for all of the last four weeks.

That's when I raise my hand and just have to ask. "Is there anything in those books we should know? What are they? And the scrolls too, how ancient they must be!"

Nefir glances at me with a blooming smile. It changes his stark, somewhat off-putting usual expression to that of animated welcome.

"Thanks for asking, Gwen. I was wondering how long it would be until any one of you would say something about these old treasures from Atlantis. . . ."

"Oh," I mumble. "I was wondering from day one, but didn't think to ask, for some reason."

"These are copies of copies of copies . . . of some of the original written records that we have brought with us from old Earth. We rescued them from destruction when we first escaped Earth and headed for the precious new habitable world in the constellation of Pegasus that later became known as the planet Atlantis. They are some of the oldest written things known to the *homo sapiens* race, older than the cuneiform tablets and most of the cave paintings."

"Oh, wow!" I exclaim, and so do many of the other

Candidates in the room.

"For the rest of this class," Nefir says, "feel free to come up here and look. I hope they might inspire you for the Semi-Finals."

I spring up from my seat to approach the desk, and I'm the first person there.

N ext up is Agility. We gather downstairs in the Training Hall gym, and Oalla Keigeri greets us with a blast of her whistle.

We line up, ready to run laps, but instead it looks like this class is going to be different too.

"Attention, Candidates!" Oalla says, pointing to a large box that sits on the floor near the weights training area. "Since you've trained for all these four weeks under the color of the Yellow Quadrant, it's time you showed your allegiance properly—not only by the color of your token but as a traditional armband worn proudly on your sleeve, as we do in Atlantis."

We stare at the box and apparently it is full of fabric swatches of yellow.

"Candidates, line up and get your armband! Once you pick up the material, I will show you how to wrap it around your sleeve. Go!"

I follow the rest of the class in line, and when my turn comes, I reach in and select a piece of bright yellow fabric that looks like all the rest of them, a wide ribbon.

We line up again, this time holding our armbands in our fingers.

"This is how you do it—watch!" And Oalla removes her own yellow armband that she always wears, so it collapses into a wide ribbon. She then again wraps it around her left upper arm sleeve twice, then tucks in the ends underneath so that they stick against each other—apparently they have some kind of special bonding edges.

"Remember, left arm! Wrap loosely so as not to cut off your circulation! Make sure that the ends are hidden away and neatly connected underneath! This is how you will wear it over your uniform on the day of Semi-Finals!"

I attach my own armband, feeling a strange sense of suddenly belonging, of being grounded and *real*. I know it's a false feeling, and nothing is certain, especially now. But it really brings everything home suddenly. . . .

I am either going to die, or I will be a space-faring Atlantean.

Agility Class is also dismissed early and we go to Atlantis Tech while it's still over an hour before lunch. Apparently they are compressing the day so that we have the long assembly only remaining to us after the last class ends at noon.

Mr. Warrenson is already waiting for us in the classroom as we come in, and before all the seats are even taken he begins talking.

"All right, folks, this is it, last class before Semi-Finals!" he says in an even more rushed and nervously excited voice than usual. "There are still so many other things I could teach you, to give each and every one of you a decent advantage, but this is all the time we have. This was a crash course in Atlantis sound technology, a practical hands-on approach was all we could do, naturally—"

Mr. Warrenson goes on and on for about five minutes, trying to summarize dozens of sound command sequences, as though he expects to cram them firmly and permanently into our heads at the last minute, yes, if only he just repeats them *one more time*.

The class begins to space out very soon, but I try to listen very closely to pick up any last minute information.

"Now, you need to understand," Mr. Warrenson says. "The keying sequence is one of your strongest tools in this. You need to be precise in each note you sing, remember the correct intervals, and do not hesitate! The first person to key an orichalcum object claims it!"

Antwon Marks raises his hand. "What can we expect at the Semi-Finals? Will we be keying hoverboards or anything else, um . . . larger?" And he throws a glance at me.

Yeah, at this point everyone is aware of my so-called shuttle levitation demo. They may not know about my role in saving Aeson Kass and landing his damaged shuttle during the sabotage incident, but they know *this*. I'm the girl with the "super voice." Poor Antwon probably wonders if that kind of thing might be on our test.

"I wish I could tell you." Mr. Warrenson sighs, wiping his

balding forehead. "I really, really do. But I am not allowed, and to be honest, I don't even know the full extent of what's been scheduled. Common sense should tell you to expect hoverboard use and some keying of orichalcum objects. Anything we learned in our class is fair game for the Semi-Finals."

There isn't much more we get out of Mr. Warrenson. Class is over while he still fusses with last minute advice and nervously repeats things we already know as we exit the room.

I turn and notice the look in his eyes as he finally trails off into silence and watches us. It is sad, sympathetic, and gentle. . . .

Mr. Warrenson knows most of us are going to die.

L ast class is Combat.

I make it downstairs to the Training Hall early, and I'm one of the first ones there. I look around and there's Keruvat Ruo and Oalla Keigeri, standing off to the side talking quietly. Their expressions are solemn and serious—even more so than usual.

As the rest of the Candidates arrive, the Atlantean Instructors finally acknowledge us.

"Candidates, line up!" Oalla blows her whistle.

We rush to stand in the two familiar double rows. By now it's second nature to assume our still, orderly stances, ready to begin Forms with the Floating Swan.

But once again, something out of the ordinary happens in this last class.

"Today we will go through the Forms drill and then the weapons—the whole thing, only once," Keruvat tells us. "But first you will learn a new and final Form for your level that is an ancient Salute in Er-Du. The Salute is done as a sign of respect to your equal or your superior."

"This means," Oalla says, "that at your stage of Er-Du training, all of you Candidates for Qualification salute only your Instructors and each other. And before Combat, you salute your honorable opponent. However—you do *not* salute if your opponent has exhibited a lack of honor. And you do *not* salute your inferiors."

I take a deep breath and raise my hand. "Who are our inferiors?"

Oalla and Keruvat turn to look at me. "Candidate Gwen Lark,

do you really want an answer or are you just being your usual self?" Oalla says.

"I really want an answer," I say, wondering what in the world is that supposed to mean, *"being your usual self,"* and why the sudden barb from the Atlantean girl.

"Your inferiors are those who have no training to match yours. That goes for any field, not only Er-Du." Oalla pauses, as though considering if she should speak any more. But then she decides to continue. "Your inferiors on Atlantis will be most native non-citizens, even though all of you too are immigrating under a non-citizen status. Is that clear?"

I nod—even as she turns away, already ignoring me—even though a dark feeling is gathering in the pit of my stomach. . . . Once more I am reminded of the strange non-equal status of citizens and non-citizens in Atlantis society.

And I am reminded of the Games of the Atlantis Grail. . . .

"Now I will show you the Salute." Keruvat's deep voice brings me out of my dark reverie.

The tall dark Atlantean demonstrates the brief Form of the Salute. It consists of four elements.

First, he steps to the side with his right foot, widening his stance, and at the same time brings two fists together, knuckles touching, arms bent at chest-level. Second, he opens the fists, palm out, and touches the tips of the thumbs and index fingers to each other so that the empty space between the two hands forms a triangle.

Third, he closes the two palms together, thumbs still pointing away from the other fingers at a right angle, and draws the "praying" hands closer so that only the thumbs touch the middle of the chest. At the same time he bends his head down so that the tips of the fingers touch the forehead, while bending the knees into a semi-bow.

Fourth, he separates the hands, lifting them outward into a sweeping arc, and returns them palms down at his sides, at the same time as he straightens and brings the right leg back in, feet together.

"This is the Salute of Atlantis! Now, repeat, with me!"

Keruvat and Oalla both do the Salute, facing each other, and all of us attempt to copy their motions.

"Again!"

And we stomp our feet and mimic the Salute, better this time.

"Again!" Third time is the charm.

"You will make the Salute perfectly on the day of the Semi-Finals." Oalla says curtly. "Now, practice!"

Lunch is an abbreviated affair also, and we only get forty minutes.

We all stampede to the cafeteria. I see Dawn and Tremaine and Hasmik at a table in the back, and join them with my own tray piled with burgers and fries.

This habit of chowing down on huge meals seems to be with us now, because of the amount of calories we apparently burn on a daily basis. No one has gained an ounce of weight even though we're eating twice our normal amounts, and in some cases more.

Instead, after a month of this boot camp lifestyle, there's a buildup of muscle. Even I feel the small new muscles in my previously wimpy, skinny arms. And my calves and thighs have new strength and some definition.

"So, what you ladies think of the Standing Score situation?" Tremaine says, with a mouth full of burger. "Any ideas how they're gonna implement this for the Semi-Finals? Heard any good rumors, at least?"

Dawn shrugs her usual. "Not really."

"Well," I say, swallowing my own mouthful of fries. "There's probably going to be some kind of advantage given to people with the best scores."

"Keep in mind, they are going to live-stream the whole thing." Tremaine shakes his head. "So it's what, death match reality TV? Will we be fighting each other or something, like gladiators in the arena?"

"I wouldn't be surprised. Otherwise, why teach us Combat?"

"There are hoverboards too," Hasmik says.

"So we fight on hoverboards?"

"I hope not," I mutter. "But hope's such a bitch."

"I got a #2,985 Standing Score," Tremaine says. "It can swing in either direction for me. What about you?"

"You don't wanna know," Hasmik and I both say together.

Dawn just stares into her plate and chews something.

Claxons indicate five minutes before 1:00 PM, so off we go to the assembly.

It's a bright sunny day, and the sky is clear, as we pour outside from our dorms, an endless stream of Candidates mingling, our tokens lit up in all four colors.

As I walk, I feel a familiar touch on my shoulder from behind. I turn around, and Logan is smiling at me. He's wearing his black jeans and T-shirt and no jacket, so the first thing I see are his olive-tanned muscular arms, beautiful and powerful. Immediately I remember the hard feel of them around me during our stolen moments together. . . . His dark hair picks up reddish glints in the sun, which gather into a nimbus of rare secret color. I stare into his warm hazel eyes, and jolts of electricity pass through me. . . . He is so handsome it kills me every time, just to look at him, just to think that *we are together*.

"Hey, you," he says, leaning close in to my ear, and suddenly his expression is intense and serious. "I missed you."

"Hey, you . . . me too," I whisper. And then his hand briefly slips into mine, pressing my fingers, then releases with a sweeping caress up my wrist—that sends more sweet electric currents coursing through me—and we continue walking, jostled by the crowd.

"What Standing Score did you get?" he asks me.

I tell him my pitiful score and he reaches out and squeezes my fingers again.

"And you?" I am almost afraid to ask this question. I really, really hope Logan's score is a good one. I couldn't bear it he got a low score.

Logan takes a deep breath before telling me, and seems embarrassed. "I got #143."

"What?" I am so excited I momentarily stop walking, and people run into me. "OMG, Logan!" I exclaim, and I'm beaming. "That's such a great score! That's amazing! You'll qualify for sure! You're like the top—the top whatever!"

I put my hand on his upper arm, feeling his warm hard muscles, and I press my fingers against his skin. . . .

He shrugs, but there's a tiny smile on his lips. "It's good, I guess, but again, it doesn't mean much. These scores are no guarantee of anything, only some kind of an advantage going into the Semi-Finals, that's it."

But I am grinning at him, and I am so crazy-happy that he cannot help but stare back at me with his warm regard that turns his eyes to sweet honey. . . .

The Arena Commons super structure is packed with over six thousand people, the whole arena floor, the track, the sidelines, everything. As we arrive, there is standing room only, and I am reminded of the assembly during the first week right after the shuttle explosion incident, when we were called in here and addressed by Command Pilot Aeson Kass.

I wonder briefly where Aeson is now, and whether he will be up there again on that platform addressing us today. And then I wonder why I should even be thinking about him. . . .

Logan and I attempt to squeeze in closer to the center of the stadium floor. I see my brother George standing with some of his dorm-mates whose names I don't know, except for one older girl, Amy Calver, a pretty curvaceous redhead with whom George's been hanging around lately. Their tokens are all blazing green.

"George!" I wave, and he turns and beckons us with his hand. Amy waves also.

"Have you seen Gracie or Gordie?" I ask nervously, pushing past people to reach him. "What Standing Scores did you all get? Mine's a crappy #4,796."

"Hey, that's not so bad," George says, while his expression is forcibly calm, and I can tell he is trying hard to make me feel better. "Mine is #3,298. Middle of the road, I guess. What about you, Sangre?"

I start to tell him Logan's amazing score, but Logan gives me a modest and quick "no" look and a meaningful brow raise. He then mutters something about getting by and skillfully changes the subject.

We chat nervously, while the crowd of Candidates grows, and we watch the elevated platform that remains empty. Finally, several Earth officials ascend the platform stairs. There are no Atlanteans among them. Moments later a microphone sounds with reverb in the great stadium space, as one of the officials speaks to address the crowd.

"Candidates for Qualification at Pennsylvania Regional Qualification Center Three. You are gathered here after four weeks of arduous training that has prepared you for the Qualification Semi-Finals. We trust you are in good spirits and good health, because the day after tomorrow will require all your effort, focus and strength. There are some things you need to know in advance of Semi-Finals."

The man pauses, as whispers pass in waves through the crowd.

"First, you need to know your *odds*. There are 6,023 Candidates in this Regional Qualification Center. Only *two hundred* of you will pass Semi-Finals to advance to the Finals. Let me repeat that. Only two hundred Candidates out of six thousand and twenty-three."

Anxious voices swell in the stadium. . . .

"These are the same odds for all the RQCs across the country and around the world. That's how many Candidates will complete in the Finals from each of the RQCs. And of those two hundred, only one half—that's just *one hundred* of you per RQC—will actually win the final spots on the ships heading for Atlantis."

There is a pause. The speaker lets it sink in, and we are stunned. For some reason, although we knew the competition was going to be tough, we had no idea *how* tough.

"Oh, well then, we're screwed," says one of George's dorm-mates.

Everyone's looking around, looking at each other, and everyone's got the same evaluating nervous stare. *Will the person next to me make it? Will I make it?*

"All right," I say suddenly. Not sure what it is, but something weird prompts me to open my usual big mouth. "We knew the odds were sucky going in. So, nothing has changed. We are still going to try as hard as we can! All of us. . . . Right?" And I look around at my brother, at Logan, the others nearest to me, at their faces full of depression.

Yeah, great going, idiot cheerleader Gwen.

Meanwhile the official on the podium is telling us more unpleasant stuff.

"I was instructed by the Atlantis Central Agency to inform you that you have one day, tomorrow, to rest and prepare for the Semi-Finals. As you know, there are no classes tomorrow, and your time is yours, up to the 10:00 PM curfew. However you will be ready at 8:00 AM sharp the following morning, which is Semi-Finals day.

"Your instructions for that morning are the following. You must wear the standard grey uniform that you were issued on your first night here. You must wear the armband with the color of your Quadrant, and your ID token. You must line up, in order of your Standing Score number, at the doors of this building at 8:00 AM. Further instructions will be given on the day of Semi-Finals, and no earlier. Do not attempt to find out ahead of time, and do not attempt to circumvent or cheat the process in any way, or you will be Disqualified."

As the official speaks, the sea of Candidates is filled with turbulent whispers.

"The Semi-Finals will begin at 8:00 AM local time and end at 5:00 PM local time, in every time zone. You will also need to know that the entire Semi-Finals process will be televised and fed to the various media, for the whole eight hours from start to finish. Every moment of your progress will be recorded and transmitted via live-feed. For obvious reasons—since there are one-thousand-six-hundred-fifty Regional Qualification Centers worldwide—not every RQC will be shown on the main prime time broadcast, with the exception of special highlights, although every site will have a dedicated pay-per-view channel and net feed available for the general public. However—and this is where it becomes important for all of *you* here present—Pennsylvania Regional Qualification Center Three has been selected for *prime time feed*, together with ten others. Which means that the eyes of the nation and the world will be on you even more so than on other sites."

The noise in the stadium swells up another notch.

"Interesting," George says. "I wonder why they chose us out of over a thousand others?"

"I have a pretty good idea." Amy Calver glances at George. I notice how she seems to stare directly into his eyes, and her own eyes open really wide every time she looks at my brother.

"What?" George looks back at her. His expression when he

meets her eyes is pretty interesting too, I note.

"It's because of that Atlantean big shot Command Pilot, whassisname," she says. "He's always here, every day, apparently. We appear to be his special project. Plus there's that awful shuttle investigation. . . . So yeah, I bet the Atlantis Central Agency has its eye on us for all these reasons."

"You're likely right," George muses.

I say nothing, but again the image comes to me, of Aeson Kass, as he's speaking in sorrow and leashed fury from the platform, surrounded by the terrifying stone-like Correctors. . . .

"Gwen . . ." Logan is telling me something and I realize I've spaced out.

"Yeah, sorry," I say, blinking.

"Let's go for a walk tonight after dinner," he says. And his eyes get the momentary intense focus that I know very well by now . . . and it sends pleasant shivers through me.

"Okay," I reply, starting to smile because I know what this is leading up to—our favorite hidden nook in the alley, and the two of us *alone*.

"Do you still have to see Kass at eight tonight?" Logan says.

"Yeah. Though, I think this might be the last time."

Logan nods. "In that case, pay special attention to what he might tell you this last time. It might be especially useful."

I nod, thinking of what to expect. As usual I get a feeling of minor shame for partially lying to Logan about what happens with me at those training sessions. But I've been asked to not talk about it, and for the sake of Blayne and his special training, I don't. And even so, keeping a minor secret from Logan, even one that's not entirely my own, feels wrong somehow. . . .

The official up on the platform is talking about the Standing Scores and the Achievement Score breakdown. This is all super important, and yet for some reason I've stopped paying attention.

Instead, I am thinking about what will happen tonight.

Chapter 30

The assembly is let out after a surprisingly long time. We have been made to listen to so much mind-boggling detail of numbers, scores and standings, and general protocol, that none of it seems to matter. Most important takeaway—a 10 breakdown score is almost never given out, and even the best scores Candidates received only range from 6 to 8. Which means that my Voice score of 10 is an outlier.

Dinner goes by quickly, as I eat in a hurry with Laronda and then go to see Gracie briefly over at her dorm. Turns out, Gracie has received a Standing Score of #4,482, slightly better than my own, thank goodness. And, she tells me with relief that Gordie has received a #1,941, which is the best of all of us Gees.

"I looked his up on the dorm smart-board," she says, pointing to the wall, as we sit in the Red Dorm Five lounge.

"Wow, it never occurred to me to just look you guys up on my own dorm board," I say sheepishly. "Okay, I am officially a total dork."

"Yeah, you are," Gracie says with a silly grin. Nearby, Charlie Venice is being extra loud with a few other guys, and Gracie looks at him occasionally with a roll of her eyes whenever their noise level goes way up.

We glance around and, even this late in the day, the smart-board is surrounded by a bunch of Candidates who are gawking at it, looking up their own and other people's Standing Scores and their own AT breakdowns.

"They're trying to figure out who got the top 200 scores," Gracie says sullenly. "Cause those people are going to make it. I know at least one guy, he got a #106—"

"Hey!" I put my hand on her arm. "Don't think that way. These crappy numbers, good or bad, don't mean a thing when it comes to your determination. You and I and all of us will Qualify," I tell her, even though I'm unsure I believe any of it myself.

"Yeah, whatever." And Gracie looks away from me. "I wonder what Mom and Dad are having for dinner tonight. . . ."

I shut that thought out of my head by force. Then I check the time. "Okay, I need to head out. Logan's waiting for me and then I have to go over to my training appointment."

"Whatever. Go. Your two dates are waiting."

"*Dates?* What are you talking about, Gracie?"

But she only shrugs stubbornly and I have no time to argue.

I meet Logan at seven-forty near our usual spot. The moment I step into the place of shadow between two buildings where the bright lights of the compound and the surveillance cameras are blocked by a small portion of wall, Logan is there, and his hands close around me, tight.

"Gwen. . . ." His words come muffled, as he buries his face in my neck, and I feel the heat of his mouth travel against my skin, as he devours me.

Yeah, I know, we are both crazy to be risking getting caught like this.

Because it would mean instant Disqualification.

And yet, it's like a compulsion. . . . I know it is for me—the strange head-spinning visceral *need* to be always touching him, to feel him holding me, to get as close as possible, skin against skin. . . . And it must be the same for him, because he keeps on coming back to this.

Minutes later we come apart, breathless and panting. He wipes his mouth with the back of his hand, and he is *shaking*. "Gwen," he says. "I need—I need to tell you something."

I watch him, as I work to slow down my own breathing. Should I be worried? "What?"

"Okay. . . ." He pauses. "This is not easy. . . . I am going to tell you something very important and I need you to *listen* and trust me. And, I need you to promise me that you will *not* speak a word of this to anyone. And I mean anyone—not your brothers or sister, not any of your friends."

"Okay," I say, my parted lips hovering near a smile. "Now

you're scaring me. . . ."

But his eyes, dark in the shadow, are glinting with intensity. "Promise me!"

"All right! I promise."

He puts his hands on my arms just below the shoulders, and I feel the grip of his strong fingers biting into me. He then leans closer, as if he is about to kiss me again, but instead speaks near my ear. "Gwen, I am not who you think I am."

"What do you mean—" A cold fear has entered my gut, and everything is suddenly very numb.

But he continues. "This is going to sound very strange, but please bear with me. I am not merely a Candidate. I am working on behalf of a government-sanctioned special operations group—"

My pulse begins to race in my temples and I am suddenly drowning in cold. "What are you saying?"

Bu he continues, speaking hurriedly and firmly in a strange cold voice. "I have been trained and planted as a high-probability Candidate who is most likely to Qualify—

"What?"

He grips my shoulders and shakes me slightly. "Gwen! Listen, *please*. Remember what I said, this is very important, and I need you to trust me. Now, I was recruited months ago, as soon as the asteroid situation started and we were informed of the Atlantean terms of Qualification."

I am staring at him, my lips parted, in absolute stunned confusion. But he continues, and his hands go up to gently smoothe back a lock of my hair that has fallen across my face. "I told you my brother is in the military. Well, there's more. . . . He's a member of clandestine special forces, a special division that was formed to deal specifically with the Atlantis situation. Earth Union was specifically formed to observe and infiltrate on behalf of the United States government and allied forces of the United Nations. I was one of the first trainees my brother Jeff brought in."

"You told me your brother was deployed overseas," I mutter, as my mind has suddenly lost much of its focus.

"It was all I could tell you," Logan speaks quickly. "In fact, I would not be saying anything at all now, and none of this would even matter, if not for my new orders."

"Your orders? Wait, are you a *terrorist?* Were you behind the sabotage and the shuttle explosion? Oh my G—"

"No, Gwen, no!" He speaks in a rush, and his hands clench my shoulders painfully. "I am far from a terrorist, believe me, we had nothing to do with the tampering! In fact, Earth Union operatives have been put at a serious disadvantage by the half-assed disaster that some idiots created here at the RQC. We were ready to intercept those stolen navigation chips—"

"Disadvantage? Innocent people *died*, it was a tragedy!" I am panting with emotion.

"I know! And it was awful and regrettable, and again, we had *nothing* to do with it! We do not operate like that. But you must know that 'innocence' is a relative thing. I am not saying those Atlanteans deserved it, but no one is innocent in this, *no one*—trust me when I tell you this—"

I stare at Logan as though he's an alien being. "Trust you?"

His eyes are fierce with emotion. "Yes! Trust me! It's the only thing I ask of you. Under other circumstances, I would still be discreetly performing my function in this and keeping everyone else I care about safely out of it, and no one would even need to know. Yes, I am sorry. . . . I am so sorry I had to withhold so much from you, but now—now I've been authorized to recruit you."

"Okay, what?" My jaw drops yet again. "*Recruit me? What are you saying? For what?*"

"Your voice," he says. "It is an unprecedented advantage. No one on our side knew about this, about the potential, even about its existence, not until you demonstrated such an impossible ability to control orichalcum devices—"

I find that I am suddenly getting sick. "So what is this, then?" I say, starting to draw away from his touch. "Why are you—why are you with me? Is it just because of my voice? Is that it? None of this is real? You and me? It's all some kind of bull—"

"Gwen, no!" He places his hand on my cheek, but I push him away. "Gwen, listen to me—I admit, at first I was only observing you, being generally friendly, following orders. But it changed. *Everything* changed. . . . As I got to know you, the real true genuine *you*, not just your voice but the girl, Gwen Lark, with her vibrant eyes and shy smile and brave opinions, I started to *feel* for you. And now, I really have strong feelings—"

"Please, just—stop it!" My vision is suddenly getting clouded with all the liquid that's pooling in my eyes. My voice cracks.

"Gwen, I *care* about you. I really do! And recruiting you is not an easy decision, because I *know* I am taking a risk here, by laying it all out for you. Please think—this is not just a deception, there is a good greater reason for it. It's a matter of life and death for all of us on Earth, not just the US government. Because what we're doing is an attempt to *save everyone*—not just the ten million so-called lucky teenagers who will Qualify, but as much of the human population of this planet as we can. Can you understand now why I am in this, why I want you to be in this too?"

"Okay," I whisper. "I understand. If what you're saying is true, then yeah, I do . . . understand. But it still hurts like hell to know that you and me, we're kind of *fake.*"

"Didn't you just hear what I said? We're *real!* Nothing about what I feel for you has changed!" He frowns and then tells me something else. "You know how we've supposedly met for the first time here at the RQC despite going to the same school for three years? Well, that's not true either. I've seen you at school before, and noticed you, long ago. . . . Maybe even from day one. I *knew* that you sort of liked me, and I knew that you looked at me, like *all the time.* . . . That time in the cafeteria when we collided and you got flustered and spilled something all over your feet, you were sweet and cute, and you made an *impression* on me. And I might have said something, but you were so incredibly shy in your crush, and I didn't want to make you feel uncomfortable. . . ."

As Logan speaks, I find my face is flushing bright horrible red, and I put my hands up to my cheeks. *Holy lord, he knows everything!*

"I—I had a crush on you for three years . . ." I whisper, trembling, while tears start to run down my face in torrents.

"I *know,* my girl, hush . . . I know." And he puts his warm muscular arms around me and holds me very, very tight, so that I can barely breathe. And again I feel his lips against my throat, and then I sort of lose it, and just bawl, silently, desperately. . . .

A few moments later we separate and I wipe the mess that's my face with the back of my hand. "I don't really know what we are any more," I whisper. "But if I am to be 'recruited,' whatever that means—not saying that I agree to anything—but supposedly if

I am, then what do I do?"

Logan exhales in some relief and smiles at me, and runs his fingers along my cheek. His expression is gentle and beautiful. "You don't need to do much of anything at all—for now. Only look and listen and pay careful attention."

"You mean, *spy?*"

"Nothing so drastic. For starters, I want you to listen very carefully to what Command Pilot Kass has to say to you, and also observe what he does—what's in his office, whom he talks to, anything that might be of interest. This is likely your last chance to do it, that's why I felt I had to tell you everything *now* . . . before you went in to see him tonight."

"Okay. . . ." I gulp and blink to dry my eyes. "I am not a spy. I hate lying. But this—this, I can try." And then I realize it must be near eight PM. "I—need to go."

"Go!" He nods, still smiling lightly, his gaze intensely focused on me.

I turn away without another glance, and everything inside me has been turned upside down.

Apparently I didn't know Logan at all. And I see now, I don't know him even more at this moment.

My emotions, my mind—everything is in impossible turmoil as I hurry to my appointment with Aeson Kass.

When I open the door to Office 512, I am a few minutes late. Blayne is already on his hoverboard, keeping it almost upright after many days of hard practice with his lower body. Part of his exercise training is to stay immobile and balanced that way, so he is already hard at work.

I am supposed to mostly watch and learn by observation. However, during this fourth week, we've tried a few LM Forms exercises using weapons, and Aeson has let me do most of the sparring in his stead. He merely watches us occasionally as he sits working at the console surveillance center where he scans the many screens and takes calls.

Tonight, Aeson does not seem to be here.

I am guessing he's inside the private rooms behind that inner door where we have not been allowed.

However, as I wait, I find I am almost shaking—that's how unsteady with nerves I am after my mind-blowing exchange with Logan. . . .

Only now is it really starting to sink in. Holy lord! *Logan's secretly in special ops, working for some government org I never heard of.* Is any of it even true? And if so, what am I going to do? What should I do?

Furthermore, Logan knows the true extent of my crazy feelings—has known that I like him, for all these years!

And now, I don't know what I feel about any of it. . . . Or if I even believe him!

As I'm reeling with all these conflicting thoughts spinning through my mind, the interior door opens and Aeson Kass emerges. He looks very grim today, a gravity that seeps through his usual controlled exterior. In contrast, there is something careless about the way his uniform has been unbuttoned on the top button, so I can see his bronze tanned throat. My eye is drawn there, as I watch the lean muscles of his neck, and the perfect jaw-line.

His glance falls on me briefly and he looks away so quickly that I almost wonder if I missed something. "Let's get started," he says, addressing Blayne. "This is the last session and there is much last-minute material we need to go over. First, I am going to show you a few evasive movements that are non-combat strategies but will come in handy. And Lark—you watch also."

Aeson explains to us a hoverboard strategy called Rainfall that involves free-falling with one's board on top of other people's boards mid-flight, and a variation called Hail where you actually abandon and jump off your board to land on the other person's.

"These are racing strategies that were not covered in your Agility Class."

"Will we need them tomorrow?" Blayne asks, after a pause, while I listen with elevated interest.

"You might."

"Wait—will we be racing?" I say.

Aeson glances at me sideways then returns his attention to Blayne. And he does not answer my question.

Or, maybe his non-answer is more eloquent than the alternative.

Holy moly! Yes! We will be racing in the Semi-Finals! I think suddenly.

We do some final sparring, then Blayne is allowed to go, with a handshake from Aeson. "Good luck, Candidate Dubois," the Atlantean says genuinely, and there's a shadow of a smile on his lips. "You will do fine."

Blayne nods, mutters his thanks in a strange, almost flustered tone, and then transfers himself back into his wheelchair.

"Rest well tomorrow," Aeson tells him, as Blayne rolls out of the office, shutting the door behind him.

And now there's only the two of us, once more.

It's the truly strange time of the night, every night—as it has been for close to four weeks—as I find myself in a peculiar state of tense intimacy with Command Pilot Aeson Kass.

Time for my voice lesson, whatever it's going to be, this one last time. And if I am to listen to Logan, I should pay special attention so that I can tell him "all about it" later.

Well, this is going to be rather awkward, considering I am already withholding some things about my (and Blayne's) training from Logan and everyone, and now I will have to withhold some of my intentions from Aeson Kass. Okay, that may not be the same thing, since intentions are personal and private anyway. . . . Who is he or anyone to judge what's inside my head?

And yet, it still feels kind of wrong to have these "additional intentions" in my interaction with him, even if I am not lying outright.

Gwen Lark, the double agent. Yeah, right.

As I think these idiotic thoughts, Aeson gives me his full attention. His deep blue eyes with their exotic fine outline of kohl darkness—eyes, which for some reason he keeps averted from me most of the time, even when he gives me direct instructions—are suddenly trained on me. . . .

And immediately I feel a strange energy charge pass through my body, as I meet his rare gaze directly, and I am once again faced with his overwhelming presence.

Before he says anything, I blurt out, "Command Pilot Kass, may I ask a question?"

"What?" He watches me, and there's instant suspicion in the

way he starts to crane his head slightly, without taking his gaze off me.

"I realize this may be the only chance I have to speak to you about this, but—what is it exactly about my voice that makes it different enough to be a Logos voice? I know there are awesome singers on Earth who have more power and volume, and others who might have more precision. So, what makes mine what it is?"

He exhales, as if he'd been expecting a more difficult question and is relieved to answer this instead. "Your voice has a certain subtle *expressiveness*. Combined with just the right amount of tonal precision and force, it becomes a power voice. It's a matter of all the elements coming together in just the right way. To put it simply, your voice is charged with the power of focused intent."

"Thank you for the explanation," I say carefully.

He shrugs. "Common knowledge on Atlantis, actually. You could have asked your Culture Instructor."

"I wasn't sure. I felt it more appropriate to ask you."

"That's fine. Now, we need to discuss what is going to happen the day after tomorrow." Aeson walks over to the sofa and sits down, then points to the spot next to him. "Take a seat."

I do as I'm told, sitting down next to him rather stiffly, keeping my hands folded in my lap. There are about five inches of space between us on the sofa cushions.

He leans back and puts his hands behind his head, rubbing the back of his neck tiredly, then straightens again, but looks straight ahead and not at me, as though musing. "All right, first—your Standing Score. It is on the low side. That's a disadvantage going in."

"I know." I purse my lips.

"However your trained voice is a huge advantage which can balance things out otherwise."

"Okay. . . ."

"So now let's take a look at what other elements there are. Your Combat skills are above average, mostly in hand-to-hand Er-Du. But with weapons, not so much. Furthermore, your Yellow Quadrant native weapon is too complex which makes it a natural disadvantage. Try not to use it."

I nod.

"Your endurance, agility, speed, and strength are sub-par and are your main weaknesses. You will be going up against some very physically advanced, agile Candidates who are faster, stronger and more resilient than you."

"Yeah, I know I am screwed," I mutter.

He glances at me in that moment and there's a flicker of something lively in his expression. "Not necessarily. Because you have one possible and obvious strategy that I strongly recommend you employ."

"What strategy?"

"Simply *avoid* everyone and everything."

I frown and stare at him.

"Avoid any unnecessary interaction and confrontation," he elaborates. "I cannot tell you exactly what you will be faced with during the Semi-Finals—don't ask me how or why, but suffice it to say that if you know anything *specific* in advance, it is grounds for immediate Disqualification, and yes, they have the technical means to discover if you *know*. But I can tell you what general course of action will best serve you. Does that make sense?"

"Yeah, I think so. . . ."

"Good, you are smart enough to figure out the rest on your own. Use all the voice techniques I taught you, if the opportunity presents itself. And no, they cannot Disqualify you for advanced technique knowledge, so you are safe in that respect."

"I see." I glance down and nervously pick my nails as I listen, which is an annoying stress habit of mine.

"That's about it," he says softly, after a pause.

I look up, and see him looking at me. There's a strange expression on his face. "Try to stay alive, Candidate Lark."

"Are those your parting words of wisdom?"

"It is entirely in my interest that you Qualify," he replies in a neutral tone. "So, yes, such is my parting advice. I will likely not see you again, unless you pass the Semi-Finals."

"That must be a relief for you," I mutter with a frown, looking back down at my nails. "Sorry for all your trouble and your time spent with me." And then something makes me look up and add, "I know you still don't believe me, but I had nothing to do with the shuttle disaster. I can swear to you I have not—I mean, not sure if you guys even swear on Atlantis. . . . And I am sorry with all my heart for the death of those three Pilots and friends of yours who were on that first shuttle—"

"*No.* You do not speak. Do not *ever* speak of them to me." He cuts me off in a voice like razors.

"I am sorry!"

"Enough. That subject is closed between us. The criminal investigation is still on-going, and you are a prime suspect. Your voice is the only thing keeping you here."

There's a strange bitter lump that starts to form in my throat, and it's choking me.

No, I am not going to cry.

Not in front of *him*.

So I steel myself and get a grip and control my breathing. "Command Pilot Kass, I will not take up your time any longer. Since we are done, am I allowed to go?" I say coldly.

For an instant, we look at each other in silence. It takes all my effort to stay composed, but I make damn sure neither one of us blinks first.

"Yes," he says. "You may go." And then he gets up and simply turns away from me, returning to the other end of the office and his surveillance consoles.

I stand also and watch his blond hair, his proud straight back.

"Goodbye," I say suddenly, after I cross the room and pause at the door. "I am sorry about everything, sorry for your pain, just sorry—regardless what caused it. May you find what you're looking for, here on Earth, and when you get back to Atlantis."

Okay, I have no idea what I just said. It is strange and surreal and it just comes out of my mouth, and I cannot stop it.

But it is so bizarre that it makes him stiffen and turn around to look at me one last time. "Go," he says, and his blue-eyed gaze meets mine with cold intensity. "Do me a favor and Qualify."

Chapter 31

Not sure if I remember what happens the rest of that evening. It all blurs in my mind, maybe because my emotions are so messed up right now. Logan walks me back to my dorm but we don't say much of anything, and then he tells me to sleep tight. . . .

I get up to the girls' dormitory floor and it feels like Friday night, even though I don't even know what day of the week it is—they've been keeping us so cut off from everything normal this past month that we've lost track of days—but it feels like a party. We all know tomorrow is a precious free day, so everyone's talking, laughing, squealing, a few pillows get thrown—as if there's no tomorrow. Which is not that far from reality.

Laronda's already in bed when I get to my cot. She looks grumpy from trying so hard to ignore the general ruckus. "Seriously, how many times and how many ways must it be said? This is *not* summer camp, girlfriends. Cut out the happy." She rolls her eyes at me, pulling her blanket up to her chin.

"Yeah, I know. . ." I say. "How are you? I think I'm going to bed early too."

"Haayyl, yeah," she says. "Tomorrow, I'm sleeping in—waaaay in. Like, all day. Anyone touches me, and they die!"

"I'm with you." I get under my own blanket and squint up at the bright overhead light that's striking right in my eyes.

For the hundredth time I think, *I really should've picked a different bed on that first night.* Yeah, I am such an idiot.

When I wake up the next day, there are no claxon morning alarms. Furthermore, it is not morning. The noonday sun is shining brightly in the large glass windows, and for the first time in weeks I am not sick to my stomach with queasy sleeplessness, and I'm actually well rested.

Wow, I've slept past noon!

And apparently I am not the only one. Most of the beds all around the hall are still occupied with sleeping girls. A few are stretching and yawning. Most others are quietly turning over or just lying there in a kind of blissful stupor that is worthy of a weekend.

And so I stretch and yawn too, then get up and pad softly to the bathroom, then come back to my bed and lie right back down again.

Screw breakfast *or* lunch.

I turn over to my side, pull the covers over my head, and fall back asleep.

When I wake up again it is late afternoon. This time half the beds are empty, though I admit that there are still people sleeping or lounging around. I get dressed and go wander the dorm downstairs. It's close to 3:00 PM. I suppose I should go look for my siblings. But I am in a strange, lazy, "relaxed" zone where everything is moving at a crawl, including time.

It's like, at this rate, if I tarry and move slow enough, tomorrow will never happen.

Because tomorrow is *it*—Semi-Finals Day.

I am hungry and thirsty but I've slept through the first two meals, and it's still more than a couple of hours until dinner. So I decide to go walk outside.

No one I know seems to be about—Laronda, Hasmik, Dawn, the guys. Wonder where they all are? A few lazing Candidates in the lounge give me uncurious glances as I pass by. A couple of teens stand before the smart-board wall with stressed looks, looking up Standing Scores for the umpteenth time. The alpha crowd is nowhere to be seen either.

Outside is a crisp afternoon, slightly windy, and my ponytail immediately becomes a mess of loose airborne tendrils. Candidates are walking past me, tokens lit up in all four colors, and no one's in a hurry today. A stream of humanity seems to be moving in the vague direction of the Arena Commons super structure and the airfield.

"What's going on?" I ask a girl Candidate with a green token.

She stares at me as if I've crawled out from under a rock.

"They're setting up the media feeds for tomorrow," she says. "All the journalists and media people have been let in to the compound for the first time, and they're mostly over at the AC Building."

"Oh," I say. "Okay. . . ."

"I'm heading to the airfield to see the other half of them setting up the huge smart walls and hologram projection stations for TV interviews."

"What interviews?"

The girl really wants to roll her eyes at me at this point. "Our interviews! Who do you think? They're going to be interviewing random Candidates, and probably those who make it. Whatever, go see for yourself." And she hurries past me.

I pause, standing with the wind tearing at my hair.

And then I start walking in the direction of the airfield.

Before I even get there, I can see the skyline near the Arena Commons Building has a different look. There are tall rectangles of stadium smart screens looming up in places where they hadn't been previously, and more are being put in position around the airfield perimeter. Helicopters are circling. The distant barbed wire fence that demarcates the compound is silhouetted against large semis and trucks and smaller vans outside, and it all looks like an ant hive out there, beyond the boundary.

I recall hearing that there are parents of Candidates supposedly camped out around the perimeter, in addition to the media, and everyone is staring at us, and waiting . . . waiting for the big event to start. Who knows how long they've been there, but now it's less than twenty-four hours remaining. . . .

As I walk together with many other curious Candidates, there are guards everywhere, in the usual grey uniforms, and they are not interfering, but definitely observing the newcomers who are now on the *inside* of the fence.

I stare at the harried looking news crews—journalists and cameramen, gofers and various technicians, as they move about, carrying equipment and network workstations, setting up hubs for their own network broadcasts.

Off to the side, near the edge of the airfield, there's a new platform that has been set up, and a small group of Candidates is being recorded and photographed by several different networks. A very tall, very fit and athletic Asian girl and boy, probably seniors, who might be related, stand in the center of a major network logo backdrop while camera lights flash around them. They appear almost bored, and have a definite cool, kick-ass attitude about them. Both are beautiful and muscular, so alike they could be twins, and both have short spiked blue-black hair and glinting smart jewelry that sparkles in the bright lights. Their ID tokens shine blue.

"Who are they?" someone asks behind me. "How come they are getting special treatment?"

"That's Erin and Roy Tsai," a guy I don't know mutters. "They have the two top Standing Scores in the RQC. She's #1, and he's #2. Brother and sister."

"So they're our main competition?"

"Yeah. And those others are also all top ten or something."

I look closer, and recognize only one Candidate from my own Yellow Dorm Eight, a smart-looking dark-haired boy my age with a street-tough stare. I think his name is Ken Fisher. Apparently he has a Standing Score of #6.

Several others are notable. A petite girl with bright red hair down to her waist seems to pose for the cameras, her brilliant smile flashing white teeth, as she tosses flirtatious looks in all directions. Her name is Isabella Saltwater, her token is as flaming red as her hair, and her Standing Score is #9.

Next to her is a tall burly older teen, Samuel Duarte, with huge muscular arms and wide shoulders, and a sharp attitude. His token is green, and his Standing Score is #8.

I pause to stare, among the crowds of Candidates, as these select top Candidates are getting all the attention. Turns out, there are more platforms behind this one, one for each of the major networks, and on each a few elite Candidates are getting interviewed or filmed.

After a few more minutes of this, it really gets to be depressing. It turns out, although I really *should* be getting to know my competition, I really don't want to hear them brilliantly answer personal questions on national TV in over-confident and sometimes-snotty voices. And I really don't want to see them with their perfectly toned bodies and cocky grins. Honestly, I just want to get as far away from here as I can and just shut off my gloom-riddled mind. . . .

So I turn away and start walking back to my own dorm, wondering where my siblings are. I'm also starving, and dinner can't come soon enough.

In fact, I am ready for this whole day to just be over, and for the nightmare of Semi-Finals to begin. Maybe because there are no other obligations on this day, the dark doom thoughts and eternal stress simmering in the background takes the opportunity to rise to the surface now, with nothing to take my mind off it.

Back home, Mom and Dad are probably in our living room right now. Dinner is already cooking. Mom has just taken her meds and is quietly resting on the sofa and Dad is in his deep chair, leafing through his reference books and lesson notes. . . .

Lost in my thoughts, I wander back, and stop by Gracie's dorm. I would really like to see my sister and the other Gees before the day is over, but I am told she's gone to the AC Building.

Next I try Gordie's and he's nowhere to be found.

I return to my dorm and consider if maybe I should go look for Logan or my brother George. . . .

Where the heck is everyone?

In the Yellow Dorm Eight lounge I see maybe three people. One of them is Blayne Dubois. Blayne is sitting in his wheelchair in the corner, a few feet from the smart-board with all the scores. He appears to be reading an ebook on his tablet, and occasionally glances up to see who walks by and who checks the Standing Scores marquee.

"Hey, Lark," he says to me, as I pause near the outside doors. And then he returns to his book.

There are so few people around that Blayne does not bother to hide the fact that he and I interact—or at least that we hang out together every night for practice. Everyone knows that I go to see the Atlantean VIP in his office on a regular basis because of my weird power voice—even though nobody knows for sure what that means and what I actually do there—but no one knows about Blayne.

I approach him, and mutter something in reply. For once I sound more like Blayne, and he sounds like me. We've traded our social moods apparently.

"Ready for tomorrow?" I say softly.

"I guess." He briefly looks up from his tablet again. His expression is bland but not off-putting. "And you?"

I roll my eyes. "It can't come soon enough. Just wish it was over already."

"With your voice, you have a decent chance," he says, without looking up.

"You too." I stand there, staring at him.

"I'm not the one with the Logos voice." He still does not look up at me.

"But you've got the LM Forms down," I say, lowering my voice to a near whisper. "The way you can ride that hoverboard is—"

"Yeah, I know, I'm amazing." His voice drips with sarcasm. He finally puts down his tablet and stops pretending to read. He looks up at me seriously with his blue eyes.

"I'm sorry," I mutter again. "I think I am—I don't know—having a bad day. Quietly freaking out. . . . I know it sounds weird, and it's actually *supposed* to be a good day for everyone since we get to rest, et cetera, but I think it makes it *worse*, all this waiting, and the endless buildup."

"Agreed. Waiting can psych you out."

"The worst part is just seeing all those media people out there, and the top Candies getting interviewed and treated as if they've Qualified already."

He glances at the smart wall scoreboard. "Whatever. I didn't even bother to go and look at the media circus. Why should I? Why should you? It's just a distraction. Nothing changed. Just because some network exec decided it's a good idea, and now some hotshot Candy is getting interviewed on TV, means *nothing*. For that matter, why aren't *you* getting interviewed up there? You're the one with the crazy outlier power voice that can bring down shuttles. That kind of wildcard stuff makes for great reality TV—exactly what they're looking for—hey, should be worth at least a thirty second newsbyte."

I shrug. "I don't think they know about it. And even if they did, I don't think it matters that much to them. The media knows squat about nuances like Atlantean power voices. What they get is numbers and stats. And my Standing Score kind of sucks, at #4796. What's yours?"

"A shocking #1,692. Have no idea how I managed that."

My mouth falls open and I smile at him with sincere enthusiasm. "Wow! That's crazy good!"

"You mean, crazy good for a wheelie boy."

"No, I mean, crazy good, period! That's better than most of the people I know!"

"You must know a whole lot of losers." But he smiles faintly as he says this.

"Blayne," I say. "Cut it out, okay? You are good, and it has nothing to do with anything."

"*Nothing to do with anything?* Way eloquent of you, Lark. Just say it already—*disabled.*"

"Okay, disabled—differently abled? I am sorry, I know I have no idea how to say it correctly without coming across like a rude a-hole. . . ."

He rolls his eyes. "Too late on that account. But I'm used to you and your big 'ole foot-in-mouth."

I take a deep breath. "In that case, why do you keep being like that? I get it, things are tough, but you don't need to put yourself down all the time, especially since you are really strong and talented and—"

"You *don't* get it. You just don't."

I feel my face flush then grow cold, as a wave of emotion comes and recedes. "Okay, yes, I don't. So, then, help me get it! Tell me! Please! I want to be your friend! But you've got to let me—"

"Actually," he says, beginning to frown, "I don't have to do anything. I don't have to explain myself to you or anyone."

"I know! But, please! Just give me a chance to *understand*—"

Blayne's frown grows. He turns away from me, letting his hair fall into his eyes. Long seconds pass as I just stand there, staring at him as he slouches in his wheelchair, breathing fast in sudden agitation. "You really what to know why?" he mutters. "Why I am like this?"

"Yes . . . I really do!"

"Because I'm *here.* I'm here at the RQC, and I *made* it this far," he snarls suddenly. "I made it as far as Preliminary Qualification, and my brother and my sister *didn't*. They're just the right age, falling within the Qualification range. They're a thousand times more deserving and talented than me. I'm just a screw-up, and here I am, given a freak *chance*, while Laurie and Jake are back home, waiting for death by asteroid."

I stare at him, and yeah, I finally get it.

It's not a self-esteem issue; it's *guilt*.

He continues: "Laurie was dreaming of going to medical school. Was gonna be a doctor, save people. Jake is really good at all kinds of things. He could've been anyone—engineer, lawyer, architect, scientist, teacher. He was going to change the world! He was going to—"

Blayne goes quiet.

My breathing has grown so faint that I cannot even hear my own pulse in my temples.

"I am so sorry," I say. "I had no idea."

"Well, now you do."

"Then for *their* sake, Dubois, you'd better Qualify!"

At some point later, it's dinner hour, and Blayne and I've been hanging out in the lounge, not particularly caring any more that anyone might see us talking. Some of the alpha crowd is now here and they've occupied most of the seating and the nice sofas. The noise level has risen. They're gossiping about the media circus and about the Qualification frontrunners, discussing everyone's chances tomorrow, and what can be expected. Everyone's hating on Erin Tsai and her brother Roy who got #1 and #2 and are all-around amazing athletes and achievers, and on some guy from Red Dorm Nine whose name is Kadeem Cantrell and who's supposed to be an amazing parkour or urban freerunner, and who got #3.

Olivia and Ashley give me and Blayne occasional dirty looks. Then Claudia walks up to the smart wall and starts looking up people's Standing Scores and making snide loud comments about everyone. She is only a few steps away from where I stand near Blayne. She tosses her long, silky black mane of hair and glances occasionally at the alpha girls and sometimes at us. Her piercings glitter with silver under the overhead lights.

"So, Gwen-baby, too bad about your crummy score," she says

suddenly, and I have to glance in her direction. "Looks like your fancy Atlantis voice isn't enough to pull you out of the four thousands dump."

I stare, and see that Claudia's brought up my own Standing Score for all the world to see, and she's brought up the AT score breakdown too, in all its low-numbered glory.

"Hey, look everyone! Our Gwen's got a 3 for Agility, Strength, Endurance, and Leadership. Way to go!"

Olivia and Ashley put their hands over their mouths and bust out in nasty giggles.

"So?" I say. "How is that any concern of yours?"

"Awww, but we're so concerned about you, Gwen. Concerned about you, you know—making it!" Olivia drawls loudly from her spot on the sofa, with her legs dangling down from the seat's back as usual.

"Why don't you worry about yourself," I say.

"I would, except my Standing Score's #2315."

"And mine's #942," Claudia says with a cruel sneer. "You're gonna eat my dust tomorrow."

I shrug. "Whatever. So I eat dust." And then I simply turn around and ignore whatever else they're saying.

Blayne watches our exchange with a slightly craned neck. He then meets my look and smiles. It's a very fine, light smile . . . just a hint, just barely there. But for the first time it reaches his eyes, and it makes everything easier for some reason. Easier to stand there. Easier to ignore the stupid comments and the bullies.

"I hear, dust tastes pretty good with a little mustard and ketchup," he mutters with a slight sarcastic twist of his lips. It's a typical dry Blayne thing to say.

Soon, more Candidates come in from the outside, and I see Dawn and Hasmik.

Hasmik waves to me, and they approach.

"So, had a good long sleep, Sleeping Beauty?" Dawn says. "You and Laronda were both still out cold, close to two PM when we got up."

"Oh, yeah." I smile. "For once, got enough sleep to make up for the whole month."

"Long scary day tomorrow!" Hasmik says. "We come from

Arena Commons Building, it's crazy there! Many, many people from the outside!"

"Yeah, have you seen?" Dawn adds. "They've got these mega-screens and holo-projection stations all over the stadium, now. Annoying TV people everywhere you turn. They all got their media event passes, so they've overrun the place like sewer rats with high-end electronics. I'm kind of amazed the Atlanteans are letting them in here."

"This is their only way to reassure the general Earth population about what's happening with us," I say. "So I don't see how they wouldn't let them."

"Okay, 'reassure' is not a word I'd use to describe it," Blayne says. "Whatever they'll be live-streaming tomorrow during Semi-Finals is probably going to make our poor parents and the rest of the global audience crap their pants."

"Ah, sweet." Dawn glances at Blayne. "Now I feel even better about tomorrow. Thanks, dude."

"Any time."

The cafeteria eventually opens for dinner and they begin serving what smells like pizza, and let us in.

By then I am so starved I'm ready to eat three giant pizzas all by myself.

After we eat and exit the cafeteria, there's Gracie, waiting for me in my dorm lounge. She waves as soon as she sees me.

In these last few weeks Gracie has toughened up somewhat, and I might even say, almost grown up—*almost*. At least she's gotten this strange hard look in her eyes, and she walks taller now, with a tiny swagger. There's some new muscle tone and definition in places where there used to be none. Plus she carries all these knives and sharp bladed objects constantly. I realize it's part of her Red Quadrant "thing," but it has added a fine layer of self-reliance to her previously anxious personality.

"Hey, Gee Four," I say with a smile, as a bunch of us walk lazily from the cafeteria doors. "Have you rested up? Hope you slept in!"

"Oh yeah," she says. "I totally did. Then I went to see all the setup happening for tomorrow. Can you believe the big deal they're making about those top ten Standing Score people? There's that jerk guy from my dorm who's at #4, Craig Beller, who knows kickboxing and karate, so he's all hotshot at Er-Du too, *and* weapons—"

I stand in front of her and look closely at my little sister. "I see. Well, screw Craig Beller and the rest of them. Don't think about them. Just, *don't*. . . . Okay, I did check up on you in your dorm, and that explains why you weren't there. Couldn't find any of the other Gees either. You look good!"

"Thanks."

"How are you feeling?"

"Okay—fine, I guess."

I put my hand on her cheek and turn her face to look at a small scratch or scar that's near her eyebrow on the left. "That's new. When did you get that one?"

She immediately twists away from me in embarrassment. "Cut it out!"

"Sorry," I say. "But you need to put something on it so it doesn't get infected."

"It's nothing. And I know. . . . Stop fussing!"

I smile. "Not fussing. Just making sure you're okay."

Gracie rolls her eyes. But she looks at me with a familiar old nervousness peeking through. I know she's thinking about the Semi-Finals in less than 24 hours from now. And she's thinking about home and Mom and Dad. . . .

Meanwhile Dawn and Hasmik are chatting with a few people from our dorm, standing aside to give my sister and me some privacy.

"Whatever happens tomorrow," I say, "just do the best you can, and you will do fine. I have absolute trust in your super awesome abilities. Just keep going, keep doing what must be done, and never, ever, *ever* give up—"

"I know," she says. "Like Dad told us."

"Exactly like Dad told us."

"If they make us choose weird, scary, dangerous things tomorrow," I continue, "take a deep breath and make the best choice you can out of sucky choices. Do not hesitate too long. There's always a best choice, even when all seemingly sucks."

"I know."

"You'll Qualify, Gracie."

"You'll Qualify too. You'd better! You have that crazy magic voice!"

"It's not magic. But I will, I promise." I smile again. Even though I don't for a moment believe it, for Gracie's sake I have to sound confident. "Now, be sure to use your strengths tomorrow, you have an excellent weapons score, and a pretty good agility one—"

Gracie bites her lip and winces. "It's okay, but not that great."

"Better than mine!" I punch her arm lightly, and again she moves away from me in a semblance of annoyance.

And then I remember other things. "Okay, are your running shoes in good condition? Got clean undies for tomorrow? What about socks? Remember, we have to put on our grey uniforms for the first time, and you know how to tie the armband, right?"

"Yeah, yeah, and yeah, Mom!" she says, punching me back on my arm. "I think you need to go tell this to Gordie, he's the one who always has gross socks and underwear!"

"Eeeew!" I cringe half-jokingly at the thought of my younger brother and his messy habits.

Eventually Gracie leaves, promising me she will go to bed early. I manage to give her a hug that's more like a close squeeze, before she twists away from me with a little smile.

"See you tomorrow, after Semi-Finals!" I say in her wake.

And then I wonder, with a sickening sudden feeling, if I will in fact ever see my sister again.

Chapter 32

Today is Semi-Finals Day.

The early morning alarm claxons cut through my crazy stress dream of running through tall grass from some unnamed pursuers in great robot vehicles equipped with searchlights while giant evil alien ships close in from above, filling the night skies overhead with more terrible blinding lights. . . .

I blink, moaning from not enough sleep, while a familiar, sickening, queasy feeling comes to grip my gut. At the same time I realize it's the overhead dormitory bright lights that have come on and mingled with my nonsense dream.

I have no idea how I've managed to fall asleep last night. Like most of us, I've gone to bed early, promptly by ten PM, back on training schedule hours, in a dormitory of suddenly quiet, serious girls. Before bed, some were meditating, others praying quietly. Only a handful continued to giggle and chat, up to the very last moment of lights out.

In that sudden darkness I vaguely remember lying awake for hours, tossing and turning, my mind burning in anticipation. Somehow I must've dozed off eventually. . . .

And now, it's here.

The big horrible day.

I take a deep breath and sit up.

Laronda makes agonized noises in her own bed on one side of me, Hasmik on the other, and everyone is stirring.

"Good luck!" we mutter to each other.

A minute later, we hear the voice of Dorm Leader Gina Curtis, who blows her whistle and barks her commands at us. "Okay, Yellow Dorm Eight, it's Semi-Finals Day, rise and shine! *Rise and shine!* Quick bathroom time, then uniforms and armbands! Downstairs in twenty minutes to get your numbers scanned! Go! Go! *Go!*"

As she is haranguing us, I quickly grab my neatly folded uniform that's been lying next to my bed, ready from the night before, plus my shoes, socks, underwear—and I rush to the bathroom. It's a zoo, everyone elbowing each other, girls fighting for showers and toilet stalls. Claudia Grito manages to kick me in the shin as I move past her, but I avoid the worst of it by moving out of the way quickly. . . .

I make it downstairs, one of the first from my floor. The unfamiliar grey uniform fits too loosely on me. It's a generic large size that sort of hangs in an unflattering way over my torso and I end up tying it around my slim waist with the provided belt. At least the pants are the right height so I don't have to fold them around the ankles like some of the shorter girls.

The cafeteria line is moving extra-fast, and there are additional guards strolling all around the dorm. Meanwhile our three Dorm Leaders stand in the Common Area, watching us anxiously. "Quickly, now!" they say. "Come up here, get your tokens scanned with your Standing Score Number, then go line up! Line starts at the doors of the AC Building!"

And suddenly we understand exactly what they mean, about getting our numbers scanned. . . . As Candidates come up to the Dorm Leaders and their tokens are scanned by the hand-helds, a large black number against a square white background appears on the front and back of each person's grey uniform. It looks like a number that marathon runners and other athletes get assigned in sports, except these numbers are not stuck on but "insta-printed" somehow on the fabric surface of our uniforms, which I am guessing is photo-sensitive or otherwise sensitive to image display.

Wow, I think, *so, it's a smart uniform.*

I get scanned, and immediately watch how my own uniform fabric fades in the front into a white square and displays a great big #4,796. I know, without needing to look, that the exact same number has appeared on my back. Ugh, how pathetic and embarrassing. . . .

Then I exit the dorm into the cold morning air outside and the pale bluish sky. Other Candidates are walking on all sides of me with grim silent determination—it's an ocean of numbers on backs and chests. I have no idea where Laronda or any of my friends are, and it doesn't really seem to matter at this point—in this thing, we are each of us all *alone*.

Soon I see tokens burning yellow, green, blue, and red, from other dorms, as we mingle, approaching the Arena Commons super structure. The doors are shut, because it is still before eight AM. However a huge line begins to snake around the building perimeter. We crowd in closer, watching each other's numbers, and I observe the familiar handful of top scoring candidates already in line directly at the doors.

Erin Tsai stands proud and deceptively relaxed, hands folded, as she watches the rest of us line up behind her. A huge #1 blazes on her uniform. Her dark head with its short spiked hair shines bluish-black, and smart jewelry sparkles around her neck and in her earlobes.

What a feeling that must be, to be in spot number one!

Next to her in spot two, her brother Roy switches from one foot to the other, as he lingers also, looking tough and bored at the same time.

Then there's the very tall skinny African American teen and parkour god who's third in line, Kadeem Cantrell. Behind him in the fourth spot is Craig Beller from Gracie's dorm, sandy blond and compact, a powerfully built martial artist, so that his grey uniform looks good on him, like a dojo sparring uniform should. Fifth in line is a girl I've never seen before, but who, I recall, is Desiree Bell, supposedly very quick, very strong. She's got dark brown skin and super-dark hair and an otherwise nondescript appearance, if you don't count her confident wide-footed stance—which changes everything about her, revealing her to be a barely leashed force of nature.

From my own dorm there's smart and dark-haired Ken Fisher at #6, followed by stocky and tattooed Jaime Robles at #7, huge and muscular Samuel Duarte at #8, perky redhead Isabella Saltwater at #9, and finally very dark, tall, and intellectually brilliant Mamraj Shahad at #10.

The rest of us start lining up, based on our own far less exciting numbers. We jostle and move around, backing up past those of the Candidates who have already found their spot in line.

Knowing how far back I will end up being, I basically walk

backward and outward past the line, seeing how as it's growing it will soon form concentric circles around the building and eventually fill the block. At some point I see Dawn get in line, and *whoa!* Girl's got a #98 on her chest! I had no idea Dawn scored so well!

My jaw falls open in surprise. I wave at her and smile as I hurry past her, and Dawn waves back, looking somewhat sheepish and embarrassed. No wonder she didn't want to tell anyone her score.

"Way to go, Dawn!" I mouth at her in passing, and she rolls her eyes and says, "Shut up!" But she smiles back at me.

The line keeps growing as more of us get into our places, and now it's snaking backward around the AC Building, going all the way around and back again, and forming another row.

Soon after, I see Logan get in line in spot #143. I pass him and he turns his head to watch me, and calls out my name. "Gwen! Remember, stay focused!" Our fingers brush past each other, and his warm hazel eyes follow me. I smile at him nervously, then move away.

As the numbers get higher, I start seeing more and more people I know. I watch Claudia get in line and toss me a sneer.

However I am more interested in seeing Blayne in his wheelchair get in line at #1,692, his toned arms moving rapidly to turn the wheels. He is remarkably fast and yet my gut sinks in worry on his behalf, since there is no hoverboard here to help him. How is he going to manage with whatever it is we have to do? The Candidates around him are staring, giving him curious, disdainful, pitiful, even stunned looks—a whole range of reactions, the works. I know he's used to it.

But Blayne sees me and gives me a light crooked smile that for him is almost a grin. He nods at me and I mutter something semi-stupid, like "Hey, good luck there."

"Hey, Lark," he says suddenly, as I am several steps away. "When all else fails, remember you can sing."

I know it's a play on my name, and yeah, I've heard it a million times before from teasing kids and bullies, all my life. But somehow this time it really works. It's the perfect expression of encouragement.

"Thank you!" I mouth the words and wave at him with a

"thumbs up."

By this point, over a thousand Candidates are now in line. There's Gordie at #1,941, looking relaxed and sleepy in his place in line. "Gordie!" I exclaim, move in quickly and squeeze his shoulder. The boy comes awake practically, and then grins at me. "Hey!"

"Be strong, and never give up! Love yah, Gee Three!"

"You too, okay, hugs, whatever, yeah . . . see you! We Qualify, yeah!" he mumbles, but I know his gaze is following me as I move away. I am suddenly crazy glad I have this unexpected, last-second chance to see my younger bro, and possibly the rest of the Gees, as we all line up.

One by one I see others—Tremaine, then my brother George who holds me, pats my shoulder and tells me to Qualify or else. Then, there's Laronda who gives me a quick hug, then Raj, Mateo, and a bunch of other people from my dorm.

Then there's Gracie getting in line. Her number is close to mine, so I know my own spot is not too far ahead. I squeeze Gracie's fingers and she clutches my hand desperately, and her eyes—oh, her eyes are suddenly again those of a very lost little girl.

"You're a *winner*, Gracie! Remember that, you just keep going, sweetie! Love you tons and tons!" I speak quickly into her ear, and we separate.

At last, somewhere in the fourth concentric row of Candidates standing in line, I find the person whose Standing Score is the number right before mine, a younger teen boy with freckles and a green token.

I take my place in line right after him.

Moments later, the person who comes next after me, a blond teen girl my own age with a blue token, gets in line behind me.

And the line still just keeps growing and growing. . . .

At eight AM exactly, the doors of the AC Building are opened and we are allowed to enter.

I am still far away from the entrance, in the outer middle concentric circles of the spiraling line, but the noise inside the building hits us, as the microphones and voices of the announcers echo and reverb through the stadium. The media film crews are in there, I recall, and oh yeah, they are beginning the broadcast. . . . Loud, up-beat theme music plays on giant super-speakers from all directions, so that the AC Building rumbles and shakes from the low bass notes of the drum track, interspersed with the announcer voices.

I even recognize some of them, the TV celebrity anchors who now speak urgently and with excitement to introduce the start of the Qualification Semi-Finals programming for the day.

Candidates are moving quickly—even though it seems they are allowing us inside in batches of six people at a time.

As we file along, exchanging nervous looks, some of us move in place with athletic exercise warm-ups, others stand stiff, frozen with an immobilizing fear of what awaits us—as all of this is happening, we can hear the announcer voices describing the events.

"Good morning to our viewers across the country and around the world, and welcome to the international Atlantis Qualification Semi-Finals! To all our eastern time zone and other audiences just tuning in, please note this presentation has a live internet simulcast and is being live streamed on ENNThisMorning dot com and on all our local affiliates . . ."

The wind moves tendrils of my hair that's been pulled back tight in a functional ponytail. I glance up at the morning sky, blue and clear, and think about how it looks like it's going to be a bright and sunny day ahead. . . .

This might be the day I die.

No, stop thinking like that . . . pull it together, Gwen Lark. . . .

" . . . The first hour portion of the program is simple sorting," says the deep and soothing voice of Bill Anderson, the Eastern National Network prime time anchor, echoing loudly from the outdoor speakers, so it is heard outside the super structure building and beyond. "The Candidates run a single lap around the track, in bursts of six teens at a time, separated by only ten seconds per set, to compete for objects and tools that will be assigned to them for the tasks ahead. . . ."

As he speaks, I can just imagine his clean-cut, bland features, the graying hair smoothed back, the neatly trimmed beard, tailored suit and subdued tie. It is unlikely he's here in person, in our own

RQC today, but rather back at the network studio—but I suppose I'll find out soon enough once I actually make it inside and *see*.

Most likely, only his hologram is being projected inside the Arena Commons Building stadium onto the media podium panel which is holo-installed here and at every other one of the nearly two thousand RQCs nationwide and globally. This virtual panel allows local and global anchors to take up prominent spots and feature only the networks of their choice that are relevant to their country or region. Other international major network anchors in other places are also holo-projected the same way. Furthermore, viewers can select what feeds to follow with whose commentary, and which language dubs.

"So explain to me, Bill, how exactly does this work, then? With only ten seconds of advantage given each group of six, plus Candidates with better scores on the inner lanes, the Standing Scores don't seem to play all that great a role, do they?" This time it's the voice of Cathy Estrada, the sassy raven-haired Latina ENN co-anchor who rolls her r's and wears bright colored tops to match her trademark fire-engine red lipstick.

"Well, Cathy, as you know, the Atlanteans don't really tell us much of anything ahead, to build suspense, one might suppose, but we *are* told to expect many surprises. After the top two hundred, might as well forget the Standing Scores, they tell us! Each lap around the track determines what kind of prizes—if you want to call it that—our teen competitors receive. For example, we know that the top ten scoring Candidates at each Regional Qualification Center will be given hoverboards automatically, but they will still have to run the lap to determine what other weapons and power-ups they get *in addition*. As for the rest of them, who knows? The farther your Standing Score, the worse are your odds. We can only watch and hope and pray on their behalf! After all, it's our children out there!—Oh, look! There go the first six Candidates around the track!"

This is hell. I am in idiot hell, I think, as I slowly approach the doors, while hearing the running commentary only, and having no idea what's really happening visually.

"Let's switch quickly to one of our featured ten Regional Qualification Centers and watch the early action at New York

RQC-One. Looks like Jimmy Wong is in the lead, with his #4 blazing in front, but ooh, this is going to be a tight one, as Angela Manwell #7 is coming up from behind—"

Shuffling forward slowly in the line, I zone out. Twenty minutes later, they've only barely processed two thousand Candidates. I know that's crazy many people actually, but it feels both insanely slow-mo and urgent-fast.

Well, I think, at least Dawn, Logan, Blayne, and Gordie have gone through. And Claudia Grito. . . . And I'm closer to going inside the building. Maybe another twenty minutes?

Only—how did Blayne manage the running part? The worry on his behalf comes to me yet again, with a pang. For that matter, why aren't the announcers saying anything about a boy in a wheelchair? Wouldn't it be something to comment on?

"So, as they run around the track," Bill Anderson's hologram says, "we see that they are getting scanned automatically at the finish line by a row of sensors. Here's an interesting note for our viewers—all those ID tokens—notice how they are lit up in one of four colors—are based on something the Atlanteans call the Four Quadrants—"

"But wait, what awaits our Candidates at the finish line, Bill? I am still confused—" Cathy Estrada's projection voice sounds whiny and nasal.

"A choice, Cathy! A tough choice!"

"What choice, Bill?"

"We are told we cannot say it on the air, in order not to influence the Candidates who are possibly listening to us speak, and so, viewers at home, watch the bottom of your display screens for the marquee with the answer! Yes, folks, this is the tough choice that the Candidates have to make at the finish line! Now, how about that, ain't that something? That should give you an idea of what awaits our Candidates in the next few hours—"

I can't tell how many more minutes have passed, but I am finally at the doors, am about to enter the AC stadium. Guards rush us inside, counting us off in batches of six, saying, "Go, go, go!"

I pick up the pace, matching the others before me, and we are greeted by a blast of noise, canned music, and lights. Officials stand at all wall perimeters and we are told to advance directly to the racing track.

We move at a run. With my peripheral vision I see a projection screen that shows what's happening on the track in real time, and in huge several-story-tall format. There is a podium bathed in light with a semi-circle holographic virtual panel of media personalities, projected at three times life-size. Bill Anderson's holo-head is huge, I think stupidly, it's the size of my whole torso. The anchors are rotated every few minutes, so that the holo-panel lineup changes constantly.

I realize the media nonsense is just a part of the atmosphere of hype, and it's apparently there to add to the sports-event flavor.

But it's absolutely, soul-sickeningly ridiculous.

Meanwhile, on the track, Candidates are running . . . and running. We approach the starting line, and I see how a signal shot goes off every ten seconds, just enough time for people to line up in the six inner lanes out of the available eight, and then take off.

There are no pauses, no waiting for each group to complete their lap—that would take too long, all day, probably, for over six thousand Candidates. Instead, it's a constant moving stream. I see that a large display smart panel awaits at the finish line, where Candidates pause momentarily, and then press some kind of lever to make a choice. Then they rush onward and disappear into the outer building, going lord knows where. . . .

"Line up! Get ready to run! Go!"

Suddenly I am in the middle of my batch of six teens, in the fourth lane from the middle, at the starting line. I place my feet in the proper places and crouch down.

This is it. . . .

The starting gun signal goes off.

I take off and run.

The previous batch of runners is still pounding the track, only about twenty feet in front of me.

I suck at running, even now, after four weeks of hard training and yes, some improvement. Very quickly, in a matter of just five paces, the boy to my left and the girl to my right both overtake me, and I am running behind them—not the last person in my batch, but definitely toward the back.

My breath starts coming hard, and my temples pound.

Ten seconds pass . . . so I hear the pop of the starting signal gun, and another batch of six runners has entered the track and is now coming up behind me.

I pump my legs and arms, moving hard.

Focus, focus! Breathe!

Another ten seconds, another starting shot. I am halfway around the track, and I can no longer tell where I am in relation to my own batch of six Candidates, since all the runners are mingling, some falling back, others overtaking the earlier group. . . .

Another ten seconds . . . another starting signal shot.

My breath is ragged, and I see the finish line coming up about thirty more feet.

Ten more seconds, another gun-pop.

I reach the finish line.

My ID token gets auto-scanned. I know this because it flickers and flares a brighter yellow as I run past the sensors.

The person just before me—I have no idea who—pauses before the smart wall panel, takes a breath, reads whatever's on it, then slams one of the five large protruding button-levers. Then the Candidate takes off running again, forward, away from the track.

My turn.

The panel is before me, and the row of five levers.

It flashes yellow, then a readout appears in black letters. . . . Just two lines.

The first line says:

Candidate Gwenevere Lark, choose your City.

And below it, the second line reads:

New York, Chicago, Dallas, Denver, Los Angeles.

My mind goes into overdrive. Holy crap, what is this? What am I choosing?

What does any of this mean?

If I am going to be *assigned* to a city for whatever next task of today's ordeal, I have only a second to decide.

Right. This. Second. . . .

And so I try to think like the Atlanteans, try to imagine what it could be. But all I can think of is, okay, I was born in California and I know L.A. I know nothing or close to nothing about the other cities. Okay, when I was six, my family had been to Dallas once on a quasi-vacation for Dad's boring university conference, for two days. That's about it.

I take a deep breath and slam the lever for *Los Angeles*.

The smart panel display changes and I see a new readout of three lines:

Candidate, you have been assigned:

Weapon: 1.   Hoverboard: 0.

Proceed upstairs to the roof of the building for further instructions.

I start moving. Now I get it—I see where the Candidates who have gone before me are heading. They are going for the stairs and elevators to reach the upper levels of the structure.

They are all going for the roof.

Whatever's there, that's my destination too.

Chapter 33

I sprint past the crowds and the noise, and the guards watching us, along the narrow open path where the others are heading. I watch the back of the Candidate right in front of me as he runs up the spiraling staircase, ignoring the elevators, and I follow him and those before him. Just as many others come behind me.

It's five flights up to the five level walkways. Our feet slam hard against the stairs, thundering, as we run upward. Fifth level is as far as I've been in this building. It is where the offices are, including Office 512. I wonder for a split second if Aeson Kass is in there now, watching us and our progress on his numerous surveillance consoles—watching *me*—as I rush past the fifth level walkway, and then head for the door that is labeled "Roof Access."

I follow the teen in front of me and we take the stairs—he is doing two at a time—and then emerge outside up on the roof, into a strange flat area of concrete, a perimeter strip that goes all around the huge building structure, and alongside which I see many people. . . .

And Atlantean shuttles.

The wind is blowing. The morning sky is clear blue above, and the shuttles hover silently just a couple of feet off the roof, massive grey-silver oval birds, with rung ladder staircases hanging off. There are five of them, and I see that overhead, about a hundred feet up, five more wait in formation . . . and then another five more, two hundred feet up. Indeed, the sky is filled with them, like weather balloons. Altogether, it's a stunning sight.

These shuttles are larger than the ones I have experienced before, at least three times greater in circumference, and I am guessing they function as mass transport buses.

Weeks from now, these same shuttles might be used to ferry those of us who Qualify up to the motherships. . . .

As I pause, still reeling in my mind, gawking in uncertainty, a uniformed official passes a hand-scanner over my token. "Shuttle number five," he says. "Over there, Los Angeles. One weapon assignment, Yellow Quadrant." And already he turns to the next person behind me.

I hurry in the direction pointed, and I see more officials with signs, each one bearing a number and city name.

I find the shuttle for Los Angeles and start moving up the rung ladder, seeing the clattering feet of the Candidate before me.

A sudden crazed stress-thought occurs to me. *What about my brothers and Gracie? What city did each of them choose? Did they spring for the familiarity of L.A. also?*

Inside the shuttle is a wide roomy interior resembling a long hallway with rounded walls of soft pale off-white color that bear faint lovely symmetrical etching designs. . . . Instantly I get a flashback to that night when I pulled Aeson Kass out of the burning shuttle, because these walls are exactly like the ones in that shuttle. . . .

"Move it, Candidate!"

I start awake and see an Atlantean whom I don't recognize, but who could as well be one of the Instructors. "Take a seat," he says, as he stands near the doors like a bored airline flight attendant, except with arms folded in a cold typical stance of his kind. His hair is long and metal-gold, and his attitude suggests he is used to command.

The shuttle hull interior is filled with rows of high-backed seats, at least twenty across, and five times that many more going back. The seats are filling fast. I hurry along the side aisles looking for open seats, find one in the back rows.

I sit down next to a much younger teen girl with a red token who looks back at me with a nervous frozen expression. As soon as I take up my seat—which is surprisingly comfortable, made with soft resilient material—another Candidate sits down next to me on the other side, another silent girl with a hard expression on her face and a blue token.

"Move it, move it, Candidates!" the Atlantean at the door says. "The longer you take, the less time you have."

"Where are we going? Are we really going to L.A.?" a boy

asks.

"You're going to get your instructions as soon as we are up in the air." The speaker is another Atlantean, this one a girl who looks a lot like Oalla Keigeri, beautiful and confident, only with a deeper tan and a more muscular built. She walks the aisles, and watches us as we take our seats, pointing to others to indicate empty seating space.

In less than a minute the shuttle is full. The two Atlanteans engage controls that raise the ladder and secure the doors. A soft hum comes to the walls of the hull, and as I sit, mesmerized, I see the etched patterns on the walls come alive with golden razor-thin lines of light.

"Everyone, look down to your right and left and see the safety harness and belt," says the Atlantean girl, lingering among us in the aisles to point things out. "Pull both sides of the harness toward you so it meets in the middle of your waist. Press the button on the side of your armrest and engage the harness lock. Do it now!"

As she speaks, the other Atlantean moves away to the door and goes to the back of the shuttle to what looks like a small command center with four seats. He takes the first pilot chair and turns his back to us.

We begin to fumble with our harnesses. I have a bit more experience with it, having seen this same harness engaged around the lifeless body of Aeson Kass. . . . I quickly find both ends, move them to the middle as instructed, then press the side button on the armrest. Immediately a strange thing happens—the two harness lines connect, then several more lines shoot forth like snakes and descend from around the back of the chair and seat from several directions, all connecting in the middle, and the round button lock captures them all and clicks in place.

I am as well secured as a birthday gift, ninja-wrapped with a dozen ribbons and a button bow. How weird!

The Candidates all around me take a bit longer, but eventually everyone is harnessed properly.

"Attention, everyone!" the Atlantean girl says, stopping before the front row closest to the door in which we all entered. "I am your Pilot Lirama Rikat, and he who sits in the other pilot chair far behind you is Pilot Mikelion Wasi. We will be taking off and on our way to Los Angeles in a few moments. As soon as we are in motion, I will give you the instructions for what you are expected to do there, in order to pass today's Semi-Finals."

She pauses, observing our tense faces.

"Take-off in thirty seconds," Pilot Mikelion announces from the back. "Ready, *daimon?*"

"Ready, Mik—proceed!" she responds, then races to the back, moving with sleek easy motions, past our chairs, and grabs the second pilot seat next to the other occupied one in the back. We hear the click of her harness, a brief complex sequence of musical tones—someone, possibly the male pilot, is *singing* them in a deep voice, or maybe it's only the sound of the alien Atlantean navigation mechanism engaging—and then the walls of the shuttle start to quiver lightly, as the general hum deepens. The golden lines of light start to move like liquid honey being poured, racing faster and faster along the etched channels in the hull walls. . . .

So, she's *astra daimon*, I start to think.

But in that moment there's a great lurch, and the floor seems to fall right from under me, while my head feels heavy suddenly, with a strange thick weight of extra gravity. I—and all the Candidates around me—we are getting *squashed*. We are pulled back deeply into our seats, and our harnesses counter-react with a buoyancy, so that there's an impossible rubber-band sensation.

"Oh, no . . . oh, crap . . ." mutters some guy behind me.

We are falling—rather, we must be rising.

"Oh God, oh God . . ." the girl on my left gasps suddenly, and she looks like she is about to throw up.

"Are you okay?" I whisper, turning slightly to look at her, as my own head is getting sucked into the headrest with the force of many g's.

"I hate planes," she mutters. "I really hate flying! I had no idea this would be—"

"Hang on," I reply. "Just hang in there."

"How long is this flight going to be anyway?" another guy asks loudly from the front.

"About ten minutes," Pilot Lirama replies with amusement.

And then the pressure on our bodies seems to ease and the gravity normalizes.

"Wow," a girl says. "This feels much better."

"That's because we are now outside the Earth's atmosphere and in orbit," Pilot Mikelion says cheerfully.

"We're *what?*" a guy says. "We're where? How? Why?"

"It is much faster and more efficient to fly through vacuum than the atmosphere, so we just go up, go around the earth, then come back down on the other end of the continent."

"But we're not weightless! How come we're not—"

"The shuttle is generating artificial gravity."

"Well f— me! We're in outer space!"

"Oh God . . . I'm in *space.*" The same girl on my left looks like she is about to die.

"Well, yeah, what did you think was going to happen eventually if you Qualified?" A girl in the seat in front of her turns around with a mean glare. "We are all competing to get off this doomed rock and get to outer effin' space and then Atlantis!"

"All right, your attention, everyone!" Pilot Lirama engages some kind of audio-enhancing tech and speaks into an amplifier, so that her voice carries crisply throughout the shuttle. "These are your instructions for the rest of the day. First instruction! We land in Los Angeles and you will be deposited and released thirty miles from the city center—commonly known as downtown. Each one of you will receive your weapons and in some cases hoverboards, according to your track sprint results. There are a hundred of you on this shuttle, but only a few Candidates will get hoverboards. Those of you who get them—hold on to them the best you can, because as soon as you're on the ground, others can and *will* try to claim your hoverboards and any weapons or other equipment advantages you might have on you. Yes, it *is* allowed."

She pauses, and we stare and listen intently, while nervous whispers move around the shuttle.

"Second instruction! Once you're on the ground with your allocated items—weapon, hoverboard—you have one simple task. You need to get to the center of the city as quickly as possible, either on foot or via hoverboard—using just these two means. Word of advice: if you have no hoverboard, start running immediately, because 30 miles is a long way to go on foot. No other means of standard transport are allowed, including no urban transport—no cars, no buses, no bicycles, nothing. Also, you may not make contact with any of the residents, nor may you receive any help or medical assistance from them, no matter how hurt you might be. The penalty for disregarding this is Disqualification.

"The Semi-Finals is a *race*. You are racing against the clock—five PM, Pacific Time—and against each other. And the Rules of Conduct are, *there are no rules*—anything goes. You may work together in cooperation with one another, or you may fight each other for weapons and advantages. You may do whatever it takes, using all your training and skills, and *you may kill*. In fact, many of you will be killed today, because there are several difficult and fatal obstacles along your way.

"The City of Los Angeles has been specially prepared for your Semi-Finals Race. It has been divided into several circular zones, hot zones and safe zones, separated with fence boundaries. To pass from one zone to the other you will have to scale the fence and get scanned by the fence sensors—so *do not* lose your ID tokens! Bright four-color light beacons are set up along the fence in short intervals, so that you will know a boundary when you come to it. As you move closer to the center, you will pass from one type of zone to the other. If it's a safe zone, you will face no additional dangers other than your fellow Candidates—each other. But if it's a hot zone, you will be faced with random unpleasant surprises. Be ready for fire, snipers, explosives, booby traps, and other tough obstacles. A hot zone will only be marked with a red stripe painted on the interior side of the boundary which contains the danger. If you are lost, disoriented, or cannot decide in which general direction to move, scan yourself against any beacon and it will rotate and point to the center of the city like a compass."

Pilot Lirama pauses for a moment, as though considering her next words. "If at any moment you decide you've had enough and want to give up—or are simply too hurt to proceed—you have the right to make the ultimate choice to *quit* the competition. To Self-Disqualify, simply remove your token ID, turn it over, and press the recessed button on the interior. It will transmit a signal and designate you as Disqualified, and also send a request for help, including a medical ambulance. I realize it's a hard choice to make, but for many of you it will be the kinder choice today.

"Remember also, media cameras are everywhere, so every move you make, everything you do, will be recorded and transmitted nationally and globally via live video-feed. If you break the rules, you will be seen and Disqualified.

"Third instruction! Once you get to downtown, in the very center of the city there is a giant deep pool reservoir filled with water. On the bottom of the pool are hundreds of batons made of orichalcum. You must dive into the pool and come up with one of the batons. There are only enough batons for twenty percent of you—thirty people competing for one—based on the number of you from each RQC, who chose Los Angeles. Each Candidate is allowed only one baton, so you may not remove more than one from the pool or you will be Disqualified. At the same time, there will be transport shuttles like this one, waiting up in the air, about a hundred feet from the ground. Take the baton up to any waiting shuttle, either by means of a hoverboard, or by voice-keying the baton itself and making it levitate upward as you hold it. As soon as you do that, you will have passed Semi-Finals. The shuttle will take you directly to the National Qualification Center for the final Qualification stage and final training.

"Word of warning—all the shuttles leave all Semi-Finals sites at five PM sharp. If you are late, even if you have the baton, you will be Disqualified."

Pilot Lirama grows silent.

We sit, stunned and overloaded with all the information.

And a few minutes later, we feel a sudden lurching sense of falling.

"All right, we are going down now," Pilot Mikelion says. "We're in orbit directly over Los Angeles. Hang on!"

And then the shuttle plummets. . . .

A very long few minutes later, we stop falling, and then come to a hover stop. The golden threads of light stop pulsing around the hull walls, the hum fades, and there is silence.

"We have arrived in Los Angeles," Lirama says, popping off her harness and getting up from her seat. "You may now remove your safety harness by pressing the button in the middle. Then, get up and come line up at the exit door to receive your equipment. As soon as you are equipped, you head out! It is 6:30 AM local time, and because you've changed time zones, you're lucky—you gained *three extra hours* of time, since the competition is based on local time. You would've had exactly seven and a half hours had you stayed in Eastern Time, but instead you have *ten and a half* hours! The clock starts now!"

"Wait, does that mean that people from the West Coast RQCs who chose an Eastern city have *lost* three hours?" a teen mutters. "Wow...."

"Yeah, it does. And—unlucky break," Pilot Lirama says, overhearing him.

Both Pilots proceed to the front, past our rows of seats, and open side compartments in the walls. At the same time the shuttle exterior door slides open silently, and Southern California early morning sunlight and clear blue skies greet us from the opening, together with a blast of lukewarm dry air, faintly tinged with exhaust and chemicals that constitutes local smog—a familiar childhood smell for me. The smog also carries fine particles of low-grade coastal radiation, which is relatively harmless for short-term exposure, but over time it can cause serious consequences— as it did for my Mom.

The ladder descends even as Mikelion begins the process of scanning our tokens. He gives a lucky few of us hoverboards, while Lirama hands out Quadrant weapons from the other compartment—various firearms ranging from automatic assault rifles and semi-automatics to small handguns to the Blues, swords and knives to the Reds, protective armor in the form of vests, arm-sleeves, and other partial wearable pieces to the Greens, webbing, nets and cords to the Yellows.

When it's my turn, I receive only a slim long cord folded like a lasso. Looks like it's the best I get based on my sub-par running score.

"One basic Yellow Quadrant Weapon," Lirama tells me. "Good luck."

I also notice that as I get scanned, the Standing Score number and white background square on my uniform *disappear*, front and back, simply fading away, and there's only the plain grey fabric. Same goes for every other Candidate who gets scanned— apparently our scores are wiped clean, and we are now anonymous blank slates.

Clutching my weapon I step on the ladder and descend

outside into the growing early light of day.

The first thing I see as I hop down from the ladder stair is a wide urban panorama with the distant dot of high-rise buildings that indicate downtown L.A., the heart of the city, straight before me. I blink and squint in the sun glare. Some mornings start out overcast in L.A. but this is not one of them. I am on some kind of elevated hillside, covered in yellowed grass and native chaparral shrubbery.

Where are we exactly? In what direction from the center? I am not too sure, all I know is, we're thirty miles from downtown.

There are other Candidates milling all around me, trying to get their bearings. I realize many of them have been deposited here by other shuttles, from many other RQCs from all across the nation. Wherever they've come from, all I know is, I don't remember seeing these Candidates on my own flight. To prove my point, there are, at present, several shuttles hovering at various intervals along the large hillside, casting great ovoid shadows upon the sloping grade. Some are still unloading Candidates, others already rising and receding to specks into the aerial distance.

The Candidates—we are a varied, mixed bunch. Some of the Candidates stand, holding only weapons, while a few have hoverboards that they hurry to key to their own voices while giving wary stares to anyone nearby. Even as I watch, two guys are already airborne, up on their hoverboards and away from the rest of us, making hover circles from a safe distance, and then speeding away toward downtown, balancing skillfully on the boards.

And then it begins.

More Candidates are still descending from the shuttle that brought me here when the first screams come.

An older muscular girl has just attacked another teen, and has taken away his hoverboard. The young kid, probably an eighth grader, sits on the ground, rocking from the pain of a hurt leg, while the attacker, up on his former hoverboard, is rising up into the air without a second glance.

"What a bitch!" another girl with long stringy reddish hair and freckles says expressively, a few feet away from me. She wears a green armband, a green token, and carries a small armor vest that she didn't even have time to put on. And her accent is either

British or maybe Australian, but I cannot tell which because, yeah, I am that much of a doofus, I know, sorry.

In any case, I agree with her assessment. For a moment I consider if I should approach the boy who's down to see if he needs help, maybe. And then I see the two Blue guys with guns about twenty feet away. They are older, hard-faced, and I suddenly get a bad feeling as one of them starts loading a magazine in his assault rifle while looking at us.

"They did say we should start running," I mutter, just as the first of the Blues takes aim in the direction of another batch of Candidates who are wisely sprinting away in the general direction of the center of L.A., which happens to be downhill.

"Run!" cries the red-haired girl, in the same moment as shots ring out and echo across the panorama.

Our own shuttle takes that very moment to swoop directly up, having released the last of the Candidates onto the hillside.

I start running downhill, running for my life.

Chapter 34

I feel my breath catching as my feet pound and slide against the crumbling gravel and dry grass, and I come rushing down the hillside in the direction of the nearest highway. The girl who cried warning is running about twenty feet away from me, her stringy hair tangling in the breeze.

More shots and cries sound behind us.

Down, down, down, I go, past shrubs, and rocky inclines, barely missing sharp branches scraping against my loose uniform pants-covered legs.

As I run, a sense of despair comes to me, together with the realization of the immense distance that is before me that I will now have to cross on foot.

Because I don't have a damn hoverboard.

Could Gracie and Gordie and George be here too, also running for their lives? Are they here now, somewhere on another distant Los Angeles hillside, maybe? Or did they choose some other cities?

For that matter, where is "here?"

From the looks of it, I make a wild guess it's somewhere east of downtown, with the Pacific directly beyond it, as I'm facing in that direction.

I need to get my bearings, and quickly. . . .

Think, Gwen, think . . . try to remember. . . . This is L.A.

A vague memory comes to me. Mom and Dad had once mentioned some kind of 30-Mile Studio Zone which is a circular area used by old-time Hollywood film studios for union work zoning purposes. If I remember it right, this is the exact 30-mile radius around the center of Los Angeles, and the boundaries of this zone run in a circle pretty much where the Atlanteans have deposited us. So, if I am in a spot along that boundary to the east of the heart of the city, then I am most likely somewhere in Anaheim, or possibly further north in Fullerton, or Pomona. Had I been even higher up north along the circle boundary, I'd be in the middle of Angeles National Forest, but I am not, since I can definitely see populated areas at the foot of the hill.

One easy way to get my bearings is to find the nearest major freeway artery. Once I see it, I will get a better idea of where I am.

Needle in a haystack, is where I am.

This is hopeless.

This is hell.

You are dead.

Breathing fast, clutching the cord lasso in one hand, I keep moving at a light run down hill, and there is definitely a freeway up ahead.

At the place where the shrubbery ends, the hillside runs into a fenced area overhanging a multi-lane freeway. A couple of Candidates are milling around, looking dejectedly at the impassable section of concrete wall overhanging the freeway. The girl with long stringy hair and freckles is one of them. She turns around at me with a nervous glance.

"Hey," I say. "Thanks for the warning back there. We almost got shot."

"Yeah, sure," she says.

The other teen is a skinny older boy with a tan, weather-beaten, sandy blond longish hair, and the vague look of a typical California surfer. He's holding a long hunting knife, and his armband and token are red. He stares warily at both of us.

"I'm Gwen," I say to the two of them. "I promise—I don't want to fight either one of you, so how about we work together? They did say we *can* cooperate. Might as well pool our resources?"

"Okay," the girl says immediately, with a look of relief. "I am Sarah. Sarah Thornwald. I certainly don't want to fight, especially not using that dreadful Er-Du."

"Me neither," says the surfer guy. "My name is Jared. Screw this, I just want to get to downtown, you know what I mean. Don't wanna fight you or anyone. Peace!"

"Ok, peace works for me. So let's team up." I wipe my forehead and squint in the hot sun. "Where are you guys from originally? How well do you know L.A.? Although I live in Vermont, I was born here."

"Me too," Jared nods. "Parents are in Arizona. But me, Venice Beach, dude."

I smile. "You look it."

He grins back crookedly. "He-he-he, like, yeah. Totally."

I cannot help smiling, because that's really old school, like fifty-year-old slang called Valley Girl slang. My grandma used to speak it back in her day.

Sarah says, "I'm from North Carolina, and my dad is British, but I lived here for many years, it's why I chose it."

"All right, can anyone see the nearest freeway overpass sign?" I stare out at the road where the cars are moving, and suddenly see something blinking colorfully along the wall fence. It's a long ovoid light fixture, made of four stacked color sections, and I realize it's a Semi-Finals zone beacon.

"Hey, I know where we are, it's the 210 Freeway, and this is Glendora!" Sarah says.

But I point at the beacon.

"There," I say. "That's a new zone indicator, the wall's a boundary, and I think we'll need to cross the freeway."

We move down closer to the wall, and now we see the rainbow beacon, one of several. They stretch out every thirty feet along the top of the wall.

"How the hell are we going to cross? Look at that crazy traffic!" Jared mutters. He then leans over the concrete wall and stares down on the other side.

Below, a stream of cars, trucks, and semis is roaring along the road in both directions. It occurs to me, there are probably hidden cameras all around.

"Um, is the red strip on the other side supposed to mean a hot zone?"

"Oh, crap, yeah." Sarah leans in to stare over the freeway also.

I pause, utterly at a loss.

Suddenly behind us I hear more noise, more shots, wild screams, and the sound of more Candidates running down the long hillside toward us.

"Okay, we need to get the hell away from here, *run!*"

The three of us start moving, running parallel to the wall, having nowhere else to go but down, more than twenty feet and into the freeway traffic.

Meanwhile, I whirl around to look, and it's the same Blues armed with rifles, and they're basically picking off Candidates one by one, since we are all equally trapped by the boundary wall, with nowhere to go. Apparently that's their technique, simply eliminate all nearest competition.

We're all on foot, and we're all screwed.

And then I get a wild idea.

I open my mouth and start to sing at the top of my voice.

Sarah and Jared stop running and whirl around to stare at me like I am insane. But my clear voice soars in the wind, and I am making a single, perfect, precise note, an F, which appears to be my trademark emergency "go-to" note. And then I follow it up by a major chord sequence of several others, sustaining each one.

"Are you crazy? What the hell are you doing?" Jared exclaims. "You want to bring everyone down on us, here?"

Indeed, the Blues have heard me and seen us, and they are coming directly at us down the hill.

Fortunately, so is the closest *hoverboard*.

It's coming from the west, the direction of the hot zone, over the freeway, past the tallest treetops. The girl riding it, a slim younger teen, is balancing wildly, barely holding her upright stance, and flailing her arms, at the same time as she is desperately trying to sing her own keying sequence to regain hover control.

Poor thing. She has no idea I just re-keyed her hoverboard mid-flight and locked it away from her with an Aural Block.

Yeah, that's my secret weapon.

"Whoa!" Jared says, seeing the approaching hoverboard. "Did you do that? Sweet!"

"Hey!" the girl on the hoverboard is screaming at me. "What is happening! Stop it! What is this?"

But I continue sustaining the note sequence, and the board comes to a stop right before me, a foot off the ground, with its rider flailing wildly.

I go silent. "Hi, I'm Gwen," I say quickly. "Sorry to do this, but we really need your hoverboard, *now*."

"No way!" The girl on the board glares at me. She is skinny, frail-looking, very young, but with a stubborn set of her angular jaw, and brave blue eyes underneath light brown bangs. "This is *my* board, I earned it fair and square! You can't have it! Give it back! What happened to it? How come it doesn't obey? What did you *do?*"

I notice she has a yellow token also, and there's a cord wrapped around her waist that looks almost identical to mine.

"It doesn't *obey* because it's not a dog," I say lightly, stepping forward.

"Don't come any closer! I can really kick your ass!"

But Sarah and Jared and I have surrounded her.

Meanwhile, behind us the Blue Candidates with guns are coming fast, now that they have seen there's a hoverboard involved.

"Look," I say. "There's no time to argue. This board can carry *all* of us, I swear to you, I know the poundage ratio for this amount of orichalcum, so yeah—"

"Shut up already and let's just take her board," Jared says grimly, and brandishes his big knife without much enthusiasm.

"No!" Sarah and I both exclaim, whirling at him.

"Whoa! Okay, whatever," he says, throwing up his arms, so that the knife he's holding is flipped back ineffectively and he almost loses his grip on it.

Then again I turn away and put a hand, palm out, to the girl in a calming gesture. "No one is taking away your board, but we can *share* it! Quickly now! Just let us all sit down on it, okay? We'll ride together! It's like a long bench, it will work great to carry us— you just sit down and hang on with your hands. We simply all straddle it, okay? Don't hit me on the head, please, let me just show you—"

And then I swing one leg over the front of the hoverboard and take a seat, risking the fact that the girl stands directly behind me and over my head, and she might take the opportunity to clobber me senseless.

Fortunately for me, the girl is a decent person. Because she pauses, then sighs in resignation. She then jumps down to the ground, with feet planted on either side of the board, and takes a seat right behind me. "Okay, this better work!"

Sarah does not lose a moment and gets behind her.

"Jared, sit your butt down!" Sarah says in her pointed British accent, turning to stare up at him.

Jared shrugs, and gets behind us at the very end of the board, and sticks the long knife back into a holder at his belt. With four of us, it is definitely a tight fit along the six-foot length of the board. "Are you sure this is gonna work?"

In reply I start to sing. That way I don't have to think about the fact that I am about to fly a hundred feet up in the air, like a witch on a broom, over a major L.A. freeway.

The broom—pardon me, the hoverboard—shoots straight up, and starts gaining altitude. Sitting behind me, the other passengers let out squeals and other noises of alarm, as they hang on. . . .

If the media cameras really are everywhere, they must be getting a seriously weird feed of us, all straddling the hoverboard, like a boat rowing crew, high up in the air.

I close my eyes momentarily, as I always do during hoverboard up-and-down riding practice to stifle my vertigo, and desperately clutch the sides with both hands, white-knuckled in controlled terror, as we soar forward into the abyss over the 210 Freeway.

My yellow token ID makes a sudden flashing blink, and I recall that the zone boundary has scanned me, and all of us, crossing it. . . .

I continue singing, mouth open into the wind, never faltering, repeating the hover sequence to move forward.

Below us at the foot of the hill, the Blues have arrived and are yelling in frustration and shooting up into the air, aiming at us.

But we are already many feet up and away, and their aim is not that great, especially with this high wind turbulence.

The hoverboard carries us deep into the hot zone, over the freeway and into a residential neighborhood. As we're flying—going about thirty miles an hour, since I don't want to risk any higher speed with a load of four people—the immense panorama of the City of Angels, covered in a delicate smog haze, is overwhelming.

I feel secure enough in our movement that I go silent at last. The hoverboard is perma-keyed to me and has been programmed to fly forward.

Which means, I can shut up and get my own fear of heights under control.

"So, yeah, this is effing awesome," Jared yells from the back, and then makes a horsey laughing sound into the wind.

"Hey, did you just pinch me?" Sarah exclaims at Jared, squirming. "Jerk!" But she seems half-annoyed, half-amused.

"So, yeah," I say, echoing Jared's phrasing, and turn my face lightly to look at the poor silent girl behind me whose board I so shamelessly appropriated. She is staring at me sullenly and her face is pinched and tense. "My name is Gwen Lark, what's yours? I'm sorry to have taken over your board like this, but it was kind of desperate there. . . ."

"That was horrible and scary," the girl tells me. "I almost fell off. You had no right."

"I agree. Again, really sorry. But this is a horrible situation we're all in. Can we just all work together, please?"

"Do I have any choice?" The girl frowns.

"Well," I say. "Sure, I suppose we can land a little farther over there and let you go on your own way on the hoverboard while we all just walk. But that would really suck for all of us—including you. Because, here's the thing—together we can *protect* this hoverboard and make sure you and we all have a chance to make it. Without us, someone else much less nicer might come along and pop you in the head with a gun or gut you with a knife and take away the board and leave you to die."

"I'm Zoe," the girl says after a pause, with the wind whipping her thick brown bangs around her eyes. "And okay, I guess. . . ."

"Great," I say through gritted teeth, as another sudden wave of vertigo passes through me, and I am suddenly reeling, clutching the seat of the hoverboard.

I close my eyes and take a deep breath of wind.

"Nice to meet you, Zoe," Sarah says mildly, maybe recognizing my discomfort. "I am so glad we have you and your board. You saved us, you know, thank you."

"Yeah, you did," I add, recovering sufficiently to speak again.

"So, are we gonna just ride this board all the way

downtown?" Jared says. "Because that would be awesome. At this rate, we'll totally ace this Semi-Finals thing, and be there in just a couple of hours, max."

Just as he says this, there's a loud whoosh in the air. A fiery projectile passes about three feet from us. And then another one, this time just barely a foot overhead. Each is about five inches in diameter, and leaves a comet-searing trail of fire in its wake. What the heck is it? A rocket grenade? A firework?

"Damn, someone's shooting at us!" Jared ducks in reflex.

"Well, yeah, this is a hot zone!" Sarah and Zoe are both "landlocked" between Jared and me, and both cringe in place.

Having crossed the freeway, we are flying vaguely alongside the path of it, next to the 210 Freeway artery, heading in the general southwest direction. I squint from the sun and wind and try to figure out where these fireballs are coming from, because it seems like they are just rising out of nowhere from the treetops and the residential areas along the way. Possibly they are coming from the several multi-story apartment or condo complexes right below us.

Since we are not much higher than the treetops anyway, it seems smart to rise a bit higher. On the other hand that might make us even more visible targets.

"How do they know where we are anyway?" Zoe mutters in my ear, still cringing away.

"I am guessing our tokens send out some kind of GPS coordinates."

"Should we fly higher? Or lower?"

"Or how about just *faster?*" Jared grumbles.

Meanwhile, the fire projectiles are coming thick and fast. I see them rising like fireworks rockets and roman candles from various random spots on the ground below—buildings, street corners, trees.

In moments, the sky is thick with them.

"We have to go lower!" I exclaim through gritted teeth, and start singing a sequence to bring us closer to the treetops, and even street level. We begin the stomach-lurching descent.

"Are you crazy?" Jared is at it again. "This is going to make it worse! They're gonna be able to hit us—"

"No, look up," Sarah says. "Compare *here* and up *there*. There's hundreds of them up there now, and if we rise back up, we will be hit for sure! She's doing the right thing!"

"There's Arrow Highway up ahead," I say, as we whistle past the trees, about twenty feet above street level. "And there's the 605 Freeway coming up, we can head southwest along the highway past Irwindale and I think there's Baldwin Park somewhere here. . . ."

As we move close to the street, it becomes visible now, residents stand outside their houses and stare at us. . . . And now that we can see houses up-close, the windows and balconies of multi-levels are also filled with faces watching.

Furthermore, we are not alone.

Apparently there are so many Candidates here today who chose Los Angeles that they are pretty much scattered all over the place. What are the chances there'd be Candidates on the same street as we are, in this huge sprawling monster of a city? Because even on this street below us I can see two teens in grey Atlantean uniforms same as ours, wearing color armbands, a Green and a Red, running with determination, slow marathon style.

They must've had a significant head start on us, because here they are, on foot, and have managed to make it this far.

Or they are just that *good*.

I try not to think about what kind of position I'd be in now if it hadn't been for my ability to commandeer this hoverboard. I might still be running several miles back, near the hillside, along the wrong side of the 210 Freeway, unable to cross it. Or I might have been shot dead by the Blues.

Stop it. . . .

I shut off that part of me and try to focus on the here and now.

We are in a hot zone. We are being randomly fired upon.

"Ok, here's the problem," Sarah says in that moment. "If we just fly low, along this street level, we will have a tough time getting our bearings and general direction."

"And if we rise up higher to look around, we'll get shot down," Zoe puts in.

I turn my head slightly, my messy ponytail rifled by the wind. "So what's the best solution?"

"There isn't one. It's all crap." Jared sighs. "Man, I could use some water now. It's getting damn hot. And we're going to be dehydrated real soon."

Oh, great . . . I didn't even think of that.

Because Jared's right. And the Atlantean shuttle Pilots mentioned nothing about food or water supplies. They only said we could not get help locally from the city population. Would getting water be considered getting help?

As I think this, I hear gunshots behind us.

"Oh, no! Go faster! Go, go, go!" This time it's mellow Sarah who exclaims.

Apparently there are other hoverboards coming our way, and the Candidates riding them have firearms.

Chapter 35

"Hold on!" I exclaim, and then I sing the sequence to increase speed, followed by variations to keep the board away from various obstacles in our low-hanging path.

The hoverboard under us lurches onward, and I feel the increased wind-drag against the skin of my face and all of my upper body. Since I am the lead anchor, the wind tears into me first.

That's another thing I didn't think of—when you're flying fast, it's impossible to look straight ahead without squinting, and your eyes dry out. What you really need is protective eyewear such as goggles or sunglasses. Bike and motorcycle riders know this. I bet Atlantean hoverboard riders know this.

It is also really hard to sing. Hard to open your mouth even, as the wind fills your lungs immediately.

So I keep my face half-turned and try to sing the notes that way.

"Can someone look around and tell me who's behind us?" I cry out.

"Two guys on boards—no, make it three. The third's a girl. They're all Blues."

"Damn these Blues and their craptastic firearms!"

We move along Arrow Highway then turn off north on some side street, because two hoverboards are coming fast from both sides behind us, to cut us off from the south, while the third begins to rise to treetop level, so that it ends up tracking us while coming down from overhead. The guys balanced on the boards are holding automatic assault rifles. So is the girl overhead.

They are now only about fifty feet away, and coming hard and fast.

The two marathon-style runners on the street with us take note and pick up the pace, then wisely disappear into the nearest side alley.

Volleys of shots ring out behind us.

I make the board swerve as we are flying too fast now, way too fast for safety and my ability to navigate it properly.

"Go up! Up!" Jared cries. "Go faster!" He's the one in the back, so if anyone gets hit, he's first in line.

Coming up directly before me is the 605 Freeway overpass. I direct the board to fly right underneath the wide concrete slab and then we turn a corner behind giant support posts and freeze in place, levitating right below the ceiling that happens to be the freeway underbelly. It's not really a hiding place, but at least it's out of direct line of fire.

"What now?" Sarah says softly.

"We're trapped," Zoe mutters.

I am breathing fast. At least there's no onrushing wind and I can breathe and think straight, if only for a moment. "We'll wait them out . . ." I say.

"How long?" Jared whispers. "They'll just take us out the moment we show ourselves. And we have no weapons that can take them on. My knife-throwing skills are crap and besides, I've only got one."

"Besides, what's stopping them from coming in under here and just executing us all? They can guess we don't have firearms," Sarah says.

"Would it be too much to hope that they just leave us the hell alone and go on their own way?" I grumble.

"Hey," Jared says. "Can you do something again to take over their boards?"

"What, me?" I say.

"Yeah, who else? You, Gwen. Do that weird singing command thing that you did before."

I frown, thinking.

Just as I consider whether or not I am capable of doing high-speed, directed, remote *keying* of not just one but two orichalcum objects at once, while being fired upon, the Blue girl Candidate on the hoverboard appears, floating from behind the concrete support slab. She is balanced easily on her board that's levitating forward in slo-mo at about two miles an hour, and she holds her automatic with practiced ease.

We're basically sittings ducks for her.

I think of Blayne Dubois practicing his LM Forms. And then I sing a sequence that creates an Aural Block and then raises the board underneath the Blue girl nose up, at a near vertical angle.

It all takes a few seconds. The Blue girl screams in surprise as she starts sliding off her suddenly-upright board, tries to hold on, then inadvertently starts firing. . . .

Her rifle goes off, and the splatter-volley hits the concrete right behind our heads, so that the wall is riddled with holes.

Behind me, Zoe cries out, and then Sarah slumps over.

The Blue girl loses her hold and falls, about twenty feet onto the concrete and asphalt sidewalk of the street level below.

Her board remains hovering nose-up in the air before me.

I look down, and see her grey-uniformed body and blue armband, as she lies broken on the asphalt.

I just killed another human being.

I did it . . . I, I did it.

. . . Killed another human being.

And then, as a wave of utter numbing cold washes over me at the realization, as I sit frozen, I feel a stinging pain in my left arm. And I see a red stain.

At the same time, behind me Zoe is screaming, while Jared holds on to Sarah's lifeless slumped body in his arms.

All it took was less than three seconds.

To change *everything*.

I start "awake" and suddenly tears are gushing down my face, while the two people still alive behind me are yelling, saying something that I can hardly understand.

"Go! Go! Go!"

In that same instant the two remaining Blues on hoverboards appear. They see the other empty board hovering, and the body on the ground below.

And instead of firing at us, they suddenly take off.

Had they stayed, I would not have been able to sing a single note in time to fend them off, because I am very slow right now, like molasses . . . slow and numb and thick. . . .

"Gwen!" Jared yells my name and Zoe shakes me. Zoe is bleeding from a light wound on her cheek where a bullet barely grazed her. Jared is apparently unharmed, but Sarah—she is dead.

"We need to go, Gwen! Land us, for a moment, please, just set us down right here," Zoe says. "We need to—we need—"

I take a deep shuddering breath to stop the tears, and the wound in my arm is really hurting now. *Good.*

It'll give me enough focus to regain control over my *voice.* Because I have to sing us down.

I start the note sequence, and my voice starts out breathy, powerless, so I repeat, forcing my lungs to cooperate. This time we begin moving, descending slowly, and hover a foot over the ground.

"We can put her down here . . ." Jared mutters, resting his dangling feet on the ground, wiping his forehead and smearing Sarah's blood that's all over him and Zoe, and me. He holds up the girl's body with a kind of horrible quiet awe for which there are no words.

"No," I say. "Not here. Not on this horrible ugly concrete, under a freeway."

And then I look up and the other board is still hovering near the ceiling of the freeway overpass.

I make a sound and it comes down to me, floating softly, and then I make it right itself so that it is once more horizontal. "Put Sarah on top of the board," I say. "We'll take her somewhere else—more decent."

"You're bleeding too," Zoe says awkwardly. "You need to press down on the wound or something. Or—or you'll bleed to death."

I look at my arm, and there are rivulets of red liquid running down my uniform. Zoe's right, it's not a bad wound but I need to stop the bleeding or I'll go weak eventually.

I point to Jared's knife. "Let me borrow it for a moment."

He hands me the knife and I use it to cut off a length of my cord weapon lasso. I then bind my arm above the wound and just below the armband. *Funny—it looks now,* it occurs to me, *that I have a yellow and a red armband. . . .* What a mess.

And then I think, *I have a bullet lodged inside my arm.*

After Sarah is laid flat, her thin body stretched out along the second board, I use the rest of my lasso cord to tie her in place. I look over her face with its stringy hair and freckles.

Sarah's eyes are still open. Someone—someone needs to close her eyes.

And then I walk over to the fallen body of the Blue girl. I try not to look at *her* face. But I do anyway. I pick up her automatic assault rifle, the same thing that killed Sarah and wounded Zoe and me. I set the safety on and sling it over my other shoulder. And then I get back on the first hoverboard.

I start singing in somebody else's *alien* voice, and the two boards rise simultaneously, three of us straddling one, and Sarah's body on the other.

We float just above street level but not high enough to engage any of the hot zone firepower that gets activated whenever we rise too high in the air.

"Where to now?" Jared asks, while Zoe just holds on to my back with one hand and the board with the other. I can feel her shaking.

I know just the place. A few miles northwest of here, beautiful and appropriate, in San Marino.

I suppose I could just set Sarah down on the first decent suburb lawn somewhere in the next block. In fact, I probably *should* do it, the smart thing to do.

And San Marino is a little out of the way.

But something crazy inside me makes me proceed. Because I can see the body of the Blue girl lying on the ground, short brown hair, ordinary features, and yet, unforgettable, fixed in my mind's eye, permanently.

I killed her. She was going to kill us all. And she killed Sarah.

It happened because I tipped her board. Had I not done that—
The thought goes around in my mind in an endless circle.

At least I can make this one other *thing right—for Sarah—as right as it can be.*

"We're going to the Huntington," I say through my teeth. "They have beautiful botanical gardens and rose gardens and a Japanese garden and a library."

"Wait, that's too far north!" Jared says. "That's out of our way, and crazy! Why? Let's just put the poor girl down over there, in that grass, it's decent enough—"

"Shut up," I say in a hard voice. "We're going to the Huntington."

We start flying just above street level along smaller streets of suburbia in a direction that vaguely follows the 210 Freeway as it's moving west in the direction of Pasadena—it's the only way I know to approach the Huntington.

To be honest, I have no clear sense of what I'm doing, where we're going. The last time I was here at the Huntington Library, Gallery, and Botanical Gardens, I was a little girl with my parents and George. I remember running through the amazing structured gardens, with manicured lawns, sudden twists and turns framed by artful plants and trees among Grecian statuary, roses and cactus gardens and natural wonder. . . . I remember looking at stern, dark-brown, faded portraits in the Gallery.

It was all so long ago. . . .

My insides are numb, starting from my gut and outward, and my circulation seems sluggish, while my extremities are cold.

"We're wasting time, this is all wrong," Jared says periodically. "We should just leave her body somewhere and go on our way. There's nothing we can do, it's not like it would make any difference for her."

Stubbornly I say nothing, looking straight ahead, with the dry wind in my face. The automatic firearm that I got from the Blue girl's body slaps against my side whenever I make an abrupt motion.

"Look, I *get* it," Jared says. "She seemed—no, she *was* cool. A good person. Too bad we didn't get to know her any better. I wish I did. I'm really sorry, okay. I am sorry she died. This sucks. But *we have no time!* We need to just leave her and go."

"Ten minutes," I say, turning my head around to glare at him fiercely. "Give me just *ten minutes*. We're almost there. Okay? If not, we'll turn back, I *promise*."

"Okay," he grumbles.

All the while, Zoe remains silent behind me.

I sing to keep us moving forward at a quick but more even pace, hoping that as we get through this neighborhood—El Monte?

Temple City?—wherever we are, we'll eventually hit San Marino and Huntington Drive where the landmark gardens and art gallery are located.

There I will leave Sarah lying, on one of the green lawns maybe, or near the glorious rose garden ached walkway. . . .

I am insane.

Jared is right, we have no time for this. And I have no right to force them to go along with me on a selfish sentimental whim. This is just me being nuts, unable to deal, to let go . . . to just let this person whom I barely know, go in peace. . . . Because I'm feeling guilt about the *other* dead person. . . .

Up ahead is some large intersection.

As I consider whether to make our two hoverboards rise another ten feet higher so that we can safely clear the busy traffic intersection, or to turn along a smaller street—or maybe to just turn around altogether and give up on this—there's a rumbling noise. It is both deep and high-pitched at the same time, like a hurricane rising. Or a tornado.

It's coming from the south, from behind us in the distance of what seems like many miles.

I turn around quickly, and so do Zoe and Jared. We stare at what appears to be a dark flock of birds approaching rapidly, filling the sky behind us. There is also a hollow advance sound of rushing high wind that precedes them.

"What the hell is that?" Jared raises one hand to shield his eyes as he looks intently.

"How weird. . . . Are those birds? Okay, no, that can't be just *wind*. Even I know the Santa Anas are not that bad," Zoe mutters.

And then we see them closer up, and it's definitely not birds.

It's Candidates riding hoverboards, dozens of them, flying crazy-fast.

They are being pursued.

And what's behind them is not a flock of black birds either but an array of *shuttles*.

They are small, compact, near-black, the smallest Atlantean aircraft I've seen yet. There are so many that they appear as a dark speckle of dots, enough to black out the sky from a distance. They fly soundlessly, but because they are moving so fast through the atmosphere, they cut the air around them, rending it apart so that a dull hurricane roar is produced. . . .

Meanwhile, the vanguard of the Candidates on hoverboards reaches us. As we hover on our two boards, levitating in place before the intersection, the boards and riders go whooshing by, some at street level like us, others higher up, and many others yet riding above the trees, and causing the hot zone firing systems to activate as they go by.

"Drones behind us! Move! Get away!" one Candidate on a board yells at us as she passes by, going too fast for us to see her face.

My heartbeat goes into overdrive. I sing the forward hover sequence and immediately our two boards lurch forward, picking up speed.

Zoe grabs my belt from behind silently, so as not to fall, and Jared cusses, taking hold of the board on his end, the best he can. The board carrying Sarah's body moves silently alongside us. I sing us ten feet higher, so that we can safely cross the intersection where the cross-traffic is fortunately stopped due to a red light.

We plunge forward and become one with the speeding army of hoverboard riders.

I don't dare look around too much, since I am concentrating on the way ahead and any street-level obstacles that might pop up, such as stop signs and light poles. But I can see enough with my peripheral vision. . . .

Most of the other Candidates are riding standing up, balancing on two feet the way the Atlanteans taught us. However, there are quite a few who are also straddling the boards while seated, or even lying flat on their bellies and hugging the boards so as not to fall off. However we're the only "crew" of more than one person riding a single board. So, others give us looks—or is it, they're looking at Sarah's body on the other board? Whatever it is, most people are going faster, so eventually they pass us.

"Hey, dude, what are these drone things after us? How come we're all running away?" Jared yells out to the nearest boy atop a board, who's balancing in a loosely hunched snowboarder stance.

"You wanna stay back and find out?" the boy yells back.

"Killer drones!" a girl cries, gasping from the force of wind resistance, somewhere several feet above our heads. "They come from the south . . . as soon as you get close to the inner end of this hot zone, the boundary fence activates them. . . ."

"How do you know they're dangerous?" Zoe cries out.

"Because I saw them fry at least three people!" the same girl answers. "They fire these flaming lasers or something, just trust me, they are bad!"

"Yeah, they incinerate you completely, so only the board remains and eventually it drops down with your ashes," the boy adds.

"All I know is, we need to get out of this hot zone," the girl says. "And since they cut us off from the south, we have to backtrack."

"Hey," I yell out to the girl. "When did the drones first appear?"

"No idea."

"Does anyone know? I mean, at what point specifically? Where do you have to be inside the zone to activate those drones?"

But the girl shrugs, and the boy is already many feet ahead of us.

And so we keep going.

Whether we like it or not, we are now going the wrong way, away from our destination downtown and north toward San Marino.

Toward the Huntington.

Chapter 36

"What time is it?" I say a few minutes later, as we approach what looks to be a large intersection, and just might be Huntington Drive. The hurricane roar is almost directly behind us. "I don't have anything with a clock app, and no phone."

"I don't either," Zoe says. "No smart jewelry."

"Doesn't matter, just keep going!" Jared is looking around constantly at the sky full of drones that are stretched out in a mathematically perfect array, approaching us with a terrible inevitability. "There's gotta be an end to this evil hot zone."

"So we get out of the hot zone," I mutter. "And then what? We'll just be back where we started, only at a different spot in the 30-mile radius around the center of L.A."

"I don't know!" Jared yells at me angrily.

"We'll have to go back in again."

"So then, *what?* What do we do? These things will kill us!"

I think and think, until it hurts. "Okay, look. The Atlanteans didn't put us down in an impossible scenario. At least I don't think they did. If there really was no way to cross that hot zone safely, it wouldn't be in the Semi-Finals."

Zoe and Jared stare at me as I glance at them, just before plunging across and just barely above the intersection traffic. Then I move our boards along Oxford Drive, in the wake of a dozen other hoverboard riders. Just ahead of me is an expansive visitor parking area, and beyond it I see the front entrance of the Huntington Library, with the venerable buildings of the Gallery in the distant background.

"I think we need to land somewhere and hide, or otherwise bypass the drones."

"We can't just stop now!" Jared looks from me to Zoe, for support.

But I am frustrated, tired, dazed, and my wounded arm is now hurting like hell plus the circulation has been slowed down where the arm is tied, so it's numb and awful, and I can barely use it to hang on. . . .

"I'll find a way," I mutter. "Give me a minute, I'll find a place, a safe place to land, to hide, to—"

There's an awful scream from behind us. It is followed by the sound of scorching fire that gets cut off immediately.

About a hundred feet down the street the first of the drones has reached the last of the hoverboard riders, those in the very back of us. I can't help turning to look. . . .

A solitary hoverboard in the very back of our lineup floats forward, still moving under its original momentum, but without a rider. Whatever happened to that Candidate must have ended with the scream and the scorching. A single black drone moves directly over the empty board, then rises and returns to its array formation.

We all stare in horror, as another sleek black drone drops out of formation and descends thirty feet to hover right over a Candidate who's now the last one of us in the back. He's balancing on his hoverboard awkwardly, and going slower than everyone else. He looks up desperately, flailing his arms to stay upright, and then we see it happen. . . .

A bright beam of scalding white fire comes from the base of the drone. The boy is engulfed in bluish flames, his scream cut off in seconds, and his form disappearing into a pile of grey ashes that floats down and around the board.

Nothing is left behind, not even bones.

His board floats forward, unoccupied.

The process repeats. Drone rises and retreats, then another one targets the next person who is now last.

The girl starts screaming even before she is hit. She cringes, straining to regain balance with her arms, falls on her stomach, then slips off her board and lands on the ground.

As we flee this, I glance back yet again, mesmerized with the nightmare scenario that's taking place. However, a peculiar thing happens. The drone that has targeted the girl and her hoverboard now moves along for a few feet directly over the vacant board, then lifts up and retreats without firing at the fallen girl or her board.

The girl who fell remains on the sidewalk, huddled with her hands over her head, screaming and whimpering, while the drones now ignore her completely and pass by over her without engaging.

In a flash, I suddenly understand.

"The drones only target you if you're on a hoverboard!" I scream, raising my voice to reach as many Candidates around me as I can. "Everybody, get off! Get off your boards now, if you want to live!"

"What?" Jared yells back. "How do you know? How can you be sure?"

"Just look at her!" I point to the fallen girl on the street. "She was no longer targeted and left unharmed as soon as she fell off her board."

"I don't know, this is too crazy, we can't be sure!"

"Okay, you want to stay on, go ahead, idiot!" I scream. "I'm getting off!"

"Me too!" Zoe says hurriedly.

"Oh, crap, crap, crap!" Jared mutters and looks bewildered.

Meanwhile I sing the sequence to pause and hover, bringing us down to a foot above street level. Then, as several other Candidates also slow down or keep going, with everyone staring at us, I get off our board and step aside. Then I approach the second board with Sarah's body and I start untying her, while my numb hands are shaking and my one arm is almost entirely without feeling now. The dratted assault rifle I am still carrying over my shoulder is not helping.

"Crap, we're gonna die . . . I'm gonna die," Jared mutters, but he too is standing well away from the board, next to Zoe. The two of them stare upward, cringing. Zoe looks white and close to fainting from fear.

"Help me!" I say meanwhile, as I am done untying Sarah. "Help me move her down from this thing, quickly! Please!"

Jared comes alive and moves in, and together we pull Sarah down—she is cool to the touch and heavy now—and I feel bile or something else rising in my gut, and I am about to retch and cry at the same time—but I don't. . . . We get her down.

And then we stand and watch the ocean of drones arriving and passing overhead.

About half of the Candidates have listened to me, and they too stand, cringing, hoping, while their hoverboards levitate nearby like docked boats.

The others who continue fleeing on their hoverboards—we hear more screams and more scorching fire, as the rearmost Candidates are eliminated, one by one, as soon as the drones reach them.

However, we are now living proof that my lucky hunch was right. And eventually more and more of the fleeing riders in the front get the hint and dismount from their boards.

The drone array flies over the Huntington grounds and beyond, hunting those who are unaware of the means to stay safe.

For the next ten minutes, we stand listening to distant screams.

And then the array of drones returns, and passes over us again, as it is heading back to its place of origin at the other end of this hot zone.

We are ignored completely.

We carry Sarah's body through the visitor parking and past the front building into the botanical gardens walkway, and leave her there at the foot of a white lovely statue near a small pond.

It is green and soft and silent here, only the warm wind moving leaves of the tall trees, and the dappled sunlight on grass. It is so easy just to go still, to space out, close your eyes and forget what *this* is, what day this is, and only know the moment of peace, here in a natural spot. . . .

I sit down for a moment, a few feet away from Sarah as she lies there, her stringy reddish hair mingling with the grass. I tell myself she looks peaceful. We've taken off her Green Quadrant weapon, the small armor vest that didn't protect her from the bullet in the chest—it was never fastened properly. Zoe ends up putting it on and keeping it, since she's the smallest of us, and it appears to fit her best.

The two boards hover nearby, while Jared lies on the grass and Zoe sits, her feet tucked sideways under her, and her arms around her knees. The armor vest is loose around her and she does not bother to secure it properly either, so it gaps open on one side. A sheen of sweat covers most of our exposed skin, and more sweat stains our uniforms, as the day is heating up.

Finally I get up and force myself to put my hand out and gently close Sarah's eyes with my fingers. Then I turn away from her face with its freckles, think a prayer, or maybe just think *peace*, and never look at her again.

"Okay, I am ready to go," I say softly.

We start walking back, while I call the two hoverboards to move beside us. We pause at a running fountain and wash our faces, then drink some of the water, cupping it with our hands, not caring how safe or drinkable it is.

Other Candidates scattered all over the lawn and the grounds, are doing the same thing. They are walking, with their boards moving at their sides like well-trained animals.

We are all heading south, by foot now.

It's a long way to go.

An older teen who calls himself Ethan Jamerson starts walking with us. He is lanky and tall and skinny, like a beanpole, with dingy pale brown hair, a slightly disjointed nose and a sharp jawline. There's a green armband around his arm. If he has any Green Quadrant body armor, it's not visible.

"Hey, you all are, what, some kind of team or something?" he asks me warily at first. "I saw you get off the board first—smart move. Is it okay if I join you guys?"

Jared gives him a sideways look. "Hey, as long as you don't plan to kill us in the next five minutes, yeah, sure."

"But in about thirty minutes, that would be okay, right?" Ethan says with a crooked smile.

I give him a tired sideways glance as I trudge along, feeling lines of pain shooting through my arm and into my shoulder. "Yeah, sure. In thirty minutes, you can put me out of my misery, if you like. And if you *can*."

"Unless you get to me first, eh?" Ethan says, glancing over at the automatic firearm I'm carrying. He raises his non-existent faded brows.

But at that point I decide that he is probably okay.

"So how screwed are we, anyone know?" Jared says a few minutes later, as we walk down some street in the suburb headed south toward downtown. "How much time do we have left?"

Ethan pops a small gadget out of his pocket. "It's close to nine AM, Pacific Time. Not too bad."

"We got lucky because of the time zone factor," Zoe says.

"Yeah." I sigh. "The three hours we gained we lost being driven in the wrong direction by the drones."

"Well, guys," Ethan says cheerfully. "Back in that botanical gardens place I saw a large visitor map, one of those 'you are here' things, and it had some info about the Huntington being located *twelve miles* from downtown L.A. So it's not as bad as you think. We're more than halfway there! Just need to keep moving southwest."

"Oh, yeah?" Jared rubs his nose with the back of his hand. "Okay, then."

We trudge forward some more. Or at least I trudge, while the others are walking at a brisk pace and I am barely keeping up. My wounded arm is numb almost completely, and it has swollen, I think. I really need medical attention. Or at least to sit down. Or—no, yeah, I *need* medical attention.

"I am going to try to get back on the hoverboard," I say.

Zoe nods. "Might as well."

"If the drones show up again, we'll just see them and hop off the boards immediately."

There are four of us, and three boards. Zoe and I straddle Zoe's original board, while Jared gets on the one that carried Sarah's body.

"Hey, Gwen, how about you un-key this board or whatever it is you did to it, so that I can command it myself properly?" Jared glances at me in expectation.

I nod tiredly. Then I take a deep breath and sing a sequence that releases the Aural Block on the second board. Of course I don't tell him what it is I am actually doing.

Jared then sings in a light tenor a new keying sequence, and gets on the board, straddling it like a horse. "Why stand when you can sit?" he mutters tiredly, shrugging to excuse himself, but no one cares.

Ethan meanwhile gets up on his own board and rides it properly, standing up, like a skateboarder. From the lanky looks of him and the effortless way he balances it, he has ridden boards before.

Regardless of our riding form, we soon make the hoverboards rise up about five feet from the ground.

Then we all fly in a close formation, one after the other, at street level, at about twenty-five miles an hour.

We are somewhere in Alhambra, a few blocks away from Atlantic Boulevard to the west and the I-10 San Bernardino Freeway to the south, when the hurricane sound returns.

In seconds, the southwest sky is blackened out with drone shuttles as they rise from their launch sites and start moving at us.

Oh, but they are moving fast!

"Drones! Get off the boards!" Zoe cries wildly, giving me a loud earful.

As quickly as we can, we sing the hover stop commands and jump off, with not a moment to spare.

We stand away from the boards as the drones pass directly overhead, ignoring us. Instead they keep moving north many blocks beyond us, where once again we hear screams and firing, as other Candidates are caught unaware.

"I bet the end of this hot zone is just up ahead," Ethan says.

"Yeah, I can't wait," I mutter tiredly, as I resume walking.

Ethan's right. We get to the intersection of Atlantic and the I-10 Freeway, and the street is marked with four-color beacons every thirty feet. The beacons are installed along the freeway and along Atlantic Boulevard, this time on street level, so all we need to do is cross the barrier in either direction to be out of this hot zone. The red stripe is painted on our side of the barrier, as though to remind us.

And the barrier itself is a simple chain link fence. Except it is at least fifteen feet tall, with barbed wire on the top.

And, judging by the "Danger, High Voltage, Do Not Touch" and the skull and crossbones sign, and—as if that's not enough—the lightning zigzag, this is an *electric* fence.

"Great, just what we need," Jared says, wiping his forehead streaked with sweat and road dust, and remainders of Sarah's blood.

We stand at the corner, evaluating the situation.

"Okay, so what options do we have?" Ethan says. "Fly over? Climb over? Find a door or a hole in the fence? Disable the electricity?"

"That pretty much covers it. . . ." I stand next to Zoe and our hoverboard. I sway slightly, feeling a head-rush from the heat of the merciless SoCal sun overhead, and from the fact that I can barely remain upright due to approaching shock and loss of sensation in my arm.

"Which fence should we try to cross? The freeway or the street one?" Jared nods at the Freeway side. "I think if we follow along and find an I-10 overpass we might be able to just walk under?"

"Not so easy." Ethan points down along the fence boundary to where the closest overpass is to our left. "The Atlanteans stuck a pesky fence continuation under the overpass too. The entire way is blocked."

"How quickly can we saddle up and fly over the fence?" Jared ponders.

"Not quickly enough," I say. "There are drone launch sites hidden all along this street, there, can you see? There are more drones waiting to fly up and incinerate us."

And I point to the dark convex spots in the concrete of the street where the tops of the drone shuttles show, sitting like recessed mushrooms. I just saw them, just made out what they are. . . .

Holy crap, they are all around us! Like, there's one two feet away on the sidewalk next to my feet!

Good thing I said something because Ethan was about to get on his hoverboard.

"No! Stop! Don't touch your board!" I exclaim.

Ethan whistles, and quickly backs away. "Wow, thanks."

"Okay, so much for flying over." Zoe looks sullen and hopeless.

As we continue standing, not knowing how to proceed, more Candidates who cleverly avoided the drones the same way we did, gradually arrive. We gather at the corner of the zone, milling around.

"Hey, what are you all waiting for?" an older teen girl with dark hair and an arrogant expression says. Her token and armband are red, and she's carrying not one but *two* long, impressive swords. . . .

Apparently, very sharp swords.

Because she stands back, then swings powerfully, and her sword crashes against the chain links.

There is a hissing sound and sparks fly. . . . The girl screams, then starts arcing with the electric charge, and is unable to drop the sword. A few seconds later, her burned body falls down on the concrete, at the foot of the fence.

A strong horrible smell of burning flesh is carried on the hot wind.

"What a stupid idiot!" some freshman-age kid says. "Couldn't she see the 'danger, high voltage' sign?"

"Shut up! Just—shut up!" another girl Candidate says, holding her hand across her mouth. "That was awful!"

"Yeah, it was. But she's still an id—"

"She *was*. She's gone now. Have some respect, man," Jared says. "We're all in this screwed up crap Semi-Finals together, you might say we're all idiots."

Chapter 37

About twenty minutes later, as we still have no solution to getting past this hot zone boundary fence, I risk doing something a little crazy.

I approach one of the "recessed mushroom" drones that's cleverly resting in its launch pad—or whatever the hole-in-the-concrete thing underneath it is. And then, taking a deep breath, I put my foot down on top of the drone.

"Hey! Watch it, there, careful," Ethan says to me. He's been observing me silently for the last few minutes.

But, nothing happens to me. So I press down harder with my foot, then take a step and stand on top of the slightly curving surface.

"Oh, no! What are you doing?" Zoe says. "What if you activate it and it explodes or starts firing?"

The drone is circular, curved slightly like an upside-down plate, or a classic warrior shield, only about four feet in diameter, like an oversized large manhole cover.

I stand with both feet on it, testing its resilience. There is lack of give, which is good.

And then I sing an F note, followed by the rest of the keying sequence.

Yeah, I've assumed this thing is made of orichalcum.

Everyone stares at me like I'm crazy. Candidates turn in my direction. Jaws drop.

With a soft lurch, the drone rises and hovers about a foot over the launch pad, with me standing up on its mushroom-cap shaped surface.

I balance with my hands, starting to flail slightly, and my usual terror of heights kicks in . . . plus I am not in my best physical shape right now. And the weight of the automatic rifle on my shoulder is pulling me off-kilter.

But I steel myself and sing the rising object sequence, my voice soaring an octave higher. The drone begins to rise, carrying me with it.

I start to close my eyes in that automatic response to the terror of vertigo. Soon I am rising over the barbed wire top end of the fence and over the beacons along the boundary.

As I pass the beacons, my yellow token flashes brightly as I get auto-scanned by the zone boundary. . . .

The choice before me is to go straight ahead and over the I-10 freeway with its *six lanes* of onrushing traffic *in both directions*, while balanced on top of a flimsy rounded slippery object not designed to be ridden. Or I can direct the "drone-board" to go to the right, over the Atlantic Boulevard traffic with half the lanes but equally-rush-hour levels of vehicles in both directions. Then I would still have to cross the freeway somehow, later, but under less pressure to stay upright on the surface of a flimsy drone. . . .

A Greek mythology reference comes to me. *Scylla or Charybdis, Gwen Lark. . . . Scylla or Charybdis.*

What would Odysseus do?

I think Odysseus would do the smart thing. . . . I bet he'd take the easier crossing on Atlantic Boulevard.

But considering that I am this close to passing out, this close to being on my last strength here, the smart thing would be just to go forward as far as I can, while I still can.

Damn, but I should have *sat* down on that drone instead of trying to balance on it while standing upright.

Well, too late now. . . .

I think this as I start moving the drone forward over the twelve lanes of freeway.

The next two minutes are the longest minutes of my life. The drone, with me riding it, sails very slowly over the San Bernardino Freeway.

I never look down, not once, only hear the roar of cars and semis below, the honking of horns, and *feel* the churn of air from the vehicles in motion cutting the wind tunnel right underneath me.

Just don't think, don't think.

Don't look down.

Breathe. . . .

Finally, after an eternity, I reach the other side. Somehow I have managed not to fall off, and now the sidewalk of the other side of the freeway beckons, is looming before me.

I sing the descent and then the hover stop sequence.

I don't so much jump off as I fall off the drone and collapse onto the sidewalk, hitting my knee as I land, and scraping my good hand that's attached to the arm without the bullet lodged in it—the limb I can still use in its entirety.

I crouch, then sit on the concrete, right next to the hovering drone, and for about thirty seconds I simply breathe and breathe and think *nothing.*

And then I look back over the short pedestrian fence railing on this side of the freeway, and I see them.

Candidates riding drones, just like me—dozens of them—crossing the freeway.

Looks like I've set a trend.

"Okay, you're officially *crazy*," Jared tells me, as he lands his own drone two feet away from me. "But in a good way. Wow! That was brilliant!"

"You're right, I am crazy." I sigh, glancing up at him. "I had no idea it would work."

"Well, yeah, who knew the drones would be dumb enough to let us ride them?" Ethan says, landing on the other side, followed by Zoe who is riding her drone while seated on it.

"Actually," I say, "the Atlanteans probably had no idea *we* would be dumb enough to try something like that. So they never bothered programming the drones against this kind of thing."

"How do you know," Zoe says, "that they didn't want us to do it? Maybe that's part of our test, to think in weird new ways to solve tough problems?"

"Yeah, I suppose," I say. "Could be."

"So, now what?" Ethan stretches his long arms, swinging them side-to-side.

"Call our boards here, I guess. And send the drones back to their manholes."

Ethan stares at me. "Huh? Can you do that? How can you call

so far across the road? Will the voice keying work long distance?"

Obviously he doesn't know.

"Yeah, *she* can do that," Zoe says, rolling her eyes.

And so I send away the drones and call our three hoverboards. My voice rises cleanly over the noise of traffic, and in moments, the boards come sailing across the freeway expanse toward us.

Again, other Candidates stare in surprise and almost in dismay. Because the rest of the boards—*their* boards—are still stuck on the other side of the freeway, inside the hot zone. At this point, if these Candidates want to ride anything the rest of the way downtown, these drones that they used to cross the boundary are all they've got.

"How in the world are you doing this?" a girl says to me.

I shrug.

The good thing is, we're in a safe zone now, and this is Monterey Park, according to a road sign. The bad thing is, I am not doing too well.

"Hey, so what was that thing you did?" Ethan asks me again as we get back on our three boards. "How did you sing loud enough for the boards to come to you from so far away?"

"I dunno, I have this talent, I guess," I mutter. And then I watch as several teens try to emulate me. A girl sings a keying sequence at the top of her voice, leaning over the freeway guardrail. But her voice is not as precisely in tune as she could make it, and so her board remains inert on the other side of the freeway. Another boy tries the same thing, belting it out loudly, and again, imprecisely. . . .

Meanwhile, most people simply give up on their boards and sit down on their drones instead, rising in the air while riding these huge, black, upside-down dinner plates made of orichalcum.

"Better than nothing!" a wiry Asian kid with a Yellow Quadrant armband exclaims, laughing down at me as he zips away on top of a drone in the direction of downtown.

Zoe and I sit down on our board and rise up in the air, followed by Jared and Ethan on theirs. And this time, we can safely go much higher, above the treetops, without dealing with a projectile firing system trying to bring us down.

My vertigo seems less acute now, as we rise thirty feet above street level. Maybe because by now I am too faint to care about anything but staying awake and upright.

I put all my effort into singing the hover commands properly, focusing on the right notes and precision of tone.

We move southwest, crossing varied neighborhoods, and in about twenty minutes approaching the 710, the Long Beach Freeway, which runs north-south and apparently designates another zone boundary.

Because, yeah, I see the dratted four-color beacons every thirty feet, festooning the top of another chain link fence that runs parallel to the 710.

"Oh, damn . . ." Jared mutters, riding his own board right next to ours, feet dangling. "How much do you wanna bet this is another hot zone coming up?"

"Where are we anyway, East L.A.?" Zoe asks me. The dry wind whips her hair at this altitude.

We all stare down.

"I don't know, not sure." I barely find the energy to answer her, that's how fuzzy my brain is at this point.

"Not quite," Ethan says. "We're just a few blocks north of it. . . . I think. It's out of our way."

"So, ready to cross the boundary?" Jared takes a deep breath and sings the notes to move forward. He's the first of us to sail over the beacons and his red token flashes as he gets scanned.

Next, Zoe and I cross over, at least ten feet above the beacons and fence top.

Then, Ethan comes after.

As soon as we pass the boundary, we check for a red stripe painted on this side of the fence, and sure enough, there is one.

Which means, we're in another hot zone.

Meanwhile, we see that many other Candidates are riding drones in the air around us. However, in addition to us, only a few are on hoverboards.

Lucky for us, the drones themselves don't seem to care. Apparently, the "rules" of this particular hot zone don't work the same way—don't activate the drones to kill the hoverboard riders.

So . . . what do they activate instead?

Great, I think. *What will it be?*

What horrible new surprises lie in store for us here, as we get closer to downtown?

It occurs to me incidentally: *At least some people figured out how to call their hoverboards remotely across that other freeway.*

It doesn't require a Logos voice, merely the ability to be both loud and precise, as Mr. Warrenson taught us in Atlantis Tech class, and as I'm sure the other Instructors in other RQCs across the country did also. It's surprising how many people must have forgotten—or at least, did not extend the notion of auto-keying objects that were simply out of reach across the table from you, to the idea of doing the same thing from very far away.

Because, yeah, this was definitely something we were taught in Tech class, but we never practiced it across long distance. And getting it to work does require practice—which I've had.

But now, not even all these long hours of practice spent under the supervision of Aeson Kass, can help me maintain my strength.

Because I realize, as I direct the hoverboard forward, that very soon I will not have the *strength* to form the correct notes for the hover commands—even the most basic ones.

At the rate I am deteriorating now, I will soon be unable to sing at all.

And so, in a faint but still precise voice, I sing the complex sequence that removes the Aural Block from the hoverboard underneath me, and I tell Zoe that she can take over.

"The board is yours," I tell her, with the dry wind bathing my face in energy-leaching heat. "I reset it, so that you can voice-key it to yourself again—before I pass out and we both crash."

"Oh. . . ." Zoe looks at me with worry. "Are you okay?"

"Yeah . . . not really."

Zoe nods, then sings the keying sequence in a sweet soprano. But she still looks at me seriously.

She lands our board for a moment so that we can switch seats, and she can move to the front. Then we rise and continue moving, this time with Zoe at the helm, singing the hover commands in her higher voice. I sit behind her, clutching the sides of the board with both hands, mostly my right hand, while my left feels like a heavy log of wood, a foreign limb mistakenly attached to me, an arm that belongs to someone else. . . .

Gracie, I think, engulfed in a wave of dizziness, *hope you are okay, wherever you are, little sis. And George and Gordie, hang in there, just keep going, please . . . you have to make it, for me. . . .*

For the first time it sinks in, the simple reality. And it fills me with darkness.

I am *not* going to Qualify.

Chapter 38

The first mystery of the new hot zone danger becomes clear about fifteen blocks into the zone as we pass thirty feet over East Cesar E. Chavez Avenue, and over what looks to be a green lawn-covered stretch of cemetery.

Snipers.

Bullets ring out all around us, and ricochet off distant concrete and buildings in the surrounding area.

"Oh, no!" Zoe shouts, and cringes automatically, pressing back against me as if I could protect her from a stray bullet. She then sings a sequence to increase speed.

From all directions I hear the shouts of other airborne Candidates as we pick up the pace and increase flying speed.

"Go faster!" Jared exclaims, as he bends forward, leaning in against the wind, and almost lies flat against his board.

About ten feet away in the air behind me, overhead, I hear a boy's shout of pain, as a Candidate gets hit. His body goes limp, sliding down from the drone he's riding . . . and he is falling. . . .

I cringe, and turn away and do not look back.

"Where's it coming from? Who the hell is firing at us?" Ethan says from his board, easily matching our pace as he bends his knees in a wider stance for better balance while he remains upright.

"I'm not sure," I mutter. Since Zoe's driving and navigating the board and cannot easily take her eyes off where we're heading, I am the one who must look around and try to get a bearing on our position.

"Do you see anything?" Zoe screams as another bullet zings nearby, cutting through the air, and almost touches us.

I look around as much as possible, but there is only a green stretch of lawn below, with tiny distant grave markers. I try not to look at what I *know* is the broken body of the fallen teen who was shot down seconds ago. Instead I observe a lone Candidate running on the street adjacent to the cemetery. *The teen's on foot, no hoverboard in sight*, I think. *Amazing that he managed to get this far simply by running. Or did he lose his hoverboard along the way?* My feverish stupid thoughts trail off. . . . I am very sluggish now, and it is very hard to maintain any sort of proper focus.

"The shots—they're coming from those multi-story buildings up ahead!" Ethan cries. "Past the cemetery!"

"Oh yeah, I see something," Jared says. "A five-tier parking structure, and on the rooftop a bunch of black figures. They look like SWAT or riot police or something. With rifles! They're the ones firing!"

"But why?" I say. "Why fire at us? That's unbelievable. Why would the local police or whoever fire at what could be their own innocent kids competing to survive?"

"Maybe they're not locals," Zoe mutters grimly. "Maybe they were brought here exactly because they're *not*, and told that by killing us and cutting down the numbers of Candidates overall—all of us competing for limited spots—they were improving chances for their own kids elsewhere?"

"That's really sick." I shake my head weakly. "But if that's so, it makes sense."

With bullets flying all around we manage to fly past the rest of the cemetery at breakneck speed, and then put some distance between us and the structure with the snipers on the roof.

Except for that one fallen boy, none of us are hit, maybe because those snipers were not trying all that hard to hit any of us—or at least that's what I hope and tell myself. Because to think otherwise is much too dark, and I don't think I can bear that line of thought.

And then I remember, *thousands of cameras all over the city are live-streaming us. Millions of people all around the world are watching. Multiply that by the number of cities involved in the process.* . . .

Maybe the snipers just didn't want to be *seen* doing what they were doing, by all those millions of people.

"Anyone know the time?" Jared calls out, as soon as we're outside sniper range.

Balancing on his board, Ethan checks his gadget again. "It's twelve-nineteen PM, local time. Lunch!"

"Heh, I wish." Jared shakes his head. "Would be nice, though. To take a little lunch break detour from this Semi-Finals hell, go for some pizza, you know, maybe sandwiches. . . . Hey, I'd even settle for some crummy tap water."

Zoe glances at him. "You do *not* want to drink L.A. tap water. Remember the yuck back at the Huntington fountain? Anyway, at least we still have plenty of time."

"We have about four and a half hours," I say. "That sounds great, and downtown is very close. But considering what might be ahead of us, I don't know if that's enough or not."

Right now, what appears to be ahead of us is a stretch of park, and beyond it, a mess of freeways. We're flying high once more, at least thirty feet overhead.

"Oh, man . . ." Jared says in awe, looking into the distance of curving and connecting roadway loops of concrete. "What the hell is that?"

"It's a big honking freeway loop," Zoe cries out. "I don't remember what it is—the I-10, or maybe the I-5?"

Ethan puts a palm up over his eyes to stare. "The sign says it's the Golden State Freeway. And the Santa Monica Freeway. I think it's both the 10 and the 5 merging with the 101 which in this place happens to be the Santa Ana Freeway."

"Holy—wow. It's . . . it's like they're *mating*."

Zoe snorts at Jared's slack-jawed surfer dude expression. "Yeah, well. This is L.A., land of concrete road beasties."

"Yeah, I know! But I've never seen 'em from the air like this. . . . Blows your mind . . . and not in a good way."

"So, are we going over them now, or what?"

"See anything firing at us? If no, let's do it."

"We basically have to," I say. "Downtown is on the other side."

We approach and sail over the freeway octopus concrete jungle from somewhere in Boyle Heights, with a low-flying bird's-eye view of the panorama, and the smog-shadowed outlines of the tall buildings downtown well within sight.

As soon as we're on the other side, something bad happens.

Our hoverboards start to *fall.*

Or, to be precise, they start coming straight down, as if some giant has pulled them from under us.

We scream and plummet. And around us, Candidates on drones are also falling.

Apparently all orichalcum objects are affected.

The sudden fall is cut short about three feet off the ground. The hoverboards and drones remain, levitating in place.

And despite our voice commands—yes, even my Logos voice—they remain inert and unresponsive.

It's as if some kind of sonic barrier has been erected around them, or maybe we entered a sonic "dead zone"—whatever that might be.

And now, it looks like we have to abandon our rides and continue on foot.

"Crap, crap!" Jared starts cussing in all kinds of ways, as he swings his long legs over the board he's been straddling, gets up and then kicks it for good measure. The board springs back a bit with a small resilient give, but remains inert yet hovering in place.

"Why do I get the sense the Atlanteans want us to move our lazy asses off these things and walk the rest of the way?" Ethan is just full of tired sarcasm.

I get up silently, feeling an immediate lightheadedness come over me. The head rush lasts a few seconds. Then I manage to pull myself up straight, and adjust the assault rifle that's slung over my shoulder. I swear, I don't even know why I am carrying that damned evil thing that weighs a ton.

It looks like we're on some kind of crummy looking street filled with potholes and cracks in the asphalt, in a rundown neighborhood. There's very little green anywhere, mostly concrete and graffiti-covered walls, and freeway overpasses nearby.

The fiery SoCal sun is beating down from overhead, and the concrete is radiating heat in short stacks, making the air pulse and warp in waves like a mirage. It's definitely over ninety degrees Fahrenheit, an average temperature for this time of day, downtown. In the heat the streets stink of old piss. . . .

Our abandoned hoverboards and drones hover vaguely along the perimeter of the freeway, just a few feet from it. Dozens of Candidates start walking dejectedly in the general direction of the heart of downtown.

Zoe and Jared walk ahead, followed by Ethan and me. We are soaked in sweat, and sullen and silent. We move at a decent pace, but compared to the others I am struggling already, after just one city block. My breath comes fast, temples pounding with the pulse-beat, and my head is light and "soaring" with weakness.

A few minutes of this, and some Candidates start jogging, picking up their pace. I see all four colored armbands, but a slight predominance of red and green. It does make sense that the high-aggression Reds and the high-endurance Greens would be the early ones near the finish.

What am I doing here? I think. I am barely hanging in.

"Hey, Gwen," Jared says, turning around. "You might want to have that rifle ready to fire, because pretty soon we'll need it. Too many Candies here all in the same place, kinda reeks of trouble."

"Not sure if it's trouble, but yup, it definitely reeks." Zoe wipes her forehead and wrinkles her nose.

"You're lucky you got that thing." Ethan nods at my rifle. "How'd you get it?"

A sick memory flashback comes to me, and I don't immediately answer.

"We met up with some Blues back there," Jared says quickly, and I feel immediate gratitude. "Things got ugly, we got lucky."

We walk a few more minutes in silence, seeing occasional Candidates running by to overtake us. Mostly, I note, they are very fit, athletic types who look like they could run a marathon. One boy, very tall and skinny African American, I suddenly recognize.

It's Kadeem Cantrell from Red Dorm Nine, my own RQC, who got the #3 Standing Score. He appears as though out of nowhere, out of what looks to be a dead end alley, and passes us on the street, running effortlessly. There are two intricate folding swords attached with a harness on his back. Unlike most other Candidate runners, he's not keeping to a street layout but moving along his own personal path, which at present takes him on a clean diagonal through the current street we're on.

Kadeem clears the road then leaps over a short fence. In seconds we watch him run up and scale a wall using only his speed and the soles of his shoes as leverage—as though he's made of rubber—and cut across through someone's back yard, and then emerge on the other side of a short chain link fence, and then beyond. . . .

"Whoa, that dude's doing parkour," Jared says. "He must've been running all this time, I bet!"

I nod. "Yeah, he's really good, from my RQC, actually. He got a #3 Standing Score."

Ethan whistles. "Oh yeah, he's gonna pass Semi-Finals."

"Unless some Blue shoots him down," Zoe whispers.

"What time we got? How much farther?" Jared asks a few minutes later as we pause before what looks like another freeway overpass.

"Let's see. It's just after one-fifteen PM. And I don't know." Ethan puts away his gadget and wipes sweat from his face. "See those tall buildings up ahead? Downtown, baby."

"I know that, but where's that big-ass swimming pool we're supposed to find? With batons or something?"

"I am guessing it's where all those shuttles are." I point up, trying to ignore the wave of nausea that moves through my body together with the lightheadedness, whenever I make sudden movements. And in the white sun glare we finally notice the dozens of silvery disk shapes hovering in the skies over downtown.

But first we need to pass this latest freeway.

Only it's not.

We walk up East Seventh Street and it rises up into a bridge over a huge concrete basin that is none other than the L.A. River.

Yeah, I know, start laughing now. It's basically miles and miles of ugly concrete dotted in places with discarded trash that people toss over the many bridges, and in the center there's a *trickle* of water. Admittedly during Los Angeles rainy season— those fabled three days of the year, unless it's drought year, in which case, forget it—during those few days when water actually comes from the sky in Los Angeles and causes multiple-SigAlert twenty-car pileups, the basin gets filled up pretty well, so there's a significant rushing torrent, and people and poor stray dogs fall in and have to be rescued by emergency services who then have to be rescued by *other* emergency services. But otherwise, this basin is a desolate and sad testament to, well, pretty much nothing but a few birds and tadpoles. And oh yeah, it works great as a wind corridor, so the Santa Ana winds use it effectively to blow throughout the city.

And here we stop.

Because the way across the bridge is blocked by a barricade. It is dull, charcoal grey, impenetrable, a twenty-foot wall of bristling metal and barbed wire and concrete erected to keep anyone on foot out—probably even a fancy parkour urban runner like Kadeem Cantrell.

"Great." Jared frowns, squinting in the sun, and looks in both directions. The rest of us who reach the barricaded street also pause.

We mill around for a few minutes, as our numbers grow and more and more Candidates arrive. Looking north along the length of the L.A. River on this side, we see another street crossing several hundred feet away, and on it towers another barricade wall. Same thing in the other direction, south.

All street crossings are blocked, so we will need to enter the concrete river basin in order to cross.

A few Candidates are already scaling the short railing into the River, and the most athletic ones are running down the steep incline of the concrete bank that frames both sides. Good thing this portion of the river basin does not have vertical walls as it does in some sections of the city. Otherwise we'd need rappelling equipment. At least there my Yellow Quadrant length of cord lasso would come in handy. . . .

"Okay, so we cross the hard way," Ethan says. And then he goes to cross the railing. Zoe and Jared follow.

I trail behind them, pressing my teeth together while waves of nausea move through me, and it is harder to contain, and to keep myself upright.

Just as I reach the railing, the screams come.

"Hot! *Hot!* It burns!"

The Candidates in the middle of the concrete basin and those who have almost reached the opposite sides are instead screaming in pain, and some jumping from foot to foot, others stumbling and waving their limbs. An unfortunate few have fallen down, and their bodies are contorting on the concrete floor amid the discarded city trash and the trickle of water that runs in the central gutter ditch that is nothing more than a thin groove gully that has been cut from the concrete.

"It's hot! Oh crap! Burning!" Teens closest to our side of the railing begin experiencing the whatever the heck it is, and start racing back to the railing and climbing back out of the river basin—that is, those of them who *can.*

The others—it's hard to describe the awful thing we get to witness.

Because the bodies of the Candidates still in the basin begin to smoke, and then their screams are cut short as they are engulfed in flames.

Ethan, who's only about five feet down-slope from the railing, exclaims in sudden pain, flails his arms and immediately turns around and runs back toward me. . . .

Zoe and Jared don't need to be told to move. They've just managed to swing their feet over the railing, hop off, take a few steps, and are paused near the edge—and immediately back they come, climbing like crazy.

"What is it?" I cry. "What's down there? What is burning?"

"Me! Everything feels like it's on fire!" Ethan yells back as he climbs the railing, moving wildly.

The moment he's over and back on the level of the street, he stops, frowns as though "listening" to something, to his own body, and suddenly it's over.

"Are you okay?"

"Yeah," he says. "*Now* I am. All right, this is insane! The pain is gone and the burning sensation all over my body, my shoes even—it's all gone."

"What the hell is it?" Jared stands rubbing his elbows. "I swear, I could begin feeling it too, a sudden warmth, and it was growing with every second the longer I was down there. But because it was gradual, it was easy to ignore, attribute it to the heat of the sun or exhaustion. If not for those other people screaming, I'd have kept moving across until it was too late to get back."

"I felt heat coming through my shoes," Zoe says thoughtfully. "And through my clothing, the sleeves, pant legs, everything. . . ."

Meanwhile, Candidates are climbing out of the basin all around us. Faces are flushed, and some look like they've been running for miles. They wave their hands to cool off, stomp their feet. Those who have come from deepest in the river basin, look the worst. They have what looks like sunburn or first degree burns on their neck and around their sleeves. For some, their skin is starting to blister.

Everyone stares at the half a dozen bodies left in the basin, now charred and smoking.

"Okay, this is bad," a boy says. "Whatever's down there—a force field or reactive chemicals or something—there's no way to cross."

And so we stand, looking over the basin, as minutes tick. More of us arrive, and the news of the danger below gets passed on.

As others mill about, I put my fingertips on the railing. It feels warm to the touch, hot even, but in a way indistinguishable from being the usual sun-heated metal and concrete stuck outside on a hot L.A. day.

I think. . . . Or I *try* to think through the fog and sluggish nausea that fills my mind.

"What time is it?" someone behind me asks.

"Close to two o'clock."

"That really blows," a Candidate mumbles. "Is there any way to go around this, maybe climb the barricade wall on the bridge?"

I stand and stare out at the river basin expanse. Sterile concrete rises for endless miles in both directions, interrupted only by thick bridge supports. A few birds circle occasionally, then land briefly to drink from the trickle running in the gully.

I glance to one side and see a pale moving spot that draws near and resolves into the shape of a stray dog running along the incline of the basin. My heart immediately feels a twinge of painful pity for the poor stray. The animal appears unharmed, and it has definitely been in the basin long enough to be affected by whatever forces that generate the killer heat.

Except, it is not.

Neither the dog nor the birds are in any way experiencing the warming effect.

I touch Zoe's arm and point at the dog. "Look, it's been running for some time and is not getting burned."

Zoe stares at the dog.

Meanwhile I take a deep breath, put my hands on the railing, and with some effort climb over.

"Wait! What are you doing?" Ethan says.

I stand on the other side, a couple of feet down the incline, and take off my yellow ID token.

"Hold this for a moment, Zoe," I say, handing it to her.

For just a few seconds I feel nothing different.

And then there's a warmth. It is definitely there, gathering around me, as though a gust of hot air has risen to sweep along my skin, underneath my clothing, inside my shoes.

And it is growing warmer.

"Okay . . ." I mutter. "So it's *not* the token."

I take another deep breath, as the warmth rises around me, becoming unpleasant. And then I begin to strip.

First, I ask Jared to lend me his knife, and I use it to cut off the length of cord that's been tied around my arm to stop the bleeding. As soon as the pressure of the cord is gone, my arm pulses with a sudden agony of restored circulation.

I grit my teeth to hold back the moan of pain. . . . And then I hand the knife back to Jared, and use my good hand to untie the Atlantean yellow armband.

The heat continues to rise around me as I drop the armband on the concrete floor of the L.A. River. Then I carefully set down the automatic rifle.

Candidates on the other side of the railing are gathering, staring at me, voices are raised in curious discussion.

I untie my uniform belt and drop it on the ground, together with the lasso cord weapon still attached. Then off comes my shirt that I unbutton with numb fingers, too tired to be embarrassed about being seen in my underwear by millions of people. Good thing I wear a tank top, and a bra underneath. The shirt falls on the ground. Then I pull down my uniform pants and remain only in my practical cotton briefs. Down go the pants, to lie on top of my shirt.

As soon as the uniform is off I feel an immediate relief from the stifling heat. It dissipates immediately. I don't even have to pull my socks off, or my shoes.

So, it's definitely the uniform, then, I think. And that makes sense—the uniform has to be made from some kind of Atlantean specially treated fabric, possibly orichalcum-based. After all, it "magically" displayed those Standing Scores, so it is definitely reactive to things.

Candidates stare at me as I stand in my underwear, holding my numb arm and watching the trickle of blood resume from the bullet wound.

I glance at all of them and say through my teeth, "It's the uniform that's causing the burn. You guys might want to strip. Zoe, can I get my token back?"

Zoe nods, watching me intently, and tosses me my token ID.

I catch it. Then I pick up my cord lasso, unravel it and tie up my uniform clothes in one bunch, handling them as quickly as possible before my fingers start to burn. Making sure that none of it comes in direct contact with my body, I carry my uniform bundle swinging from the cord attached to the end of the rifle and walk across the river basin.

I step over the gully at the halfway spot, glancing at the tiny bit of running water. I try to ignore the charred bodies lying every few feet. . . . At one point I turn to see if the poor lonely dog is still there, but he's gone far along the riverbank.

And then I keep walking coolly to the other side and up the incline.

At the end, I slowly climb over the railing and pause, looking back.

Behind me, Candidates in their underwear, some carrying their uniforms at the ends of swords and rifles, others suspended on cords just like me, are beginning to cross the river basin.

Chapter 39

"I did mention previously that you're absolutely nuts, didn't I, Gwen?" Jared says, walking up to the railing on my side of the river. His uniform is swinging from the end of his knife blade, and he's in nothing but his baggy boxers.

"Yeah, you did." I give him a pained smile as I start putting my clothes back on.

"Well, let me repeat it. You're way more cray cray than anyone I know."

"Thanks, I think. . . ."

"It's a compliment."

I smile again, weakly.

A few minutes later I am dressed, with my armband once more around my sleeve, tied awkwardly with one shaking hand. And then I cannibalize another piece of my cord weapon to tie my arm off again, using my good hand and my teeth. This time I nearly pass out from the pain.

Zoe, who's gotten dressed while I am still fumbling, watches my slow and difficult movements. "How are you hanging in?"

"Okay." Because, really, what else can I say?

But Zoe steps closer to me and looks into my eyes, so that I am staring down at her very young face with its angular jaw and fierce blue eyes framed by the brown bangs.

"No, you're not, I can tell."

I shrug.

Zoe takes my arm—the good one that's not hurt. And then we begin walking together, with Zoe supporting me lightly.

I admit, it does help, a little.

By now, we've pretty much nearly there.

We walk a couple of blocks, heading slightly north

toward the Arts District section of downtown. Why? Because that's the general direction of the spot over which the Atlantean shuttles seem to be hovering in the skies. At this point, I admit, my mind is a muddy mess, and I am only thinking about putting one foot ahead of the other.

Other Candidates soon overtake us, and I watch the more athletic ones again take off at a light run. But Jared and Ethan continue walking next to Zoe and me.

"Why don't you guys go on?" I say, nodding tiredly at the way ahead. "I am only slowing you down."

"Are you kidding?" Ethan flashes me a slightly crooked smile. "Without you we wouldn't have made it even half as far. I'm not dumb enough to go off on my own when I've got a good thing going here. Right, man?" And he glances at Jared.

Jared just nods tiredly. "Oh, yeah. Gwen's the man."

"Besides, we have plenty of time." Ethan checks his gadget for the zillionth time. "Looks like it's only two-thirty PM. We've only got a few blocks."

At the corner of South Alameda and East Sixth Street, we see familiar four-color beacons and only a light, short picket-height concrete divider fence that runs just a couple of feet off the ground. It serves more as a marker boundary than a way to keep us out. And the red stripe that indicates a hot zone is drawn on our side.

Candidates ahead of us race up to the fence, and easily step or jump over it. Everyone's unharmed, and apparently they're out of the hot zone.

When it's our turn, I put my foot over the concrete line and my yellow token flashes as soon as I scale the boundary.

I glance back, and this side is not painted red.

So, a safe zone.

Zoe exhales with relief. "Good. We definitely could use a break."

I look up, squinting from the sun, and the Atlantean shuttles are hovering there, a dozen silvery disks, not too far off the ground, just about the height of the venerable Westin Bonaventure Hotel with its cylinder towers looming in the vicinity and out of our way.

"The pool must be thataway," Jared mutters. He then almost

gets knocked over by a big bulky runner with a red armband who passes us.

"Hey, watch it!"

But the hulking teen gives him a hard glance. He's got a heavy, mean-looking blade attached at his belt.

On the other hand, I've got an automatic rifle hanging over my shoulder.

The Candidate sees my rifle. And he wisely keeps going.

He has no idea I can barely stand upright, much less fire.

A few more blocks, and we're in an area that used to be Skid Row.

This is where the city homeless had their own makeshift city-within-a-city, and there were several missions and other charitable organizations located within these blocks.

Now, it's still Skid Row. But it's also something else. And in some ways it's even more desolate, hoary, trash-filled. Even more run-down. . . . A place of despair. Even the once-vibrant graffiti murals have faded, and it has grown neglected, now that the taggers no longer bother to ply their art here.

Instead, the homeless residents shelter here like shades, stooped human figures sitting in alleyways, watching us pass with dull hopeless eyes.

And the Atlanteans chose this forsaken area to uproot, and built a giant multi-block water reservoir.

The pool—I should stop calling it that and just say an artificial urban *lake*—begins at what used to be Towne Avenue and spans two blocks to South San Pedro Street—so that what used to be a block of Crocker Street is now underwater—and is bordered by Sixth and Fifth streets, forming a great urban rectangle.

The waters of the lake sparkle like razors, white fire in the blazing sun. It sits like a strange watery mirror in the middle of a concrete forest of urban high rises and decay. Its calm surface does not ripple, since there is little wind here, so it reflects the remote oval disks of the shuttles directly overhead, as they levitate a hundred feet in the sky above.

We stop at the shore of this lake and stare.

The lake basin is yet one more thing made of concrete. It is deep, but not so deep that we cannot look down and see the strange almost luminescent shapes sunken on the floor. The water is translucent, with a greenish tint.

Piles of batons rest underwater, and if I didn't think I was hallucinating, I'd say they were *glowing* . . . or maybe just weirdly reflecting the sunlight.

"Holy lord! We have to dive in that?" Zoe whispers, letting go of my arm. "I can barely swim!"

I stand there, and watch as the first of the Candidates take brave running leaps and splash downward into the lake. A few decide to take their shoes off, and some again strip down to their underwear.

The mirror water of the reservoir is now broken, a mess of splashing and white spray churned by swimmers.

We watch them, to see if there are any surprises to be had at this point in the Semi-Finals.

The first boy to emerge with the baton makes a hard splash and then pulls himself up from the water to stand at the street-level shoreline. The baton is about two feet long and three inches thick, a smooth, slightly oval shaped rod, its orichalcum surface the usual gold-flecked charcoal grey. He holds it up proudly and makes a "woot" sound, pumping his fist.

And then he shouts out again, this time almost in surprise. . . .

And drops the baton on the ground.

The baton is definitely glowing. It is obvious now, as with every passing second it is becoming dull incandescent pink, like a branding iron that has been just removed from the flames. Except it is glowing *hotter*, not cooling down.

Soon it begins to smoke, charring the asphalt underneath it.

The Candidate who retrieved the baton stands over it, with a dropped jaw, and begins to cuss loudly.

The baton is burning. It is a wicked red-hot thing that is impossible to handle.

"Oh, crap, crap, crap!" Teens everywhere are exclaiming and gathering to look.

Meanwhile, more of the divers are returning from the bottom with batons, splashing forth from the water triumphantly. . . . And in moments their triumph turns to pain and horror.

Because everyone's batons begin to grow hot and

incandescent the moment they are out of the water.

Some people immediately drop theirs back in the pool, screaming in pain as their hands are scalded. Others manage to throw their batons down on the street, and then stand around watching them inflame more and more, and burn like live torches on the asphalt.

"What did the Goldilocks sadists want us to do with these things?" a boy cries, watching his baton roll and scorch the ground. "This is hopeless! How are we supposed to hold them and levitate up to the shuttle?"

"Hey, dude," Jared asks the closest person who drops their baton near his feet. "When you were underwater, did you feel this thing being hot or something?"

"No," the teen replies. "I didn't even notice anything. It felt cool, just like the water around it."

"Okay," Zoe muses. "So when submerged, the baton is not burning. Does that mean it has to be kept in water in order not to burn your fingers? And it reacts with the air to burn?"

Meanwhile I stand and watch a tough Latino boy who remains in the pool, treading water, and holding his retrieved baton submerged. "Hey," I say. "Does it feel hot now, when you hold it like that underwater?"

The boy spits, shakes his head negatively. He then looks up at the shuttle that's hovering overhead.

And then he starts to sing the keying sequence in a tenor voice.

Nothing happens.

The orichalcum is underwater, it occurs to me. *The sound waves cannot reach it the same way.*

"Damn . . ." the boy says.

"I guess you'll have to take it out of the water."

He nods then takes a big breath, quickly lifts up his hand with the baton. And again he sings.

This time the baton begins to react. The boy follows up the keying sequence with the rise command, sweeping up an octave.

And then I watch him grimace in pain, as the baton starts to hover and rise, at the same time as it begins to grow hot and glow.

The boy keeps singing and stoically holding the baton as he is lifted out of the pool, and then continues gaining altitude.

Ten feet, twenty feet, thirty. . . .

The boy stops singing and screams.

He continues screaming and yet holding on, and the baton is still lifting him higher and higher, and from my vantage point it is red-hot now.

About halfway up to the shuttle, the boy either lets go—or maybe his hand is simply too damaged, burned off and he can no longer maintain the hold—and he plummets down.

The boy's body strikes the surface of the pool from a distance of nearly sixty feet, and he goes under like a rock.

Then, a few moments later his body floats back up, limp and motionless.

People around me scream, or gasp. Zoe puts her hands over her mouth.

"Wow," Ethan says. "Damn. I think that guy is dead."

"It's official," a girl says behind me. "We're all screwed."

About a half hour later, there's a sizeable crowd of Candidates gathered around the water reservoir. Teens sit on the ground, some dangle their feet in the cool water. A few pace nervously. Several retrieved batons are lying on the shore, scorching and burning still, burning non-stop. . . . They are now not merely pinkish red but *white-hot*.

Jared stops his pacing and turns to me, as I sit on the ground, cross-legged, holding the barrel of the rifle with my good hand. My fingers pass lightly over the black metal, stroking it absently, as I think.

"Okay, Gwen," Jared says. "What do you think? You're the smart and clever one. What solutions are there? What options do we have? Let's do it, man!"

"Yeah, Gwen, what should we do? C'mon, don't clam up now. Open your brain-pan up for us." Ethan joins in, plopping down next to me.

Right now I'm too weak, numb, and out of sorts, to even roll my eyes at them.

"There's always the one option," Zoe says, sitting a few feet away from me at the edge of the reservoir, with her feet cooling in the water. "Instead of dying a horrible burning death *today*, we can simply turn over our ID token and press that recessed button to Self-Disqualify. Then we can die a horrible burning death a few months from now when the asteroid hits. And today we can just go out for pizza."

I frown and turn in her direction. "Don't, Zoe. Don't think that way, don't give up. There has to be a solution. We'll find it."

"No," Zoe says. "Maybe *you'll* find it. We only have about two hours left. That's two hours to feel like we have a *choice* in our life."

Jared sits down near Zoe and puts his hand in the water. "True. Just two frigging hours to continue having *hope*. Okay, this line of thinking seriously blows."

I shut up and stare silently out at the lake, as my vertigo returns, and waves of pain and nausea move through me. . . .

All this while, Candidates attempt to retrieve batons from the lake and try all kinds of mostly useless, different things to achieve the final task of Semi-Finals.

One girl removes her uniform shirt and tries to fill it with water like a balloon, before tossing her baton in there. However, the fabric of the uniform is permeable, and the water quickly drains away. In moments the baton begins to steam the uniform fabric, which then bursts into flames. The girl screams as the baton falls through and lands on her foot, giving her instant severe burns.

Another teen levitates his baton in the air before him without touching it, and uses a Yellow Quadrant cord weapon to make a loop from which to suspend himself with both hands. The boy rises about ten feet in the air before the heat of the baton melts the cord, and down he falls, landing awkwardly on his hands and knees, and gaining a bunch of painful scrapes.

"This is horrible," Zoe mutters. "I can't bear to watch."

Ethan frowns. "Then, don't." He gets up then and begins pacing once more.

I feel my eyelids closing as I nod off in a daze. I sway slightly, as I continue to sit cross-legged, then jerk awake at the splash sound of what seems to be water cannonballs—several Candidates falling back into the lake with screams after attempting more variants of levitation with the batons.

"What time is it?" I whisper.

"About three thirty." Ethan's voice sounds behind me, and I

am too dazed to bother to look.

And then Ethan returns to sit down next to me and leans in to stare closely at my face. He snaps his fingers. "Hey, Gwen, wake up! You look like sh—"

He is interrupted by a loud squealing girl's shout.

"*Gwen!* Oh my God! Gwen!"

And with a jolt I recognize my little sister's voice.

In seconds Gracie tumbles into my arms, exclaiming and chattering and speaking *something*, pulling me by the shoulder which agitates my wound and I moan in pain—and I let her chatter away because I can hardly *understand words* at this point, only know the familiar little girl face that's trying so hard to be all grown up, with her raccoon eyeliner makeup and her heart-wrenchingly intense expression.

Maybe I'm just hallucinating Gracie?

My sister, staring in my face, shaking me . . . framed by the background noise of splashing water, floundering teens and screams of pain.

"*Gwen!*" She shakes me solidly and this time I regain awareness, wincing in pain.

"Is it really you, Gee Four?" I mutter through cracked dry lips. "You made it! I was wondering if you chose Los Angeles—"

"Of course I did!" Gracie says. She looks hardcore, with her hair in a tight ponytail, dark eye makeup, and two very sharp blades stuck at her belt. She also looks exhausted, sweat running down her face and neck, several minor bloody scratches, and a grim expression.

"How did you make it past the hot zones?"

"Don't ask—we had a few hoverboards, and then I lost the group I was with and went with another, and then we ran into a few fights, and then—"

Gracie chatters on in her usual quick anxious voice, and I just watch her with a sudden gathering of warmth. I put my hand up and fix a tendril of her hair that's stuck on her forehead.

"Hey, cut it out, Gee!" But Gracie gives me another sudden hug. That's when she notices my automatic rifle and the wound in my arm.

"Oh, no! What happened? You're hurt!" Gracie's mouth falls

open.

I try to smile and it barely comes. "It's okay . . . never mind. What we need to do now is figure out how to get up to that shuttle."

And then I point to the lake and the splashing Candidates and explain to Gracie the burning baton dilemma.

"So what can we do?" She wails, rubbing her nose angrily with the back of her hand.

"Nothing," Jared says, frowning, as he listens to us.

"What we really need is a hoverboard," Zoe says suddenly. "Then maybe we can sit on it and put the baton on top and then ride up with it, hoping it doesn't melt the hoverboard. Would be nice to have a bowl that's big enough to hold water and a baton inside it."

"Except all of the hoverboards are stuck back in the beginning of the last hot zone, where the sound dampers are." Ethan shakes his head in disgust.

"How do we know?" Gracie looks around at them, then stares back at me.

"You can try calling one again, Gwen?" Zoe looks at me meaningfully.

I nod, then take several deep breaths to quiet the ringing in my ears, and expand my lungs. Then I start to sing the sequence to call the nearest orichalcum object and auto-key it in the process. My clear voice rises powerfully over the sound of water and the human screams.

Bad move. . . .

In my dazed state I forget that the closest orichalcum objects are the *batons*—those that have been retrieved from the water.

About five batons immediately come hovering toward me, torn away from the Candidates trying to handle them. More follow, from all directions. They pause, levitating three feet above ground, and growing incandescent pink, brighter and brighter.

"Hey! What the—"

Candidates begin yelling angrily.

I stop the auto-key sequence and sing the release.

Batons rain down to the ground.

I am a blasted idiot.

"I am sorry . . . really sorry!" I hurry to say.

"What the hell did you do that for?" a boy asks me angrily, coming up to me, and kicking one of the batons that's still not too hot, with the rubberized toes of his running shoes. He then kicks it some more until the object rolls over the concrete ledge and back into the water.

"Thanks a lot, now I have to dive back in and get it *again*."

"I'm so sorry . . ." I say quietly, avoiding his eyes and looking down at his shoes.

His shoes.

Okay, now I know I am absolutely crazy to be thinking this. But it makes sudden horrible sense.

I get up, moving weakly, and stand up then pause, while a head rush passes.

Ethan immediately notices. "What?" he says. "Did you think of something?"

I nod. And then I shake my head, as though trying to shake away the *crazy*.

Because it really is—absolutely bonkers crazy.

"What?"

"Think about it," I mutter. "The Atlanteans would not have made it entirely impossible. The solution exists. And it has to involve us using whatever means we've got, whatever we *already* have on us—"

I have several people's attention now.

"Yeah. . . . Like, what?"

"Like," I say, "maybe what we're carrying and wearing."

"We already know the uniforms burn quickly, even when wet," Zoe says sadly. "And they don't hold water."

I slowly turn to look at her. "But shoes do!"

"Huh?" Jared frowns.

"Our *shoes!*" I say. "They hold water."

"I don't get it." Gracie stares at me with her own intense form of frown wrinkling her forehead.

"How's that gonna help us? The batons cannot be keyed when submerged." Jared makes a dismissing gesture with his hand. "What are you gonna do? Stick a baton in a shoe filled with water and then what? The part that sticks out of the shoe will still burn. You can't get a solid grip on it!"

"But—but—" I say. "We have *two* shoes. If we fill both shoes with water, and stick each end of the baton in one shoe, the *middle* part will still be exposed to the air. Then we tie the shoes together tightly with the shoelaces—do all this while holding the whole contraption down underwater. Then, we take it out of the water, holding on to it by the shoes from both sides. The ends will still be inert and cool underwater, and you just key the middle part, even though it burns—"

"Holy crap! That actually makes sense . . . stoned-out-of-your-mind-but-remotely-possible kind of sense. . . . And it just might work!" Jared exclaims, his eyes coming alive in excitement.

I nod, a kind of mental peace coming to overwhelm me in that moment. "Yeah, I really think it will work. Just be sure to keep the shoes turned and angled just right, so the toes are filled with water, for as long as possible, until you make it to the shuttle.

Suddenly Ethan snorts, then begins to laugh. "This is wild! You know, the old-school tech geeks used to call this kind of absurd brute-force solution a *kludge*. It's so sick I love it! So, who's going to try this first?"

But a boy nearby, who's been listening to us, is already moving. He pulls off his sneakers, sets them on the ledge near the water, and jumps into the lake. Moments later he comes back up, with a baton in his hand.

Wasting no time, the boy sits down on the bank, keeping the baton submerged and pressed under his knees. He sets to work filling his sneakers with water, then sticks the baton into the toe area of each shoe while underwater. Next, he ties the shoes together with shoelaces, mostly for temporary stability—since the laces will likely burn away as soon as the middle of the baton is exposed to the air.

Carefully the boy lifts the contraption out of the water, keeping the shoes angled so that as much of the water as possible fills each one. He grips each shoe tightly with both hands, and then begins to sing the keying sequence . . . and then the rising sequence.

We watch him in amazement.

The baton rises, carrying the boy upward. He continues singing, holding on to his shoes, and he is now twenty, thirty feet up, and still rising. . . .

VERA NAZARIAN

I blink in the sun. Everyone around me stares also—everyone stuck on the ground.

The boy is more than fifty feet up now, and keeps going.

Several long breathless moments later, the speck that is the boy reaches the shuttle. There is a dark opening in the silver ovoid disk that must be the door portal, and he disappears inside.

He is the first Candidate who has successfully completed the Semi-Finals.

Chapter 40

From this point onward, it's a wild stampede. Bodies of Candidates bombard the water. People pull off their shoes, dive in, emerge. Moments later, Candidates rise up into the air, successfully holding on to their baton-plus-shoes bundles, as they ride the things up to the shuttle.

Now it comes, the actual life-and-death struggle for the batons, now that we *know* what to do with them. . . .

I stand still momentarily, dazed, watching others around me move. It all seems like slow motion, a strange urban melee.

Gracie's expression is desperate as she takes my arm—the good arm that's unhurt—and she pulls me. "Let's go! Gwen! We need to hurry! Everyone's grabbing those things, there won't be any batons left—"

I nod, and begin taking my shoes off. Gracie pulls off her sneakers and then she watches Ethan and Jared dive into the water, followed by Zoe who jumps in holding her nose.

Gracie's expression is anxious. I remember how Gracie has never been much of a swimmer. When we were very little back here in California, there was a backyard pool we all used over at a neighbor's house. Gracie tended to splash around in the shallow end when the rest of us kids swam laps or dove into the deeper bowl part.

And now that I think about it, I don't recall Gracie ever diving, or going underwater for more than a few floundering strokes.

My sister cannot dive or swim submerged.

The grim realization hits me.

And yet, knowing we both have to do it—according to the Semi-Finals rules I cannot do it for her—I know she is gathering herself, getting ready for the inevitable.

"Gracie!" I say, fighting my own dizziness. "Listen, take a deep breath, okay? Just hold it and push forward with your hands! It's not that far down, okay? As soon as you grab a baton, start rising, it will come naturally—I will be right behind you—"

"Okay . . ." she mutters. But I can see a dangerously lost look in her eyes, a kind of resignation.

We stand at the ledge before the water, while teens jump in all around us. Water splashes up, cool spray striking us.

"Gwen . . ." Suddenly she looks up at me. "I don't think I can."

My pulse is pounding and my head is heavy like a brick, and light at the same time, while the sky seems to spin. "Yes, you *can.* Just hold my hand, Gracie . . . Hold my hand and we will go down together. Don't let go until I let you go! Now, deep breaths! On the count of three!"

We count and then we jump, holding hands, and the cold shock of water surrounds us. . . .

I am a decent swimmer, and I start moving downward, pulling Gracie's hand, grasping it with all my strength. But in seconds I realize that I am using my *other* hand—the wounded, semi-useless, numb hand—to do the bulk of the hand stroke swimming motion.

An instant of panic fills me, together with pain and weakness, and that in turn results in an overwhelming rise of pressure in my lungs, and an urge to exhale and inhale. But I continue holding my breath and swimming downward, about seven more strokes, and thankfully Gracie is helping along with her own free hand.

On the bottom, the light is shimmering like in an aquarium. The batons lie before us in a rapidly shrinking pile, glittering softly in the greenish-blue water and fractured sunlight. Agitated bubbles rise everywhere, from all the sudden bodies in the water. I see five other Candidates closest to us reach for the nearest batons, and kick off to rise again.

Abruptly I feel Gracie's hand jerking mine, and realize she is short of air and beginning the drowning panic. . . . I reach out clumsily, and take hold of the nearest baton, feeling my useless swollen fingers close around it.

At the same time I pull Gracie's floating, panicking body forward, propelling her deeper and right onto the pile, so that she grabs out wildly and has a chance to get one. As soon as I see she has taken hold of a baton, I let go of her hand, and start rising.

I break air with a shuddering gasp, and tread water, seeing others break out to the surface also. I keep my baton submerged.

Five seconds later, there's no sign of Gracie.

Oh, lord, oh, no . . . Gracie!

I glance back to the street shore, and see Zoe back out of the water, and Jared sitting on the concrete ledge next to her. They are both fiddling with making their baton-and-shoe contraption. And there's Ethan, filling his shoes with water.

"Zoe!" I cry. "Please hold on to my baton, for just a second! I have to get my sister, she's still under! She's—"

"Hey, no, it's okay, I'll get her . . ." Jared says immediately, and I watch his tanned body slide back into the water. "Here, watch my stuff for a sec!" He shoves his shoe-baton bundle at me—it floats in the water due to all that rubber on the shoes—and he dives in.

"Thanks!" I mutter, but Jared's already gone under in easy surfer strokes.

I float in the water, holding on to the ledge with one hand, and to Jared's floating stuff and my baton with the other. I tremble and blink in the sun glare.

What am I doing up here? I should go back under myself. . . . Gracie is down there! She is drowning . . . she needs my help!

As my thoughts race wildly, Jared comes back up. He is pulling Gracie's limp body after him.

"Gracie!" I cry in a broken voice, and let go of my baton. It sinks back underwater—to hell with it—as I propel myself toward my sister.

Jared and I pull Gracie up over the ledge, and just like that, she is suddenly sputtering and coughing up water and then *screaming.*

While underwater, she must've stuck her baton through her belt. But now that it's been exposed to the air, the heating reaction has started and the pain of it must have shocked her into consciousness, a really crazy-impossible form of "CPR."

"A-a-a-a!" she screams, and Jared and I pull her back into the water, so that she floats, together with the baton still attached to her belt. The baton cools back down immediately. "Holy lord, that hurts!" Gracie gasps out, coughing and splashing water with one hand, and holding on to the concrete ledge. "I thought I died!"

"Never mind, you *didn't!*" I pant, while tears and water mingle in my eyes. "Just start making your shoe thing, do it now, Gracie! I'll be right back!"

And with a deep breath I sink back underwater.

This time I have the use of both my hands to swim, making it somewhat easier. On the other hand, I am on my last strength, short of breath as it is, so my weakness acts to slow me down. . . .

This time as I reach the bottom, there are just a few batons left. Apparently it took just a couple of minutes for everyone to grab theirs and reduce the great big pile to nothing. As I move through the aquarium-green water, I see three batons rolling around on the floor.

Just *three* batons left!

And *four* other Candidates are swimming down there with me, all headed for the batons. What happened? How did it come to this?

I spot one baton closest to me and move toward it, stroking through the water as quickly as I can . . . which apparently isn't quick enough. An older teen girl moves like a predatory shark before me, shoving me away with one hand, while with the other she closes in on the last baton. She kicks off and rises, and I am left reeling, holding my breath.

One last baton remains, but it is many feet away in the reservoir, and even as I consider it, two other Candidates rush for it, and fight, tumble and struggle underwater, sending up clouds of air bubbles. . . .

I don't bother to stick around to watch.

I rise back up to the surface with a kind of solemn quiet peace that comes when you *know* it's all over.

I see Gracie waiting on the reservoir ledge, squatting over her pair of shoes and baton—everything tied together and floating, all ready to go. Zoe is already rising in the air, holding her shoes awkwardly and hanging on for dear life, as she sings the sequence. I am guessing Ethan has already gone up, and so has Jared.

I remain in the water to catch my breath, and watch Zoe, and then I look up.

The sky is filled with Candidates, bodies retreating into dots, like tiny strange specks of rising birds as they approach the available shuttles.

Meanwhile the Candidates who remain on the ground are still jumping into the water, most of them not realizing yet that they are all *done* and out of the running.

And then it occurs to me, *Oh, no! Gracie is the last person left with a baton, she is alone and vulnerable.*

My pulse pounds and heartbeat goes into overdrive as I swim the few strokes to reach the shore, and grab the ledge. My rifle is still lying there a few feet away. *I should probably take it now. . . .*

"Gracie!" I exclaim, and my voice is trembling. "What are you doing? Go!"

My sister stares at me, and in a flash she understands. "Where is your baton?" she screams at me. "*Gwen!* Where is it? Where is *your baton?*"

"Shut up, idiot!" I scream back, and then I pull myself out of the water with one good hand, and end up on my belly. "Go! Right now! Damn you, you little idiot, *go!*"

"No! I am not leaving without you!"

"Yes, you *are!*" I grab her, shake her, so that we both end up rolling on the concrete, and her shoe-wrapped baton gets pulled out of the water.

Gracie begins to cry, sobbing wildly, holding on to me.

It's then that we hear the first shots being fired.

Several late arrivals in possession of Blue Quadrant firearms have gotten the grim picture. And they are firing up at those Candidates who are airborne.

Screams come, from high up in the air, followed by several falling bodies. Automatic weapons on the ground fire volleys of desperate rounds, and many hit their targets. . . .

They're so focused on the people escaping to the skies that they haven't noticed yet that there's *one last baton* here on the ground, next to Gracie.

I crawl on my belly and take hold of the automatic rifle, while holding on to Gracie who is still a weeping mess and in no condition to act. I check the magazine and reload the rifle, make sure the safety is in the correct position, and keep my trembling fingers near the trigger.

I haven't had to fire it yet, but after four weeks of weapons training I can at least perform the basics—if I have to. This way I can at least buy Gracie a few precious moments once she pulls herself together enough to sing the keying sequence.

Next to us a body falls. . . . A dead boy still holds on to his shoes while the water pours out, and the baton inside it is already smoking—just like Gracie's.

"*There's* my baton!" I exclaim. "Quickly, refill the water in yours, and go! I'm right behind you!"

Gracie nods, still sniffling, clearing her throat, and plunges her shoes and baton into the water.

"Go! Go! Go!" I scream, as I toss away the rifle over the ledge into the reservoir, then desperately fling my body forward and grab the fallen dead boy's contraption with both hands. Meanwhile, Gracie begins singing the keying sequence, her voice cracking a few times, loses it completely, then restarts again.

There's no time to make my own new "shoe-baton holder." I plunge the existing one into the water to refill it the best I can, then pull it out, and sing the keying notes as I grab the big rubber shoes of the dead boy, sloshing with water. . . .

Shots ring out all around us, and several other Candidates are running to grab at us as we hover and rise in the air.

I feel someone pull at my own legs, and I kick out . . . and then I am twenty feet in the air and rising, with Gracie directly overhead.

Vertigo takes hold of me, and the world is turning like a carousel. My head goes into a wild spin, while I continue rising, through the explosions and bullets, my eyes narrowed against the sky and sun and only Gracie's dark shadow directly above . . . while my lips mouth the words, this time directed only at myself.

Go . . . Go . . . Go . . .

Just go.

We are about seventy-five feet up in the air when I realize the muscles in my arms are erupting in fine spasm-tremors. There's a sharp ripping agony in my armpits, and my wounded arm cannot fully support me. My hold on both the shoes begins to slip. . . . Furthermore, the shoelaces tying the two shoes together have now burned away, because the middle portion of the baton exposed to the air is red-hot.

That's when I hear Gracie screaming.

And the next instant, she plummets on top of me.

Whatever has just happened, Gracie is no longer supported by her own baton. Her panic reflex causes her to grasp at me, and as a result I almost lose hold of my baton also.

Gracie screams and holds on to me around my neck and waist. We wobble in the air, like two skydivers trying to share one parachute.

My hold on the baton slips, and I have no idea what I do, but as my one hand slips I grab out wildly, and suddenly there is *no shoe* on one side. It goes spinning down.

Instead, my fingers clasp the orichalcum surface that's newly exposed to the air, and immediately I feel warmth followed by severe heat and then . . . *white-hot agony.*

I scream from the pain in pure instinct.

The pain, it is *indescribable.* My palm, my fingers, everything is on fire.

This is happening to the hand that's attached to my one *good* arm.

And yet, because I know it is the only thing holding me—and Gracie—because Gracie is hugging me in a choke-hold, *I do not let go.*

The Atlantean shuttle—one of the last ones hovering over downtown L.A., looms before us.

We are now a mere twenty feet from the hatch opening, a black soothing void against grey-silver. Gracie's own abandoned incandescent baton is bobbing in the air right near the opening, like a piece of aerial flotsam.

Screaming, I try to force my mind, to force my vocal chords to *sing.* I have to sing the new sequence to change direction and bring us closer in and enter the hatch. If I don't—we miss the shuttle and it will all be for nothing, and we will plummet anyway.

I force myself to shut up. And suddenly, in my own silence and Gracie's whimpering, I can hear a crackle and smell my hand smoking, charred near the bone.

I will not let go.

With a gasping breath, I open my mouth and I sing.

I put all my being, all the remainder of my *drowning self,* into the note sequence to stop the ascent and instead move forward.

We pause the rise and slowly hover in the direction of the shuttle opening.

Five feet... three feet... one.... There goes Gracie's baton.... Now, just a few inches more....

My voice breaks. There is now only tearing wind at this altitude, and silence.

Do not let go.

At the doorway a man stands, leaning into the wind, watching us approach. I see him, a wild tangle of long metallic-gold hair, lapis-blue eyes lined with sharp darkness of kohl. A stark chiseled face stilled in intensity. Around his uniform sleeve, a black armband.

Aeson Kass stands before us at the opening of the shuttle. As we levitate within reach, he puts out his bare hand and places it directly upon the incandescent white middle of my baton.

He never flinches as he makes contact with the fire, simply pulls us inward into the soothing darkness.

"You can let go now," he says softly, staring directly into my eyes.

And as my mind plummets into darkness, I do as he says.

Chapter 41

I wake up out of a deep mind fog into soothing sterile twilight.
Such an impossible sense of *peace*.

Amazingly there is no pain, nothing at all. It's as if everything
has been erased into a bad dream that happened somewhere far
away and long ago.

I lie on a soft bed—or what feels like a bed, or maybe a cot.
There's a comfortable pillow under my head. There's a soft hum of
equipment in the background. What appears to be a hospital
curtain on rollers is hanging from overhead on one side to give my
bed-space privacy.

My body is relaxed . . . everything, all my limbs, I can feel
them.

I feel *both* my arms and my hands.

Oh wow, my hands! My wounded arm! They are whole and
unharmed!

Last thing I remember is the fire agony of a burning terribly
charred hand on one side and the dulled ache of a bullet-wounded
arm on the other. What happened? How did I regain both limbs
entirely?

I stir and make sounds. And apparently it is enough to bring
someone by to lean over me, up-close, and examine me. I blink,
attempting to keep my heavy eyelids open.

The stranger looking down at me is an unknown Atlantean.
He observes me with an impassive gaze, and then moves away.

"What . . . what happened? Where . . . am I?" I whisper,
barely moving my lips.

But the next moment I see two familiar faces. George and
Gracie are at my bedside, both rushing toward me. George leans in,
grins and presses my arm very gently—yes, my fully functional
arm!—and Gracie comes around from the other side to rest her

head against my chest and hug me with both arms.

"Gently, gently!" An unfamiliar voice sounds, and I see it is the Atlantean man speaking. I am guessing he is a doctor or a med tech, because he comes to check the IV line in my arm—which I notice only now, because again, I have a fully functional arm there, amazing. "Don't get her agitated, don't suffocate her, now."

"Gee Two!" Gracie mutters, raising her head from my chest.

"Finally!" George says. "Welcome back to the world of the living, Gee Two."

"George . . ." I mumble. "Oh, thank God . . . you made it. What about Gordie?"

"Don't worry, knucklehead's here too. He stepped outside to get food. He's fine."

I start to smile in relief. "Typical Gordie. . . . So, where are we exactly?"

"We made it! We're at the National Qualification Center!" Gracie says.

George pats my arm and hand lightly. "Yeah, and the Atlanteans fixed you up real good. See, all perfect."

"But—" I say. "What about the bullet wound? And the burned hand, I thought it was all ruined—"

"Apparently they have medical technology we can't even begin to dream of." George lets go my hand and adjusts the covers around me. "When the L.A. shuttles came in and they brought you in to the NQC, their medical team took you away—"

"They were taking many others too, all the hurt and wounded Candidates who passed the Semi-Finals, hundreds of people—" Gracie interrupts.

"Yeah, and they took you and worked on you for a couple of hours. Then they told us you were sleeping it off."

"How long?" I lift my hand that was burned to a crisp and look at the healthy skin and muscle and nails, open and close it, flex my perfectly formed fingers, as though nothing had happened to it. "How long was I under?"

"Hmm, let's see. . . ." Gracie looks around for a wall clock. "It's close to eight PM now, so it makes it a day plus three hours."

"A *day*?" I say. "Wait—"

"The Semi-Finals were yesterday." George grins.

"I was out for *that* long?"

"Yeah, well, you needed the rest, so all good."

I stir some more, and try to sit up weakly, and feel a sudden stabbing head-rush. Immediately the Atlantean medic who is not too far away, returns. "You need to lie back down," he says calmly. "Just an hour more, and I take out the IV. Then you're free to move around or sleep it off—your choice."

"Wow," I mutter, and sink back on the pillow. And then I stare at my brother and sister. "So, what happened? Tell me everything."

In the next half an hour, I listen to George and Gracie speak, laboring to keep my eyelids open, even though my mind is clear and hungry for news.

It turns out we're somewhere in the Eastern Plains of Colorado, or at least we think that's where the huge National Qualification Center is located. They don't tell us for sure, and they don't tell the public, in order to keep all of us precious Finalists safe from any possible terrorist actions or other threats from the turbulent world outside. . . .

The NQC, George tells me, is the size of a goodly city, self-sustaining and completely enclosed from all sides with seventy-five-foot tall impenetrable steel and concrete walls like a fortress. It is supposed to keep us safe for another month until we train and get ready for the Final phase that will determine our Qualification status.

"Right now we're in the medical building, their hospital, I guess," George says. "Yesterday as soon as our respective shuttles brought us here, we got sorted into sick and not-so-sick and then assigned to our final dorms. There are only four dorms here, based on the Four Quadrants, and they are huge—I am talking, each one the size of a mall."

"Oh," Gracie puts in. "And we also get to have three days off, to rest and heal and whatever, until the new training sessions begin. So we are all just kind of hanging out."

"Did you—did you have a chance to contact Mom and Dad?" I speak in a faint voice that sounds awful even to me.

George signs, frowning. "No, still not permitted to do that. They have similar firewalls set up here as they did at the RQC, e-dampers everywhere, so we can't call out. But they tell us the global situation outside is getting rougher every day, riots, et cetera."

"So we can just imagine the worst," I whisper.

"No, don't . . . just, stop!" Gracie says, putting her hand on mine, and immediately I see her eyes begin to glisten with tears.

"You're right," I say, immediately, to humor her. "I am sure Mom and Dad are just fine, things aren't as bad in Vermont as in some of the other places. . . ."

As I speak, George gives me an intense meaningful look, so that I know he knows I'm speaking for Gracie's sake. Truth is, I have no idea—none of us have any idea how bad things are, and whether our parents are even alive. . . .

We mutually change the subject, and George and Gracie tell me more things.

Apparently George chose New York for his Semi-Finals, and so did Gordie. They had different kinds of hot zones there, and most of their difficulties involved tall buildings, skyscraper high rises, and crazy vertical flying.

"Then, good thing we went with L.A.," Gracie says. "Because we both suck when it comes to dealing with heights."

"Oh, yeah," George says with a light smile. "I really can't see the two of you handling a few of the circus trapeze things they made us do in New York City—and I hear it was just as bad for those Candies who picked Chicago. They also had to walk tightropes across buildings and run on narrow ledges in the high winds—"

In that moment Gordie shows up. He's chewing a sandwich and carrying a drink and a bag of chips. "Hey, Gee Two, you awake!" he mumbles with his mouth full and a sloppy smile, and then comes in closer to bop me on the shoulder, dropping a bunch of chips on the blanket covering me.

"Oh," I say. "Look who showed up! Gee Three, good to see you, little bro!"

We chat and I take a peek closer, to see that Gordie's old facial bruise has healed completely—turns out he was slightly hurt during Semi-Finals, his face scratched up by knives and grazed by a bullet, so he too got taken into the hospital and received medical treatment that incidentally also cured his older bruise.

"There's a huge machine, like one of those full body scanners," Gordie says, swallowing, then slurping the drink. "You lie down on it, they cover the glass top, and some blue and purple lights go on and there's this light buzzing sound. . . . You get a little dizzy, and maybe zone out or sleep for a few seconds . . . and the next thing you know, you are all healed! Like, my face got fixed completely, skin and everything, no scars. Nothing hurts. Pretty slick!" And Gordie's grinning. "I bet it's the same machine they put you in, to fix you too and reconstruct your hand. They have dozens of them. . . ."

I reach out with my brand new reconstructed fingers to touch Gordie's cheek. "You look good, Gee Three."

And then I remember suddenly, and with amazement at my own self, at how I could've even forgotten. "Hey! Who else made it? Oh, lord, please tell me that you saw other people we know! Laronda! Dawn! Logan! Hasmik? Who else? Anyone?"

"Hmm," George says. "Well, I can tell you your friend Laronda made it, because she came by to check on you when you were asleep. So, yeah, Laronda's here."

"Thank God!"

"Yeah, and relax, Logan is here too!" Gracie laughs and tickles me lightly. "He came by this morning. I was here and George was not. He said he's okay and to tell you he will be by again later. He looked way tired but not hurt—at least not so much that he had to be put in that medical machine."

A great weight suddenly lifts from me, and I exhale in relief.

Logan made it!

"Oh, and let me think, I am pretty sure there are a few more people we know from our RQC, there's Greg Chee and Charlie Venice from Red, and I think I saw your other friend Dawn Williams, though not sure—"

"What about that other guy?" Gordie says, loudly crunching a handful of chips he stuffs in his mouth. "You know, that Atlantean a-hole. You said he came by."

"What?" I mumble.

"Oh, yeah," Gracie says. "The Phoebos guy, he was here too. Came in first thing this morning, looked at you for a few minutes, said nothing, and left. I was passed out in the chair near your bed and barely noticed him, he was so quiet—kind of creepy."

My mind is suddenly in turmoil. I turn my head and frown, thinking. *So, Aeson Kass came to see how I am doing. . . . Strange.*

Or maybe, not so strange. I suppose he has to make sure I'm okay, with my precious Logos voice and whatever it means for them. Not to mention, he has to keep tabs on a potential terrorist. Because, yeah, that's still hanging over my head.

"He did pull us into the shuttle at the last minute, Gracie," I mumble. "We should be grateful. Makes sense he'd check in on us."

"Oh, he definitely came in to check up on *you*. I don't think he even noticed me."

"Well, yeah." George pats me on the arm again. "She's his special project with the super duper voice."

"Teacher's pet," Gordie teases.

"He's not my teacher, and I am definitely not his pet," I say, raising my voice and finding it steady for the first time. My irritation apparently gives me strength. "I think I'm like an investment of some sort. Besides, he can't stand me."

George raises one brow meaningfully and looks away.

"Hey!" I say, slapping the covers with one hand. "What's that eyebrow thing supposed to mean, Gee One?"

"Nothing." George shrugs. "I don't know, whatever."

"Just, well, you know," Gracie says. "He does seem to spend an awful amount of time dealing with you, considering he's one of their top VIPs."

"I told you, he's invested in *my voice*," I mutter angrily. "They need my voice for whatever reason. So he's keeping tabs on me. Furthermore, I am still under major suspicion for that shuttle sabotage incident—or have you guys forgotten? These Atlanteans are not just going to let it slide, there is going to be permanent surveillance and inquests until they find the real guilty party."

"Yeah, you're right, sorry." Gracie looks down on the bed covers near my arm and smoothes the edges of the sheet. "Didn't mean to tease you. Besides, the guy's too intense and scary to joke about."

"It's okay, Gee Four. And yeah, well, he's just military. I actually don't blame him for being suspicious, it's his job."

We talk some more about other things, speculate about what's to come in the next four weeks, and who else survived the Semi-Finals. Meanwhile I feel my strength slowly coming back. . . . By the end of the hour when the Atlantean med tech comes to remove my IV line, I am strong enough to sit up in bed and have some yogurt and ginger ale.

Just before ten PM lights-out, Logan Sangre comes to see me. My brothers and Gracie tactfully make themselves scarce and leave us alone in the room, exchanging little smiles.

Logan stands before me, pausing momentarily near the privacy curtain. The low light falls on the lean hollow planes of his cheeks and jaw, highlighting every perfect feature. My heart once again constricts painfully at the sight of him, the fall of his super-dark brown hair, the way his warm hazel eyes seem to be full of sweet honey as he looks at me. . . .

And then comes his heart-stopping smile.

"Logan!" I exclaim, and almost drop my cup of ginger ale.

Thankfully he moves in, just in time to intercept me, takes the cup out of my trembling fingers and sets it aside. He then puts his strong hands around me in an embrace that is hard and gentle at the same time. With a kind of wonder he sweeps my messed-up hair aside, strokes my cheek, and suddenly he is kissing me. . . .

And all at once, I am bursting with *wildness*. . . . My pulse is racing, and warm electricity mixed with languid weakness fills me as I sink back against the pillow and let him *touch* me, let him do to me whatever it is we're doing that makes me forget where I am and who I am and why.

We come apart gasping for air, our lips bruised and sweet and desperate for more.

"That's enough. . . . You need some rest, Gwen," he whispers in my ear, then ruins the effect of his own words and kisses me deeply again, on the lips, then on the neck, rubs his face against me, skin to skin, his faint stubble sending more electric pangs coursing through me.

He is breathing fast and his eyes are very, very dark when he finally moves away while I lie trembling, like a puddle of flesh and no bones.

"I didn't know what I'd do if you didn't make the Semi-

VERA NAZARIAN

Finals," he says, looking into my eyes.

"Same here," I whisper. "But then, I always knew you'd make it."

He smiles, shakes his head slightly. "You always have such amazing faith in me."

"How was New York? I heard it was pretty bad."

"Oh yeah, terrifying." He makes a short tired laugh sound. "Same goes for L.A., I hear. I also hear stories about a certain Shoelace Girl saving the day multiple times. They say, if it hadn't been for you, most of the California Candies in La La Land would not have passed the hot zones or the Semi-Finals."

I make a sound that's halfway between a snort and a cough. At least it gets my mind off Logan's sensual proximity.

"How do you feel?" he says.

"Better. Definitely. And I have hands and arms." I smile. "And you—you look perfect, as always."

"Oh, boy. . . ." He cringes slightly and I find that he is actually blushing. "No, I had a few scratches—nothing serious that some Atlantean meds wouldn't fix. They have some amazing tech there, you know? Very interesting stuff."

And I am momentarily reminded that Logan has his eyes on things in his clandestine ops capacity.

We talk some more, but the mood is gone because I am suddenly very tired.

"I'll see you tomorrow," he tells me at last, seeing my drooping eyelids. "Now, sleep!"

And with a brush of his hand against my cheek he is gone.

In the morning I am up early, after a great night of sleep. I am issued a fresh new uniform and armband, receive back my yellow ID token, and Gracie is there to see me as I am discharged from the hospital building.

"Come on, I'll take you to your Yellow Quadrant dorm, you'll need to check in," she tells me, as we walk through the long sterile corridors of the building with pastel walls and medical personnel wearing grey uniforms and Atlantean four-color armbands.

Outside, the skies are cornflower blue and the morning air crisp. The wind blows in from the plains, and I stand staring at the sheer *immensity* of the compound I am in.

When George called it a whole city, he wasn't kidding. Large buildings stretch for blocks in all directions, all multi-story, each bearing a color square designation of some sort. I see rows and rows of connected mall-like structures marked with squares that are color solids. And each long structure is interspersed by another that is designated as common area by its four-color square logo.

Candidates, guards, and other compound workers are everywhere, walking from building to building. There are even occasional vehicles that look like patrol cars or delivery vans. The Candies are all mostly aimless like myself and Gracie, wandering around, staring in curiosity around them, while the guards and workers move with a purpose. There are far more Atlanteans in this NQC compound than back at our Pennsylvania RQC-3.

"You're gonna need a map," Gracie tells me, taking my arm, as I stand gaping. "Don't worry, it's pretty overwhelming, I know, plus you are still a little woozy."

"No, I'm not," I retort, with a light smile. "I am just taking it all in."

"Okay, see how this whole row of linked buildings is all marked with a square red logo?" Gracie points. "That's the Red Quadrant Dorm. That *whole thing*. It stretches at least two miles down the line."

"Wow."

"Yeah, I know. . . . And next you get the building row with the rainbow logo, the one with the hospital we just left, that's the Common Area number One—one of *three* such. After it, you'll see yet another long dorm, that's the Blue. Then another CA, number Two, then the Green dorm, and another CA, number Three, and finally, your Yellow Dorm. Each one is like two miles long. It kind of blows your mind."

I shake my head, snorting.

"Every teen in the United States of America who will Qualify is being housed in this place right now," Gracie exclaims. "Isn't it wild? And they say every country in the world has a similar NQC for their Candies. Though I bet ours is bigger."

"Not as big as China's, I bet," I say. "Or even United Industan."

"Oh, yeah, you're right." Gracie giggles. "They must have

four or five times as many people as we do. . . ."

As Gracie continues to chatter with a mix of nerves and excitement, we walk along the wide thoroughfare street area between buildings, until we reach a glassed-in walkway inside the CA-1 structure. The walkway allows us to cut in perpendicularly through the miles-long structure, since there is no easy way of walking around it, and we end up on the next street and across from the next dorm structure which is Blue Quadrant Dorm.

We repeat this several times, crossing the street, finding a glassed walkway, going through, until we reach Yellow Quadrant Dorm, which is last.

Gracie enters first, and takes me directly to an info desk near the doors. We're in a very large hotel-like lobby that stretches along the entire first floor like an airport terminal. It is filled with noise and teens, mostly all Yellow Candies such as myself.

The official at the desk scans my token and informs me I am on the third floor, which is all girls' dormitory space, in Section Fourteen, bed #172.

"Your personal belongings from your RQC have been brought over by freight shuttle last evening together with all the others who passed Semi-Finals, after the end of the event. Your belongings are now waiting for you next to your bed," he tells me, handing me a small check-in packet that includes a paper map of the complex and a general conduct and instructions checklist. "Be sure to locate and introduce yourself to your Section Leader who will give you the next instructions and answer any questions. Good luck, Candidate."

And the official turns away.

I go to find the nearest stairs, and Gracie and I go up to the third floor that resembles another airport terminal row, except instead of airline terminal check-in areas there are dormitory Sections along an endless hallway. Each Section is the size of an RQC girls' dorm floor, and has double doors marked by a Section number.

We walk past endless doors and many girls I don't know moving past us through the hall in both directions, until we come to Section Fourteen.

We enter the dormitory which is another sea of neatly placed rows of cots—most of them slept-in but empty because their occupants are elsewhere—and Gracie helps me find bed #172 that's somewhere in the back.

My bed is pristine, and my two duffel bags sit on the floor before it.

"There's your stuff!" Gracie says with excitement. "You might want to check to see it's all there."

But I am hardly listening. Instead I glance around the huge room to see who my bed neighbors are, and who else is here.

And that's when I see Claudia Grito. She's three beds down from me, her metal piercings glittering in high contrast against her silky black hair, sitting on her cot with her feet up and going through stuff in her bag. As though she senses my presence, she happens to look up in that moment, and our gazes lock.

Oh, great, just great. . . .

Claudia frowns and glares at me. "Look who's decided to show up, Gwen-baby! Didn't think I'd ever see your skinny ass again, loser face."

Gracie immediately turns around and her jaw drops in outrage. "Who the hell do you think you are? Don't talk to my sister like that!"

"It's okay, Gracie." I glance at her. And then I turn back to Claudia. "Sorry to disappoint you." And then I look away.

Meanwhile, I notice a few other girls in the room, and they all look vaguely familiar. And then . . . the bathroom doors open and I see Laronda! And there's Dawn behind her, and Hasmik too!

"Girlfriend!" Laronda shrieks, and rushes toward me, and practically jumps in my arms with a huge choking hug. "You're alive! You look *good!* Way, *way* good, compared to yesterday when you were half-dead in the hospital!"

"Hey!" I exclaim. And then the others reach me, and I am hugging Hasmik and Dawn simultaneously, who both look tired and excited and generally healthy except for a kind of slight air of additional gravity and resignation that all of us who've passed the Semi-Finals now seem to have. It's an imprint of tiredness, of suffering, of *death*, that stamped us all, deep underneath the veneer of "happy."

"Can you believe, I make it!" Hasmik says in a high-pitched tone, and repeats it. "I, *I* make it this far? No way, huh? I still don't believe it! Complete accident!"

"Shut up, girl," Laronda turns and punches Hasmik lightly on the arm. "Of course you made, it, I told you, you would! Good thing you picked Dallas, too—no big deal, just an obstacle course in the middle of burning oil wells! I picked New York like an idiot and got to climb ledges and fall down from skyscrapers like some kind of caped comic book heroine—ugh!"

"New York, eh?" I say with a grin. "Yeah, I heard the horror stories."

"Yeah, another New York here," Dawn says in her usual calm deadpan manner. "Though Los Angeles was pretty rotten too, eh? What was it, you crazy Wild West cowboys rode explosive *drones?* Whose bright idea was it?"

"Oh, well," I say in a somewhat flustered voice. "I didn't really want to actually, it was the only thing we could do, to get over the—"

"Hey, hey, whoa! Kidding you." Dawn rolls her eyes at me, with a quick, sly smile. "It was a brilliant thing to do. Color me way impressed . . . Shoelace Girl."

"Oh, crap. . . ." But now I'm the one grinning and rolling my eyes.

We chatter back and forth, and it turns out, Section Fourteen is basically all the girls from our Pennsylvania RQC-3's Yellow Quadrant, so no wonder everyone's here, and no wonder the girls in the room look familiar.

"All right, we have tonight and tomorrow to relax, before hell resumes," Laronda says, sticking her finger out to poke my shoulder. "But now, I say we talk trash and gossip while we go have a good look at this huge National Qualification Center! Who's in? You can tell me all about those flying shoes and drones and other absolutely insane junk you're single-handedly responsible for, while we walk. Tell me *everything*, girlfriend!"

Chapter 42

The rest of the free day we spend wandering the immense sprawling compound and learning where everything is—the Quadrant Dorms and the Common Areas, which include more cafeterias, training gyms, classrooms, not one but three arena stadiums with track and sports training equipment, and three double-Olympic-length and extra-wide swimming pools.

"I hear we'll be doing swimming training in addition to other types of classes," Dawn says as we walk through yet another glassed-in walkway between building structures to cross to the other street that runs parallel.

"Interesting," Laronda says. "I wonder why. Does Atlantis have a lot of oceans and water?"

"It could also be their tradition," I say, "stemming from the Earth's original continent of Atlantis. So much stuff related to the sea, oceans, water. Like the name of their ancient city, Poseidon, who's the Ancient Greek god of the sea—though it's earlier than Greek, we now know, it's in fact Ancient Atlantean. . . ."

"Glad you're still such a smarty-pants." Laronda smiles.

In that moment, Grace—who's been tagging along with us on the walk, and has been somewhat inseparable from me since the trauma of Semi-Finals—looks up and points.

Four Atlantean shuttles plummet down from the sky, and land somewhere beyond the buildings, their aerial activity generating a sonic boom.

"That way lies a huge airfield," Dawn says. "Want to go see?"

"Um," I say, as my expression darkens. "Not sure . . . I think I've had enough Atlantean shuttles and airfields to last me a lifetime."

"No! Don't say that!" Gracie immediately tugs my sleeve. "If we Qualify, we will have to deal with them all the time."

"Okay, I know," I reply tiredly. "But seriously, let's just—not."

Dawn shrugs comfortably. "Okay."

So instead we walk toward the nearest cafeteria to get more free food for as long as they're still feeding us.

As we stroll down the street between buildings, Gracie pulls me aside for a moment, while Dawn and Laronda and Hasmik walk ahead.

"Gwen . . ." Gracie walks at my side with a strange closed-up expression and stiff posture, hands nervously clutching the bottom of her uniform shirt. "Gwen, I . . . I have to tell you something."

Okay, this does not bode well.

"What?" I say, glancing at my sister carefully.

Gracie does not say anything for several long moments.

"Promise—" she says. "Promise me you won't go crazy when you hear this, okay?"

"How can I promise when I don't know what you're talking about?"

Gracie bites her lip, takes a deep breath. "You know that awful night when they found that chip in Laronda's jacket?"

"Yeah. . . ?" Suddenly I feel cold. And I'm really beginning to dislike what this is leading up to.

Gracie stops and looks up at me. Her face is full of anguish. "I put that chip in her jacket! I am so sorry!"

"What?" I stop also, while cold waves of fear pass through me, one after another, and I am reeling with it.

Gracie grabs my sleeves and her hands are shaking. "Please, don't freak out, oh, don't freak out, *please!*"

"Gracie, what are you saying?" I take hold of her, and my fingers dig into her shoulders, at the same time as my voice grows very hard and very quiet. "Are you telling me *you* planted that navigation chip on Laronda? Oh my God, what are you involved with? Who gave it to you? Who told you to do something like that? Do you realize what you've done? You got so many people in trouble—you—"

"I know! I *know* it was awful and wrong, now, okay! But at that time I didn't know what it was, just a stupid little chip! I was supposed to just hide it temporarily, they told me—drop it in someone's pocket—any person I knew and dealt with casually— and I could get it back later from them, after the Correctors finished searching our dorm. It was supposed to be for one night! That's why I came over to have dinner with you and went up to your dormitory floor, so I could find a safe spot to hide it overnight. The guys were all passing it around like a game of hot potato, they were saying that was the best way to keep it hidden—" Gracie's face is red and she is on the verge of tears.

"The guys? What guys? *Tell me!*" I shake her, hissing in her ear, while glancing before us where up ahead the girls are still walking and laughing and talking loudly. They didn't notice yet that we're lagging behind.

"The guys were from Red, they were some kind of rebel group, and they were doing all these crazy secret things to get back at Atlanteans and to steal their secrets. . . . And I thought I might be cool if I did something wild like that, and Daniel might think I am—"

"*Daniel?*" I am filled with sudden rage. "Is it *Daniel Tover?* Did he put you up to this, Gracie?"

"No!" Gracie whimpers. "No, not Daniel! He had nothing to do with those guys, he is not one of them, I swear! But—but I didn't know it at the time! I *thought* he was, and I thought I would do this one awesome thing for them and he might notice me and—"

"Oh, Gracie!"

"I screwed up, okay! I had no idea! I didn't want to hurt anyone either! And turns out, Daniel is not even one of them, even though he hangs out with many of them—that's why I thought he was with Terra Patria, but he's not—"

"Hush!" I hiss again, and look around, wondering what kind of surveillance cameras and maybe audio surveillance they might have in this compound.

And then I take a deep breath and force my voice to calm down as I speak to my little idiot sister. "Gracie, listen to me. You *have* to keep your voice down. This is bad, you cannot be screaming all this loudly."

"Okay. . . ."

"Now . . . I am not going to tell you now that you did

something stupid, idiotic, and horrible that could have gotten you and all of us Disqualified, hurt, punished, and possibly killed. You already know all this. What I want to know is why didn't you *tell me*—or George—any of this earlier? Have you any idea what kind of position you've put so many people in?"

Gracie scrunches her face and big fat tears roll down her cheek. "I am sorry! I am so sorry! I was scared! I wanted to tell you, and I kind of tried to, before, but I just couldn't! And then, when they took Laronda away and then locked you up, it was too late! I didn't know what to do! And now—I still don't know what to do, what if they find out? Will they Disqualify me and lock me up? And what about you guys—"

I squeeze Gracie's shoulders again. "Look at me. . . . *Stop.* You did the right thing telling me. And now, just hush, okay? Let me think. . . . We need to figure out what we need to do. Okay? Stop crying! Okay? It will be okay!"

And then I hug Gracie, and I feel her completely shaking and falling apart into a weeping mess in my arms. Might as well let her cry it out, and then she'll get a grip. Eventually. I hope. . . .

"What's going on here?" Laronda and the others have backtracked and now look at Gracie crying and me hugging her. "Is she okay?"

"Oh yeah," I say. "She's having a delayed-reaction nervous breakdown, I think. The Semi-Finals—she remembered bad stuff that happened then, and it's getting to her." And I pat Gracie's hair gently while she quiets her sobs and wipes her nose on her sleeve.

"Oh, poor baby," Laronda says to Gracie. "Here. . . . Girl, let me give you a hug too!"

Of course at that, guilty Gracie weeps even harder, since it's Laronda she wronged in the first place. And me, in second. And herself, ultimately.

My poor fool baby sister!

I tactfully let everyone do their hug thing, and then change the subject.

For the rest of the day, Gracie follows me around—continues following me like a puppy, wherever we go.

And now I know why.

She's not just feeling vulnerable, and lost, and clingy-dependent on me after our hell experience in Los Angeles, as I originally thought. No, she's also one helluva *guilty* puppy.

I continue to think about what Gracie told me all evening, and wake up the next morning and it hits me hard, like a bucket of cold water.

Gracie can get in huge trouble because of this. If anyone finds out, she can and likely *will* be Disqualified—and probably worse.

I feel sick to my stomach as I go to breakfast with the people I know from the Pennsylvania RQC-3, Yellow Quadrant—including some guys who I am glad to see, such as Mateo and Jai and Tremaine—and then I go to look for my brother George, who needs to be told as soon as possible.

Instead I run into Logan.

Logan is standing outside the Red Quadrant Dorm structure in a small crowd of Candidates from all Four Quadrants, near what looks to be a news media van and truck lineup. Compound guards pace idly, blocking off most of the area, while a portable platform has been erected right on the street. A major network news channel crew of holo-projection techs and cameramen is arranging a brightly lit interview area. A familiar news anchor's hologram has been projected directly from their studio into one of the chairs to interview selected Candidates about their Semi-Finals experience.

Someone is occupying the other chair, a brown-haired boy I've never seen before, with a cool manner. He is talking while a sound tech moves a studio microphone in his face.

"Logan!" I say in a loud whisper, waving and leaning in toward him past a guard who blocks my approach. "What's going on?"

Logan hears me, glances in my direction, and nods with an immediate light smile. He then raises one hand and mouths "ten minutes" to me. And so I wait at the periphery with a few other gawking passerby Candies, while he in turn gets briefly interviewed about his experience in New York, climbing cables and scaling the side of a tall building.

I watch Logan take a seat easily, lean back in his chair and speak with effortless confidence into the cameras, and I realize he was born for this—calm yet outgoing, composed, friendly, making great eye contact.

"And really," he concludes with a self-depreciating bittersweet laugh, looking directly at the various media feed cameras. "It was a tough marathon and I am glad it's over—at least this Semi-Finals phase. We may never forget how many of us got hurt, and yeah, many teens *died* out there. Manhattan is a floating graveyard for so many. But at least they died trying, having hope, up to the last second. And I am hardly the only one who managed to make some rather lucky and solid decisions that helped me survive."

He pauses, and his gaze suddenly searches the surrounding audience and settles on me. "For example, right here is a Candidate who is far more interesting than me and should really be interviewed, if you want to get the best of us here in this chair. You all know her from the Los Angeles live feeds. I believe some have used the term 'Shoelace Girl'. . . ."

My mouth falls open as everyone turns to look in my direction. The hologram anchor stares at me, and suddenly his expression lights up with recognition. "Oh, my, that's right! How incredibly lucky we are, there she is! My dear, you are Los Angeles Shoelace Girl, the clever amazing girl who commandeered hoverboards, rode the drones, and then created the flying contraption with the shoes!"

He waves energetically toward me. Two techs approach, and suddenly I am directed past guards onto the brightly lit media platform. Logan sleekly moves aside and gives my hand a quick squeeze, while I am seated in the interview chair, and the microphones point at me.

"We are absolutely privileged to have you with us, Shoelace Girl!" says the anchor. "Which is of course, not your real name, I realize—so what *is* your name, dear, for our audience? The nation wants to know!"

"Gwen . . ." I say, in a breathless voice. "Gwen Lark."

"And where are you from?"

"Highgate Waters, Vermont."

"Fantastic achievement, Gwen—may I call you Gwen? And may I be the first to congratulate you on passing the arduous Semi-Finals! Now, how did you ever come up with all those incredible clever ideas?"

My mind is going into a light version of deer-in-the-headlights panic and my temples pound. What is this? What can I say? I don't know anything! *Logan, how could you do this to me?*

Instead I say, "Well, I just got really desperate, I guess."

"Is that so?" The anchor prompts me encouragingly with a smile. "Go on, tell us. How was it that you survived the brutality of the attacks and obstacles that left many of your fellow Candidates helpless and even worse, dead? I am sure everyone remembers the way you managed to carry on with the horrible army of explosive drones—"

I flash back to the fallen Blue girl underneath a freeway overpass, her shattered body . . . Sarah Thornwald's perfectly still glass eyes as she lies on the grass of the Huntington. . . .

"I don't know," I say in a wooden voice. "I don't know how I managed. I think no one knows, not when it's happening. You just do what you can, that's all."

"Brave words of wisdom, Gwen, very well said." The anchor nods. "And yet, the question remains for many of our viewers—how is it that you came up with so many clever solutions to what seemed to be impossible problems?"

"They weren't, not really . . . clever, I mean. They were actually kind of crazy and not even well thought out. Stupid, you might say." I pause, feeling like a fool before an audience of millions. "But—with all factors put together, they *worked*—for the circumstances. It's like—you know that old myth about the bee? That, according to 'physics,' a bumblebee is not 'aerodynamic' enough, is not supposed to be able to fly—it just does because it doesn't know any better? Well, that's all nonsense. A bumblebee flies just fine! It flies according to physical laws, only *different* ones, because it *itself* is different, using other complex variables for its flight method—for example, something called 'dynamic stall' comes into play. . . . Anyway, what I did wasn't clever but kind of *all over the place*, using everything at my disposal . . . like the bee. It's like—if you move fast enough and just the right way—if you do some things quickly and desperately enough, hoping they don't have time to fall apart on you—you can make the seemingly impossible happen. And it's not 'before it knows any better.' It's *before the whole unstable construct falls apart.* Move fast enough and you can walk on water. . . ."

The anchor claps his hands, nodding at me with a brilliant smile. I've just babbled him to death, but he is loving it.

"Gwen Lark, I had no idea you're such a wonderful science geek! Whatever you just said there—wow! You must get straight A's at school, am I right?"

I blush, feeling my cheeks start to burn. "Yeah, mostly," I mutter.

"Aha!" the anchor exclaims. "No wonder you came up with all these wild solutions! Tell me, and our audience, do you think these are the exact specific qualities that the Atlanteans are looking for? Because it's still the big question—what do the Atlanteans want? Someone like you? A clever bright young lady who can solve tough problems?"

"I don't know," I say. "But I think they want people who don't give up. Because that's the only way to Qualify. And if you give up—you don't."

The anchor asks me a couple more specific questions and I answer. And then, "Well, Gwen, I must say it was a delight, so glad we caught up with you here at the National Qualification Center. Your parents must be so proud! I'm sure they're watching. Would you like to say something to them before you go?"

My heart, my breath, my pulse, everything goes into overdrive. I gulp, and a lump begins to gather in my throat. "Yes!" I say in a mad rush of joy. "Mom, Dad, we are all okay! Gracie, George, Gordie, we are here and we made it! Please stay safe! Love you always!"

And then I am done.

I get off the media platform and Logan waits for me. I am shaking slightly from the nerves, the emotional overload, so he takes my hand, and we walk away down the street where I lean over the side of a building to get a grip on things.

"Okay," I say. "Logan, *thank you*. Admittedly, I wanted to kill you at first, for putting me on the spot. But then I got it, I know why you did it. . . . It gave me a chance to say something to my parents, something that might actually get to them. At least now they'll know we're okay, at least for the moment!"

He smiles lightly, and his fingers run up my wrist and arm.

"You're welcome. I figured this was a good opportunity for you."

And then I tell him about Gracie.

Immediately our light mood changes.

"Come on, let's walk," he says.

And once we're on the move, we discuss, in quiet careful voices.

In a nutshell, Logan tells me to keep it quiet. Not a word to anyone else.

"Not even George?" I ask, with a grim expression.

He shakes his head. "If George knows nothing, he can be perfectly honest if he ever has to deny something—if he gets questioned."

"Do you think that might happen again? Didn't they question all of us like half a dozen times?"

Logan's hazel eyes watch me seriously. "Anything can happen. Incidentally, have you seen Command Pilot Aeson Kass recently?"

"Not since the Semi-Finals."

"If you see him again—which I have a feeling you will—be very careful. Because now you are in a position to *lie*. Your sister's unfortunate confession has just made you a knowing party to her actions."

"I don't care about that," I say. "I care about Gracie and keeping her *safe!*"

"I know you do. But what I'm saying is, you will now have to lie, and *he* will see right through you."

I frown.

"Gwen," he says gently. "You are not the best liar. . . ."

"And you are?"

"Better than you." And suddenly he smiles cockily at me.

I punch his arm with a loose fist. But he catches it, and holds my fingers, stroking them until a jolt of warm electricity travels down my arm.

Chapter 43

That night I dream about being seven or eight years old again. It's a warm spring day and our parents have taken George and me to the Huntington Gardens in San Marino, California. Little Gordie and Gracie are with a babysitter, while we get to spend the day walking through amazing gardens and staring at paintings in the gallery.

As dream logic goes, I wander and somehow end up alone in the gallery room that houses the two most famous paintings at the Huntington. "Pinkie" painted by Thomas Lawrence hangs in a great hall directly facing, on the opposite wall, "The Blue Boy" by Thomas Gainsborough. The two Thomases painted their unrelated subjects years apart, and yet they seem to have a magical emotional connection, and fit together like a mated pair. . . .

I know, I am just a kid. . . . But that's the kind of kid I was—staring at art was fun, and I remember being in awe at the fact that I was in the same room with them, like being in the presence of two classical celebrities.

And now, in this dream, I look up, and *Pinkie*, whose real name is Sarah Barrett Moulton, looks down at me from the distance of the eighteenth century. Only, her face changes and now she is a different Sarah . . . she is Sarah Thornwald and her open eyes are stilled in death and accusation. . . . And when I turn around in sudden terror, feeling a ghostly prickling on my back, there's *The Blue Boy*—only now he's the Blue girl whom I killed, and the Blue girl is watching me, looking at me with an absence of life, of sight, an empty *vacuum* that is somehow more terrifying than intensity. . . .

The morning claxon alarms peal and I am torn away from the terror—I wake up, and it is 7:00 AM, the first day of training here at the NQC, and I am lying in a cot, and somewhere out there an asteroid is blazing through space on its way to end the world.

The horrible dream is gone, only its ugly sickening residue remains.

And the grim reality.

The Candidates assigned to Section Fourteen—both from the girls' and boys' dormitory floors—are called to gather on the first floor in a lounge area that's similar to the Pennsylvania RQC-3. Except this so-called common lounge is just one small part of the miles-long "airport terminal" portion of the huge Yellow Quadrant Dorm structure.

Our Section Leaders stand ready to explain our final four-week training here at the NQC. I recognize only some of them as Dorm Leaders from the other Yellow Dorms, but feel relief to see two out of three of our own Yellow Dorm Eight DLs, Gina Curtis and Mark Foster. However, the third DL, John Nicolard, is not here, because apparently he did not make it through the Semi-Finals. . . . The sobering news hits home again, a reminder of the precariousness of all our positions here.

Section Leader Carlos Villa blows the whistle to call us to order—and at the same time we hear numerous other such whistles going off all through the endless lounge terminals, as other Sections get ready to be briefed.

"Attention, Section Fourteen!" Carlos says in a loud strong voice. He is a large muscular guy with dark hair and prominent biceps. We crowd around him and the other Section Fourteen Leaders, at the same time as we throw nervous glances at each other, to see who else of us is here, who made it, whom do we recognize. . . .

Who, from Pennsylvania RQC-3, is still left in the running.

I stand next to Dawn, Hasmik, Laronda, and the guys—Tremaine, Mateo, Jai. Looking around, I see several other familiar faces of Yellows. Yes, there's Claudia, and unfortunately I see the familiar tattooed thick neck belonging to creepy Derek Sunder, before he turns around and notices me and gives me a cynical stare. So, Derek, the A-list a-hole, made it. And so did Wade Ruthers apparently, and a few others of the alpha bullies.

On the other hand, I see in the back of our Section crowd the familiar wheelchair, and then get a glimpse of sloppy dark brown hair mostly covering a boy's eyes.

Blayne! Blayne Dubois made it!

I am stunned. . . . I am also so unbelievably happy all of a sudden, as if a dark burden has lifted from me, one I didn't even know was there. It occurs to me that, despite all the time spent together, all the hours of specialized training, and seeing how well he was progressing, I never quite had enough faith in Blayne, never expected him to make it this far. And the ugly doubt had been there in the back of my mind, causing my time with him to seem surreal and doomed—in my own stupid head.

And now, Blayne has proven me wrong, and I am so full of "happy" that I am ready to burst.

I start to edge toward him, and wave my hand enthusiastically, but Blayne does not see me through the crowd. And besides, Laronda pulls me on the uniform sleeve, because the Section Leader is telling us important stuff and I should be paying attention.

"Listen up, everyone!" Carlos continues. "You are all here because you have proved yourself capable of basic survival. And now the final stage begins where you train twice as hard to prove that you meet the advanced criteria for Qualification. Let me warn you in advance, it's going to be *brutal*. The Finals will take place four weeks from now, at an undisclosed location, and in that time you will have continued your training in Combat, Agility, Atlantis Culture, Atlantis Tech, and a fifth additional track which will involve Water Survival and Swimming."

Waves of stressed whispers travel the crowded space, as Candidates take in this latest news. I can hear people around me start to groan.

"Oh, no . . ." Hasmik says. "I cannot swim very well!"

"You're not alone, girl," Tremaine mutters. "I think this brother's gonna sink."

"Come on, man, don't say that," Jai replies. "We're gonna learn, we'll get better, we have four weeks!" I glance at Jai and notice that his ever-present smile has been toned down recently. Jai looks existentially tired these days, and I think I like him better that way. No more jolly smiling serial killer vibe.

Carlos Villa turns to another Section Leader. This one is

Shontae Smith, an older brown-skinned teen with a do-rag on his head, who picks up and continues: "You will attend five classes every day. And yeah, your schedules will be scanned every morning as previously. But the big difference is, this time you're all working in *teams*. Let me repeat that, you will be divided into teams for a lot of the stuff you have to do! There will be some tasks you do on your own, but others will be counted as group tasks. So yeah, that means that there will be group credit and individual credit. Now, you might wonder what kind of teams I'm talking about. Wonder no more—your Section is your Team! Let me repeat that—your Section, Section Fourteen is your Team! Congratulations, you are now officially Yellow Quadrant Team Fourteen!"

"Great." Laronda looks at us and rolls her eyes. "I always wanted to be drafted."

"Furthermore," Shontae says, "you all will be assigned points. Each one of you gets one hundred starting points. In order to pass the Finals, you will need to have *over* one hundred points at the *end* of the Finals Day."

Carlos speaks again. "Now, let me explain points. Starting today, every Candidate is assigned points that can be reduced with demerits, or increased with credits, at the discretion of your Instructors, for the four weeks of training. You can check your points total every day when you get your ID tokens scanned. That sum total is what you take with you into the Finals. And you will have the chance to earn additional points during the actual Finals competition. However, during the Finals, your accumulated points become *your personal property*. You can decide to keep them all in order to Qualify. Or, you can share them with others—let's say, if you have more than enough. For example, a portion of your points, or the entirety, can be transferred to the team as a whole or to other individual team members."

Hands shoot up. "What does that mean, exactly?" a boy asks.

"It means, that during Finals, your remaining points are to do with as you please. More details will be given on the day. But for now you need to be aware how *important* these points are. And you also need to know that your fellow team members and their Qualification chances are important too, and there is a *team score* that will make a final difference to your fate."

"Sounds insanely complicated," Dawn whispers to us.

Laronda again rolls her eyes and puts up her hand. "Girl, don't even begin. I am trying to tune out most of this baloney right now before I go craaaaay-zee."

Section Leader Gina Curtis—our own former DL—picks up where the others leave off. "Okay, now we need to talk about Water Survival and Swimming, or Water SAS for short as we've come to call it. There are three huge, twice as long as Olympic-size and extra-wide swimming pools located in each of the Common Area structures. Your Water SAS classes will be held there, and during Homework Hour you may practice swimming there. You may also practice swimming in the smaller pools that are located in all the dorms—up to you, first come, first served. Your Instructors will give you more info on that in class. If you have any questions, come talk to any one of us later, individually. And now, we're done! Please get your ID tokens scanned for your daily schedules. Your first class starts in fifteen minutes!"

Fifteen minutes later, I am standing at the edge of a truly immense and long pool located inside the CA-3 structure. Yeah, lucky me, I got Water SAS as my first class, and none of my friends did. . . .

The pool is rippling gently, throwing off pale aqua shadows against tiles, and the enclosed roof overhead is a translucent ceiling many feet above, letting in a diluted amount of sunshine through tempered shaded glass.

About forty more Candidates are gathered here, and we are all wearing unisex swimming trunks, with the addition of tank tops for the girls. No pretty swimsuits or bikinis here. We grab whatever we're given in the back of the hall at the showers and lockers section. And what we're given is this plain grey colored stuff, probably made of the same orichalcum fabric as our regular uniforms.

Our Instructor is a tall willowy Atlantean with the usual metallic gold hair who introduces himself as Qurume Ateni. However, his blond mane is gathered behind him in a tight multi-segmented ponytail that resembles a loose braid.

"Good morning!" he tells us in a pleasant tenor voice, getting right down to business. "First thing you must do is put your hair up if it's long. Tie it, braid it, do whatever you need to get it out of your face. Otherwise you will end up tangled in your own seaweed."

So, I think, *the guy has a sense of humor.* That's a first.

"What about swimming caps?" a younger girl with long blond waves asks.

Qurume glances at her and raises one dark brow. "What about them? There are a few swimming caps available in the back, but not for people with hair as long as yours. Get it tied, or better yet, get it shaved. In fact, shave every square inch of your body, and then come back here when you're sufficiently aerodynamic."

"No!" the girl exclaims with a frightened look.

"Relax," the Atlantean says. "You can do absolutely nothing and still take this class." And then he winks at her with a shadow smile.

Yes, this guy *definitely* has a sense of humor.

"First thing we'll do today is discover how well you can swim. You will simply do a lap all the way down the length of this pool. The pool stretches for one hundred meters, so there's plenty of time for you to collapse and drown and clear out a lane for the next person."

"Jeez, what a jerk . . ." someone whispers behind me.

I turn and there's Zoe! She's standing right behind me, and smiling. I instantly flash back to Los Angeles, and my mouth parts, and my jaw probably drops.

I am so insanely *glad* to see her. . . . But because I pause and freeze like a dork, Zoe cranes her head and whispers, "Gwen! Remember me, Zoe? It's Zoe Blatt!"

"Zoe!" I whisper back. "Of course! I am so glad you're okay, you made it!"

"Yeah, me too!"

Meanwhile the Instructor continues talking, ignoring our loud whispers even though I am pretty sure he heard us. "As you can see, there are twelve lanes. You will enter the pool twelve people at a time, so please line up before each springboard." He pauses, and this time he throws Zoe and me a sarcastic glance, then moves on to extend the disdain to the rest of us.

"As far as swimming stroke," he continues, "do whatever you

can. Use whatever style you feel most comfortable with. Or don't. I am just as interested in observing you at your worst stroke possible, even if it is your only one. Which is to say, I am not interested at all, but here we are. . . . You must swim and I must teach you."

The Atlantean's mouth quivers and he maintains his deadpan expression.

A few minutes later we're all splashing in the water.

And then for the rest of the hour we do some long, boring freestyle laps to build endurance. Qurume walks along the edges of the pool, back and forth, and looks at us closely, giving occasional form and breathing advice and comments, which turn out to be very astute.

This guy definitely knows what he's doing.

Good thing I don't suck at swimming. Because there's plenty of homework laps to do later, and that takes strength and a huge amount of resources.

Meanwhile, there are still four other classes to go, and I am already exhausted.

Chapter 44

The rest of the day at the NQC is not particularly different from the RQC Semi-Finals training, except for the difference in location, scope, and individual Instructors. Suffice it to say that by the time dinner hour comes around, I am tired and starving.

I meet up with Laronda, Dawn, Hasmik, Zoe, and a few others to eat in one of the ten cafeterias scattered throughout the first floor terminal area of our Yellow Quadrant dorm. Zoe is in Section Thirty-Nine, so she would have to make a minor hike to meet us at our own nearest cafeteria. We decide to compromise and aim for a cafeteria that's halfway between our Section and hers.

As we mill around downstairs below Fourteen, waiting for a few more people before we head out to eat, I see Blayne's wheelchair roll out of an elevator.

"I'll be right back!" I say to Dawn, and then quickly walk toward him.

"Blayne!" I say, stopping before him. "Hey! Good to see you made it!"

The boy tosses his hair back out of his face and looks up. "Hey yourself, Lark. You're alive. . . . Obviously." But he has a lively expression. Since our training sessions with Aeson Kass, Blayne has taken on Aeson's way of addressing me by my last name, and I find it kind of comforting.

"Yeah, it was touch and go there toward the end." I make a snorting sound. "L.A. almost killed me. So, what city did you do yours in?"

"My personal hell was in Denver," Blayne says calmly. "I chose it figuring I'd get mountains and heights, and hence more chance of flying at high altitude as opposed to being on foot. Which would have been the end of it for me."

"Wow. I can imagine. . . ."

"Well, no, you probably can't imagine it, not really, but I'll humor you." He gives me a crooked smile.

"So how was it?"

"Peaches and cream. No, it blew chunks the size of the Rockies. *Literally*. We were taken to the mountains and had to contend with sonic-boom-induced man-made avalanches. Yeah, those damn Atlanteans and their sound tech. . . . Overall, after hearing what kind of obstacles they had in the other cities, I still think I made the right choice—I'm here, aren't I? By the way, I did beat out three guys for one hoverboard, using, amazingly enough, the LM Forms. Happened right at the get-go when they unloaded us from the shuttles and suddenly it was all 'Lord of the Flies' meets the Battle for Helm's Deep. Not even five minutes in, I think they ate a guy. . . . Anyway, if I hadn't, I'd be screwed. The hoverboard saved my ass . . . and the rest of me."

"That's so cool you made it!"

"Yeah, amazing." He smirks. "I'm pretty stoked about it myself."

Is there just a hint of sarcasm there? I never know, with Blayne. The boy oozes sarcasm and dry commentary, so probably, yeah.

We pause, and there's one awkward moment during which I want to say more things, while he just kind of looks at the wall or the people walking by.

"A bunch of us—we're going to eat at Cafeteria Five," I say at last. "I'd ask you to come with, but not sure you want to deal with rolling all that extra distance. Do you? Wanna come? Cause that would be great, if you like—"

Blayne cranes his neck slightly. His expression is slightly closed up, proud, calm, as he considers me. "Maybe another time, Lark. But—thanks for the invite."

And with that he turns away and starts rotating the wheels with his hands in his quick easy manner. I notice he's bulked up even more and his strong arms show it.

I sigh and return to where Dawn and Laronda are waiting for Hasmik and Tremaine to show.

In that moment I hear someone yelling my name. I turn and there's a petite brown-haired girl with a red token running toward me, whom I vaguely recognize as Mia Weston from Red Dorm Five back in Pennsylvania—she hung out with Gracie.

"Gwen . . . Gwen Lark!" she barely manages to gasp out, and I see she's struggling for breath. "Your sister! Oh my God! You need to come! Grace has been arrested! These Correctors showed up and took her away just now! She was just—she was—she told me to run and get you—"

Mia stops, then bends over to catch her breath, while I suddenly grow very, very cold and my own breath stops.

It just cuts off. . . .

And then my heart *restarts* with a crazy lurch. Temples start pounding, and I breathe in with a shudder and exclaim, "What? Where? Where is she?"

"Come!" Mia cries. "She's being taken to CA-2 . . . there's a correctional facility there in the back of CA-2 . . . it's right near the airfield."

Which means it's all the way at the end of the compound, two miles away.

I start running.

A s Mia and I—followed by Dawn and Laronda—cut through several huge building structures, then race past the foot traffic along the street that stretches between Green Quadrant Dorm and CA-2, Mia tells me in short gasps what happened.

Gracie was at her girls' dormitory floor in Red Section Fourteen. She was about to come down to eat with Mia and a few others, when suddenly four Correctors and several guards came in, and there was a Section lockdown. That's when five people got arrested—three guys, and another girl, and Gracie.

Apparently, after the Semi-Finals, some of the sore loser Candidates who did not advance, went to the Atlantis Central Agency authorities and confessed to being a party to the sabotage of the shuttles at Pennsylvania RQC-3. And they named names.

All names.

Why did they do it? Probably because it was a last-ditch effort to get rescued, a kind of twisted attempt at getting a plea-bargain— information in exchange for Qualification. Or maybe, they were just dumb enough to think that they would be incarcerated on Atlantis, and get to escape the asteroid apocalypse in exchange for life in prison. Or maybe it was just pure malice. . . .

In any case, Gracie was named as one of the secondary conspirators, one of the Candidates who handled and passed one of the navigation chips around.

The Correctors took Grace Lark and Becca Marlin, the other guilty girl, away. At the same time, other Correctors were arresting the three guilty boys, one dorm floor below.

Gracie had barely time to cry out to Mia to get me—or get our brother George—before they took her away in handcuffs.

"Oh crap, oh crap, oh crap," I keep muttering, as I run. "Did they say where exactly she is being held? Or what will they do to her?"

Mia shakes her head, barely keeping up with me. "Not sure—but I think she may be Disqualified."

Oh, crap!

A bout twenty minutes later, staggering and gasping for air, we arrive at the end of the long CA-2 building. The glass walkway leads us into a rear portion of the building that is dedicated Atlantean office space on all four floors, while the correctional facility space begins in the very back, its end wall facing the huge airfield.

I burst through the double doors and into the short sterile lobby with a guard behind a glassed-off security area. He stops me with a calm glance away from his computer screen.

"I must see my sister, Grace Lark!" I exclaim. "She was arrested, and I need to talk to someone in charge *right now!*"

"Your name?

"Gwen Lark!"

The guard gives me a scrutiny then looks away and checks his console. I hear the keystrokes he makes through the crazy pounding in my head.

A moment later he looks up. "Grace Lark has been detained until tomorrow morning when she will be taken from this compound together with the other Disqualified Candidates."

"What?"

"I believe her belongings are being picked up right now. Fortunately for her, her charges were secondary, so she will not be prosecuted by the ACA, simply discharged to return home."

"*No!*" I exclaim, while my throat starts closing up with the pressure of tears. "No! She cannot be Disqualified! She can't be! This is just—*no!* I must talk to *someone* right now! She is *twelve!* She's just a stupid little kid who made a bad mistake! She is not a terrorist, she didn't even know what she was doing! Look, she was trying to impress a boy! That's all! Just an idiotic prank! She has no idea about any of this—"

"I am really sorry, Candidate," the guard interrupts my tirade, and his gaze softens slightly seeing what a mess I am. "But your sister—she has committed a serious criminal act that is punishable. There's nothing I can do, she broke the law."

"Is there any—any kind of thing—or process—or *anything* that exists to—to—"

I find that I am crying. . . .

Tears are running down my face and my nose is full of snot, and suddenly I can't *see* anything. . . . Someone's gentle hand presses against my back lightly—Mia? Laronda?

I stand, taking in deep shuddering breaths while the guard watches me kindly. *He might have kids of his own*, it occurs to me, *he probably knows what it's like. . . .*

"If you want to come and see your sister tomorrow morning around eight AM, before they put her on the shuttle bus, that should be okay," he says.

I take in another deep shuddering breath and I stop crying.

A wall of silence slams down.

"No," I say. And my voice is suddenly very steady. It belongs to someone else.

I wipe my face with the back of my hand and look at the guard with a dead expression.

"No, *I do not accept this*. I demand to see Command Pilot Aeson Kass."

Chapter 45

The guard's previously sympathetic expression closes up and he looks at me as though now I've become an annoyance.

"Okay, what?" he says.

"I must see Command Pilot Aeson Kass!" I repeat. "The one they call Phoebos!"

The guard looks at me for several long seconds. "You do know what you're asking?" he says coldly. "That's a very busy man, very high ranking in the Atlantean Fleet. He isn't going to have time to talk to you, especially not now—"

"Look, he *knows* me, okay! Command Pilot Kass knows me, and he *will* talk to me!"

How do I know this, I have no idea. But I persist, with the full confidence fueled by insanity that comes from desperation. Will Aeson agree to see me? It occurs to me, I don't really know. I might be overreaching. But at the same time, there's a strange feeling in my gut that no, *I am an asset*, my Logos voice and I. . . . And Aeson Kass *will* give me the time of day.

As the guard continues to stare at me with a growing frown, I hurry to add: "Look, just tell him my name, please! He will agree to see me, you'll see! Just call him now! *Please!*"

The guard shakes his head, and lets out his breath in frustration. He then presses one hand to the smart-set in his ear and punches something on the console. After a few seconds, he turns to me and says, "Okay . . . Command Pilot Kass is currently unavailable. Sorry, Candidate."

"What do you mean, *unavailable?*" My mouth falls open. I suppose I expected to get some kind of instant response, at least an answer of one kind or another, but—nothing?

"I mean, he is unavailable."

"But how? Maybe you can ask again? Where is he? I will go

to his office right now—"

The guard shakes his head at me. "He is unavailable because he is not *here*—not in this compound, not on Earth." And he points with a finger up.

The meaning finally dawns on me. "Oh . . ." I say in despair. "He's gone up to the Atlantis mothership."

The despair deepens. I freeze for a few seconds in silence, my mind spinning, while Laronda and Mia and Dawn stand watching me with grim sympathetic eyes.

"When—when is he coming back?" I try again.

"That information is unavailable."

"Can you please check?"

"His personal schedule is outside my clearance level." The guard looks at me hard.

"Okay . . ." Desperation makes me relentless. "But—"

"Candidate—Gwen, is it? Candidate, you need to leave now. There is nothing more I can tell you. I am very sorry."

"I—I don't accept that," I repeat again like a stubborn idiot. And then more wild ideas pop in my head.

"What—what is his office? Where is it? Is it here in this building?" I say. "It *is* general knowledge, isn't it?"

The guard bites his lip. "Yes, it is. Office #7, CA-2, first floor. You can get to it if you go outside and then use the next walkway entrance for the general offices. But again, he is *not* here—"

"But he *will* be, tomorrow morning! Right? *Right?* He'll be there eventually?" I interrupt in a high breathy voice that is again about to crack with tears.

The guard shakes his head again, and then softens up. "All right, yes, he will be here tomorrow. This is not his specific schedule, but *in general*—he is usually here by seven AM local time, sometimes as early as six-thirty. But again, no guarantees. He may not even show up—"

"Okay . . ." I say, crying once again. "That helps very much, thank you. *Thank you!*"

The guard only nods, but already I've turned away, and I am walking out of the front lobby.

I stop as soon as I'm outside, and stare into the early twilight, taking shuddering breaths.

"I am so sorry," Laronda says, holding my shoulder. Dawn is right there too.

Mia watches me. "What are you going to do?"

I wipe my face with the back of my hand and look at them. "I don't know. . . . No, I *do* know. I'll go to his office. I will wait there all night if I have to. And I will talk to him—Aeson Kass. Even if I have to go and wait at the airfield. . . ."

"Want me to go look for your brother George?" Dawn mutters.

I nod, silently.

"Want me to get you some food, girl?" Laronda squeezes my shoulder.

"No thanks, not hungry. But—thanks."

"You need to eat something! It's gonna be a long wait. And then there's the sucky ten PM curfew, what will you do? If you don't make it back to our dorm—"

"I—don't know," I say again, hearing only partially what is being said around me, as I stare ahead and up at the darkening clear sky. There are a few stars out already, and I wonder if any of them are *their ships*, up in orbit.

Aeson Kass is up there right now.

He has Gracie's fate in his hands.

A few minutes later, I am in the large business office area of CA-2. Laronda and Dawn have gone, to get George, to get me food—Laronda insisted—and Mia went back to Gracie's dorm to see what's happening there.

After inquiring at the front desk, I am told that Office #7 is right around the corner and down the hall, one of the first ones on this floor, which is the VIP area.

"But, we are closing for the night, hon, and sorry, but you cannot stay here," a woman guard tells me. I need to lock up this floor. The Atlanteans work late sometimes, but we cannot have any unauthorized personnel here—"

In a dead voice I explain to her what has happened with my sister. And then, "I am just going to wait in front of his office, until Command Pilot Aeson Kass comes in," I say. "I can sit on the floor. Please!"

But the woman shakes her head. "I'm really sorry, we cannot let anyone stay here after hours, not without permission—"

"But he knows me!"

"Sorry, no, we can't do that. Go on now, dear, come back first thing tomorrow morning. . . ."

I turn around and exit the building.

And then I start pacing at the front entrance.

My mind is an absolute, swirling, numb mess. I—the girl who always comes up with solutions—I suddenly have none.

I don't know how much time goes by, and then I see the entrance doors open and someone exit. Probably an office employee or guard, leaving for the night.

I glance up with a clouded gaze, and it's Nefir Mekei. I recognize his somewhat shorter-trimmed metallic hair and Atlantean features, the slightly blunt chin with a dimple, and his skin tone that's the dark red hue of river clay.

My Atlantis Culture Instructor from Pennsylvania!

He pauses, looking directly at me, and then there's recognition. "Candidate Gwen Lark!" he says with a shadow of a smile. "Glad to see you passed Semi-Finals."

"Oh, Instructor Mekei!" I exclaim. "Please, maybe you can help me! It is urgent, I need to see Command Pilot Aeson Kass!"

And then I explain to him what happened.

Nefir listens to me with an expression that is so hard to read, as always. And then he nods. "I don't have a direct line for him, but a general one to his command deck. I will relay a message to Command Pilot Kass for you. He may not get the message until tomorrow morning, when the regular ship-to-ground relays are opened, but at least it will be there waiting for him."

"Thank you!" I say. "Thank you *so much!*"

Nefir takes out some kind of gadget, and then punches what looks like Atlantean text into it. I recognize the strange hieroglyphic-and-phonetic-alphabet hybrid that is Atlantean script, which looks remotely like Ancient Egyptian and Sanskrit rolled into one. In moments he is done, and hits their equivalent of "send."

If I weren't in such a state of mind right now, I might have gotten a kick out of seeing someone texting into orbit.

Instead I nod, looking at him numbly.

"It's done, Gwen," Nefir says. "Now I suggest you get back to your dorm and get some rest, and then come back here in the morning. Six-thirty to seven should be a good time to catch him. Kass is never late."

I thank him again, and start walking.

Overhead, twilight has deepened into night, but down here it is dispelled by the bright street illumination of the compound.

The rest of the night is a mess. I remember almost none of it, only that I get back to my dorm and go directly to bed. I don't think Dawn ever finds George. And Laronda leaves a small plate of food next to my cot before heading over to her own that's on the other end of the large girls' dormitory hall of Section Fourteen.

I wake up with a start, just before dawn, and get dressed in the dark, pull my hair into a messy ponytail, then slip out and downstairs, then outside.

The sky is turning to pale silver on the eastern edges, as I quickly walk through the street. Soon, my walk turns into a jog. I run in the crisp dawn air, and in about fifteen minutes I am back at the farthest end of CA-2.

It's just after 6:00 AM. . . . Should I risk checking the airfield first? His shuttle might be landing soon.

Or maybe I need to head directly to the offices and wait at the door of Office #7. . . .

I grow still for a few instants of painful indecision. And then I decide not to waste any time and head directly to the airfield.

Around the corner, the CA-2 structure ends. Immediately beyond the building is an open street space and then the endless row of hangars begin, interrupted only every hundred feet or so with alley passageways between each structure. On the other side of the hangars, the airfield stretches into an immense paved expanse fading in the distance into a tall imposing wall that marks the edges of the NQC compound.

I pause again, considering my next move. Should I linger here and watch for *his* arrival, or advance forward and walk through the hangars?

To my luck, as I watch the lightening skies, already I can see several Atlantean shuttles approaching. They fall from heaven—

grey pinpoint specks that resolve into vaguely oval saucer shapes—and their purple plasma underbellies glitter like cabochon jewels.

Please be on one of them, please be on one of them, I chant silently.

I walk quickly forward, moving through the narrow walkway space between two nearest hangars, past a solitary guard who glances at me but does not stop me.

The first of the shuttles lands, then hovers lightly several feet above the ground, but does not pull inside the hangar. It is one of the smaller models, exactly like the one I entered on that fateful day of the sabotage explosion. . . .

I hold my breath, clutching my fingers until my knuckles are bloodless with tension.

This has to be his, I tell myself. It's the one closest to his office. It would make sense he would park it here.

The shuttle hatch opens and the auto-stairs descend. It's open in the opposing side facing the airfield, so all I can see are booted feet descending, then someone coming around.

A man emerges, and I can see long metallic blond hair, but it is not *he*—the armband is red, and the face, when he turns toward me, is Atlantean but unfamiliar. Meanwhile more people descend, and I stare as two pairs of booted feet come down.

The next one is a woman, also Atlantean, tall, slender, typically beautiful, but not anyone I have seen before. She wears a green armband.

The third man is Aeson Kass.

My heart does a very painful, hard, extreme lurch, so that my throat closes up, and at the same time it feels like I am going into cardiac arrest. . . .

I see him come around, with his usual controlled and confident posture. I see the crisp lines of his uniform, the fall of his pale metallic hair, and the half-turned lean jaw-line with its hollowed cheeks and darkness of kohl-outlined lapis-blue eyes and dark brows.

Once again the crazy myth-thought comes to me, *he is Phoebos Apollo descended from the skies in his divine chariot. . . .*

And then Phoebos raises his face and looks directly at me.

For a moment he pauses.

And then his face becomes like stone, and he walks toward me.

At the same time I start to race toward him, meeting him halfway from the hangar to the shuttle. And then I stop right before him, breathing hard, and I know my eyes, my expression, it is absolutely crazed, wild. . . .

"Command Pilot Kass!" I exclaim. "Please, I must speak to you! It is urgent! It is about my sister—"

"Candidate Lark." His cool voice interrupts me. "I received your message."

"Oh, thank God!" I find that I am trembling.

"We'll talk in my office."

Aeson nods to the other two Atlanteans, curtly acknowledges the guard's greeting, and begins to walk quickly toward the CA-2 building. I hurry at his side, barely able to keep up with his long stride.

We move in absolute silence, crossing the short distance to the offices, and he never once looks at me but stares directly ahead, while I throw quick desperate glances at him, and also say nothing.

It's as if, for some reason, all of a sudden, cat's got my tongue. . . .

We walk through the front area lobby, past the guard—a different one—who buzzes the security glass door open as soon as he recognizes Aeson Kass. I follow him, almost stumbling on the anti-static floor mat because I am not watching my feet.

At the doors of Office #7, Aeson takes out a key card and opens the door.

"Come," he tells me, flipping on the overhead lights. I see basic office space with various consoles similar to what he had back in Pennsylvania, except there is no lounge area here, nowhere to sit but his one high-backed chair behind a wide desk. The console panels line the walls behind him. It's basically a desk inside a machine room.

I take a step inside.

"Close the door," he says.

I do as I'm told, and then turn toward him and stand with my hands at my sides, shaking with fine tremors. My hands—what a horrible betrayal of me. . . .

I am suddenly terrified.

Aeson Kass goes to his desk and sits down in the chair. He leans forward, puts his hands on the desk surface, palms down.

What surprises me, in that surreal moment of intensity, is that I can sense *he is tense* also, by the way he holds his hands—straight, composed, under such an excess of control.

Too much control.

"Speak," he says. And he looks directly at me.

I begin to talk. Strange halting words come out of me, stumbling phrases. . . . Logic out of order . . . a torrent. "My sister Gracie—Grace Lark—she is only twelve, and she is an *idiot*. I mean, a complete little fool, trying to impress a boy. She did not mean—she is just a kid who screwed up, was part of a prank that went horribly wrong—no, okay, I mean she wasn't really part of it, of anything. She just made the wrong decision, and she is completely innocent—"

"Innocent?" Aeson Kass interrupts me and his voice cuts like a blade. "Innocent implies true ignorance. I reviewed the circumstances of her case just now, and she knew *exactly* what she was doing. Her Disqualification is the direct result of her criminal action."

"But she is just a *stupid little* twelve year old girl! A kid! I swear to you, she did not mean to harm anyone!" I exclaim, and my voice starts to lose its resilience. . . . I feel a painful lump gathering, and I know that in seconds I am going to crack, and I am going to bawl. "That chip—she only handled it after getting it from someone else—someone who was really responsible! She dropped it in Laronda Aimes's pocket, and she didn't even think how much trouble it would cause for everyone. Can't you see that it was not malice? It was *not* intentional! You cannot Disqualify her for something like that! She does not deserve such—"

"Do you know how many other teens—kids just as young as your sister, and far more deserving—have been Disqualified already, when they simply did not pass the Semi-Finals? And what about all those millions of younger children who did not meet the age requirements for Qualification? Or the older ones? Or the rest of the adult population of your Earth? What have any of *them* done to *deserve* being excluded from rescue and left behind to *die?*" Aeson speaks with measured precision. His eyes are tragic.

"*No one* deserves to die!" I say in a voice that ends on a whisper. "And yes, I *know*. I know exactly what you're saying. But—this is *my sister*. Do you understand? All justice, all fairness, all comparisons can go flying out the window! Because *I don't care*. All I know is, I am not going to let my sister go, and I will do whatever it takes to save her!"

He looks at me silently, and the intensity between us is unimaginable.

"I am sorry," he says. "There is nothing that can be done. She is Disqualified and she is returning home."

"No," I say, and my voice rises in strength. *"I do not accept that."*

But as soon as I speak, I can feel it—a prickling sensation along the surface of my skin—I can tell something is different.

There is something definitely strange going on. . . . My voice, it sounds *tangible* somehow. As though the acoustics of it cause a ripple in the air and a reverb in the walls.

Aeson Kass frowns. He then turns his head slightly, while his gaze remains locked on mine. It's a strange automatic response, as if he's shaking off an invisible touch. . . .

"Candidate Lark, what did you just do?"

I frown. "I—what?"

"You just used a *compelling* power voice on me?" he says, in amazement and rising anger.

"I don't know what you mean!"

"Oh, I think you do."

And suddenly I do remember, from one of the earliest Atlantis Culture classes—the discussion of various power voices and how they could be used, among other things, to compel others, and how that was considered unethical, not to mention was highly illegal in Atlantis culture.

Aeson Kass narrows his eyes, and his expression closes off completely. "This has gone far enough. We're done." He gets up from his chair and stands before me, pointing to the door.

That's when I begin to tremble. . . . Suddenly I am so light-headed, so impossibly numb with despair. My breathing becomes so shallow that I cannot hear it. At the same time, those same helpless, disgusting, pathetic tears start flowing down my face, and

I am doing it—*bawling* in front of *him* in great big shuddering sobs.

At the sight of it, he blinks. I know him enough by now to know that it is his one and only "tell"—a crack in his perfect armor, an expression of vulnerability. A single blink.

"I am truly sorry," he says quietly.

I continue choking on my tears, and raise my hands to wipe my disgusting face with my sleeves.

"There is also something else," he continues in a strange voice. "Because of this unfortunate incident with your sister coming to light, you are now formally cleared of all charges. . . . There are no more suspicions regarding your actions in this. Therefore, I owe you an apology."

I stop crying. And suddenly I look up. My expression is probably crazed—or blazing—or what you want to call it. "No," I say. "You owe me a *life*."

He blinks again. And then he takes a step toward me.

"That is true . . ." he says softly.

"I saved you from that burning shuttle," I say in a wooden voice drained of all emotion, only driven by single-minded focus.

"Yes. . . ."

"So you *owe* me! A life for a life! Give me my sister's life!"

He exhales suddenly.

I stare up at him, breathing fast, waiting.

There is a long pause. . . .

"Okay," he says unexpectedly, and then returns to his desk. He pushes forward one of the mech arms that extends a console-and-monitor unit, lowering it over his desk surface. And observing the screen, he starts keying in something.

"The Atlantis Central Agency has Disqualified your sister and removed her Candidacy—the entirety of her ID data and all her current points as of yesterday. I cannot reverse the decision, not even with my level of authority, but I can try to reinstate her ID. Grace Lark will be given a new blank ID token and there will be nothing on it, only her name and basic background, vital stats, and residency."

"What—what does that mean?" I whisper.

"It means—" He looks up at me with a serious expression. "It means Grace Lark will have to earn her place from scratch. She will be a 'new' Candidate, with no points and no history. She will be allowed to remain at the National Qualification Center and attend training classes. She will be allowed to participate in the Finals, but without any starting points going in."

"Oh, but then I can give her my points!" I exclaim with a burst of relief.

Aeson Kass shakes his head. "No. You will not be permitted to transfer your points to Grace Lark. It is one thing I will *not* allow. In fact, I will set a safeguard on your ID, so that you will be unable to do that—so that you don't throw your own life away in exchange for hers."

"But what if I *choose* to do that, for her?" I exclaim, as the horrible despair returns.

"I do not permit it," he says. "We need you and your voice—on behalf of Atlantis."

"But it is *my* choice!"

"Not entirely—not if your choice affects far more than you or your sister."

I stare at him, stunned.

He in turn watches me with a careful, unreadable expression.

"But—" I say, as outrage starts to build. "I don't understand! How can you tell me what I can or cannot do with my own life? Don't you have a *heart?* What about basic human compassion? Have you no clue what it's like to stand by and not help your own family—the people you most care about—when you absolutely have the means to do it?"

As I speak, I notice his face takes on a strange new expression. I simply don't know what it is, don't understand it . . . maybe it is not human after all.

He is not human.

"Are you finished?" he says after a terrible pause. His voice has grown low, and very soft, like the slither of a serpent. Its chill makes the fine hairs on my skin stand up in goose bumps.

But like a stupid fool who doesn't know when to stop, I take a step, nearing his desk, and lean forward and exclaim, completing my humiliation entirely, "Please! I'll do anything you want me to do! *Anything!* Just let me help her! Look, I am begging you! Anything you want! Take it! Tell me if there's anything I can do, anything I have that I can give you. . . ?" At this point, even I am not sure what it is I am saying, what it is I am offering him in my desperation. . . .

We face each other at close proximity, our gazes locked in intensity.

"You have *nothing*," he says suddenly, and a faint line of derision comes to his lips. "There is nothing you have that I want."

Once again I am stunned. "What about my Logos voice?"

"Your voice has value for Atlantis, which is already a given. If you Qualify, we have you." He pauses, and again there's that fine subcurrent of disdain. "I thought you were offering something for *me*."

"I—" My words trail off.

He is right, what *am* I saying?

"Look," he says in a milder tone, after that unbearable pause during which my mind is reeling. "You got what you wanted, Lark. I reinstated your sister, and she has a fair chance of earning back most if not all of her points. Under the circumstances, it is absolutely *the best* I can do for her—or for you. In fact, I think you should be grateful right now. What do you say?"

I exhale, as general numbness returns, and I am suddenly worn out, depleted completely, emotionally wrung out. There is nothing of me left here, nothing to offer, nothing to barter with. . . . He is right.

"Thank you," I say.

He nods. "I am glad this is resolved. In the next hour your sister will be discharged, and her belongings returned to her dorm."

"For real?"

"Yes. Now I strongly recommend you get back to your own dorm and schedule. Strange as it may seem, I have other things to deal with than Lark family drama."

I nod, then mutter something that sounds like "Okay."

He watches me as I turn around and move to the door. Just before I step outside, he says, "Before you go—we need to continue your regular voice training. Be here tomorrow night at eight."

Startled, I glance again at him. "But—I thought you have other things to do?"

"Lark," he says. "Just be here at eight."

Chapter 46

On my way back I run into George halfway between the Atlantean offices in CA-2 and Yellow Quadrant Dorm Section Fourteen.

George looks like he's been pulled out of bed, or else he hadn't been to sleep at all, his dark hair standing up in a tousled mess. He is breathing fast from running and his expression is grim. It's the closest to being panicked that I've ever seen my brother be. With him is Logan, equally stressed and serious.

"Gwen! Where's *Gracie?* Where is she?" George cries. "What the hell is happening? What has she done? I can't believe any of this!"

I remember with a minor delay that up to this point George knew nothing about Gracie's involvement in the sabotage incident. I am guessing, he has just been told by Mia and the others in Red Quadrant Dorm, Section Fourteen.

"It's okay! Gracie's okay!" I exclaim in a hurry, putting up my hands in a reassuring gesture. "She will be released! She—they Disqualified her but *he*—Aeson Kass—I talked to him and he somehow reinstated her, so she is being let out soon—"

And then in a jumbled torrent I explain what happened.

George and Logan stand listening to me, and George regains his breathing. "What an absolutely *stupid*, flaming ass!—Oh man, Gracie, what an insane fool! How could she do this thing?"

"I know," I say, and my own temples are pounding from renewed stress. "She's a stupid little idiot and I'm ready to strangle her, but thank God it's going to be okay!"

George shakes his head. "Why on earth would she even do it?"

"Get this—she was trying to impress Daniel Tover!"

"What?" Logan says. "What does Daniel have to do with

this?"

"Apparently nothing." I glance at him. "But Gracie has a little girl crush on him, and she thought she'd look cool or something."

"Great. . . ."

I notice that meanwhile Logan has been staring at me closely, and I am not sure if it's because of what I am saying, or if he is just worried about me.

"Logan," I say with a light smile. "It will be all right. Really!"

"It's amazing that you convinced the hard-ass Atlantean—Kass—to do this for Gracie. Seems to me, he didn't do it so much for Gracie as he did it for *you*."

"Huh?" I say. "I stalked him, begged and pleaded, and gave him every logical—and illogical—argument under the sky. I think I even went a little crazy there, not even sure I remember the insane stuff I said. But in a nutshell I reminded him that I saved him from that burning shuttle, and I think he realized he owes me."

"Well, good," George says. "Because, he does. You saved his Goldilocks ass."

An hour later, when we're back at the dorms, namely Red Quadrant Dorm, Section Fourteen, Gracie shows up.

She looks awful. Her hair is a slept-in mess, jacket barely pulled on, smeared eyeliner and mascara streaks on her cheek. A guard is walking with her, carrying one of her duffel bags, while she has the other, slung over her shoulder.

The moment she sees us, Gracie drops her bag, rushes forward and throws herself silently at me, and then at George. Her hug is so tight that she is choking me. Then George holds her in a bear hug, while she mutters something unintelligible, at the same time as I gently pat down her messy, dirty blond hair, and run my fingers through it in a calming way.

"You're okay, Gee Four . . . all is well . . . you're fine, you made it!" I repeat over and over.

"I am . . . so sorry . . . so sorry!" Gracie keeps repeating, and her face is muffled against George's chest.

"You should start by thanking your sister," George says. "If she hadn't busted her ass to convince the Atlantean VIP to give you another shot, you would be back home by now."

Gracie tears herself away from George and turns to me, and

her eyes are big and brimming with liquid. "Gwen! Thank you, I love you!" she mutters, and then she's back hugging me.

"It's all right, Gracie, all right, sweetie! Love you so much!" I press her against me and feel the little girl skinny body shuddering. "It's *over*," I say. "No more horrible bad moves like that, *ever*, okay?"

She nods. "Okay. . . ."

"Promise me you will never do something like that again. Promise me you will think before you act, and you'll remember why we're here, and what's really going on," George says. "Or I swear, you'll never live it down. I won't let you forget it, brainless ditz! You'll see—"

"I promise!"

We go on like that for the next five minutes, doing the "good parent, bad parent" thing to parallel the "good cop, bad cop" thing they do on TV (Mom and Dad would be proud of us now if they saw us in action), and then we help Gracie settle back in and reclaim her cot and dorm space. Other Reds from her dorm stare at us curiously, as this is all happening. . . . Fine, let them. Neither George nor I care.

"Be smart, Gee Four! Remember, you're a Lark!" we tell her, before we head back to our own scheduled classes that are starting in about five minutes.

As we leave Gracie's dorm, George turns to me, grim and thoughtful. "You think she'll last?" he says softly.

I frown. "She has to. We'll do everything we can to help her regain points." And then I explain to George the full extent of the situation, and how I have been forbidden from giving any of my own points to her.

George exhales and bites his lip. "If it comes down to it, I'll let her have mine," he says.

My heart constricts painfully. I knew that was coming. "Look," I say. "Let's not go there yet, okay? Please . . . I can't lose *you* either!"

"Hey, I hear yah. I can't lose me either," my brother quips bitterly, running his hand through his messy dark hair. But I see the darkness has taken hold in him, and the despair is back—all that despair that's been there all along, simmering under the surface, temporarily eclipsed by the hope that we still had a chance to Qualify, to make it out alive somehow. Because now George knows that even if he Qualified, he still would have to do this thing—the right thing, for our younger sister.

In fact, the whole "points dilemma" has been hanging over all our heads as soon as the situation was explained to us by the Section Leaders on our first day of classes yesterday. Points are now like currency. They can be earned, bartered, given away, et cetera.

I can just imagine the kinds of dealings that will start happening on the day of the Finals when we will finally have full control of our points and the ability to hoard and keep them or to disburse them as we please. . . .

I try to put all this out of my mind as I go to my classes. After my nearly sleepless night and the ordeal with Aeson Kass, I am exhausted, so it's a very long day, followed by a blah evening. It doesn't help that the temperature has been unexpectedly warm, even for mid-spring in the Eastern Plains of Colorado, where most of us suspect we are. The huge dorm structures are air conditioned but not enough to keep up with the unusual balmy weather outside.

The heat doesn't let up overnight, but I'm so tired I manage to sleep anyway. And the next morning I wake with a much clearer head and the beginnings of a plan for Gracie—at least I hope so. Laronda and I make it to breakfast at the closest cafeteria, and there, along with Dawn and a few other people we know, we talk points and teams and what can be expected for the Finals.

"Hey, you gotta remember," Mateo says, chewing his eggs and hash browns. "This thing is going to be unlike anything we can imagine, and it's going to be *international*."

"Oh, yeah," Dawn says. "You're right, easy to forget." And she rolls her eyes.

"No, really. Actually it *is*." Mateo takes another big bite and continues seriously. "I mean, think about it, we all know what's coming, and that the competition is only getting tougher and tougher, and that now the odds are fifty-fifty, and only *half* of the Candidates in this NQC are going to Qualify. But that's just still old thinking, as in, only all of us, United States. Now we have to deal with everyone else on this frigging planet!"

Now that he says it, it does kind of hit home.

"Well, let's think for a moment, what are we training for—endurance, power, fighting skills, general Atlantis tech and social knowledge," I say. "And now, they've added swimming—all the Water SAS stuff. Put it all together, and up the odds on an international scale, and what does that imply?"

"I'm thinking, a big-ass ocean," Tremaine says. "And hey, maybe the Atlantic, cause, you know, Atlantis?"

"Hey, you're kind of a smarty-pants too." Laronda turns to him and tugs the long sleeve of his uniform around the arm. It has fresh sweat stains on it—as all of ours do, because, yeah, it's hot. . . .

"So, we're gonna be what, swimming across the Atlantic?" Jai says with a sigh and a widening of his eyes. "That would majorly suck."

"Not to mention that would be kind of impossible," Tremaine mutters.

"Hey, man, with our Atlantean overlords, nothing is impossible." And Jai flashes his white teeth in a world-weary grin.

After a grueling day of Combat, Agility, Tech, and Culture, swimming is almost kind of a relief from the muggy heat. Today we meet at a different giant larger-than-Olympic pool, this one located in the CA-2 structure, because we are doing mixed swimming with the Green Quadrant Dorm. Our last class for the day is a combination of team swim relays plus handling weapons in the water—Green shields and Yellow nets.

So yeah, we get to learn how to spar in the water.

Zoe is once more in my class, and as we splash around, I explain to her what happened the other day and why I didn't show up for dinner, because of the Gracie situation.

"Less talking, and more floating," Instructor Qurume Ateni tells us in his deadpan manner as he walks past us on our side of the pool. "Naturally, you may carry on doing whatever it is you are doing, as soon as I am on the other side and cannot see you." And then he keeps moving.

Which we in fact do—as soon as he is out of hearing, Zoe tells me she's sorry about Gracie's close call with Disqualification and relieved she is okay after all.

"Wow! How did you ever convince Command Pilot Aeson Kass himself to give your sister a second chance?"

"It's a long story," I exclaim, splashing her as I cast my net weapon at the approaching opposite team swimmers with green tokens who use their shields as flotation devices.

"I bet!" Zoe says with a laugh, splashing me back as she tosses her lasso weapon in turn. "But then I should know you're always kind of full of surprises!"

Soon, Water SAS class is over, and okay, I admit it, it was actually *fun*. What a weird thing to say about any aspect of Qualification. But we've all been so stressed and tired for so long that swimming seems to really work well for most of us—except for those of us who could not swim before, and are getting a crash course now. . . .

A fter class, I make plans with Zoe to attempt dinner once more, and maybe introduce her to my other friends.

"How about, see you at the cafeteria closest to this pool in an hour?" I say as we turn in our Quadrant weapons and get dressed at the lockers. "That way, after dinner we can use Homework Hour for messing around in the pool again, and yeah, okay, some laps?"

I don't bother to disclose the fact that I also have to see Aeson Kass at 8:00 PM tonight, and it's right here in the CA-2 building. I can sneak off for half an hour and then come back and get in the pool afterwards.

Zoe agrees, and so I hurry back to my Yellow Section Fourteen to round up some people while she goes in the other direction toward Section Thirty-Nine.

When I get back to my Section, Logan is down in the "airport terminal area" first floor lobby, waiting for me. He is leaning casually against the wall, and I watch his sleek powerful body as he comes toward me. Glancing into his hazel eyes, I get the familiar warm jolt of electricity.

"Gwen!" he says with a smile. "Hey, Yellow Candy, I've been meaning to see you. Classes have been insane, or I'd have been here for lunch."

"Logan!" I hurry to approach him.

He immediately pulls me by the hand and we come closer,

slide against each other body-on-body and *almost* touch—not quite but almost, because again, surveillance cameras are everywhere and there is still the "No Dating" rule being enforced.

"I *really* miss you . . ." he whispers in my ear, leaning in casually as though to adjust my uniform collar, as his hair brushes against my cheek.

Oh, how badly I want him to hold me! And how much I want to just reach out and run my fingers against his arms, his chest, his soft wavy hair. . . . My skin is prickling with goose bumps, and it's not the heat of the late afternoon, but the heat that's rising between us, as we stand in such impossible near proximity, tantalizing each other with our bodies.

"Hey . . ." I say, looking up into his eyes, while my own are in a dreamy haze. . . . And then I tell him about the dinner and then swimming plans.

"Oh—forgot to mention, I still have to see Command Pilot Kass at eight, for the voice training, again," I add.

Logan's expression immediately hardens. "Oh, yeah? Did he—tell you this when you were seeing him about Gracie?"

"Yeah."

Logan exhales then nods. "Okay. Then you do that." But he glances away and looks cool suddenly. . . .

"What?" I mutter. "What's wrong?"

"Nothing," he says. But I can tell he is upset somehow.

And suddenly it occurs to me in that bizarre moment, *Is it possible that Logan is jealous?*

WTF? Seriously? My mind is reeling.

"Logan!" I say. "Hey! You know I *have* to go see him, for my voice! Remember? It's not a *choice!*"

"Of course, I know." He glances at me briefly, and there is something odd and vulnerable in the way his eyes meet mine for just an instant, before he again looks away. "But I still don't have to like it."

Logan *is* jealous!

I am absolutely amazed! And at the same time, I feel a weird perverse stab of pleasure. It is wrong of me, but it's what I feel, just for a moment. . . .

And then I tell him softly about the pool, as a kind of reward.

"Afterwards," I say, in my most ridiculous attempt at a *seductive* voice, "when the voice training stuff is over, and I get out of there, I will see you at the pool . . . in all that sweet cool water. . . ." I briefly run my fingertips over his hand.

At my feather-light touch, I can feel him shudder slightly. *Okay, wow.* I did not expect that. . . .

And then he looks directly at me, and this time his gaze locks onto mine with intensity, and the hazel eyes are very, very dark, his pupils wide. "Do you know that normal surveillance cameras are not going to see very reliably what's happening underwater. . . ?" he whispers.

"I know," I whisper back, feeling a slow, strange, languid pulse-beat awakening in my head. "And there's very little chance that there are underwater cameras, though with the Atlanteans we never know."

His lips curve up sensuously. "I think we can risk it. . . ."

"I think so too." And I smile also.

My lord, I am flirting!

Chapter 47

After a large and loud group dinner in a huge and noisy CA-2 cafeteria, during which Zoe Blatt gets to know my friends and we exchange Semi-Finals horror stories, we all make a beeline for the nearby pool. However, it's seven forty-five, so Logan and I excuse ourselves, and pretend we're going for a brief walk together.

"Hey! No fooling around, you two!" Laronda wags her finger at me and Logan. "Remember, they catch you, you be screwed, but not the way you'd like to be, if you know what I mean—"

"Oh, shut up, jeez!" I say with a grin.

And then Logan and I head outside, walk down the street briefly and find the glassed-in walkway that leads to the Atlantean offices section.

"What will you do while I go in there?" I say, pausing with him before the lobby entrance. "It'll be at least half an hour."

He shrugs with a brief smile, putting hands in his pockets. "No worries. I'll find something to do."

And then he turns and saunters down the street into the balmy night, waving at me.

"See you soon!" I yell back.

And then I go inside.

I tell the guard in the front secure area I am here for an appointment to see Command Pilot Kass, and he only asks my name, then buzzes me right through.

At the door of Office #7 I pause momentarily. Already my pulse is starting its familiar pounding race in my temples—ragged and wild and dangerous, in contrast to the languid sensuality I've just experienced with Logan. . . .

I knock, then hear *his* calm voice. "Come in."

I open the door and a blast of slightly cooler air hits me. I see the now familiar machine room office, and Aeson is sitting at his desk.

His face is weary and dispassionate as he stares at a console screen, half-turned from me. But as I enter, he looks up immediately. I notice the slightly damp tendrils of his metallic gold hair and a sheen of sweat at his temples.

"Lark, it's you—good," he says, as his dark blue eyes immediately overwhelm me with their unblinking regard. And after a tiny pause, "How is your sister?"

"She's okay, thanks," I reply, and my voice sounds teeny and uncertain. "She is—doing her best, I suppose."

"Come on in, come closer." He motions with his hand.

I take two steps, and then there's his desk.

There's no other chair in the room.

I think he only realizes it just now. It occurs to me, he must not have many visitors in this relatively small crowded office. Else there would be another seat?

"Well. . . . There's nowhere for you to sit, Lark, sorry about that." He raises one brow, in an expression that comes closest to minor amusement I have ever seen him display. "For now, you may sit on the end here, if you like." And he pats the surface of his desk lightly. "I'll have a chair for you next time."

I bite my lip and then use my hands to lift myself up. I perch on top of his desk, at the end farthest from him. My legs dangle down. Good thing I am wearing the baggy uniform pants. It feels surreal, and for that reason I forget to be uncomfortable.

"Let's get to work," he says, looking away as he reaches for a small box in a drawer under the desk, which I recognize as an orichalcum sound damper box—a soundproof container that neutralizes the effect of keying on orichalcum objects.

"You know what this is?"

I nod.

"Open it, and take out a piece."

I do as he says, opening the box and seeing several small pieces of orichalcum inside. I pick one out and take it.

Aeson watches my movements as I sit on the desk, and my legs and feet dangle involuntarily. "Now, close the box. Then set an Aural Block on this piece, so that no one can again key it. If I recall, you had much success with setting Aural Blocks back in Los Angeles."

"Oh, yes," I mutter. And then I clear my throat and sing the complex sequence to key the orichalcum to me and make it obey no one else.

"All done," I say almost proudly, while the orichalcum piece hovers in the air in front of me, now my little perfectly obedient servant.

Aeson looks at me, craning his neck slightly. "So, you think this piece is now impervious to anyone's commands?"

"Well, it should be—at least that's what I've been told. And what I saw happen in practice. So, yeah."

In reply he parts his chiseled lips and sings a very strange intensely piercing tone that combines in it a low rumbling vibrato.

The sound is so rich, so tangible, so *awful* somehow, that it scrapes along the surface of my skin. . . .

And the next instant my "perfect little servant" piece emits a brief flash and falls down, inert and dead, on the surface of the desk. It also appears far more dull in color than normal orichalcum—the usual patina of gold flecks is missing from the charcoal grey.

"Oh!" I say. "What just happened?"

"It's fried." Aeson makes a light sound similar to a snort.

"Wait! What?" My jaw drops as I stare at the piece. "It's *fried?* What does that mean?"

"Try re-keying it."

I frown and then sing the basic sequence.

Nothing happens.

I try again, this time loudly, and focusing as I've been taught, to not only key an object but to set an Aural Block on it once more.

Again, nothing.

"What did you do to it?"

Aeson watches me with a trace of amusement. At least it's what I think it is, because there is *something* there, underneath the surface.

"Seriously, what just happened?"

"In plain English, I broke it—scrambled and messed up its quantum atomic structure. It is no longer orichalcum, but something else. So, yes, it's fried."

"Okay, wow." I stare at the dead piece of now-unknown material, with growing disturbance. "I didn't know you could do that with sound. That's mind-blowing."

"It is an advanced technique. You will learn it," Aeson Kass says.

"Me?" My lips part again. "Okay, that sound sequence sounded impossible, but I suppose I need to try. . . ."

"Few things are impossible if you know what needs to be done," he tells me. "And knowing how to completely neutralize orichalcum technology will come in handy for you during Finals. This will be your homework assignment for the week. Show me how quickly you can master this technique. I believe you can do it, especially after what I've seen you do the last time we talked."

I feel my cheeks start to burn. He is talking about the compelling power voice that I accidentally used on him. . . .

"I'm sorry about that power voice, I didn't mean it, I was just so upset—"

"I know," he says. And he glances away. "Now, enough for today. Candidate Lark, you're dismissed."

For some reason the way he says it feels very abrupt, so that I start to slide off the desk then pause. I watch him as he takes the damper box and leans down to put it away into a lower desk drawer. His pale strands of hair fall forward over his face, like a golden curtain.

When he straightens, I find that I haven't moved, and I am still looking at him.

"You know," I say, because yeah, my crazy big mouth takes over. "I really do mean it, I am truly sorry. And—maybe if I had any idea how to control it better, you might teach me so that I don't do that kind of rude thing again—"

Aeson Kass grows even more still, and slowly looks at me. "You have no idea what you're asking, Candidate Lark. It's not rude—it's *illegal*."

"Then maybe you should tell me more so I do know? Teach me what I need to know, please!"

The Atlantean shakes his head. "No," he says, and his tone is hard and cold and implacable. "The less you know of it, the better. Maybe if you Qualify eventually, and spend time on Atlantis,

you'll get the opportunity to explore this dark aspect. But now—
you are a raw beginner. And this conversation is over. *Dismissed!*"

"Okay! All right!" I exclaim with irritation, getting off the
desk surface. And then I mutter, trailing off. "Don't need to yell at
me like I'm one of your Fleet cadets. . . . What an uptight—"

"What?"

"Oh, just chill, take a break, already!"

Too late I realize what I've said. "Damn . . . I'm sorry!" I put
a hand over my mouth.

But he is staring at me, and he is out of his chair. . . .

"Candidate Lark, any comparison with you is an *insult* to my
cadets," he says in a soft voice that sends prickling fear along my
skin. The intensity of his gaze . . . it cuts through me and I
suddenly feel completely transparent, vulnerable.

I take a step back and find that my heart is pounding.

"But you are correct about one thing." He takes a step toward
me. "I need a break, and I intend to take it as soon as you *vacate*
my office."

This time I say nothing and bolt for the door.

As I shut the door, I turn back briefly in a kind of visceral
inexplicable terror that is also electric and wild . . . and I see him
stand, watching me.

I hurry from the VIP offices hallway of CA-2, almost at a run,
turn the corner and there's Logan. I am a little surprised to see
him on this interior side of the glass security barrier and not in the
front reception area. How did he get in here past security?

And then I see he is talking with someone. Hearing me
approach, he turns, and I see the person behind him is Nefir Mekei.
Both of them grow silent momentarily and then Nefir nods to me
with a light smile.

"Oh!" I say, because my heart is still pounding. "Hi,
Instructor Mekei. And Logan! What are you doing in here? How'd
you get in? Okay, ready to go?"

"Just waiting for you," Logan says, smiling. He then nods to
Nefir, and the Atlantean turns away and walks to his own nearby
office.

Logan turns to me. "How was everything?" he says, as we

start walking.

"Stressed! Hot! Pool!" I say, because my heart is still pounding. And then I tell him an abbreviated version on the way.

We get back to the CA-2 pool area, and looks like everyone has the same idea. The huge pool is packed with swimmers. Some Candidates are doing laps, but most of the teens are just splashing in the water, and there is the sound of happy squealing and laughter.

It's a sound I've almost forgotten, over these past weeks of the Qualification ordeal.

The sound of kids having fun.

And, as I glance around some more, I see there's quite a number of Atlanteans in the water too, male and female. They are doing sleek elegant laps, their long blond metal hair tied back, their bronzed bodies skimming the water with a noticeable skill level far above our own. They don't just swim—they appear to be flying. . . .

We hurry to the lockers and change out of our uniforms into the unisex swimming gear. Logan puts on the swim shorts, and I immediately feel my cheeks flush at the sight of his amazing bare chest and the definition of his hard abs, his beautiful muscled arms and runner's legs.

Oh dear lord, good thing there's cold water!

I've slipped on the shorts and tank top, and now, with a squeal, I jump in ahead of him.

Cool water closes over my head. The soothing bliss of it surrounding me is indescribable!

And then Logan's sleek body strikes the water next to me in a clean dive.

I emerge to the surface, then spit and sputter, treading water easily. . . . The pool has no shallow or deep end; it's all the same equal two-meter depth so you have to keep floating. The overhead canopy of glass near the distant ceiling is translucent so you can see the night sky. However the entire area is well-lit with overhead and wall lights. Pool water shadows shimmer along the tiles and reflect in the distant ceiling.

"Gwen!" someone shouts. "Hey, over here, girlfriend! Par-ta-a-ay!"

It's Laronda and a bunch of people from Section Fourteen—in

other words, our Pennsylvania RQC-3.

"Race you!" I exclaim to Logan, and start swimming in decent freestyle strokes in their direction. For once I am not completely incompetent when it comes to a physical activity, so for a few seconds I give Logan a run for his money before he overtakes me.

We reach everyone, and for the next ten minutes it's just carefree silly stuff, and then someone points out the various swimming Atlanteans as one by one they pass by in various lanes, doing their impressive, elegant laps.

"Okay," Laronda says in a loud whisper, finger-gathering the water around her teasingly into froth. "I don't care what anyone thinks, but these people are *hot!* Just look at all those gleaming bods, the perfect muscles, the sleek, oozing, tight booty hotness. . . . Yum-yum! Mrrrow! Oh lord, thank you, thank you! I can die happy now, if the Asteroid takes me."

"Hey, their girls are super-hot too!" Jai says with a silly giggle in a high tenor voice.

Meanwhile, Logan gives me a slow smile and then submerges and glides smoothly underwater next to me. And the next second I feel a deep stroke of his palms against my waist as he holds my sides and then pulls me down lightly. It's just deep enough that my mouth and nose is still above water, but now we are both closer to the edge of the pool that has a small shaded overhang.

Logan remains under a few seconds longer, as his fingers move up and down my waist. And then his hand quickly slides under my tank top in the water, brushing up against my front. I suck in my breath as his fingers barely touch the underside of my breasts then move away. The wonder of it is, the whole thing is almost invisible under the surface waves set in wild motion by all the swimmers. . . .

I make a small sound, just as he comes back up, deeply inhaling air, and his dark hair is plastered to his forehead in wet curls. But he is still holding me closely, with both hands now sliding up and down my sides and back, and snagging the curve of my waist, my hips, occasionally bumping into me with his torso, the full length of him. . . . When it happens, we both seem to freeze momentarily, floating, while sweet languid honey fills me all over, a rich spreading warmth despite the cool water.

I know he cannot kiss me here, cannot do anything more overt, but he can touch me underneath the waves. . . .

And he *does*.

"Gwen!"

I start, coming apart from Logan, because I think we've managed to sort of embrace while upright in the water, our hands all over each other, without making it too obvious what we're doing.

"What?" I say to Laronda.

"Stop petting, and look!"

I splash-turn to where she's pointing and Dawn swims up to us in the same moment to mutter, "Hey, look, Gwen, it's your Atlantean a-hole, Phoebos! Isn't that him, over there?"

"Wow," Hasmik says. "He's—"

"Amazing!" Laronda finishes.

I stare . . . and my gut does this weird thing where my heart kind of lurches then dips down into my other internal organs and then hammers against my diaphragm or lungs or whatever—it feels like an internal war is going on inside me, and there's this crazy drum-beat. . . .

Aeson Kass is walking along the distant opposite side of the pool. He is wearing nothing but swim shorts, and his long sunmetal hair is pulled back into a segmented tail, the kind of hair fashion that other Atlanteans use when swimming.

His body is perfect . . . just as I suspected. His skin is tanned to a deep-bronzed sheen, or maybe it is the natural coloration of his body. Wide shoulders and chest tapering into a slender waist, tight hips encased in shorts, gorgeous defined abdomen, powerful legs, muscular arms.

And he still wears the black armband around one bicep.

Aeson turns his head and says something to a couple of other Atlanteans walking behind him. I recognize them immediately as our RQC Combat Instructors, Oalla Keigeri and Keruvat Ruo, also wearing standard issue swimming gear and showing off spectacular bodies. Oalla laughs, and Keruvat leans in to say something else, at which point Oalla shoves him back lightly with her hand, followed by more laughter.

In that same moment Aeson takes a step to the edge and dives into the pool. His body hits the water like an arrow, and he disappears under the surface. I blink and moments later I see him surface many feet away, and then begin moving with powerful effortless strokes that hardly break the water, as he swims laps in one of the farther lanes.

At some point he passes by us, six lanes away, and he never breaks his stride. I freeze and hold my breath in suspense, but I don't think he even sees me. . . .

So, it occurs to me, *Command Pilot Kass decided to take that break after all.*

Twenty minutes later—during which I find I am absolutely distracted and unable to hold a proper conversation with my friends, as I am constantly *hyper-aware* of *his* presence wherever he moves in the pool, even when I am intentionally looking away and pretending to be interested in the people around me—twenty minutes later, Aeson Kass gets out of the water.

He walks along the side of the pool, slick and dripping, his golden hair plastered to his scalp, and heads for the lockers.

At some point, he passes by where a bunch of us tread water, and never looks at me. I catch a glimpse of his striking face, the dark shadowed blue eyes outlined by such a perfect sharp line of kohl, the proud angles of his jaw as he observes the panorama of all of us Candidates in the water. He is straight-backed, tall, and infuriatingly confident.

"Stop drooling!" Dawn punches Laronda on the arm as they both watch the Atlantean walk by.

Logan gives me a long scrutiny as I maintain—what I believe—a perfectly casual expression at the exact moment that Aeson Kass moves past.

"You know," I say—seemingly to no one in particular—staring in his wake, and feeling a little crazy and still worked up just then, so that my voice carries. "What is it with Atlanteans and *eyeliner?* They must use waterproof or permanent eye makeup that it doesn't get smudged in the water, even after all that swimming. Talk about vanity!"

"Good point," Laronda says.

"And what's up with all that ridiculous metallic hair dye?" I continue. "So okay, it doesn't run in the water. But really, eventually it would—wouldn't you think?"

"I bet they probably need to re-apply touch-ups every time they wash their hair," Dawn says. "That kind of metallic hue must be really difficult to make permanent."

I watch Aeson's retreating back, and somehow, weirdly, have a feeling he *heard me*. How do I know this? Did he stiffen momentarily?

I am not sure. . . .

But in that moment I know that someone else definitely heard. Oalla Keigeri, also dripping wet, walks by, and turns at the sound of my voice. She raises one brow and then gives me a peculiar intense look before she too moves away in the direction of the lockers.

Chapter 48

We get out of the pool eventually, cutting it too close to ten PM lights-out curfew. Dripping wet, we pull on our clothes and race back to our dorms, laughing. At the entrance to Section Fourteen, Yellow Quadrant Dorm, I squeeze Logan's hand as he turns to me with another lingering look before heading back to his own Red Quadrant Dorm.

"I'll look in on Gracie for you," he says.

"Thanks!" And I smile at him as he goes.

"Hurry, hurry, gotta hop in bed in five minutes," Laronda says, as other late Candidates all around us race up the stairs to our sleeping floors.

I run after her and Hasmik, and as we hit the bathrooms, there's a minor stampede and a decent line. That's because Claudia Grito cuts right in front of us with a sneer, together with a few other alpha girls.

Dawn gives Claudia a withering look, but it's no use.

"Gotta pee, gotta pee," Laronda sing-songs to us, shifting from one foot to the other. And then she pulls my sleeve. "So, Gwen, I had no idea that Aeson Kass guy is so red-hot—as in, sexy, on a purely physical level. Must've been fun—"

"What?" I bite my lip and start to frown at her.

"You know—fun to have that special voice training thing you had to attend back in Pennsylvania."

It occurs to me, I didn't mention to Laronda that I am still doing the voice training.

"Yeah, well," I mutter. "He's mostly kind of scary. . . ."

Laronda shines me a wicked smile. "But it didn't stop you from drooling all over him back at the pool, just now. Cause, yeah, I *saw* that!"

I am suddenly angry and agitated. "You saw *what?* What are

you talking about?"

But now Dawn raises one brow and nods. "Uh-uh . . . I noticed it too."

"Wha-a-a-at?" My mouth falls open at them both.

"Come on, even with your sweetie Logan there, and right after the two of you were messing around, even so, the moment the Atlantean VIP showed up, you went all *weird*. You changed."

I stand, lips parted in outrage, shaking my head at them. "But—that's just crazy! You guys are seeing things! How did I go 'weird' and change? What's that supposed to mean?"

"Well, you were flirting with Logan more loudly than normal. Less like a normal you, and more 'fakey' and exaggerated. And whenever Kass swam by, you, I dunno—you kind of acted *different*, kind of hyper."

I stare at everybody, and even Hasmik is nodding now.

As all of this is being said, I feel my head, my cheeks, flushing. . . .

Oh, no. . . .

But now I am angry for real. I shake my head, as if to shake off this stupid stuff they're saying, and I roll my eyes at them.

Fortunately I am saved from further embarrassment and need to explain, or even *think*, by the vacancies in the next few bathroom stalls.

In the morning, the first thing I remember when the claxon alarms go off is that I do, sort of, have a half-baked plan to get Gracie's points built up. It involves asking a whole bunch of people to sacrifice just a few of their points on her behalf, when the time comes for the Finals.

Now, *how* will I ever convince them to agree to this thing, is still a big question mark.

The second thing I remember is what happened at the pool last night. An uncalled-for image of Aeson Kass, dripping wet and toned and beautiful, walking at the side of the pool, haunts me as I get dressed, get down to breakfast, and put some unidentified food in my mouth while my friends talk at me—and apparently, past me.

Okay, this needs to stop. . . .

I don't know what it is that is happening to me, but when I see him later tonight, I will *deal* with it.

The classes and the rest of the day are generally tedious and uneventful. We swim, do extensive Combat sparring and practice Er-Du Forms over at the large CA-3 Training Gym. Later, a new Atlantean Culture Instructor gives us a lesson on Atlantean early history, including the original colony establishment on the planet later called Atlantis. And finally a Tech Instructor, this one also an Atlantean, unlike Mr. Warrenson, teaches us some new tone sequences for controlling orichalcum—basic stuff that I know already from my voice training with Aeson Kass.

After dinner, when I finally take a deep breath and knock on the door of Office #7, Aeson Kass acts as though nothing happened the previous time I was here. . . . However, he is possibly even more remote and reserved than usual. For half an hour we go over the exact tonal sequence to restructure orichalcum on the quantum level. In the process, Aeson "fries" at least three more chunks of the metal, showing me how it's done, and I am still unable to replicate it.

"We'll continue tomorrow," he tells me dryly, without meeting my eyes.

And then I am again dismissed.

I get back to my dorm and go to bed with a dismal feeling of peculiarity, and always, underneath, is the undercurrent of despair. I think of Gracie with a nervous sick feeling in my gut, and then George, Gordie, and Logan, and the rest of the people I care about, and how Finals will affect all of us. . . .

The unseasonal heat wave continues, and I fall asleep all sticky with sweat. Then I dream of strange old paintings at the Huntington, with Sarah as Pinkie watching me with glassy dead eyes, and opposite her, the broken Blue girl. . . .

The fact that *I took a life*—was responsible, however indirectly, for killing not one but two people in Los Angeles—is haunting me subtly in that vulnerable time between waking and sleep. It's the only time I let it get to me, since the rest of my time is occupied with stress and exertion and usual despair.

Then, for the next two weeks, maybe three, time blurs. All I know is, we're deep in the middle of May, and days are flying by in a flurry of training activity. There is so much and yet so little to tell. We, as Candidates at the National Qualification Center, continue our arduous classes. But for some reason—maybe because it's become such an ingrained part of out lives—it seems less unbearable and more routine.

My sister Gracie manages to do as well as I had hoped in all her training classes, and she has been slowly earning back the points that had been stripped from her. The rest of us Larks each have more than the baseline 100 points required to Qualify. I get scanned each morning and I find I have at least one or two more credits every day, mostly from Culture and Tech where I get to display my geek brains as opposed to physical prowess.

By the middle of week four at the NQC, with only four days remaining before the official day of Finals, my cumulative points average stands at 157. George has earned 179, and Gordie eclipsed us all by scoring a whopping 213 points. Meanwhile Gracie has 67 points, which puts her more than halfway in the right direction.

"Hey, Gee Four can totally have like a whole hundred of my points," Gordie announces with a proud crooked smile, pushing his glasses up his nose.

"You are awesome, bro!" I tell him. And George nods and even abstains from trying to finger-snap his little brother's forehead, or calling him a monkey.

In short, we think we have this whole points dilemma figured out, for the most part.

Now, all we have to do for the rest of the time before Finals is actually keep up our strength and endurance, and then, Qualify.

Meanwhile, Logan and I continue to meet up wherever we can, and yeah, we do a lot of homework running and witty clever banter during which I learn how truly smart and clever Logan is. But mostly, we cannot keep our hands off each other. Only, it's all brief, stolen touches . . . a few squeezes . . . and once, a hungry kiss while pressed between a shadowy door and a wall that blocks us from the nearest surveillance camera.

Not once does Logan bring up again the fact that he does not approve of my meeting Aeson Kass on a daily basis for my voice training. We basically treat it as an untouchable subject, an unspoken prickly-weird thing between us.

And as for Command Pilot Kass—I honestly don't know what

it is, what happens every time I enter his office. We are both on pins and needles, and there is a strange explosive *atmosphere* of charged electricity and ragged wild energy that builds and builds . . . and yes, there's a whole lot of repressed anger and frustration.

At least that's what I think it is.

I believe Aeson Kass actively dislikes me on a personal level. He definitely regards me with the greatest disdain. . . . And I in turn find him irritating, frustrating, annoying, rigid and pompous, and more often than not, a smug a-hole, especially when he is right about something and *knows* it.

Not to mention, he's overbearing and ruthless and implacable.

But I strongly believe he is the only one here who can teach me the full extent of what I need to know to use my Logos voice.

And so, I *deal* with it.

At some point, with only three days left before the Finals, I suddenly realize that tomorrow is my birthday.

Holy lord, I am turning seventeen!

And when I mention the fact that the next day is May 25, my birthday, Laronda squeals and says, "That's it, girlfriend, tomorrow we're giving you a Birthday Party!"

Chapter 49

I'm not sure what Laronda was thinking when she thought to throw me a party. I mean, how in the world are we supposed to do that at the NQC? And where, exactly? Surveillance cameras are everywhere. . . . And we're not supposed to be "fraternizing" too much, even in the platonic friendly meet-ups sense.

"Don't worry, Birthday Girl, I'll take care of everything, you'll see," Laronda whispers to me as we sit down for breakfast at the cafeteria on the morning of my birthday. "I'll get everyone you know to show up, and you'll see, we'll even have cake!"

And she turns to Dawn. "Girlfriend, you're in charge of dessert-gathering."

"Huh?" Dawn says, raising one brow. "You mean, like prehistoric hunter-gathering?"

"As in, you grab a few pieces from the food bar, now—just whatever they might have, pie, cookies, jello, you name it— whatever can fit in a napkin and in your roomy uniform pocket."

"Jello? Hell, no! That's disgusting."

"Okay, whatever, just grab something, Dawny-baby-poo, and tell a couple of people we know to do the same."

"Baby-poo?" Dawn punches Laronda on the arm, and Laronda says, "Aww!"

"You're serious?" I mutter with a snort.

"Oh, yeah." Laronda cackles, rubbing her hands together. "We will have the best, yummiest bunch of asteroid-end-of-the-world-compound-cafeteria yummies gathered in one place."

"And what place will that be?"

"Let me think about it, let me ponder, and I will let you know by lunch!"

"O-okay," I say. But I'm shaking my head, because I know how crazy this whole thing is.

A nd so, for the rest of the day I am exposed to the "crazy." Candidates of all Four Quadrants from my own Section Fourteen whisper "Happy Birthday!" as they pass me by in the halls, in the classrooms, outside in the long streets between our dorms, and pretty much wherever I turn.

I swear, I don't even know most of these people!

At one point, just before lunch, when Charlie Venice from Red Quadrant Dorm slides by me on the street and gives me a genuinely painful pinch on my waist, accompanied by a very breathy falsetto "Happy You-know-what, Me-e-ez President!" I've had just about enough.

"Yo, Charlie!" I say. "What's up with this already? How many people know about my birthday? Who told you?"

But Charlie grins widely, and makes a horsey laugh noise, and runs along to wherever the hell he's going.

"Little dummy jerk!" I say to his retreating back.

When I turn around, there's Logan.

My heart does a happy jump, and my pulse starts racing as soon as I see his warm hazel eyes and the slow smile.

"I hope you don't mind," Logan says, falling in with me as we walk back to my dorm. "Gracie told a couple of people at our dorm about your Fun Day. Oh, and—Happy Birthday." And with that Logan takes my hand briefly and brushes his fingers against my palm, so that now my pulse is *really* racing. "I don't have a present for you here with me, but I will have something for you at the party."

I can't help smiling. "Thanks. As far as presents, don't be silly, you don't have to! I mean, where will you get presents? And, yeah, I can't believe I'm seventeen. Heh. . . . One more year, and I can vote. Not that it means anything. Or, like, who needs a driver's license these days? Or whatever."

"One more year—" He briefly leans near my ear and I can feel his warm breath on my neck. "And you'll be *all grown up*. . . ."

My smile deepens and I look down and bite my lip. "Yeah. . . ."

And then, with a jolt of sharp clarity, the despair returns.

One more year, and I will most likely be dead.
I, and everyone I know and love.

But I force myself to continue smiling and then we go in through the closest glass walkway to the lobby of Section Fourteen.

"Okay, girlfriend," Laronda tells me as we meet up for lunch. "Right after your last class, at five-thirty PM, you need to go to the big Training Gym in CA-3. Got that? That's where the party is. Don't be late!"

"Laronda! How many people are going to be there? This is nuts! What if they catch us?" I shake my head at the girl, but she's implacable.

"Just get your skinny smarty-pants booty over there at five-thirty! Don't make me have to use deadly force on you! Oh, and if any of the Instructors or guards ask you where you're going, tell them it's 'team-building homework exercises' for Section Fourteen!"

My mouth falls open, but I am laughing. "Seriously?"

"Asteroid-impact seriously!"

"Ugh . . . don't remind me," I say.

And then I endure lunch and two more classes, with people giving me winks and coy little looks. Generally I'm feeling even more self-conscious than usual.

The weird thing is, the alpha bullies give me looks too, but none of them make the nasty usual comments. Could it be, Derek and Wade and Claudia have given me the day off from their a-hole behavior? Nah, must be something else. And the thought of what that something else could be gives me a cold feeling in my gut. . . .

At around five-thirty, I make it to the CA-3 Training Gym, huge, sterile, and sprawling, that has a full-size running track and tons of exercise equipment and what looks like a mile-high ceiling. I turn the corner, overcome with sudden uneasy shyness, and enter the main hall area past weights and rowing machines.

There's a whole bunch of people all over the gym. At a glance, could be at least fifty, if I had to count. And no one yells "Surprise!"—thank goodness for that.

Instead, I see my brother George. Behind him is Gordie, and

then Gracie. They are smiling widely, and at the same time other people at the gym turn away from whatever they're supposedly doing, and all give me meaningful looks.

"Happy Birthday, Gee Two!" George takes me in a brief hug, then whispers in my ear, "We all have something for you. . . ."

And the next instant I feel something being placed in my fingers. George closes his big hand over mine, and I see . . . a shoelace!

My jaw falls in a silent laugh.

But I have no time to react, because Gracie comes to hurl herself at me and she squeezes me in one of her crazy hugs, and then her cold little fingers are fiddling in mine. . . .

Another shoelace!

I turn around and Gordie tickles me, and punches me multiple times—because again, he is not the hugging type. And then he places a third shoelace in my hand.

Then there's Laronda. "Happy Birthday, Shoelace Girl!" And she hands it to me.

She is followed by Dawn, Tremaine, Jai, Hasmik, Mateo, and a whole bunch of people, who each abandon their exercise equipment and then walk by me as though casually, and whisper a greeting followed by a shoelace.

As I stand there, giggling and counting shoelaces, someone taps me from behind on my arm. I turn and it's Blayne in his wheelchair. His head is craned to the side slightly, his blue eyes are full of unusual suppressed energy, and he's offering me a shoelace. I glance down and notice one of his pristine-looking shoes is missing a shoelace for real.

Wow. . . . For some reason seeing his feet like that, I get a sudden lump in my throat and my eyes start itching.

"There you go, Lark. Happy Birthday," he says with a shadow of a smile. "Now, I'm heading for the cake."

And with that he starts rolling toward the nearest wall, where I suddenly see in the back is a small stack of boxes. On it are several unrolled napkins, and on top of the napkins is a bunch of pieces of cafeteria desserts of all kinds—cookies, pieces of crumbling pie, and a few actual cake chunks. It's a sorry looking gooey mess, but several people are gathered around it, and they are all grinning at me . . . and holding more dratted shoelaces.

"Go get your cake, so we can sing!" Laronda nudges me forward.

I walk over to the cake "table," followed by more and more people, some of them looking vaguely familiar, until suddenly there's Jared Holder and Ethan Jamerson—two of my Semi-Finals buddies from Los Angeles! Zoe is next to them, naturally.

"Hey, Gwen!" Ethan says. "Or should I say, Shoelace Girl!"

Zoe shrugs laughing. "I had to tell them about this, Gwen."

"Oh, hey!" I exclaim, and feel an indescribable pang, as a whole bunch of memory flashbacks come to me. . . . Things both good and bad.

And then another vaguely familiar teen comes up to me, and offers the shoelace. "Thanks," he says to me. "If it hadn't been for you, the drones would've killed me back in L.A."

"And thanks from me too, man," another guy says. "I copied you when you did the underwear thing, and didn't get burned crossing the L.A. River bed."

"What underwear thing?" I hear Logan's semi-amused voice as he suddenly comes up behind me. "Should I be concerned?"

"Oh!" I exclaim, turning to him, and blushing a deep red. "It's nothing! You really don't want to know."

Logan raises one brow. But he is laughing.

"Not to mention, your insane shoe-baton rig saved a whole bunch of us in the very end, that day," a slim girl says. I've never seen her before, but apparently she knows me.

"You're welcome, I guess," I say, smiling sheepishly.

"Okay, cake! Now!" And Laronda shoves me at the dessert spread.

I pick up a crumbling piece of some kind of white cake with a bit of frosting on it. Before I can take a bite, everyone in the Training Gym starts to *sing*.

And I mean, *everyone*.

I put my hand up to cover my mouth, because I don't know how else to react, as from every spot in the hall teen voices rise. . . .

Since the surveillance cameras are on us, most people remain where they are, "using" the exercise equipment, or pretending to stretch and look in another direction away from me, or walking around the track perimeter. But the birthday song is overwhelming, and it gets so amazing, because it's a given that everyone here can *sing really well*, and many people start doing gorgeous harmony.

I stand, with shivers going up and down my spine. . . .

And then it's over.

"—And many, zany, granny mo-o-o-re," George intones, finishing up with our own family twist on an extra add-on line to the popular song everyone knows.

My brothers and sister and my friends grow silent. They stand looking at me.

There are no candles to blow out. No wish to make.

And it occurs to me, in a strange surreal moment of existential awareness, *this is probably my last birthday.*

And for many of them, it also occurs to me, *this is probably their very last party or celebration of any kind.*

The moment is interrupted when a small commotion happens at the doors to the gym, as we hear voices and more people approaching. And then I hear Claudia Grito's obnoxious loud tone as she says, "There she is! They are having an illegal gathering! They're breaking the rules!"

The room is instantly silent and many people either turn away in haste to pretend-exercise, while the rest stand around me and the cake table, looking vaguely guilty.

I look around with worry, and see Oalla Keigeri walk into the gym hall. She is followed by Claudia and Derek and a few others of the alpha crowd. Oalla walks closer, and her boots ring with angry loud echoes against the linoleum floor until she comes to the mat-covered area and stops. She glances at all of us coldly.

"There it is! They stole cake and food from the cafeteria too!" Claudia points gleefully.

"Attention, Candidates!" Oalla exclaims. "What's going on? Is it true that you removed some food from the cafeteria? What are you doing here?"

"Nothing, we just got a little hungry," Laronda mutters, stepping forward to block me from Oalla's wrath.

"So what are you doing?"

"We're having a team bonding exercise for our dorm

Section," Dawn says suddenly, taking a step forward also.

"Is that so?" Oalla raises one brow. "And which class is this for?"

"It's for all of them," Zoe says. "We are practicing teamwork for the upcoming Finals, since we know teamwork will be required."

I push forward past Laronda and start to open my mouth to basically come clean and take the blame. But Laronda shoves me painfully in the gut.

I remain quiet.

Oalla turns to stare at the rest of the room, and no one else meets her withering gaze. "All right. Those of you near this unauthorized pile of snack junk, step forward. You get a single point demerit for whatever it is *this* nonsense is." She pauses to include everyone in her scrutiny. "Come up and get scanned. Anyone else in this room who's possibly involved, you may also step forward to get your demerit. However I will not bother to go over to where you are, so it's all up to you."

I bite my lip and sigh, while my friends shuffle forward and Oalla Keigeri scans their tokens rapidly with a blank expression that could be boredom. When it's my turn, she scans my ID token and doesn't even bother to look at me.

No one else seems to take her up on her invitation to approach. So then Oalla turns around to look at the bully crowd who came with her. Claudia is whispering with Derek and repressing giggles.

"And you!" Oalla Keigeri says suddenly in a loud sergeant drill voice, addressing Claudia. "All of you get demerits too—*two points each*, for snitching on your fellow Candidates! Come up to me now, to get scanned! *Move!*"

Claudia's expression goes from smug to priceless. Her jaw drops with outrage and she starts to mutter in protest, but Oalla passes her handheld over Claudia's token. And then she does the same to Derek who looks ready to kill someone—*me.*

"Now, get out of here!" Oalla tells the alpha bullies ruthlessly. "Back to your dorms and actual homework!"

They stampede out of the hall.

Oalla turns to us in the meantime. As we stare in amazement, she walks up to the dessert table and picks up a messy chunk of cake. "Okay, I am not a big fan of this cloying sweet stuff that you eat here on Earth, but I think I can have one for the occasion," she says, looking at me with a crafty, amused expression.

Holy lord! Humorless drill sergeant Oalla is human, and furthermore, she is amused! I have never, ever seen her like this. . . .

"Oh, and Happy Birthday, Shoelace Girl," Oalla tells me, as she bites into her cake.

And so, for the next few minutes it looks like the party is still on. My siblings and friends exhale in relief and then crowd around the dessert stuff, and everyone starts to giggle and talk louder than usual. Even the people "hiding" behind exercise equipment come out eventually. Oalla talks to a few of us casually, as she chews a small bit of cake.

"Candidate Lark," Oalla says, turning to me, and her kohl-lined beautiful eyes are somewhat cool. "As you can see, I'm cutting you some slack here. But it's not for *you*."

I watch her, not sure how to respond.

"It's for all the rest of *them*," she says, nodding at the room in general. "Look, I get it. You are all letting off steam, because it's what happens in a situation like this. It's like before going into battle. . . . On Atlantis, people celebrate hard before they have to do something where there's a good chance they will die."

"I—I think people on Earth do that too."

She nods. "Exactly. So, we're not unlike in that sense."

"Okay."

Oalla continues to look at me, and I do not look away, do not cringe from her direct, hard gaze.

There's a strange little pause.

"You still have your special voice training later tonight, don't you?" she says.

"Yeah," I say. I am a little surprised she knows about it, but then, why not? Apparently Aeson Kass and the other Atlanteans talk about us in detail. So yeah, she would be informed of my ongoing schedule. Besides, they're all *astra daimon*, and there are probably many things they share in general. . . .

Oalla looks at me closely. Not sure what she is trying to see, but the weight of her scrutiny is almost tangible. "Only two more times left—for your voice training," she says, watching me. "And then, Finals. I think you and I are going to have a little talk before Finals—but not just yet."

"What do you mean?"

But the Atlantean girl simply nods at me with her composed unreadable expression, and then starts to move away. "Enjoy your party, Lark, everyone. And, thanks for the cake."

And she exits the Training Gym hall.

Ten minutes later, the party is still going strong. Sure there's no booze, the last pitiful crumbles of cake and cookies are gone, and there's no music or pretty much anything else you get at teen parties. But the *people* are here, and that's what counts.

And yeah, I have a whole bunch of mismatched shoelaces in my hands. I stand grinning, and Laronda says, "So, whatcha gonna do with all of them?"

"Make a really *long* cord super-weapon of the Yellow Quadrant?" Gracie giggles.

"Hmm, I could do that, I suppose." I tickle Gracie. "But—don't you guys all need them back at some point? I mean, it's not like you can run to the store to buy new ones. . . ."

And then I glance at George with an uncertain smile. "So, was getting the one point demerit worth it?"

"I think it was," my older brother says matter-of-factly, as he rubs his hands together to wipe the cookie crumbs off his fingers.

"Oh, yeah, definitely," Dawn adds with a single wiggle of her brow.

"Okay, then," I mutter. "As long as you guys don't regret it."

Logan takes my arm in that moment, and pulls me away. "I have your present," he whispers, leaning near my cheek.

I turn my face to him, smiling with a flush of excitement. "What?"

Logan reaches in his pocket, and after a small strange pause, takes out his knife. I recognize the small penknife—it's the one he's always fiddling with, playing with the blade in his fingers whenever he is abstracted.

"Here, I want you to have it," he says, handing me the knife. "It—it belonged to my brother Jeff and he gave it to me before he went on . . . assignment."

"No!" I say, looking down at the knife with a sudden jolt of emotion. "I can't take that! I know how much it means to you."

"Please, keep it. . . . It's my birthday gift to you," he says, watching me with serious, intense eyes. "Sorry it's not much, but I think it will come in handy. Might even protect you during the Finals—who knows? In any case, no arguing with a gift, okay?" And he puts it in my hand so that his fingers close over mine, lingering momentarily.

"Wow, okay . . ." I say. *"Thank you!"* And then I give him a swift deep hug, regardless of any surveillance cameras.

A lump is building in my throat and this time is does not let up.

Soon enough the party is over.

Chapter 50

After that, time gets all weird, really. . . . And the two days before Finals fly by in a blink. They give us the last day to rest, just as they did for Semi-Finals. No classes on the day before, just sleep in, wander around, take advantage of whatever freedom remains. There's also the media presence as they once again allow news crews into the huge NQC compound. But this time there is heightened security, because supposedly the global situation outside has grown even more turbulent, as the world is rioting, and we're told it's all for our own protection. . . .

During my last evening of voice training with Aeson Kass, I finally manage to sing the complex set of tones that rearranges the quantum molecular structure of an orichalcum object to make it something else. Aeson watches me as the transformed lump of metal falls to the surface of the desk, dead and fried.

"Good work," he tells me. And I can tell by the glimmer of something lively in his otherwise reserved expression that I did well indeed.

And then it's time for me to go.

"No final advice?" I say with an excess of composure, turning to glance at him, while my pulse hammers in my temples.

"Stay strong and focused," he says softly. "I know you can Qualify. Simply do what you always do best."

"And what's that?"

"Be yourself."

And with those words Command Pilot Aeson Kass looks away from me, and I see only the austere line of his lips and his stark perfect profile. Whatever is—or was—in his eyes in that moment is hidden now, as he returns to his machine consoles.

Our classes are done.

On the morning of the Finals, the alarm claxons go off an hour early. We've been told to expect a 6:00 AM wakeup, but it still feels abrupt, sickening, terrifying.

I open my eyes to bright overhead lights and groaning or silently terrified girls waking up all around me. . . . I don't really hang out with the two girls in the beds to the right and left of me, Annie and Blair, and so we merely exchange momentary glances of solidarity between near-strangers, wishing each other luck. We will likely never see each other again, and with luck or without it, we will probably all be dead in a few hours.

Well, this is it.

Today is the day I learn if I live or die. Or at least so I'm told. Nothing is known about Finals. . . . *Nothing*. They've managed to keep it a secret.

The day before, there were no general assemblies. This NQC compound is so huge that there is simply no way to fit all of us in one stadium anyway. So instead we got briefed in our specific Sections throughout the day and evening. Section Fourteen had a meeting at night, and our Section Leaders gave us very minimal and mysterious information on what to expect on Finals Day.

"First thing tomorrow morning, you will get up, get dressed and come down here to the section lobby by 6:30 AM to get your ID tokens scanned. Your final points will be tallied and announced. These are the points with which you will be going into Finals. At this juncture you will also be given your official team designation for the Finals—remember it well.

"Then you will have less than fifteen minutes to eat. And at 6:45 AM, you will exit your dorms and go directly to the airfield.

"Arrive no later than 7:00 AM. Proceed to board the Atlantean shuttles according to your team designation. Further instructions will be given once you are on-board. And that's about it, good luck, Section Fourteen!"

After that meeting, no one's in the mood to do anything, including sleep, even though it's near curfew. I remember running over to briefly see Gracie and my brothers, just to give them final squeezes and hugs, and possibly to be in the same room with them for the last time. I remember asking them about their points and then repeating their numbers in my head like a mantra, all evening.

Gracie has over 70 points at this moment, which is good and hopeful. . . .

At some point, yes, there was Logan. I know we kissed, hard and desperate, in the shadow of a doorway, just before I went upstairs to my sleeping floor. Logan has decent points, 204 as of last tally, so I tell myself I needn't be worried about him.

And now—now it's Finals morning.

My head is spinning with queasiness and lack of sleep after an almost sleepless night, as I get dressed, adjust my Yellow Quadrant armband over my uniform sleeve, and then come down to the ground floor to get scanned and learn part of my fate.

I see Laronda and Dawn and Hasmik running down the stairs, and we all go together.

On the ground floor "airport terminal" lobby, the crowds are thick. Sections are getting processed simultaneously, as far as the eye can see in both directions, for the next two miles of floor space. Our Section Leaders stand grimly, scanning everyone and announcing our status and rank.

When it's my turn, Section Leader Shontae Smith passes the handheld over my token and tells me I have 185 Final Points, and I am assigned to Team USA Fourteen-C.

I stand aside to let Dawn get her turn, and meanwhile there's Laronda who apparently has 189 points and is on my team, Fourteen-C.

"What does that mean, I wonder?" I mutter. "What's Fourteen-C?"

"I got Fourteen-D," Hasmik says. "And I have 106 points."

We all turn to Dawn. "Okay, girlfriend, what did you get?" Laronda says, poking her arm. "And no hiding your numbers this time!"

Dawn shrugs. "You asked for it. 201 points, Team USA Fourteen-A."

"Okay," I say. "Sounds like A is the highest points scorers. Then probably come the B's, which none of us are, then the C's, that's two of us, and finally D."

"I am the lousy D, I know, I not too good," Hasmik mutters, as we all hurry to get food in the cafeteria.

"Hey, you guys all better chow down," a Candidate we don't even know says in the food line to everyone in general. "This could very well be our last meal, like *ever.*"

"Great," Dawn says.

But hey, he's right and we all eat, because it makes good sense to do that, and really, we never know.

Fifteen minutes later, after scarfing down breakfast eggs, orange juice, and who knows what other stuff—and mostly gagging on the food since no one is really hungry—we rush outside. There, in the dawn light we jog in the direction of the distant airfield two miles away.

"Wow, chicas, look up!" Dawn says, as we move quickly down the street. We look at the sky and it's full of Atlantean shuttles. They are like dark floating marbles, balloons and circles, polka-dotting the sky in the direction of the airfield. I know that up-close many of them are huge, and that these are oversized freight transport shuttles, not the small passenger personal flyers like the ones the VIPs use. But it still looks surreal to see them like that, all gathered here in the same general five-mile radius in the skies above the NQC.

"So, any ideas where we might be getting shipped out?" Laronda says, breathing quickly as we run.

"Your guess is as good as mine," Dawn replies.

Hasmik just runs silently next to me. I give her a sympathetic look, because neither one of us can run all that well, even now after two months of training. But, at least we can manage to keep up without falling apart completely.

When we get to the airfield, we are overwhelmed.

The crowds of Candidates here are amazing. Everyone is here. And I mean, everyone—Candidates, guards, news vans and media people running around taking image feeds and photos and setting up last-minute projection anchors. Up-tempo music is playing through network studio speakers, and holograms announce the events in artificially bright voices.

The closest transport shuttles hover three feet off the ground, while other shuttles wait their own turn, hovering about fifty feet directly above. Candidates are already boarding them. . . .

We glance around, lost momentarily, overwhelmed by the ocean of teens, adults, general humanity.

And then we see the large fluorescent orange signs. They

show the Section number followed by letter designations. We are all Team USA here at the NQC, but there are at least a hundred Sections, likely more, and we wade through the crowds looking for ours.

Toward the back, we finally find Section Fourteen, with four shuttles, one for each letter designation.

Here we say an unreal, numb goodbye to each other. . . . Dawn and Hasmik proceed to A and D, while Laronda and I go together to the hanging staircase leading up to the hatch for shuttle C.

As I start to go up the rung stairs, I sigh. . . . At least I have Laronda with me on this one. As far as I can guess, Gordie is probably somewhere on shuttle A with Dawn and Logan, George is on B, and Gracie is on D with Hasmik.

May luck be with all of them . . . with all of us.

"Candidate Gwen Lark!"

Through the noise of the crowds, I hear my name called and I turn around, even as I'm about to enter the shuttle.

Oalla Keigeri is standing on the ground near the ladder. The wind stirs her metallic strands of hair, and in the morning light it seems to glow like a halo of pale fire around her composed face.

I pause, in surprise.

Oalla motions with her head. "Come down for a moment. I have something to say to you."

My gut feels a stab of worry. Other Candidates are jostling behind me, but I back up and return to the ground.

I stop before Oalla, and we are evenly matched in height. "Yes? What is it?"

"Candidate Lark," she says, as we stand aside somewhat, to let other Candidates pass on their way to the shuttle. "I've been considering whether or not to say anything at all, but I feel, after all, I must."

I look at her in expectancy, and my blood pressure is rising.

"I am not doing this for you," Oalla says quietly, so I can barely hear her above the din. "I am doing this for *him* . . . Command Pilot Aeson Kass."

"What? What do you mean?" Now my turmoil is indescribable.

Oalla pauses, looking away from me, and gathering herself—

for something, I don't know what. "Look, there's little time, and this is not something that is said easily. And the only reason I do say it, is because it is only fair. If you Qualify, you will learn it soon enough anyway. But if you *don't*—if you don't make it—I think it would be right for you to know . . . *he* would want you to know."

"Please, just tell me!" I say, as the numbing cold rises inside me.

"Remember that time, weeks ago at the pool, when it was very hot, and we were all swimming? It was then that you said something very loudly as we were walking by—Command Pilot Aeson Kass was walking past you. . . . You said some cruel things about 'eyeliner' and 'hair dye' and something about 'vanity.'"

I start to frown. "What?"

"You raised your voice and made damn well sure he heard you. . . . Well, he *did*. And it affected him—it *hurt* him, deeply."

Now I'm reeling. "What? Oh! But—I didn't think it would—I mean, I am sorry! They were just words, silly words, I didn't mean to—"

"Oh, I think you meant it, precisely. You meant for him to hear it. Or you wouldn't have spoken." Oalla shakes her head at me in cold, implacable disapproval. "And now, Candidate, you might wonder why any of this matters, why I bother to tell you this trivial thing as you're about to go to your possible death."

I stare at her as she points to her own golden hair.

"See this?" Oalla says. "Yes, you are absolutely correct to guess. It is gold metal dye, and I wear it proudly to show my respect and loyalty to Kassiopei, the Imperial Family of Atlantida. It is my choice, and I make it willingly. And so is this—"

She pauses and points to her eyes, an unusual shade of turquoise blue, outlined in dark kohl. "This is my mark of respect also, as I wear our traditional colors in solidarity with the Imperator."

"Okay . . ." I mutter. "So it is true then, that the hair color and eye makeup are traditionally and culturally important to you, not just for looks. . . . I am truly sorry to have offended—I feel awful now. I did not think . . . I was in a strange stupid mood and I really did not think—"

"I am not done," Oalla interrupts me in a hard voice. "As I said, it is my choice. The hair color, the eye decoration—vanity or tradition, it is *my choice*. Command Pilot Kass does not have that choice. His hair—did you maybe notice it looks a little different from the rest of ours? Just a tiny microscopic difference in lightness, a purer, more fragile gold? Well, because it is *not* hair dye. It's his natural hair color."

I listen, and suddenly my breath stills. . . .

"And his so-called *eyeliner?*" Oalla continues. "The dark 'line' that runs around his eyelids? You think it's *vanity?* Have you any idea that Kass is the most humble, self-negating individual I know? No, it is not paint, and neither is it a permanent tattoo. It is natural also—he was *born* with it. It's a part of his DNA, a unique ancient physical trait that runs in his family, was there for ages, long before Atlantis the Earth continent sank and we left for the stars."

"So what are you saying?"

"I'm saying that Kass—which is merely short for Kassiopei— is a great ancient royal line, and Aeson Kassiopei is not only my commanding Fleet officer, not only my fellow *astra daimon* and heart-brother, but he is also the son of the Imperator of Atlantis, and the heir to the Imperial Throne."

I look at her, and I no longer hear the noise of the crowd. There is no sound left in the world around me.

"I have told you all this because *you matter to him*, Lark. And every action, every word of yours makes a difference. If you do not survive the Finals, you will carry this secret with you. And if you Qualify, then you will be all the wiser for it. And now—go on in, your shuttle is waiting."

"But—I—" I open my mouth and . . . not sure what's coming out now.

But Oalla Keigeri nods to me. She then reaches out with her hand and shakes mine in a firm grip—it's a greeting used on Earth and not Atlantis. Her fingers are warm and strong.

"Best of luck, Gwen Lark," she tells me. "I sincerely hope you Qualify—for everyone's sake."

And then the Atlantean girl disappears in the crowd.

Chapter 51

I feel like I've been dealt a hard blow to the head as I climb back aboard the stair rungs and enter the shuttle.

. . . You matter to him, Lark . . .

The words go round and round, ringing inside my mind. Even now, I don't dare understand what it means.

I am so numb that the unfamiliar Atlantean standing at the doors has to repeat himself as he scans my ID token. "Move along, Candidate, take a seat! No stalling!"

I stagger inside, and the interior looks familiar, a transport shuttle identical to the kind that we rode to L.A. during the Semi-Finals.

Candidates are filling the seats fast, and I see Laronda a few rows to the back. She hurriedly waves to me.

"Hey! What was that about, girlfriend?" Laronda says, as soon as I reach her and take the seat next to her that she's saved for me.

"Oh," I mutter. "Nothing. Just spoke with Instructor Oalla Keigeri. She came to say goodbye—or whatever."

"Oh, really?" Laronda can see my strange, dazed expression. "Wait, she actually *showed up* just to see you? How come? What's wrong? Did she say something?"

Quickly, I try to get a grip. Laronda is too perceptive for her own good. I need to tone my emotions down, and fast. "Oh, no biggie! And yeah, no, of course she isn't here for *me*, she's just seeing all of us off. She happened to see me. . . ." I trail off, hoping the line of vague bull is sufficient.

Because there is simply no way I can say anything about what just happened—to Laronda, or to anyone.

Instead I try to put my mind in a calming zen state. *Focus, focus, Gwen!*

I need to concentrate on the here and now, because this is Finals. This is life and death. So I need to get a grip and push everything else out of my mind and pay attention.

And somehow, after several deep breaths, during which I and everyone else fiddles with our seats and our individual safety harnesses, I am sufficiently calm and clear-headed that I can think once again.

. . . You matter to him, Lark . . .

No, just stop it.

About five more minutes pass, and our shuttle fills with Candidates. Every available seat is taken.

There are two Atlantean pilots on board. The one at the hatch entrance introduces himself as Pilot Ekit Jei. He is metallic haired, compact and muscular, and his skin is river-clay-red, which reminds me of Nefir Mekei.

As soon as we are in our seats, Pilot Ekit tells us to make sure we are buckled in, and then proceeds to check us, walking our rows.

The other pilot, a female Atlantean, sits in one of the four command chairs up in the back control and navigation center. "I am Pilot Radra Vilai," she announces over a voice amplifier in a rich alto. I glance back and can only see her profile and the back of her gilded head.

"Good morning, Team USA Fourteen-C," Pilot Radra tells us, as a familiar resonant hum begins to rise in the hull of the shuttle. "This is your Final Test for Qualification. Your instructions will be given to you as soon as we take off. You are going to be taken to the site where you will begin the task that will Qualify you. And now, Pilot Ekit, please, lift-off on your count—"

Ekit quickly moves to the back of the shuttle to take the adjacent pilot seat next to Radra. At the same time, the razor-fine lines of golden light that slither throughout the hull start racing with motion. . . .

And then the walls—or the Pilots—or the shuttle itself—begin to *sing*.

"Here we go, baby. . . ." Laronda grips her chair armrests and glances at me with a nervous toothy smile.

"Oh, yeah," I mutter, then look straight ahead and momentarily close my eyes. . . .

And the next instant, I am being pulled back into my resilient chair by the forces of gravity. . . . Candidates' voices, soft muffled exclamations and other sounds come from all around, as we are pressed, squeezed, flattened by g-forces.

A few gruesome moments, and you can even hear someone retching in the back.

And then it all recedes and gravity is back to normal.

"Are we—are we in space now?" someone asks pitifully.

"Yes, we have successfully achieved orbit," Radra replies in an up-beat manner. "Next up, your destination."

"So what is it? When do we finally find out where we're going, already?" a boy asks.

But the question is ignored. Instead, Ekit's deeper voice now comes through the amplifier.

"Attention, Candidates! First, a quick explanation: thousands of years ago during the time of the original Atlantis here on Earth, we—that is, our Atlantean ancestors—built a major transportation network between the continent of Atlantis and the other continents bordering the Atlantic Ocean. A complex system of subterranean caves and tunnels was designed to allow secret travel *underneath* the ocean from Atlantis to other lands.

"The tunnels connect a series of sunken chambers that get flooded and drained by means of locks and floodgates. This is necessary for tunnel integrity, in order to avoid cave-ins—this way, only a few chambers are filled with air at a time. The mass of water in all the rest keeps the tunnels and caverns intact under the immense weight of the earth and the ocean.

"Now, the entry points to these tunnels are located at numerous places all around the shores of the Atlantic. And they all connect in the center, right underneath Ancient Atlantis itself—the modern-day area spanning Bermuda and the Bahamas."

There is a brief pause, letting it sink it. We sit petrified in our seats, as things begin to coalesce in our minds.

"Uh-oh . . ." Laronda whispers next to me. "I don't like the sound of this."

And now Pilot Radra picks up where Ekit left off.

"These are your instructions for the Finals," Radra says. "Today you will be taken to one of these entry points along the shores of the Atlantic. We will dive underneath the ocean and emerge in a subterranean cavern that will be drained of water and filled with air, initiating the ancient transport system of locks and floodgates—"

"Oh, man, this is *bad*," a boy mutters behind me, while more whispers start in nervous waves all around the shuttle.

"Once inside the first cavern, you will exit the shuttle. Each Candidate will be provided with a hoverboard, a single weapon of your Quadrant, a flashlight, two flares, and a small pack containing food and water for one day. Control of your final points will also be released to you, to be used at your own discretion. From that moment on, you will act both as an individual and as a team. To transfer points, you initiate the transfer—press and hold your token and the other person's, and speak the number of points to be moved. It is one-way only, you cannot take points from others, only receive them if they are given.

"Your task for the Finals is simple. You have approximately 33.3 hours to cross the distance of 1,000 miles underneath the ocean floor, on hoverboards, which is achievable if you are going at the minimum rate of 30 miles an hour—"

"Oh, good grief!" a Candidate exclaims. "That's insane!"

But Radra continues, ignoring the outburst. "Every half hour, the locks and floodgates activate, starting a new 'lockout wave'— removing water from the next chamber in the sequence and flooding the chamber you are presently in. At that time the gates between the two adjacent chambers are open, allowing passage from one to the other, while the water drains. You must time your movement so that you are always *ahead of the floodgates*, because if they close with you inside, the chamber will flood and you will drown—"

"Oh no, oh no!" There are more outbursts of protest from everywhere in the shuttle.

"The floodgates are marked with four-color beacons, and your ID tokens will be scanned as you pass each one. It is recommended you stay close to your team members and work together. For each team with the most surviving members, you will get a cumulative score that will figure in the formula that determines your final Qualification standing. Therefore, it is in your best interest to keep other members of your team *alive*.

"Next instruction—once you have reached the last of the cavern chambers, which happens to be the central hub underneath Ancient Atlantis, you will need to rise to the surface through a wide tunnel carved out of an underwater mountain. The original tunnel opening is unfortunately many feet underwater. But we have retrofitted it so that it extends to the surface of the Atlantic Ocean, and it is the last leg of your journey. You will go through the opening and rise to the transport shuttles that will await you.

"The final difficulty you will encounter will be in that major central hub cavern. That's because *every single team* of Candidates from all the countries around the world will be converging into the same cavern. And the final sprint race for Qualification spots will happen there. Remember—only *one half of you* will Qualify. That means that you must move as fast as you can in those final minutes and fight for your place on the shuttles.

"Even if you arrive at the shuttle early enough, you will still be scanned at the entrance and allowed entry only if you have sufficient points—a minimum of 100 individual points plus a minimum average number for your entire team—the higher, the better. This team average number will include missing or dead members whose points will be subtracted as negatives and will bring down the team average. As soon as the last shuttle is filled to capacity, the doors will close and anyone not onboard will not Qualify. Which means that, a day from now, at eight PM exactly, the shuttles depart Earth."

Pilot Radra pauses and then Pilot Ekit takes over. "Candidates!" he says. "Here is where I need to explain your team roles. All the Sections have been divided into four teams, A, B, C, and D, in order of achievement, as measured by points. And this determines your time of entry into the cavern system. Everyone on this shuttle is in team C. This means that you get to go in third in your Section. The first team A has an hour advantage over every one of the rest of you. Then comes team B with a half-hour advantage, then you, then team D that will go in half an hour behind you. Once we set you down in the entrance chamber, you will wait your turn."

"But that's unfair!" a girl in front of me says. "Even if we move as fast as we can, those other teams will still get to the central hub ahead of us, so what chance do we even have?"

"It's true, you will be in a later floodgate 'lockout wave' than teams A and B." Ekit acknowledges the girl's statement. "However once you're in the central hub, you will be surprised how much time you can make up in the struggle to advance to the surface."

"This sounds absolutely horrendous," another girl says. "What if we fall off the hoverboard, or get hurt, or get stuck in some awful dark tunnel?"

"Then you die," Ekit says. "Sorry."

"Oh, wow. . . ." The girl is rendered speechless.

A few seconds pass and Radra speaks again. "We are now about to return to Earth at your designated entry point. Everyone, brace for transitional gravity."

And in the same instant we start to fall. . . .

I close my eyes and keep my head turned straight ahead as vertigo renders me close to passing out. Fortunately it lasts only a few minutes. The sensation of falling ends, and then the shuttle hull seems to absorb and then resonate with a heavy impact that sends the hull lights flying even more rapidly. Meanwhile, the sensation of motion is changed, *thickened* somehow. . . .

"We have now submerged underneath the surface of the Atlantic Ocean, somewhere off-shore between Jacksonville, Florida and the former location of your long-flooded ancient Florida Keys," Radra announces.

And for about a minute more we move at a vague angle through what we have been just told is the thickness of water, until the shuttle lurches sideways then slightly up, and finally comes to a hover stop. The golden threads of light stop pulsing around the hull walls, and the musical hum fades into dead silence.

We sit, frozen in our seats, breathing faintly.

Pilot Radra gives us a moment to recover and then speaks again. "It is now nine-thirty AM Eastern, local time. We have lost two hours due to time zone transition from Colorado Mountain time. However, it has been accounted for—the exact starting times at all international points around the Atlantic have been synchronized. You all have 34 hours to complete the task. The clock starts now."

"This is a tough moment of decision, Candidates." Pilot Ekit speaks to us, as he disengages his seat harness. "It's the point of no return. As soon as you step outside into the network entrance cavern, you will have formally agreed to proceed with the Finals competition. You forfeit your lives and your choice in the matter. However—right now is the time to Self-Disqualify. If you genuinely feel that you are unable to compete in this Final Test, it is not a reflection on you. You have the right to give up. Simply remove your ID token and press the recessed button on the back. Then, remain in your seats and wait. You will be returned back to the National Qualification Center and discharged to go home. There is no shame in it. But please note that you *may not* Self-Disqualify once you step off the shuttle. Unlike the Semi-Finals, we have no means of rescuing you from the middle of the tunnel system once its sequence is activated, so if you get in trouble, you will not survive."

He pauses, and the silence in the shuttle is overwhelming.

It occurs to me, *everyone here, including me, is considering this option . . . considering whether to give up now or proceed into living hell.*

So easy to just give up.

Press a button and go home.

I shudder, taking a deep breath. And then I think of Mom and Dad, and the asteroid flying through space on its way to burn us alive.

I've come this far, and I simply cannot give up now. Besides, Gracie and Gordie and George might need me in this thing. Not to mention, Logan, and Laronda and the rest of my friends. After all, we are a team.

. . . You matter to him, Lark . . .

And *he* might need me.

I blink, and then begin to unbuckle and get up, together with the rest of the Candidates who make the choice to keep going.

Laronda and I both stand, and we move toward the hatch exit, where the line is forming and the two Atlantean Pilots are handing out our gear and hoverboards.

"I'm so gonna regret this," Laronda mutters.

"I already regret this," I reply with an exhalation of breath.

Curious, I glance around at the shuttle to see if anyone stayed behind.

Sure enough, there are at least three people I can see, sitting motionless in their seats. One young boy is crying. Another girl looks like she is in shock. Their ID tokens are no longer lit.

One boy gives me a glance of despair as I pass by him and his lifeless token.

They have chosen, I think. *It's their free choice, to die here on Earth, with their families, later. At least they don't have to go through the nightmare Finals now.*

A fair choice.

And then I turn my back on them and share a look of sorrow with Laronda.

Moments later we're at the doors, and receive our hoverboards and supplies.

"One Yellow Quadrant net weapon, one hoverboard," Pilot Radra tells me. "Flashlight, flares, and food are in the backpack. Good luck, Candidate—may you Qualify."

I nod silently, receive my stuff, and go down the shuttle stairs after Laronda.

Cold, musty, damp air hits us. We emerge into a place for which I have no words.

First, eerie, greenish-blue light, a general glow, and twilight.

When they said huge cavern, they meant it! Holy lord, this is immense!

The Candidates crowding ahead of us stand on a slippery cavern floor with smooth water-eroded rock formations jutting out all around us. The cavern is at least three hundred feet across, likely more, because the chamber is segmented into lesser ones in all directions, and the ceiling overhead is covered with descending stalactites hanging like icicles of ancient sediment.

The floor of the cavern ends about fifty feet behind us, and there is an expanse of lapping ocean water. The large transport shuttle hovers partially over the water and over the floor, since there is really no place for it to set down, even if it had to—good thing it does not.

Since we are apparently well underneath the ocean, the light does not shine from the water which appears black as ink. The only source of light in the cavern is the plasma lights on the underbelly of the shuttle. They are the ones creating the eerie glow and casting shadows.

No, I take that back. . . . As I glance directly ahead, the cavern wall reveals a row of four-color light beacons, six in total, spaced three feet apart. They appear to be attached to the walls, but if you observe closer, they are actually installed in a horizontal line to the bottom half of a vertical lift-gate.

"Attention, Team USA, Fourteen-C!" Pilot Ekit says loudly, using a voice amplifier, as he stands at the shuttle doors. His voice sends up immense echoes that resound in the cavern. "On my count, I am now activating the tunnel gate system! Water will begin to flow out as soon as the gate opens, so get up on your hoverboards *now* or prepare to be drenched if you're still standing on the ground. As soon as the gate opening is of sufficient height to allow you through, do not waste time and enter the tunnel. Fly as fast as you safely can, until you see the next row of six beacons. That would be your next floodgate. Wait for it to open, then repeat."

As we scramble to voice-key our hoverboards, Pilot Radra's disembodied voice sounds from the amplifier, since she is still inside the shuttle. "Please be aware there is no other light inside the tunnel system, except for the beacons to mark each gate. Use your flashlights wisely. Also, do not get distracted by any seeming detours, and stick to the main tunnel. Yes, there are off-shoots, and you do *not* want to take them, because they are not a part of the main system. Always stick to the biggest tunnel and cavern."

"Finally," Ekit says, "if you must rest or stop, do it only when you get to the next closed floodgate. That's the only place you can be certain you are not losing precious time. Rest and eat as you wait for that floodgate to open, in the few minutes you earned by moving fast."

Pilot Ekit ends and then disappears into the shuttle. The rung ladder retracts and the hatch closes behind him.

Sickening tension starts the pulse racing in my temples. I sit down on my hoverboard, straddling it, and quickly open my backpack to find the flashlight. Everyone else is also feverishly rummaging through theirs. . . .

A disembodied voice sounds through the amplifier, echoing through the cavern. "And now, good luck, Candidates! The next shuttle carrying Team D is waiting to enter after us, so we must vacate the cavern. Beginning gate sequence count now . . . *One . . . Two . . . Three.*"

And suddenly a low rush of water comes from ahead of us, as the horizontal lift-gate parts and the top portion starts rising slowly, with a dull sound of rock grinding against rock.

Black churning water enters the cavern and in seconds the floor is covered. We are all hovering, and those of us with feet dangling low, feel the spray against our legs. . . .

"Oh, holy Jesus!" Laronda cries, as she lies forward on her belly, gripping the hoverboard close to her with both arms, clutching her flashlight in one hand, while her backpack sticks up like a small lump from her back.

I'm lying on my own board right next to her, still zipping up my pack, and then quickly pulling the two straps through my arms to adjust it tightly on my back. I loop the lead cord from my flashlight around my right wrist, and clutch it in my trembling fingers.

The gate opening grows larger and it is now at least three feet up. Water continues rushing into the large cavern, creating a fall, and all around, the echoes mingle with the sound of singing voices keying hoverboards and directing them forward.

I throw wide glances around to see who else is here with us, looking for other familiar faces. After all, we're supposed to be a team. In the low flickering light of many flashlights, it is hard to see who's who.

"Okay, go! Go!" a boy near the front cries, because there's a traffic jam up ahead. Teens lie flattened on hoverboards, ready to burst forward as soon as there's enough clearance between the top and bottom portions of the lift-gate.

And then they begin to move. The front-most Candidate in line sings the "go" sequence and his board springs forward and disappears into the maw of darkness over the churning black waterfall. Immediately two more hoverboards go in after him, and then it's an endless stream of Candidates and hoverboards, taking the entrance two and three at a time. . . .

We rush onward like desperate salmon swimming upstream into the great unknown. There are about one hundred of us in Team USA Section Fourteen-C, judging by shuttle capacity. We come from all Four Quadrants, so the majority is unfamiliar to me.

Laronda and I are somewhere in the middle of this chaotic lineup. When our turn comes, I take a deep breath and sing the hoverboard sequence, feeling cold air and wet spray hit me as I pass the gate, hovering about ten inches over the rushing water. My token flashes momentarily as I get scanned. I glance to my right, and there's Laronda, flying next to me, clutching her board for dear life.

"Hang on tight, girlfriend!" I yell out to her, as the stale ancient air of the tunnel whooshes past us.

"Oh, yeah, mama!" she yells back. "You and I are gonna be flying out of here in no time!"

The first few minutes are the most intense. We have to get our bearings and navigate the tunnel that is generally circular, with a dripping ceiling. The whole thing's hewn of rock that has been smoothed by centuries of water, and feels intensely claustrophobic—and I've only been in it for about two minutes.

The fact that there are other people with flashlights, flying ahead of us in a vague formation of about two or three people per row, makes it a little easier. They are basically lighting our way.

"Watch out! Big rock thing ahead!" someone yells several rows before us. We see hoverboards swerving, right and left and then the rock is right there, a half-formed stalagmite rising up from the tunnel floor, that must have developed over the eons since the tunnel was first built. Water is churning on both sides of it as it flows around it.

We go around it, singing the correct bypass sequence, and continue forward.

"Anyone know how fast we're going?" a girl's voice sounds behind us. "Because we have to go at least 30 miles an hour—"

"Yeah, yeah, we know, bitch," a familiar hard voice retorts several hoverboard lengths ahead.

It's Claudia Grito.

Oh, great. I am stuck in a narrow tunnel deep underneath the ocean in the same damn team as the *bruja* from hell who hates my guts. . . .

Next to me Laronda grimaces and throws me a look. She's not a big fan of Claudia either.

"Seriously, how fast are we all moving? Anyone?" a guy says from further back behind us.

"Thirty-four miles an hour, according to the speedometer on my GPS, a worthless piece of crap that died two minutes ago," another boy replies up in front. "Happy now?" And I recognize the sarcastic voice belonging to Derek Sunder.

Oh, no, Derek. . . . Why, lord, why?

"Well, now we know how badly this road trip's gonna suck," Laronda mutters.

We keep moving forward in general silence, except for the sound of cold air whistling past us, and the water flowing a few inches below, then a few feet below. The deeper we go, the less water there is, until the tunnel is nearly drained completely.

And then we come to the second closed floodgate. The six beacons glow with what feels like holiday cheer in this damp awful place. We arrive, gather in close formation, hovering in place, crowding forward, some of us closer to the ceiling, others near the floor.

And now we wait.

We know that as soon as the water has left the current tunnel chamber entirely, only then will this new gate open, releasing its water and starting the process again.

About five minutes later, a now-familiar, slow, deep sound of grating stone comes, and a thin horizontal slit appears in the floodgate as the top begins to rise.

Immediately water gushes forward, and we move back a bit, letting it drain away until there's room to enter.

"Well," a Candidate boy says with a snort. "One gate down— or should I say, *up*—and only about a billion more to go, till Bermuda, baby!" And he plunges forward into the newly revealed tunnel.

We follow after.

About five hours and ten floodgates later, we have fallen into a boring routine. We fly in formation, maintaining an even speed of about 30 to 35 miles an hour, having now learned our pace and familiarized ourselves with our "neighbors"—or at least their feet and the backs of their hoverboards. We have also come to expect a floodgate about every fifteen miles.

An eternal drip-drip of water comes from the ceiling upon our backs and our heads, and soon we are as thoroughly drenched as if we had been swimming. There's also a slow leaching weariness in my limbs, and I know Laronda and others around me are feeling it too. . . . It seems like no big deal, but just try lying on your stomach on a hard surface for five hours, without moving hardly at all, while clenching a stiff board underneath you, all your muscles tense and constantly in a state of alertness.

Eventually you go numb. . . . Every limb feels atrophied. Muscle groups ache, itch, tingle, you name it. Everything becomes unbearable. Crap, everything just hurts.

Whenever we come to a gate, most of us get off our boards, waiting for it to open. We jump around, stretch our limbs, move or jog in place. Some of us open our backpacks and pull out something to eat, drink from the water bottles.

"It's not like I'm even hungry," Laronda mutters with her mouth full of granola bar. "I just need to get energy, you know. It's so damn cold here!"

She's right. The *cold*, it is the most overwhelming sensation of all, down to our bones. So far deep underground, beneath the ocean, the thousands of tons overhead pressing down upon us, we're basically inside a huge natural icebox. And we're *wet*. Ugh. . . .

Pretty soon, our teeth are chattering. Every gate stop becomes a few moments of vigorous exercise as everyone gets to work, to get our blood pumping. And then we cram food calories into our mouths, and wash it down with a few gulps of drinking water. It's ironic that in this wet place, we have to conserve our water.

Only about twenty-eight hours to go. Who knew hell could be such a boring monotonous, cold thing?

"Okay, you know what really blows?" a boy says, as we fly through the tunnel in the middle of our seventh hour. "The fact that we cannot get any rest. Not gonna be sleeping for more than a day."

"Everything blows," another guy says. I think his name is Emilio Flores and he's from Yellow. "Just don't fall asleep, man. You fall asleep on your board, you fall off, you're screwed."

And I admit, it's getting harder and harder to stay "awake."

The longer you fly, the more you enter this weird zen state that's neither sleeping nor awake, and you cannot do anything but think. And being cold and numb, it's mostly delirium.

"People, anyone know any word games or something?" a girl calls out. "Cause that would be good, now."

I jerk awake, coming out of the zen state, and good thing too—there's a slight curve in the tunnel ahead, and unless I navigate the hoverboard properly I'm about to crash into a wall of rock.

"Wake up!" I exclaim, and I think Laronda starts too, and all of us maneuver our boards around the curve.

"Ouch, close call," Laronda says, trying to shift and stretch on top of her board as best as she can.

"Word games are good," I say loudly to whomever brought it up. "Anything to stay conscious."

"Who knew the main problem would be falling asleep to our deaths?" a guy mutters right behind me.

So for the next couple of hours, we play "Simon Says" or yell out random crazy phrases like, "I like eating Mindy's boogers!" Laughter works too, to keep us awake.

But even that gets stale. By the time we're on our tenth hour of flying, no one listens much to anything at all, and when a Candidate says something, it's like a murmur intruding upon a nightmare dream.

By hour eleven, many of our flashlights start going out. The batteries are running out, and we don't have spare ones.

"Oh, crap! Mega-crap!" people start exclaiming, and that gets us awake and alert faster than anything.

"Okay, everybody, take turns using your flashlights!" some guy yells up ahead.

Really, we should've thought of this in the first place. Heck, *I* should've thought of this. . . . *I am Gwen numbskull Lark.* . . .

"Most of us should turn ours off," I call out. "Just have one person in each row keep theirs on until we get to the next gate, and then another person at the next gate. That should be enough light."

And in moments the tunnel goes a few degrees darker, as most of us turn off our still functional flashlights. I nod to Laronda to turn hers off and keep mine on until the next gate.

By hour twenty, many more flashlights have gone out, despite our efforts at battery conservation. Good thing our eyes have gotten used to it, because now we fly in near-darkness, and mostly watch for the six rainbow beacons up ahead to indicate an upcoming gate.

And when the gate opens, during hour twenty-two, together with the in-rushing water we get the first floating dead bodies.

Chapter 52

The first one comes as the biggest shock. A boy's waterlogged body washes up through the opening in the floodgate. We know he's a Candidate, because he is wearing the grey uniform, and there's a red armband on his sleeve. He's floating face down in the current.

"Oh my G-g-god! There's someone d-d-dead in there!" a girl cries through chattering teeth, seeing him first as he tumbles out of the gate opening.

And those of us who are up in the front, crowd in closer to see.

"Anyone want to check if he's dead, for sure?" says a boy from Blue, straddling his hoverboard.

"How can he not be dead?" Derek says meanly. "Come on, he's been in a water-filled tunnel for the last half hour at least, probably longer. You wanna touch him? On the other hand, move over, hey, maybe he's got something useful on him." And Derek actually gets off his board, wades through the incoming water and kicks the body with his foot, then bends over and goes through the dead boy's backpack.

While Derek's looting, the rest of us get on our hoverboards and plunge into the tunnel. The nightmarish mood of despair has just gone darker by at least another degree.

"Did you see that?" Laronda whispers. "What happened to him?"

"Probably fell asleep, fell off," the guy behind us says. I believe his name is Jack, and he's got a blue armband. "I didn't see any blood in the water, or on the body. So probably just fell off, maybe got knocked unconscious."

"Everyone, stay alert, people!" a girl directly in front of us says. I've been staring at the deeply grooved hot pink rubber soles of her running shoes for the last three hours at least, as she's lying on her board in front of me.

And then, as we watch the water, more bodies float by. A girl with long pale hair, which fans in the current around her, passes right underneath my hoverboard. She is young, looks a bit like Gracie, which sends a stab of pain through my gut. And then she floats away.

Pretty soon, there's a body every ten minutes, it seems. . . .

And then the tunnel we're in widens suddenly, and we find that we are in a huge natural cavern. The cavern is even taller than the one we entered in the beginning of Finals. And there are several smaller chambers stretching in multiple directions, and the current is flowing haphazardly here. Hard to tell where it's coming from.

"Okay, this might explain the bodies," Jack says behind us. "This place is huge, and people got lost and could not find the next floodgate in time! Crap!"

"You're right," Emilio says up ahead, as we break formation and sort of sit there, levitating, staring around us. "I have no idea which cavern or tunnel is the right one. Where do we go?"

"Usually, the direction from where the water is flowing should tell us," I say. "But it kind of does not seem to be flowing from anywhere at this point, it's standing like a lake. Or at least, hard to tell."

"Whoa, look up, guys!" a girl says, lifting her face toward the ceiling, and directing her board to rise a few feet. "Check out the amazing stalactites! Those are the biggest I've ever seen!"

"You just keep checking out junk on the ceiling, and you'll end up floating face down in the water too," Claudia says from a few feet away.

I glance at her with a frown. For a moment our gazes lock, and ugh, Claudia has a fierce expression on her face. . . .

"I think we need to break up into small groups or pairs and go check out each of these sub-caverns," Jack says.

Meanwhile I am staring at the very still water below us, and the three or four additional bodies floating in it. There's no current, no movement.

Think, Gwen, think! What is going on here?

And then it hits me.

"Wait!" I exclaim. "Don't go off anywhere! I think that's what killed these people! They wasted time looking around, wandered too far into the sub-tunnels and by the time they got back to the actual gate it was too late!"

"Ooh, Gwen-baby! So why the hell are *you* in charge, *puta?*" Claudia snarls at me, turning her hoverboard around aggressively.

I flinch at the ugly word, but before I can open my mouth, Laronda exclaims, "Because she's the smarty-pants! Don't you know, she's Shoelace Girl? In case anyone missed it, if it hadn't been for girlfriend here, most of you in L.A. wouldn't have passed the Semi-Finals! So if you know what's good for you, you listen to her!"

"Oh, yeah? You're Shoelace Girl?" Emilio says with a small grin. "Okay, you got my attention."

"Here's the thing," I say tiredly, ignoring the annoying fact that I've just been outed as that minor NQC "celebrity" I am trying very hard to live down and forget. "The water is not moving because I think this is a permanent lake here—it's not going to drain, *ever*. So if we judge by the water level here it might seem like we have plenty of time to explore, but in fact, this is as drained as this chamber is going to get. Which means, the new gate is about to open any moment."

"Okay, so what do we do?"

I bite my lip. "We listen. We need to be very quiet, stay exactly where we are, and just shut the hell up completely, and *listen* for a sound of rushing water. That would be the new gate opening."

"Okay, I think that works for me," Jack mutters.

Laronda meanwhile glances around at the cavern with all the Candidates in our team flying around everywhere, tired voices raised in echo-raising chatter, and then she yells, "Everyone, over here! Right now! And be quiet! As in, effing *shut up!*"

Some people turn briefly in our direction. And then, most of them decide it's worth checking out whatever's happening here in our group.

"Listen to Shoelace Girl!" Laronda keeps repeating, as more and more Candidates converge.

And then I have to repeat what I just said. I do, and everyone,

VERA NAZARIAN

surprisingly enough, *listens to me.*

The cavern chamber is suddenly very quiet, except for the soft drip of water coming from the ceiling.

"So how long do we listen?" a girl whispers.

"S-s-s-sh," I say.

Because, in that moment, I can hear it. A sudden remote sound of a waterfall, barely audible in the distance, and coming from one of the larger sub caverns off to the right.

"Over there!" I exclaim. "Quickly! That's the new gate!"

"Go! Go! Go!"

And we fly in the direction of the sound.

We reach the six beacons about five minutes later, when the top half of the floodgate has lifted up all the way, which means it's far ahead in its cycle.

"Faster, go faster!" everyone cries, as we fly past the gate, and see our tokens being auto-scanned, and then we continue through the normal-sized tunnel from that point on.

"Phew, that was a close call," Laronda yells out to me as we're flying in our usual formation. "Okay, my turn to use the flashlight."

"How much time do we have?" someone asks.

"Just keep moving!"

And so we keep going for about fifteen minutes at high speed, until we see the next floodgate. And yeah, it's already open too, so we missed the most optimal entry time, which means that we have to make up time again, and go really fast to reach the next gate before it opens. . . .

Things kind of blur at that point. I grit my teeth and hold on to the hoverboard with numb hands, and I know I am going way too fast, just like everyone else around me is.

Unsafe fast.

Because, yeah, a few minutes later someone runs into a tunnel wall.

There's a yell, and the boy falls off, hitting his leg against a rock, so it's bleeding. His hoverboard spins out and slams into two more people, who also collide with another three right behind them. Because, again, we're all going *very fast.*

Seconds later, it's a team disaster.

"Stop! Stop! Everyone halt! Stop!"

Those of us who can, sing the stop commands to bring our hoverboards to a levitating pause. We breathe fast, waiting for people who have fallen on the floor to get back up on their boards.

"Are you okay?"

"Yeah. . . ."

"What about you?"

Candidates are checking each other, and two guys help a girl get back on her hoverboard because she sprained her ankle badly. A couple of minutes later everyone—including the original teen who capsized and caused our train wreck—is back on the boards, and we are off again.

But we've just lost about ten minutes.

Crap . . . crap . . . crap.

We approach the next gate with a significant delay again. Which means we have to fly just as fast through the next chamber. We've entered a horrible cycle that we must break out of, or we will not be able to maintain this high level of pace for much longer.

"Go, go, go!" Voices sound from all directions.

"But *carefully!* Watch the walls! Watch the tunnel curve, watch for any obstacles!"

And so we stare with dilated eyes at the way before us, watching for any changes in the tunnel.

The terrifying thing is, the floor of the tunnel now barely has a trickle of water left. Which means that this chamber segment is almost empty and the next gate will open and begin pumping water here and transferring air out, long before we can reach it.

"Go! Just go *really* fast! No time!" Everyone's screaming, and we lean into our boards, flying so fast that the walls of the tunnel become a twilight blur.

Our ugly suspicions are justified. Water begins rising again as the next chamber is emptying here into ours.

"Go! *Go!*"

But—there it is. The six rainbow beacons glow in the distance of about a hundred feet, water lapping over them. And the water level on our side of the chamber is very high up now, so we have to fly closer to the tunnel ceiling, flattened as much as possible.

"Oh God, it's *closing up!* The gate is closing up!" someone screams up ahead.

We hurtle forward, reaching the beacons just when there's a clearance of only three feet remaining between the top and bottom of the lift-gate—and it's narrowing with every second. Candidates start throwing themselves through the slit opening. By the time Laronda and I are at the gate, we have to glide through carefully, keeping our hoverboards perfectly horizontal, and I even feel the top of the gate scrape against my backpack.

The people right behind us barely make it. And the last person literally *crawls* through the closing slit, while his backpack gets snagged. So he pauses, pulling hard until the bag is un-jammed, and then barely misses his hoverboard getting crushed in between the closing "jaws" of the gate.

"Damn! That was the closest damn thing ever—" the boy cries, breathing fast, and then we continue onward, picking up speed again.

Because there is simply no time. We have to compensate with high speed to break out of this doomed cycle.

We are approximately on our twenty-sixth hour. *Where* we are exactly, no one knows. The last remaining speedometer and mileage tracker on someone's otherwise non-functional GPS has stopped working due to water damage pretty much after the first ten hours—which is ages ago—so we can only guess that we are now well in the middle of the Atlantic, deeper than anyone really wants to imagine, and more than two thirds to our destination.

I honestly don't know how we've even made it this far. I think it's the grueling physical endurance training over these past two months that is saving us. Without it, I've no doubt most of us would be long dead, due to a gazillion factors—shock, extreme tension, impossible exertion, oxygen hunger, too much carbon dioxide or carbon monoxide, calcium carbonate or limestone and other freaky chemicals in the limited "air pocket" we're traveling in, extreme cold, and ultimately, hypothermia.

Hypothermia is a constant danger. Everywhere, I can hear teeth chattering. . . . Even now, I suspect our bodies may be too far "gone"—messed up, damaged by the environmental stresses and the cramped position we maintain—so that we can not recover enough for the final sprint to the end, once we arrive at the central hub mega-cavern underneath Ancient Atlantis... blah, blah, blah....

The flashlights are mostly off now. We fly by the light of a single one that the person in front holds like a headlight to illuminate our way. Surprisingly, it is enough for our dark-acclimated eyes.

One thing is different though. The tunnels here appear to be of a more roughly hewn nature, less streamlined. Many of them contain weird "cutouts" or pockets in the walls, on all sides, like ancient lava bubbles or cavities, pockmarking the tunnel interior with holes like Swiss cheese, ranging from small to huge. The presence of these bubble pockets creates an additional difficulty for us as we try to navigate as cleanly as possible in a straight line and avoid the tunnel walls.

I shudder to imagine the antiquity and the amazing natural consequences that *might* have caused the formation of these tunnels—because yeah, I have an odd gut feeling these are no longer artificial but natural veins and arteries running deep through the crust of the Earth. And the ancient Atlanteans—and now *we*, crazy kids—are just using them after the fact, fully formed and minimally retrofitted for our wacky human purposes.

Incidentally, does the air we're breathing even have enough oxygen anymore? What is this musty, stinky miasma?

Okay, can you tell I am delirious and rambling?

Yeah, Gwen, the uber-nerd, only you would be thinking about ancient rock formations and atmospheric chemical compounds at a time like this. Focus, Gwen, focus!

"Does anyone know how many hours we have left?" a Candidate yells at some point as we arrive at the next floodgate, having somehow managed to regain our good timing.

"Hey, man I lost track. Maybe seven or eight hours left?" Emilio says in a voice that cracks with exhaustion.

"If this were a bus ride," Laronda mutters, "we'd be singing songs to pass the time. Too bad if we try that kind of thing here, we'd screw up our hoverboards programming. No singing!"

"Yeah, yeah, no singing!" a girl Candidate says and starts to giggle drunkenly.

It occurs to me, we really are experiencing oxygen deprivation, and who knows what other poisoning by breathing this crap air for so long. Now, I am assuming the Atlanteans have a minimally functioning air filtration system of some sort here, or we'd be long dead by now. . . .

"Hey, guys," Jack says behind me. "Wanna hear something scary?"

"Hell, no." The moan comes from Laronda. "This is all scary enough, no, thank you."

"No, I mean, just think—what if the whole tunnel gate system collapses? Like, it breaks down and stops working all of a sudden? I mean, how ancient is this place? Must be thousands of years old! All that time, and the effing gates still work? Wow! Just, wow!"

"Okay, you're right," I say. "That *is* the scariest thing you can say right about now. So just shut up, okay? Seriously!"

The guy goes silent, thank goodness.

And minutes later we reach the next gate.

As we pause and hover, waiting for it to open, a few of us take out our drinking water bottles to take small precious sips, and eat a bite or two of something. In the shadows a couple of people use the deep bubble pockets in the tunnel walls to answer the call of nature.

And then the familiar grinding sound begins as the floodgate starts opening. The usual black fountain of water gushes in through the growing slit from the next chamber.

We wait, ready to plunge forward.

But the top of the gate rises about a foot over the opening and then it just *stops*.

It sits there, making an awful deep grinding noise, as the wall of water flows and flows into our chamber, with no way to squeeze through because of the force of current and water pressure. . . .

The damn thing is *stuck*.

We watch the stalled lift-gate. As the reality of our situation sinks in, I feel a stabbing cold pang of absolute despair in my gut.

"Oh, no, oh, sweet, dear lord, no!" Laronda mutters, clutching her hoverboard with trembling ice-cold fingers.

"Oh crap, oh crap!"

People begin to cuss. And then someone says to Jack, "Well, f— you, man, just f— you! You jinxed it! If you hadn't said anything about these tunnels breaking down, you stupid ass—"

"Oh, we're so dead! We're *dead!*" Claudia exclaims not too far behind me. Her voice, it sounds terribly high, on the verge of crying. It's the sound of a terrified lonely little girl, and I have never *ever* heard Claudia like that. . . .

Me? I am numb. The cold fear spreads like a paralyzing agent in a drifting cloud to make me barely able to breathe.

"Oh lord! Oh, mama, please, oh, please, help us! Sweet Jesus, help us!" Laronda is crying. She is not the only one.

People cry and people cuss.

A few throw stuff at the walls, watching it bob away in the current. Because, who cares now? Water bottles and gear and dead flashlights are no good now; nothing matters anymore.

We watch the water fill our chamber and slowly equalize with the stuck lift-gate between this and the next chamber.

"Is there anything? Anything we can do?"

"Un-jam the gate?" I say in a dead voice. "I don't think so. We could try to squeeze through that slit, but it's tricky with all that water current. I don't think it's possible."

Laronda turns her face to me suddenly with a crazy light of hope in her eyes. They glitter black and wild in the twilight. "Gwen! You have to come up with something! You're *Shoelace Girl!*"

"I—I don't know—"

"But you have to!"

"I said, I *don't know*, okay?" I yell back at her in a sudden burst of fury that is caused by numb despair. "I don't have an answer! I just don't!"

But Laronda, and a few of the others have all turned to me. I see their eyes like blinking jewels in the near-darkness.

I think, then. Feverishly think. . . .

"Okay," I say. "Maybe if we wait it out, and try to squeeze through when the current is at its slowest?"

"Can't we un-jam it somehow? We can try pushing up? All of us, together?"

And in the next few seconds, we all get off our hoverboards, and wade through the icy horrible water toward the gate and try to raise it all together.

We give it our all.

It does not even budge. Not with a dozen or more of us pushing and lifting.

"Okay, so much for that exercise in stupidity. Anyone else want to try squeezing through?" Derek says, after straining his thick muscled neck in an attempt to lift, and then trying to stick his feet through the slit.

A skinny tiny girl wades forward, her teeth chattering, and tries to go through the opening. Her body makes it halfway, and then she is stuck. So we end up pulling her back out with some difficulty.

"Damn it, the space is just too small," Emilio mutters. "Just a few more inches could've done it—"

We get back on our hoverboards and out of the cold water. And yeah, we are out of options. The water continues to flow into our chamber and now it is higher than the beacons and a foot over the slit between the top and bottom gate halves.

In about ten minutes this chamber will be flooded completely.

And then we will drown.

Chapter 53

Minutes later, I am lying flat on my back on top of my hoverboard, relaxed in that weird painful way that can only come from absolute despair added to absolute exhaustion. My eyes are closed, and I am listening to the water rise around us. What else is there to do?

"I really didn't think I was gonna die like this," Laronda says, lying on her stomach against the hoverboard, propped up by her elbows. "I mean, I knew I was probably gonna die, but not like this. Drowning is a crappy way to go."

"Every way to go is a crappy way to go," Jack mumbles.

"It's like, I wish we could plug this seeping hole in the gate somehow?" Laronda rolls her eyes and coughs. "Wish we could just board it up somehow and, well, you know, keep this air in this chamber, until maybe we can figure a way out—"

With a start I open my eyes.

"What did you just say?" I mutter, turning my face to stare.

Board it up.

Board, as in hoverboard!

A strange crazed sequence of thought explosions happens in my mind. Bam! Bam! Bam! Idea! A chain of ideas!

I sit up, then stare wildly around us—at a bunch of other dazed, freezing people levitating on top of their boards, as we slowly inch up toward the tunnel ceiling, forced by the inevitable rising water level.

"Holy crap!" I say. "We can use our hoverboards! We can use them all kinds of ways!"

Laronda whirls to me. "What? What! Did you come up with something?"

"Yes!" I exclaim. I am suddenly shaking. "But—but it's kind of insane, it's gonna be a bunch of weird things, and I'll need everyone's board for this—" I continue speaking in a crazed rush of words, as the idea takes hold and flowers, and other "baby idea" offshoots come, rapidly, wonderfully. . . .

Oh, if only I'd thought of it ten minutes earlier, it would have been so much simpler!

"Okay, everyone, first, I need you all to look around at the tunnel and find the deepest largest bubble pocket in the wall with a kind of small opening, just enough to squeeze through, but not bigger than the length of a hoverboard! Also it should be enough to hold several people with air to spare," I chatter in a crazed voice. "But make sure it's above water!"

"Okay, so, what are you thinking here?"

But other Candidates are already looking around, and moments later we have found a large, deep, cave-like pocket that recedes into the wall of the tunnel like a small appendage or auxiliary tunnel. Water has almost reached it, but not quite.

"Okay," I scream. "Everyone get off your boards and get inside! Hurry! I have work to do!"

"What? What?"

"Just trust me on this, damn it! Go! Go! Go!"

"Listen to her!" Laronda picks up. "She is Shoelace Girl!"

Candidates start hovering closer to the bubble pocket, and teens get off their boards, and huddle against the soggy slimy surface of the bubble. I stand on the ledge and look out, and make sure that the last reluctant person gets inside, including Claudia and Derek, who are no longer protesting, because, pretty much it's this or die.

"What next?"

"I am going to board us up here," I say. "For the next half hour, we will wait out this cycle and then Team D will be here and this chamber will have air again."

"But how are you going to board us up? That's crazy!"

"And what about the next cycle? Even with Team D here to help or whatever, we're still just gonna drown because that gate will still be stuck!"

"No, it won't be!" I say. "Because we'll use hoverboards to lift it!"

"Oh, crap, yeah!" Emilio says, as the idea finally dawns on

him. But then he adds, "Wait, how come you can't do that now?"

"Because hoverboards can't accept voice commands when fully submerged underwater. No sound!"

"Oh. . . ."

"Yeah. But once the water level cycles again, and it's back down to its starting position, the gate opening will be exposed to the air. Then we can send hoverboards in there from our side and give them voice commands. Makes sense?" And then I step back. "Okay, now quiet please, I am about to board us up."

"Wait! How will the boards keep the water away? Who or what will hold them tight enough to seal the opening?"

"The force of directional vectors!" I exclaim. "I will voice-key each board to be moving in a certain direction against immovable objects, and it itself will create a tight seal!"

"Huh?" a boy says.

But I ignore him and look out into the tunnel where a whole herd of riderless empty hoverboards now levitates in the dwindling air. I start by setting individual Aural Blocks on every one, so that no one but me can move them out of place and accidentally mess up the crazy toothpick-and-house-of-cards structure I am about to erect. . . .

And then I start singing each board into place.

First, I call all the boards inside the great big bubble cavity in which we are huddling. And then I begin by lifting them one by one so they "stand up" and hover upright. Next, I stack them vertically with a "go forward" command so that they advance, smack hard against the walls, and cover the opening. Basically I am forcing them to move away from me and fly—while still in a vertical position—in the direction of the opening.

Each board hums with angry force as it strains against the rock holding it back from its direction of movement, snagging it around the top and bottom ends. As the rows fill, I make sure the boards are as tightly squeezed against each other horizontally as they are against the edges of the cave bubble, so that there are no slats or openings for water to get through. But of course it's likely insufficient to keep the water away, so I erect a second row of boards as an additional insulation wall, and then a third layer.

When I am done, boards are pressing tight against each other, each one programmed to move, and unable to comply. The force of each board trying to *move forward* holds them all in place and against each other.

"Okay," I say, turning to the others. "Hope that holds. I think it will. Cross your fingers. . . ."

"How the hell did you do that? What did you do?" a girl asks.

"Hello? Shoelace Girl," Laronda says. As if that explains everything.

"Okay, that's enough," I say with a sigh. And then I add, "Now we need to shut up, conserve air, and wait for the cycle to complete."

"But—how will we know when the water is gone again?" Claudia asks with a frown.

"Easy. We will hear Team D in the tunnel. That should be a dead giveaway."

"Ugh, please, don't say the word 'dead,' girlfriend," Laronda mutters.

Well, so far so good. After about ten minutes of trying to breathe slow and shallow, we hear only an eerie silence on the other side, which means that water has completely filled this chamber of the tunnel.

And then we see tiny droplets and rivulets starting to seep through and creep down at the edges of the bubble opening where the boards struggle to "pass" and so keep the water out.

"Oh, no! Water is coming in!"

"Not too badly. It's just a few drops. Should be enough to last us till the gate re-opens."

"You'd better be right, *chica!*" Claudia says. But her tone has grown milder, significantly so. I think Claudia is too frightened out of her head to do the alpha mean girl crap.

And so we wait.

Ten more minutes later, we hear the first voices outside, and the sound of rushing current.

Team D has arrived, and so is our chance!

I sing the command to remove the Aural Blocks and release all the hoverboards back to their "owners."

As it happens they all start falling, like a suddenly broken house of cards.

As the boards fall away, ending up levitating inches off the floor, the tunnel is revealed. We see a whole bunch of Candidates flying past. The moment they see us, there are a few startled screams and a collision or two.

And then we all come out and explain what happened. "USA Team Fourteen-C, here! You guys are Team D, aren't you?"

As we get back on our boards, Team C people start re-keying them, while everyone stares at each other. Team D looks exhausted as much as we are, and possibly more.

And then I see Gracie.

"Gracie!" I scream, as my bedraggled shivering little sister moves forward, lying flat and hovering low over the water.

"Gwen!"

And then we come together, and hug ridiculously across our boards, hands wrapped awkwardly around each other, patting down, checking each other's limbs, making sure we're all in one piece.

But there's no time for a proper reunion.

Hastily I explain everything again, this time to Team D, about what's going on with the defective lift-gate in front of us.

Apparently it must have closed back down during the completion of the previous cycle. However, it is now back up to its small slit opening level, and the water is starting to pour in.

"Okay, everyone!" I exclaim. "Now we move our hoverboards in there and program them to rise. This will lift the gate—I hope!"

And in seconds Candidates get off their boards and everyone's using the basic forward motion commands to guide their hoverboards into the narrow lift-gate opening, and then execute the rise command.

At first there seems to be no effect. But after about twenty boards all jammed in between the gate, each one *pushing upward*, we hear a slow strange creaking of gears, as immense stone begins a deep low rumble.

And then the ancient lift-gate makes a jerking motion, and then starts slowly rising.

Candidates yell out happy woots, pump fists in the air, and people clap.

And then at last, we retrieve our hoverboards, climb back on, and continue into the next tunnel chamber.

The next few hours are relatively uneventful, a cold painful daze. Once again we all fly at a high speed in order to gain time that we lost while group-lifting that one defective gate. The fact that we have now fallen back to the Team D timeframe and schedule matters far less than just making the next gate at the right time in its cycle.

On the bright side, at least Gracie's with me now. She's flying in the middle of our formation row, sandwiched between me and Laronda. That way I can be sure she is as safely away from both tunnel walls as possible. If anything happens, at least she'll have us around her as a safety cushion. . . .

As we move, Gracie can barely form words, but manages to tell us how their team's been doing. The rest of Team D has integrated into ours, forming a single larger group, and it's both a good and a bad thing. Good, because there's strength in numbers. Bad, because, um . . . *numbers.* Now there's twice as many of us and we still have to pass through each gate at a reasonable time, which now takes twice as long, with twice as many people. . . . Not to mention, it means we've got to maintain a higher average speed from now on, *permanently*, just to get all of us through every chamber.

As I glance around, during each now-crowded stop we take while waiting for the next gate opening, I see more people I know, including Hasmik and Jai, both looking like they're ready to keel over, but still hanging on, somehow.

"*Tsaveh tanem, janik,* Gwen!" Hasmik mutters, reverting to her native Armenian from sheer exhaustion. I squeeze her in the same awkward board-to-board hug that involves reaching across to the other person's board and sort of touching whatever part of them you can reach. It's the best we can manage under the circumstances.

"We'll make it," I mumble back. "You'll see!"

"I know! We totally will!"

Team D also has Blayne Dubois, and I am happy to see him lying stoically on top of his board, keeping up with everyone else and then some. I think, as a well-practiced flyer in this position, he

QUALIFY 583

actually has an advantage over all of us here.

"Hey, Lark, fancy meeting you here," he deadpans, through slightly chattering teeth.

"Hey, Dubois," I reply, grinning through my own clenched teeth. "What can I say, it's a small underworld."

And then, somewhere around hour thirty-two, just when it seems that we'll be in this hell race forever, we pass yet another floodgate and emerge into a huge cavern filled with amazing, blinding, artificial light, blaring noise, and other teenage voices, speaking in various *foreign* languages.

It's the central hub super-cavern underneath Ancient Atlantis.

We have arrived.

I shoot out of the tunnel and into *white*, a horrible brightness. As I blink, squint, putting one hand up over my eyes that have been in the dark for thirty-two hours, my vision finally grapples with the overload and I can see stuff—many floodlight projectors illuminating every part of this monster cavern, and oh, the *thousands* of people!

What am I saying? When all is said and done, there have to be *millions!* Probably more are arriving soon, while others might have already left.

I quickly sing a stop command to pull up my hoverboard, in order to not collide with the closest people nearby.

Because Candidates on hoverboards fill the very air around me, jostling so close that we could be on parade, as we hover, "stacked" on top of each other, just to be able to find an inch of space.

The din! And oh, lord, the *screaming!* In every frigging language on this planet!

As the rest of Team USA, Section Fourteen-C and D pour out of our tunnel, I realize that our tunnel is *just one of thousands* that cluster on the walls like honeycombs in a beehive. And more and more people are arriving from other cells of the great honeycomb.

The cavern itself—honestly, I am not really sure how big it is, because so many people are blocking my field of vision, all the way up to the remote ceiling. All I can tell is, there are floodlights shining on us, and that there's a cavern *ceiling* generally above, and a *floor* far below.

VERA NAZARIAN

"Oh, man, this is crazy-huge!" several of my teammates exclaim.

I see Laronda and Gracie and Hasmik levitate in formation next to me, as we stare around us helplessly.

A foot away and right below me, a brown-skinned boy wearing a Middle Eastern keffiyeh on his head points up with his finger at the ceiling and makes brief eye contact with me before looking away. Next to him is a pale blond boy who looks Scandinavian. Another board over, I see a girl who is speaking either Polish or Russian to another girl next to her.

Everyone is overwhelmed. And it really is impossible not to be.

"What's next?" Jai yells.

"Who cares! At least we made it out of the tunnel from hell!" a girl from Blue says.

We stare upward, and after a few moments it begins to make sense.

Somewhere high up, in the general middle of this super-cavern, the cathedral ceiling disappears upward in a conical shape. That has to be it—the way leading up to the surface, the one we were instructed to go through.

"Okay, so we go up. What's everyone waiting for?" Derek grumbles.

"Maybe we wait our turn?" I say.

"What turn? There are no 'turns' here, Gwen-baby! We just push and shove, and blast and *kill* our way up, and go!" He stares at me in dark, street-tough sarcasm.

"Okay," I say. "Then *go*."

Derek shrugs. And then he in fact sings his hoverboard to rise and starts shoving his way past other people hovering over him. A few exclamations and a stream of what sounds like juicy cursing in French comes from overhead, and I see Derek start pushing aside boards and then clobbering another guy. . . .

"Oh, jeez," Blayne says in disgust, moving in near us.

"Whatever, let him go, good riddance," Laronda says.

A few minutes later, as we wait, stuck in a strange holding pattern, we manage to learn what's going on.

According to a Candidate from New Zealand, the way up is a

relatively narrow tube, about twenty feet in circumference. The bottom portion, making up about one third of the way up, is a natural stone tunnel of volcanic origins, formed by lava eons ago. But it ends well below the surface of the ocean, so a concrete extension has been built to accommodate us, and this is the part that we have to navigate to reach the surface.

So, what's the problem?

The problem is contained in that first one-third, the natural tunnel. Not only is it convoluted like a tree branch, but it takes frequent curves and sharp side-turns while generally narrowing then widening again while moving up, so it is impossible to rise at a decent speed to pass through it without hitting the walls or getting hurt against the sharp rockside. Nor is it possible to go through it for more than six people at a time.

Supposedly the original volcano channel was more straightforward. But with time and erosion and the shifting of the earth itself all around it—plus the immense weight of the ocean water, with no water on the inside to compensate, unlike the floodgate tunnel network we just traversed—it had been seriously degraded, and in places nearly collapsed on itself.

So, basically, people really *are* waiting for their turn to get through. Even at the rate of high-speed hoverboard flight, it still takes a while for so many Candidates to pass the small, convoluted tunnel portion of this underground-to-surface chute.

"Yo! How much longer do we have?" Claudia says, kicking a guy from Team C to make him check his clock app.

"Less than two hours," Emilio replies instead, glancing at the smart pin on his sleeve.

Laronda snorts, wipes her mud-covered forehead with the back of her hand, then rummages in her backpack for food. "Great. Might as well have dinner while we wait. If these smarty-pants Atlanteans had time to install fancy-pants electric lighting in this joint, plus build a concrete tunnel, why couldn't they just make it all nice and easy? And for that matter, some vending machines wouldn't have hurt either . . . or a mini-mall. . . ."

Many of us follow her lead and eat whatever stuff we have left. Every five minutes or so, there's slight movement and new space clearing overhead as Candidates rise, a little burst of a few feet at a time, inching closer to the exit chute overhead.

"Okay, stupid question," Jai says, taking a huge bite of some kind of dried fruit bar. "But, what if you have to take a leak? Or what if you have to, you know, do Number Two? Are people going to be pissing on our heads now, as we wait?"

"Oh, disgusting! Jaideep, you are so disgusting!" A girl makes a face at Jai.

But he laughs like a neighing horse, and grins at her with a crazed expression.

A few minutes later, a miracle happens. Suddenly, there's my brother George followed by Gordie and Logan and Dawn, plus more, all levitating in a group, only a few feet to the right of us. Apparently it's not that much of a miracle after all, since we all came out of the same tunnel hole, and Team A and B were only about an hour ahead of us. In this crowd, its not like they could scatter far and wide and go sightseeing. . . .

"Gee One!" Gracie yells, with a burst of enthusiasm. And then, "And Gee Three!"

I feel a wild smile coming on. . . . Joy bursts from inside of me as I see so many of the people I care about all present and accounted for, and reasonably safe!

"Hello, ladies!" George says in a tired but flirty voice, maneuvering his board in our direction. We all collide and mingle and hug. Under the bright lights, everyone looks sickly, covered in wet mud-like gunk from the water in the tunnels, and just tired messes.

After I practically squeeze George and then Gordie to death across our hoverboards, I turn to Logan. His warm dark eyes sparkle with renewed energy as he sees me, and we reach across and hold icy-cold hands, pressing hard, and not willing to let go. . . .

"Dawn!" Laronda squeals. There is more hugging and touching and patting, plus a little bit of bodily displacement past a bunch of dark-haired frowning Candidates from what might be Team Greece, or Albania, or possibly Turkey.

Looks like most of Team USA Section Fourteen is gathered here—in other words what's left of the Pennsylvania RQC-3. We blab, share horror stories, and talk about bodies in the water and close calls.

"Yeah, that was us, Team B, in that multi-chambered cavern from hell," George says grimly. "I lucked out, just barely made it to the floodgate before it closed. So many other people didn't make it out on time. . . ."

"Oh, yeah, we had a rough time there too," Logan says, taking a swig from his water bottle.

But then I tell them about our stuck floodgate and how we barely made it with the hoverboards contraption.

Logan gives me a triumphant steady look of admiration until I blush.

"Gwen's the man!" Jai exclaims.

Gordie snorts, and attempts to lick dirt off his horribly smudged glasses. "Heh! Shoelace Girl, yeah. Nice going, sis." And then he puts a granola bar wrapper in his mouth and sucks it.

"Ugh! Stop eating paper, Gee Three." I smile and shake my head, patting him on the arm.

"Yeah, I'm hungry," Gordie says, raising one eyebrow.

"Then eat!"

"He ate everything in his pack." George rolls his eyes, but shows a crooked smile.

I shake my head then reach in my own backpack and pull out the last chunk of a granola bar and hand it to Gordie.

"Nah, it's okay, you need it," he says.

"No, I don't," I insist and press it in his cold sticky fingers.

And then I remember. "Oh! Points!" I exclaim. "Quickly, Gordie, time to transfer some of your extra points to Gracie!"

"Oh, yeah. . . ." Gordie shoves the chunk of granola in his mouth, wipes his fingers, then reaches out to Gracie and puts one hand on her ID token and the other on his own.

"Wait!" I say worriedly, while George gives me an intense, equally worried look. "You do have enough points, right, Gee?"

"Oh, yeah, tons. Two hundred-sixteen as of this morning." Gordie talks with his mouth full then swallows the rest of the granola.

"So, if you give your sister about sixty points, that should be enough—"

"I can give her more, like a hundred."

"No!" both George and I say at once. "Don't screw up your

own score. That's too risky."

"Okay, sixty then."

And Gordie says, "Transfer, sixty points to Grace Lark."

His token and Gracie's both flash.

"Done," Gordie says.

"Thanks!" Gracie mutters with a smile, and reaches across to board-hug Gordie. He skillfully evades her.

"Phew. . . ." I exhale a long-held breath. "I guess that's settled then—"

"Terra Patria!"

The insane shouts come from about a hundred feet ahead, from the general direction in the middle, right underneath the surface escape chute. They are followed in a split second by a horrible *sound.*

The mega-cavern is rocked by a great explosion.

Thousands of teens scream all around us—above, below, everywhere.

I cringe and close my eyes, while Logan suddenly hurls himself on top of me, covering me bodily from the impact of flying rocks, debris, supply packs, people falling, more screams, general chaos. . . .

The whole world seems to be swaying, rotating, as we barely hold on—as everyone around us latches on to their wobbling, spinning out, scattering hoverboards, or hangs by their hands, dangling in the air.

"Oh my God! Go, go! Go! Just go!"

George is yelling at the tangled mess that's me and Logan, and we get our bearings, and then there's what looks like an opening directly overhead.

"Everyone, go! Get the hell out!"

Dawn is pulling Laronda back up onto her hoverboard. Gracie is lying flat on hers, while Gordie is already above us, and he is yelling something in an incomprehensible voice, while the side of his face is bleeding.

"Up! Up! Go! Go!"

"What happened?" I gasp out, while Logan rights us, then transfers himself back on his own board that is floating next to mine.

In answer he cusses, then says, "Goddamn lowlife terrorists! No time! Go, Gwen, we have to get out of here! Rise, *now!* I'm right behind you!"

"Okay!" I scream. And then, "Gracie! George!"

I have no idea what is happening.

The earth is shaking around us, and it feels like the deep rumbling of an earthquake as cavern walls start collapsing far out along the edges.

I grab Gracie by her shirt, as she is reeling, and scream at her. 'Gracie! Sing! You have to go! Up!"

And then I sing my own command to rise, while screaming people and objects fly all around me, and picking up speed I hurtle upward.

Toward the ceiling, and the opening to the surface chute.

Toward the distant sky.

Chapter 54

The volcanic walls of the narrow vertical chute tunnel are pressing in around me, and there is no light, except the distant flickering shadows from other people's flashlights far up overhead, and the receding white glow of the huge cavern below.

It occurs to me to pull out my own flashlight that still has a faint amount of charge left in the battery. The flashlight casts an erratic, sickly yellow glow on the walls of the chute around me, as I rise and rise . . . up, up, up . . . angling my board at a slightly elevated position on a 30 degree slope, nose up, as I straddle it.

"Logan!" I cry out a few moments later. "Gracie? You there?"

"I'm here!" I hear Logan's strong voice coming from directly below me. "Keep going!"

And then a few seconds later, I hear Gracie reply.

"Watch for a hard curve up ahead!" The voice belongs to George.

Oh, thank the lord! George is here, is okay!

For the next few minutes we yell out things in the near-dark, just to hear each other's voices, just to know we're all still *there*.

The curves are wicked. The chute branches here and there, so that it is so easy to run head on into a wall or rock incline. I sing new hover commands every few seconds to correct for the changes in direction and movement.

This crazy vertical roller coaster ride goes on and on for interminable moments. . . .

At last, about fifteen minutes later, the chute tunnel straightens out and we are inside a long and wide concrete tube that rises like an arrow straight up, piercing the Atlantic Ocean.

With the end to the old volcanic portion of the chute, the rise becomes easy, and we all pick up speed.

The air whistles around us as the boards meet wind resistance. I have no idea how fast I am going now, but it's *fast*, and the rounded tube walls of concrete blur into a streak around me.

The air is still frigid cold, but there's a new freshness to it, as the musty depths of the earth are left behind.

I close my eyes momentarily, reeling with exhaustion and remember that I am supposed to be afraid of heights and that I suffer from vertigo.

It is gone now.

The stunning realization comes to me—the fact that I am no longer bothered by height, by any of this at all, that *fear* has receded because of so many other things taking its place. . . .

And just as I realize it, I suddenly burst through, out of the great tube chute, and into a great wide expanse of sky, filled with golden light. . . .

And orange sunset.

I soar up heavenward, my eyes blinking in the sudden radiance, my lungs bursting with the fresh, clean, balmy air. Dots of Candidates on hoverboards fill the sky all around me, like rising distant birds. *Or maybe*, it occurs to me in a silly flash, we are Halloween Witches, riding crazy brooms, straddling the boards in black silhouette against the sunset.

I let out a wild laugh, followed by a scream of exultation.

"Gracie! Logan! George! Gordie!" I scream out names, and laugh, like I am insane.

And then I turn my head and look higher up in the direction of the Eastern darker portion of sky, and see the hundreds of Atlantean shuttles.

In the same instant I see right below me, Blayne is flying next to Gracie, and she is clutching him by the hands and barely hanging on to her own board with her legs.

"Gracie, what happened? Are you okay?" I yell, as the happy drunken joy deflates from me, just like that.

Gracie sobs and makes little terrified noises, while Blayne voice-commands both their hoverboards to hover in place and then nods to me. "She's okay, I got her. She spun out, started to fall just now, as we were flying out of the tube, but I grabbed her mid-flight. Remember, Grip of Friendship?"

"Oh my God! Blayne, *thank you!*" I exclaim, but he just nods at me tiredly, and sort of disengages himself from Gracie's desperately clutching grasp. I see his blue eyes flash with some kind of quiet satisfaction as he then rises up and speeds away toward the distant hovering shuttles.

"See you on the flip side!" he yells in our wake.

I turn to Gracie, and hold her, silently, as together we rise up to the shuttles, right behind him. Gordie is soaring overhead, and George, just a few feet below.

A t the door of the nearest transport shuttle, an Atlantean stands with a faint smile. He passes a scanner over my ID token, then Gracie's. They both flash a bright yellow and red light, respectively.

"Qualified," he tells us. "And, Qualified. Proceed inside."

I pause, breathing deeply, in utter serene disbelief . . . while Gracie lets out a tiny scream of joy.

Gordie is already inside, seconds ahead of us. He is leaning from the hatch opening, grinning widely, waiting for us. "I Qualified!" he announces. And then Gordie just laughs.

I turn back, and see George, as he hovers before the shuttle entrance, coming in for his turn. There's a strange solemn look on George's face.

"Hurry up!" I tell him.

George nods. And then he floats toward the Atlantean who scans his green ID token.

There's a brief flash of green.

And then the light goes out and George's ID token goes dark.

I freeze.

The Atlantean looks at George, and his faint smile changes to a blank look with just a shadow of sorrow. "I am very sorry," he says. "Not Qualified."

"What?" I cry.

Behind me Gracie and Gordie's voices have gone out.

There is wind and perfect silence.

"Yeah," George says, breaking that silence. "Yeah . . . I didn't think I would."

"But—this has to be a mistake!" I stutter. "You—you are here, you made it! Your score is great! What's going on?"

"It's your *team* score," the Atlantean says softly.

"Unfortunately it is below the minimum."

"What? No! *No!*" Now I am crying, big sloppy sobs and fat tears running down my ugly mess of mud-covered face.

George sighs. "Most of Team B died in that cavern. I suspected this would happen. Too many of us gone, not enough for the team average. . . . The only reason I even bothered to continue this far here was to make sure you guys were all okay, that you got loaded in safely—"

"No!"

I stand and bawl, hearing Gracie also crying behind me, while George hovers silently at the entrance, looking at us.

"It's okay," he says. "Really."

In that moment Logan arrives, and his expression is serious as he pauses there and hovers next to George. He does not appear surprised that I'm bawling, doesn't need to ask why. . . .

The Atlantean passes the scanner over Logan's red token. It flashes and remains lit. "Qualified, proceed inside," the Atlantean says, nodding at him, almost with relief.

Logan gets off the board and steps onto the shuttle. He then holds me silently as I shake with weeping, and only acknowledge his own glorious moment of Qualification with a nod and a pitiful grimace that is trying to be a smile.

"George!" I cry, freeing myself from Logan momentarily, like a crazed maniac. And then I hurl myself at George, pulling him in, drawing him to me and smashing my face hard against the front of his dirty wet uniform shirt as he leans in tight against me.

We remain stilled this way for a few long seconds, while Candidates crowd the entrance.

"You need to make room for others, sorry," the Atlantean tells us.

"Just one more second! One more *stupid tiny* second! It's my *brother!*" I cry, holding George's shirt, his arm, his shoulder.

"Okay, but say your goodbyes on that side of this door. Move back and make some room for other people to pass," the Atlantean says.

I let go and move back, to now let Gracie bawl all over him. Gordie moves forward and presses his brother on the shoulder, and just leaves his hand there.

Finally George disengages from all of us. His eyes are moist, but he grins, and it's the familiar, wily, Cheshire-Cat George-smile, and it's painted bright by the orange sunset.

"Hey, hey, now! Listen, I'll be okay!" he says, getting back on the hoverboard. "Mom and Dad will be glad to see me, and honestly, I think we'll manage somehow! Screw the blasted asteroid, it'll all be okay in the end!"

"No, George! I am *not* letting you *die* here, I don't accept this!"

"Come on, Gee Two, no one's dying here, you'll see—in a couple of hours they'll send a bunch of ships or choppers to pick us up and take us back home—"

"That's not what I mean!" I scream.

But George is starting to move away, singing the hover command to descend, and now he is two, three, five, fifteen feet away, painted bright orange gold . . . a magic wizard flying on a hoverboard broom in the sunset.

"I love you!" I scream, and my knuckles bite against my mouth.

And then, for one crazy moment, George spreads his arms wide and starts to sing on top of his lungs:

> *When that I was and a little tiny boy,*
> *With hey, ho, the wind and the rain,*
> *A foolish thing was but a toy,*
> *For the rain it raineth every day.*

It's the fool's song. . . . A song we all know, something that Mom used to sing both with a harp accompaniment and a cappella, and we kids joined her in harmony. It's music from Shakespeare, of all things, "Feste's Song" from *Twelfth Night*. Only the Lark family would sing something like that and not bat an eyelid.

And now, here we are. . . .

George's gorgeous baritone soars in the air, and I take a deep breath, swallow shuddering tears, and then join him, because I must.

> *But when I came to man's estate,*
> *With hey, ho, the wind and the rain . . .*

I sing. . . . My voice begins breathy and quaking, and then it grows steady and gains power. Soon it's deep and rich like the sun setting in the Atlantic as I sing the second verse without stumbling. As I do so, I see George nodding to me, because, yeah, for the first time in years, I am singing again.

I am *singing.*

Suddenly Gordie joins in, and his tenor is clean and perfect like the air around us:

> *But when I came, alas! to wive,*
> *With hey, ho, the wind and the rain . . .*

And oh, but then Gracie does too! She picks up the next verse, and her bright soprano soars like a morning lark on the wind:

> *But when I came unto my beds,*
> *With hey, ho, the wind and the rain . . .*

And in the end we all sing the last verse together, and our harmony rings in strange wonder. . . .

> *A great while ago the world begun,*
> *With hey, ho, the wind and the rain.*
> *But that's all one, our play is done,*
> *And we'll strive to please you every day.*

And then there is silence. George is so far away now, a distant speck far below. He turns around one last time, and waves vigorously, and then he flies away, like a blazing meteor.

I stare for a long moment, then I go inside the shuttle. There's Gracie, and Gordie, and Logan, solemn, shaken. Gracie is weeping softly, again. The rest of my friends are getting on board other shuttles.

In a few moments we will rise high up and cut through the miles of atmosphere, and we will be in orbit. Sometime soon after that, we will be inside monolithic ships, heading for the stars.

Even now, *he* is on one of those great ships—he, the golden-haired sun god, son of Kassiopei, and of an ancient empire, and somehow I *matter* to him. . . .

No, no, no . . . I told you, I don't accept it, George, silly, silly, I mumble, for many endless minutes afterwards, as I am strapped into a harness. Then I sit in a daze, as the sunset fades and probably the sky outside turns indigo, but I don't know any of it, since there are no windows to look out, here in this damn *alien* shuttle.

As the Earth recedes, and gravity squeezes me into a bottomless abyss, I think of Mom and Dad . . . of Vermont autumn foliage . . . of maple syrup.

"I promise you, the Lark family will Qualify, hands down, all four of you!" Dad had told us, on that last day, two months ago.

Qualify or Die.

But, no, I whisper in the silence of my own mind, *I reject it. . . . With hey, ho, the wind and the rain . . .*

There is no "or" for any of us. Because there can be no "Die."

George, Mom, Dad—I am coming back for you somehow.

All of you.

I will win the Atlantis Grail and turn worlds upside down and inside out, and I will come for you.

There is only one acceptable answer for anyone human.

Qualify.

The End of QUALIFY: The Atlantis Grail, Book One

The story continues in . . .

COMPETE: The Atlantis Grail, Book Two

About the Author

Vera Nazarian is a two-time Nebula Award® Finalist and a member of Science Fiction and Fantasy Writers of America. She immigrated to the USA from the former USSR as a kid, sold her first story at 17, and has been published in numerous anthologies and magazines, honorably mentioned in Year's Best volumes, and translated into eight languages.

Vera made her novelist debut with the critically acclaimed *Dreams of the Compass Rose,* followed by *Lords of Rainbow.* Her novella *The Clock King and the Queen of the Hourglass* made the 2005 Locus Recommended Reading List. Her debut collection *Salt of the Air* contains the 2007 Nebula Award-nominated "The Story of Love." Recent work includes the 2008 Nebula Finalist novella *The Duke in His Castle,* science fiction collection *After the Sundial* (2010), *The Perpetual Calendar of Inspiration* (2010), three Jane Austen parodies, *Mansfield Park and Mummies* (2009), *Northanger Abbey and Angels and Dragons* (2010), and *Pride and Platypus: Mr. Darcy's Dreadful Secret* (2012), all part of her *Supernatural Jane Austen Series,* a parody of self-help and supernatural relationships advice, *Vampires are from Venus, Werewolves are from Mars: A Comprehensive Guide to Attracting Supernatural Love* (2012), *Cobweb Bride Trilogy* (2013), and *Qualify: The Atlantis Grail, Book One* (2014).

After many years in Los Angeles, Vera now lives in a small town in Vermont. She uses her Armenian sense of humor and her Russian sense of suffering to bake conflicted pirozhki and make art.

In addition to being a writer, philosopher, and award-winning artist, she is also the publisher of Norilana Books.

Official website:
www.veranazarian.com

Acknowledgements

There are so many of you whose unwavering, loving support helped me bring this book to life. My gratitude is boundless, and I thank you with all my heart (and in alphabetical order, cause in any other way lies madness)!

To my absolutely brilliant first readers, advisors, topic experts and friends, Anastasia Rudman, Cindy Couch Cannon, Jeremy Frank, Susan Franzblau, and Susan Macdonald.

To the lovely and wonderful group of Vermont writers and friends, Ellen Jareckie, Jeanne Miller, Lina Gimble, and Valerie Gillen.

To everyone at the White Lotus Kung Fu Studio in Los Angeles, Master Douglas L. Wong, Sifu Carrie Ogawa-Wong, and Sifu Phil Jennings for the discipline and Forms-based inspiration to create "Er-Du," my own imaginary martial art of Atlantis, stemming from the Tai Chi Chuan and Kung Fu traditions, and of course Sifu Travis Wong for the Parkour inspiration—I love you all and miss you constantly!

Finally, an immense thanks to the awesome and all-knowing Facebook friends who helped me brainstorm geeky science and general research details such as canal locks and floodgates, automatic firearms, the sport of running, songs, terms, and provided helpful responses to all the other crazy questions I asked at all hours:

Abigail Reynolds, Abrigon Gusiq, Al Sirois, Alan Levi, Alex Hunter, Alexa Adams, Alice Massoglia, Alison DeLuca, Alister Cameron, Allen Parmenter, Alma Alexander, Amira Bencherif, Amy Bisson, Amy C. Berger, Amy Herring, Ann Gimpel, Anne Hutchins, April Epley, Barbara Denz, Bobbie M. Smith, Bobo Lee, Brian Holihan, Brian Lane, Brian M. Logan, Brook West, C Allyn Pierson, Candra Jones, Caro Soles, Carol Kennedy, Carol R. Ward, Catherine Lundoff, Cathy Georges, Christy Wong-Langstaff, Concetta M Payne, Corwin Brust, Dan Robelen, David Bellamy, David Krieger, David Suitor, Debbie Ledesma, Debbie Moorhouse, Deborah Flores, Deborah Millitello, Deej Garden, Diana Birchall, Diane Sciacca, Eden Mabee, Elaine M. Brennan, Eleanor Skinner, Elisa Difino, Elyn Selu, Farah Mendlesohn, Gayle Surrette, George Kramer, George L. Dziuk Jr., Gerri Brousseau, Graham England, Gregg Mitchell, Harold Chester, Hasmik Davtian, Helen E. Mercier Davis, Hervey Allen, HP Waugh, James Flanagan, James Stevens-Arce, Jan Goeb, Jane Tanfei, Janet Jia-Ee Chui, Janice Lijek DeRossett, Jeff Corkern, Jeffry Dwight, Jenn Brissett, Jenn Reese, Jess Molly Brown, Jessica Saunders, Jessica Wick, Jo Allen, Joe Clark, Joshua Villines, Julia H. West, Julia Mary Breidenbach, Julie Marin, Juliette Winterer, JC Noir, Kari Sperring, Kate Savage, Katy Sozaeva,

Katharine Eliska Kimbriel, Kathy Hurley, Kathy Watts, Ken Schneyer, Kenneth Fields, Kurtis Roth, Larry Bonham, Leslie Tolbert, Lillie Thom, Linda Dunn, Lindalee Stahlman Volmert, Lisa Deutsch Harrigan, Lisa Mieth, Lisa Moore, Liz K. Burton, Liz O'Donnell, Lou J. Berger, Louise Turner, Luis Arrojo, Lyn Croft, Margaret Organ-Kean, Maria Grace, Maria Vagner, Marian Allen, Marilyn Holt, Mark Breuer, Michal McKee, Michelle Hufford, Monica Fairview, Nic Grabien, Pamela D Lloyd, Pamela J. Lorenz, Pamela K. Kinney, Patricia D. Novak, Patty Rains, Paul Nagai, Paula Fleming, Paula Helm Murray, Paula Lieberman, Paula Whitehouse, Peggy Wheeler, Persiphone Hellecat, Philip Brewer, Phyllis Irene Radford, Piera Chen, Rachel S. Heslin, Raechel Henderson, Rama Dixit, Rebecca Newman, Regina Jeffers, Rhondi Salsitz, Rhys Hughes, Rich Puckett, Richard Suitor, Rigel Ailur, R-Laurraine Tutihasi, Robert Brandt, Robert Brown, Robert M. Brown, Robert T Canipe, RobRoy McCandless, Ron Collins, Ron Dee, Rouben Sulahian, Ruth de Jauregui, Sam Long, Sara Cooper, Sarah Liberman, Scott Vilhauer, Sharon Lathan, Shelley Hunt, Stacey Helton McConnell, Stacey Miller, Stacey Nomura Wood, Stella Bloom, Stephen Ormsby, Stig Carlsson, Sue Burke, Sue Martin, Susanne Meyer Brown, Suze Campagna, Sycerith H R Krishna, Tera Decky Clare, Terri Bruce, Terri Bryan, Thomas Thurston Thomas, Tony N. Todaro, Tora K. Smulders-Srinivasan, Torbjørn Rasch Pettersen, Trent Walters, Valerie Howarth, Vee Stolesk, Wendy Delmater Thies, West Yarbrough McDonough.

If I've forgotten or missed anyone, the fault is mine; please know that I love and appreciate you all.

Finally, I would like to thank all of you dear reader friends, who decided to take my hand and step into my world of the Atlantis Grail.

My deepest thanks to all for your support!

CPSIA information can be obtained at www.ICGtesting.com
Printed in the USA
BVOW04s1133030916

461073BV00003B/9/P

9 781607 621348